The author, John Emslie, aged 53, has worked as a journalist for over 30 years. He is the editor of three trade magazine titles.

He divides his time between his principle home in South West Scotland, a Tudor beamed apartment in the ancient Cinque Ports town of Rye, famous as a smugglers' haunt in days gone by and the South of France.

He shares his life with his partner of nearly 20 years, who provided the inspiration for this, his first novel.

Together they share their lives with two dogs (both very badly behaved), who travel with them everywhere.

BENIN

John Emslie

BENIN

Vanguard Press

VANGUARD PAPERBACK

A CIP catalogue record for this title is
available from the British Library.

ISBN 978 184386 488 2

Vanguard Press is an imprint of
Pegasus Elliot MacKenzie Publishers Ltd.

www.pegasuspublishers.com

First Published in 2009

Vanguard Press
Sheraton House Castle Park
Cambridge England

Printed & Bound in Great Britain

This book is dedicated to the person who, in the book, is called Jo.

Disclaimer

All reasonable efforts have been made by the author and publishers to trace the copyright holders of the material contained in this publication.

In the event that any of the untraceable copyright holders come forward after the publication of this edition, the author and the publishers will endeavour to rectify the situation accordingly.

Book I

1897

Chapter 1

Mary shivered; a long, cold sliver of ice slipped down her spine. She awoke to a dark February night. A film of frost glistened at the edges of the window panes, like the work of a dozen or more miniature spinning wheels operated by spiders too frozen to emerge from their lairs and unlikely to catch any passing prey on such a bitterly cold winter's night.

It could not have been later than nine o'clock. The coal fire in the cast iron grate had long ceased to give off any heat. She had little enough coal anyway, having placed the last dying embers into the copper warming pan, before smoothing it over the crisply starched sheets to rid them of their immediate chill.

It had been a hard day, working a double shift in the Queen Hotel in Edinburgh's New Town. She had collected the laundry from her younger sister, who had a job in one of the wash-houses and who helped by taking care of Mary's two children on the days when the elder sister worked as a housekeeper at the grand hotel.

After working a ten-hour day Mary felt quite exhausted. She had little appetite, but still she forced herself to warm a bowl of broth on the range as an evening meal for herself and for her young daughter, Anne – a quiet child who, although only approaching her fourth birthday and at an age when most children were inclined to be precocious, was content to help her aunt stack and fold the linen brought in for washing from the large hotels in the city and to help her mother with the task of caring for her baby brother.

Finally, after feeding baby Robert and tucking little Anne into bed with a short story and a warm "Goodnight" kiss, she had made herself comfortable in the threadbare armchair, with the baby in her arms.

Soon the child's sagging eyes were mirrored by her own and she stirred herself to rise from the chair and settle the baby to sleep in the rough-hewn cradle that her husband, Alex, had originally constructed from a couple of discarded wooden orange boxes when Anne had been born and which now rested beside the brass and iron bedstead, in which the older child already lay asleep and which Mary herself climbed into gratefully at the end of the day.

Mary fell asleep almost the moment that her head touched the bolster.

She had been in a sound state of unconsciousness for probably no more that a couple of hours, when she awoke suddenly and, inexplicably, in fear of the darkness of the attic bedroom.

She looked at the black marble timepiece on the mantel shelf, squinting through sleep drenched eyes in her effort to focus and to make out the exact position of the hands on the clock. She had imagined it to be later, but it was only half past ten.

Baby Robert was gurgling, so perhaps it was no surprise that she had been awoken, but why did she feel so apprehensive? Maybe it was simply a mother's instinct – instantly aware of her child's cries of distress.

No, this was something more – a deep-rooted anxiety, which clung to her like the twisting stems of a vine, a fear that she could not shake off simply by the action of opening her eyes.

Baby Robert cried again, deep, vibrating sobs escaping from his tiny body in bursts, as if disturbed by something which had touched his cradle unseen in the shadows cast by the moonlight.

Mary leaned down and touched the baby's forehead, anxious for any sign of the fever, which had swept the Stockbridge streets over the winter and taken many a child to an early grave.

Here the small dwellings did not share the same sanitation as the elegant Georgian town houses of the nearby New Town and childhood diseases took a regular toll of young lives in the poverty-ridden, depressed dwellings of St Stephen's Street.

Mary sighed with relief to find the child's head dry and to discover that it was only tears which had dampened his little round face. She lifted him to her breast, hoping that the child would find comfort in her body's warmth and that he did not want feeding, for she did not wish to have to expose her breasts to the chill night air, allowing him to nuzzle into them and begin suckling.

Soon the baby quietened, comforted by her maternal presence and Mary returned him to his crib, gently settling the blanket loosely up under his chin, before returning to bed for the sleep that she so desperately craved.

Still she felt uneasy and her attempts to dispel the strange thoughts that she was experiencing proved more of an effort than she would have liked.

Eventually she felt herself drifting back towards an all too welcomed slumber, unaware of any pervading presence within the room. Her mind began to swim in that half-conscious state between wakefulness and the deep-seated care-free satisfaction that only sleep can bring.

Anne, the little girl who occupied the bed with her mother, murmured momentarily in her sleep, obviously disturbed by no more than her mother's return to the warm cocoon behind the rough blankets, which itched and scratched at her soft, pale skin, when they rode above the sheets. She alone apparently remained unaware of the cause of any disturbance.

Mary touched her daughter's tightly curled blonde hair, barely conscious of her own motherly gesture.

Mary's tumbled thoughts were soon interrupted once more just as she had begun to plunge headlong into a deep sleep, which promised to cure her aching limbs.

On this occasion she awoke with even more of a start. She sat bolt upright in the bed. Her bare arm brushed against the brass bed knob, as she tossed aside the counterpane and one foot touched the cold iron bed-rail.

She shivered against the freezing temperature of the room but, more than that, because of the cold, all pervading atmosphere that enveloped her.

Baby Robert was crying, sobbing in deep breaths that had made him gulp in the unfathomable darkness, filling his lungs with fear, his tiny fingers clutching uselessly at the cold night air.

Queen Victoria's portrait hung above the fireplace in its sombre black ebony frame. Clearly she was not amused by the cries of the tiny baby. The slightly disgruntled look on the monarch's face marked her disapproval.

On the mantelpiece, the black marble clock struck midnight, like a wake up call for the dead.

An icicle of fear flowed freely down Mary's back. Cold and slivering, it settled at the base of her spine and remained there like a coiled serpent, feeding on her fears. She knew for certain that there was someone in the room.

Instinctively too she knew that it was not her children who were in danger – not her flaxen-haired daughter, nor the baby boy born less than six weeks ago and whose father was right then battling through the forests of West Africa. Somehow she knew with a wife's instinct that it was her husband, Alex, whose life was threatened.

Mary's wide eyes caught the slight movement of the cradle, as if rocked by a hand unseen: a movement which provided no comfort to the boy child, who cried out as if gripped by sudden anguish.

A cold, icy draught swept across the counterpane and caught the thin net curtains at the attic window, seemingly causing the very panes of glass to rattle in their slightly rotting, unpainted frames.

A spider which had braved the cold night air, scuttled into a corner – no longer intent on making a meal of the moth which had stumbled into its trashed web.

Mary swept the baby up out of the crib into her arms and clung to the tiny infant, gaining solace from the cessation of its sobbing cries.

Somehow, if she protected Robert, then she could protect her husband – the man whom the child would soon learn to call "father".

She girded the grey army blanket to her bony frame, which lacked a single ounce of spare flesh and to the child, as if for protection against the unseen presence.

Her eyes searched the darkness of the small room, with its bare floorboards, which creaked when anyone walked across them, but which had not made the slightest sound when whomever it was had stolen silently into the bed chamber.

Again she caught the swaying movement of the crib, as it rocked gently, soundlessly and empty on the uncarpeted floor. Someone had a hand on the cradle and Mary gripped the baby ever more tightly to her bosom.

A shaft of moonlight ducked from behind a cloud, causing a glimmer of light to puncture the dark, unlit interior of the attic bedroom. For a brief moment it shone its incandescent light, illuminating an ashen figure, blackened features barely visible, like the last charred remains of the coal fire which had burnt itself out in the grate.

Mary found herself wanting to scream, but no sound would escape from her fractured throat, rendered hoarse by a mother's inherent fear for her child.

If only she could reach the hearth first, the brass poker, which stood in the fireplace, its tip blackened and twisted by the flames of a thousand fires, would provide her with some measure of protection against the intruder.

17

As if reading her thoughts, slowly the figure drifted towards the fireplace – ghosted away from the frightened child and its mother, as the moon slid once more into oblivion.

Plunged once more into darkness, Mary could barely fathom the features of the phantom, but she was aware that they were as dark as the night in which they sought to conceal themselves.

The fact that the phantom's hair was piled high should have made it easier for Mary to have a clearer view of the face before her, but the blackened face was seemingly devoid of features.

No sparkling eyes – just empty sockets. No pink mouth, just a slash across the face; flared nostrils that would never inhale another breath and coral studded ears unhearing of centuries of sound.

It was a face where a face should be, but the like of which Mary had never experienced in her life before.

Black! It was totally black!

Mary knew of the existence of people whose skin was the colour of coal. An uncle who had worked down the mines years ago would sometimes frighten her as a child when he had emerged from the pits.

Underneath she had always really known that a pallid skin lurked ready to reveal itself after a cold sloosh at the village pump on his way home from work in one of the Fife coal mines.

No, but this was totally different – mischievous and mysterious. In the dim light, the face of her intruder would always remain the colour of witchcraft and no amount of ducking in the village pond, or splashing at the village pump would ever change that.

A witch? Perhaps, because there was something about this apparition that marked it out as female. How Mary was able to define the sexuality of the sorceress, she had no idea.

Maybe it was the unseen hand rocking the cradle, the need to reach out towards an infant child. Or maybe it was the voice, which had begun to call to her and which seemed to resonate around the attic room with its gabled ceiling.

> *Thou taketh my head*
> *And blood will be shed*
> *A spear in the heart*
> *The thief will depart*

Two horrible rhyming couplets that were repeated over and over again. Two meaningless phrases which struck at Mary's soul and prodded at the heart of both her absent husband and her tiny infant son, Robert. She knew not what they meant. Were they a threat? She had never heard the words before and their significance was totally lost on her.

Still she could not see the face of the witch who taunted her, the face that seemed to float above a shroud of cloth, enveloping a body, which had no hands to rock an infant's cradle, nor feet to walk across a bare, uncarpeted floor, which normally creaked and groaned at every step.

18

Mary took one careful step towards the fireplace, as her antagonist wafted towards the window in a movement that was both effortless and surreal.

Summoning her last vestiges of courage, Mary turned towards the window, still clutching baby Robert, whose weight hampered any thoughts of swift movement.

She was too late!

The threatening presence was present in the room no longer, swept away in a tangle of the tattered net curtain, enveloping the shroud in lace, until only the white punctuated curtain remained.

Two paces took Mary to the window, where the fine filaments of a dozen, or more miniature spinning wheels remained undisturbed by arachnid, or apparition.

Wisely, from her statuesque position above the mantelpiece, Queen Victoria looked down on the séance-like scene being enacted below her.

Perhaps she recognised that this visitation was being made by no ordinary person, but none other than the ancient queen of Benin in West Africa – a queen who had reigned for more years than Queen Victoria herself in this her Diamond Jubilee year. A queen who had been dead for centuries!

No living person had ever dared touch the queen of Benin, nor looked upon her image, fearing that she would strike back, for such was the ancient myth that anyone who spied upon the queen would pay dearly for their act of obsequiousness.

Glance upon the queen of Benin and she would strike back in vengeance at the heart of any man who cast his eyes upon her, spearing him in cardiac arrest, whilst his son looked on in horror at the death of his father.

Mary's husband, Alex, was in West Africa as a member of the Benin Expedition of 1897 and right now he was tramping through the rain forests, heading for the City of Benin and a confrontation with the Benin king, whose chief protector was his long dead royal predecessor.

Thou taketh my head
And blood will be shed
A spear in the heart
The thief will depart

Chapter 2

'It's utterly preposterous. king or no king, he cannot expect demands like that to be met,' announced the Acting Consul General. 'He's only expecting the British Government to supply him with twenty thousand sheets of corrugated iron for roofing his damned mud huts.'

Alexander Seath, a trader's clerk with Miller Brothers of Glasgow, was listening to the words of James Phillips, the eldest son of an Archdeacon, a fellow of Trinity College in Cambridge and whose grandfather had commanded a cavalry regiment during the Battle of Waterloo – three facts about the Acting Consul General's upbringing that Alex knew by rote, having heard them enunciated to anyone who was prepared to listen on many an occasion since his arrival in the kingdom of Benin in West Africa in late November 1896.

'And I wonder exactly when His Royal Highness will see fit to reply to my letter?' the Acting Consul General thundered. 'Do you realise, he's already stopped Major Copford-Crawford and Captain Maling reaching Benin City.

'I understand they reached Gwatto and were turned back by the Benin City soldiers on the instructions of King Oba Overami. With an attachment of only twenty troops and some Jakri carriers, I suppose they had no option. God damn the Oba, just who does he think he is?'

'If they were simply turned back, sir, I take it that there was no fighting,' replied Alex, his own indignation aroused by the thought that the British detachment should have demurely returned to their barracks, without a single drop of African's blood having been spilt.

'I don't mean they were simply stopped in their tracks and turned back. No, Seath, I don't mean anything of the kind! What I'm saying is that they could advance no further without the certainty of having a battle on their hands and our lily-livered Consul General has issued strict orders that there is to be no fighting.

'God only knows what's wrong with the man, I'd have gone in there with a party of Blue Jackets and a battery of seven pounders and blasted the bastards to oblivion, if it had been up to me.'

Alex was inclined to agree with the Acting Consul General. Peaceful tactics were best left to the politicians and men like his friend, Charlie Paterson, who had arrived in Sapele from Liverpool just ahead of Alex to take up his position as a member of the trading post, shipping back to Britain a variety of goods, including elephants' tusks, to fuel the popular demand for ivory, as well as sacks of pepper and barrels of palm oil from the former slave trading centre.

As fellow traders, the two men had become friends and often joined the Acting Consul General and Major Copford-Crawford, either at Mission Hill in Old Calabar where James Phillips lived in somewhat regal splendour in the Consul's residence – a barn-like building, much admired by visitors, or at the Major's consulate quarters at Warri, where they would be wined and dined in style, for the military man's hospitality was well renowned.

In the dining room, in the shadows cast by the Major's array of big game trophies, Alex and Charlie would often listen to the older man's entertaining, if somewhat tall tales long into the night.

Afterwards, they would return to Consulate Hill for one last drink with Phillips, who would sometimes even summons his African cook, Baddoo to prepare them a little light refreshment to accompany their brandy, as if to infer that the Major's grand hospitality had been in some way lacking.

Cleared of the bush and with properly drained roads now running in all directions, the area had been renamed Consulate Hill and there a whole series of wooden, double-storeyed houses had been built for the British and European officials among whom the Acting Consul General occupied the highest rank and the most splendidly appointed abode, situated some two hundred feet above the riverside.

Situated in what, in West Africa, passed as a picturesque little square, were the well-scrubbed headquarters barracks of the Niger Protectorate Force, which fronted Soldier Town – a native village built by the soldiers themselves for the accommodation of the ladies and children of the regiment.

Once he had put aside sufficient money, even the lowest ranking recruit would take on a "wife", who would be employed to cook his "chop", usually making a little extra money on the side for herself and her "husband" by not keeping to the rule that single men should not be allowed to visit the married quarters!

In the barrack square there was even a cricket ground and although the boundaries were a little too close for any batsman who proclaimed himself to be a big hitter, it served well as a Saturday afternoon meeting place, where a brass band would play and cups of tea would be poured by ladies from the local mission, who were not adverse to reminding some of the serving officers of their manners.

A game of lawn tennis or, perhaps, a gentle game of quoits could be called upon to while away the evening and even a round of golf was not beyond the possibilities of what the day had to offer. Often a good drive, or an excellent putt would result in arguments and celebrations in equal measure when the nineteenth hole was finally reached.

In addition, the capital of the Protectorate now boasted a European hospital, to which all the white men, officials and traders were taken when they became ill with blackwater fever, dysentery and other tropical diseases that beset the area.

It was presided over by four English lady nurses and it was here that Charlie Paterson first met his wife to be, Muriel, who was to save his life when he had finally emerged from the jungle after a harrowing escape on foot from marauding natives, with gunshot wounds in his leg and an assortment of septic sores.

Charlie had always been a pacifist, preferring to talk his way out of a situation, even when the two men would hit the pubs down by Edinburgh's Leith Docks on a rare night out in the Scottish capital and where there were usually plenty of sailors and dockers all too ready for a fight.

At the initial sign of a brawl, Alex would be the first to throw a punch, but Charlie was always more reticent to join in the fray, which would often spill over on to the cobbled streets and finish up with a bloody nose for Alex.

Despite their different characters, together the two men had strengthened a bond, which had begun when they had both been posted to the Gold Coast some years ago.

Alex had always worked for Miller Brothers in Glasgow. Charlie, despite his Scottish upbringing, had originally been employed by Crooks in Liverpool and then by John Swainson – a trader with the Liverpool firm of Pinnock's – an old "coaster", his skin yellowed from years of swallowing too much quinine to ward off the fever.

Alex and Charlie's friendship had continued when Charlie had been taken sick soon after his arrival in West Africa and the more robust Alex had been forced to double his work load, whilst his friend made his recovery – even if Alex had been a little jealous at the amount of attention that Charlie had been receiving at the hands of one of the pretty young nurses!

'So what do we do now?' asked Alex, returning to the subject of the Oba's reluctance to acquiesce to the British request and secretly hoping that the Deputy Consul General's answer would be an antagonistic one.

Maybe it would at last herald a return to the drawing up of battle lines – not that this was the Africans' way of fighting from all that he had heard!

'I suppose we give the Oba to the end of the week to send his messengers back with a reply,' sighed the Acting Consul General, 'but, mark my words, Seath, I will not be ignored by some tinpot African despot.

'I've told him that we will be returning to Benin City in the New Year and we will be paying His Royal Highness a visit, whether he likes it, or not!

'We certainly intend to re-open the trade routes, I can assure you. So have no fear, Alex, my friend, you can tell your bosses back in Britain that you'll be able to take as much ivory as you like out of this goddamn place.

'There are plenty of elephants here in the Protectorate and the Oba's storehouses are stacked with tusks,' boasted the Acting Consul General over their usual brandy one evening.

'There's many an old tusker, who's met his end in these parts, let me assure you,' asserted Phillips.

'And there's no need to arrange any shooting parties either unless you enjoy the sport,' he continued. 'Why bother? The beasts are difficult to track down in the bush; there might be a whole herd of them no more than a quarter of a mile away but, believe me, thanks to the density of the scrub, they can be hard enough to spot. They might just as well be a couple of hundred miles off. Leave the hunting to the natives is my advice.'

'The Portuguese had it all their own way for far too long. It's time we marked the Oba's card for him and let him know that he can't meddle with the British.

'We'll have him singing "Rule Britannia" before the Queen's Diamond Jubilee next year, even if I have to teach him the bloody words myself!' concluded Phillips.

It was strange to consider that the people of the ancient kingdom of Benin, who had seemed to be civilised in the sixteenth century, with a grand city and broad avenues that had excited the admiration of visiting Europeans should, by the end of the nineteenth century, have lapsed into a state of barbaric behaviour.

Here what had once been a wonderful city had become little more than a disorderly collection of half-ruined mud huts. Many leaked like sieves and were in a very dilapidated state.

Benin may have been a kingdom since time immemorial, but its occupants, and especially its monarch, were still savages at heart.

Some of the serving army officers and officials had witnessed ritualistic human sacrifices.

Suspended from the ubiquitous crucifixion trees – the silk cotton trees, in whose branches witches, wizards and any victim of the monarch's choosing were spread-eagled after execution, bore witness to a particular brand of savagery in the form of mutilated, dangling bodies left to provide sustenance for the gods.

If it was the anniversary of the death of the Oba's grandmother's aunt's second cousin, then slaughter another dozen or more slaves; if a new trading market was opened up, hell, damn it, that was ample excuse for another mass execution. In fact, there seemed no possibility of having a proper celebration without the ritualistic killing of yet another batch of unfortunates.

'God, you've no idea how barbaric these people can be!' said the Acting Consul General, discerning the certain amount of relish with which Alex met his words and, at the same time, noting Charlie's shiver.

'It's time we went in there and put a stop to some of their horrible habits. What it needs is a strong-armed expedition. Instead we pander to their king with presents and all he ever expects is more and more "dash".

Maybe Alex would feel differently when he encountered such wholesale slaughter at first hand, but listening to the Acting Consul General's tales of the tyrannical Oba and his fanatical juju priests, right now he could not help but agree with Phillips' particular preference for forceful imperialism.

Alex's boss had already regaled his clerk with some of the dealings he had experienced with the man, who now sat in front of him in a comfortable wing arm chair, swirling his alcoholic nightcap in a large brandy balloon. There was no doubt in Alex's mind that, where the Benin king was concerned, the Acting Consul General meant business.

He had even been told by Charlie that Phillips had been heard in his club in London's Piccadilly – just a short walk from the Foreign Office late one night, boasting of his plans to overthrow the Benin ruler "by fair means, or foul".

Unlike Alex, Acting Consul General James Phillips was a well-connected man of great ambition and he had not taken long to prove himself to be a strong and ruthless deputy, with his eyes firmly set on rapid promotion.

The possible threat that he posed had not escaped his superior, Sir Ralph Moor, whose position and rank Philips so desperately aspired to.

As his superior recognised, his deputy feared no one and often proceeded with foolhardy recklessness.

As a newly appointed official, Phillips had even taken it upon himself to address the British Prime Minister, Robert Cecil, in a dispatch, sent without the knowledge, nor the approval of his superior.

In it he bewailed the recent loss of trade and clamoured for the British Government to act against the Benin king, ending his note with a direct plea for the use of force:

"I therefore ask for His Lordship's permission to visit Benin City in February next, to depose and remove the king of Benin. I do not anticipate any serious resistance from the people of the country – there is every reason to believe that they would be glad to be rid of their king – but in order to obviate any danger, I wish to take up a sufficient armed force," he had written, adding that he had every reason to hope that sufficient ivory would be found in the king's house to pay the expenses incurred in removing the king from his stool.

Alex was impressed that Phillips had displayed the guts and determination to get to the root of the problem and didn't doubt the assurance that there would be little, or no opposition to their plans, as long as they brought with them plenty of gifts to bestow upon the natives, unaccustomed to sharing the customary "dash" with their ruler and his favoured chiefs.

'Why when one of their chiefs was disappointed not to have received a present from our queen of a carriage and a pair of horses, he cut off all the trading routes, with threats of juju and other witchcraft,' said Phillips one night over dinner.

'They have traded with the Portuguese since the days of Queen Elizabeth I. Let us have their ivory and they can have all the bloody corrugated iron they want!'

Chapter 3

In the weeks leading up to Christmas, James Phillips sat apprehensively awaiting a reply from the British Foreign Office and canvassing for companions to accompany him on his proposed, unauthorised expedition.

Not surprisingly, his first success was in persuading two of the important Glasgow and Liverpool based traders to join him, accompanied by their clerks, Alex Seath and Charlie Paterson.

Alex's boss, Harry Powis, was a popular agent, who had lived and traded in the area for some years, even learning to speak a few words of the local language and he, in turn, had persuaded Thomas Gordon to join them, along with Alex and Charlie.

Captain Allan Boisragon, the commandant of the Niger Coast Protectorate Force also agreed to go as the senior army officer and he, in his turn, was joined by Ralph Locke, another serving officer, who had first arrived on the West African coast some five years previously.

At the age of thirty-two, Ralph Locke was five years younger than his senior officer. Slight of stature, he was, nevertheless, probably the more handsome of the two men, lacking the balding Boisragon's piggy eyes and with the knack of charming the ladies, who were sometimes heard to comment on the younger man's good looks.

Immaculate in appearance, his thinning, but meticulously combed hair bore a parting down the middle. His carefully trimmed moustache, whilst not displaying the exuberance of the other man's more luxuriant facial hair, marked him out as someone who was no stranger to the verandah of the barber's shop in Old Calabar.

He would visit most days, enjoying the administrations of the African barber, commanding him to wax and trim his whiskers, so that the points struck out fashionably in exact parallel to his surprisingly pale skin, which was in sharp contrast to his dark, slightly hooded eyes.

Charlie shared a little of Locke's elegance and always tried to dress as well as he could, within his limited means. On the other hand, Alex cared little for his own appearance.

Indeed, he was often chided by Mary for his vagabond look. She would tell him that his clothes marked him out as more like the local coal man, warning him that he should watch out for the St Stephen's Street urchins. If ever they chased him, it was probably in the hope that he might drop the odd knob of coal, as he made his way home on cold winter nights.

Alex was a big man and normally had a hearty appetite, although he suffered with his stomach and belched repeatedly after meal times, much to Mary's disgust and to the dismay of Charlie, his more mild-mannered friend.

And so on Christmas Day 1896, when the small gathering of gentlemen and traders sat down to dinner and to make the final arrangements for their impending departure on Boxing Day, Alex was reminded by Charlie to mind his manners and also to endeavour to curb his prodigious consumption of alcohol, which normally did nothing to limit his more exuberant excesses.

'We are starting tomorrow on a perilous expedition from which some of us may never return,' the Acting Consul General announced ominously but, by that time in the afternoon on Christmas Day, they had all had eaten their fill of the festive fare that the African cook, Baddoo and his boys, had prepared and drunk a little too much good French brandy to really care.

Charlie's gentle jibes to Alex about his excessive appetite and even more excessive intake of brandy were long forgotten. Everyone was in high spirits, regarding Phillips' prophecy as little more than a joke.

'Hey, if you're going to start making ominous predictions like that, we'll string you up and hang you from one of the cotton trees down by the river, along with the rest of the soothsayers. This place needs its very own crucifixion tree,' said Alex, drunkenly.

'What's good for the king of Benin is good enough for us. Come on chaps, let's get him! String him up! One minute he's a warmonger, the next minute he's a warlock! Get him lads. He deserves to die!' added Alex light heartedly, after his brandy balloon had been filled yet again, urging the other men to grab an arm, or a leg, lifting the Acting Consul General high above their heads and threatening to "hang 'im high". The Acting Consul General took the ribald behaviour in good spirit, cracking open another couple of bottles of fine spirit, with which to announce yet another toast to the success of their forthcoming expedition.

He had heard nothing from the Foreign Office by way of a reply to his request to travel up to Benin and take the city by force. He had therefore contented himself that the next best objective was to persuade the Oba to allow white men to come up to Benin City as often as they wished.

Only in this way could the sacrificial rights, which so horrified the British colonists, be stamped out and, more importantly, the trade routes be re-opened.

A message had been sent to the Benin king giving him notice that a small party of white men would be coming up river to Benin City itself – a distance of only some 14 or 15 miles, but a journey that was fraught with hazards. For weeks the African king, like the officials at the Foreign Office, maintained his silence, much to the frustration of the British Acting Consul General.

Finally, the expedition had set off on the day after Boxing Day, sending ahead a small gift for the king. It was not until the visiting party had reached Gwatto that the Benin king had sent messengers to inform the party that, whilst he was extremely pleased to receive the present, which he did not expect, he could not see any white men just then, as he was celebrating the "custom" of the anniversary of his father's death.

Quite simply, what that meant was that he was otherwise engaged in the ritualistic sacrificing of hundreds of unfortunate slaves, whose deaths would allow the departed monarch to continue on his path into the afterlife and prove his predecessor's great wealth and standing.

No one but a member of the Benin ruling family could afford to maintain such a vast number of slaves, taking them to the grave and sacrificing many more on each subsequent anniversary of the royal funeral.

Acting Consul General Phillips was outraged, especially by the addendum that the Oba would let him know in "one or two months time" when he was ready to set up a meeting with the British official and that, at the king's bidding, no other white men would be made welcome.

Arrangements for a large party to arrive at Benin City were too far advanced to be halted by the intransigence of a despotic African monarch and James Phillips would not hear of putting a stop to the expedition.

Any delay would have meant that the party might have been caught up in the rainy season, which usually began with a succession of thunderstorms at the beginning of March and would have made the expedition's progress on foot up from the creek well nigh impossible in such heavily forested terrain.

Here the total annual rainfall was reckoned to be the heaviest in the world and it would have undoubtedly have meant postponing the trip by as much as a further six months.

In West Africa these rainstorms could last until the beginning of November and James Phillips, his patience almost completely exhausted, had absolutely no intention whatsoever of waiting until then. Besides, Kenneth Campbell, who had once helped his family run a large estate in Argyllshire and who was now in charge of over two hundred carriers, had worked like a slave himself to get everything ready for the expedition, grouping a small number under a headman and issuing each carrier with a number.

Alex had his camp bed carried by No 13 – an ill omen! He had tried to persuade Campbell to dispense with the number altogether and skip to No 14, but the pragmatic District Commissioner would hear nothing of it.

James Phillips had every intention of putting on quite a show to impress the Benin king. His entourage was to include the drum and fife band of the Niger Protectorate Force.

He remembered how, years before him, Sir Richard Burton had gone up to Benin City, with an accompanying missionary in an attempt to put a stop to the number of human sacrifices.

With him the missionary had taken a small harmonium and had entertained the Oba by playing a popular tune of the day, "We shall meet to part no more", whilst Sir Richard, for his part, had effected an Arabian dance before the king.

And there was no way that he, James Phillips, was performing a jig and reel in front of some heathen despot!

The departure from Old Calabar in the closing days of 1896 had meant that James Phillips had been forced to forego a concert being given by the brass band, who were playing selections from Gaiety Girl and other comic operas of the day.

The performance was scheduled to celebrate the passing of the Old Year and it had been planned that the band was to play dance music at two balls, which were to be staged in Calabar at the start of the New Year.

The Acting Consul General was no opera buff, preferring his musical entertainment on the lighter side, but he had been looking forward to having the chance to dance with Mary Slessor, one of the lady missionaries from the Scotch Mission at Old Calabar.

She lived in Oloyon, some way inland from Old Calabar and James had met her twice before at one of the polo matches staged in the old town.

He had been greatly smitten with Miss Slessor from their first chance meeting and had a great deal of respect for the way in which she had apparently tamed many of the natives, learning to speak their various tongues.

This was no mean feat in itself, considering the large number of different tribes, all with their own languages and dialects.

However, her main achievement was that, single-handedly, she had brought about the prevention of the wholesale slaughter of any child unfortunate enough to be born as one of twins.

The killing of twins was yet another example of the wretchedly insane customs that had been perpetuated for centuries by the natives in and around Benin City.

A twin birth was considered to be the work of the Devil and when a woman gave birth to a pair of infants, the babies were immediately put to death, or simply thrown into the bush and left to die.

The unfortunate mother was driven out and never allowed to return or, indeed, to come anywhere near any town, or village again. Most probably, she would die of starvation in the bush.

Meanwhile, the house into which the twins had been born and everything inside it was destroyed by fire, as only the cleansing flames could purge the unnatural production of two babies out of the same womb.

Such was the edict of the ancient Queen Oba Eeeni who, centuries ago, had given birth to twin baby boys. Both had died, bearing, it was said, the mark of the Devil and leaving the Oba without an immediate heir.

She had been the Oba's favourite of his many wives and he had been bitterly disappointed that she had never again been able to produce him a son.

It was therefore decreed, by ancient custom, that no twin child born of a mere subject of the king would be allowed to live and the mother would be driven out of the city, so that the king would never be forced to look upon a woman who had given birth to twins.

The father would be spared the fate of the mother of his children, but he would be forced to pay sacrifices of sheep and chickens by way of purifying the village of the evil, which had been brought upon it.

After the banishment of his former wife, he was free to take another woman, but he was never allowed to take his first wife back, nor was he ever allowed to see her again.

Miss Slessor had organised the building of "twin villages", where the unfortunate mothers would be allowed to go and live, whilst their babies would be spared from death and brought up by someone else.

When such twins were born, Miss Slessor would be called for by the people, by whom she was now held in high regard. She would set about the task of purifying the house and its contents by washing down the walls inside and out and, likewise, washing everything inside.

She would then be allowed to save the woman who had given birth to the twins and to take the babies back to her own house – a comfortable wooden property some way from the Old Calabar River, which she had fashioned and built almost entirely with her own bare hands.

In the opinion of James Phillips she was a woman much to be admired. Not only was she feisty in her approach to taming the barbaric behaviour of the natives, so steeped in their juju beliefs, but she likewise commanded the respect of all the officials and traders in the Protectorate.

She was also an accomplished bridge player and would attend the cricket matches and tennis tournaments staged at regular intervals at the club houses, which had largely replaced the hard-drinking carousals at various points up and down the river.

Yes, James Phillips was determined to get to know her better on his return from visiting the Benin king. At thirty-four years old, it was time he settled down and finding a suitable wife was high on his agenda!

He had his sights set on the Consul General's posting for the Gold Coast Colony and having a suitable wife by his side would certainly not impede his ambitions.

As comforting as it was to think about the admirable Miss Slessor, his present task was to concentrate on the progress and comfort of the small party of officers and traders that he was determined to lead into Benin City for an overdue audience with the Oba. However, as far as he was concerned, there was no point in sacrificing creature comforts.

No, this party would travel in as much style as possible and, to this end, each of the white men was allocated three carriers – two to carry baggage and one to carry a camp bed. In addition, a vast number of porters was needed to carry extra food and water and rations for the carriers themselves.

In total some two hundred and forty carriers were to be employed in order to provide the visiting contingency with as many home comforts as possible – a hundred and eighty of them were Jakris, supplied by the different Benin and Warri chiefs and the remainder was to be made up of around sixty Kroo boys supplied by the Government Consulate at Sapele.

Unlike other natives in this part of the world, James Phillips had observed that the Kroo boys were particularly hard working.

Consistently cheerful, they were so unlike many of their West African brethren, who had little relish for toil and labour.

Typically they would leave their own country in their thousands, returning maybe a year later, with their wages in the form of clothes, vests and hats in many strange and wonderful shapes, calculated to arouse the aspirations of their fellow countrymen on the Kroo Coast and which they would subsequently exchange and barter.

Alex left Old Calabar with the Acting Consul General on the morning of Sunday December 27th after celebrating the festivities with Charlie, getting totally drunk on palm wine on Christmas Eve and again repeating their Bacchanalian revelry on Boxing Day.

They had spent Christmas Day together, but it passed them by in a hangover that Alex described as like having being hit on the head with a poker.

On the Sunday that Alex and Charlie joined the small party of British officials headed by James Phillips, they embarked on a twin-masted steam yacht called the Ivy – an apt name, as Alex soon found himself clinging to virtually anything he could grab hold of for most of the short voyage and wanting to be sick over the side, as they made their slow progress up the New Calabar River.

It was luxuriously appointed, with every possible comfort, boasting both electric lighting and air conditioning. Indeed, the boat was the pride of the New Marine Department, although many of the Liverpool traders had questioned the need for such luxury and extravagance paid for out of their profits.

Some had even queried her suitability for river work and had succeeded in persuading their local Member of Parliament to ask embarrassing questions in the House of Commons, such as "whether her bottom is only wood sheathed in copper, from which fact she is likely to suffer by the least grounding, causing exposure of her timbers to the actions of worms".

James Phillips saw no reason at all why a man of his newly appointed standing should not enjoy all of life's creature comforts.

Now that he was mixing with men of greater substance, he had joined several of the Gentlemen's clubs in Piccadilly, taking full advantage of the capital's many attractions and he had soon grown to be an advocate of Lord Wolseley's theory that:

"If you are fond of the theatre, you can find any amusement in music halls and in the society of women whose character has long ceased to be doubtful".

No, life on board the Ivy suited him very well, with his own private cook and servants seconded from the Consulate and if, per chance, they should encounter any resistance, whilst making their way up river, the steamer was fitted with a battery of twelve and six pounders, which were made to withstand any amount of knocking about.

They were also fashioned in such a way as to be mounted and dismounted in a very short space of time, should the need arise.

They were hated by the natives, being called "them gun that shoot twice", referring to the explosion of the shells, which they considered most unfair, taking place so far away from the gun itself and, most inconveniently, close to their target when, as they might have thought, they were completely out of range.

Another weapon that they particularly abhorred was the war rocket, which the natives looked upon as the invention of the Devil, failing to understand how the wretched thing was capable of working its way through the thickest forest, as if searching for them everywhere.

Harry Powis and Thomas Gordon, like Alex, a fellow Scot, who hailed from a tiny fishing village in the Highlands, headed the quartet of traders.

The four men who made up the trading contingency had little in common with the army men and Consulate officials, as Harry came from the North London borough of Stoke Newington and Charlie originally came from a family of steel workers in the North of England, although his father had begun to make his mark, rising to the position of work's foreman by the time that Charlie had left school at the age of fourteen to become an apprentice clerk.

On the other hand, Captain Copland-Crawford was an old Harrovian and the rest of the army officers and officials were mostly from public school backgrounds.

Alex, with his crude manners, was often made to feel inferior in such exalted company, even if Charlie did his best to cover up his friend's shortcomings, reminding him how to hold his cutlery and the appropriate glass from which to drink on the occasions when Alex would have been happy to take his port straight from the pitcher and booze his brandy from a beer tankard.

John Swainson, the agent for Pinnock's in Liverpool, had excused himself, on account of the fact that his rheumatism was playing up and other traders, perhaps a little more wary of the expedition's prospects, had declined to make the trip for a variety of reasons.

Harry Powis, who had been to Benin City on two or three previous occasions, had joined them at the embarkation point and, like Locke, had proved to be a jovial companion, caring less about his physical appearance and more about the opportunity of arming himself with a decanter of fine French brandy – preferably paid for at someone else's expense.

Unlike James Phillips, Captain Boisragon was not optimistic about their success and had challenged the Acting Consul General to a wager, betting him the large sum of £1 that the expedition would never reach Benin City and that they would be turned back, probably at Gwatto.

The Acting Consul General was, as usual, far more sanguine about the likely success of the enterprise and Charlie, ever more of the pessimist, had persuaded Alex that they too should have a wager on the outcome, betting his more bombastic friend a packet of cigarettes that the captain was likely to win his bet.

'If we do get stopped, it will almost certainly mean that the next expedition to Benin City will be an armed one sanctioned by the Foreign Office,' said Alex, adding that they should have gone up with an armed force and been prepared to fight, if they had met with any opposition.

He knew that the Ivy was armed and he knew that Phillips would have been under strict instructions not to deploy any means of force, but then again, the expedition had not been sanctioned by the Foreign Office anyway.

'Instead, what are we armed with when we reach dry land? Bloody walking sticks! What happens if we are attacked? How are we supposed to defend ourselves?' asked Alex, in a rare moment when he wasn't being sick over the side of the Ivy.

Captain Copford-Crawford was hanging over the rail with Alex, whilst lighting his pipe. He still walked with a limp from a wound received some years ago and he strongly believed that, if local opposition was quelled by force, the Whitehall civil servants would retrospectively condone the act after the event. He leant heavily on his hardwood walking stick, allowing it to take the weight of his not inconsiderable bulk.

'It's my birthday on January 6th, Alex. I'll be forty-one. You know how I would like to celebrate it? In Benin City, with their bastard of a king showering me with gifts and bending down to wash my feet.

'We pander to him, with presents and patronage and he snaps his fingers and closes down the trade routes. Meanwhile, we sit around waiting for His Majesty to condescend to open them, as and when he sees fit.

'Her Majesty Queen Victoria undertook to extend to Benin her gracious favour and protection. It's time we forgot about protecting him and his subjects. Let's get in there and have the bastard out is what I say.'

James Phillips passing the two men huddled in conversation heard the last words of Captain Copford-Crawford's tirade and tapped him gently on the shoulder.

'Well spoken, Captain, there is only one king in this God-forsaken country and that is the white man.'

Chapter 4

On December 29th the Ivy called in at Brass to land a number of British troops, who were relieving a detachment there and Lieutenant Arthur Maling joined the boat, before they set off again the next day up river with the intent of arriving at New Benin later that afternoon.

The whole country near the coastline was little more than a network of creeks and mangrove swamps, adjoining one tributary with another; any villages bordering the river were hidden some distance away inland and the path to each settlement was often so insignificant and well concealed, that it could so easily be missed altogether.

The river itself was usually busy with the canoes of local tribesmen, going about their daily routine of bringing casks of palm oil to the trading posts, or "beaches" as they were known.

All along the thickly forested river banks, the British trading companies had established their outposts, each with a little jetty for pulling up canoes and a trader's house with a high, corrugated iron, or thatched roof, a wide verandah to dissipate the heat and wire gauze to dispel the hordes of biting insects that gorged themselves on human blood at every opportunity.

Meanwhile the chiefs and wealthy traders went about their daily business in gaily painted gigs with candy-striped awnings, manned by six, or sometimes eight, native paddlers, with an extra servant to waft a large palm leaf over them, if the heat became too much even under the canvas.

Strangely, on this trip up river, the water was quiet and the Ivy's passage was seldom interrupted by a passing canoe. The river banks were virtually deserted, although how many pairs of eyes lay hidden in the dense vegetation, no one could hazard a guess. For many of the natives, the white man was still a source of fascination … and the fear which was a constant factor of their lives.

Steeped in superstition, many of the villagers had never encountered white men before. By virtue of their belief in the king of Benin and his juju men, they were forbidden to leave their country, or even to cross the water so, consequently, they were not allowed to climb into a canoe for fear of invoking the wrath of the very powerful spirit, who was personified by their juju king.

Here juju was everything, religion, superstition and custom all rolled into one. In its wake came human sacrificial rites, cannibalism and witchcraft, with the Great Queen Oba Eeeni held in awe as the Great Witch Queen and the Mother of all Damnation.

Even the big chiefs of the district were in the habit of sending annual subsidies on account of the juju and, as a result, the Oba was very rich in ivory.

It was considered bad luck for any man to hold a pair of tusks, just as it was considered an ill omen for any woman to give birth to twins and so, in order to diffuse the bad fortune, the king received one tusk for every elephant shot.

This tribute was usually transported up river to be stacked in his storehouses, with little effort being made to trade it for European goods.

It was Alex and Charlie's appointed task to change all that.

Access by water from the Atlantic was difficult, for like most of the rivers on the coast, the mouth of the Benin River had a mud bar, which only shallow draft vessels could cross. Besides, Gwatto Creek was no more than three-quarters of a mile wide.

Gwatto itself had suffered from the falling trade of recent years, and all that was left for Alex and Charlie to see of the former trading station was a rotting wooden jetty, which extended out into the creek, serving only as a lookout post for the herons; the factory visited only recently by Harry Powis was completely gone, its timber frame and weatherboarding no doubt purloined by one of the river chiefs seeking to repair his own residence.

Finally, the creek narrowed to only forty or fifty yards wide, much of its width criss-crossed with mangrove roots. Here it was completely surrounded by mangroves. In places the water's flow narrowed still further, as it dwindled away from the source.

It was not the healthiest place in the world! Charlie had already been hospitalised in Old Calabar with blackwater fever, being nursed back to health by the pretty young Muriel, whom he had yet to pluck up sufficient courage to ask out on a date.

Many of the tradesmen who had travelled this way before had come away suffering from dysentery. Malarial fever was rife. At low tide the swamps of black mud seemed to ooze out malaria.

At low water any number of oysters could be gathered from amongst the mangrove roots, but no one was prepared to consume them as a delicacy, as there was a general belief that, far from increasing sexual prowess, the mangrove oyster was one of the main carriers of malaria.

Hordes of biting mosquitoes buzzed and droned in the failing hours of daylight, taking mouthfuls of warm, human blood.

Feasting on human blood was apparently not something restricted to the voracious appetites of the local insect life and after dinner on board the Ivy, Phillips would regale the party with some of the more lurid tales of cannibalism.

On one occasion he told the tale of the son of one particular chief, who had recently returned from England where, for some years, he had been educated at a missionary college. Soon after the boy's return, a successful raid on one of the neighbouring towns had resulted in the capture of a number of Kroo boys.

'And do you know that this educated, supposedly civilised son of the local chieftain could be seen waltzing about the town with a Kroo boy's leg over his shoulder,' announced Phillips with relish, whilst handing out cigars to his travelling companions.

'When he met the French father from the local Roman Catholic Mission, he generously proffered the offending leg, with the words "Father, would you like a bit?" ' concluded Phillips, taking another slug of his brandy in the smoke-filled atmosphere and laughing uproariously at his own joke.

On board the Ivy the small party passed many of the daylight hours without so much as seeing a sign of another human being on the river banks.

Indeed, there was little of any interest to be seen, apart from the depressing monotony of mangrove and swamp, sometimes relieved by a solitary kingfisher, or an occasional heron flying overhead. Strange, haunting calls could be heard from the dense jungle canopy above them, but seldom could anything be seen to justify the unnerving sounds.

Great blue touracos flashed through the fig trees, their iridescent plumage catching the shafts of sunlight and green vervet monkeys peered curiously at the intruders from another world.

The smell of the effluvial mud assaulted the white men's nostrils and, for Alex, once again vomiting over the side of the yacht, the stench only served to increase his alcohol-induced misery.

Hippopotami wallowed in the shallows, with black crakes that rode piggy back, or padded gingerly across their ample, leathery rumps, like moorhens picking their way through lily pads in the hope of finding a juicy parasite to extract from the thick hides, as the hippos emerged from the muddy waters of the creek.

Occasionally Alex, or another member of the party, would amuse themselves by taking pot shots at the crocodiles, or the hippos, but seldom did a carcase float to the surface.

The crocodiles, which abounded on every river bank, seemed to have developed a mean reprisal to being hit, struggling into the water and disappearing, often to be torn apart by their fellows. Only those which were not consumed by their brethren would eventually float to the surface.

Even the hippos seemed to adopt an amused attitude to any attempt being made to shoot them, sinking beneath the level of the water at the first sight of a raised rifle barrel.

On New Year's Day the Jakri carriers braved the crocodiles by jumping into the water to be sent ahead of the party in their canoes. Alex had once seen a Kroo boy bathing in water that scarcely reached his knees, being snatched by a crocodile and dragged into deeper water.

His screams only subsided when the water ran red with his blood, as his captor twisted and cavorted in the muddy river, tearing limb from limb, before being joined in the feeding frenzy by a posse of the hungry reptiles, who fought and snapped as they tore the flesh from the dead boy's body.

It had not been a pretty sight and even leaning over the side of the boat to be sick, Alex was careful not to lean too far forward, lest one of the beasts rose out of the water and made a meal out of him – vomit and all!

Splashing about in the water, as they waded their canoes ashore, the Jakri carriers and the Kroo boys seemed totally unaware of what dangers might lurk in the muddy waters of the creek, which swirled around their bare feet and legs.

Seldom did the Kroo boys stop laughing, apparently finding amusement in such simple pleasures as swopping hats with their companions, poking and prodding each other until Kenneth Campbell shouted them into line, addressing them by the numbers that were painted in white on their bare backs, with orders to meet up with the British contingency at Gwatto the following day.

They took with them the presents intended as gifts for the Benin king, together with surprise items, such as bottles of soda water. The natives had proven to be much impressed by the corks popping out of the bottles, with apparent ease – thus proving the white men to be the possessors of "Big juju", or powerful magic.

Photographic cameras too proved to be the cause of great delight, with their exploding flash lights, operated by men who disappeared, magician like, under a black cloth, only to re-appear apparently unharmed by the explosion of light.

Alex was still lamenting the fact that the party was to be unarmed, when they reached landfall, with only their so-called white man's juju to protect them in the event of an attack.

Still by way of small compensation, he was rejoicing in the fact that Charlie had been forced to part with his last whole packet of cigarettes, when no effort was made to prevent their onward progress to Benin City.

Altogether the white men numbered twelve in their party; mostly they were a fit and lean looking lot, having, in many cases, survived the rigours of malarial fever and other tropical illnesses.

Malaria seemed to attack all manner of men, making no differential between consuls and their consorts. At low tide the swamps of black mud seemed to pour out doses of the deadly disease.

As they approached the estuary which led up to the city, the remains of the old slave barracoon were clearly visible. With the abolition of the slave trade, one immense source of wealth had disappeared and, on account of the Oba's stupidity in preventing his people from trading whenever he saw fit to do so, many of the towns and villages lay virtually in ruins.

The great City of Benin was a mere shadow of its former self, with its high surrounding walls having crumpled and decayed. Even the once enormous broad streets running through the length of the city – so long that it was virtually impossible to see to the opposite end – were now little more than a tangle of back street alleyways.

Once the king of Benin City would boast as many as six hundred wives, but now their numbers were reduced to a mere eighty or ninety!

In the past the gentlemen of Benin City would ride to court on horses, with a man on each side to hold them on. Other slaves carrying big bronze shields would accompany them to keep the sun off the courtiers' heads, whilst yet more slaves provided a musical accompaniment, striking hollow irons, horns and flints, blowing ivory flutes and with a striking drum beat booming along behind them to precipitate the progress of the procession and announce its entry into the palace courtyard. With all this cacophony of sound it was little wonder that the horse riders had to be held on to their mounts.

However, all this was in the past. Benin was no longer a boom town.

Now there was but one horse in Benin City and on this the king himself rode, being held astride his mount in much the same fashion as his predecessors. Benin City was definitely now a one-horse town.

The Oba himself was a sight to behold on the rare occasions that a ceremony permitted him to emerge from his palace and allowed him to be seen amongst his people.

He was still a young man, adorned in a mass of gold from head to foot. He wore a kind of fireman's helmet and his golden sandals alone must have been worth a small fortune.

He was always surrounded by his priests, usually paunchy and potbellied, dumpy of stature and easily mistaken for fat women at a fair, had it not been for their black faces.

His glorious golden attire would be polished to a rich lustre by those slaves who were fortunate enough to be appointed to menial household duties.

In Benin the life of a slave was not highly valued and for the Oba and his courtiers it was difficult to appreciate why the white man should raise any objection to a few dozen of them being killed for a rich man's funeral, or an occasion, such as the Ceremony of the Royal Coral Beads, which always followed the last downpour of the first rains of the season.

The Oba's palace was separated both physically and symbolically from the rest of his subjects by a massively thick wall, some twenty feet high and about a quarter of a mile long. It measured about four feet thick at its base. The palace was roofed with thatch and corrugated iron to protect it from the torrential tropical rains.

Fixed to the great wooden gates of the palace were bronze plaques, depicting leopards and other creatures of a more mythical nature, including a huge curling serpent, its fanged mouth reaching downwards, eager for prey.

The Benin kingdom had existed for over a thousand years, since the long ago, but not forgotten days of the original Oba and his favourite African Queen, Oba Eeeni, whose juju still held sway, cursing the lives of babies who shared the same womb.

Her sacred bronze head sat on the stone altar in the king's palace with its flint carved inscriptions of ancient curses, sanctioning sacrifices and demanding the quenching of her thirst with the blood of her people.

Ancient tradition forbade the Oba to leave his palace, except for religious celebrations. On such rare occasions as the king emerged from his royal seclusion behind the great walled palace, he would always first pay homage to his forefathers and the queen who had not lived for a thousand years, laying a bronze trinket at her head, with the promise of a blood-spattered coral necklace and a dish of warm blood from one of the human sacrifices that had been ordained to mark the day's proceedings.

After paying due accord to his ancient ancestor, the Oba would finally emerge from his palace, his shoulders bowed by the weight of his regalia.

Around his lower limbs he wore an elaborately embroidered cloth, adorned with the emblems of his great authority; on his upper torso he wore a shirt with countless knots, each furnished with a red coral bead and around his neck and wrists he wore strings of coral beads that clicked and rustled softly together, with every movement of his head and hands. On his head he sported a massive coral head-dress.

Making and embroidering the coral head-dress and the coral knotted shirt were the responsibilities of his son and heir, who alone could look upon his father whilst he hoisted the heavy regalia on to his head and which no servant was allowed to see until the king was fully adorned in his regal costume.

On leaving the palace in all his finery, for the procession around the city, accompanied by his many retainers, the king's personal servants, or "emada" went naked except for a bronze anklet – for it was their place to be, and to be seen to be, totally subservient to their master, who would have been presented with them as children by their fathers as gifts to mark their obsequiousness to the king.

His favourite two servants were required to stand either side of him, to support his arms, such was the weight of the regal robes.

Others cooled him with leather fans as he walked and servants bearing the swords of state ran before him, whilst the palace chiefs followed the regal procession, bedecked in bronze and ivory and surrounded by their own retinues.

Court musicians precipitated the procession, with haunting tunes played on ivory flutes, shaking bead-filled gourds and banging on beaten bronze gongs, whilst a choir accompanied by the drums sung the praises of their regal master.

At the climax to the ceremony, there would be a human sacrifice in the principal palace compound, around the walls of which were arranged the shrines of dead Obas past, each mounted with carved ivory tusks and bronze figures fashioned in the shape of crouching leopards and serpents.

In the middle of the compound, on its sacred stone sat the bronze effigy of the Great Queen Oba Eeeni, her hollow head filled with palm oil wax, died blood red and hardened by centuries of the baking sun.

There she sat for three hundred and sixty-four days of the year, only being removed from her throne by the High Priest on the summer solstice, when the heat of the sun threatened to melt her waxen plug.

On the day of the Ceremony of the Royal Coral Beads she sat on her stone, awaiting her share of sacrificial blood, watched by the priests and chosen members of Benin City society, who lined the long sides of the palace compound, while the Oba took his place at the main altar.

There he removed the coral regalia from which he drew his great strength and, in deference to the long dead queen, bowed solemnly to her image and offered up to her a bronze bowl of sacrificial blood.

Only in this way could the king renew his spiritual power. Only in this way could he receive the ancient queen's blessing. Only in this way could he retain power over his people!

Once, at the close of the year, when the summer solstice has passed its zenith and the bronze effigy of Queen Oba Eeeni was safely returned to her altar stone, the sacrificial victim had not been the customary criminal, selected slave, or an enemy of the state, but an unauthorized trader captured by Benin soldiers and brought back to Benin City for execution.

He was a so-called "white black man", who had not only traded with white men, such as John Swainson of the Liverpool trading company, but had even adopted the customs and dress of his peers.

His name was Thompson.

He arrived as no lamb to the slaughter, arguing vociferously for his life, condemning the Benin people and their king and making no attempt to hide his contempt for their customs.

Nevertheless, Thompson was brought to the sacrificial altar, struggling and fighting with his captors, whilst the Oba voiced the ritualistic words in readiness for offering up the captive's blood to the Great Queen Oba Eeeni.

The king called upon the man who was about to die to carry a message to the gods but, instead, as the victim was held ready for the executioner to cut off his head, Thompson cried out:

'The white men that are greater than you or I are coming to fight and conquer you,' as the ceremonial axe fell, scattering his blood over the coral regalia, according to ancient custom.

The thousand year-old dead Queen Oba Eeeni drank his still warm blood from the bronze bowl held to her lips by the king. Later the servants gathered his body parts to boil up for a meal.

For the onlookers, the final words of the sacrificial victim cast an uncustomary gloom over the proceedings. Words which were soon to be remembered, words which James Phillips had related over the dining table that night with a certain amount of glee and anticipation.

Charlie listened aghast to the tales of capture and cannibalism, heralding the savage death of a fellow trader. He was anxious that neither he nor Alex should gain first hand experience of the witchcraft and wicked ways of a people with whom they hoped to trade.

Alex, for his part, seldom tired of hearing the ghoulish anecdotes of his fellow shipmates that he was stoically happy to stomach – far more than he was content to stomach the movement of the gently lapping waters, which caused the Ivy to rock and roll and add to the nausea he felt, not as a result of the Acting Consul General's lurid tales, but simply from a wretchedness borne of an excess of fine French brandy.

The next morning they awoke at Sapele, situated about fifty miles from the river mouth, where there was good, deep-water anchorage. For the British contingency of traders the town had become an important port of call and they had come to know it well as the headquarters of much of the trade that was conducted along the Benin River.

It had a splendid background of huge forest trees in the various clearings along one of its banks, whilst the opposite bank was a dense, impenetrable mass of foliage and undergrowth, which reached right down to the waterside.

Here the water was crystal clear and studded with masses of dark-coloured water lilies, which formed small green islands, bobbing just above the surface of the water.

Some eight miles below Sapele was Warrigi, where the main column of the Naval Brigade was concentrated prior to its subsequent advance on Benin City.

To the north lay Ciri on the Ilogi Creek where the Niger Coast Protectorate troops were garrisoned and from where the inhabitants of the nearby Benin City drew their water supplies.

Nana was the head chief of the Benin River natives and the leading African middleman in the palm oil trade. A Jakri tribesman, he was an extremely rich and powerful man, with headquarters at Brohoemi – a town built on land reclaimed from the mangrove swamps, using millions of canoe-loads of sand.

Brohoemi had been captured and destroyed by a combined naval and military expedition three years earlier, during the course of which Captain Copford-Crawford had sustained the leg injury that necessitated him walking with the aid of a stick.

Nana was the greatest and most powerful of the trading chiefs along the Benin River and both Alex and Charlie had previously visited the markets under his control.

His prestigious position was well known to the king of Benin, yet he still paid a yearly tribute on account of the powerful juju of Benin City to ensure that the trading routes were kept open.

Neither Nana nor his men would ever have dared to have launched an attack on the king of Benin whom they held in the utmost awe. After Nana's fall to the British and following the desperate words of the sacrificial trader at the Ceremony of the Royal Coral Beads, the people of the City of Benin were in fear that they too would be attacked and began making preparations accordingly.

Several previous attempts had been made by a detachment of troops to reach the city and each time they had been halted by Benin City soldiers.

James Phillips was not a man to be stopped in his tracks, but neither he nor any of his small British party could ever have countenanced the treacherous cruelty of the massacre which was about to take place!

Chapter 5

It was in the middle of the January morning, as the Ivy was steaming down river that the British party encountered Chief Dore, the head chief of the Benin River, paddling a small dug-out canoe.

Strangely he was dressed in what looked like a fireman's helmet. At first sight it glinted like gold in the reflecting shallows but, on closer inspection, it was probably brass. Nevertheless, he presented a spectacular image, as he sped through the water towards the steam ship.

He was bringing a message from the king of Benin that James Phillips and the contingency of British visitors were to proceed no further, as the king was observing the rites of passage of his predecessor and busily sacrificing slaves to accompany his father on his onward journey through the after world, as presages of the dead monarch's prestigious position.

It was also made clear to the Acting Consul General that parties of Benin soldiers had been sent to all the waterside towns, but as this was normal procedure whenever any white men arrived in the vicinity of Benin City, the African military presence was not considered to pose a threat to the small assembly of officials and would-be traders.

Indeed, the Acting Consul General was keen to point out that this was a good omen and that the visitors could expect a warm welcome. He immediately dispatched a messenger to the Oba to thank him for his kind words and to announce the impending arrival.

'The Acting Consul General has received the king's message and is very pleased to hear that his friend, the king of Benin, has been gratified with the present given to him. As he had accepted this gift, it proves that the king is the white man's friend and the Acting Consul General is now coming to visit the king with eleven other white men. With him he is bringing a much larger present for the king,' Phillips informed the monarch's messenger.

He added that he regretted that he could not wait two months, as the king suggested, but he had so much work to do in other parts of the Protectorate. He was therefore obliged to come now, as there were several important matters he wished to discuss.

With these fateful words, the messenger left at once and another message was sent to the headman of one of the larger Jakri villages.

Dudu Jerri was a great friend of the Benin king and, unknown to the Acting Consul General, he had long been suspected of passing information on any expedition setting off from Gwatto, with the object of reaching Benin City.

Dudu Jerri duly arrived, declaring that Gwatto was full of Benin soldiers and equally full of forebodings that they were armed and ready to fire on the British, if they made any attempt to land.

His warnings were dismissed and, encouraged by James Phillips, some of the British contingency, including Alex, laughed openly in the face of such predictions.

Only Charlie remained quiet on the matter, urging caution and suffering the admonition of the would-be Consul General for his cowardly attitude and the fact that he would not countenance a forceful approach.

'You're a spineless, yellow-bellied wonder, Paterson,' Phillips growled, chided him into submission. 'You can't be namby-pamby with these natives, otherwise they'll walk all over you. What do you want to do then, my man? I can put you back in a canoe with the band, if you like, but they'll be no ivory for you to take away from the Benin storehouses, you chicken-hearted fool.'

When it became clear that Acting Consul General Phillips had no intention of acquiescing to this request, both Captain Boisragon and Charlie had suggested that it would be advisable to send back the two dozen men of the drum and fife band in Chief Dore's canoe to avoid an immediate confrontation.

Owing to their brightly-coloured uniforms and ceremonial swords, the Benin soldiers might have been led to believe that this was a military detachment, rather than a source of musical entertainment whose intention was merely to put on a performance for their king.

It had taken a great deal of effort to persuade the leader of the British expedition that discretion was the better part of valour but, eventually, he had reluctantly agreed to forsake the extraordinary musical extravaganza that had been planned to delight the king of Benin and his court.

Four and twenty blackbirds baked in a pie.
When the pie was opened, the birds began to sing.
Wasn't that a dainty dish to set before the king.

It wasn't only the bandsmen who were attracting attention in their brightly garbed attire. The two coloured Government interpreters, Herbert and Towey, who had been with Chief Nana when Brohoemi had been captured by the British raiding party, were quite a sight to behold.

Both were resplendent in bicycling costumes, which comprised blue knickerbockers, stockings and cloth tennis shoes in which they swaggered about the bush like mannequins on parade.

Their linguistic skills were needed to ensure the success of the trip, there being so many different languages and dialects within the Protectorate. Indeed, a Jakri from the Benin River would often be as hard pushed to comprehend the words of a visitor from Old Calabar, as he would be able to understand a white man.

And so it was essential that they remained with the party, along with Basilli, a scoundrel who had fled from Benin City some years previously and who had been appointed as guide for the expedition.

Unlike his coloured brethren, his choice of clothing was a trifle more sombre.

One of the Jakri messengers informed the Acting Consul General that the Oba had spoken to him privately and told him that if the white men were not to be deterred from their proposed mission, then he should return as quickly as possible to Benin City and inform the king, so that the necessary preparations could be made for receiving his guests!

Before his departure in the canoe with the bandsmen, Chief Dore tried once more to persuade Phillips not to continue, insisting that he believed that the British party would be fired upon, if they persisted with their foolhardy mission.

'It be monkey palaver, it no be man palaver,' was the advice given, but Phillips was in no frame of mind to listen. It was not until days afterwards that the true meaning of the old chief's words came to be appreciated by the more deep thinking Charlie.

Quite simply the Benin chief had found it difficult to believe that the Benin king could have ever behaved so treacherously as to plot the ambush and massacre of the men whose skin was of a different colour and who came trekking through the jungle for nothing more than peaceful palaver.

Acting Consul General James Phillips would countenance no form of advice from any quarter and proceeded down the Benin River as far as the entrance to Gwatto Creek.

He would heed no warning. It was an act of obstinacy that would cost him his own life and herald the deaths of many of those around him.

* * * * * * * * *

The party arrived at Gilli Gilli, the first Benin village on the Gwatto Creek at around four o'clock that afternoon. Here the muddy waters of the creek narrowed to no more than fifty yards or so wide but, at ten feet or more in depth, whilst by no means bottomless, it still provided ample room for the launch.

At Gilli Gilli the party caught up with the Jakri carriers, who had arrived in their canoes with the stores of bully beef and bottled stout to sustain the white men on their march through the jungle.

Gilli Gilli was a tiny village comprising no more than a dozen half-ruined mud huts but, what was surprising, was that they were all totally deserted, with the exception of one that contained an elderly native woman.

Towey, the interpreter, greeted her in a polite manner, making three circles with his right hand closed and his stubby thumb pointing upwards over the palm of his calloused left hand, which was held open, before rubbing his two open palms together, like two blocks of sandpaper.

At the same time he nodded slowly and seriously to the old woman, who returned his form of salutation, nodding gravely in turn to each of the white men, before explaining to Towey in a strange sounding dialect that all the men of the village had disappeared into the bush, as they were frightened and did not know what to expect of the white men's arrival.

The British party returned to the awaiting launch that evening, a dozen men arranged on both sides of the ship's dining table, with Acting Consul General James Phillips at its helm.

It proved to be a cheery dinner, for they had decided to celebrate Captain Copford-Crawford's birthday a few days early. It was a wise decision, as the forty-year-old captain was never to witness his forty first birthday.

* * * * * * * * *

43

The next morning Dudu Jerri returned to the launch to announce that one of the Gwatto chiefs had extended a warm welcome to the visiting white men and had even prepared a house for them all to sleep in that night.

It wasn't until around midday that the party finally set off in the wake of the Jakri carriers, who had been sent ahead with their machetes to clear the creek of its tangle of weeds and to chop down any overhanging branches, which might interfere with the onward progress of the Ivy.

With any impeding vegetation slashed away from their path, it only took about twenty minutes to reach Gwatto in the beating, dazzling sunlight, which filtered through the mangroves. However, the decision was made not to land until later, when they could do so in the relative cool of the afternoon.

Charlie and Alex were on the lookout for a signboard denoting the location of the Old Miller Brothers of Glasgow factories, which had been forced to be abandoned when the king of Benin had put a stop to all trading activity some few years previously. However, they failed to find even a vestige of the twin waterside buildings.

True, they weren't quite sure on which side of the river they should be looking for, as with all Benin villages, there were two habitations, one of each side of the river, but both bearing the same name.

One was built for the Benin City men and was usually constructed some distance from the creek on top of the bank and the other was situated by the edge of the water on the opposite side of the river and comprising a few huts where the Jakris would live.

Only a few of the Jakri tribesmen would be found on the Benin side of the river to collect the palm oil and other trade goods, paddling them down to the factories on the river.

Once arrived at its destination, the oil would be processed for use in lubricating the burgeoning amounts of machinery to be found in the factories of the Midlands and the industrialised North of England.

Together Alex and Charlie peered intently into the dense vegetation that bordered the thirty foot high banks of the river, forming a dark green, seemingly impenetrable forest.

Each of them took turns with Alex's binoculars, but there was no sign of any remnant of the former trading post.

Charlie had brought along a camera, hoping to take photographs of what remained of the abandoned buildings, but there was nothing at all to be seen.

Like some of the other members of the party, who had also brought along their cameras, he had to be content with photographing the vervet monkeys that chattered and screeched, as they ran along the mangrove branches, snatching at anything edible that caught their eye, fighting furiously over the fulsome, ripening figs.

At other times they would focus the lenses of their binoculars on the hippos that raised their rumps from the muddy shallows.

Before they landed, James Phillips summoned the entire party on deck, issuing strict orders that he himself was to lead the party, marching at its helm, preceded only by Basilli acting as guide and either Herbert or Towey to serve as an interpreter between himself and any tribesmen that might be encountered en route for the City of Blood.

He also issued orders that whilst the officers would be allowed to carry revolvers, they must not show them, for fear of frightening the natives.

Alex and Charlie had only their walking sticks with which to beat a path through the dense undergrowth, which bordered the narrow trails through the forest, if they needed to step off the track at any time to relieve themselves.

Typically, Alex was not pleased. He had secretly brought with him an old army revolver, which was in his cabin trunk, but walking in the damp, sticky heat in the middle of the day, meant that the only practical thing to do was to dispense with his coat and any excess clothing, leaving little opportunity to conceal his revolver from Phillips' prying eyes.

* * * * * * * * *

They landed at four o'clock and set off with the long line of carriers being brought up at the rear by Kenneth Campbell, trying to keep them in their groups and, ridiculously, in numerical order – a task which proved both impractical and impossible.

The path led along the dried out bed of a stream, with perpendicular walls of blood red clay ranging nearly twenty feet high on either side.

It stopped almost as quickly as it had begun, terminating after two hundred and fifty yards or so in another perpendicular wall, which could only be scaled using a roughly fashioned ladder, made up of tree branches, by way of rungs, fastened to strong, sturdy uprights, using twists of liana as bindings.

It took the weight of the Jakri carriers with no trouble and the more energetic members of the British party climbed it with relative ease in the wake of the Acting Consul General, who had insisted that he was the first man up the ladder, which had creaked and groaned under the weight of his stocky frame.

Captain Copford-Crawford, with his lame leg, had struggled defiantly, but finally had to admit defeat and was hoisted up the ladder on Alex's strong back, with Charlie in charge of his walking stick, clutching the two canes in his left hand, as he used his right hand to grasp the rungs of the roughly assembled, makeshift ladder.

As a defensive tactic it served its purpose well. Before they left the path leading up to the ladder, any invading force would have had no chance whatsoever of returning enemy fire from tribesmen waiting to ambush them on the banks, as soon as they had mounted the last rung.

On arriving at the top of the ladder, the British party had its first encounter with the men of Benin City. The juju priests promptly welcomed their guests with traditional salutations, making three circles with their right hand, bowing and nodding their heads and then, through the auspices of one of the two interpreters, bestowed upon each member of the white men's party the "freedom of their country" by washing the men's boots.

Not content with this preliminary and suffering already from an aching corn, Phillips enquired through Herbert whether the African priests might prefer to wash his bare feet, urging the rest of the party to remove their boots and socks and to have their feet washed.

Sweaty, stinking feet relieved of their stench and damp socks wrung dry of perspiration, the priests asked for the customary "dash", or backsheesh as a reward for their labours, but were told by Phillips that they would have to await the arrival of the "treasure chests", which were still being unloaded from the Ivy.

Charlie, always anxious to avoid any unpleasantness, had begged a couple of cigarettes from Alex and quietly slipped them to the head priest by way of a small reward.

Somewhat refreshed, they made their way towards Gwatto, passing another juju in the form of a newly-killed chicken, which hung from a tree bordering the narrow path, its twisted neck drooped, blood still dripping from its severed head and entrails bursting from its bloodstained body.

Blood red clay was the basic building material of the forty or so dilapidated mud huts which formed Gwatto village, with the invasive bush growing up between them.

The chief's house where the British party had been invited to sleep for the night was at its centre. It was a more elaborate construction, with thicker walls, that had been buffed and polished to a glass-like finish until they shone, reflecting the sinking sun, filtered through the magnificent trees of the great forest that surrounded them, with rich dark mahoganies and canwoods forming a glorious backdrop.

The chief himself was away at Benin City, but he was represented by his eldest son, who provided a warm welcome. A young man who had only recently reached manhood, he wore several narrow coral necklaces, which were the mark of the ruling classes and were highly prized by the chieftains and rich men of the Benin River.

He walked to the sound of jangling hawks' bells, attached with little leather throngs to his ankles, swishing a horse tail against flies and other insects, which buzzed and droned around his head, surmounted by a black top hat, no doubt presented to him by some former missionary, or a trader anxious to bestow favours and impress with gifts from another world.

Most striking of all was the strange mark on his right hand, which left a circle of pink on his otherwise jet black skin. Charlie was the first to notice it and, through one of the interpreters, he questioned the young man as to how he had sustained the injury.

He learnt that it was a "birthmark", not naturally imprinted, but branded on the upturned hand of the child when it was only a few hours old by the elders of the village to mark out the eldest son of the headman of the village and a boy child born to be a future chief.

It looked for all the world like a leopard's head, its open mouth snarling and bearing its teeth, whilst piercing eyes glowed and glowered from the young man's knuckles.

Another member of the expedition, Lieutenant Arthur Maling, a man in his late twenties, a little older than both Alex and Charlie, even met up with an old "friend" called Mary Boma – a Benin City chief, who must have known about the murderous preparations being made but, who, despite his protestations of friendship, uttered not a single word of warning of the fate which awaited the party the very next day.

Chapter 6

James Phillips was extremely angry that the Gwatto Chief had left only his eldest son to meet and greet such an important official as the Acting Consul General and his entourage of traders, army officers and officials and took it as a slight.

However, after spending some time talking with the Chief's son, he was appeased to learn that the king had sent down three "Big men" from Benin City to provide an escort for the visitors.

The three courtiers from the Oba's palace were rather elderly and, with their wizened features, had the appearance of left-over prunes.

Their demeanour was grave, but the Gwatto tribesmen and women obviously held them in high esteem, serving them and their white men guests a whole host of delicacies, some of which Alex, with his weak stomach, was keen to avoid.

The elders had arrived to inform the party that the Benin king had sent them to serve as escorts, but that they should all remain at Gwatto for another two days, so that the Oba would have plenty of time to make all the necessary arrangements. If only they had known just what those arrangements were to entail!

By way of reply, James Phillips was insistent that, now they had come this far and as the Benin king was such a friend – not only to himself, but also of the Great White Queen, on whose behalf he was to make an additional, much bigger gift, they should delay no further, adding that he could not afford to lose a single day.

After some argument, the "Big men" finally agreed to accompany the party the next morning and to send a messenger to Benin City to announce their impending arrival, packing him off with a lamp, a bottle of gin and a length of cloth by way of reward, together with Captain Boisragon's silver-topped malacca cane walking stick as a sign that they were genuinely on their way.

The Jakri carriers were summoned by Kenneth Campbell and shown where to gather kindling, wood and water in readiness for an early departure the next morning.

Despite the amount of palm wine that he had imbibed, Alex found that sleep evaded him and Charlie, stretched out in a makeshift bed beside him, also felt uneasy.

Somehow he did not believe that the Benin king would give in so easily and resign himself to the need to welcome white men into his city – especially when he had more important things to do, such as sacrificing slaves in memory of his father and presiding over the initiation ceremonies of the young tribesmen, as they passed into manhood.

Their dark, ebony skin was branded with the mark of the leopard and their initiation rites were watched over by the ancient queen of Benin, whose bronze head occupied the sacred stone in front of the altar where the high priests would conduct their age old, ritualistic branding of generations of her subjects.

Charlie also had his doubts that the "Big men" would turn up the next morning to accompany the party on to the city where so much blood had been shed over the past centuries.

He doubted too the motives and loyalty of Basilli, their guide, who had behaved none too well five years previously when another British contingency had visited Benin City.

Charlie couldn't put his finger on it, but there was some strange reason why Basilli was not talking to his own people, except when helping the two other interpreters to clarify matters for Phillips. No, Charlie did not trust Basilli.

Something was wrong.

Twelve men were seated at a richly polished mahogany table surrounded by mud huts in the middle of the West African bush. At Phillips' insistence, the burnished table top had been carried from the steam yacht moored close by.

It was delivered into the African night and deposited on upturned boxes, illuminated by tiny lamps floating in clay dishes, containing palm oil into which the servants had floated thin strips of cloth saturated with oil each acting as a wick.

No one could have guessed that for many of the twelve men, it was to be their last supper!

All around them, squatting mostly cross-legged on the earthen floor were the Jakri carriers and Kroo boys, giggling, their bellies full and warmed by any one of a number of big wooden fires, which sent sparks dancing up into the African night, like a hatching of fireflies.

No, something was wrong!

The Acting Consul General had been the last to retire to his camp bed that night, sitting on his campaign chair, writing to the captain of the Ivy by the light of a few candles and the still lively light of the surrounding camp fires.

"I think we shall be back in a fortnight", he wrote, admitting that, "we have been threatened and solemnly warned at every step that the soldiers of the king of Benin are waiting to fire upon us, if we dare to land at Gwatto. So much so that, in a moment of panic, I sent back the band, for which I am sorry now.

"We have had a palaver with the representatives of the Benin standing army, which ended in great hilarity and general goodwill. They propose to accompany us at daybreak to the City of Benin. Chief Dore did his level best to frighten us out of going but, so far, we have had no opposition and I don't think we shall have any at all".

Alex had already turned in to bed, but sleep evaded him. He drew the rough army blanket up under his chin, just as, hundreds of miles away in the tiny Edinburgh attic, his wife, Mary, drew a similar blanket over herself and Alex's daughter, Anne, at the same time comforting baby Robert, as the mother and her two children struggled to find warmth.

Unlike Mary, living in abject poverty, sharing little more than a bowl of broth with her eldest child, having for months not seen a farthing of her husband's wages from Miller Brothers, Alex had enjoyed an African feast, even if some of the items it contained were not of his choosing.

Beset with chronic indigestion, he finally settled to a sleepless night. A chill wind blew through the cloudless African sky; the Harmattan wind blew down from the great Sahara Desert, bringing with it clouds of soft sand, which seeped into open pores and dried the throat, cracking lips and cheeks and mixed with as yet unshed tears, gluing eyes tight shut and unable to be prised open in the morning light.

Unshed tears for some of the men who slept and snored around him – tears as yet to course their way in tiny droplets down his wind-cracked cheeks.

Tears for the dying.

Tears for the dead.

* * * * * * * * * *

At seven o'clock on January 4th, the assembled carriers were lined up ready for departure and checked that none of their number was missing before being allowed to continue the journey.

The Acting Consul General was beseeched by many of the Gwatto people for "dash", or small presents as a reward for all that they had done the day before.

Most vociferous in their demands were the juju men, who had washed the feet of the travellers as, one by one, they had emerged at the top of the ladder for their first meeting with the men of Benin. In every single case and to each protestation, Phillips replied that they would receive their reward on the return leg of the trip.

Many of the men looked extremely disappointed by this steadfast refusal to reward them for their efforts. Maybe they knew what was in the wind.

It was the wind that had blown so sharp and cold the night before – the same ghostly, howling wind that had swept through an Edinburgh attic.

Nearly everything that the white men had brought with them would end up going to Benin City – unlike most of the members of the ill-fated expedition, who would never set foot in the City of Blood.

At half past seven that morning no trace remained of the large visiting shebang, save for the dying embers of the camp fires. With the exception of Charlie, the party set off in high spirits.

Alex's friend seemed to hang back, as if reluctant to finally make the departure for their final destination and for their ultimate destiny.

Charlie felt uneasy.

Something was definitely wrong!

It remained coolly comfortable at that time of the morning, as it was still the dry season. For Alex, the early shafts of sunlight penetrating the treetops made for a pleasant walk.

It seemed more like an afternoon stroll in the Royal Botanics where he had first shared a long, lingering, kiss with Mary than a tedious trek through a tropical rainforest.

The path along which they made their way was slightly broader than usual. Still it only permitted a single file procession, headed by Basilli, followed by James Phillips' orderly, a civil policeman called Jumbo dressed in a smart blue uniform and holding aloft a blue ensign – the Consul General's flag, decorated with the Protectorate's crest in its corner.

Marching behind the flag came Herbert, the interpreter and then, of course, at the head of the white line, James Phillips himself stepped out, followed by his minions – both black and white.

Everyone kept to his place, with the exception of Kenneth Campbell, who kept walking up and down the long line of carriers, often finding it difficult to squeeze past them on the narrow path, constantly checking that they were keeping up.

Gradually gaps would open up between them, as one man, perhaps with a particularly heavy load, would lag behind his companions in front and the whole of the remaining line would be forced to slow.

As a result, and much to Kenneth Campbell's annoyance, the two hundred strong assembly of carriers must easily have straggled for nearly a mile backwards along the track.

Unencumbered by the heavy loads hoisted on the heads and shoulders of the carriers, the rest of the party found the going relatively easy. For the most part the path itself was smooth and flat and free from creepers and roots which snatched at the legs, anxiously trying to entrap unwary feet, plunging their owner flat on his face.

Most bush paths in West Africa were hideously overgrown on all sides so that, whilst trying to prevent a twig from gouging your eye out, you often ran up against the hidden trunk of a sapling tree, bruising your forehead and, if you were particularly unlucky, causing a shining black eye.

Trees both large and small intermingled their branches, all woven together in a tapestry without beginning or end. Below a dense carpet of shrubbery concealed lengthy, evil-looking thorns, which pierced all but the stoutest pair of leather breeches, whilst flies emerged, as if from nowhere, to feast on the oozing blood.

At each of the three villages passed through during the morning's march, the line of carriers was halted to allow everyone to catch up and drink from the rainwater reservoirs, made from smooth, heavily beaten clay.

Appreciating the health danger of drinking from such fly-blown sources, extra carriers had been employed to allow Phillips and his party to take with them a sufficient supply of clean drinking water to last the whole of the ten-day expedition.

At all three stopping points, some of the village men came out to greet the strangers, grinning their often toothless smiles from round, boot-black faces. They seemed genuinely welcoming, offering nuts from the huge kola trees, which grew around the perimeters of most West African villages.

Great crowds would gather, including some of the village women, anxious to cajole pinches of tobacco and cigarettes from the white men and even finding a use for their empty bottles of stout.

One chief, dressed in an old red tunic, with white metal buttons and carrying an ancient black umbrella with several of the spokes broken was particularly welcoming and went into a long speech which, as Charlie observed, Basilli's few scant words could not possibly have served to translate.

To Charlie's maybe over-cautious mind, the chief was scared. Maybe he was offering a warning.

Something was undoubtedly wrong!

* * * * * * * * * *

At eleven o'clock the decision was made to halt and have breakfast. By Lieutenant Maling's calculations, they had marched for maybe seven or eight miles.

At this point the party was joined by the "Big men" of Benin City, together with Mary Boma, who Charlie noticed was led away by the village men for what seemed like a very long and secret discussion.

Charlie voiced his suspicions to James Phillips, who sat on his campaign chair, with the African guide, Basilli, squatting on the ground at his feet.

'I've told you before, Paterson, we've come here for what the natives call a "peaceful palaver". Now away with you and your suspicious mind,' he said angrily.

'We will not be attacked, I can assure you! Besides, we represent Queen Victoria – the Great White Queen. The Benin king has accepted our gifts and knows that we come in peace. No harm will come to us this day, or any other day.'

It was nearly one o'clock before the party made a move again, passing two more villages at which they stopped for a few minutes to allow the carriers to close ranks.

Soon afterwards the party must have walked past nearly a mile long line of Benin warriors lying in wait no more than twenty, or thirty yards from the path, waiting for the chance to launch their attack, their presence undetected, hidden in the lush vegetation, as silent as a leopard stalking its prey.

In places the muzzles of the natives' guns reached almost to the path, but they were so well hidden that even Phillips, at the head of the column, walked past most of the awaiting ambush, totally unaware of its existence ... and its threat!

A short distance from the path lay Egbini, the war camp on the Gwatto Road. All the senior chiefs had sent men here, among them the chief responsible for the capture of sacrificial victims.

At Egbini some of these soldiers had been living in makeshift mud huts for many months, waiting for their orders to launch an attack on the British.

At this point the bush had grown sparse, although it bore no signs of recent cutting. Here the path was cut deeper, with the banks on either side extending to a much greater height, stretching upwards towards the sky, which was no longer so completely blocked from view.

The vegetation had been carefully cut, so as not to reveal its sparsity to the uninitiated, but throughout the area, which ran parallel to the main path from Gwatto to Benin City, a series of ambush paths had been cut by order of the chiefs.

According to Lieutenant Arthur Maling, they had tramped a further five or six miles since stopping for a breakfast of bully beef, accompanied by bottles of Irish stout. Altogether they had travelled a distance of maybe thirteen miles.

By his own reckoning, it was another thirteen miles to their ultimate destination – an unlucky thirteen miles to what, for many members of the party, would be their ultimate death.

Chapter 7

By this time, everyone was pretty well convinced that the Acting Consul General's assertion that, the next day, they would reach Benin City and even Charlie, for all his pessimism, was reluctantly resigned to parting with his last full packet of cigarettes to Alex as the loser of the bet.

The discussion centred around how they would all drink Her Majesty's health for the first time that it had ever been celebrated in Benin City in this her Diamond Jubilee Year or, indeed, at any time before by such a large party of white men in this God forsaken place.

Tripping over a stray bramble which crossed his path and had entangled itself in his bootlaces, Alex bent down to free himself, allowing Charlie and the rest of the party to overtake him.

Bending low, he heard a single shot ring out behind him, ricocheting against a nearby fig tree, before winging its way harmlessly through the dense, wild woodland.

It was followed by a fusillade of gunfire.

Strangely, the Benin warriors had allowed the first column of white men to pass unharmed, especially as they had been told by the Benin City chiefs that if they did not kill all the white men, then they themselves would be killed instead.

It was only the dawdling Alex, plainly visible in his white shirtsleeves, who formed a possible target, as the ambushers opened fire on the head of the carrier column.

Maybe it was a salute in honour of the visiting band of white men, who had travelled so far to reach the outskirts of the African city.

However, any such thoughts were rapidly expelled by the bloodcurdling screams of pain and horror as, one by one, the African carriers began to fall, as volley after volley of bullets rained down upon them, smashing through soft skin and sinew before ricocheting off in all directions and burying themselves deep into the boles of the forest trees.

Alex kept low, ducking beneath the level of the undergrowth, anxious to find Charlie and even more eager to seek out his revolver locked up in one of the trunks being transported along the jungle track by the Jakri carriers.

He dared not raise his back above the line of the dense vegetation that bordered the path that was masked in gun smoke for fear of providing a clear target.

He pushed past Lieutenant Arthur Maling sheltering behind a fallen tree trunk at the edge of the path, which had begun to rot and was providing food for an army of ants, swarming through the soggy, rotting pulp like a miniature black horde – just like the black army surrounding the members of the expedition and hungering for blood.

'We've got to get our guns!' whispered Maling, addressing no one in particular, anxious that his words travelled no further than to Alex and Kenneth

Campbell, who was next in line, crouching in open-mouthed fear behind a bush, which offered practically no protection at all from the singing bullets.

It was left to Alex to make his way on hands and knees to the front of the line, for he knew that it was the Acting Consul General who held the key to the trunk containing their revolvers and who, quite possibly, held the key to their survival.

'No revolvers, gentlemen,' came the authoritative voice of their leader.

Alex was at a loss to understand Phillips' orders and also concerned to know what had happened to Charlie.

Maybe he had been shot in the first volley. Maybe he lay wounded somewhere and was unable to move.

Maybe he was dead.

Alex called out for number 13, the Kroo boy who carried his camp bed. Unknown to the Acting Consul General, Alex also carried a small hand pistol wrapped in his bed roll, but the young boy had bolted at the sound of the first shots, disappearing into the dense undergrowth, discarding his bundle, as he sought to save himself from the Benin brutes, who were all around them.

Alex never saw the boy alive again. Maybe he would be taken captive and taken back to the City of Blood, for enslavement, ritualistic torture and eventual sacrifice on one of the crucifixion trees draped with the dead and dying.

Maybe he would be one of the lucky ones and would be killed outright, as he searched for his own salvation.

Alex inched further down the path to try to locate the discarded bed pack containing his pistol, or maybe even to find the trunk containing the revolvers, with the idea that he would break it open, using his bare hands if necessary, despite Phillips' forbidding instructions.

Making his way slowly forwards, Alex was sickened at the sight of the result of one of the first attacks. Half a dozen bodies of the Jakri carriers lay in a bloody, mangled heap on a strip of road about fifteen or twenty yards long.

They had been shot dead, their bare bodied, black, glossy upper torsos peppered with bullets, which had punched crimson holes through their chests and their heads had been sliced off with machetes.

Sticky blood oozed from a multitude of tiny, glowing craters in their pockmarked skin, like the eruptions of miniature volcanoes. Each neck, unsupporting of a head, spilt treacly blood on to the earthen floor, as swarms of flies gathered to celebrate the dance of death.

Alex wanted to be sick, to puke his guts out to mingle with the dismembered body parts that littered the path ahead. He tripped and fell as his boot touched a head which had rolled across the red clay soil, streaking it with rapidly congealing blood.

He picked himself up again and found himself looking straight at the brass-bound trunk containing the guns. His way into it was guarded only by the sentry who sat bolt upright and dead, his bodily weight lessened by the lack of a head.

Alex roughly pulled the carcase to one side, looking all around him for any movement in the trees, which would announce the lurking presence of a would-be attacker.

He searched around for something with which to burst open the lock, but found nothing but short lengths of branches, snapped off from the overhanging trees and now littering the forest floor. They offered no way into the trunk.

Alex was joined by Lieutenant Maling. Together they dragged the blood-spattered trunk into the undergrowth. The lieutenant had lost his own revolver and was hoping that the firearms contained within the trunk might offer them some scant protection from the outnumbering marauders, who surrounded them.

'Are you sure, that's where the guns are?' asked Maling, mouthing his words, through dried, cracked lips.

'I think so and sod Phillips and his orders not to shoot.'

'Don't worry about him. He's been shot dead.'

'What do we do now? Do we try to make it back to Gwatto?' asked Alex, realising at once the folly of his suggestion, for if the survivors kept to the paths parallel to the surrounding bush, the Benin warriors would have no problem at all shadowing them and shooting them down, one by one, as they went along. They would be sitting ducks.

Herbert, the interpreter, joined them, along with Baddoo, the Acting Consul General's cook, who would make his master's meal no more. As the three of them melted back into the shelter of the rainforest, a slender Jakri carrier hurtled past them, bleeding from a long slash down his right arm.

Hoisted on his back was a Kroo boy of a similar age, who had been badly wounded in the foot and who was obviously incapable of taking a step for himself. His left ankle was a mass of blood and his foot was twisted at right angles, torn off and hanging by its tendons.

As he ran, the Benin men began shooting at him and he fell with the heavy load of the dead weight on his back. The injured Kroo boy's body was peppered with bullets.

Some of the bullets had passed through his frail, slender frame, also piercing the body of his rescuer, who had managed to crawl away across the damp forest floor, filling his fingernails with earth, as he grasped the leaf-strewn ground, stricken with agonising pain and desperate to escape.

Kenneth Campbell had been urging his Jakri carriers onwards to plug the gaps in the line when Alex had heard the first volley of shots ring out, so there was little doubt in his mind that poor Kenneth had quickly met his end.

The Benin fiends kept up a running fire at the dwindling ranks of carriers, scything them down in repeated bursts of gunfire, like the blackened heads of over ripe corn that was only fit for silage.

Where was Charlie?

Unable to make good his escape, one member of the British party was deploying desperate measures to avoid his impending fate. He was trying to stop being fired at by going through the form of the Benin salutation.

Alex spotted him standing some way into the bush, nodding his head like a wise old Chinese mandarin and rubbing his hands slowly up and down, muttering "Adoo, Adoo?" which, in the Benin tongue, amounted to "How do you do?"

By way of an answer, a Benin soldier crept up behind him and severed his head with a machete.

Alex's boss, the fellow trader, Harry Powis, the only member of the party who could string together a few words in the native language was seen pleading with the attackers.

He disappeared around a bend in the path. Alex never saw him again and could only imagine his fate.

Towey, the African interpreter, was captured, screeching and howling fit to shit his bright blue knickerbockers. He was quickly put to death, presumably because he spoke the white man's tongue and had effected their dress.

He squealed like a pig, as the machete-wielding warrior hacked off first one arm and then the other, before chopping his legs off at the knees, leaving him screaming in agony, as he stood upright for a second, balanced precariously on the stumps of his knees, his blood and brown-stained knickerbockers suddenly reaching the ground, before he toppled backwards, presumably left in the bush limbless and in limbo, awaiting death.

Lieutenant Maling and Alex made another effort to break the lock on the trunk, which contained the revolvers, scrabbling with broken, bloodied nails to force the lid open, but it refused to budge.

Basilli, the Benin City guide, was unhurt and soon Alex saw him approaching one of the Benin soldiers, who was cold-bloodedly blasting the remaining Jakri carriers into oblivion. Basilli calmly whispered something in his ear. It was obvious that he was in no fear of any threat to his own life.

So Charlie was right to suspect him of treachery, but where was Charlie?

Their attempts to arm themselves were useless. There was no way of breaking the lock. Forest floor sticks were no match for toughened Sheffield steel.

There was only one thing left to do – charge into the bush whenever any of the Benin City soldiers looked set to fire armed with the only weapons they could lay their hands on – stout sticks plucked from the forest floor.

Surprisingly, the tactic worked and invariably the ambushing army took to its heels and fled. Captain Boisragon came upon one warrior, who was chasing some to the last remaining carriers through the bush.

He quickly collared his gun and machete.

The captain gave the gun to Baddoo and the machete to Herbert, before bravely rushing off to repeat the performance and provide the sorry straggle of survivors with more weapons with which to defend themselves.

Captain Boisragon came next upon one of the Benin messengers, shouting manically, as he waved a machete around his head. He chased him into the bush, but the African's long, athletic legs outpaced the thirty-seven year-old captain, who eventually had to give up the chase.

Alex was hit by a volley of small shotgun pellets, several of which struck him in the forehead, one just missing his right eye. He dug into the pocket of his breeches for a handkerchief, which was soon soaked with his own blood.

Much of the ammunition being used by the Benin troops was pot leg, made by smashing up iron cooking pots into small, rough, jagged pieces.

Captain Copford-Crawford had a whole volley of pot leg discharged into his groin from close quarters and died in agony, after being carried away from the scene of his ambush by two of his comrades and imploring them to leave him to die.

Together in a small clearing Captain Boisragon and Alex came across another injured member of the party; both his legs had been blasted with pot shot and a jagged wound gaped from his thigh.

It was obvious that he was unable to walk and clearly he understood the gravity of his situation, imploring the two men to leave him and make good their escape.

The last Alex saw of him was some few minutes later, when he was surrounded by Benin soldiers, who had gathered around him like a flock of sheep.

Alex did not want to think of what happened next, but from the single English curse and the bloodcurdling cry of anguish that rung out though the forest, he could well imagine the other man's fate.

These sheep were dressed in wolf's clothing.

Somewhere in the distance Alex heard the beating of a big drum. Maybe it wasn't far away at all. Echoing through the forest scene of this bloody massacre, it seemed to come from all sides at once – a drum dance of the Devil, mysterious and weird, resonating all around like a call from the depths of Hell.

'My God, the war drum!' said Herbert in an announcement that hardly needed making, for this was war – there was no doubt about that!

He clapped his hands over his ears, as if the act of masking his hearing would save him from the fate that had already befallen so many.

Where was Charlie? Had he fallen too? Had he gone like a lamb to the slaughter?

Alex crawled on his belly, stalking through the undergrowth like a big cat intent on catching its prey. He stumbled upon one of the Kroo boys, who he recognised by dint of the number 13 painted ridiculously on his back and the multi-coloured woollen knitted hat that he wore.

The young African boy had carried Alex's camp bed and had proved a particularly jovial character, urging Alex to teach him a few basic words of English and bumming the odd cigarette.

He lay beside the dried up bed of a tiny forest stream, lined with fair sized boulders that had not been immersed in water for many months.

He lay on his side, writhing in agony, with his stomach ripped open.

The number 13 had not proved lucky at all!

Blood and gore spilled on to the forest floor, staining the stones and seeping into cracks in the dried out bed of the stream.

Alex searched around for Baddoo, who held the only gun, anxious to put a bullet through the boy's brain and end his agony, but realised that he was completely alone.

Besides he could not fire off a shot, even if he had the means of doing so, for he did not dare to run the risk of attracting the Benin beasts to his place of relative concealment.

Silently, Alex picked up a fist-sized flat rock and slammed it into the back of the boy's skull. It was all he could do for him.

Now Alex really was on his own, bleeding profusely from the pot-shot wounds in his forehead, his blood-soaked handkerchief no longer able to absorb any more of the lifeblood that flowed from him.

He felt dizzy. His legs began to crumble beneath him. He fell to his knees and crashed into the dried out bed of the stream, on top of the dead boy, whose blood mingled with his own. He tasted black man's blood. He tasted his own.

He raised his head, painfully, as the swirling tops of the rainforest trees cavorted and spun around him, kicking up their skirting foliage like music hall dancers.

Who was dead? Who was still alive?

Was he himself among those who were still living, or was he slipping slowly, inexorably towards his own death?

Thoughts swirled, memories twisted in his mind, passing sails in the setting sun of his own consciousness, until all was pitch-black darkness.

And where was Charlie?

Chapter 8

Alex awoke to darkness and to the bitter taste of blood, dried and caked around his lips in a crust that sealed them together, moulding his mouth into silence. He had no idea how long he had remained among the pebbles and boulders of the dried out stream bed.

He felt something beneath him, soft, black, velvet skin, now taut and stiffened and starched in death, a body once soft and pliant, now rigid and rock hard – as hard as the rocks that shielded him from view, that had shielded Alex from certain death.

Maybe it was the way he had fallen – in a tangle of legs and arms that had entwined his bloody with that of the dead Kroo boy. Only his white skin gave credence to the fact that there were two bodies – not one, but so little of his dirtied, blackened skin remained its normal colour.

Likewise, his once white shirt was now the colour of the clay floor. His arms, caked in the blackening, congealed blood could so easily have belonged to a black man. His dark-coloured breeches were of a similar hue to the dead Kroo boy's bare legs and his face was a mass of dirt and debris.

Only the eerie sounds of the African night punctuated his waking thoughts. Strange, haunting sounds rang through the tree-top canopy, as unfamiliar creatures proclaimed their territories.

Alex listened to the sounds of the night, alert for any sign of a human voice or, more threateningly, the sharp crack of a dry stick under a man's footfall.

His mouth was parched, dry and sore, as if he had been coughing through the night. His head pounded with the steady war drum beat of the Benin marauders.

His breeches were stiffened and his legs were chaffed, as if he had slept on rough horsehair bursting out from a hole in a mattress.

How long had he slept? How badly was he injured? What length of time had he been there? Was it night, or was it day?

Slowly, Alex began to ease his bulk from the dead boy, stretching his aching sinews, flexing his calf muscles and extending his toes into socks which smelt of damp, death and decay.

His brain wasn't functioning properly, but slowly he began a methodical inspection, first of his aching legs and then of his other limbs.

He could sit up, despite his dizzy demeanour, slowly focussing, as his sight grew accustomed to the darkness. He rubbed dirt and debris from his eyes with hands that fingered his face, in an anxious exploration of his visage.

He pressed his tongue, first against his teeth, working its way along the rows of ivory coloured molars and then against his blood caked lips until it stuck out from his mouth, as if in a childish taunt.

Alex wanted a drink, to assuage his desperate thirst, so he reached for his water bottle and shook its last dripping contents down the back of his throat and ran his moistened tongue across rough, cracked lips that tasted bittersweet.

He staggered to his feet, resting his bulk against one of the boulders, which had hidden him from view and probably saved his life. His whole body swayed, as the first rays of morning light penetrated the overhead canopy.

Something nestling among the leafy debris on the forest floor caught the light, sending diagonal shafts of shimmering reflection off in every direction. He bent down and picked up his compass, its glass face cracked and splintered, but with its little dial still bobbing and bouncing.

It had been given to him by Mary as a Christmas gift the year that little Anne had been born. She had worked long extra shifts, helping her sister out at the wash-house, scraping together the pennies before spreading them out in a long, triumphant line on the counter of the pawn shop in Morningside, so proud to have achieved her goal.

He clutched the little round, gold-plated directional globe in his fist and tears of relief began to flow, coursing their way down his cheeks, channelling a path through congealed blood and dirt, until he tasted their saltiness on his cracked lips.

He lurched to the ground, clutching Mary's gift, rolling himself into a tight, defensive ball, protecting himself from the unknown horrors that surrounded him. He rejoiced in finding the precious compass, which might prove his only saviour in this God-forsaken land.

He had never cried before – at least not since the age of six or seven, when the local policeman had caught him stealing oat cakes from the back of the horse-drawn delivery cart and given him a sharp clip round the ear, before marching him off by his collar to the blacksmith's shop where his father, availed of the tale, took off his belt and gave his son a damn good leathering bent double over the anvil, unheeding of the youngster's screams.

Alex Seath was not an emotional man, but right now he cried for his own salvation, for the lives of his companions hacked to death by a cowardly gang of savages on foreign soil.

He cried too for his special friend, Charlie, no doubt butchered and quartered like a side of pork, poked like a pig, chopped to pieces and left to die in the dirt.

He alone had survived – somehow he was sure of that and, remarkably, apart from the pot shot wounds in his forehead, he was unscathed.

The blood which drenched his outer clothing and the guts which had been spewed over him, were not his own. Only the sodden handkerchief, which he had held to his forehead, was soaked with his own blood.

He could walk and he could speak – only there was no one to talk to here in this inhospitable forest of fury, where furious fighting had broken out with an enemy who had purported to be a friend.

Here there was no one who spoke his own tongue, no one who hadn't had his tongue ripped out, or his head sliced through with a sharp machete.

Alex had to get back to Gwatto, to return along the road he had come, but taking such a route was fraught with danger. If he attempted to retrace his footsteps, the Benin soldiers, or their lookouts, would surely report the existence of this sole survivor and his destiny would be no different from that of his friends, who had already been dealt the hand of death.

He remembered being told that the Gwatto Creek bent round to the right and eastwards so that, with the aid of Mary's compass, if he steered a northwesterly course through the thick jungle, there was just a chance that he could find his way back to the creek and to the awaiting steam yacht.

Going to Gwatto itself was out of the question, as the Benin soldiers were always sent to guard the waterside towns. They would surely deduce that any survivors would make their way there. It was the obvious destination and, therefore, one to be avoided at any cost.

Without a machete, or an axe, it was virtually impossible to walk more than a few yards in any one direction in the bush without coming up against one obstacle or another.

True, Alex had his pocketknife, but that was it – a pocketknife, a small compass and a water bottle that he had already drained dry of its contents.

In places the vegetation was like a thick, impenetrable wall. Often Alex was forced to resort to crawling on his hands and knees, dragging himself along the ground like a sick and ailing serpent, tearing the palms of his hands and scratching his knees on tiny flints embedded in the clay floor.

Occasionally, a fallen tree would create a patch of clearing, which opened up the sky above, but Alex did his best to avoid such intermissions in the overhead canopy, forcing his way through the tremendous mass of undergrowth beneath, crouching and slithering for fear of being seen.

Sometimes when the underlying shrubbery was just too thick, he managed to get through by jumping as far as possible into the middle of it and emerging on the other side.

From time to time, exhausted by his own efforts and where the undergrowth was particularly thick, he would reward himself with a brief rest before tackling the obstacle, always aware that unseen eyes might be observing him and tracking his every movement.

He proceeded in a northwesterly direction, guided by Mary's small compass. Sometimes he was forced to deviate from his intended route, especially at the borders of the plantations, where all the cleared vegetation had been heaped together at the edge, forming an effective barricade to his progress.

At the edge of these plantations, with their black walls of undergrowth and rotting vegetation, he was particularly wary, not wishing to show himself in the open.

Trails of thorns lashed his already bloodstained face and soon there was barely an inch of his anatomy that wasn't cut and torn – sometimes by the hardened palm-tree thorns, with their razor sharp tips as thick as a darning needle and at other times by the smaller, pricking prongs of the creeper that straggled over the undergrowth. These thorns were like the barbs of a fish hook, casting in every direction, like miniature mantraps with Alex as the catch of the day.

Sometimes he would even be forced to proceed backwards against the tide of undergrowth, picking the thorns from the exposed parts of his flesh as he went.

Soon his khaki riding breeches were a mass of tiny tears, as if someone had set about them with a razor blade. What remained of the original fabric might have been woven into narrow sheets of corrugated iron – just like the mass of material demanded by the Benin king to repair the roofs of his stores, as they were perfectly stiff and starched hard by the blood and gore which had penetrated them when Alex had laid for so long on top of the dead Kroo boy.

Alex's gaiters saved him from the worst of the onslaught below the knee, but his cuts attracted a multitude of biting insects and mosquitoes, which came to feast on his blood, biting into his knees where a single stray pot-shot pellet had grazed his knee cap, creating a deep furrow in the sparse flesh around the bone.

Thinking about the carnage that he had left behind him only added to the hopelessness of Alex's position. It weighed on his mind, like a giant fairground sledgehammer that only the strongest man in the world would ever lift.

Occasionally, the bush would thin out for a stretch and Alex would find himself running for a while, anxious to put as much distance between himself and his would-be attackers, but never certain from which direction the next attack might come.

Once he thought he could hear the yells and shouts of the Benin soldiers close behind him. It was as if he was being followed, as if he was being tracked down like a rat in a trap. Perhaps they had taken their fill of blood for the time being.

Perhaps the opportunity to loot and steal from the abandoned bundles and to smash open the cabin trunks to reveal what treasures they held had proved too much to resist.

A bale of cloth was worth more than any white man's head, a pouch of tobacco more eagerly twisted between the fingers than a Kroo boy's intestines; a bottle of soda water popped open and allowed to spill its foaming contents more readily than the contents of a macheted stomach.

The Benin men were obviously anxious to remain close to the main path, where they could pick over the spilt loot, arguing and gesticulating over a favoured length of cotton, or keen to be the first to burst open one of the boxes with a swipe at the lock with a well-aimed machete, sometimes resorting to smashing through the lid in their impatience to get at its contents.

At one point a fresh volley of gunshots resounded through the forest, probably indicating that a small group of escaping Jakri carriers had been caught up and slaughtered, belying any thoughts that Alex might have had that the bloodthirsty bastards could ever satiate their blood lust.

It was difficult to determine what distance he might have travelled, stumbling over fallen tree trunks, zigzagging his way through the jungle in an attempt to avoid detection. He had been on the move since dawn and, judging by the height of the sun, it was now approaching midday.

Alex doubted whether he had journeyed more than two or three miles, when he came across a plantation larger than any that he had seen before.

With every possibility of being seen and sudden death a consequence of any such observation, he ran across the open space as quickly as his tired legs would carry him.

On the opposite side he met one of the black walls of cleared vegetation and thick, impenetrable undergrowth. He looked anxiously around for some form of gap, or a relatively easy place to thrust his aching limbs through to the other side. It was like Hadrian's Wall, seemingly stretching for mile upon mile.

He had no option but to charge his way through at the nearest point, tearing the tattered remains of his filthy shirt to ribbons. Its ragged remains clung to his sweating back like mussels clinging to their shells awaiting their fate at the hands of Newhaven fishwives.

Finally, in the failing light of the late afternoon, he could go no further. As darkness descended, it brought with it a kind of calm, as if the Benin warriors were temporarily rendered incapable of acting like stalking cats in the night, like leopards ready to leap.

Alex sat, supporting his back against the broad circumference of a hardwood tree, close to one of the clearings studded with slightly luminous mounds of parasitic growth, like a button-backed Victorian mahogany armchair with its small leather upholstery studs.

He remembered the last time he had sat in a chair like that in the Acting Consul General's study in his house on Plantation Hill in Old Calabar, a whisky and soda in his hand and a log fire burning in the highly polished lead blacked grate.

Now he was uncomfortable, tired to the point of exhaustion, hot and thirsty. What he would have given right now for a sparkling tumbler half full with old malt poured from a silver-topped decanter, ice cubes gently jangling like the sound of the cut glass stopper chinking against the Edinburgh crystal.

His swollen lips and mouth were rough and as dry as coarse grade sandpaper and in the fading light, the mosquitoes began to swell the ranks of biting insects, which were already intent on making him even more miserable than he could have ever imagined possible.

Oh God, if only he had anything to drink.

He had felt the need to urinate earlier in the day and had peed into his water bottle, carefully directing the flow, so that not a single drop had been wasted; raising its contents immediately to his cracked lips and supping the strong tasting yellow liquid.

If only he felt the need for another piss, maybe he could still produce enough to wet his lips and dribble his own foul tasting urine down his throat.

Occasionally he had found a squashed fig that the forest floor fauna had yet to forage and gratefully he would squeeze its last remaining juices on to his sun-struck, blood-baked lips.

In a tiny tree hollow close to the ground, he had squatted, lapping the water that Nature had provided, in the form of a makeshift wooden drinking bowl, spitting ants and other insects that had come to drink and drown from his mouth. He felt like a cat that had found the cream.

As Alex sat resting his broad back against the tree, he began to daydream of the back street bar in Edinburgh where he had gone with Charlie to wet the head of his newborn daughter, Anne, born six months after his marriage to Mary.

He recalled how everyone in the bar had insisted on buying him a drink and he had rolled home drunk, with Charlie propping him up at every step and singing the ditties of the day.

Mary, opening the door and smelling his distasteful breath, had made him spend the night in the coal-house for fear that his ribald behaviour would awaken their newly born daughter – not to mention the rest of the neighbourhood.

He shivered at the thought of that night, cold and dark, but which registered little on his scale of suffering, compared to shivering in the rapidly chilling African night air, devoid of little bar the scant remains of his shirt and with only a blood-soaked handkerchief to serve as both sheet and blanket.

He had not eaten for more than twenty-four hours, but he had no appetite. Any thought of food made his stomach heave.

Any thought of his own stomach made him think of the poor Kroo boy's intestines, sliced and quartered and seeping their vile, vomiting contents from great suppurating wounds.

He wanted to be sick.

Alex had only been sitting for a few minutes when he distinctly heard the sound of other voices. Strangers whose eerie whisperings rang softly through the night in words that he failed to recognise. Undoubtedly, the words uttered were those of an unintelligible Benin babble.

He froze.

The hairs on the back of his neck rose against the remains of his collarless shirt. Now he wanted to pee – now at last he could assuage his thirst, but fear froze him to the spot. He dared not move an inch.

With a looming certainty he knew that the time for his own inevitable death had ultimately arrived.

The voices appeared to be coming from the edge of the plantation, barely thirty, or forty yards from where he sat slumped against the tree.

A thick wall of undergrowth was all there was between them – all there was to prevent the Benin warriors from the execution of their duty – his execution.

Alex's time had come – he was quite certain of that. He would not allow himself to be taken prisoner – that was a fact that he clung on to with grim determination.

No, he would do something to make them shoot him, leap out and attempt to throttle them with his bare hands, if necessary. He crouched as low on the ground as possible. The sound of voices grew louder, as they made their approach.

Two men emerged together into the clearing, their heads bowed strangely, looking both left and right, as if they too had something to fear from the night. A rough blanket was draped over one man's head, shielding him from immediate sight.

He walked with a stick, a silver-topped malacca walking stick, no doubt looted from the dead body of its owner and the other man held a gun!

* * * * * * * * * *

Alex sat his ground, ready to leap forward in a last desperate effort to save himself from torment and torture. He would rather die here and now, than be dragged off into the bush for a ritualistic beheading, or to watch his own empty stomach being torn apart.

True, there were only two of them and one of them appeared to be walking with a limp, but the other man, the one whose face was not covered in a blanket was brandishing a gun and it was pointing straight at Alex, grasped steadily and unflinchingly in the African's fist, his finger poised on the trigger.

65

'Oh God, please let him shoot! Please let him shoot right now!' Alex whispered to himself in almost silent prayer.

He began ripping at his torn and tattered shirt with his left hand, gripping the cloth remnants in fear, tearing the cloth still further, exposing even more of his bare, bitten torso, offering a clear target – a clear bull's eye view of his heart, an explosion of his lifeblood, a death dealt swiftly and painlessly, as he breathed his last.

He closed his eyes, waiting for his final breath but, after a few moments, found himself still breathing and alive. Maybe it was a bluff.

Perhaps the gun was out of ammunition. Maybe the gun-totting warrior, so intent on proving his manhood, had already fired off every last bullet.

One bullet representing every token of his bravery, with nothing left but bravado.

In what would surely be the last moments of his life, Alex recalled the tale told to him by the late Acting Consul General, who had once sat a friendly African chief down with him to demonstrate the working of the maxims – the weapons that the native called "them guns that go pop, pop, pop, pop".

The old chief had been so delighted by the spectacle that he had insisted on wasting nearly five hundred rounds of ammunition, before he could finally be induced to stop pressing the trigger.

Strange the thoughts that came unbidden, when one was close to death. Instead Alex could have thought of his soon to be widowed wife, tucked up safely in their Edinburgh attic, but his mind ran only to his own helplessness and the lack of any weapon with which to defend himself.

If he rose to his feet and took a run at his adversaries, maybe he would live to tell the tale, then again maybe he wouldn't live another minute.

If he struck out at the weaker man first, the one who walked with the aid of a walking stick, then maybe his stronger companion would be forced to react, pumping bullet holes into Alex's scantily covered chest, soaking the last remaining scraps of white cotton with a splattering of bloody crimson.

Maybe, just maybe, if he launched himself at the man with the gun, he could smash his head against a tree, just like he had crushed the head of the Kroo boy with a rock from the stream.

If he could strike out silently, he could take on the limping warrior, who didn't appear to have a gun and murder him with his bare hands, without the sound of gunshot reverberating through the forest to alert the rest of the Benin army.

Yes, Alex had made his decision.

He pressed his back hard up against the tree, hoping to achieve maximum propulsion. In one bound he was on his feet, tackling the fitter, taller man in a flying rugby tackle, that brought his victim tumbling to the ground before he had any chance to regain his balance.

Alex clawed at his neck, like a leopard sinking its talons into his prey, pinning his would-be attacker to the ground, as the gun struck the earthen floor with a soft thud.

The other man, his head half concealed under the blanket, took a swipe at Alex with the silver-topped walking stick, striking him on the temple, which already ached with pot shot wounds.

It was a fairly feeble blow and Alex fended off the threatening walking cane, whilst grovelling in the dirt for the gun.

Ignoring the man armed only with the stick, Alex struck fists of fury into the face of the fiend who had surely sought him out with the intention of slaughtering the last survivor of the ill-fated Benin Expedition.

He was going to kill the bastard who, with his companions, had cooked up such a treacherous and final feast, whilst the twelve men ate their last supper at Gwatto, unaware that whilst they were enjoying a convivial banquet, the "Big men" of Benin, guided by Basilli, were taking the opportunity to inspect their stores, quickly discovering that the party had neither guns, nor swords with which to defend themselves.

Alex's fists continued to pummel into the face of the prostrate form, until all movement ceased. At last, he was able to scrabble for the gun, cocking the trigger and aiming straight at the man with the gun's lame companion, snatching the rough army blanket away from the hooded head and hunched shoulders of the second, smaller man, who stood in the gathering gloom, armed only with a silver-topped walking stick.

'What the fuck do you think you're up to?' demanded the normally more demure Charlie. 'You've just nearly killed the Acting Consul General's cook – the man who saved my life!'

Chapter 9

Alex clung to Charlie in utter relief, stunned into silence that his friend had survived the massacre, with no more than a fairly nasty gunshot wound in his leg. The two men hugged each other, finding solace and reassurance in the knowledge that they were both alive.

Alex luxuriated in sharing another man's warmth, as they wrapped their arms around each other in an embrace which contained no embarrassment.

Their faces were blackened with dirt and streaked with blood. They held each other close, like two lovers whose very lives depended on each other.

'I can't believe this,' spluttered Charlie. 'How are you my friend? I never imagined that anyone but Baddoo here had survived and now look what you've done to him. Is he going to be all right?'

'I guess he'll live,' intoned Alex.

'What about you, Charlie? How did you get away? Phillips is dead. So is Copford-Crawford. Campbell and Maling too. I saw Locke escape, but the bastards may have caught up with him. I don't know about the others. It was an absolute blood bath.

'They killed most of the carriers, murdering and mutilating them, the bastards. Charlie, you've no idea of the carnage they wreaked. It was like nothing I've ever seen … or would ever want to see again.'

'I witnessed most of it too,' replied Charlie quietly.

'Have you got any water?' asked Alex.

'Yes,' replied Charlie, 'but, first things first!'

Baddoo, the African cook, who had saved Charlie's life after he had been hit in the thigh with a whole charge of pot leg, fired from a distance of no more than half a dozen yards, had done his best to bind the white man's wounds with palm leaves, tied at the waist and knee with lengths of vine, the whole stitched as tightly as possible together, using a palm thorn as a needle.

The force of the blow had been sufficient to knock Charlie off his feet, bowled over like a shot rabbit, tumbling down an embankment before coming to rest hidden away from the scene of devastation and mass execution.

There he had remained for what seemed hours, until the horrors of the massacre had been pushed to the back of his mind, only to remain forever etched in his memory.

Charlie must have passed out, for he had no idea when the African cook had found him, cradling his head in his arms and offering him water from his own hip flask.

Now Charlie's saviour had begun to stir. Without another word and anxious to return the favour, Charlie bent beside his new-found fallen friend, his injured leg struck out at an awkward angle, as he filled the silver-plated cup, which formed the cap of his hip flask with all but the last few remaining drops of water, holding the vessel gently to the tall African's lips and cradling his head, as he allowed him to drink virtually all the remaining water supply.

'Hey, save some of that water for me,' chided Alex, only to be ignored by Charlie, who placed his hand over the long black fingers, grasping them lightly, as if to say "sorry" for the attack that Alex had just launched on his rescuer.

Meanwhile Alex checked the revolver, noting that it contained just two last bullets – one each for Charlie and he to hold at their heads, if they were attacked and captured.

Charlie said nothing.

Alex took the hip flask from his friend's hands, grateful for the last drops of liquid, savouring them on his tongue, before allowing them to drizzle down his parched and aching throat.

He was alive. Charlie was alive.

There was hope!

Together they would forge an alliance from which they could both grow strong, gaining strength and hope from each other.

Alex looked his friend over. He was in a pretty sorry state. His improvised palm leaf bandage was caked with dried blood. What little that was left of his thin serge trousers was quite something to behold, with a mass of tears that had left them even more shredded than his own shirt.

Some of the torn pieces were roughly stitched together with lengths of bush straw and joined in other places by the thick stemmed thorns of the palm trees – no doubt also the work of Baddoo.

Dressed in rags, Charlie looked like a Grass Market beggar, pleading for pennies in the gloomy shadows of Edinburgh Castle. And Alex didn't even have a good luck silver threepenny bit to offer him!

At last, Baddoo sat up, shaking his head, in an effort to rid it of the blows that Alex had rained down upon him. Urged on by Charlie, Alex bent down in supplication, finally seeking to say he was sorry, but all the while thinking that the African probably offered them their best means of salvation, for he would be better able to help them find a way back to the river and a way to survive with little or no water and without supplies. Baddoo placed his large hands on Alex's, smiling gently, as if to indicate that he understood.

'No palaver,' he murmured breathlessly. 'White man good. White man afraid,' he added, indicating that nothing more needed to be said.

Together the three men squatted on the ground, huddled in a heap, with Charlie drawing the protective blanket closely around them. They made for a sad and sorrowful trio but, at least, they were alive – for the time being!

Charlie groaned softly every time he was forced to move his injured leg and the banging sensation in Alex's head struck up a resonating drum beat, like the war drums that had echoed through the forest the day before, beating in time with the carnage as, one by one, heads had been hacked off in a harridan's hell of harrowing slaughter, each drum beat heralding the cessation of another heartbeat.

Alex shivered through the night. At one point he must have dozed and awakened to find that his hands were wrapped around Charlie's chest in an involuntary quest for warmth.

He withdrew them and felt the chill night air tingling his fingertips, his nails still full of dirt, as he had scrabbled along the forest floor in his earlier bid to escape the extermination of his fellow white men in a not so distant past, but one which now seemed like a lifetime ago.

When, at last, dawn broke and first Alex and then Charlie emerged from the grey army blanket that the three men had shared during a fitful and wakeful night, they found that there was no sign of Baddoo.

Maybe he had reckoned that he had a better chance of survival without the crippled Charlie and Alex, who lashed out with his fists first and asked questions later.

He had been their hope – perhaps their only hope of reaching the steam ship Ivy, which languished in a deep water channel, with Captain Child and his men unaware of the fate which had befallen the members of the expedition.

Alex cast his eyes around the gloomy forest punctuated by the early morning rays of sunlight, at times dazzled and unable to see; at other times his vision was fogged by the ethereal mist that rose, ghost-like, from the low lying vegetation. A phantom-like figure walked towards him, emerging from the swirling haze.

It was Baddoo, carrying two immense, dark, glossy green leaves, which he presented one each to Alex and Charlie. On their surface was a mass of tiny filaments to which drops of the morning dew clung precariously.

Baddoo squatted down on his haunches and mimed a licking action to his two comrades, before disappearing back into the mist again in search of more leaves, which he carried carefully back to the two men, repeating the exercise a dozen or more times, until they had licked their last.

Pointing to Charlie's hip flask, he indicated that he should be allowed to take it, disappearing for maybe twenty minutes or more back into the misting forest before returning with it, miraculously almost full to the brim with water carefully harnessed from overhead leaves, which he had bent low, funnelling their contents into the narrow neck of the leather bound container.

Finally, he disappeared once more, returning with a handful of overripe figs, dropped from the giant forest trees by a passing troupe of monkeys and for which he had been forced to do battle with a wild boar and her piglets in order to gain the prize, threatening them with a stick, but anxious not to use it to beat the bark of a nearby tree, for fear of alerting any remaining Benin soldiers to their presence and their plight.

After breakfasting with Alex and Charlie on the squashy fig pulp, Baddoo made a move to examine the latter's leg wound, carefully removing the layers of palm leaves wrapped around the other man's leg to reveal the cratered flesh, with its peppering of pot shot, around which hot, fiery blisters had already begun to form and from which a yellow, oozing pus had flowed.

Gently Baddoo squeezed each of the pustules between his thumb and forefinger, making Charlie wince, as the thick, putrid, creamy liquid discharged from each of his wounds, which Baddoo then dabbed clean with a damp leaf.

'Come!' he said at last. 'We go!'

Alex helped Charlie to his feet and Baddoo handed him the silver topped walking stick. Charlie wrapped his left arm around Alex's shoulder for support, leaning his weight heavily on both his friend and the cane, which he grasped tightly in his right hand.

Baddoo led the way, as Alex, in his turn, clung tightly to Mary's compass, like a precious partner, which they would follow to the ends of this hell on earth. Alex noted the course in which Baddoo struck out, observing too that the tiny brass hand pointed in exactly the same direction.

Charlie's body weight rested heavily upon him and soon his shoulders began to ache, but he said nothing, for fear that his friend would feel that he was becoming a burden.

Progress was slow and Alex often wondered how they managed to make any headway at all. Some of the undergrowth they battled through was like scaling a steeplechase and, at times, Charlie had to be carried over their heads by the two men to whom he owed his survival.

Alex had to summons all his strength, marvelling at his own stoicism.

It was remarkable what he could still manage to do when it came to saving his own life and that of the friend whom he had been so sure that he had lost.

Charlie was the only real friend he had ever had. He was the godfather of Alex's baby daughter, Anne, and got on well with Mary, for whom he would sometimes buy little gifts – a tiny bunch of violets from the flower seller at the Waverley Station, or maybe a bar of her favourite lavender soap, bringing a little unaccustomed luxury into her life.

When Anne had been born, he had presented the child with a hallmarked silver dressing table set, which cost far more than he could really afford.

Together the three men struggled through the jungle, avoiding the footpaths and maintaining an uneasy silence, for words could cost lives – their lives!

Their very existence hung so precariously in the balance in this dank, inhospitable world, where a snapping twig would resound through the forest like a fire cracker, revealing their whereabouts.

Here and there a disturbed troupe of monkeys would run screeching up into the forest canopy, broadcasting the presence of the interlopers into their world; these men who did not belong, who did not even want to belong for a moment longer than necessary to an environment in which they were the alien presence, one in which they were probably being hunted down at this very minute.

When darkness finally fell, Alex figured that they had probably covered no more than two or three miles, zigzagging around the obstacles which abounded in their path.

They had been forced to make frequent stops to permit Charlie to rest up and for Alex to allow his weary shoulder blades to untangle twisted muscles, tense and taut, like his forehead over which he had draped his blood-soaked handkerchief in an effort to prevent the perspiration from mingling with his pot-shot peppered skin, mixing salt with open wounds, which had yet to form scabs.

With no means of telling the time, they guessed it was about five o'clock when they eventually sat down to rest for the night. Alex had lost his favourite pocket watch, which he had left in his discarded jacket.

Charlie's own timepiece had rested useless and unwound in the remains of the trousers which Baddoo had ripped away from the white man's thighs when dressing his wounds and it had eventually fallen from his shredded pocket.

71

It now lay somewhere along the track that they had forced through the undergrowth, scrambled over by forest floor ants dragging away to their nest their insect victims whose time had come.

Hot, tired and thirsty, their water supply from Charlie's hip flask long since evaporated down parched, eager throats and with no dew-soaked leaves to quench their thirst, the two friends would have given anything for a cup of water, willingly trading all the worldly possessions from the world to which they sought to return for just a few sips of the substance upon which all life depended, aware that only the coming morning would provide them with a tiny well of water from which to drink.

They thought of little else, dropping their thoughts into the wishing well of their own desperate desire.

Suddenly, Baddoo held up a hand in silence, running his finger vertically down his lips, bidding the other two men to remain silent, as voices rang out through the surrounding bush from the edge of a plantation, which was only separated from where they sat by a thick wall of undergrowth on slightly higher ground.

'Benin!' Baddoo whispered almost silently.

Benin soldiers were cutting their way through the bush with machetes and the party was heading in the direction of the three recumbent men.

Alex fingered the trigger of the revolver, remembering that it only held two last remaining bullets – one each for Charlie and him.

He would hand Charlie the revolver and let him blow his brains out, before taking it in his own trembling hands, blasting his own grey matter into the black hole of oblivion.

It was all he could hope to do for his friend, one last favour, that would save them from an unholy end at the hands of the evil savages.

Baddoo would have to make his own way to eternity.

No words were spoken, but Charlie, seeing the glint of the metal revolver, sensed his friend's intention, for he too knew that their turn had finally come.

He thought for a moment about Alex's pocketknife, wondering if he plunged it into the Baddoo's racing heart, whether it might save him from the agony of torment and torture, but he was too weak to carry out the foul deed.

Besides the small blade was blunted, as it had been used too often in the day to hack away at the vines that lay across their path and to rip away the leafy dressings from Charlie's leg, each time they had been tenderly replaced by the attentive African cook.

Alex and Charlie crouched on the ground as low as they could, hearts beating fast, pulses racing inexorably towards the final curtain. Here the music hall show of their lives was rapidly drawing to a close – a final performance that would win no applause from anyone, as a party of about a dozen Benin soldiers approached their hiding place.

All of them were armed, some carrying the looted boxes and bundles, cutting their way through the bush, inching ever nearer to a last act of vengeance, a last, final beheading, a blast of bullets and a machete slashed across the white men's stomachs.

Alex handed Charlie the revolver, knowing that the first chamber contained one of the two precious bullets. Charlie took the pistol in shaking hands.

'Good-bye, Charlie. Good-bye, my friend!' whispered Alex.

Chapter 10

Baddoo broke cover. For a moment, as Alex quietly handed the revolver to Charlie, neither of them were aware that the two of them were quite alone, with just two bullets and their own fateful thoughts. Charlie put the gun to his temple, his finger twitching on the trigger.

He couldn't do it.

He didn't need to do it!

Baddoo had leapt to his feet, screaming and hollering, as he rushed headlong into the bush, leaping over fallen branches and crashing through the undergrowth whilst, in his wake, boxes and bundles were swiftly thrown to the ground, as the war-mongering natives set off in hot pursuit, machetes raised in an unholy alliance.

Charlie lowered the gun from his temple, unable, at first, to appreciate the full horror of the situation and unable to comprehend that Baddoo's bravery could herald a lucky escape for himself and his friend, as well as certain death for the African cook.

Alex had recognised one particular discarded trunk amongst the hastily deposited spoils of war. It was the one that held his revolver and its extra rounds of army issue ammunition.

Its domed top was already splintered and shattered. Instantly he recognised their good fortune – their one chance to arm themselves properly. Maybe it was their one and only chance to stay alive.

He left Charlie with the gun and crawled out into the clearing, scraping his knees on some rough stones that lay concealed amongst the leaf mould, but with his prize firmly in sight. No sentry lay in wait for him – all dozen Benin soldiers had rushed off into the gathering night intent on one more act of brutal savagery.

Alex hauled himself to his knees, feeling around inside the trunk, until his hand touched something cold and metallic, nestled in the folds of his jacket. He grabbed the bundle, clenching it in his right fist, as his other hand searched for something warm and woollen.

He located a couple of blankets and snatched them up, returning quickly and quietly to Charlie, aware that the snapping of a single twig underfoot would sound like a gunshot and could easily bring their would-be attackers racing back towards them in a raving rant, hell bent on his extinction and to deal the hand of death to his crippled friend.

Alex and Charlie huddled together in silence, pulling the two hastily snatched blankets around them in an effort to stop their teeth from chattering in fear of the fragility of their own continuing existence and in deference to the chill night air.

Alex checked the newly acquired gun and, finding it empty, quickly filled its chambers with bullets from the box, which he clutched in his left hand. He handed the fully loaded gun to Charlie, exchanging it for one that held only the two bullets intended for their own suicide pact and rapidly inserted more ammunition.

Now they were fully armed and ready to face their attackers. Twelve bullets with which to thwart a dozen men and probably no chance to reload. Every bullet was accounted for. Every bullet counted.

It was a blood-curdling shriek coming seemingly deep from the bowels of the earth that rent the night and which proclaimed that the Benin soldiers had begun their own gruesome gratification as soon as they had cornered their victim.

Baddoo fell to his knees, awaiting an ultimate meeting with his maker, as first one soldier, then another, swung down upon him the slashing blade of a machete, hacking at his body like demented butchers, crazily intent on slicing off the best cut of meat for themselves.

Tears ran down Charlie's face, spotting the metal gun barrel with salty wet splashes. His hand shook ever more violently, as he tried to control the trembling fingers that rested on the trigger.

He dropped the gun among the fallen leaves littering the forest floor, unable to trust the tremor of fear that run through him and the shock waves which threatened to tighten his finger on the trigger, blasting out an announcement of their presence into the bloodstained night.

Pragmatically, Alex picked up the weapon, anxious to arm himself to the hilt and ready to protect his friend who, at that moment, didn't seem capable of defending himself.

Charlie had developed cramp in his foot and longed to stretch out and change his position, but felt Alex's warning pinch, as he was urged to maintain his silence.

As quietly as he could, he shifted his position, whilst every dry, crumpled leaf in the vicinity seemed to crackle and snap beneath his weight.

At last the death cries of Baddoo were drowned in the night and the Benin soldiers drifted back to collect their stolen booty, taking up the trunks and hoisting the burgled bundles on to their shoulders.

Tensely, Alex and Charlie marked their passing, afraid to move, reluctant to even breathe, lest the air that they exhaled into the cold atmosphere of the African night left a telltale cloud of exhalation.

Slowly and silently, Alex and Charlie counted them as they gathered up their ill-gotten gains and left, one … two … three … four … five … six … seven … eight … nine … ten … eleven.

One Benin soldier remained, posted sentry-like, no more than fifty yards from where the two friends huddled together. Somehow he sensed that there was a valid reason to stay, a chance to shed more blood, be it black man's or white!

He wandered around the tall trees, coming so close at times that Alex and Charlie could almost feel his warm breath, as they, in turn, held theirs. Reluctantly, Charlie accepted the second revolver once more, gripping it with grim determination, knowing that a single shot would start a war – a battle which, whilst they remained so heavily outnumbered, would surely not be theirs for the taking.

It was obvious that this last man had no intention of leaving, settling himself into a squatting position, with the butt of his rifle resting on the ground, its barrel pointing upwards into the night sky, as if solely intent on blasting the fruit bats that had emerged from their nocturnal roosts to feed on the figs – as if he didn't care a fig about slaughtering the last two survivors, grouped so closely in front of him and whose one false move would belie their presence.

Alex rested his head on his elbows, tucking the revolver close to his body, feeling its cold metal butt against his bare chest. With a blanket apiece and a spare one to wrap around Charlie's injured leg, they should have felt more comfortable, but both men were exhausted and horrified by the additional carnage that had been wrought in the setting sun.

Much to his surprise, Alex found himself dozing off to sleep. Charlie remained awake and alert, nudging Alex whenever his gently snuffling snores shook his body, filtering their sound through the night.

Charlie could not sleep.

His nightmare thoughts rang with the blood-letting genocide of Baddoo, the gentle giant, who had laid down his life for the two white men he had sought to protect.

At one point Charlie must have drifted off to sleep and woke suddenly, feeling a hand at his boot, creeping up his gaiter. He yelled out a silent scream, convinced in that split second of wakefulness, that they had been discovered by the sentry and that the Benin soldiers had returned to confer upon them the same fate as that which they had employed to deal the last of life's pack of playing cards to the African cook.

However, it proved only to be Alex, shifting his position quietly and searching to ascertain Charlie's whereabouts.

It must have been around four o'clock in the morning that more voices could be heard. Charlie made out the sound of a second sentry soldier, returning to join his companion.

Charlie listened in silence for a few moments unable, at first, to detect the exact location from which the voices emanated, but certain that they were very close. He nudged Alex awake.

Alex shouted out his displeasure at having been awoken and the secret of their safe hideaway was no more. Any further attempt to conceal themselves was useless.

Charlie gripped the revolver, unable even to stagger to his feet, as Alex shook himself awake, taking a second or two to understand the situation.

Alex had been dreaming of Edinburgh and the tiny attic bedroom where he and Mary had shared a narrow bed. He dreamt too of the local bars where he and Charlie had enjoyed a gallon of beer together on those nights when the whisky chasers too had flowed and he had stumbled home to his bed, helped by his friend, who would protest their shared innocence to Mary in the hope that Alex would not be forced to spend another night in the coal-house.

Now he faced the ultimate threat, from which Charlie was in no fit state of health to help protect them. No night in the coal-house beckoned but, instead, endless nights in the dark of the Devil, thrown into one of the sacrificial pits in the City of Blood to await their sacrifice to an unknown goddess.

Maybe Baddoo's death, as horrific as it was, had not been so bad after all. At least he had escaped days of horrendous anticipation of his own ultimate fate.

It had been twelve black men against one, with Baddoo as the unlucky thirteenth – just like number 13, the poor Kroo boy, who had carried Alex's bed through the jungle and had his stomach sliced open for his trouble.

Here though, it was two men against two, even if Charlie could barely stand and, unlike Alex, had never before fired a gun in his life. Strange thoughts whirled around in Alex's sleep-befuddled brain.

Why hadn't the Benin men shot them as they slept?

Was their need to savagely dismember and disembowel their living victims so acute that they would risk their own life and limb in pursuit of their bloodthirsty goal?

Alex had no answers, but he did have a weapon, a gun whose echoing shots might bring another dozen, or more of the marauders out of their jungle hideouts.

Could he risk firing off a volley of bullets into the night?

Could he chance the consequences of not doing so, certain in the knowledge that there was no way that Charlie could take to his feet and run for his life?

Alex had plenty of deaths to avenge; killing the two warriors, who had probably delighted in hacking one of their fellow countrymen to bits just a few short hours ago, would be all too easy – all too pleasurable. Perhaps they had been amongst the fray that had beheaded the limping Captain Copford-Crawford.

Killing them in cold blood would do nothing to trouble Alex's conscience. Why, given the chance, they would undoubtedly set about his lame friend, without any further thought, returning to the Oba's palace, parading their triumph, seeking recognition of their "bravery", perhaps bringing with them Charlie's head hacked from his body, with a stick gag in his mouth.

Alex very much doubted that they possessed any reluctance about shooting a man as he lay on the ground. These beasts were no less decent than the so-called sporting gentlemen who lined up for a pheasant shoot on the moors on Boxing Day.

Occasionally joining his blacksmith father as a beater on one of the large country estates, he had watched birds being blasted from the air, after the beaters and their dogs had aroused them from sheltering tussocks to await a long line of tartan clad gentry, whose bellies burst from their waistcoats, having taken their fill from overladen dining tables in the shooting lodges of the Scottish Highlands.

Shoot the bastards and be damned!

Charlie, staggered to his feet, ready to fight with his friend, ready to fall, maybe as the final victim, ready to meet his maker in a pact that was not of the Devil's making.

Like Alex, Charlie had witnessed so many deaths. Now it was his turn to pull the trigger.

Two single shots blasted through the darkness. Two men fell to the forest floor. It was all over! Death had dealt its hand once more!

Neither Alex nor Charlie had fired a single shot.

Chapter 11

Both Alex and Charlie stood in amazement, as the two Benin warriors fell just a few feet away from them, shot in the back by two dead men's ghosts. Two men who had died in the massacre of the white men. Two men who had been dead for two days.

Two men who weren't dead at all!

Captain Boisragon and Ralph Locke stood, shoulder to shoulder, a short way off into the bush, stepping out from behind the cover of a tall, forest giant behind which they had sought to conceal themselves in an attempt to weigh up the situation.

So intent had the Benin soldiers been on facing their newly-awakened adversaries that they had failed to realise that the hunters had become the hunted, as two deadly adversaries had crept up on them, wide-eyed, fully awake and alert and ready to shoot the natives in the back.

The two warriors hadn't stood a chance, blasted into oblivion by the desperate fugitives, who had long since given up lying low in any attempt to deny their whereabouts.

Their presence in the forest was the reason why the majority of the Benin soldiers had made off to track them down, leaving just the two sentries to patrol the area close to where they had killed Baddoo, in case the murdered cook had been acting as a guide to any remaining members of the Phillips party.

It was a joyous reunion. Now there were four survivors from the ill-fated trip – a quarter of the original deputation, whose companions had been quartered and beheaded or, if they had been among the lucky ones, shot in the back and dispatched with the same speed and alacrity as the Acting Consul General.

Like Alex and Charlie, both Captain Boisragon and Ralph Locke now sported the beginnings of stubbly beards to accompany their once trim moustaches.

Locke had experienced a close shave with death. He had been in a group, including Arthur Maling, when a party of Benin soldiers had crept up on them and shot them in the back.

Miraculously, he had only been shot four times in the arm and once in the hip, but none of wounds had been able to stop him and they seemed to trouble him comparatively little.

Captain Boisragon, even more astoundingly, seemed to be almost completely unharmed, complaining only of a grazed knee, the result of a ricocheting pellet, together with the inevitable scratches and insect bites.

They too owned a toy-like compass, taken from the dead body of Arthur Maling. It was housed in a little gunmetal casing and its dial seemed to stick from time to time.

However, the silver pocket watch which they were careful to keep fully wound afforded them extra hope, for they knew that, even without a compass, they could have fore-guessed their intended route fairly easily by the time of day and the direction of the sun.

Just as with Alex and Charlie, their clothes too were a mass of tears, which testified to similar trials and tribulations.

How they had obtained their revolvers, Charlie at first hesitated to ask, but soon noticed that they were the same army issue as the gun that Alex had secreted in the folds of his jacket packed away in the trunk.

Maybe they had come across another of the hastily abandoned wooden cases and had ransacked it for weapons.

What they brought with them too were some dry, hard ship's biscuits, taken from one of the bundles carried by a dead Kroo boy. They had been soaked in rank palm oil to give them flavour. Charlie and Alex accepted them hungrily.

Mixed with the smell of acrid oil and the taint of blood, they tasted disgusting and soon the two hungry men realised that it was impossible to swallow them with their dry, parched mouths, stowing them away in what remained of their trousers pockets for later consumption when, at last, they found a decent supply of water.

Charlie turned away from the pockmarked backs that lay face down in the mud before him. He could stomach neither biscuits, nor bullet blistered bodies. He felt the bile rising in his throat and would have been sick, if there had been anything left in his stomach.

Alex meanwhile kicked out at one of the prone forms, anxious to confirm that no last life remained, that all existence had been extinguished, striking out with his foot at the second hastily dispatched body to likewise confirm the demon's demise.

After a few brief handshakes, they decided that the better part of valour was to make an immediate departure from the scene of their own defence, for fear that the commotion would attract unwanted attention.

They wanted to put as much distance between themselves and any possible pursuers as quickly as possible, without waiting for the break of day.

It was not easy to fulfil this ambition, stumbling over obstacles unseen in the gloom, but they made their way as well as they could in the dark.

Captain Boisragon, who was the most able bodied of the sorry looking quartet, took the lead. He had made his way through the African forests under cover of darkness before and, with his keen night-time vision, which had already been put to the test, he proved worthy of the task.

At every excruciating moment of their onward passage, they expected to hear gunfire ringing out of the bush, which they had already put behind them.

Perhaps they were still being watched by Benin soldiers a little more wary now that they knew that their quarry was armed and ready to shoot to kill.

As day broke and light began to shimmer through the forest canopy, they halted for a few minutes. Charlie and Alex took pride in demonstrating to their companions how to lick the early morning dew from the broad-leafed plants in the way that Baddoo had taught them.

Neither of their two recently re-united companions had managed to bring a water flask with them and had confided that they had not quenched their thirst for nearly forty-eight hours.

Charlie carefully made a limping, stumbling tour of the larger leafed foliage, funnelling the liquid into his hip flask, instructing each of the others to make it last, like a parent trying to persuade a child not to down a whole bottle of pop in one go.

By now they had lost all cognisance of how far they had travelled, disappointing themselves every time they thought that they had, at last, reached the creek.

As they passed through each plantation they saw the line of trees ahead suddenly disappearing as if at the water's edge, only to re-appear again like a magician's rabbit, popping their fluffy foliage above a limited horizon, like a man whose top hat top had slipped below the level of his eyes.

With the aid of their twin compasses, they tried hard to maintain their northwesterly direction, attempting to push their way through the thick bush.

Captain Boisragon and Alex took turns to assist the disabled Charlie, both of them lifting him high above any major obstacles they encountered, whilst Locke remained the keeper of his walking stick.

The four men struggled on in this fashion until nearly midday, when tiredness forced them to stop. They set up a makeshift camp beside a tiny trickling stream, at the side of which Alex, Allan Boisragon and Locke knelt to lap its muddy waters, like cats at last locating a saucer of milk, or a source of cream. Alex filled Charlie's hip flask, allowing him the luxury of drinking its whole murky contents.

Alex was even able to wash his bloodstained face in the running water and rinse the handkerchief, which was saturated with his own blood.

In the heat of the day, three men slept, the fourth acting as sentinel. For several hours they dozed under the shade of a spreading fig tree, taking it in turns to share sentry duty, each man waking the next, as the hands of Ralph Locke's pocket watch marked out the hour of the next man's period of observation.

As the sun begun to lose its heat, they set off again, measuring their progress by the amount of time that they had travelled, no longer oblivious to the passing of the day, as Charlie and Alex had been before they had Locke to act as their timekeeper.

Shortly before dusk, they came upon one of the old Benin roads and, not having encountered any opposition throughout the day, chanced their luck, following it for a mile or so, before Charlie, happy to be limping on level ground, but ever cautious, urged them to strike out into the bush again for the sake of their own safety.

Eventually they lay down for the night among the roots of a large tree, three men to a single blanket, pressing hard up against each other for added warmth, whilst the sentry enjoyed the luxury of a roughly woven covering all to himself – a reward for his observation duties and his struggle to remain awake and alert for danger.

Alex took the first turn, taking Locke's pocket watch, with its four-leafed clover fob as his talisman and as a timepiece with which to measure out the hours of darkness and the execution of his duty as night watchman, waiting to hand the silver time traveller on to the next man whose turn it was to keep watch.

As Alex's thoughts ranged widely and wildly over the events of the previous two days, he wondered if news of the massacre had, as yet, appeared in the newspapers back home.

He imagined Mary picking up a discarded copy of *The Scotsman* in the lobby of the hotel where she worked and reading of her husband's likely demise, worrying her with the prospect of early widowhood and the thought of not having the support of a man's wages.

Hardly had he dismissed these thoughts from his aching brain than he detected the earthy smell of a native situated somewhere behind him. It was a very old man, sitting squatting like an ageing wood nymph on a log not ten yards distant.

Alex kept up an animated, silent, one-sided conversation with him, until the wizened little old man vanished back into the forest and to his place in the realms of Alex's imagination.

Hunger was driving Alex's thoughts and he reached into his pocket for one of the dirty, dankly smelling ship's biscuits, taking a single bite out of it and spitting the contents of his dry mouth out into the bush. The crumbs caught in the back of his throat, for he had little, or no saliva with which to wash them down.

He began coughing and choking, waking Charlie, who struggled out of the shared blanket and limped awkwardly forward to perch beside him. The sores on his injured leg had begun to fill with putrid pus again and they throbbed with pain.

Charlie sat in silence with his friend, quietly seeking his assistance to unwrap the makeshift bandage, so that he could sit and squeeze open the sores, oozing out their foul smelling pus in the way that Baddoo had taught him.

It was not a task to be observed by the squeamish onlooker, but Alex seemed not to care. It certainly wasn't going to put him off his foul tasting biscuit and there was nothing else to eat, not so much as a discarded fig, not even a morsel of fruit deemed unfit for consumption by some forest creature.

Together they sat in companionable silence, until Charlie, finished with his stomach churning, self-appointed makeshift medical skills, plucked at a flesh leaf and urged Alex to help him bind his wounds.

Ham-fistedly Alex began the task of re-attaching the thick palm tree thorns, lacking the dexterity of Baddoo and making a poor job by comparison.

As they sat together, the old man re-appeared again, sitting this time cross-legged on his log, like a wise old monkey, playing monkey tricks with their minds.

All their water had long since gone, a mouthful to each of the four parched throated men. Hunger and thirst drove their hallucinations.

Fear continued to forage along the backs of their necks, rasping at each stubbly chin, as every slight gust of night air seemed to bring with it another quietly howling demon from their horrific and recently shared past.

They were the lucky ones, Alex, Charlie and the others – the chosen champions of a brand of barbarism that had spread its unholy tentacles like an eight-armed octopus, each snatching and grabbing at one unfortunate member of their expedition, leaving eight men dead, or dying, an octet of singers singing only a song of death.

Forearmed and forewarned of exactly what to expect, now they could take comfort in a certain strength – the power provided by the feel of gun metal in their hands.

Alex urged his friend to take a share of the comforting blanket.

Together they sat out the duration of Alex's watch, waiting for the moment when they could retire to the tangled tree roots, leaving another man to take over the night-time vigil.

Alex had now become the fortunate recipient of Ralph Locke's singlet and he had used one of the last scraps of the tattered remains of his shirt to form a rough bandage around his head wound.

Its frayed cotton ends caught in an occasional gust of air, acting as some small measure of deterrent against the hordes of biting insects that emerged in the night.

Alex shivered through the watchful hours of the night. They had not dared to light a camp fire, although its flames and belching smoke might have provided them both with warmth and with some respite from the marauding mosquitoes, but knowing that its telltale plumes would provide a smoke signal summarisation of their situation. Besides, they had no matches and none of them had learnt the knack of striking flints and harnessing the sparks.

At daybreak they arose, waking almost as one man, as the sun began to rise over the treetops, pausing momentarily behind a passing cloud.

Gradually they were beginning to master the art of dew drop gathering, selecting only the broadest, widest leaves and becoming quite expert at the task, moistening their tongues and allowing the wondrous well of water to drizzle down their throats.

On other occasions they would lap at a small water-filled hollow in a tree, clenching their teeth together to act as a barrier against the bitter tasting drowned insects.

In the plantations they fared better with the big plantain leaves which, although mixed with ants and dirt, held much larger drops of dew than any of the bush vegetation. Locating a well-moistened leaf was like being served by an inexperienced barmaid, who had misjudged a measure of scotch in their favour.

Alex and Charlie sampled some of the plantain fruit, but found them bitter and inedible. Their dryness only served to increase the men's thirst. They dreamed of finding bananas and pined for pawpaws, or pineapples, but their search was fruitless.

Besides, any time taken looking for food meant that they were postponing their chances of reaching the river and increasing their chances of coming up against another party of Benin warriors, unperturbed at wading in against the wounded white men.

They prayed for a shower of rain. They longed to luxuriate in its cleansing, cascading free fall, to kick off their boots and let it splash over their feet, unwashed since they had emerged from the top of the ladder and accepted the administrations of the priests supposedly as a gesture that all was well.

With their cast off boots serving as water butts, they could even have drunk from them, enjoying a pint or more of water that would have tasted sweeter than the richest, darkest Irish stout.

82

Fearful of the fever and their lack of warm clothing, maybe it was as well that the rains never came, as they struggled through the bush, their bodies growing ever weaker from lack of proper food and water.

From time to time they stumbled upon a hunting path, which provided a welcome break from the monotonous slog through the undergrowth, but sometimes lead them in the wrong direction.

Charlie would always urge them back into the safety of the forest and they all knew that it was only sensible to heed his words of warning.

When they were on the move, they felt so exhausted that all they wanted to do was rest and when they rested, they were restless, anxious to get going again, lest their whereabouts were discovered. When they slept, nightmares threatened.

As soon as they awoke, they wanted to fall back to sleep again to rid their minds of the seeming hopelessness of their situation and memories of their fallen friends, left murdered and mutilated along the way.

When they drank from Charlie's hip flask, they begrudged themselves every tiny mouthful, knowing that, before long, thirst would once more grip their throats and there was no remaining water to rely upon … no sip of liquid to leap upon their lips and provide momentary relief.

If they tried to nibble on one of the foul tasting ship's biscuits, it dried their mouths, depriving them of precious saliva, which they slugged back down their throats from time to time, retching to return it to the dried out river bed of their mouth before, irretrievably, it descended into their stomachs.

By ten o'clock in the morning all the dew had disappeared, bowling down into the bowels of the earth, like a rabbit running for its burrow.

Charlie taught Ralph Locke how to squeeze the pustules of suppurating matter from his wounded arm to ease the pain.

At one point, Locke even thought that they might provide the means of lubricating his cracked lips, spreading the evil smelling ooze over his upper lip, so that the cream-coloured residue lingered in his moustache, like some ghoulish lip balm.

In one of the plantations they found an old woman, gathering plantains, but she seemed not to take any notice of these other worldly visitors, as if discovering a dishevelled, disparate band of white men wandering seemingly aimlessly in the wilderness was an everyday occurrence.

As the midday sun arose, they sought shelter from its sweltering rays.

Alex, who had been up half the night before and whose turn of watchful duty was not pending, fell asleep the moment his aching head touched the ground.

Charlie lifted his head gently, placing a ball of dried grass under the side of his friend's face, before lapsing into sleep himself, whilst Ralph Locke snored gently beside him and Captain Boisragon struggled to keep his eyes open and maintain his eagle-eyed watch.

At around three-thirty that afternoon, when the men began to stir in preparation for their onward passage, Charlie gave in to the question that was forming in his mind, proposing that they bide the night, for they were all too exhausted to go on. Reluctant though he was to admit it, he felt that he simply could not abide the pain in his leg a moment longer.

Locked in pain from the pot shot wounds in his right arm, his fellow sufferer, Ralph Locke, was keen to offer his support for the idea, but Alex and Captain Boisragon, who more agile and in better physical condition, as well as having more superficial wounds, were keen to press on.

It was two men against two, with no one to decide who held the casting vote. Without a coin between them, they detached the lucky four-leafed clover fob from the silver watch chain, tossing it into the air to see if it landed hallmark up or down in the dirt in order to determine their fate.

Unbeknown to the weary travellers, if they reached the waterside before dark, they would then have been met by a party of Benin soldiers lying in wait for them. Charlie cast the tiny medallion into the air.

Four leaves. Four men. Four lives waiting for a four-leafed clover to decide their fate.

Chapter 12

In the company of Captain Boisragon, Alex set off in the late afternoon in search of Gwatto Creek, where they clung to the hope that the Ivy would be waiting for them.

The tiny silver four-leafed clover watch fob had fallen hallmark down in the dirt and, with its descent, the decision was made.

As the two most able-bodied survivors, he and the captain would strike out together, hoping to reach their would-be waterside rescue point before darkness fell.

By their hastily made calculations, the creek was no more than two miles away and a royal blue kingfisher flashing through the forest seemed to confirm their hopes.

If they struck out on their own without their wounded compatriots, they could return at first light, bringing with them fresh drinking water, food and proper dressings, together with a hastily assembled team of deckhands from the Ivy to swell their ranks and, hopefully, deter the enemy from launching any further attack.

Charlie's leg wound was now severely septic and Locke's arm was little better. Both had passed the point of merely smelling badly, emitting an acrid, nauseous stench that Alex stoically avoided commenting on.

It filled the air around them, forcing Alex to wrinkle his nose into his bloody handkerchief every time he helped Charlie to change the pus dripping leaves that were the only available form of dressing.

Flies descended in great hungry hordes, whenever the rotting carrion was exposed, swarming and balancing on the festering limbs in their hundreds like acrobats in an abattoir.

Charlie had taught Ralph Locke how to purify the putrid epidermis by squeezing the gunk and gunge, but many of the bullet holes were too deep and crater-like for the forceful pressure of his fingers to have any effect.

As dusk descended, the attacking swarms of flies were replaced by furious, biting mosquitoes, like miniature leopards muzzling into the bloody wounds that their fellows had created, each intent on gaining an ample share of the bloody booty.

Left alone, Charlie and Locke spoke very little, spending most of their time swatting insects in a vain attempt to quell the hungry marauders, scraping off the ooze from their respective wounds, which now flowed even faster, dripping on to the forest floor, like a tap that needed a washer. It poured from their flesh almost as fast as they could wipe it away with the big, broad leaves which were their only desperate disinfectant.

If they exposed their flesh to wipe away the oozing pus, the insects descended to flit and feast around them, like hungry parishioners at a vicarage tea party. If they covered themselves and allowed the skin to rot, the throbbing pain became almost unbearable.

If they spoke to one another, driven by the combination of fear and thirst, they soon became argumentative. Charlie swigged a small mouthful of the precious water from his hip flask and in the tetchy tsetse-infested atmosphere, Locke complained that he had imbibed more than his fair share.

Before they settled for the night, they learnt to dig small holes around them with their bare hands, allowing a tiny amount of extra dew to settle in the hollowed out clay bowl, to which they lowered their lips and drunk gratefully the next morning, even if it caused great pain to Charlie when he tried to manoeuvre his injured leg into a suitable position in order for him to reach the water. Nevertheless, it proved less tiresome a task than gathering a sufficient quantity of leaves to lick and marginally more rewarding too!

It was Charlie's task to dig out the molehill mounds of clay, as his companion now had very little use of his right arm, which had grown stiff and useless, as mortification began to take its toll.

Meanwhile, Alex and Captain Boisragon began their slow descent towards Gwatto Creek. They could hear its splashing waters, as several crocodiles slithered silently from the muddy banks, twisting and turning and thrashing the water's surface in a feeding frenzy that greeted the crocodilian news that a dead hippo, its body bloated and balloon-like, had floated downstream to provide the dish of the day.

On a log, a strikingly coloured giant kingfisher sat, beating and battering its catch, which looked far too big for its mouth, its keen eyesight proving bigger and better than its belly.

A portly mother pig had come down to drink by the water's edge, bringing with her a bevy of stripy-bellied piglets, which drank in no fear of being snatched by one of the floating "logs" that normally cruised the riverside, their eyes resting just above the water's surface, for the crocodiles, feasting on the dead hippo, had bigger and bulkier bloated flesh to flay and a tiny, stripy piglet would prove little more than a pork-pied snack.

At last the two men sighted the river, but the embankment was overgrown with bush, so they climbed up the bank again and located a rough pathway, which led circuitously down to the water's edge. In front of them were a few roughly hewn huts. If they entered a village, who knew what lay in wait for them?

Maybe there were Benin soldiers watching their every move, carefully biding their time, until they could cut off the exit route, butchering the white men by the river, as they finally achieved their goal.

If they met opposition, Alex and Captain Boisragon had their two revolvers and a reasonable amount of ammunition, but was it sufficient to save them, if they were heavily outnumbered?

If the Benin produced weapons and they were clearly outgunned, they would make a rush for the waterside, plunging headlong into its murky depths, in a desperate bid to make it unharmed to the other side, perhaps even summoning their own British troops, before venturing back in a bid to rescue their ailing companions, before septicaemia set in and their injuries and lack of food and water overcame them.

Water would provide Alex and the captain with a relatively safe barrier, for it was part of the Oba's edict that no Benin man was permitted to paddle a canoe and cross the river, contrary to their juju beliefs.

There was activity in the village, but Alex, without his binoculars, was unable to tell whether its occupants might be friendly Jakri tribesmen, or Benin foe.

A forest twig snapped behind the two men, like a sudden explosion of gunfire. Both men turned to meet the party that emerged from the tangled undergrowth. It was to be their last step towards the gently lapping waters of the creek.

* * * * * * * * * *

Charlie and Locke spent a miserable night huddled together. They had both of the blankets and had the rare luxury of one apiece. The sounds of the night still jangled their nerves, coupled with the uncertainty of what had happened to Alex and the captain.

True, they had not heard any guns being fired, but whether that was good news or bad, they had no way of telling. Maybe, they had been stalked and had their throats cut silently before they had even had time to draw their guns.

They had no idea whether the morning would bring rescue, or further worry. Charlie bitterly regretted allowing Alex out of his sight, clutching at the four-leafed clover, hoping that it would bring luck to all four of them.

Perhaps the leaf of life had already been cruelly plucked. Maybe his friend had already had his head sliced off, like a bobble-headed purple clover flower snapped off at its stem.

And what if they were now on their own, with only one tiny compass to guide them forwards to the unknown dangers of their destination? By now Charlie was barely able to walk and Locke was in no position to provide support and succour.

Together they sucked the moisture from the damp leaves. Together they bent double to quench their abiding thirst from the contents of the hollows that Charlie had dug the night before, supping their liquid contents like thin, workhouse soup. Scotch broth without the barley, altogether light on the lentils and with only a drowned bug to serve as both mutton and meal.

Charlie was barely fit enough to join in the spartan breakfast. He was scarcely able to move. His body stiffened and weakened, he could hardly stand.

Hunger heralded his thoughts but, most of all, he reflected on the fate of Alex and the captain, sure of the fact that they were condemned men, perhaps already awaiting execution and certain too that, as condemned men, they had not enjoyed a hearty breakfast.

He was wrong.

Charlie's would-be savours had yams for breakfast and all the water they could drink. They had even managed a quick wash in the river.

Alex and the captain had been found by friendly Jakri carriers from a trading village on the opposite side of the creek and had been carried triumphantly back to their village and welcomed by having their feet washed by way of celebrating their survival.

Alex even noticed the telltale signs of the white distemper still etched on one man's back. number 77 – one of the late Kenneth Campbell's numerically ordered crew, was a survivor who owed his life to luck and who was now a hero among his own people, especially as he had been the first to spot the two white men, as they approached the creek.

The two British survivors were treated regally. Their arrival was greeted with joyous, if somewhat raucous, approval and they enjoyed copious amounts of celebratory palm wine for breakfast!

It was far from fresh and tasted sour and potent, but it would have been impolite of them to have refused, for these unshaven, bloodied white men covered from head to toe in black thorns were the toast of the village.

The Jakri chief even produced a packet of Egyptian cigarettes, inhaling deeply, before passing it to his guests. The strong tobacco burnt its way down Alex's throat, making his mouth feel even more parched, but he accepted it eagerly, passing over his dirty, but once brightly coloured gaiters to the chief by way of a return gift. Apart from the revolver and Mary's compass, it was all he had to give.

With no shared language between them, somehow they had to get across the notion that there were two more white men survivors in the bush, who still depended upon them for their lives.

Thus began an elaborate mime, with Alex and the captain as the principal characters and with two of the Jakri carriers seconded from the gathered audience to play the parts of Charlie and Locke.

Inventively, Alex rubbed the features of the two black men with the pulp of the boiled yam, rendering their faces a paler hue. He took out his revolver, quickly emptying its barrel of bullets to assure their rescuers that he meant them no harm and pointed the empty gun at each man of the two men in turn, loudly clapping his hands together to mimic the sound of gunshots.

Gently, he forced the men to topple over backwards on to the sandy floor, urging them to remain still. Afterwards he began tearing thin strips from his bloodstained handkerchief, draping them over first one man's leg and then the other man's arm, forcing the forearm gently against the second man's chest and making his other "victim" stretch out with one stiff leg before him.

He pointed back towards the forest, beckoning his onlookers to follow, eternally grateful when the village headman seemed to pick up the message, organising a team of two dozen or so men, carrying with them water-filled gourds, more yams and bravely arming themselves with stout sticks that were surely no match for the Benin brigade.

With Alex's pocket compass to guide the way, Alex and Captain Boisragon, as the only two armed men, returned the way they had come, fortified by the thought that now, at least, they had numbers on their side and food and water to consume along the way.

Armed with a machete, one Jakri, who Alex believed to be the headman's son, led the way, clearing a path before him and allowing them to push their way through the bush with relative ease. With only two miles to go and walking in the coolness of the early morning, they made good progress.

They had strength in numbers, if not in firearms. With so many willing hands, Alex was sure that they would succeed and be able to carry his injured friend and Locke back to relative civilisation.

Alex knew the exact spot to look for, beneath the tremendous trunk of one of the largest mahogany trees he had ever seen. Underneath he would find the two injured men, huddled together, perhaps picking at their sores, but alive and, if not well, at least not further harmed.

He spotted a patch on the forest floor rubbed bare by the movements of the men who had tried, in vain, to succumb to sleep the night before.

Charlie was missing. Locke too.

Alex bent down and picked up the broken links of a silver watch chain, dangling it from his dirty fingers. Its little fob was snapped in two. Just two lucky leaves of clover remained.

Chapter 13

Feeling utterly deflated and totally defeated, Alex picked up the broken fob. What message it told, he had no idea. It glinted in the early morning sunlight, filtered through the huge, thick branches of the broad mahogany, which had stood sentry over his friend and Locke.

Two leaves were left. Himself and the captain? Where was the watch? Where were the two men?

True, there was no sign of a struggle, but then neither man had been fit enough to fight. No bloody trail led through the undergrowth and the grey army blanket bundled beneath a bush bore only the congealed marks of its recent bloody past, with no signs of having witnessed the spilling of the lifeblood of the present.

Dare he risk shouting out for them?

Alex cleared his throat and called the names of those who had outlived the harrowing events of the past few days, lamenting Locke, whom he hardly knew, a little less, but rushing through the bush chasing after Charlie, his booming voice echoing back at him, with only his own clearly enunciated calls returning his words in response.

At any moment, he was sure that his friend would come limping out of the undergrowth having, perhaps, relieved himself in the bush, not bothering to fasten his fly, as the last remaining buttons had been torn away days ago.

No one came.

Alex pocketed what was left of the four-leafed clover – the hallmarked half. He dared not think that the Benin brutes had come and robbed the four survivors of the chance of a joyous reunion. Slowly, he turned to face the captain, whose face belied his thoughts.

The Benin beasts had obviously struck again and had taken their captives by surprise – and all without a single shot being fired. Charlie and Locke had been left with two of the revolvers, but there was no sign that either of them had ever had the chance to fire them.

Just where should he start looking? How much more could he endanger the lives of the peaceful Jakris who had brought them this far?

Alert for any signs of trampled undergrowth, the Jakri son of the chief gesticulated, as he began to discern the telltale signs of another path that led down to the river in a broad, sweeping circle.

Alex and the captain began to follow it, but it soon became apparent that no lame man had ever managed to manipulate his exhausted, injured frame through such dense undergrowth, with only Locke's one uninjured arm to clear their passage.

As Alex picked up the path, one of the Jakri carriers spotted tracks and began a babble of excitement. By the expressions of joy on the Jakri men's faces, they were tracking others of their kind and not the feared Benin warriors.

Alex clutched at the broken watch chain links that he had plucked from the forest floor, suddenly rejoicing in their finding. It was a sign that all was well.

When, a quarter of a mile or so further on, as he proceeded along the recently flattened path, his eyes cast low in constant search for other telltale signs, he spied a scrap of Charlie's once white shirt, dangling from a wicked palm oil thorn, he clasped the two remaining clover leaves, at last recognising them as a good luck sign.

He'd heard of a four-leafed clover of course but, maybe, two leaves were even rarer than four! He pocketed the talisman and hope began to fill his heart.

How Charlie had managed to break the little good luck charm, he had no idea. Perhaps, he was leaving some sort of message, pointing the way to a small creek bordering the Gwatto river and the fact that he had been transported there by another small posse of Jakri carriers.

Along the path the friendly Africans encountered one of their number, sent as a messenger to relay the good news that, somehow, Alex already knew and understood.

The messenger placed the other half of the silver fob into the hands of the Jakri chief's son, who led the party and who, in turn, passed it down the line.

Alex was only too happy to re-unite the two pieces, noting that the tiny hinge pin that mounted the two halves together was missing, either deliberately, or not – it no longer mattered.

A four-leafed clover was definitely a sign of good luck and meeting up with a good friend deemed deceased was fortune beyond Alex's wildest dreams.

Emerging into a small clearing and sheltering in a tiny river inlet, his back propped against an upturned dug out canoe, rested Charlie, his injured leg washed clean of the dirt and debris, with Locke by his side, likewise looking relatively wholesome.

It was a joyous reunion, but one which they were encouraged not to prolong, as the four men were quickly installed in the canoe, with two Jakri paddlers, who furrowed them through the murky waters, like willing carthorses ploughing a muddy field.

Charlie had already had a drink from one of the spilling, hollowed out gourds and now he eagerly stuffed some mushy boiled yam into his mouth, extracting great handfuls of the stuff from the enveloping palm oil leaf, which acted as both parcel and plate.

Ralph Locke let his arm trail through the water, rinsing it clean of some of the impurities and bringing instant relief to his wounds.

When the paddling tribesmen slowed their efforts for a moment, Alex leaned over the side, unheeding of reptilian retaliation. He let the water flow over his lowered head, helping to clear the hangover he was beginning to feel from an over-indulgent intake of palm wine, exhilarating in the rush of water and the freedom brought about by their escape.

Re-united, the four white men, together with their Jakri paddlers, made good their escape, travelling down river to a village comprising maybe thirty huts. It was called Aketti and was inhabited by more Jakri, who met the survivors, greeting them like long lost friends.

They had been unreliably informed that all the white men had been killed and had never expected to learn otherwise nearly five days after the bloody massacre had taken place, which had resulted in so many of their fellows slashed and slain, their beheaded bodies left to rot in the rainforest.

Whilst a larger canoe was prepared for their onward journey, the small party of white men was shown around to the back of the huts, where they quickly realised they were supposed to remain hidden, lest any Benin men were observing the cause of such excitement from the other side of the river.

Once again much palm wine was drunk and both Charlie and Locke used some of the alcohol to flush out the pus-filled craters in their injured limbs, soaking it into their skin, so that it stung like the attack of a hundred angry bees, but left their flesh reeking of its pungent aroma, which smelt so much better that the suppurating wounds.

Men, women and children from the village crowded around the four sorry looking refugees, bringing with them fresh fruit picked from the forest that morning.

The four men ate like royalty, enjoying a regal banquet without crockery, or cutlery. It was not their first of the day, but they were still starving and every mouthful tasted like heaven after their heathen-enforced fast.

They gathered what few cigarettes they had left between them and gave them to those who brought them their breakfast, along with the two tiny compasses, presenting one each to the village chief and his eldest son.

Alex was at first reluctant to part with Mary's hard-earned Christmas gift, but threw it in with their other meagre offerings, knowing that she would understand, not regretting for a moment the hours of extra toil that she had worked to earn it for him.

The chieftain spoke a little fractured English, but all he could tell them was how all the others had been slain and that, no other white men had escaped the bloodbath.

He urged them to be on their way, for not only was he anxious for their safety, but he was also worried about what reprisals might be heaped upon his people for harbouring the fugitives.

A great war would soon be fought with the British, of that he was certain and he did not want his people caught up in it.

Enough Jakri blood had been spilt these last few days and with the creek only about forty or fifty yards wide at this point, he feared that, if spotted, they might be shot at from the other side.

One old woman, with wizened, drooping breasts, launched into a tirade of unintelligible abuse at the four bedraggled white men when she learnt that her son was to be one of the paddlers appointed to take them on their onward journey, fearing that he might be shot and killed by the Benin men, as they made their way down the creek.

A couple of cigarettes, which Alex had already handed over to the headman, silenced her, quelling her fears with the thought of a rare taste of tobacco.

As Alex later learnt, she was a Benin woman outcast from her own people many years ago, as the mother of twins and, subsequently, taken in by the Jakri.

She was yelling to any of the Benin brutes who might hear her from the opposite bank of the river in the hope that her duties as a spy might be rewarded by her being accepted back in Benin City and by the husband, who had long since taken another wife.

Alex, Locke and the captain were anxious to get down to the water where the canoe was moored to a tiny, rotting wooden jetty.

Alex supported Charlie who, in turn, still enjoyed the support of his silver-topped walking stick, which the headman of the village had viewed with envy, but which Charlie clung on to for both physical and moral support.

Such progress, unheeding of any danger which might lurk on the opposite side of the creek, set alarm bells ringing for the Jakri chief, who urged caution.

He instructed the paddlers to take the canoe out of the water, carry it on their broad shoulders up to the small clearing behind the huts, ostensibly for a running repair to its hollowed out frame, but allowing the white men to steal aboard, lying full length and flat out in the middle, packed tightly in its uncomfortably tight confines, with a covering of rush mats to conceal their presence.

The survivors proceeded down the river under the blazing sun, sweat mingling with the tattered remains of their clothing, plastering the fabric tightly to their torsos and their outstretched legs, unable to move, quickly developed cramp.

Their heads ached from a combination of unaccustomed breakfast time alcoholic indulgence and the earlier exposure to the full heat of the sun. It was anything but a comfortable journey.

Their full stomachs rumbled and groaned, unaccustomed to such bounty. Alex belched repeatedly and wanted to be sick, whilst Charlie did his best to snooze, despite the pain in his wounded leg which, from time to time, made him want to scream out in pain.

After travelling in this way for maybe three or four hours, hidden from view, their presence protected by the roughly woven rush matting, they reached Gilli Gilli, eventually emerging from Benin country. Only then was it deemed safe to remove the itching, irritating matting.

They sat upright in the small dugout canoe, still barely able to stretch their aching limbs, where they dined on fu-fu, a doughy bread-like substance made from pounding yams and plantains together.

It tasted dry and somewhat unappetising, but they learnt to follow the example of the Jakri paddlers, swigging it down with fresh palm wine, poured straight down the back of the throat from a straw-covered demijohn, the rim of which tasted slightly of its original rum contents.

All four men shed their boots and socks, untying their mud-encrusted laces, heedless of the stench that their rotting feet created in the small canoe, soaking their socks in the passing waters and joyously wringing them out over each other.

Charlie made a more meticulous inspection of his bullet-blasted leg, anxiously looking for the first signs of gangrene, sponging away yet more of the revolting pus with one of his river rinsed socks, revealing a series of punch holes, some of which were almost deep enough to hide the full length of his forefinger.

Locke's wounds were lighter, peppering his forearm in a series of little craters, which contained less pus and which had already begun to sprout miniature toadstool-like scabs, still soft as the edges, but beginning to form a crust.

Perhaps the worst of Locke's wounds had been caused by a palm oil thorn in his leg, which had festered furiously, no longer cut open at regular intervals with the aid of the little pocketknife which Alex had presented by way of a gift to the headman of the band of Jakri rescuers.

One of the five paddlers was himself a survivor of the massacre; the number on his bare back was still faintly visible, although it was no longer possible to see the original three numbers.

Presumably by dint of his high number, he had been at the back of the line, dumping his load and escaping into the bush with his life, as the first volleys of shots rang through the forest, whilst his comrades began to fall.

He had arrived at Aketti two or three days after the massacre but, with no knowledge of English, had been unable to relate the tale of his escape.

Other canoes ferried up and down the creek – mostly going in the opposite direction and all manned by Jakris, bravely going up river in an attempt to search for abandoned belongings.

The decision was made that the party of British survivors would seek shelter for the night with Chief Dudu, before attempting to reach the safety of Sapele. However, they did not arrive there, for as they emerged into the creek, which served the friendly chief's village, they were surprised to come upon one of the Protectorate launches, which had just dropped anchor.

Fearful that the ship might up anchor before they could reach it, they urged the Jakri paddlers to hurry towards it, as Alex and the captain dug their outstretched palms into the water, acting as extra oars to quicken their pace.

Captain Boisragon snatched the remains of Locke's battered straw sun hat, flourishing it frantically as an S.O.S signal, waving it for all he was worth, before a gust of wind finally caught it, blowing it out of his hand, scudding across the water, before settling unseen amongst the mangrove roots.

Charlie upended his silver-topped walking stick, extending it high above his head, fearful that the last three hundred yards to the ship would prove to be a bridge too far.

Such desperate measures to draw attention to themselves proved to be unnecessary, for very soon their frantic attempts to be seen were rewarded by a flourish of waving handkerchiefs, billowing out from the bows of the launch.

Two white men, one of them a fellow trader and half a dozen or so Africans crowded on to the deck, screaming, shouting and cheering like football fans on the terraces after the home team had scored a goal.

It was Charlie's waving walking stick, flourished like a demented orchestra conductor's baton, that had attracted their attention.

Those on board the Protectorate vessel could scarcely believe their eyes at sighting the four white men survivors, having given up all hope of finding any refugees from the bloody massacre.

Charlie choked back the tears of relief. Salvation was at hand. Their long ordeal was at its end ... but for Alex the battle had not yet begun!

Chapter 14

Locke was the first to be lifted aboard the launch by a sea of helping hands and, whilst it was immediately clear to anyone that his right arm was wounded and sorely troubling him, the multitude of septic sores that covered his legs and arms generally were not so readily apparent.

He objected to the slightest touch, so much so that he screamed in agony when he was somewhat unceremoniously hoisted up on deck from the canoe, which lay low in the water.

All hope had evaporated of there being any white men survivors of the ill-fated expedition, even if the four vagabonds who had emerged from the jungle, virtually unscathed, did look as if they were competing with one another in a competition for the world's worst dressed scarecrow.

What remained of their clothing was filthy and ripped to shreds, like bonfire night guys emblazoned with their own blood.

Charlie was close to tears, whether as a result of his wounded leg being accidentally slammed against the side of the launch, as he was hoisted on board, or whether he was weeping tears of sheer relief, even he was unable tell.

A bottle of champagne was produced from nowhere and, as if by magic, a glass appeared in each man's hand.

Charlie was shaking so much that he dropped his glass, snapping its stem in two like a bent, frosted twig. He looked down at the broken shards of glass, poking them around in a tiny circle on the deck with his walking stick, unaware that the tears of abject relief that flowed down his face were mixing with the celebratory champagne, like rapidly crystallising diamonds.

The glass of champagne had been meant for Alex, but his friend had been happy to hand it over, needing no excuse to swig the remaining liquid straight from the bottle.

'God save Her Majesty the Queen and to hell with the king of Benin,' announced one of the well-wishers.

Charlie could not help but feel that it was they who had languished in a hell that had so nearly heralded their own swiftly executed passage into eternal damnation.

He felt so completely exhausted, so totally drained that he could have laid down on the deck there and then, curled himself into a ball and slept like a hibernating hedgehog.

Certainly with the mess of prickles and thorns that covered his aching body, he could have passed for a small, spiny, nocturnal pig-snouted creature, shunning the daylight and rolling himself up into a ball by way of defending himself against the barrage of well-meant, but all too exhausting questioning that he was forced to undergo to satisfy the curiosity and the quest for knowledge of those on board ship.

Alex, on the other hand, seemed to be relishing all the attention that was being heaped upon him, happily grooming himself with his own self-importance; it seemed as if he would have awarded himself a medal of honour on the spot.

Instead, he settled for a proffered tumbler of whisky and soda, keen to scotch any notion that the four men's survival had not been almost entirely down to him.

Together with Captain Boisragon, Alex continued to toast his own bravery long into the night, clinking glasses with the captain long after Charlie and Ralph Locke had retired below deck to have their wounds nursed and to doze fitfully in comfortable armchairs.

At frequent intervals they would be awakened by the cheering crowds, both black and white, who lined the river banks as they passed, all anxious to express their delight at the rapidly spreading news of the survivors' miraculous escape from death.

It was dark before they finally docked at New Benin. A company of black troops had turned out en masse, lining the rickety wooden boarded jetty, which promptly collapsed under their weight, so that their cheers and joyous greetings were suddenly swamped by their own enthusiasm.

Despite their wet and bedraggled state, they were insistent that the "heroes" should be hoisted head high above the gathering crowds and it took all Charlie's efforts of persuasion to convince them that both he and Locke, at least, were in too much pain to gain any enjoyment from such a boisterous welcoming.

Luckily for the injured duo, a doctor was on hand to dress their wounds, after the sorry looking pair had been put into a carbolic bath in an attempt to remove the worst of the ingrained dirt from their drained, weakened and weary bodies.

Packed off to bed, Charlie fell asleep immediately. He found himself dreaming first of Muriel, the pretty little blonde-haired nurse, who had first caught his eye at the hospital in Old Calabar.

However, strangely, waking up in the middle of the night, he became immediately aware that the object of his affections had metamorphosed into Mary, and that it was Alex's darkly attractive wife who occupied his thoughts!

At one point he remembered being woken up to sup a bowl of meat extract. He peered through bleary eyes at the African servant who nervously stood by the bedside, a silver spoon in one hand, his dark-skinned arm overlaid with an impossibly white napkin, starched and crisp to the touch and neatly folded in a simple triangle.

Charlie recalled how he had spent one rare relaxing Sunday afternoon with Mary and her daughter, Anne. He couldn't remember where Alex had been at the time, but Mary had been glad enough to see him anyway.

Afternoon had passed into evening and, with no sign of Alex returning, she had cooked him a scanty breakfast the next morning with all that she had in the larder!

Anne had been entertained for a good part of the afternoon, being taught by Charlie how to fold the napkins that had been collected from the wash-house where Mary's younger sister worked, ready for delivery to the Queen Hotel in Edinburgh's New Town.

Charlie had formed them into fans and had pretended that he was from China and in need of wafting away the warm air. On other occasions he folded them into little coronets, which he placed on the girl's head, telling her that she looked just like a princess.

Most of all, he had entertained her when he had fashioned one into a rather chubby looking mouse and then chased the child around the attic room with it, with Anne squealing in delight every time the white linen rodent, held between Charlie's thumb and forefinger, trapped her in a corner and made her pay the forfeit of having her bare toes tickled.

Meanwhile, whilst Alex and Charlie languished in the comfort and company of their rescue ship, back in Edinburgh Mary had already heard the news that not only were her children "fatherless", but that Anne had lost her precious "Uncle" Charlie.

Robert, of course, was too young to understand anything of what had happened. Little Anne knew immediately that something was wrong the moment that Mary had arrived at the wash-house to collect her that cold, chill January afternoon, when the vapour from the hot tubs had filled the air like the smoke emanating from a well-stoked steam train.

Mary had sobbed and Anne's aunt had pressed a replacement handkerchief into her sister's hands, gathering both her sister and her niece around her in an embrace that needed no words to express their shared grief.

Both women had seemed surprised when Anne had cried for poor "Uncle" Charlie and had expressed no similar sorrow at what had been reported in the newspapers as the deemed demise of a father she barely knew.

It was nearly a week later that the news finally broke in Scotland that four white men had survived the bloody massacre and that Anne's father was one of them, but still the child's first words were:

'Is Uncle Charlie all right? Will he come back and make a little mouse for me again?'

It was white linen of a rather different kind that was figuring largely in the life of "Uncle" Charlie during the days that followed their final rescue.

Dr D'Arcy Irvine, whose job it had been to dress his wounds was pragmatic in what he told his patient, informing him that another day spent out in the bush with no proper supply of food, or water, would probably have resulted in the flesh on Charlie's leg mortifying.

Furthermore, he advised him that, if that had happened, it would have been doubtful whether he would have survived and certain that, at the very least, he would have lost his leg.

Nicknamed by Locke as their "Chief Tormentor", the doctor proved to be both skilful and delicate when changing their dressings. Although Alex and the captain commanded comparatively little of his medical attention, all four men would jostle for position, always endeavouring to get one of their opposite number taken first for treatment.

However, Charlie soon learnt that it was best to get it "over and done with", giving him the opportunity to jeer and jest at the screwed up, pained faces of the others as, each in turn, they tried to disguise their medically applied torture.

Perhaps the most excruciating pain for Charlie was having the wound in his leg probed for any remaining pot shot. He found himself barely able to stifle a scream, as he felt the cold metal instrument being twisted and poked around inside the gaping hole that the doctor swabbed clean of pus every morning and afternoon.

The need of continuing treatment did have certain compensations however, for when Charlie arrived back at Old Calabar and was transferred to the European hospital at Old Calabar, he found himself being delivered into the care of four young nurses, including the delightful Muriel, who had first taken his fancy when he had become ill with dysentery on his initial arrival in West Africa.

He was particularly pleased that she seemed to take it upon herself as her appointed duty, and hers alone, to change and dress his wounds each day, apart from Wednesday afternoon, which appeared to be her only time off.

Charlie made a mental note that, when he was well enough, proposing a mid-week meal at the tennis club probably afforded him the best opportunity of a first date.

Muriel always brought a smile to his face and she would chide him light-heartedly that she had known many a five-year-old that was not in the habit of making as much fuss as he did, when it came to having his dressings and bandages changed.

In response, he would suggest that, if he was indeed a little boy, she would probably try to "kiss it better" for him and she would blush and turn her attention to pumping up his pillows, reaching out from behind the head-rest of the metal-framed hospital bed, so that he could not see her face, as it blushed bright pink.

In this way he could not see her embarrassment, even if it did allow him a better chance to sniff the sweet scented bouquet of the lavender toilet water, which she was apt to dab around her neck in the morning, running the little glass stopper over her wrists in an attempt to mask the smell of hospital disinfectant, which seemed to adhere to her hands, no matter how vigorously she tried to scrub them at the end of every shift.

Slowly, as Charlie began to make his recovery, Muriel would tease him that if he exercised his wounded leg more and walked a few yards further than he had done the day before, then she might just consider giving him a little kiss on the cheek.

However, whenever he tried to claim his reward, she would quickly answer that he had not walked far enough and that maybe tomorrow …

Alex visited Charlie most days, bringing with him news that the Benin king had sent back two rings that had belonged to Captain Copford-Crawford and how the more gruesome story that they still had the poor man's fingers attached had appeared in several of the English newspapers.

Such was the reply from the despotic African leader, when asked if there were still any white men alive and being held captive. The poignant and all too implicit message that they alluded to in response left the British in no doubt that the Benin king meant business.

And so when the Oba announced that he would send down to the waterside as many of his soldiers as it took to wipe out the white men and that he would carry on enlisting more of his troops until they had killed every white man who dared set foot upon his kingdom's soil, the newly appointed successor to the slaughtered James Phillips began the organisation of the Punitive Expedition.

It was an act of retribution, in which neither Captain Boisragon nor, Ralph Locke were deemed to be sufficiently fit to take part, despite the former's protestations. However, it was a call to arms in which the now fully recovered Alex was to play a crucial part.

Alex desperately wanted to go, if only to avenge the cold-blooded murder of his friends and to vindicate the fact that Charlie had been told that he would never be able to walk properly again.

For Charlie the silver-topped walking stick, with which he had stumbled through the forest when he and Alex had made good their escape and with which he had summoned the attention of their final rescuers, was to become a part of his daily routine for the rest of his life.

It was quite obvious that Charlie would never be fit enough to take part in the bloody battle which was to reach its gory height in the February of 1897 as, by the beginning of that month, he was scarcely able to limp from one end of the hospital verandah to the other with, or without, the ever more coquettish Muriel waiting at the end with words of encouragement.

With her lips pursed in a tight cupid's bow, she would drive poor Charlie on to greater and greater endeavours until, finally mustering all his strength and casting his stick to the floor, he had swept his arms around the pretty young nurse and planted a kiss on her cheek, nearly falling over backwards in the process.

Muriel had blushed scarlet, especially as Charlie's bold move had been witnessed by Cameron, a Scottish lad, barely out of his teens, who had arrived in Old Calabar just a few weeks earlier intent on gaining a military posting, but who had finished up spending his first weeks in the hospital, suffering from blackwater fever.

Now almost fully recovered from his illness, he was due to be discharged from the hospital later that day. He was a cheeky, cheery lad and his brash brand of humour drew many a smile from his fellow patients.

Muriel had a soft spot for him too and although she would often rebuke him for his remarks, she often found herself smiling inwardly, being reminded of the older brother she had lost in the South African Boer War.

Cameron had wolf-whistled his appreciation of Charlie's lovelorn efforts to entrap the young nurse and had been scarcely able to wait to relate the whole tale to a visiting Alex later that afternoon.

'That friend of yours, Charlie, is well-smitten with the pretty blonde nurse. Have you got any idea why he thinks so much of her?' he had asked.

'I can't understand why he should think so much of her. She stuck a bloody great needle in his arse the other day,' continued Cameron, giving the visitor a broad wink, tossing his head slightly to one side to indicate to Alex that Muriel was standing right behind him at the time and could hardly have failed to hear every word.

'And guess what, I've got an even bigger, rustier one and I've been saving it especially for you, my lad,' Muriel had retorted, having recovered from her earlier embarrassment.

Alex smiled, first at Charlie, and then at the youngster. He was not normally so astute when it came to assessing a fellow human's thoughts and feelings, but there was no doubt in his mind that Cameron held him in a great deal of esteem.

Why, his young hero worshipper had even taken to addressing him as "Alex the Avenger", when the older man had announced his intention of joining the Punitive Expedition, which was heading back to Benin City with a military force reckoned to be more than sufficient in terms of numbers and well equipped to teach the Benin king a lesson he would never forget.

At thirty years old Alex was ten years older than Cameron, but he was still far too young to remember a time when Britain had not been ruled over by a sombrely clad monarch dressed from head to toe in black these last many years.

It was sixty years since Queen Victoria had taken her place on the throne and now the clock was ticking towards the celebrations planned for her Diamond Jubilee.

For a black African queen of a blood-spattered kingdom, time was also ticking ... ticking towards a British reprisal against a civilization that had survived for centuries, followers in the horrific wake of a long dead Devil queen.

Yes, time was ticking ... like a wakeup call for the dead – a ticking time bomb of murder and retribution.

A queen who so often drank the blood of her sacrificed victims from a bronze bowl was baying for more blood. She who had an unquenchable thirst could be denied no longer. It was time for her to arise again from centuries of slumber.

Alex was on his way to fight – to do battle in a war that would continue throughout the generations that followed him, bringing with it trial and tribulation, happiness and heart-ache, death and damnation.

For little could Alex understand, but his actions, when he finally reached the City of Blood, would have implications for Mary, for Charlie and for Cameron too – three people for whom their own lives and the lives of a whole generation of their children and grandchildren would become inextricably interwoven for over a century that was yet to come.

Chapter 15

The advance on Benin City began on February 12th and, although he had no military skills to offer, Alex was gladly taken on as a scout, for there was virtually no one alive who could claim such intimate knowledge of the treacherous stretch of forest that the hastily assembled armed forces would be forced to penetrate, if they were to have any hope of victory.

Orphaned when he was barely out of nappies, Cameron had been raised by an elder brother, who had emigrated to Canada. He had been anxious to escape from his upbringing during his early teens.

Cameron lied about his age and had signed up for army service shortly after his sixteenth birthday. He had been all set to join the Blue Jackets, but for the fact that he had failed to gain a clean bill of health, due to the blackwater fever, which he had suffered soon after his arrival in West Africa.

He was therefore all too happy to join forces with Alex and was taken on despite his inexperience, even if he did have a good deal of difficulty in persuading Lieutenant Turner, who was in charge of the forty strong team of Hausa soldiers, to give him the chance to prove his worth.

Cameron had come to know Alex quite well, looking up to him both as a hero and as a father figure.

Together they had enlisted and, as soon as Rear Admiral Harry Rawson had learnt that Alex was one of the four men who had survived the previous mission, he had insisted on meeting him.

Cameron, much impressed that Alex was to have an audience with no less a person than the leading naval officer of the Benin Punitive Expedition, had inveigled and cajoled Alex into allowing him to tag along.

Big, bluff and bearded, the Rear Admiral was a typical Yorkshireman, with a ruddy complexion, whose presence commanded respect and whose opinions, whilst not always accepted, or agreed with, certainly had the knack of gaining the attention of anyone in authority.

Never afraid to speak his mind, he had once offered the opinion that, in order to save the amount of time and money that he felt was wasted in Parliament, apart from the party leaders:

"All others may only speak as long as to take up three columns of Hansard when reported and if they desire to continue, a charge of ten shillings a column should be made."

Such open and radical thinking made him both popular and unpopular in equal measure. He was well liked by the men who served under him, as he prided himself on caring about every one of them.

At the same time, he was equally unpopular amongst British statesmen in whom he held little regard. Indeed, it was said that if it hadn't been for the fact of having "friends in high places", he would never have reached the rank he had achieved, despite his loyal service to the Navy for over forty years.

At the age of fourteen, when he had been just a few years younger than the impressionable young Scot who had befriended Alex, Harry Rawson had witnessed his first action in China.

Now in his mid fifties, the Rear Admiral had twice before led successful punitive missions on the East African coast – one of which had gone down in the record books as the shortest war in history, lasting as it did just thirty-two minutes.

The Admiral's ships had bombarded the Sultan's palace in Zanzibar for a little over half an hour to dislodge a usurper of the throne, who had been deemed unacceptable to Queen Victoria's Government and to British interests generally.

Years earlier, whilst serving on the royal yacht, Victoria and Albert, Harry Rawson had formed a life-long friendship with Queen Victoria. It was a friendship that, not unnaturally, he closely guarded and he would not hear a word spoken against Her Royal Highness by any man who served on his ships. Later upon the queen's death in 1901, Harry Rawson was to command the naval escort at her funeral.

It was even rumoured that, for years, he had been secretly infatuated with the monarch, despite the seniority of her years and her unattainable position.

True, she was more than twenty years older than him and, for her part, still remained very much in love with her beloved Prince Albert, whose early death, in 1861, had left her widowed and bereft, but to Her Majesty's loyal servant, Harry Rawson, such trifling impediments mattered very little.

In 1882, just short of his fortieth birthday, he had been awarded a medal for his part in the Egyptian Campaign. He had been placed in command of the Cape Squadron in 1895 – just eighteen months before being recalled to lead the naval expedition against the king of Benin.

'You'll be well rewarded for your services and you'll be treated well. No short rations, I can assure you!' he had told Alex.

'Ask any man in my service. I've seen for myself the results of inadequate supply arrangements on Wolseley's Egyptian expedition where sick and wounded men died of starvation and the advance guard went without food for forty hours in the desert heat. No, Seath, you'll find I'm a fair man. I don't hold with meagre rations and frequent floggings.'

As if to confirm his point, he called upon one of his deputies to annunciate details of the rations, which had been packed on board the warships – supplies which were meant to last a thousand men for ten days, soldered into the tin inner cases of thirty pound biscuit tins, secured to wooden pallets for easy head-loading.

Each tin contained rations for twenty-four men for one day – preserved meat, rice, onions, biscuits, tea, coffee and sugar and, of course, a tot of rum and lime juice to be doled out to every man on a daily basis. Each tin also contained two candles, two boxes of matches and portions of salt, pepper, mustard and curry powder.

'Curry powder?' Cameron had intoned curiously, but not too loudly to avoid being heard by the Rear Admiral.

'That'll put the shits up the men, if nothing else will,' he added, smirking at Alex through the forest of lightly tanned freckles that were scattered across his pale-skinned face.

'Yes, indeed, young man and making sure that every man has his bowels moved regularly is as important an aspect as any of our military campaign, let me assure you. Medicine is available, if necessary, so have no fear, on this expedition the medical officers will have your backside as loose as your tongue,' commanded Harry Rawson bluffly.

'Here take one of these each of you,' he added, issuing both Alex and Cameron with a list of written instructions headed "For the safety of Troops".

Along with dictates to take daily doses of quinine, to wear a cholera belt, only to drink boiled water and for socks to be removed and washed following each day's march, Alex was more keen to take note of the daily ration of rum and the fact that each man was to be issued with a pint of stout during their time on the river.

Meanwhile, Cameron sniggered at the instructions as to how each man in camp was to make use of the latrines and how, when on the march, they were to go off a short way into the bush and be careful not to commit a nuisance by shitting too close to the path.

'What about water supplies?' asked Alex, knowing only too well from his recent first-hand experience that licking leaves as the dawn light of day filtered through the canopy tops was no substitute for an adequate supply of clean, fresh drinking water.

'There will be a quart of water issued every day to each officer, soldier, sailor and scout and a pint each to the carriers,' answered the Rear Admiral's deputy.

'Apparently the best way of carrying water supplies in these parts is in scoured-out paraffin tins, fitted with a wooden base to prevent buckling when carried head high,' he added officiously, letting everyone appreciate that he knew his business and was experienced in such matters.

'In the past, gallon glass demijohns have been used transported in wicker baskets, but the traders tell me that they break easily and the glass fragments cut the bare feet of the carriers on the bush paths,' Rear Admiral Rawson interjected, displaying a little more of his customary humanity, as Cameron, in his naiveté, wondered why the black men were inclined to drink less than their white counterparts.

Had Cameron been taken on as a Blue Jacket, he had looked forward to wearing their smart customary uniform, but now he had to content himself with the blue serge, red fez and cummerbund, with its black leather and other accoutrements as worn by the members of the Niger Coast Protectorate Force, who were to be in the front line and who it was intended would bear the brunt of the fighting.

In all, the NCPF force numbered four hundred and fifty well-trained and battle-seasoned troops led by fifteen officers, mostly seconded from the British Army, but with one African officer amongst their ranks.

Like Alex, the officers of the NCPF had a reputation for heavy, riotous drinking in the club houses, which were constantly springing up, along with the whore houses, around the headquarters at Old Calabar and the barracks situated at Sapele.

Muriel had often complained that she and the other young nurses dared not go out after dark on their own, or even with a female friend, for fear of having to forcibly remove the groping hand of a passing officer from running up the inside of her starched petticoat, halting momentarily on his drunken, zigzag path to make some lewd suggestion as to how she might care to join him, as he staggered home to bed.

Generally speaking, she found the men of the Navy more courteous and easier to deal with, lacking the rough manners of their military counterparts, whose idea of a night out invariably meant learning the colour of the lady's knickers and scrabbling to undo the multitude of laces which served as much to protect the virtue of the wearer and prolong their undoing, as much as they served to increase the prettiness of the undergarment.

Muriel was pleased that Charlie was still too unwell to give any consideration to joining up with the more fool-hardy Alex for a second confrontation with the Benin king and his troops.

She had been told by the surgeon, who had operated on him when he had first arrived at the hospital, that he would be unlikely ever to walk again without the aid of his trusty malacca walking cane.

When it had become obvious to the other nurses that she harboured a soft spot for him, Matron had taken her aside one morning and asked her if she really felt the need to hitch up with a cripple.

It was this remark that made Muriel think that it was time to relinquish her hospital duties for a while, to get away from such bitching and sniping interference in her life and to devote herself a little more to what she had come out to West Africa to do.

It wasn't long before the opportunity to make herself more useful presented itself.

Such was the reputation of the West African coast for fever that a hospital ship was chartered to join the warships, which were being prepared for action.

Appropriately enough named after Charlie's saviour walking stick, it was the P & O Steam Ship *Malacca*, which had been on the point of leaving London, its cargo already loaded, but which had been rapidly recalled to the docks, her cargo discharged and fitted out as a hospital ship.

With its own operating room, sterilising apparatus, ice-making machinery to reduce the temperatures of patients suffering from fever and beds for up to a hundred of the anticipated wounded, it had set sail from London's Thames Docks staffed by a surgeon and six doctors.

All that was needed was a sufficient number of suitably qualified nurses to attend to the likely casualties of war.

'You'll have to get one of the other nurses to pick up your walking stick every time you drop it from now on, Charlie,' announced Muriel one morning.

'What do you mean?' he had enquired anxiously.

'What I mean is that I'm leaving you and I don't want to hear of any of your hanky-panky either, while I'm away. I'll pick it up for you now, but it will be the last time for a while. I'm off to work with the doctors on board the *Malacca* – it's to be the hospital ship for the Punitive Expedition.'

'You can't go and leave me,' replied Charlie, all child-like and imploring.

'You can't just up and leave. What will I do without you? I'll be so lonely. And just what will you do without me?' he added roguishly and with a twinkle in his eye.

'Oh, I guess I'll find some kind of diversion,' Muriel intoned by way of a mischievous reply.

'I'm told there's going to be a detachment of a hundred and twenty Royal Marines on board and I guess they'll all be missing their girlfriends back home,' she had teased him.

And so the hospital ship, with Muriel on board, joined the six ships of Rear Admiral Harry Rawson's fleet – the *St George, Philomel, Phoebe, Barrosa, Alecto and Widgeon,* all steaming at full speed and joined by the *Theseus* and, finally, by the older, smaller *Forte*, labouring behind the faster, newer ships.

Their destination was a rendezvous five miles offshore from Brass, where they were due to gather on February 3rd, 1897.

A joint venture between the Army and the Navy had been under discussion, but the idea of such a combined force was soon dropped, since relations between the two armed services were not good and there was a general reluctance to mount a major military expedition, on account of the expense, the risk of disease and all the necessary organisation.

However, the Admiralty had been in more confident mood and when Rear Admiral Harry Rawson had cabled from Cape Town that he believed that it was possible to take the City of Benin inside a period of just six weeks and at a cost of a mere £50,000, he was recalled almost immediately from the Cape of Good Hope, with the objective of capturing Benin City, ending the bloodbath and avenging the deaths of those who, unlike Alex and Charlie, had not been lucky enough to escape with their lives.

News of the massacre had broke in the British newspapers a month before the planned advance on Benin City. In Liverpool the trader, James Pinnock, had called for immediate retribution, being quoted as stating that:

"Apart from all considerations of commerce on both sides, the depopulation of the country by human sacrifices would be a sufficient reason for Her Majesty's Government stepping in to suppress horrors more atrocious than anything depicted in the history of any country in what is practically British territory."

It was even rumoured that Queen Victoria herself had voiced more of an opinion in the matter than was normally her wont. It was also said that the appointment of Harry Rawson to lead the expedition was greatly influenced by Her Majesty's stated preference for what she considered to be "the right man for the job".

It was whispered in Court circles that the time that they had spent together on the royal yacht had not all been "plain sailing" between Her Majesty and the well-educated Yorkshireman and that the favour of the granting of his appointment to lead the expedition might have been in response to certain other "favours" which Her Majesty had enjoyed.

Thus it was that Rawson's flagship, the *St George*, left Simonstown with a fleet of seven other steam ships in its wake barely a week after news of the ill-fated Benin Expedition had reached British shores.

By coincidence, it had set sail at exactly the same time that Mary had picked up a copy of *The Scotsman* in the lobby at the Queen Hotel and learnt that she was not a widow after all.

Meanwhile, at another hotel in Cannes, the ageing Queen Victoria, was spending a quiet winter in the Hotel Excelsior Regina before the inevitable exertions of her Diamond Jubilee year.

She was eagerly awaiting news that an additional, hastily assembled detachment of naval vessels had been dispatched from the Mediterranean Squadron in Malta's Valletta harbour to join the other ships being assembled under the auspices of Harry Rawson – Her Majesty's naval admiral, friend and admirer.

Many of the officers serving on board the vessels harboured on the tiny Mediterranean island had, at their own expense, brought their wives out from Britain, as the Malta season had been about to begin and the prospect of a rigorous and, quite possibly, dangerous expedition several thousand miles away in the steamy West African tropics had not been viewed with any enthusiasm.

With the news that, first Alex, and now both Cameron and Muriel were off to play their part in the taking of the City of Blood Charlie, left alone in the hospital without his close friends, had only one occasional visitor – Captain Boisragon.

Charlie felt sick at the thought that, of the quartet, there was every possibility that not all four would return unharmed, or even live to tell the tale.

Muriel would probably be safe enough from the fighting on board the hospital ship, but what if she contracted a fever and what of Alex and Cameron?

As scouts they would be placing themselves in the most dangerous position of all, making them easy targets to be picked off by the Benin foe.

Charlie knew that Alex had received a letter from Mary, rejoicing in her husband's safety and enquiring too about his own welfare. Alex had not replied, professing not to have had the time to do so.

Instead, Charlie had sat up in his hospital bed and scribed a long letter to Mary, describing their hazardous escape and detailing how his days of rest and recuperation had been brightened up by the playful, cheerful antics of young Cameron.

It was not until he had given the envelope over to one of the nurses for posting, that he realised that he had not even made mention of Muriel to her in his letter!

Chapter 16

So with Alex already departed for a brief training session in the use of the newly acquired Snider rifles, along with the forty or so Hausa scouts, who had been hastily recruited from Lagos Colony, Charlie was left alone in the hospital where he hardly knew anyone.

He missed Alex's visits and missed too having no cheeky chappie in the person of the young Scottish lad to help him pass the days. Even Captain Boisragon, who had occasionally called to visit him, had now departed.

Much to his own chagrin, the captain had learnt that his intention to lead a party of troops into battle against the Benin king had been thwarted and he was ordered home, ostensibly on medical grounds.

However, the newspapers in Britain had begun suggesting that, as the senior serving officer with the earlier, ill-fated mission, he deserved a court martial for not having taken the necessary precautions against attack.

Alex had no doubt in his own mind that, as scouts, theirs was to be a most hazardous role. In the company of his young protégé, he was to be among the first landing party of seven hundred men, comprising both Blue Jackets and a marine battalion, to be transferred from the steam ships to the smaller awaiting steamers, which pulled away from the shore one early February afternoon, whilst the ship's band played a rousing version of "Auld Lang Syne", as they made their departure.

As they left the safety of the ship, rain began to fall in torrents, accompanied by the furious roar of thunder and lightning, whose forked tongues penetrated through the forest in an unholy uproar, giving many of the sailors and marines their first taste of a tropical rainstorm.

Huddled together and unsure of their first move, they shivered and shook on the banks of the creek, their teeth chattering, as they assembled in a crocodile line, uncertain as to whether they were more likely to become the prey of hungry reptiles, or be shot in the back by a sniper's bullet.

Their passage through the muddy creeks was beset by thunderstorms, drenching rain and intense, humid heat, which soaked their uniforms in a mixture of penetrating rain and their own sticky, foul-smelling sweat.

Although the dry season was expected to last until the end of February, the rain gods had other ideas for their amusement, warning the expedition leader just how easily the weather might wreck even the best laid plans.

As Rear Admiral Harry Rawson knew only too well, expeditions on the West African coast commonly took place in the dry season between October and February, due to the simple reason that, at other times, tropical rains made the movement of large bodies of men virtually impossible along the primitive bush paths.

At Sapele the advance party found two hundred and sixty hastily assembled Niger Coast Protectorate Force troops crowded into a barracks that had been built to house just sixty men.

Here the officer in charge was supervising the construction of a jetty, built from logs cut from the hardwood trees that grew right down to the riverside.

Six miles further north lay the village of Siri, which was intended to be used as the expedition's jumping off point into hostile country. Here, the landing party spent an uneasy night, under a dull, cloudy, brooding sky. Swarms of mosquitoes danced around them, keeping the men awake long past the twilight.

It was Cameron's first chance to consider what the future might bring, as he tossed and turned, his bitten flesh screeching and squealing, wrestling for sleep atop a waterproof sheet.

He had no view of the pitch-black of the African night from his shelter beneath the overhanging tarpaulin sheet, whose scant protection he shared with Alex and four other men.

He desperately needed a pee, but didn't know which he feared most – stepping unwarily on a poisonous snake, or a Benin bullet in the back.

With just five days to prepare a camp for the naval landing party, it was an early morning bugle call for the work to begin of clearing an area of high ground above the village.

Whilst some of the men were engaged in erecting simple banana leaf shelters, others began damming up a stream for drinking water and others still, including both Alex and Cameron, set about the task of laying a three hundred yard long track of hardwood logs between the village and the creek, where the roughly hewn jetty was nearing completion.

One surprise visitor at Siri was Captain Boisragon, who arrived professing himself fully recovered and eager to resume command of his troops, but he was dismissed and left the camp after three days spent hanging around, hoping that the decision against him would be overturned.

Alex, who knew of the rumours of cowardliness which were circulating in the British newspapers, listened to the nightly lament of a soldier, who seemed to know that his military days were over, attempting to soften the blow of his friend's dismissal by informing him that many of the men would have been proud to have served under him, if it had been possible and that nobody had ever reckoned that he would have been fit for duty.

After the arrival of Rear Admiral Harry Rawson on an initial inspection tour of the camp, before the troops arrived en masse, a battle plan began to emerge, with the main difficulty being that the exact location of Benin City had never been accurately determined on any map.

The preferred plan of attack was to cut through the forest from Siri along the left bank of the Ologi Creek to within striking distance of Benin City, thus ensuring a good water supply throughout the march.

However, with no readily available information as to the condition of the creek, the practicality of such a plan was very much in doubt.

And so it was that, with such a lack of knowledge of the terrain they were facing, Alex found himself volunteering for the dangerous task of taking a canoe and a team of paddlers on a rain-soaked, cloudy night in an attempt to survey the territory and assess the likelihood of the success of such a course of action.

It came as no surprise that Cameron wanted to go with him, volunteering to accompany his hero, "Alex the Avenger", but the young man's presence in the canoe was thwarted by the Intelligence Officer, who was keen to point out that the youngster's talkative nature might well prove more of a liability than an asset, as they endeavoured to slip past the sentry soldiers patrolling the banks of the river at Ologbo.

And so Alex disappeared quietly into the night with the British Intelligence Officer and an assembled crew of Itsekiri paddlers, whilst Cameron paced around the camp, kicking out at the dwindling embers of one of the camp fires in his anger and frustration at not being allowed to accompany his hero on the mission.

Unable to employ flashlights, for fear of drawing unwanted attention to themselves, it proved too dark for any accurate survey work to be undertaken at the dead of night.

However, they only had to travel a few miles under cover of darkness to realise that both the river banks and the water itself was too heavily entangled with vegetation and fallen trees for there to be any hope of the expedition being able to make its approach by this route.

Meanwhile, the steamers containing the remainder of the officers and men lay at anchor off Goshawk Point. Sleeping accommodation on board was limited, with the officers dozing in deck chairs and the men languishing on deck.

Soon after supper, a heavy thunderstorm blew up, as if from nowhere, heralding the passage of another angry god. The tempers of both officers and men began to fray as, yet again, everybody and everything that was not under canvas, was soaked within seconds of the first crack of lightning, whose forked tongues emblazoned the sky, sending a cascade of fire crackers into a fiery descent through the forest.

On their return, a messenger was dispatched to impart the news of the impracticality of the preferred attack plan to the Rear Admiral, who had returned to his ship, carried back there in a litter to the comfort of the state rooms on board the Ivy moored at Warrigi.

Apparently the six-mile trek through the forest had exhausted the fifty three-year-old naval officer, despite the fact that he had discarded his uniform in favour of lightweight trousers and a thin cotton shirt, a wide-brimmed sun hat and a stout walking stick.

Sitting musing over the problem with his pipe, Rear Admiral Rawson was forced to devise other plans. Soon he came up with an alternative objective of throwing a wire suspension bridge over the creek, enabling his men to cross and capture the village of Ologbo, before making their ultimate onslaught on the City of Benin.

He knew that he had to act quickly, as the weather was already turning against him and he sat through the thunderstorm, pondering over his problems.

Overhead the angry gods whipped themselves into a fury, as bolts of thunder crashed their way through the night sky, rampaging through his thoughts and inflaming his mind, as he wondered just how he would take the city and, perhaps, more importantly, musing as to how he would find its ultimate prize!

110

For it was known that Benin – the City of Blood – was the home of a legend – a legendary gift originally bestowed upon a queen, who had been dead for over a thousand years – a priceless object that was there for the taking, if only it could be found.

And what better present could there be to bestow upon another queen in this her Diamond Jubilee year? His queen, his darling queen, who deserved nothing but the best.

Harry Rawson would not rest until he had presented her with the gift to end all gifts!

Chapter 17

Sitting in their deck chairs in the early morning sunshine and calm of the following day, which gave no hint of the thunderous weather conditions of the previous night, the naval officers were able to enjoy the dewy cool of the daybreak, before the energy-draining heat of the day began to assault them.

Steaming against the fast flowing current of the creek, in the cascade of early morning light, it seemed strange to imagine that they were on a mission which would bring death and destruction to this eerily beautiful place, where brightly coloured kingfishers flitted amongst the water lilies and palm fronds flailed their reflections in the clear, rushing waters.

It was hard to imagine that they had not come here simply to relax and marvel at the steamer captain's ability to negotiate the sharp twists and turns in the creeks as, each in turn, they were navigated with the utmost skill, ramming the bow into the bank and allowing the current to carry the vessel round each steeply curved corner.

By late afternoon they reached Warrigi, where an opening had been made in the dense bank of massive forest trees fringing the waters of the creek.

Here a rickety pier jutted out at right angles from the river bank, its planks of roughly sawn wood no longer a mass of splinters, for they had long been worn away by the countless passage of hundreds of bare feet.

Beyond the pier, camp fires were beginning to spark and twinkle between the shadowy trunks of the huge hardwood trees, their boughs festooned with giant creepers, like Christmas decorations of mistletoe and holly. Here instead of candles, tiny fireflies flitted amongst the foliage, as if by way of illuminating a Christmas tree.

Excited, yelling crowds of natives swarmed around the docking steamers, anxious for a small gift of a few cigarettes, whilst naked children begged for boiled sweets.

Noisily, the lately arrived steamers lay at anchor blowing off steam, whilst the shrill call of the cicadas rose above the whole cacophony of carnival sounds, adding their screaming demands for attention to the still of a calm African night – a calm that was soon to be shattered by so many more deaths.

Here was the lull both before and after the storm; a cool breeze blew gently through the mangroves – calmly and contentedly, as it whispered through the lush vegetation, which rustled and swayed so peacefully.

It provided a welcome relief from the intense heat of the day, but there was a mounting certainty that the storm clouds of battle were about to break.

There was nothing left to do, but to cross the creek by boat, seize the village of Ologbo and from there onwards to march into the surrounding forest and capture the capital City of Benin.

It was a bold plan and one for which the opposing troops of the Benin king were ready and waiting.

* * * * * * * * * *

Advancing towards Ologbo, along the unmapped bush paths meant that the British forces had to move in single file, making them vulnerable to attack at any time.

Alex and the forty-strong team of scouts probed ahead of the column, ready to provide an early warning of any enemy presence.

Cameron was seconded as one of the messengers, whose task it was to quickly pass back along the track and convey any news of a likely ambush.

It was a dangerous game of hide and seek, in which a skilfully laid ambush might easily pass unnoticed. Often the troops in the main column would find a tree, or a bush concealing an enemy sniper only a few feet away.

The front line troops of the Niger Coast Protectorate Force were harassed by snipers, but they were used to shooting crows out of the trees and most of the Benin sharp shooters were quickly picked off, falling from the branches like the dead leaves of autumn.

Those in the front line deployed a technique of searching the bush with volleys, as a means of driving the enemy off, or forcing them to open fire prematurely, thus revealing their whereabouts, but this involved expending prodigious quantities of ammunition which, very soon, was in short supply.

Cameron stumbled quite literally upon his first dead body, as soon as the thick gun smoke, which hung in the still air, began to lift. It was a gruesome first encounter with death; the sniper had been shot in the head, with a bullet passing right through his eye, so that all remained of his sight was one horrifically staring eye and a bloody hole where the other eye had once been.

At times it was difficult for the British troops to pick out the path ahead of them in the oppressive gloom, especially since the Benin soldiers were deploying banana leaf wadding for use with their guns.

It produced a thick, acrid, black smoke when fired and the dark clouds of gun smoke seemed to cling purposely and resolutely to the sticky oppressive heat, which lingered in the atmosphere, clinging to clothes and choking the throats of the men, who gagged and spat out the foul tasting air.

Any thoughts that the capture of Benin City might be easily achieved, due to the perceived cowardly reluctance of the Benin troops to come out into the open and fight were quickly dispelling as, one by one, the naval columns advancing through the surrounding forest came under heavy fire.

The sound of men screaming in excruciating pain became a regular occurrence. One man close by Alex's side was hit by a bullet, which entered at his right elbow and exited at his wrist.

The wound was agonising and he was dragged into the bush by Alex and Cameron, helped by a naval chaplain and another man who had lost his helmet after a bullet had blown it off the top of his head but which, luckily, had done no further damage.

Benin had no standing army, but its young men were expected to become warriors and to learn the art of warfare from the age of puberty.

Each war chief maintained his own private army, made up of kinsmen and slaves, hunters and farmers – all were encouraged to fight in order to gain honours and to enhance their status in society.

The main advantage that the British had over their Benin opponents was their modern weaponry, especially their repeating rifles and machine guns, which were unmatched by the Benin soldiers' breechloading rifles and muzzle-loading smooth-bore guns, mostly used to fire iron bolts, or "pot leg" when proper bullets were not available.

In recent years the Europeans had restricted and even banned trade in modern firearms to West Africa and, as a result, many of the guns in use were antiquated and unreliable and, fortunately for the British, the thick bush reduced their effectiveness.

In the 1880s the Maxim Gun Company from Erith in Kent had begun manufacturing a lightweight, single-barrel machine gun, in which the force of recoil automatically loaded, fired and ejected at a rate of eleven shots per second.

The Navy had adopted the use of these guns just five years beforehand and their deployment had transformed the nature of late nineteenth century warfare.

With the Benin forced to clear whole areas of bush in order to obtain an unobstructed line of fire for their ancient weaponry, this exposed them to the devastating fire power of the maxims, which would strip away any form of concealment by scything through the undergrowth and maximising the effects of the enemy fire.

Jungle warfare was a particularly harrowing and unnerving form of fighting, but British military thinking had yet to produce a systematic approach to the vagaries of bush fighting.

Rear Admiral Rawson had recommended his officers to read the relevant pages of Wolseley's Soldiers Pocket Book for Field Services in preparation for their onward advance towards the City of Blood.

However, no book of words could prepare young soldiers for the devastating horrors of war, as they shrieked at, cursed and damned the natives.

It was impossible to imagine how they could possibly cope, transported thousands of miles from home, maybe from a barracks at a quiet English seaside town in the depths of winter, only to meet a violent death, hot, dirty and dishevelled in the steamy African jungle.

One man, obviously in absolute agony after having been shot in the stomach, had implored Alex to return his revolver, so that he might shoot himself.

As Alex leaned over him, trying to offer what comfort he could, the wounded marine, unseen by Alex, pulled his comforter's revolver from its holster, pressing his finger to the trigger and raising it to his head.

Alex was just in time to knock it out of his hand, but wondered immediately if he had done the right thing. Perhaps, it would have been better to have allowed the man to end his own suffering there and then, as soon afterwards he managed to get hold of a rifle and terminated his own life in a shotgun blast that blew off his face.

As the number of British casualties mounted, all around Alex the wounded and dying were shrieking for water, damning their adversaries and crying for help. Other comrades tried to intervene, binding their wounds and trying to staunch the bleeding until medical assistance arrived.

So often, it seemed almost a curious sight to witness those who had yet to fall with their arms around the necks of their injured friends, talking to them in softly soothing terms, often uttering words that meant nothing at all, but which provided the only form of comfort that was available.

Terms of endearment normally reserved for their nearest and dearest became the verbal currency of the day, as death spread its tentacles in a forest of fear.

At night the men slept close-packed in blankets on the ground, under canvas tarpaulins to keep off the worst of the heavy dew, but still exposed to the myriads of night-time insects, which made their lives all the more miserable.

Battle stained and filthy, they had not washed for days, but that was the least of their problems, for by dawn on the February 18th news was broadcast throughout the ranks that the final battle for Benin City was about to be fought.

Chapter 18

The march to Benin City began shortly after daybreak. The bush ahead had previously been cleared by a bombardment of rockets and maxim fire.

It was hard to imagine that a place once so beautiful and tranquil was so quickly to become a scene of death and devastation and that a civilisation (if civilisation be the right word) that had existed for centuries could be destroyed in a single day.

Alex had already taken his cocoa shortly after the wake up bugle at four o'clock that morning, storing his biscuit away in his haversack for consumption later that morning, although with what he was about to witness, he would have little stomach for food of any kind.

Cameron, with the all-consuming appetite of a teenager, had begged his biscuit, the moment he saw it being stowed away but had, at first, been rebuked.

Alex rested his tall frame against a seven pounder, smoking a final cigarette before the long, hard march began and before the horror of what they had come to do finally dawned.

Today would be a day of death, a day upon which the crimson clay soil would run even redder. It was also the day upon which many of his comrades would never live to see the setting sun.

As Alex drew on the last of his cigarettes, his thoughts turned to Mary and, for a moment, he wished he was with her, safely tucked up in the cramped Edinburgh attic.

From the letter that Charlie had read to him, he had learnt that she had borne a son – a boy who, quite possibly, he would never have the chance to acknowledge as his own flesh and blood.

Flesh and blood – yes, there would be plenty of that this day. Flesh that would never normally be revealed, cut to the bone in bloody battle.

And blood, yes, there would definitely be plenty of blood.

Alex bent down and scooped a can of rainwater from the tarpaulin which lined the hollowed out trench containing the closely guarded water supply.

He recalled how one of the Blue Jackets – a young man, whom he had known simply as Chris – a boy no older than Cameron, had been shot in the head by a sniper whilst guarding the precious water tins, as they had pitched camp the night before.

It was such a waste of a life, a young man whose lifeblood had mingled with the water he had been commanded to protect.

Alex almost imagined that he could taste the youngster's blood tainting the tin mug of water as he drank – not the Holy Sacrament, not the Blood of Christ, but simply the blood of Chris.

It was at this point that he had finally given in to Cameron's demand for his breakfast biscuit, scant crumbs of comfort offered to another young man whose fate lay in what the day ahead held for all of them.

Why was he here? What was he doing?

Alex was a trader's clerk, not a man of the military. He had come to barter goods, not to barter his very existence. Did he have the right to put his own life at risk like this, when his wife, Mary didn't even know that he was putting their future together on the line, simply to avenge the lives of men she had never known?

He had a responsibility to her. He was surely accountable to the children she had borne and he also owed a debt to Cameron, who held him as a hero and who expected so much of him.

It was no use worrying any further. He was here now and all he could hope to do was to stay alive, to return to Old Calabar and sink a few celebratory pints with the convalescing Charlie, introduce the young Scottish lad to his first taste of a decent bottle of scotch and perhaps his first female acquaintance.

He hoped he would return in one piece, fit to mount the steep attic staircase that Charlie would never again manage to climb without the aid of his trusty malacca.

Alex's thoughts also turned to the pretty young nurse whom Charlie so obviously had his heart set on. How was she coping on board the *Malacca* hospital ship, dealing with bits of bodies no longer attached to their previous owners?

She had said that she wanted to experience some "real" nursing, but what was real about what any of them were doing right now?

Here they were hacking their way through a foreign forest, from which death could leap out at them at any moment, where wounds would undoubtedly be inflicted too horrific for the sight of a young woman like Muriel, forcing her to witness unbelievable atrocities and to have to offer whatever comfort she could give to the dying.

Alex bent down and scooped up another tin can of water, pouring it over his head. Water was rationed and he knew that, had he have been seen, he would have been reprimanded, but it didn't bother him.

Somehow he had to dispel the morbid thoughts that were spinning around in his brain, like fairground horses, chasing each other's tails and never quite catching up with one another.

It was time for action – bloody action!

Time to draw blood and exact revenge. He shouldered his rifle, tossing the tin cup into his haversack and settling the canvas bag more comfortably on his broad shoulders.

'Come on, young man,' he said, turning to Cameron and slapping him on the back, making the youngster gag on the last of a dry mouthful of biscuit.

'We're off to war. May God be with you, for he certainly can't be on the side of these bloody savages, that's for sure!'

At about eleven o'clock that morning, the advancing column found fresh human sacrifices on the path – men, women and children, all of them slaves, who had been left, murdered and mutilated.

They had been discarded in a bloody, sick-making heap, their rotting flesh already beginning to fester and stink, as a horde of flies danced around the dead. It was a last, desperate designation to the British troops to keep out.

Soon afterwards Alex and the rest of the team of Hausa scouts found a dead Benin soldier on the path shortly ahead of them. He had been armed only with a bow and arrow.

They approached the dead man stealthily, for they knew that the Benin soldiers were not beyond slaying one of their own kind as bait with which to attract a scouting party, luring the white men into a trap of a dead man's making.

As they advanced along the narrow path, snipers were a constant danger and one officer was killed by a single bullet to the head, dropping to his knees, as his body folded on to the forest floor.

He had been standing close to Alex when he was shot – with a bullet that could so easily have passed instead through Alex's forehead!

Alex was lucky, for the victim had been a big man, with a large, ginger beard and had probably been singled out as a target.

By noon, in the searing, oppressive heat of the midday sun, the innermost wall of the city was finally revealed. It was an awesome sight, measuring some fifteen feet high, with a twenty foot wide ditch in front of it.

Cameron imagined how it should have been filled with water, like the moat surrounding a Scottish castle. Instead, it formed part of a complex network of dried earth embankments erected over many centuries to defend the city from attack.

However, Cameron's imagination did not extend to the cannon arranged behind a wooden stockade, defended by a party of Benin riflemen. Instinctively, he drew back into the protection of the bush, seeking solace beside Alex, his breath rasping in fear.

There was no turning back. Now there was no escape from the adventure that had suddenly turned into a nightmare.

Three ancient, ornately decorated, smooth-bore cannons, all bearing exquisite filigree work and probably brought over by the Portuguese over three hundred years ago, but long since disused, they had been rescued from where they had lain half buried in the ground after generations of neglect.

Threatened with attack, the Benin chiefs had given instructions for them to be dug out, restored to working order and mounted on the stockades of the south-facing gates in the city wall, where they were lined up before the opposing British troops.

And the advancing scouts represented their first likely victims.

'Get your bloody head down and keep it down, you idiot,' Alex brusquely chided Cameron, who had crept up beside him.

'You, young man, get a message down the line that we've reached the stockade and we need the Blue Jackets to bring up some fire power,' commanded Lieutenant Turner, who was in charge of the Hausas.

As Cameron disappeared into the backdrop of vegetation, the Benin riflemen began shooting. Alex was stung in the face and blood began to course down his cheeks.

At first he thought he had been winged by a ricocheting bullet, but then he realised that it was simply a lump of tree bark that had smacked him in the face, flayed from the tree beside him by one of the singing bullets, which whirled through the air like the first of a deputation of angry bees – anxious to protect their queen, the long dead African queen, hived away in the royal seclusion of a busy, swarming palace, which occupied the very heart of the City of Blood.

As the Blue Jackets and the men of the Niger Coast Protectorate gathered their weaponry, their ranks rang out with the screams of one young soldier, who had his foot crushed under the wheel of a seven pounder, as it was hastily set to roll.

It was an eerie, blood-curdling scream, which echoed in intensifying agony, as the sound of it reverberated back and forth, encouraging the Benin soldiers who guarded the south-facing gate into a further bombardment of bullets.

Cameron returned to Alex's side; he was shaking from head to toe, his knuckles whitened and his face frozen and bleached to the colour and texture of a starched white sheet.

He had watched, at first hand, the horror of a soldier lifting his revolver to the temple of his best friend and pulling the trigger – the last desperate favour he could bestow upon a body raked with bullet holes belonging to a man who was screaming in agony and begging for the mercy of extermination.

'Do it for me, Alex. Promise me, you'll do the same for me, if I receive a blast like that,' Cameron blurted out to Alex.

Alex didn't know exactly what his young friend was talking about, but he could certainly guess, for death was all around them, spreading its red cloak like a dying opera singer on a Covent Garden stage.

He had just seen Doctor Roth scuttling past, bent double, almost scrambling along the forest floor on his hands and knees, as he crawled towards yet another victim, offering first aid at first hand and doing whatever he could with his scant supply of bandages and tourniquets, before the orderlies arrived with their hammocks and stretchers to cart the injured off to the mobile hospital.

'Don't be ridiculous, I'm here to protect you. I'll not let the bastards get you, you stupid fool,' replied Alex, his words rough and ready, yet meaningless in this world of singing bullets and rattling gunfire, where death was only at the distance of a single tug of the trigger and blood ran as easily as turning on a tap.

Alex grabbed Cameron's hand, feeling the tautly stretched muscles that made the flesh almost rigid beneath his touch. He felt the youngster cling to him, a long, slightly gangly arm wrapped around his waist in a lover's affectionate hold – a manly embrace which spoke of shared danger and one which held no embarrassment for either of them.

Together, they clutched at each other, Alex holding on to the boy mentally, whilst he, in his turn, remained cemented in a physical encircling of which neither of them were probably aware.

From their vantage point they watched, as a demolition party ran forwards towards the stockade and the maxims and seven pounders began their devastating disintegration of the defending city walls in a thunderous combined attack of maximum military machinery fire power.

Hidden from view, Alex and Cameron observed in relatively safe seclusion, as the defenders were driven off and a mine was detonated against the stockade, blasting all manner of debris into an explosive avalanche, which left a trail of acrid smoke in its wake.

With no time to withdraw the British troops to safety, many of them were knocked down, brought to their knees in a volley of tree branches, splintered planks of wood and shattered pieces of rusting corrugated iron, which had been used to form the stockade.

With the walls to the compound finally breached, the last, bloody battle for the City of Blood could now begin.

It came almost as a relief for Alex and Cameron to scramble to their feet and join in the headlong rush of troops, as the rocket party fired a volley of shells and rockets at an extreme elevation in the direction of the city.

Two of the rockets travelled nearly a mile through the air and dropped into a compound close to the Oba's palace where hundreds of the townsfolk were gathered apprehensively waiting for their leader to tell them what to do and to guide them away from the hell which had suddenly been unleashed upon them.

As the two hissing, spitting thunderbolts fell from the sky into the heart of their sacred precincts, they ran panic-stricken from the city, with the Oba and his chiefs fleeing in their wake.

Only one royal personage remained to protect the city, to provide for her people, as she had done for a thousand years.

She who had been queen in a century long past. She sat on her sacred stone, unmoving and immovable, the ancient demon queen who had, for so long, cast her bewitching spell.

Chapter 19

Entering the City of Blood through the shattered stockade, Alex, with his young friend at his side, spilled out unexpectedly on to a broad avenue, which separated the town from the Oba's palace.

Here was an open, grassy space, bathed in glaring sunlight and contrasting sharply with the shadowy bush paths that they had tracked for so long.

Alex foraged in his haversack for his water bottle, finding a single biscuit in the bottom of the bag, which Cameron had not managed to snaffle from him at breakfast time.

He bit at it hungrily, rapidly spitting out a mouthful in disgust, as he spied a dead leper woman gagged and pegged out on her back, her suppurating flesh oozing in the sunlight lying not ten yards in front of him, whilst a goat, with broken legs, lay nearby nibbling the grass around the prone woman's form.

Suddenly Alex had lost his appetite!

Cameron too had spotted the woman and was squatting at the side of the path being sick, vomiting in helpless ignorance of the immediate and far more threatening danger of the snipers arranged along the roof of a nearby building.

Instantly aware of the danger, Alex threw himself against his young charge, urging him to his feet and scuttling him into the leeway of another building, as the teenager dribbled sick along the path, dirtying Alex's boots with his foul-smelling vomit, as he allowed himself to be pushed and propelled to safety.

Meanwhile, an ancient cannon commanding the entrance to the bush path was being loosed off, but its charge of nails and stones inflicted no casualties among the increasing number of British troops, who were now storming the inner sanctum of the city.

By now Rear Admiral Harry Rawson had entered the city himself to take command of the situation, advancing his troops down the broad avenue in loose square formation, holding the carrier column in the relative shelter of the bush path, until the enemy's resistance had been broken.

It was whilst the square was being formed that the heaviest toll of casualties was wrought, the red uniforms of the marines making them easy targets in the strong light, as the swirling mists of gunpowder fire began to fade.

Dr Roth was in the midst of the carnage, dressing the men's wounds and staunching the bleeding to the best of his ability. Here the Benin soldiers had used large-bore elephant guns against their enemy and they had inflicted terrible, large, gaping wounds.

As the grass was relatively short, he was obliged to crawl on his hands and knees from one victim to another, urging the more able-bodied to seek their own protective cover by the bole of a large cottonwood tree, which stood close to the entrance to the bush path and which served as a place of shelter for the wounded, as they awaited the arrival of the stretchers.

Once they had subdued the worst of the enemy resistance, the troops moved off slowly down the left side of the avenue in the direction of the Oba's palace, driving the last of the king's soldiers from the field of battle and taking possession of the palace compound.

Alex and Cameron emerged from their hiding place, intent on not missing any part of the action and anxious to join the victory column that was to be paraded at three o'clock that afternoon.

After every man had had his water-bottle filled, the naval commander addressed his troops, proclaiming how satisfied he was with the turn of events and how pleased he was that the number of casualties had been fairly low. Following his address, the systematic destruction of the City of Blood began.

Alex was not surprised to encounter the remains of hundreds of human sacrifices, some still draped from the crucifixion trees and others lying in deep pits all over the city.

The observation of such human carnage was to have a deeply disturbing effect on Cameron. It was a sight which was to return to haunt him for many years to come. It lead to bouts of depression and an over-dependence on alcohol to help him through the day. Despite his show of bravado, he was badly affected by what he saw and for once he was struck dumb by the atrocities ranged all around them.

In one large, open space, there were hundreds of dead bodies in various stages of decomposition, mixed with the skeletons of their brethren, causing such a terrible stench that Cameron was not alone in suffering badly from nausea, as the city began to be opened up.

Abominations spread throughout the city. In the open pits lay the living, the dead and the dying – all thrown on top of one another in an indiscriminate manner.

Some, who yet lived, had their arms tied behind their backs, their mouths gagged with short lengths of stick. They had been macheted down and across their chests and stomachs, so that their entrails were left hanging, providing a feast of blood and gore for the hordes of hungry insects, which buzzed around their remains, like the participants at a children's party all eager for their share of the birthday booty.

Before the king's palace, were the seven large juju compounds, which the men entered each in turn. Occupying some two or three acres apiece, here was where most of the sacrifices had been performed and where the Benin people used to sit and watch the regular spectacle of death.

Here the large grassed enclosures were surrounded by high mud walls and in every one, were the sacrificial altars, suspended with carved ivory tusks standing upright, mounted by bronze heads, which formed hideous gargoyles.

In front of each ivory effigy to the gods was a small earthen mound, the rich coloured clay stained even more red, like butchers' blocks that had been used for centuries and upon which each wretched victim's head was placed for ritualistic execution by a rudely carved mace. The altars themselves were caked and covered with streams of dried human blood.

The stench was overwhelming and even the grass beneath the feet of the horrified British onlookers was bloodstained – browned and blackened – not parched by the sun, but bloodied at its very roots, so that even the newly-formed shoots rose from the earth, dark stemmed and damned from the moment that they had sprouted from the ground.

In the corners of each of these compounds were the death pits. Into one of these a few of the hardier NCPF troops were lowered on a length of rope to rescue seven emaciated and starving survivors, who had been carriers on the earlier, ill-fated expedition.

Outside the compounds on the field of death were the bodies of criminals and paupers, left unburied, if there was no relative to claim the body.

At the foot of one of the crucifixion trees, Alex saw the severed heads of what looked like two white men. Doctor Roth was called upon to verify the nature of their identity, although he found it impossible to discern whether they were white men, or pale-skinned Africans, because most of the flesh had withered from their hands and feet.

The overall impression was that of the stench of human sacrifice. The abiding smell of rotting flesh was omnipresent. Alex had the stink of death and blood so firmly fixed in his nostrils that he could smell nothing else.

Every compound they entered seemed to reveal atrocities more diabolical than their predecessors. Many of the crucified bodies had been made to sit up and assume a jocular air, but this was no laughing matter for anyone, as seasoned men of war turned their mouths into their handkerchiefs to gag and vomit and surreptitiously wipe away their tears.

Alex wondered if he would ever feel clean again and, as for his appetite, he felt as though he would never be able to consume another mouthful.

Such horrors of the recent past were made all the more poignant by the desperate ritual killings carried out in the last days before the fall of the city, when hundreds had met their death for no apparent reason, other than to appease the gods and whet the appetite of their ancient demon queen.

During the final battle, when the square formation was moving along the broad avenue, which led up to the king's palace, an Itsekiri carrier, captured during the massacre of the Phillips' peace party, had run screaming towards the British troops, crying out that the Benin soldiers were murdering their Itsekiri slaves.

From a distance, members of the avenging troop were forced to watch helplessly as a dozen or so Itsekiri captives were swiftly beheaded in front of the Oba's palace, as all around them the battle raged.

At the end of the broad avenue outside the king's palace were the two crucifixion trees, where witches and criminals were normally sacrificed, underneath which some fifty or sixty recently beheaded bodies lay in a tangled heap of unfathomable body parts.

In the sacred compound closest to the palace the gates were guarded by a slithering bronze serpent. Beneath its large head and gaping mouth lay about a hundred decaying bodies mounded in pits from which a great swarm of flies arose in a black cloud, momentarily darkening the bright luminosity of the African afternoon sky.

Entering the king's palace by way of huge double doors embossed with brass proved to be a revelation in itself. Alex's eyes and those of the men about him stared out in disbelief at the magnificence of the despotic ruler's treasure trove.

Most striking were the magnificent brass castings – the heads of royalty arranged in serried ranks according to their seniority. Intricately carved with adornments to fit their social standing, their eyes sparkled briefly as the huge palace doors were thrown open to the light, like re-awakened ghosts, who had known a lifetime of darkness, waiting for their brief moment in the spotlight of a sinking African sun.

And so the looting began.

In a frenzied orgy of acquisition, men scrambled over wooden benches, reaching up to the clay walls, which were polished to a glass-like finish, snatching at the finely figured bronze plaques, which covered the vanquished king's quarters, little knowing what they would do with such blood-soaked artefacts.

Many of the bronze plaques bore testimony to ritualistic sacrifice and to other events of a torrid past – a bizarre amalgamation of fine art and barbarity, whose representative imagery was now being heaped into discarded piles outside the palace gates.

Bronze leopards which had stalked their prey across the sacrificial altars for centuries were wrenched from their dark lairs and a sea of serpents entangled in each other's bronzen coils were swept into the haversacks of those who cared little for their artistic merit and far less for what they represented other than the possibility of an exchange for a gold sovereign or two from the hands of some aristocratic collector of all things heathen.

Heads rolled as the bronzen effigies of kings and queens, which had stood proudly for centuries, were swept unceremoniously from stone altars, clattering on to the earthen floor in an unholy metallic mountain of decapitated heads of state.

It was a wrecking party which had not been sanctioned by Rear Admiral Harry Rawson, for there was something very special that he wanted to claim as his own from the mounting pile of discarded treasures – something that was fit to be given to a queen and something which, in the turmoil, he was now never to find.

Alex turned his attention to Cameron, who was rummaging through the treasure trove, selecting a small jointed, carved ivory leopard for himself, knowing that it could easily be stowed in his haversack.

'Here, Alex, you may as well have something too,' he shouted, tossing him a bronze head hastily snatched from the pile.

Little did Alex comprehend, but what he had taken was the head of the great queen, which normally sat alone and unrivalled on the great stone altar within the king's palace.

She had rested there for centuries, on top of the stone altar with its flint carved inscriptions of ancient curses, sanctioning sacrifices and demanding the quenching of her thirst with the blood of her people.

She had been a queen. She was still a queen – the Great Queen Oba Eeeni. She was the Great Witch Queen. She was revered as the mother of all Damnation.

And she had not quenched her thirst that day.

The bronze bowl from which she usually drank lay overturned outside the king's palace, trodden into the ground by a stampede of looters, as the warm blood of the human sacrifice which it had contained seeped slowly into the clay.

'What do I want with this?' asked Alex, taking the head in his hands presumably to play with.

'Go on take it!' urged Cameron.

'I'm no thief, you know!'

'Go on take it. We're all helping ourselves to something. Give it to your little girl. Tell her it's a doll and it's lost its legs. Its body and arms too! Here I'll even wipe the blood off it, if you like,' replied Cameron, brandishing a far from clean handkerchief in a moment of over-excited bravado.

'Hey, Clever Dick. How about you keep it! Who knows, in years to come it could even finish up in the hands of your grandchild?'

In spite of the banter, Alex took his share of the loot, gazing thoughtfully for a moment into the face of the bronze effigy, which he held before him, curiously running his rough fingertips over its features, probing its moulded bronze surface with clumsy, battle-weary fingers and thumbs, surprised at how cold and death-like it felt in his grasp.

No sparkling eyes – just empty sockets. No pink mouth, just a slash across the face; flared nostrils that would never inhale another breath and coral-studded ears unhearing of centuries of sound.

> *Thou taketh my head*
> *And blood will be shed*
> *A spear in the heart*
> *The thief will depart*

Chapter 20

The explosion erupted like a cannon ball from hell, flaring up like a vomiting volcano, issuing forth from the depths of the Earth in an inflamed outbreak, spreading a furious fire in its wake, a blazing inferno seemingly of the Devil's making.

It was the start of the Great Fire – not of London, but of another city – a metropolis of murder, a city which had set the scene for centuries of sacrifice – Benin, the City of Blood, which fire alone could purge of its pagan past.

In the calm of the afternoon heat three days after the storming of the city, a fire storm was raging, sweeping before it the atrocities of countless years of human suffering.

Spreading its fiery fingers and fanned by a strong breeze, it pursued its path through the city like an army of housewives each equipped with a new broom.

Within minutes the whole town was ablaze. Flames hurtled higher and higher, chasing towards the gods. Like Olympic athletes they hurdled across every obstacle in their path, leaving nothing but charred remains in their waspish wake, as everything was turned to yellow and, finally, blackened and burnt to a cinder.

Like golden rain, a deluge of sparks descended, feeding on the inferno, before spurting upwards again in a series of all enveloping flashes of flaming fury.

Brilliant glowing yellows crackled and grew crimson, feasting on one building after another, as the frontiers of flame claimed yet another victim, erupting once more and flaring up into a tempestuous rage, hungry and angry in their livid livery.

Against the dwindling daylight, a crackle of sparks shot towards the sky, like fire crackers on Bonfire Night, as clouds of thick, black smoke draped themselves over the townscape. It was like a blackout curtain in a theatre announcing that the performance was at its end.

It was a stage which had supported the theatre of death for so long and it was now being destroyed by a crimson red army, advancing at a rate that was almost impossible to imagine, raging roughshod over the native mud huts and intent on purloining a palace which stood in its path.

Here was the final act of purification, played out to an armed audience drawn in to witness the last act of retribution against a merciless, murky past that was now finally being vanquished and laid to rest.

Alex had been attempting to re-pack his kitbag, finding room for the bronze head that Cameron had insisted was his for the taking, along with a number of other small bronze and ivory trinkets, which might buy the price of a pint or two, if he took them down to the pawnshop, where Mary had purchased his lost compass.

The assembled troops had been due to go on parade at five o'clock that afternoon, holding a Sunday service by way of a memorial to the dead and to give thanks that on this holy day of the week, they would be marching out of this hell hole of a place in which so many had laid down their lives.

After raising the Union Jack and offering a rousing three cheers to Her Majesty the Queen, there wasn't a man left standing who wasn't glad to be on his way ... not a single soldier injured and incapable of standing to attention who wasn't pleased to be stretchered away.

Cameron, for all his earlier show of exuberance, had grown tired of poking around to see what he could find for both himself and Alex to take back home with them as souvenirs of the suffering which had been experienced by so many.

He had even resorted to teaching some of the carriers a few simple card tricks, after Alex had refused to play blackjack with the younger man, for fear of losing his last remaining cigarettes, which were the currency of the game.

Cheap trade brandy was in abundance now that the fleeing Benin king's store-room had been made to give up its secret stash of ivory and the spoils of frequent warring with other factions.

Benin was beaten.

Its Oba was overrun and its unholy priests were no longer able to practise their dark deeds. The riches of its treasure houses were now open to those whose urge it was to plunder them.

Drunk on a mixture of palm wine and cheap brandy, two of the carriers who had no place to be in one of the huts, which was being used to store ammunition and firepower, had accidentally let off some gunpowder.

It had ignited in a thunderous explosion, setting light to the thatched roof, as drifts of burning straw, caught on a late afternoon breeze, settled on top of the roofs of adjoining houses, bringing about a conflagration, which very soon engulfed every building within the vicinity and which quickly threatened the field hospital.

Trapped pockets of air in the flaming thatch exploded like igniting cartridges and here and there, as the fire found fresh supplies of ammunition and gunpowder, a series of almighty explosions rocked the scorched air.

Alex threw aside his kitbag, shouting to Cameron to join him, as a party of Blue Jackets tackled the task of carrying the sick and wounded to safety, even as the makeshift dormitory began to burn all around them.

By fortunate chance the roof was made of corrugated iron instead of thatch, but that did not prevent it from caving in on top of them, as the last man was dragged clear of the burning building.

A shard of falling metal dug into Cameron's boot, piercing through the leather and embedding itself in his foot, as blood began to trickle through the eyelets, mingling with the mud which caked laces baked hard in the blaze.

It seemed as if the ground itself had caught fire and was burning bright. Its clay turned to a molten lava-like substance, which clung like quicksand, making mere movement a hazardous operation, as the stretcher bearers struggled even to gain a foot-hold and escape the blaze with their injured charges.

Benin City had been surrendered into the hands of the British troops, steeped with a brand of blood, which had seeped into every pore. Now the bowels of the earth appeared to be opening up, drowning the city in a diarrhoea of its own dreadful detritus.

It seemed like a legitimate end, as the centre of bloodshed burnt before the eyes of the men who had laid their lives on the line to hasten its exit from the world.

Countless lives has been wilfully sacrificed within its precincts and now, at last, they would be cremated in a funeral pyre that spanned the city walls.

It took little more than an hour for the flames to die away, having fed hungrily on everything that lay in their path. Once the fire had finally burnt itself out, the expedition was left in a sorry state of affairs.

Water was the main problem, for many of the water tins had become crumpled and distorted in the heat, shedding their precious contents in puny spurts, which could do little to avert the flames, but would have done much to quench the thirsts of men whose throats stung with smoke and who choked, coughed and gasped for both water and fresh air.

The bronze serpent which had coiled its way over the top of the entrance gates to the king's palace had bled its corpse into the ground, a sorry puddle of molten metal, its blackened ivory fangs all that remained of the horrific, venomous thrusting of its enraged lusting for blood.

As night began to fall, so the reality of the situation began to strike home. A thunderstorm was brewing up and, with virtually all the buildings destroyed, there was little shelter.

Even most of the canvas and tarpaulin sheets, which could have been put to use as makeshift tents, had melted, mingling their material with the mud.

In their tin boxes, candles had moulded themselves to the tin casings, their wicks trailing uselessly in the molten mess. In the gathering darkness, all was gloom and despondency, lacking a light to carry the avenging troops through the night.

Alex struck a match, igniting a spare length of bootlace, dropping it into a pitcher of palm oil which, miraculously, had managed to survive the blaze.

It illuminated the area around about for just long enough to shed light on the nature of Cameron's wounded foot, which had now become swollen and was beginning to blacken into a bloody bruise.

The youngster had screamed out in pain when Alex had unlaced the pierced boot, revealing a wet, blood-soaked sock from which a shard of metal still protruded.

Alex borrowed a pocketknife, and cut through the woollen sock to reveal the extent of the damage, calling for medical assistance for his young friend, who screamed all the more when the offending piece of metal was extracted, which caused more blood to flow.

Even as they surveyed the wreckage wrought by fire and the almost total destruction of their supplies, a company of Blue Jackets marched into the devastated city, with four days' provisions, a supply of water and the first mail which had arrived from Great Britain since the initial landing.

In a hastily written note, which had obviously been written by Mary in the New Year, Alex learnt that she had taken upon herself to name the newborn child, with less reference to Alex as its father, than he might have expected, naming him Robert Charles Alexander Seath.

Still, as Alex reckoned, it would cause less confusion in later years, for he remembered well the number of times that he would answer a call from his mother for his blacksmith father whose name he bore and, for his part, his father would do likewise.

Accompanying the supply column were several newspaper reporters, who had hurried to West Africa and sought passage to Benin in the hope of being the first to report the fall of the city.

As a representative of the Illustrated London News, a rather rotund, jovial looking character hailing under the unlikely name of Seppings Wright had arrived with a party of Blue Jackets.

He rode a donkey and arrived with a vast amount of luggage. A great train of servants and carriers trailed in his wake.

As the foremost war correspondent of his day, he commanded attention, distributing his largesse upon the Rear Admiral and the naval officers, bringing with him bottles of champagne and a vast joint of ham, which looked to have suffered the worse for wear.

His carriers also brought with them many boxes of cigars, with which he sought to gain an audience with the senior officers.

As far as the troops were concerned, he treated them with the utmost disdain, as if only the officers in charge had played any part at all in the winning of the city.

A day later, after a breakfast of cocoa and biscuit and the ceremonious hoisting of the Union Jack, the entire naval column left the ruined city, along with the man who had traded his position as a trader to become both a scout and in many eyes, a hero.

With Alex went the young Scottish lad, whose foot injury now meant that he could no longer walk, forcing him to leave the City of Blood on a bloodstained stretcher.

The return march along the path from Benin City back to Warrigi took three days, hindered by the slow movement of the carriers, dragging their feet under the weight of hundreds of huge ivory elephant's tusks and by the large number of stretcher cases.

In many places the path had to be widened to allow the passage of both stretchers and hammocks – one of which contained Rear Admiral Rawson, whose health and fitness had deteriorated along the route.

Nevertheless, the regal transportation of the Rear Admiral afforded him plenty of time to contemplate what he perceived to be the failure of his own personal goal and with it what seemed like the complete failure of the Punitive Expedition – not as a military exercise in deposing of a despotic ruler, but in the foundering of his own personal agenda to endear himself to his own beloved queen.

The Benin expedition was to go down in history as one of the most successful, albeit relatively little publicised, wars fought in the name of Her Majesty, Queen Victoria.

A force of some twelve hundred men had been hastily assembled from a variety of different locations, many of them several thousand miles apart, equipped and landed on the West African coast – all within the space of just one month.

In just seventeen days, having more than triumphed in all that they had hoped to achieve in destroying the city, the force was re-embarked and ready for future action.

However, Rear Admiral Harry Rawson was not a happy man, for he was going home, if not empty-handed, without the very thing which he had so desperately wanted to find.

If anything, the telegram waiting for him on his return to Ologbo addressed to him personally and sent by no less a person than Queen Victoria, only served to deepen his disappointment.

She wrote:

> "The Queen is most anxious to hear that the wounded, and indeed
> all, are doing well, for the climate, the privations and the horrors
> they have witnessed must have been most fearful."

Queen Victoria had expressed a particular interest in the Benin campaign, falling as it did in the year of her Diamond Jubilee.

She always had a ready sympathy for the sufferings of her soldiers and sailors at times of war and the naval officer, who had led the victorious troops in the routing of such evil had long been a personal friend ... and, as far as he was concerned, maybe more!

When his flagship, the *St George*, returned to Portsmouth, she rewarded him by inviting both him and his crew to her home at Osborne on the Isle of Wight.

It was the first time in naval history that any monarch had personally received the officers and crew of a British warship.

If only he could have offered his queen something by way of return.

Something very special. Something which would never be rivalled. A gift that was fit for the greatest queen who had ever lived.

Instead, he had nothing to offer which he considered remotely worthy of her. Nothing at all.

She was a widow, mourning a prince, but who held him as a dear friend. In his own mind, he had always wanted more – so much more.

What he had failed to bring out of West Africa with him was the one thing which he wanted so much to give. Harry Rawson wanted to give her a heart that only beat for a queen.

Chapter 21

Charlie was pleased to have his cheery companion, Cameron, back in the hospital ward to brighten his days. However, having made as good a recovery as he was ever likely to, he was being discharged the next morning. Alex was due to collect him at eleven o'clock.

Besides, with Cameron once again confined to a hospital bed (this time with his injured foot), it gave Charlie more than sufficient excuse to pay a daily visit to the youngster … and to a certain young nurse, who had returned from the hospital ship to take up her duties once again in Old Calabar, caring for the sick and wounded from the recent Benin Expedition.

To Charlie's surprise and delight, when Alex arrived at the hospital in Old Calabar the next morning, he had brought Muriel with him.

The two of them met up with Charlie on the verandah, where he had been sitting reading a newspaper report on the successes, trials and tribulations of the taking of the City of Blood.

Muriel was not due to be back on duty for the next couple of days. It was the first time that Charlie had ever seen her out of her starched white pinafore uniform and in a pretty, pale blue cotton dress. With her blonde hair left long, instead of being tied up in its usual bun, she looked stunning.

Caught in the sunlight, her skin was youthful and lustrous and her eyes sparkled with the same intensity as her hair, which flew and danced in the breeze, frequently forcing her to have to pat it back into position with a delicate sweep of her slender hand.

Charlie had a rucksack containing his belongings at his side and hastened in amongst its tightly packed contents, extracting a greetings card.

Its ill-fitting envelope was slightly creased and bent. On it Charlie had scrawled her name in great big swirling letters, ending in a flourish, as he looped the final letter backwards on itself in an exuberant display of calligraphy.

Inside, he had simply written the words "Welcome back", but the picture on the front of the card – a bouquet of red roses, intertwined with lace and a miniature length of pale blue ribbon, which almost seemed to match her dress, told a different story.

Muriel had blushed in her habitual fashion, but she had bent down towards him, placing a gentle kiss on his forehead – a kiss willingly, albeit shyly, given.

Charlie felt his pulse race, as a thrilling sensation coursed over his whole body, making him tingle with delight.

'Hello Charlie, I see you're looking much better,' she smiled, as Alex, in a rare moment of awareness, managed to find something of great interest to observe in the middle distance, taking a step backwards to concentrate for a moment on whatever it was that had grabbed his attention.

'You've been in the best place, Charlie, my old mate, let me assure you,' Alex advised roughly, thumping his partner in survival on the shoulders, causing Charlie to gulp and catch his breath.

'I had better go and say "Hello" to Cameron,' said Muriel, taking herself off and leaving the two men together.

Charlie noticed that she clutched the card tightly, as she left.

'I bet it's really meant to be a late Valentine's card,' shouted Cameron, cat-calling after her, once Muriel had left his bedside and he could be certain of an audience.

Charlie cursed Cameron yet again, as soon as he learnt that the youngster had urged her to check the number of blooms on the card.

Cameron had counted them earlier when, recklessly, Charlie had taken the teenager into his confidence and shown him the greetings card, which betokened the pleasure he felt that Muriel had returned.

'You can tell it's from a Scotsman. Check and you'll see he's short-changed you, Muriel. Look how many roses are on the card and you'll find there's only eleven of them. I know, I've already counted them. He's a typical mean Scot! You should insist on a dozen and that he should make it the real thing, if he's trying to woo you. You'll have to watch it! He can move pretty fast now that he's mastered the use of that walking stick!'

'Shut up, Cameron!' Muriel rebuked the lad, smiling to herself and wondering if, now that he was on his feet properly again, Charlie would finally find the courage to ask her out.

Secretively, she took the card from its envelope again, caressing the cardboard cut-out flowers with her sensitive fingertips, letting them run over the embossed basket containing its blossoming cargo, toying with the scrap of white lace and the tiny length of pale blue ribbon.

It didn't matter how many there were – the message was perfectly clear!

She didn't bother to count the roses there and then, although she did tot them up later that evening in the privacy of her own lodging house, placing the card under her pillow as she slept.

Sure enough there were only eleven.

It was quite apparent that Charlie had missed her while she had been away and, if she cared to admit it, she had missed him too.

She wondered how he had come by the card, for such things were surely not readily available here in West Africa. She searched it minutely back and front looking for clues, until she found the miniature script on the bottom of the back fold of the card.

It had been printed in Glasgow – that was all she knew and, yes, she guessed that it had been produced as a Valentine's card.

Charlie hadn't been able to pluck up sufficient courage to send it to its intended recipient and had carried it in with his belongings for over a year.

It had travelled with him all the way to Africa and weeks ago, he had toyed with the idea of sending it, when one of the nurses came round asking if any of the men had post to be sent on board a ship bound for Great Britain.

What Muriel couldn't possibly have known was that its original envelope had been screwed up and tossed into a hospital wastepaper basket.

Had she found the crumpled up envelope, she would have found that it bore the address of the woman for whom it had originally been intended – the address was that of an Edinburgh attic. And the name on the card was that of the wife of Charlie's best friend.

* * * * * * * * * *

Muriel got her wish and sure enough, Charlie did, at last, summons the courage to ask her out the following Saturday night. He invited her to a dance at the Old Mission Hall – a strange choice perhaps for their first date, as he was hardly in any fit state to sweep her on to the dance floor.

Instead they seconded a quiet table in the corner, their heads bowed together in the candlelight. Lately, she had begun to question him about his past, but he always seemed anxious to change the subject.

A man of his age, someone in his late twenties, surely had past triumphs and failures in his life – past loves too, she figured, but what did it matter?

She guessed that his past was so remote as to be best left beyond the reach of her imagination and certainly far beyond her caring. What mattered was right now.

He had survived a tremendous ordeal, escaping from what had seemed like inevitable death at the hands of those who had wrought the Benin massacre.

Now it looked as if the couple might have a future to build together. As far as Muriel was concerned, she could wish for nothing more.

Charlie topped up her champagne glass, which glowed in the candlelight – just like the warm glow, which was beginning to creep over her whole body, as his fingertips stretched across the small divide of the little corner table, meeting hers, until their fingers folded together, one set entwined with the other.

He lent forward and, slowly, gently, their lips brushed together, as a spark of passion ignited between them, overcoming their mutual shyness, lips locked momentarily, as they became lost to a world which contained no one but themselves.

Their wedding took place at the end of March. It was a riotous affair and far more was made of the day than Muriel or Charlie had ever intended.

In Old Calabar it was an excuse for the whole township to celebrate, for the brass band to play and for a grand reception to be laid on for the new bride and her man – all paid for by a hastily organised collection, which had given Alex the excuse to trail his hat around the clubhouses for days and nights, seeking for everyone he met to donate whatever they could afford.

Nobody would ever have guessed that what the bride wore on her wedding day was an assembly of three hospital sheets, all embroidered with an assortment of lace, begged and borrowed from a variety of sources.

Muriel's young female friends, who worked with her as nurses at the hospital, had toiled on making the gown for days during every spare minute of their time.

No one would have been any the wiser, if it had not been for the repartee of the now fully actioned Cameron, warning Charlie to keep his hands to himself and not to go anywhere near his new wife's breasts, as he didn't know how many bedpans had been spilt over the sheets, which now formed Muriel's bodice.

Alex, of course, was best man and Cameron, wanting to know what role he was due to play in the proceedings, was promptly advised by Charlie that there was no part in a wedding party for a court jester.

Muriel was nervous about her wedding night. Although as a fully qualified nurse, she had spent several years attending to all manner of male bodily parts, nevertheless she felt anxious that everything should be right between them.

She had no mother to offer her words of advice for the wedding night and to prepare her for what was expected of a young bride.

She hoped that she would not fall pregnant too soon after the wedding, wanting to wait until they returned to Scotland before starting a family.

She knew that the birth of twins ran in her family; her mother had told her that when she had still been alive.

However, the thought of having to cope with two babies demanding her attention at the same time in the oppressive African heat was not a prospect that Muriel viewed with any relish.

What she longed for was a little girl. Maybe she would call it Agnes after her mother. Please God, though, not yet!

She was at the height of her fertility on her wedding night and she could hardly forbid her husband his conjugal rights. She was a virgin – of that there was no doubt – for the next morning the sheets on the bed were puddled and stained with a quantity of blood that Charlie had not witnessed since the slaughter and bloodshed of the innocents who had died, slashed and slain on the paths that led through the West African bush, towards the City of Blood, which now lay in ruins, finally purged of its pagan past.

Strangely, and although he would have been loath to admit it, Charlie, drunk on an excess of champagne and still suffering the effects of an almighty hangover, didn't even remember making love to his new wife that night!

Instead he remembered only his dreams – a vision which focused on a future in which once again, he was walking up the aisle – not with Muriel, but with a woman he had once shared a fish and chip supper with, perched on the end of a bed, whose sheets had been starched and whitened in an Edinburgh wash-house and which bore no stains of a virgin's blood.

* * * * * * * * *

It was the morning after the wedding that both Charlie and Alex received news from Millers of Glasgow that they were to return to Great Britain on a steam ship bound for Liverpool that was departing at the end of the week.

Charlie was pleased to be returning to the country he knew best of all, but unhappy to be leaving Muriel behind, for she had agreed to another six-month stay of duty and would not be allowed to join her husband on his home-bound trip, although she begged and cajoled the hospital authorities to allow her to do so.

It was a fond farewell that she received both from Charlie and from Alex. She had managed to persuade one of her friends to cover for her, enabling her to accompany the two men to the port.

Alex carried with him some of the spoils of war, which he hoped would put a shilling, or two in his pocket when he finally arrived in Edinburgh.

Knowing that the news of the successful Benin operation had spread like wildfire through a country hungering for its revenge, one which had beaten the bloodshed, quelled the crucifixions and put a stop to the sacrifice of countless souls, he guessed that any artefacts from the blood-spattered city would be likely to change hands for a fair price.

The passage back to Liverpool was tedious and tiring, with little for Alex or Charlie to do but play endless games of cards on board deck, as the steam ship ploughed across the Atlantic.

With its assorted cargo of plundered treasures bound for museums and art galleries throughout Europe – mostly due to be sold to defray the cost of the Punitive Expedition, the ship contained many thousands of art objects and West African antiquities, which comprised the most important cultural achievement of the people of Benin City.

Most striking were the magnificent brass and bronze castings – the heads of royalty, pendants and plaques, figures of men and animals and, almost as remarkable, the intricately created ivory figurines – masks and massive elephant tusks all carved with complex, masterfully executed designs.

Jointed ivory leopards and carved medallions of leopards' heads, which mimicked the hallmarks embossed on centuries of silver crafted by London silversmiths, jostled for space in the packing crates with bronze beasts of every species known to inhabit the jungles of West Africa.

The casting of brass was an art which had been controlled by the Benin king himself and anyone found casting brass without royal consent faced execution, for the material, which resists corrosion, was thought to mirror the permanence and continuity of kingship and of the royal family itself.

The existence of the Benin Bronzes was fundamental to the people's belief and the veneration of their ancestors, whose spirits were believed to protect the living.

The cast effigies and commemorative heads of deceased kings and queens were displayed on altars at numerous shrines throughout the king's palace.

Bronze sculptures dating back for centuries were amongst the items, which would be most highly prized among European collectors.

The head of Benin's Devil queen, who had not lived for a thousand years, was probably the most valuable of all the stolen treasures on board the ship and right now it was languishing in a brown paper parcel in the bottom of Alex's rucksack and stowed away under his bunk.

Thou taketh my head
And blood will be shed

* * * * * * * * *

135

Finally reaching Liverpool late at night after a storm in the Irish Sea had delayed their arrival, Alex and Charlie were too late for the night train that would take them to their eventual destination at Edinburgh's Waverley Station.

They spent an uncomfortable night on a bench on the station platform, trying to steal whatever sleep they could, until the huffing and puffing of the first of the morning trains aroused them from their slumbers no more than an hour after they had finally managed to drop off to sleep, with their kitbags clenched protectively between their knees.

Thoughtfully, Charlie had telegrammed ahead to Mary in the certain knowledge that she would want to be waiting on the station concourse to greet the home-comers.

The message had arrived just in time to stop her trailing out into the bitterly cold April air, with its scrawly showers that would have saturated and soaked through to her very skin, whipped up around her shawl in a typical Edinburgh eddy of constantly cold, blowing wind, combined with lashing rain.

Obviously she would have had to have taken the children with her – Robert, a babe in arms who had never been seen by the man who had sired him – and dragging behind her a reluctant four-year-old, Anne, to whom the word "father" meant so little – a stranger from a past that she could barely remember.

And so Mary settled for an early night, hoping that the morning would bring better weather. Instead a storm of thunderous proportions, accompanied by scorching lightning, whirled up on that cold April night, howling across the roof tops like a screaming dervish, taking with it the occasional tile and whistling through the narrow Stockbridge streets, so that she too had a sleepless night.

She had been interrupted in the early hours of breaking daylight by young Anne crawling into bed with her mother, as fear took hold of her four-year-old daughter.

Braving the elements that whipped and danced around her the next morning, blowing her best black shawl into her face, so that, for a moment, it blinded her, Mary set off for the Waverley Station.

At times she had been forced to cling to the railings to prevent herself from being blown off her feet. In the blustering wind she had scuttled down the steps from Princes Street, holding on to the hand of little Anne for dear life, with baby Robert bundled into her breast.

She didn't have long to wait, as the train, with its weary passengers, was just pulling into the station. Its wheels screeched on its metal rails in a high-pitched announcement of its arrival, belching great clouds of smoke, which were rapidly swept away on the wind that howled around the concourse, harassing those who came to wait and who, like Mary, couldn't afford to indulge themselves with a piping hot cup of tea upon which to warm their hands and which, in Mary's case, might have helped to quell a strange feeling of apprehension.

Butterflies that should have been blown away on the wind fluttered inside Mary's empty stomach. Anne was crying. The child didn't want to be there, to feel the wind in her face and smell the strong, sooty smell that pervaded the air and all for the sake of meeting this stranger, whom her mother had explained she would have to grow to love and respect.

Mary caught sight of Charlie first, as Alex was left to struggle with both his and his lame friend's rucksack. Her husband was being jostled by the crowds and, in the confusion, the tightly packed contents of one kitbag burst forth, spilling over the station platform, forcing Alex to stoop to retrieve them. It was for this reason that, at first, he didn't even see his waiting wife.

Mary stood with her back to the flower stall, its striped overhead canopy lashing backwards and forwards, like the untied sails of a little sailing boat, but which provided some small measure of protection from the draught that swept across her back.

Charlie hadn't seen her for nearly a year. She stood with the children waiting for him in front of an assortment of galvanised buckets containing greenhouse blooms – the preserve of rich gentlemen, who would present a bunch to their wives as a treat or, maybe, as way of assuaging their conscience after some real, or imagined cheat.

Scudding across the open station concourse, a gust of wind caught one of the galvanised buckets, sending it clattering to the ground, where it rolled away on to the rails beneath the train from which Alex and Charlie had so recently alighted.

Water from the bucket washed the concrete concourse, as maybe a dozen red roses were scattered in all directions. One lay close to Mary.

With the baby wrapped around her, she had her hands full, but before she had the chance to urge little Anne to bend down and pick it up, a woman running towards the newly-arrived train, squashed it underfoot, grinding its scattered petals into the ground, like drops of blood.

Alex, gathering their belongings around him and hoisting both rucksacks on to his broad back, at last espied his wife, his daughter and the half-hidden bundle, concealed and comforted by the extra warmth provided by her shawl.

He waved with his free hand, as Charlie, already a dozen stiff paces in front of him, hobbled over to greet Alex's wife, stepping into a soggy mess of rose petals and, unconsciously, stabbing one with his walking stick.

Charlie planted a single kiss on each of Mary's chilled and chapped cheeks, tweaking the bonnet of the little girl who stood beside her.

Little Anne seemed to resent his interference, tossing her head to one side petulantly, as she attempted to pull herself away from her mother's grasp and away from the man with the limp.

Delving into his pocket Charlie produced a handkerchief mouse that he had fashioned for her before alighting from the train. Suddenly the little girl remembered him with delight and smiled at him, ignoring his friend, her father, who continued to struggle with the heavy load of both rucksacks.

Alex offered Mary a cursory kiss. The child that walked beside her mother shied away from him in fear of the unknown. Together the small party ran the gauntlet of the howling wind that wrapped itself around them in a chilling embrace, rendering their tracks towards the blustery Waverley Steps almost impossible.

Charlie limped up the steep steps, feeling his walking stick being dragged out of his grasp, until, as he reached the summit, a particularly strong gust caught it and sent it clattering down the stairs, where it rested at the bottom in a puddle of water, awaiting retrieval.

Alex, dragged down by the weight of their combined luggage, had no free hand to offer to his wife, or to the little girl, who seemed intent on keeping as far away as possible from him.

At the top of the climb, he spotted the new Edinburgh Northern Tramway cable car coming along Princes Street towards them. It was emblazoned down its side with an advertisement for Rising Sun stove polish and another for Broughton Market.

It was heading for the Botanic Gardens and then on to Inverleith Row, in the direction of its final destination at Goldenacre.

Alex had a few coppers in his pocket which would pay for their fares.

If they boarded the tram here, they could alight fairly close to the Stockbridge attic flat and soon be back in the warmth, without the long downhill walk through the New Town with the wind in their faces.

Alex stepped out, as a sudden ferocious gust of wind, lifted him off his feet, snatching at the rucksacks, casting them to the ground, as he was blown straight into the slipstream of air created by the advancing tram.

It blew him across the road, lifting him up into the air and impaling him on one of the spikes of the rusting, broken cast iron railings, which had been bent forward.

He screamed in momentary agony, as the piercing iron spike, thrust straight through his back and out the other side, driving right through his heart.

Mary's mouth dropped wide open in speechless horror, at the same moment that the baby, which had clung to her breast, opened its eyes and let out a chilling cry.

Anne huddled into her mother's wind-lashed skirts, whipped up into a fury, revealing her mother's petticoats. Fearful of looking out, Anne buried her head, seeking her mother's reassurance, as Mary grasped her instinctively and protectively.

Blood leapt from the front of Alex's jacket, oozing from his mouth and coursing down his collar, turning the stiffly starched white hardness to a pulp of gushing gore.

He choked, just once, before his head lolled over to meet his shoulder, his neck muscles slumped and defeated in death.

One forcibly discarded rucksack lay on the rain-soaked pavement. A brown paper package tied up with coarse, hairy string had spilled out from beneath the leather holding straps.

Its loosened wrapping paper had unfolded to reveal an ancient bronze image of a long dead African queen, whose head bounced and rolled into the rainwater gutter, whilst the man who had taken her, but had proclaimed himself no thief, lay dead just a few yards away.

Thou taketh my head
And blood will be shed
A spear in the heart
The thief will depart.

A soldier coming up the steps behind him handed Charlie the walking stick that had been blown out of his grasp. Charlie had reached the top of the steps just in time to witness the full horror of what had just happened and stood rooted to the spot.

For no apparent reason, Anne had left the protective envelopment of her mother's skirts, wandering in a childish daze towards the severed head, retrieving it from the gutter and placing it into Charlie's unbelieving hands.

The seconds widowed Mary, the one true love of Charlie's life, turned and fled into the arms of the married man she had for so long realised that she loved so much more than her husband, who had just died a tragic death in front of the pair of them.

Holding on to her lover for support and comfort, she found herself passing into his care the baby boy that she alone knew was undoubtedly his.

Anne may have just lost her father, but Robert was being held for the very first time by his true father.

Book II

1947

Chapter 22

Jo stood stock still, sturdy little legs stamping the floor in dreaded anticipation of what was to come. Andrina had swiftly exposed the child's bare buttocks and Jo had run into a corner, cowering away from her, knowing exactly what would happen when she caught up with her half-sister's child.

Jo's very existence seemed to provide ample excuse for the manner in which Andrina was wont to issue a constant stream of admonishment, especially when no one, but she, was around to witness her actions.

She raised her hand, ready to rain down the first of a series of blows, which would cut into Jo's little round buttocks, each of which was barely bigger than the hand which sought to mete out the punishment.

Immaculately and imposingly dressed, Jo's aunt had rolled up one sleeve of her bright yellow blouse, with its crisp ruffle of silk surrounding her neck, all the better to be able to bring the outstretched palm of her hand slicing through the air in a deftly executed action.

It would bear no lasting mark, other than a reddening of soft-pink skin, as the two fleshy protuberances began to glow crimson and livid in the light of her dark, sadistic deeds.

Jo hated her, but wouldn't cry, for even at just three years old and wise beyond the duration of a comparatively recent admission into the world, Jo had learnt that welling tears only brought an extra blow raining down by way of good measure, especially if a teardrop, or two, should dare to drip down and dirty her perfectly pressed and pleated black skirt.

Andrina's waspish behaviour towards the adopted child belonging to her elder half-sister seemed to be mirrored in the clothes she was wearing.

Black and yellow spelt danger and when Andrina was about, danger always stalked the draughty corridors of the Carlton Hall Hotel, just outside Edinburgh.

It was a vast edifice of a building, built in the time of Queen Victoria.

Jo had been brought there as a toddler, when Grandmother Mary and her husband had purchased the hotel in 1947, just as the first shuttle service linking Edinburgh and London had begun operation by British European Airways.

No questions had been asked about the mother, who had given up her child and, in doing so, had assuaged the brooding needs of Andrina's half-sister, Anne, who had long ago walked out on her own child and who now longed for another, despite her advancing years and her subsequent inability to produce another child of her own.

Jo stood trembling, knowing that no one was there to witness the indignity of hastily exposed buttocks, understanding only too well that Grandmother's abiding love and protection were not available that afternoon to provide a safe haven and that a doting Uncle Robert had disappeared with his golf clubs.

Andrina, of course, had known that the coast was clear, for Anne had taken to her room for her normal afternoon "nap", which usually lasted until the hotel bar opened again in the evening and she could once more make free use of the optics, helping herself to drinks that no one had bought for her and usually taking a double just for good measure.

Jo had been caught red-handed and now a red bottom would be the reward for the sugary red and green sticks of sweet vermicelli that the child had carefully picked off each and every one of the fairy cakes that had been neatly arranged on paper doilies, ranked amongst the other tray bakes, set out in the residents' lounge for afternoon tea.

Improvisation was the order of the day, with so much still on ration and the chefs at the hotel were often hard pushed to come up with a tempting selection of delicacies, with so much of their stock of baking materials still difficult to obtain, because of continued rationing.

Each little sponge cake had borne testimony to Jo's mouth-watering taste buds as, one by one, the child had picked off the sticky little sugary-tasting sticks, popping them into an eager mouth and salivating at their gooey sweetness.

Every dollop of white fondant icing sitting on the summit of a mound of light yellow sponge was cratered where its crowning glory had now slipped deliciously down the throat of the tempted three-year-old.

Moira, the waitress who enjoyed the company of the hotel's gentlemen guests and her "little helper" in equal measure, had tried to hide the evidence of Jo's undoing, after a tutting rebuke and a threat to tell Grandmother.

However, she too had been caught red-handed, with a flat knife in her hand, leaning over the three-tiered glass plate stands, smoothing over the icing and repairing the damage in an attempt to obliterate the evidence of Jo's greedy indulgence.

She had urged Jo to disappear out of sight as soon as possible, but she was unaware that Andrina had witnessed the whole performance from the shadows of the vast, high ceilinged room, with its ornate plasterwork and rich velvet drapes.

Jo's tormentor had been in the process of drawing the rich velvet curtains against the failing winter afternoon light and had stepped out unseen to allow herself to watch and observe until she deemed it time to announce her threatening presence.

Moira had immediately scuttled back into the hotel kitchen, knowing that her own admonishment would quickly follow, but helpless to say anything to plead for young Jo against the woman who was the waitress's immediate boss and who spoke to both the staff and her own family in short, snappy sentences, which cut through the air like a cheese wire.

No, Jo would not cry the tears that welled up at the corner of those dark, sparkling eyes, which were the child's greatest asset and main disadvantage whenever they were forced to look upon Aunt Andrina.

Jo's cheeky cheerfulness was as much responsible for the love and affection that was bestowed upon the child by everyone working in the hotel, as it was liable to call the owner of that flashing, fleeting smile into account with the woman who seemed to harbour nothing but hatred and resentment for the child, who had been brought into the family for no apparent reason.

Jo lacked feminine charm and possessed boyish resilience in equal measure.

Jo was intelligent and forever questing for information; the barrage of questions which there was seldom any answer grew out of a fertile imagination.

Spending the first three years of a mostly over-indulged existence in the company of adults, who occupied the child's every waking moment, Jo was a child alone in a world that was bereft of playmates.

True, this was made up for in fairly sound measure by the sometimes child-like indulgence and antics of Uncle Robert and the stern, but kindly way in which a hard-working grandmother, who had never really had the opportunity to gratify the wants of her own children, now had both the time and good fortune to be able to pander to her grand-child's every whim.

Grandmother Mary was Jo's protector and in whose salvation, solace was sought whenever Anne, her first-born daughter, was too drunk to barely even notice her adopted child's existence.

Grandmother was Jo's "playmate" whenever Uncle Robert who, as a tiny baby, she had passed into the hands of Charlie Paterson all those years ago when her first husband, Alex had met his untimely death, was busy – usually doing very little at all.

Grandmother was the person to whom Jo always turned for attention, when Agnes (or Nan, as Jo was wont to call her), Charlie's dutiful daughter by his first wife, Muriel, had her head down, pouring over the thick leather-bound ledgers at the hotel's reception desk. Only in her case, she genuinely had very little time to indulge the tiny tot, who constantly craved her attention.

Jo liked Nan and, unlike Andrina, she, in her turn, quite obviously shared a deep affection and a certain affinity with the child, who never ceased to demand the answers to questions of a nature that even Auntie Nan, with her shrewd, business-like brain, sometimes found difficult to answer.

Nan was kind to Jo, but never over-indulgent, reserving most of her affections for the dashing fifty-year-old bachelor, who won so many female hearts, but who had never settled down to marriage.

Sometimes Agnes felt that Robert hardly noticed her at all and then again he would take her completely by surprise by inviting her out to one of his golf club dinners, or appearing at the reception desk and producing a box of her favourite dark chocolates, causing her to wonder how he could possibly have obtained such luxuries, so soon after the war, when rationing was still a feature of every day.

She would hide them away quickly in the bottom drawer of her desk, daydreaming that, one day, she and Robert might have their very own bottom drawer of another kind.

On one occasion, Jo had found her secret stash and had picked out the biggest and best looking of the box, only to spit it out again, after the sharp, bitter taste had spent just a moment or two testing young taste buds.

Jo didn't bother dipping little fingers into the box again and Agnes, for her part, aware of the true identity of the rifling "rodent" remained as quiet as a mouse on the subject.

Jo gulped in a final effort to suppress the tears that were so desperately needing to be shed, retching up the last couple of slivers of the red vermicelli that had landed unceremoniously in Andrina's lap, spotting her skirt with an untidy glob of saliva mixed with half-eaten candy.

It was at this point that Auntie Nan entered the room.

'Andrina! Enough! Come here Jo. Now get to your room, whilst I speak to your aunt,' she announced sternly, as Jo bolted for the tall pitch pine door and ran up the staircase as fast as little legs would go.

Raised voices echoed up the wide staircase, as Jo crouched behind the banisters, peeking nervously from out between the spindles, anxious to hear what was going on and to listen to the harsh exchange of words below, but not daring to creep closer in order to be able to better grasp anything of what was being said.

Words that were mostly beyond the understanding of the adopted child drifted up the thickly carpeted stairs, as Jo began to make a minute inspection of a mound of fluff that was trapped behind one of the brass stair rods.

After all, even at such a young age, Jo wouldn't see anyone else getting into trouble for disobeying Grandmother's strict rules on cleanliness throughout every last nook and cranny at Carlton Hall.

Jo decided to set about the task of picking out every bit of fluff that could be found protruding from the highly polished, golden yellow coloured brass stair rods, settling down to the self-appointed venture like a conscientious Victorian housemaid.

With a bottom that continued to sting, it soon became uncomfortable to sit on the stairs for a moment longer.

A single tear escaped from the corner of Jo's eye, unbidden but, more importantly, unobserved. It dripped on to one of the brass stair rods, leaving its salty mark.

Jo quickly rubbed it away with a tiny handkerchief, which bore a picture of Minnie Mouse embroidered in its corner.

Andrina's attack had not been the first on Jo's bare backside. That had happened just over three years ago at the hand of a more caring woman, when a tiny scrap of life had emerged from a womb that had never before been stretched in child birth and belonging to one of the women currently working in the hotel whom no one would ever have guessed was Jo's natural mother!

* * * * * * * * * *

It was Jo's first slap, stinging and biting. It had cut violently and unexpectedly across Jo's bare backside, causing the newly born child to yell out in pain, as well as shock.

It was like nothing that Jo had ever known before, but then Jo had known very little at all previously in a life that had begun only moments ago.

Jo had emerged from the womb after some degree of effort on the part of the woman giving birth to her first child in a private Glasgow clinic, where no one was likely to recognise her.

Here there was very little by way of creature comforts in the austerity, which continued throughout the final years of the Second World War.

Yet here was the one advantage that Jo's mother craved so much – total anonymity, for she had hidden the latter stages of her pregnancy well, allegedly going off to do her war duty as a land girl and escaping from those who knew her.

She had eked out a meagre existence in a small lodging house, reserving as much of her Post Office savings account as possible to pay the bill that would be presented to her after the birthing.

Here in the sparsely furnished private clinic there was not a living soul who knew anything of her past life and that was just the way she wanted to keep it.

It was in the early morning half-light of a grey November's day that Jo made an initial entry into the world. It was one of those cold, miserable Scottish days when the wind whipped around the church spires, whistling through narrow alleyways and chilling the very soul.

It reminded Jo's mother of the day, nine months earlier, when she had waved goodbye to the child's father and the wind had nearly thrown her up the Waverley Steps and straight into Princes Street, had it not been for the barriers recently erected by the City Council.

Little did she, or the child's father know, just what joy and sorrow their short-term relationship would bring upon themselves in the unforeseen future.

It was the thirteenth day of the month and the year was 1944. Some would have said that Jo got off to a pretty unfortunate start in life – born under the sign of Scorpio and with the unlucky number 13 forever featuring in the marking of Jo's subsequent years.

Jo's mother had been a virgin. It had been her first time, although she was old enough to know and understand the consequences of a Saturday night spent in the arms of an Air Force man, who subsequently knew nothing of her pregnancy and probably would have cared little enough, even if the facts of his fatherhood had been made known to him.

Where was Jo's father now?

Probably somewhere across the Atlantic – not like Jo's mother, flat on her back and writhing in agony, as she tried to expel the burden that she had carried for nine long months and which, for the last few weeks, she had been at such pains to avoid exposing to the world from which she had come – a world in which no young woman who lacked a husband begot a fatherless child.

Now she was tired, so very tired and the nurses who had delivered the bloodstained bundle of apparent joy seemed to little realise the degree of exhaustion that she felt, urging her to hold the newborn child, when she didn't even feel that she had the strength in her arms to prop herself up on one elbow to view the blotchy, reddened creature, far less take it in her arms and wrap it in motherhood.

Her eyes felt heavy and her pelvis felt that it had been split in two. Her head ached and she wished that her heart could ache in the same way, but she knew that any show of feeling on her part would be a mistake.

It would be an error of judgement that she could not afford – not for the newborn child and especially not for herself.

All she really wanted right now was sleep and all she felt was guilt – not just guilt for allowing herself to become pregnant in the first place, but an overwhelming feeling of unworthiness about herself and what she knew she had to do.

Ignore it – yes, that was the answer, but just what was she supposed to ignore? Her own natural maternal instincts to nurture and cherish the fruits of her womb?

She simply had to neglect the wrinkled and, it had to be said, slightly ugly-looking creature, which had just emerged from between her legs.

Its arrival had caused her such pain anyway.

How could she possibly contemplate keeping the child? It would be like keeping a bottle of aspirin unopened in her medicine cupboard and continuing to suffer the headache, one which would last for the rest of her life, to say nothing of spoiling all her plans for the future.

Yes, that was the best thing to do – ignore it. Then she could just turn over and go back to sleep again and the pain would disappear. Yes, every part of it – both mental and physical.

Ignore the pain!

If there was no child to care for, she could be her own person again, free from the burdens of motherhood and free to take her place in society, seemingly untouched and unblemished. To all the world she would regain a virginity that she knew in her heart was forever lost.

One night of unbridled lust, sex with someone who was virtually a stranger and her most precious feminine treasure was looted as surely as the tombs of ancient Egypt.

She had given herself in an act of sexual self-betrayal and now she suddenly realised she didn't even know the sex of the child which had resulted from that brief, but passionate liaison.

'It's a g ...' began the more matronly of the two midwives, who flanked the hospital bed.

'I know it's a good weight. I felt every bloody ounce,' said Jo's birth mother wearily.

She was not normally given to swearing, but she was exhausted and bad tempered, interrupting the other woman and leaving the mid-wife's traditional announcement of the sex of the child unspoken.

'It must weigh more than a sack of potatoes,' she added, remembering the cloth sacks she had lugged across the muddy fields of Ayrshire, during the early stages of her pregnancy, until a spreading stomach had forced her to stop work, leaving her with nothing else to do, but while away her days in the small guesthouse, far away from the comforts of the more privileged life she had grown accustomed to, as she waited for her time to give birth.

'Have you thought what you're going to call the wee mite?' asked the mid-wife, who had heralded Jo's entry into the world with a harsh slap across the backside.

Whilst holding, unceremoniously, on to Jo's ankles, Nurse Bapty had noted the strange mark on the back of the child's right hand. Strangely, it looked for all the world like a leopard's head.

On closer inspection it resembled the City of London hallmark on the back of the silver St Christopher that she had inherited from her grandmother.

Her elderly relative had died earlier that year in the so-called Little Blitz, when the development of pilotless V-1 flying bombs and V-2 rockets had allowed the Germans to attack London and other major cities with weapons launched from long distances across the Channel.

Nurse Bapty peered closely at the mark, which seemed to be slightly raised from the back of the child's hand. She even imagined that she could discern the tiny pinpricks, which marked the leopard's eyes and the whiskers, which extended from its cheeks.

No, it was ridiculous. Her imagination was obviously running riot. How could such a mark possibly be discernible on the tiny infant's still reddened, blotched and slightly wrinkled skin?

However, the notion remained, distracting her from the fact that the mother had supplied no answer to the question of naming the child that bore the mark that was surely no real mark at all.

Jo's mother was hardly aware that the question was being directed at her. She was tired of what seemed like a constant barrage of questions, in which she had no interest in giving answers. Tired too of well-meaning platitudes.

Why couldn't she just be allowed to sleep?

She wanted so much to silence the banal chatter of the nursing staff, who blustered and busied around her. Surely one of the other expectant mothers on the ward would be more welcoming of the banal pleasantries of the stiffly starched duo and their endless stream of cosy mother and child bonding.

If only she could shut them up. If only she could find a way of diverting their attention.

If they had been working at the hospital down at Edinburgh's Leith Docks during the bombing raids, like the sister of one of the land girls she had befriended, then these two chattering starched and bleached storks would have had far more to have concerned them than the naming of babies whose fathers did not even know of their existence.

'Oh God! Please don't let them suggest that the father might like to name his child,' mused the newly birthed mother, her thoughts at one moment coherent and alert and the next drifting away on clouds of longed for sleep.

'Come on now, my dear, it's a bonny wee soul. Let's be having a name for the wee mite. Surely you'll have given some thought to what to call the babby?' asked the kindly Nurse Bapty.

In truth, she had given no thought at all to the question of a name. In desperation she opened her weary eyes and searched around the clinical surroundings of the maternity ward for something – anything that might provide her with inspiration.

She found nothing.

Not a single flower was there to mask the disinfectant scent of the bare, utilitarian furnishings of the ward, not a single colourful bloom to brighten the peeling paintwork and the occasional blistered patch of damp on the walls.

No Rose, no Iris, no Violet, no herb scent of Rosemary, no sprig of lucky Heather even.

And what if she had been married to the child's father and had fulfilled every man's dream by producing a son for him as his first-born child?

What choice of boys' names was brought to mind in the strictly feminine domain of a hospital maternity ward?

What could a mother call her son?

What could she call her daughter?

All she wanted was for her eyelids to close in sleep and all this domineering duo wanted from her was a name – any name!

She scoured the well-scrubbed floors and permitted her drooping eyelids to rest for a moment on the bare walls devoid of any form of decoration apart from the irregularly spaced wall charts depicting details of the human anatomy.

Nothing inspired her tired thoughts – nothing at all!

She had wasted far too long thinking about naming the child, but what did it matter anyway?

She checked out the clock on the wall to her left. Over an hour had passed since that last excruciating pain when the child's head had finally emerged from her pain-wracked body, drenched first by the bursting of her waters, soaking the lower part of her anatomy in her own bodily fluids and then the warm flow of her own blood.

Underneath the clock was a print of the baby Jesus, with Mary and Joseph watched over by the three wise men, a gathering of shepherds and a donkey.

After all, it was only just over five weeks to Christmas and any form of decoration to mark the festive season provided a useful means of papering over the cracks in the walls and diverting the attention of both patients and visitors from the unhealthy spreading patches of damp.

Was there a clue in this depiction of the birth of the baby Jesus? Was there anything to indicate what she could possibly call her own newborn child?

'Just call it Jo,' she mumbled wearily, shortening the name of the man whom the Infant Jesus would come to know as his father.

Conversely, her own child would never know its father – nor its mother either, for that matter. She was quite certain of that!

She hoped that the hastily considered monicker would satisfy the nurse, who had been so insistent that the child should have some form of personal identification.

'That's good, my dear. No child should be without a name,' replied Nurse Bapty.

'Apparently my grandmother was christened Josephine but, as a child I always called her Granny Jo. It's simple and it does the job. Come along now, young Jo, your mother needs some rest. You just get some sleep now young lady, the baby will soon want its first feed and then, my dear, the real work will begin, let me assure you.'

Jo's mother turned on one side. Exhaustion beckoned her to escape into its dark, enveloping folds. It was what she craved more than anything in the world.

She was barely able to recall the taxi ride to the hospital. The previous nine months of back ache and morning sickness were all but forgotten and those fleeting moments of passion with the child's father were little more than a passing memory.

Names?

She simply could not remember names. What had she just decided to call the child? She couldn't remember.

What was the name of the child's father? She couldn't remember that either. What could she recall about him? Not very much at all really – only that they had hurriedly had sex during the blackout.

His voice, yes, that was it! It was a strangely different voice, which had spoken to her as the couple had made their way out of the darkness together – only to depart from each other as little more than two strangers who, for a brief interlude, had come to know each other so intimately.

She struggled to remember his name but, mysteriously, all she could recall about him was that he had told her that he was only five years old!

No, that couldn't be. It didn't make sense! How could a five-year-old possibly have been her lover?

She was exhausted.

She wasn't making sense.

She remembered how he had appeared to be amused when she had asked him anxiously to "be careful". He had simply laughed and said he couldn't possibly make her pregnant – not with him being just five years old!

She remembered how together they had giggled and he had pressed her up against the wall. Now, she couldn't erase that one seemingly impossible memory from her confused mind. He had spoken little to her and none of it had made any sense at all.

How could a five-year-old have fathered her baby?

Her baby?

No, it was not to be her baby. That she could not allow! She could hardly bring herself even to look at the tiny infant. It would never be hers. It would never share her life.

She had obligations to fulfil and they did not include becoming a mother of a fatherless child. She was not going to have her future blighted by one night of passion with a young man whose name she couldn't even remember.

What had she decided to call the child? Again she struggled to remember. Yes, Jo – that was it. Just Jo. Plain and simple. Two letters of the alphabet. An easy tag to attach to a child that very soon was to have no mother to call its own.

Would she even been allowed to see the new baby? Did she even want to? Probably not.

Here was a child – a child called Jo, born into this private clinic, with its peeling paint and antiseptic smell. A newborn mite, who would receive nothing more from her than to be given a name.

She knew for certain that there was no way that she could ever consider keeping the baby to which she had just given birth.

Yes, Jo would be put up for adoption.

It had all been arranged weeks before the birth; the clinic had found a woman who was prepared to take the child. No questions asked. No questioned answered.

An older woman, herself past child-bearing age, a woman who, hopefully, would learn to love the baby, bottle feeding it in between the times that she too took to the bottle. Her name was Anne. That was all that was known about her.

No surnames were needed.

No there was no need at all for Jo's adopted mother to ever have occasion to come in contact with the woman who had given birth to the tiny bundle that was exchanged for a thick bundle of Scottish pound notes.

Cash on delivery!

It would surely mean that the woman right now resting in the maternity clinic would never see the child ever again.

She turned to face the wall, hugging her pillow, as tears began to roll down her face, softening the crisply starched white pillowcase, staining it with her grief, as the wept for her child, her mysterious five-year-old lover and a future that simply could not be.

Here in the metal hospital bed, Jo's true mother's identity would be kept a tightly guarded secret – one that, hopefully, would never be revealed.

Chapter 23

Robert cared deeply for his sister, Anne, who had been just four years old when he had entered the world in the closing years of the nineteenth century.

He knew that nowadays her reputation as a lush preceded her and that her love affair with a bottle of Gordon's Gin was the most long lasting of her relationships.

However, somehow he understood her and would always try to take her side, especially when his younger half-sister, Andrina, would wring Anne's character out to dry, mouthing off against her elder half-sister with all the acid overtones of a lemon squeezer.

As a child, Anne had been a quiet and prodigious worker, normally content to occupy her own little world, which revolved around Mary's sister's place of work, helping her aunt fold and stack the piles of clean linen ready to be delivered back to the city hotels.

She had also always been happy to help around the house, tidying and cleaning the tiny Edinburgh attic, which had been home to the little family both before and after Alex's tragic death.

Andrina had not been born until 1911, sired by Mary's second husband, Frank Finlay, who had died in the Great Gretna Green train crash of 1915, when his daughter had been just four years old – the same age as her half-sister had been when Alex had met his own untimely end.

Three trains had been involved in the crash, which had claimed so many lives; a special troop train, a local train and the night express travelling north from London's Euston Station.

Andrina's father was a big man like Alex. However, unlike Mary's first husband, he wasn't averse to beating Mary about on a Saturday night, when he would return to the little Stockbridge attic flat after a heavy bout of drinking and rebel rousing.

At the time of the crash he had been a member of the Leith-based Seventh Battalion of the Royal Scots bound for Liverpool on their way to Gallipoli during the First World War.

At Quintinshill, the signalmen, who were later imprisoned for their duplicity in the tragic events which followed, had quite simply forgotten the local train. It should have been shunted on to a loop line but, instead, it was sitting directly outside their signal box.

Once the all clear for the troop train to come through had been given, it had proceeded at normal speed.

The impact of the crash had been tremendous. Indeed, it was so great that the troop train was crushed to less than half of its original length and the overturned wreckage was littered over the northbound line for a huge distance.

Minutes later, the northbound express from Euston had ploughed into the debris, almost immediately bursting into flames and rapidly turning into an inferno. In all thirty-two officers and 182 soldiers were killed in the crash, or were burnt to death in its aftermath.

Mary never learnt whether her second husband had died instantly in the crash, or whether he had suffered the lingering agony of being burnt alive.

Robert, although not usually one to bear grudges, had always liked to think that the latter fate had been the final end for a man who was happy to treat another man's son with the same degree of cruelty that he frequently bestowed upon his wife.

Robert was nearly six months past his eighteenth birthday when news of the fateful train crash reached the Edinburgh newsstands. He had not long been called up to serve his country, but had failed the medical examination, due to his weak heart.

At the age of twenty-two, when her stepfather was killed, Anne had enjoyed no shortage of admirers, shedding them like confetti until, five years later, in 1920, a forty-year-old Scot had entered her life, in the person of one Lieutenant Cameron Thompson of the Royal Canadian Artillery.

Cameron suffered from arthritis, despite the fact that he was a mere thirteen years older than the young woman whom he was promptly to sweep off her feet in a whirlwind romance.

By then Anne was twenty-seven years old, having been made old beyond her years by the horrors of war. She had acted as an auxiliary nurse at one of the Edinburgh hospitals, where many of the soldiers had been taken to convalesce after the atrocities of the First World War.

It was there that she had witnessed the horrific injuries and mental suffering of the dozens of shell-shocked casualties of war.

One victim who had endured, at first hand, the realities of trench warfare, was the man whom, quite by coincidence, she learnt had also shared the suffering, which had been witnessed all those years ago out in West Africa by her father and his then young companion.

Anne remembered very little about Alex, recalling virtually nothing at all, except for his violent death, which she had been forced to witness as a four-year-old, holding her mother's hand and not quite fully comprehending her mother's grief at the death of a man who was almost a complete stranger to her and who had said nothing more than a brief "Hello" to her before being hurtled to his death in the path of an oncoming tram.

After Alex's death, Mary had stoically got on with life, raising her two children in the best way that she could, with seldom a word of mention of the man who Anne understood to be her father, but about whom she comprehended very little else.

Anne knew that he had been returning from a war in West Africa at the time of his death and, somehow the word "Benin" featured in her consciousness, so that when she had heard the shell-shocked soldier uttering a strangely familiar account of the City of Blood to a similarly convalescing army officer, she had tried to draw him out on the subject, discovering, at first, that he was reluctant to talk about any of his wartime experiences, either recent, or long since past.

As the days continued, she found herself drawn towards him. With no knowledge of his past bravado, she found the man greatly withdrawn into himself.

It took much coaxing before he was able to relate to her the experiences, both of the four-year-old period of the First World War and of his trials and tribulations in West Africa before the turn of the century.

She had no idea that he had even known her father and it came as a total surprise one day when he related the story of how his friend and companion had helped to extract a piercing shard of burning metal from his foot, referring to him as "Alex" and mentioning the fact that he was married to a woman called Mary, whom he had lived with in a tiny Edinburgh attic, along with his daughter, Anne.

What clinched the true nature of his identity and the fact that he had known her father was when he had told her about the letter Alex had received, informing him of the birth of a boy, who was to be named Robert Charles Alexander …

'… Seath,' she added, to Cameron's astonishment.

And so began the gradual merger of two souls – one who had already lost a father and a stepfather and one who now learnt that his hero, companion and mentor of all those past years ago lay in a cemetery just off Morningside Road.

Listening to Cameron's tales of dreadful wartime sufferings and understanding a little of the occasional mental instability that now pained him in regular bouts of depression, Anne began to grow fond of the man who, in so many ways, fulfilled the role of the father she had never known, filling in too the blanks about her father's character and behaviour that Mary had always seemed reluctant to speak of to her daughter.

Their common ground and shared experiences of a war that had left so many dealing with depression and coping with truly horrific injuries made for a genuine feeling of mutuality between them, a shared notion that life was sometimes short and that whatever enjoyment that existed was to be grasped gratefully with both hands clasped firmly together and with a definite reluctance to ever let go.

It was only a matter of weeks after their initial encounter that Anne announced her engagement to the soldier, who had both provided and been given a shoulder to cry on in equal measure.

Her brother, Robert, had been pleased to see his sister finally poised to settle down to a comfortable, caring existence with a man who, whilst he didn't excite her passions, nevertheless offered her some sort of stability, despite the sometimes unstable nature of his own rambling mind.

After a brief engagement, their wedding was announced. It was attended by a small handful of guests at the Registry Office in Edinburgh's Montrose Terrace.

It was a quiet, low key affair, which took place in the late summer of 1921, on the day in August when the newspapers were full of the news of how the ill-fated test run of the R38, the largest airship to be built at the time, had ended in disaster.

A total of forty-nine people on board had lost their lives, as the structure tore in half on its maiden flight, bursting into flames in shades of the train crash, which had heralded the death of Anne's stepfather.

155

The news cast a shadow over the day's other more humdrum proceedings, marked in their own way by nothing more dramatic than ten-year-old Andrina flouncing off in a huff, because her second-hand bridesmaid's dress was ill-fitting and pinched her at her arms.

She had flexed her chubby little arms, throwing grains of rice as confetti and the fabric had ripped asunder, forcing Mary into making an emergency repair with a couple of safety pins.

At Anne's marriage ceremony Mary had been one of the two chief witnesses, the other being her brother, Robert, who filled the place of the father she no longer had.

Anne had hardly ever known her male parent. However, in some ways, she missed the only man she had ever known as a father. He was the man whom her mother, Mary had married when Anne had been a pretty 17-year-old. Unlike the way in which he treated her mother and brother, Frank Finlay had never been unkind to her.

After an evening spent at the pub with his drinking mates, he would often come into her room at night, breathing his beery breath at her, waking her from her sleep to wish her "goodnight" with a gentle kiss that sometimes strayed too close to her lips.

Once he had even snuggled into bed beside her, his presence undetected by the sleeping teenager, who awoke the next morning to find herself, as usual, alone in her own bed, but with her fleecy nightdress ridden up around her midriff.

Its woolly material was strangely stained in the area corresponding with the upper reaches of her thighs and it sported a strange white, flaky, powdery encrustation.

Anne had been sure it had not been there the night before, but it washed off easily and harmlessly from both her legs and her nightgown and she never mentioned it to her mother.

The wedding ceremony of Cameron and Anne had been followed by a simple wedding breakfast at a corner pub in Morningside. Afterwards the couple had departed for a two-night honeymoon at St Andrews, returning with the surprise announcement that they were quitting Scotland and bound for a new life in Canada.

Cameron had a much older brother living there. He owned a remote farmstead. Alistair Thompson was a tall man, stooped low from a lifetime of hard toil on the windswept Canadian prairies. His thinning silver-grey hair made him look old beyond his years. Cameron had not encountered him for almost two decades.

It was a strange decision to forge a new life for themselves in a land which they knew virtually nothing about. It was also a decision which Anne would soon come to regret.

Cameron's brother had long since taken to the bottle and his younger sibling soon began to join him in bouts of drinking, which could last for days, whilst Anne was left to go about a series of daily chores on the remote farmstead, which were both alien and abhorrent to a young woman, who had been brought up to know nothing of country life and its hardships.

Within two years she had had enough, not only of the lonely life that she was forced to live far away from the nearest neighbours, but also of the increasingly maudlin behaviour of a husband, who had gradually begun to ignore her more and more.

Her one saving grace was the two brothers' costly drinking habits, rolling back from the nearest one-horse town twenty odd miles away in an open top truck, which veered and clattered off the road at frequent intervals, seldom having anyone other than a drunk behind the wheel.

When they arrived home and clambered into bed, Cameron beside her and his elder brother stretched out and snoring loudly on a makeshift bunk beside the dying embers of the evening's fire, Anne would lie awake, listening intently.

Soon, Cameron would join his brother in a rousing attempt to bring home the pigs in great snorting breaths. Then she would slip from their shared bed, nimbly at first, but with more and more difficulty over a nine-month period.

She would rifle the men's pockets for any loose change and the occasional bank note. By the time that morning came, she was certain that they would have forgotten how much they had spent between them the night before.

Slowly, she began to amass the necessary amount for a single, third class ship's ticket to Liverpool. She knew that, once there, she could rely on her brother to take the train down from Edinburgh to meet her with her baggage and pay for her onward fare.

She was travelling light, for behind her, back in Canada, she had left perhaps the biggest and heaviest bundle of her possessions and responsibilities – a baby boy not yet two months old, which she had deposited on the steps of an orphanage conveniently located within no more than a mile of the train station from which she had made her hasty early morning departure.

* * * * * * * * * *

In the closing months of 1944 and at the age of fifty-one, it had been no less than twenty years since Anne had last held a newborn baby of her own in her arms and now there was no possibility of her ever doing so again.

True, she was now re-married to George, a travelling liquor salesman, who was in the best possible position to provide the liquid lifeblood that she now yearned for most in life.

As far as Anne was concerned, she had everything she could possibly want in life – everything but the child that she was no longer capable of producing.

Mary had bought a run down corner pub in Morningside and with the help and added attraction of the cool brunette, who was personified by Anne's half-sister, Andrina, the business had begun to thrive.

True, Robert, did little by way of lending a hand, or helping to run the pub in any way other than bringing in the punters – from an increasingly affluent band of black marketeers whose night-time company he usually sought.

If there was anything that couldn't be easily obtained on rationing then Robert was your man, albeit that his help came at a price, which certainly did little to reflect the true value of the goods that, somehow, he was always able to produce, so often with little more than an hour, or two's notice. If Robert couldn't supply whatever it was that you wanted, he invariably knew a man who could!

Anne never therefore found herself wanting for very much – mostly thanks to Robert, who she still considered as her darling baby brother.

Mary's corner pub was always stocked with a sprinkling of life's luxuries, many of which had not been enjoyed by the local clientele since the outbreak of war in 1939.

Soon the back street ale house gained a reputation for being somewhere where something more than a pint of beer could be obtained – albeit always at a price.

With her good looks and raven black hair, always so immaculately groomed, Andrina pulled in the punters too, although they soon learnt not to overstep the mark, for she was the mistress not so readily of the mattress as they supposed, but the mistress of a mouth that could be full of both vitriol and charm, as she passed from one drinker to another, treating each to her own special brand of sarcasm, laced with the occasional burst of flirtatiousness.

As a result, those who paid to have their pints pulled came back for more night after night in the hope that, one evening, she might pull more than a pint for them after closing time.

It was a world very far removed from the depressing deprivations of life on a rundown Canadian farm, and it was one which Anne slipped back into with consummate, if seldom consummated, ease.

Even after her second, albeit bigamous, marriage to George, sex was rarely on the nightly agenda. Usually he sought his pleasures elsewhere, whilst his wife sought solace in alcohol.

Occasionally, Anne stopped to wonder why she had abandoned her baby boy to an unknown future, but taking on another man's child was not the usual habit of the type of men whom her brother brought to the bar and in whom she had sought to find herself another husband – one whose connections with the breweries and distilleries meant that the object of her most frequent and daily desire was constantly on tap.

One thing was still missing from her life – she wanted a child, a replacement for the discarded infant that she had abandoned on another far distant continent and one which now she was too old to provide for herself.

So it was not unnatural for her to prick up her ears and listen intently to a conversation in which she was not meant to play any part.

Listening from her bar stool and straining to hear what was being said, one lunchtime she overheard a discussion between two of the men who occupied one of the quieter corners in the public bar.

They were running over the arrangements for supplying a wealthy, childless New Town barrister and his wife with a child that, officially, they would have been deemed too old to have been allowed to adopt.

It was a conversation that tugged at Anne's heartstrings and she was determined to find out more.

* * * * * * * * * *

158

Late one night in mid-November, Anne heard a gentle tap on her bedroom door. She was all alone.

Surprisingly, she had drunk nothing at all at the bar that evening, which found Andrina remarking that she must have turned teetotal overnight!

Anne's husband, George had not returned home. Probably he was sleeping with the improbably busty blonde, who was a secretary with one of the local distilleries down by the Leith Docks – but Anne wasn't really bothered by his antics.

She didn't care very much at all about his whereabouts for, as far as she was concerned these days, sex was for procreation rather than for pleasure and for her, procreation was very much a thing of the past.

Anne drew back the pink candlewick bedspread, reached for her dressing gown from its hook behind the bedroom door and slipped her toes into her slippers.

She turned the key in the lock and opened it up to the smiling, slightly younger man who stood before her, with a tiny bundle wrapped in blankets from which the identifying label of a private clinic in Glasgow had been carefully, deftly, removed.

'Oh my God, you've got one! You've got one for me! Thank you. Thank you. How can I ever thank you?'

The man who stood in the half-lit doorway remained silent, pressing a finger to his lips by way of encouraging her silence and an end to the protestations of eternal gratitude that he found somehow rather endearing.

Anne, of course, assumed that what her brother had presented was out of the generosity of his heart and not for his usual price. For her there was no payment to be made.

No, a thick wad of banknotes was already secreted within the lining of his overcoat, but what was the point of his sister ever being made aware that there had been a price to pay – even if she had not been the one to pick up the tab.

No, right now there was no cash on delivery for the man who had sat huddled in the corner of the bar that afternoon, deep in conversation with one of his band of contacts for whom nothing at all was impossible to achieve.

Now his hands were stretched out towards her, his black leather gloves contrasting sharply with the brilliant white of the little shawl, which almost completely hid its contents from the outside world.

Here was a man whose black market connections knew no limitations and he was standing in front of her with the gift that she longed for so much. Here stood a man she had known for almost a lifetime.

'Is it a boy, or a girl?' Anne whispered.

'It's a surprise!' he mouthed almost silently and in that moment he was gone, cast back into the shadows in the unlit hallway of the upstairs room above the Edinburgh corner pub.

Anne was left cradling the tiny, sleeping bundle, as one pink arm slipped out of the encircling shawl.

Attached to the short, chubby little arm was a large, brown parcel tag. On it was written in big letters, which occupied three simple lines of text:

To my sister, Anne.
This is Jo.
Love Robert.

One of Scotland's most notorious black market dealers had given her what she wanted most in all the world. In what might otherwise have been taken as an act of incestuous love, Anne's baby brother had given her a baby.

Chapter 24

'It's obvious she simply cannot look after the child,' proclaimed Andrina, addressing her mother, Mary in sharp tones.

'And if you think I can work in this hotel with that little brat running round under my feet all day long, then you've got another thought coming! So I suggest you do something about it and quick too, because I've had enough.'

'Now, now, Andrina. Calm down. I'm sure we can sort something out,' replied Jo's grandmother.

'Well, sort it out and sort it out now. I'm telling you, I'll walk out of here tomorrow, if you don't promise me you'll do something about that dreadful child. And who will you get to run your precious bar then – Anne, I suppose? And she'll drink the place dry within the space of a week!'

'I'll have a look in the Edinburgh Evening News for a nanny,' Mary replied in an attempt to placate her youngest daughter.

'Who for – the child, or its mother?' came the sharp retort.

'Don't be smart with me, Andrina. I wish you'd remember who you're speaking to sometimes. I am your mother, don't forget!'

'No, I don't suppose you ever forget you're a mother. It's just a pity that your other daughter doesn't think likewise.'

'Your sister loves that child, who you so delightfully refer to as "that little brat" and so do I for that matter.'

'There's only one thing my sister loves and it's not that absentee husband of hers, nor the child that my dear brother so thoughtfully decided to bring into our lives and burden us all with. No, Mother, let me assure you the love of Anne's life is anything alcoholic, not a bloody two-timing workaholic, like that stupid husband of hers.'

'Andrina! I won't have language like that spoken in my drawing room. Now get out and leave me in peace to read my newspaper.'

'Don't just sit there reading it. Try filling in an advert for the Situations Vacant column. You can either advertise for a head barmaid, or a nanny, the choice is yours!' Andrina retorted, leaving her last words on the matter hanging in the air with all the implicit threat of a hangman's noose, before flouncing out of Mary's private upstairs sitting room in the Carlton Hall Hotel.

She slammed the door behind her, so that the ornaments on the pretty little inlaid walnut what-not rattled and shook and Ming and Mitzi, Mary's two little Pekinese, ran at the door, barking in her wake.

Although Mary hated to admit it, Andrina was right. Something did need to be done – at least until the child was of school age. It wasn't that Jo was naughty, merely inquisitive, she told herself in defence of the grandchild that she had grown to love so much.

And as for her eldest daughter, yes, it had to be said, her moments of sobriety were becoming rarer as the months stretched by.

Anne seldom arose for breakfast these days, usually wandering down the lengthy staircase in an apparent daze a little before eleven o'clock each morning and sometimes later.

Meanwhile, Jo was always awake and looking for mischief the split second that tiny toes reached for Minnie Mouse, or Donald Duck slippers, running down the stairs, with an exuberance that greeted each day as both a challenge and an adventure.

Mary reached for her spectacles and a pen and turned her attention to the jobs section. She wasn't going to waste money on advertising: there was no need.

She ran a bony finger up one column, pausing first at "Nurserymen", then at "Nightwatchmen". She peered intently at the small script. Surely her eyesight wasn't becoming that bad, or was it just that the newspaper text was becoming smaller?

Underneath the required heading "Nannies" there were just three small classified advertisements, one for a couple living in Gloucester Place looking for a "fully experienced, live-in nursemaid of good character and above average intelligence" in return for a "suitable remuneration" and two others from young women seeking employment.

She took her pen and made a neat circle round each of the two advertisements, cursing herself when the Waterman fountain pen slipped in her arthritic grasp, laying an inky line over the address of the first of the two candidates and making it impossible to read. It meant that there was just the one choice left to write to. Mary walked stiffly over to her bureau in the square bay window, taking out a blotter and a piece of the hotel's headed note-paper. She didn't have a name to write to, so was forced to begin on a formal note:

Carlton Hall Hotel
Edinburgh

February 28th 1948

Dear Madam

I am aware that you are looking for an engagement as a nanny and trust that you are suitably qualified for the post, as you claim in your advertisement.

I am seeking a lady of trustworthy integrity to take care of my three-year-old grandchild, whose mother, my dear daughter, suffers from frequent headaches and is finding the care of the child a little too much of a burden for her, especially as her husband spends much of his time working away from home.

Should you wish to avail yourself of the invitation to afternoon tea on the afternoon of Tuesday of next week at 3·30pm, I shall be pleased to speak with you and to allow you the opportunity of meeting my grandchild.

Yours faithfully
Mary Seath Finlay Paterson

She read the short note back to herself, making sure that she was happy with what she had written, glossing over the cause of her daughter's "frequent headaches" and the nature of her son-in-law, George's "working away from home", which usually involved taking some of the women he encountered at the breweries and distilleries he visited in the different Scottish towns out for a late evening supper, and which somehow so often meant that he missed the last bus or train home, and was forced to avail himself of "board" and lodgings for the night.

Yes, she was quite happy with that. It contained all that was needed to be said and the neatly embossed logo of the hotel printed at the top right hand corner of the vellum paper struck a note of added dignity, marking her out as woman of substance.

Although she had so very recently come to rise to such elegant surroundings, Mary had managed to shake off the trials and tribulations of her past life within a very short space of time since her marriage to a man in his mid-seventies, who walked with the aid of a malacca walking cane.

* * * * * * * * * *

On the appointed afternoon, Mary, dressed to impress, sat in the most comfortable armchair in her private sitting room, awaiting the tap on the door, which would announce the arrival of the woman, who had come seeking hearth, home and employment.

She sat with a bone china cup of Earl Grey tea and a plate containing just two shortbread biscuits on a little table by her side. A second empty cup and saucer sat close by, with a teapot muffled by a woollen tea-cosy topped by a multi-coloured woolly bobble, which Jo had helped to fashion.

Alongside was a small silver dish containing a tea strainer. Little lumps of sugar contained in a bone china rose patterned sugar bowl awaited the grasping grip of a pair of silver sugar tongs and a gentle stir of a silver teaspoon.

Opposite her, directly facing the comfortable armchair, was a high-backed Queen Anne style dining chair brought up from the downstairs restaurant by one of the bellboys.

Its hard, slatted back encouraged good deportment and its padded drop in seat promised little by way of prolonged comfort. As far as Mary was concerned, it suited the job very well.

At precisely twenty-nine minutes past three came a sharp rap on the door, which she answered immediately with a request for the caller to "wait a minute", as she settled herself back into the comfortable wing chair, taking another sip of her tea and watching the little filigree hands on the china-cased clock on the mantelpiece measure round to exactly half past three, before she bid the job seeker to enter.

Into the cosy private quarters walked a small, squat, slightly rotund little woman of indeterminate age, but who was probably approaching her thirtieth birthday – from the wrong side!

She smiled nervously, waiting for Mary to bid her to sit down and making no effort to remove her long gaberdine overcoat, which would have been much better suited to a woman of at least six inches taller.

Her eyes, which Mary could barely discern, squinted beneath a little pair of wire-framed spectacles, which rested lightly above her rosy, blushing cheeks, as if they were likely to take off and fly across the room at any moment.

'Good afternoon, Madam, I've come about the job,' she announced nervously, as if her arrival at the appointed hour might have been totally unexpected.

'Yes,' replied her would-be employer. 'I gathered as much. Would you care for a cup of tea? Earl Grey, of course. Milk? Sugar?'

Taking the newly poured cup from Mary, the woman declined both, believing that decorum dictated that she should not put her interviewer to any more trouble than was strictly speaking necessary, but eyeing the sole remaining piece of shortbread, which Mary made no effort to offer her.

'I have a written reference for you to take a look at. You may keep it for now and return it to me later, if you wish.'

Mary took the brown paper envelope from the other woman, extracting the twin sheets of paper just far enough out of the top of the unsealed envelope to enable her to read the name of a Glasgow establishment, which meant nothing at all to her. She shuffled the two pieces of paper back into the envelope, without making any attempt to read the words that they contained.

'Tell me about yourself, will you and, if I like what I hear, I'll introduce you to my grandchild.'

'And the child's mother,' came the slightly nervously uttered suggestion.

'I don't think that will be necessary,' replied Mary through tight lips, knowing full well that Jo's mother would be tucked up in bed at that time in the afternoon as "tired" and as tight as the stretched skin on an overcooked rice pudding that one of the hotel chefs had forgotten to take out of the oven in time.

Of all the applicants that Jo's grandmother had the task of interviewing that afternoon, the woman who sat in front of her seemed by far the most suited, even if, in truth, there was no competition for the job anyway.

Apparently she had worked as a mid-wife in a private clinic and, with her quiet demeanour, was frequently put upon and bullied by matrons and staff nurses alike.

She was a gentle soul and Mary's only worry was how she would stand up to Andrina, but she did not give voice to her thoughts.

Instead, she suggested a gentle amble around the hotel grounds for, although it was only early spring, it was an uncharacteristically warm afternoon and one upon which Jo would be sure to be found outdoors getting into some mischief or another.

It didn't take long for Jo to be found, for the child would always answer to Grandmother's calling, just as the best thing to do was always to run away and hide at the sound of Andrina's raised voice. Jo was kneeling besides a little white painted picket fence, surrounding a small flower garden containing an assortment of snowdrops and early flowering primroses in the middle of a vast expanse of lawn, knees stained a verdant shade of green and hands grubby from playing with dirt.

Grandmother's two Pekinese accompanied Jo. The two dogs shuffled over to Mary, wiggling their bottoms in anticipation of receiving half each of the last remaining short bread biscuit, which Mary held surreptitiously in one hand.

'Hello. What are you doing?' the little round-shaped woman asked kindly, bending low to crouch at Jo's level.

'I'm planting my hamster,' replied Jo, looking up with wide, appealing eyes.

'You're planting a hamster? How come? I don't understand.'

'Grandmother, you know why I'm planting my hamster, don't you?' replied Jo, imploringly.

'Yes, Jo, but why don't you tell the lady.'

'All right, I'll explain. This is my garden. Grandmother said I could have it all to myself. My hamster died this morning and Grandmother says that when an animal dies, if you plant it, after a few weeks, it will turn into a pretty flower. My hamster is going to be a daffodil.'

'I didn't know that,' answered the woman. 'Perhaps you'll show me the flower later, when I'm staying here and looking after ...'

The woman, who Mary instantly recognised was at one with her grandchild, paused. In a horrible moment of realisation, she knew that she had already said too much. Perhaps her presumptuousness had just cost her the job.

'It's all right,' said Mary, as a smile spread across cheeks which, years ago, had become wrinkled and lined.

'Jo will show you in a few weeks' time, when the daffodils are in bloom. You'll be employed as Jo's nanny by then.'

'You're going to be my nanny?' asked Jo.

'Yes, I think I am. And I can assure you that when I am, I won't be allowing you to come to the tea table with hands looking like that!' she rebuked the child squatted by her side, anxious to prove to her new employer that she wasn't all soft-hearted indulgence.

'What's your name?'

'My real name's Nancy – Nancy Bapty, but you can call me Nanny Bapty, if you like. Now come let's have a proper look at those dirty hands.'

Jo extended outstretched palms towards the nurse who was shortly to leave her employment in a private Glasgow clinic, first allowing her to scrutinise the earth-caked fingers and the grubby little palms, before turning them over, as if to prove that the reverse side was not as ingrained as the front.

It was the strange looking birthmark that took the woman so completely by surprise. She noted the weird looking brand on the back of the child's right hand. For all the world it looked like a leopard's head.

It reminded her of the City of London hallmark. Unlike the last time she had noticed it, now she was certain of what it appeared to depict – a leopard whose eyes glowed like a predator prowling in an African jungle.

No, her imagination was not running riot – this time she was sure of that. No, the child did indeed bear a mark – one she had remarked to herself over three years ago, after she had held a tiny baby aloft and slapped life into the little mite with a sharp, stinging blow on its backside.

She tried to stifle a cry of shock, stung by her own surprise, but her words rang out, cast through the open French doors of the restaurant, which looked out over the rolling landscape of the hotel gardens. Four female faces appeared at the opening, each curious to ascertain the reason for the penetrating cry, which had reached their ears so suddenly.

Mary's youngest daughter, Andrina, Charlie's daughter, Agnes and Moira, the young waitress had all been busily setting up the restaurant for the evening.

Meg, the simple girl who worked in the wash-house, had just been delivering a supply of freshly laundered table cloths and napkins.

Nanny Bapty, the nurse who had first brought Jo into the world, didn't need to be introduced to the child's mother. She had no need of an introduction to the woman who had given birth on that foggy November day and who had proved so reluctant to name her child.

No, they had already met and right now she was one of four women who were staring straight at her.

And in that moment too, the newly-appointed Nanny Bapty knew that, for as long as she hoped to remain working at the Carlton Hall Hotel, caring for her young charge, she was sworn to secrecy.

Chapter 25

From the age of four and before starting primary school, most of Jo's time would be spent with Nanny Bapty. Jo liked nothing better than to sit on Nanny Bapty's knee whilst she read the *Tales of Beatrix Potter*, happy to have the same stories read over and over again.

Sometimes, at bedtime, Jo would even insist on having the same tale read that poor Nanny Bapty had been called upon to recount over high tea that very afternoon.

For her part, Nanny Bapty never seemed to tire of relating the same accounts and always relented to Jo's insistent pleas. Sometimes she would try to interpose and suggest a different narrative, "Peter Pan" perhaps, but the child's choice was always the *Tales of Peter Rabbit* and his clan of furred and feathered friends.

Tucked up in bed by eight o'clock and by which time Jo's mother, Anne, would be far too drunk to string the words of a sentence together, the task inevitably fell to Nanny Bapty – not that Jo minded that one little bit!

Jo's favourite was Jemima Puddleduck and Nanny Bapty would be forced to include the character in adventures in which the bird was never meant to play even a paltry part, embellishing the author's original work, so that the duck would flap her way into the story at every possible opportunity.

Nanny Bapty never ceased to be surprised by Jo's inquiring mind and the sometimes strange questions that Jo would ask, gazing intently into her grey-blue eyes behind her unflattering National Health spectacles and imploring her for answers to questions that few four-year-olds would ever think to ask.

'What does "puddled" mean?' Jo once asked inquisitively, tucked up beneath the candy-striped sheets, head alone poked above the pink candlewick bedspread.

'Puddled?'

Nanny Bapty wasn't too sure how to give the answer, for she too had heard Robert, turning to Agnes earlier that evening with the words: 'Good God, my dearly beloved sister is puddled again and it's not even eight o'clock!'

Anne had hit the gin bottle with a little more gusto than was normal even by her liberal standards of insobriety and Jo had watched as one slice of lemon after another had slid its citric acidity into yet another drink that was more gin than tonic.

'Does it mean that Mummy's drunk again?' implored Jo all too perceptively and wise beyond such tender years.

Nanny Bapty shied away from giving Jo a truthful answer, trying, as normal, to shield her charge from the harsh realities of Jo's mother's wayward drinking habits.

'Now Jo. No more questions. Hush, now, it's time that little children were fast asleep,' said Nanny Bapty, bending down to sweep away Jo's unruly mop of curls, kissing the exposed forehead "Goodnight" in an attempt to change the subject and avoid imparting information that Jo had no need to know.

'What the child needs is others of the same age to play with,' Nanny Bapty would gently berate Jo's grandmother from time to time, as playmates were never invited into the refined and genteel atmosphere of the Carlton Hall Hotel – a strange 1950s bastion of times gone by where the gentlemen retired to the smoking lounge to light up their cigars and sip their brandies and their ladies were left to exchange the feminine gossip of the day.

Jo did have friends however during those formative years – secret ones whose presence in the hotel was not shared with anyone other than Nanny Bapty and the kindly Uncle Robert, whose indulgence Jo was always keen to seek.

Isolated from other children in that huge, rambling Victorian red sandstone edifice to Queen Victoria, even after the child began at school, Jo's only real friends of the same age occupied a place half way up the ornately winding staircase and in Jo's vivid imagination.

Here they would sit quietly waiting for Jo's return from infants' class, poking their heads out from between the pitch pine spindles and splendidly carved balustrades, never daring to slide down the highly polished banisters in their eagerness to come out to play with their young friend.

It was Nanny Bapty who had taught Jo that a friend is something very precious and who would always speak to the other "children" as if they were something far more than a figment of Jo's imagination.

'A true friend is something far rarer than a perfect diamond,' she would say.

'When I was a young girl, I imagined that everyone I ever met was my friend, but I soon learnt differently,' she added a trifle sadly.

'Little do we understand, Jo, that, if we are very lucky, we will gather only a tiny handful of true friends around us throughout our lifetime. And, if we are very, very lucky indeed, we may find that one special person who we want to spend our life with, someone whose friendship matters above all else. Someone who dictates everything we do, everything we say and our every waking moment. One day I hope that you find someone like that, Jo. And if you do, treasure that person, whoever they are!'

Jo would always listen intently to Nanny Bapty's words of wisdom.

However, right now, Jo was happy enough with the friends whose presence in the hotel seemed to escape the notice of Grandmother and who, had they been witnessed at all by Jo's mother, would no doubt have been seen in drunken duplication.

Jo understood well enough that there was one person, above all others who could be relied upon to share those moments of triumph and despair caused by a mother who could walk into a room and barely notice the presence of her child.

For Jo that very special person was Georgina, who was always willing and ready to share her true-life friend's secrets and special confidences.

Georgina understood that Jo always had to change out of school uniform before coming out to play and before the two of them could escape from the rigidly imposed correctness of the hotel and spend time together.

Georgina would understand when Andrina would mutter and complain, taunting the child with the fact that Jo so often seemed to occupy a dream world in which reality seemed to play but a small part.

Sometimes it almost seemed as if Andrina would encourage Jo to disobey Grandmother's orders in a simple act of defiance, giving her the opportunity to tell the child off, or lash out with an outstretched hand and a sharp rebuke when neither Agnes, nor Nanny Bapty, were around to bear witness to Jo's anguish.

Jo's grandmother was a formidable character straight out of a Charles Dickens novel, but there was no doubt in Jo's mind that she loved her grandchild very dearly, imposing her strict regime in an effort to ensure that Jo was brought up in a proper manner, learning to respect those who had the child's welfare at heart, constantly seeking to provide protection against the way in which Anne would drunkenly ignore her offspring and in opposition to Andrina's open hostility.

Grandmother would insist that Jo's coat and satchel were hung away neatly in the closet, as soon as her grandchild returned home from school.

Every afternoon Jo would be sent to the boot room situated behind the hotel kitchen, picking a careful route through the countertops used for preparing that night's vegetables and the gas burners with their steaming pots and pans.

Jo would always be in stockinged feet, brown leather sandals in hand, ready for cleaning, if they showed the slightest signs of scuffing. Jo's little hands would work away with a series of horse hair brushes and bright yellow polishing dusters, until the shoes shone with a mirror-bright finish, carefully picking any polish out from in between the buckles.

Only when every last scrap of playground dirt had been removed would Jo be allowed to tread through the hotel reception's plush, deep red carpeting and up the stairs which the maids never seemed to cease vacuuming to meet up with Georgina and her friends, who sat huddled on the turn of the stairs.

Grandmother set standards. She did so for every member of her family. She did so for the staff and, most of all, she set stringent standards to which she herself adhered to throughout her long life.

She had long since given up on her eldest daughter, Anne who was such a disappointment, with two failed marriages behind her and a bottle of Gordon's Gin always to hand.

It was Robert, as her only son, who, in many ways was the centre of her world but, above all else, he cared for Jo with a level of indulgence that caused the old lady to mellow whenever Jo looked up at her with those dark, puppy dog eyes under an unkempt mop of shaggy hair.

'Go and fetch the comb from my silver dressing set in the bedroom,' she would say. 'And do tell Nanny Bapty to use a brush on your hair in the morning. You look as if you have just been dragged backwards through a privet hedge. Whatever will the guests think? They'll suppose they've arrived at an orphanage full of ragamuffins, not a hotel where only ladies and gentlemen come to stay.'

'Leave the child alone!' Robert would interpose. 'You never had time to comb my hair very often when I was that age.'

'Come along Jo, we'll go for a spin in the MG. Get the wind in your hair and your grandmother can comb it all over again when we come back.'

'Can Georgina come too?' Jo would ask and, indulgently, Uncle Robert would utter his normal reply.

'Only if she sits tight on your lap and doesn't fidget.'

169

Sometimes Uncle Robert would take them to Edinburgh Zoo for an hour or two in the afternoon, with Jo bouncing up and down in the passenger seat on warm summer days, when it was possible to drive with the hood down. Georgina had to squash in besides Jo but, of course, there was always plenty of room.

On other occasions, they would set off before lunch, with a picnic prepared for them by one of the chefs. Everything was packed up in cream-coloured tin sandwich boxes, with tightly fitting dark blue lids.

Inside there would be ham sandwiches and small fairy cakes topped with big blobs of coloured icing – sometimes white, sometimes bright lemon and at other times pink.

Each would be contained in a corrugated paper case, to which some of the sponge mixture would adhere and Jo would lick it in an attempt to get at every last morsel, whilst Uncle Robert turned a blind eye, figuring that table manners didn't matter when there was no table involved.

Usually they would stop off at the dairy and buy a small third of a pint-sized glass milk bottle, filled not with milk, but orange squash, which Jo would suck at noisily with a straw, blowing bubbles and making hollow, echoing noises into the bottom of the empty bottle, until Uncle Robert would adopt a stern face and remind Jo how cross Grandmother would be if Jo repeated such mildly disgusting antics in her presence.

Agnes would seldom find the time in the day for any such outings, sitting behind the brown marble-topped reception desk juggling figures and totting up columns of figures from the thick, parchment-bound ledgers, rapidly calculating an assortment of sums, such as five pounds, ten shillings and three ha'pence and six shillings and eleven pence, with other amounts denoted in guineas. Sharp-witted and intelligent, Nan seldom failed to balance the books at her first attempt.

Uncle Robert always appeared to have time on his hands in the afternoon. At other times, he seemed to be very busy, but quite what he was occupied doing remained a mystery.

A golf fanatic, he would also regularly play tennis during the summer and badminton in the winter months. For a man in his early fifties he had managed to maintain his physique very well.

In looks, he bore a passing resemblance to Clark Gable and cut quite a dash with the ladies in the lounge bar of the hotel. Surprisingly, for so handsome a man, he was also popular with their husbands, who would invariably include him in any round of drinks they were buying.

Little did they realise that what they would be purchasing was a glass of expensive tap water, although what he would always order was a rare Russian vodka with a dash of soda water.

Behind the bar, one optic was kept exclusively for his use for, unlike his sister, Anne, Robert liked to keep a clear head and, in reality, only ever drank an occasional glass of champagne, whenever he felt that there was the need for a celebration.

Sometimes, he would slip Willie the chauffeur a pound to bet on a horse. He never put his money on the favourite and it never ceased to surprise Willie the number of times that a rank outsider would romp home first past the finishing post, swelling the thickness of Robert's wallet and resulting in a good tip for the chauffeur, provided that he kept his mouth shut and didn't tell Grandmother, who was commonly referred to behind her back as "the Boss".

As the child began to grown up, it was in and around the stables that Jo chose to spend much of the school holidays, for although the horses and carts had long since been replaced by Grandmother's heavily horsepowered Bentley and Uncle Robert's MG roadster, this was an adventure playground that fuelled the imagination.

Here Jo would get behind the wheel of the MG, despite the fact that Jo's little legs in ankle length white stockings would struggle to reach the pedals. With Georgina in the passenger seat, together they would set off on adventurous journeys whose destinations were never beyond the huge stable doors.

As far as Jo was concerned, sitting behind the wheel of the open-topped tourer was pure indulgence and it never crossed Jo's mind that their journeys out into the wide, wide world were nothing more than pure fantasy.

Sometimes, when Uncle Robert returned from his golf match in the Bentley with Grandmother's chauffeur, he would bring with him chocolate bars from Duncan's chocolate factory in Powderhall, or maybe a bag of boiled sweets, which somehow he had managed to obtain despite continued rationing.

At other times he would make the driver stop the car at Woolworth's on the corner in Princes Street and West Register Street, almost opposite the Waverley Steps, and rush in for a bag of broken biscuits, whilst the big-engineered car idled beside the statue of the Duke of Wellington astride his horse in front of the steps leading up to the impressive building, which housed the Scottish National Archives.

Robert would creep up behind the young driver of his car, placing one finger against his pursed lips and produce the bag from the pocket of his herringbone-patterned suit. Jo was naturally sworn to secrecy and would accept the bounty with wide-eyed enthusiasm.

Then Uncle Robert would delve back into his pocket, finding an extra couple of blackjacks, hand one to Jo and pop the other into his own mouth, sucking furiously and noisily, until it blackened his tongue, which he would poke out at Jo from beneath his neatly clipped moustache.

Jo found this hugely funny, giggling delightedly and would squiggle and squirm in the driver's seat, whilst Uncle Robert would make funny faces before launching a tickling attack from behind. Meanwhile Jo would chide him with words that were barely audible between fits of giggles.

'Please, please, don't do it! Stop, Uncle Robert! Stop! You're frightening Georgina!'

'I'll tickle her too, if she doesn't behave herself,' came the smiling retort.

At last when Uncle Robert stopped pulling faces and his boot black tongue slid back behind his slightly thin upper lip, Jo would recover sufficiently to delve into the bag in search of a favourite toffee, or rummage for a mint humbug, sliding nimble fingers into the man's trousers pocket, proffering the sweet that was known to be Uncle Robert's own weakness.

'Don't forget now, if there's any sherbet lemons in there, save them for your Aunt Andrina. With her sharp tongue a touch of citric acid won't do her any harm!'

Jo rummaged Squirrel Nutkin-like into the small, white paper bag once more, professing not to be able to find any of the bomb-shaped, bright yellow-coloured sweets which, when sucked for a minute or two, would suddenly explode their contents on to the tongue.

'Don't worry. If there's any acid drops in there, they'll do instead!' replied Uncle Robert, amusing himself with his own repartee.

Sometimes Jo would try to save a last sweet for bedtime and if Nanny Bapty caught the sound of a scrunching noise, as Jo bit impatiently through the hard outer casing to savour the soft chocolate, or toffee centre, she would chide the child and insist that Jo braved the cold, tiled bathroom floor in bare feet and a little winceyette nightgown.

Jo would stand on tiptoes to reach the sink, cleaning teeth once again with a Mickey Mouse toothbrush and pulling faces in the slightly damp spotted mirror, with its fashionable surround of alternate black and nail varnish pink-coloured ceramic wall tiles.

One by one those same teeth would finish up under the pillow at night, awaiting the arrival of the fairies, who would exchange a bright silver sixpence for a pearly white molar, which Jo had wobbled loose with a tongue that was rarely ever still.

One night, pretending to be asleep and anxious to catch a glimpse of the fairies, with their fluttering butterfly-like wings, Jo spied Nanny Bapty entering the dimly-lit bedroom and quietly slipping her hand beneath the pillow on which Jo's head rested in apparent slumber.

Jo, of course, realised that it was Nanny Bapty who was the real Fairy Godmother, but wisely said nothing the next morning, for fear that the supply of cherished silver sixpences would run out, each of which represented an orange-coloured goldfish to add to the glass globe on top of the toy chest in the bedroom with its Beatrix Potter inspired wallpaper and curtains depicting a host of woodland creatures.

From time to time, Nanny Bapty would feel the need to excuse the absence of the woman who Jo knew as "Mummy", especially on the days when Anne rarely left her room and a chambermaid would be summoned to make up the bed, whilst Jo's mother continued to lie there in her drunken stupor, unaware of the efforts to make her more comfortable. Sometimes too it would be necessary to change the sheets, if Anne had vomited and failed to reach the bathroom in time.

Whilst Anne remained totally oblivious to any presence in the upstairs apartment in the west wing, where the family had their own accommodation and guests did not get to go, Agnes would take the opportunity to search through the cupboards, removing half empty bottles of gin as she went.

In her more sober moments Anne would try to recall the whereabouts of her secret stash and bawl out her displeasure at the loss to no one in particular, sometimes frightening Jo, who was convinced that she had come to some harm.

One or two at a time, Agnes would discover the secret hiding places, thus forcing Anne to become ever more inventive in her choice of less immediately obvious points of concealment. It soon became a game of wits between the two women.

172

Agnes would recover bottles of Beefeater and green glassed Gordon's sometimes stuffed down the back of the sofa cushions, or jostling for space among the bottles of bleach and disinfectant under the kitchen sink in the family's private quarters within the hotel.

On other occasions, they would be suspended from lengths of string, under the lid of a toilet cistern, or secreted behind the rocks in the tropical fish tank in the residents' lounge.

Once Agnes had even discovered an opened bottle of gin buried in a jardinière, whilst she was watering the mother-in-law's tongue. The displacement of the topsoil had revealed the distinctive logo of a rather rotund Beefeater on a bottle-top staring up at her from the earthen crater that her watering had created.

Agnes resolved not to say a word to Grandmother. Instead she took the three-quarters full bottle and, in a moment of exasperation, poured its contents down the sink.

Grandmother would not have approved and would happily have used it to top up one of the optics, but then her own upbringing had been dogged by early years of poverty and long hours of daily drudgery and she despised any form of waste.

She had buried two husbands before reaching her early forties. Her life had only really begun to become easier after her marriage to Charlie Paterson in 1947.

Charlie already owned a couple of hotels in the Scottish Borders. His wife, Muriel, had died during the closing months of the Second World War.

Agnes, his only daughter, was unmarried and had rapidly risen to fill her mother's shoes, taking on most of the daily administrative grind, having learnt, from an early age, a degree of independence beyond her tender years.

Nan, as Charlie was wont to call his beloved only daughter, had long understood the need to work hard in support of her parents, as they struggled in those early days to establish their hotel business and now that her mother was dead, she accepted that it was expected of her to fill Muriel's shoes.

Mary, likewise widowed, when her second husband, Frank Finlay, had been killed in a rail accident, had struggled to raise his daughter, Andrina, who was only seven years old in 1918 when the First World War was finally over.

Foot-loose and fancy free and yet to meet Agnes, Robert had been little help as a breadwinner, spending most of his money on girls who craved his good looks, but who weren't afraid to expect a port and lemon or two in return for their company.

Like Nan, whose teenage years were marked by toil and tiredness, Mary's life before she married Charlie was dictated by her working day and making sure that the chambermaids and domestic staff at the Edinburgh city centre hotel, where she was employed as a housekeeper, all knew their place.

As far as material possessions were concerned, her children had very little at the turn of the century and during the early years of Edward VII's reign.

Anne had turned to the bottle in an attempt to ignore the bitterness that she felt on account of the failure of not one, but two marriages and the secret child that she had left behind in Canada, which no one in her family knew anything about.

Robert had never known Mary's first husband, whom he had always presumed to be his father. Indeed, he had lacked a father-figure to look up to until Mary's second marriage in 1910 when Robert had been at the impressionable age of thirteen.

Deemed unfit to be called to the Front to join his peers, Robert passed into early manhood with few male companions, apart from his band of black marketeers.

Somehow he felt that that he had failed his country, because the Army had rejected him on medical grounds, but he wasn't going to allow his sensitivities to prevent him from profiting out of any situation that might arise and which he could turn to his advantage.

It was no wonder therefore that the termination of the First World War and the emergence of the carefree attitudes of the Roaring Twenties, proved to be a landmark for a young man whose face was his fortune and who was fortunate enough to be adored by the ladies.

Andrina, as the baby of the family and who had never married, regarded Anne and her drunkenness with loathing and Robert with his carefree attitude towards life as a waster.

Andrina was very beautiful, with her raven black hair, piercing blue eyes and full lips. However, it was her waspish tongue that made men shy away from her, fearing the whiplash of her cutting remarks.

Grandmother had little time to lavish love on her own children. She had indulged them with her care, but had little time, or energy after a hard-working day to indulge them with her love.

She sometimes felt guilty about the reserve in which she had held her own children, especially in view of the amount of love that she reserved for Jo – her adopted grandchild. Jo was quite simply the child that she had the time to cherish, the chance to enjoy.

Indulgence was not something Mary could afford – at least not when it came to her own three children, and not during those early years of monotonous grind when she was forced to eke out a living on her own meagre earnings.

It was bad enough trying to make sure there was enough food on their plates! It was the survival of the fittest and only those who were fit and willing to work survived.

Perhaps the survival of the small family was a testament to Mary's strength of character and her willingness to work long hours, often leaving young Anne in charge of her baby brother.

As a teenager, Anne was often relied upon to be a surrogate mother towards her baby sister, making her resent the responsibilities that were heaped upon such young shoulders.

Surprisingly enough, it was immediately after the Second World War, that Grandmother's fortunes began to change. Tired of years of working as a low-paid hotel housekeeper, she invested the small amount of money she received from a maturing life insurance policy that she had been paying at the rate of half a crown a week for many years in purchasing the lease of a corner grocer's shop in Morningside.

She spent every spare moment of each early morning dawn and late into the night baking bread and pies and the occasional "fancy" to sell from wooden trays displayed in the tiny shop window.

Little by little, her culinary prowess became more widely known and by putting in even longer and longer hours, she was able to salt away a few pounds.

When the corner pub went up for sale two years after she had begun her little enterprise, it seemed like the sensible thing to do to purchase the premises, thus expanding her little empire.

She soon learnt that offering pies and cheap workmen's lunches, together with pints of beer drawn straight from the keg, proved to be popular. Quite simply, pies sold pints and pints sold more pies.

From the point of this simple discovery, there was no stopping her ambition to provide her family with everything that hard work and long hours could provide, steadfastly ruling over all their lives with her work ethos, which held no time for a mixture of work and play.

It was not altogether surprising then that Anne had quickly flown the nest, migrating to a foreign land and Robert, who considered baking and pulling pints to be woman's work, was more than happy to develop other entrepreneurial talents.

Never one who was prepared to devote himself to hard work, he left his mother to her ovens and his flirtatious half-sister to the task of pulling in the punters from behind the bar, whilst commanding a small team of barmaids, with a tongue that would cut and slice a lemon before the port was poured.

Mary met up again with her late first husband's best friend from their escape together from the Benin Expedition, when he walked into the snug at the Morningside pub quite unannounced late one Saturday night.

He had arrived just before closing time, explaining to the widow of his former trading partner that he himself had not long since been left a widower and left to run the family business with his daughter, Agnes, who aged with Andrina, but lacked the latter's striking good looks.

'I can guess where Andrina gets her looks from,' said Charlie, leaning on the bar that night, his voice raised above the usual rowdy Saturday night crowd and drawing Mary close enough towards him, so that he could catch the faint whiff of her perfume, whilst gazing intently into her eyes from the other side of the bar.

'I see you're just as much of a flirt as you ever were,' responded Mary, immediately taken by the unexpected amount of attention being paid to her and remembering too a night when Charlie had turned up on her doorstep in Stockbridge in the spring of 1896, when Alex had been away from home in the African colonies. He had bought with him a fish supper for two and in return she had cooked his breakfast porridge the next morning!

Little had he realised that he had left her with more than a belly full of supper and she wasn't about to tell him even now after all these years that Robert, his son, was living testimony to that night of illicit passion.

Charlie ordered a scotch, propping his weight against the bar and leaning on his silver-topped walking stick. He was told that it was "on the house". He knocked it back in one swift movement, giving him the chance to order another and to insist that not only was he paying for his next drink, but one for Mary too.

'A sweet sherry, isn't it, if my memory serves me correctly?' he asked, adding, 'why don't you come and join me? We've got a lot of catching up to do, you and me, Mary.'

Mary was flattered.

It was a long time since she had enjoyed any male company during an evening and the thought of sharing a sherry and another Black and White with Charlie produced a warm glow.

She moved to the optics, "accidentally" adding an extra measure to the tumbler, when her back was turned away from her unexpected visitor.

'I suppose you're going to leave me and the girls to get this lot out of here and clear this place up,' snapped Andrina sourly, tossing her jet black hair back in disapproval, like the Scottish terrier depicted on the bottle of whisky, barking at both her mother and the stranger.

'That's right, my dear, I'm leaving everything in your capable hands.'

'It's a busy looking place, you've got yourself here, Mary,' said Charlie, looking about him and taking in the bustling bar. 'You've done yourself proud.'

Looking at the cut of Charlie's coat, his expensive brogues and his immaculately groomed silver grey hair, there was no doubt in Mary's mind that he too had come up in the world since their last encounter all those years ago, when she had bumped into him in a small café off George Street.

On that occasion, they had only had enough time to share a quick cup of tea together and exchange a brief history of the intervening years, before each of them rushed off to catch their trains and return home to their respective spouses.

'I guess you haven't fared too badly either, Charlie,' replied Mary, sipping her sherry and already wondering if she would pour herself another.

'No, I suppose you could say that life has been fairly kind to me since coming through that ghastly war. I've got myself three hotels now – all in the Borders.

'There's The County Hotel in Dumfries, The Crown in Hawick and The Royal in Galashiels. So, yes, I would say that you're right, Mary. Sure thing! Charlie Paterson's come up in the world.'

'And what about Mrs Paterson?' Mary asked boldly, squeezing back into the oak settle with Charlie and a second glass of sherry, blushing slightly as she formed the words. Either she was embarrassed by her own forwardness, or the sherry was already going to her head.

'Nope!' replied her would-be suitor. 'There's just me and my daughter, Agnes. I guess she must be about the same age as your Andrina. A good pair of workers they are too from all accounts.

'I really don't know what I'd do without Nan. She keeps me on the straight and narrow and stops me from spending too much money on myself.

'If it wasn't for her, I wouldn't have built up the business so quickly.

'It's a pity Muriel isn't still around to see how well our daughter's turned out. She would have been well pleased with the girl.'

Together they stayed in the bar, long after Andrina had emptied the smoke-filled room of its regular clientele. Mary set a bottle of scotch down on the white marble-topped table and soon Charlie had felt sufficiently relaxed to slip off his brogues, stretching and flexing his toes against the wrought iron table legs.

'You two can stop up all night, reminiscing on old times, if you like, but I'm off to bed,' announced Andrina. 'Lock up after you've chucked your old friend out will you, Mother?

'That is, if you're intending to give him his marching orders tonight,' she added with a wicked glint.

'Andrina! How dare you say such a thing! Have some respect! I'm far too old for any of that sort of hanky-panky,' Mary scolded, but somehow she did not feel too deeply shocked by the implicit implication of her youngest daughter's words.

She remembered how the two of them had come together all those years ago. The warm glow that she had felt earlier wrapped itself more snugly around her, like a shawl that would provide comfort and protection against the coldest, windy Edinburgh night.

'Here, hang on a minute. There's life in the old dog yet, you know!' proclaimed Charlie, with a twinkle in his eye.

At the same time, he raised a wrinkled eyebrow, as he too recalled what had gone on before.

Charlie became a regular caller at the Morningside pub over the ensuing weeks. Sometimes he would arrive with a bouquet of freshly cut roses as a gift for Mary.

She would delight in their scent and marvel at the variety and range of colours – glorious pinks, subtle creams and glowing sunshine yellows, until one day he arrived with a bunch of rich, ruby red blooms.

Mary had smiled inwardly and knowingly to herself.

Charlie claimed that the flower seller at the Waverley station had sold out of any other colour. Besides when Mary counted them there were only eleven blooms – one short of a dozen, as if her suitor was somehow holding back. She had teased him about it, asking him if he couldn't afford a dozen which, undoubtedly, was not the case.

'Perhaps, he doesn't think you're worth the full dozen,' interjected Andrina spitefully.

Later that evening Mary ventured outside the double swing doors with their glass etchings to dash to the corner shop for wicks for the oil lamps that she still insisted in using in her bedroom, despite the installation of electricity many years ago.

As she hurried along the pavement in the rain, she was stopped in her tracks by something red lying in the gutter.

At first she thought it was a bloodied handkerchief, as fights were not unusual after chucking out time in the public bar and bloody noses were often the order of the night.

She bent down, careful not to muddy her dress on the glistening, rainwashed cobbles. She found not a bloodied scrap of linen, but the blood red petals of a single rose, squashed and stripped of its beauty; its sodden, bruised petals trapped amongst the gratings of a drain cover.

She poked them with her foot and the gushing rainwater swept all but one last petal away down into the subterranean network beneath her feet.

Mary straightened, standing erect for a moment, surveying the last remaining petal, still slightly furled, which had seemingly suffered less in the torrent than its companions.

She stooped to pick it up out of the gutter – a tiny part of the last red rose that had made up the dozen.

She was touched to realise that it had surely been discarded from the bunch by Charlie. Obviously, he had been too embarrassed to march into the busy pub with a bouquet of a dozen red roses, which he had secreted under his overcoat.

It was plain to her that he was far too sensitive to reveal the gathering nature of his feelings for her – a tenderness of heart which he had first felt over 50 years ago.

She smiled.

Maybe she should make an issue of it and tell her daughter of her find, but she thought better of it. No, she would not stoop to emulate Andrina's cutting remarks.

Instead she would wait for Charlie to make his move, perhaps marrying her at last and joining their two burgeoning empires in holy matrimony – her little corner pub and his expanding chain of hotels.

She knew that he was planning to add to his business interests with the purchase of Carlton Hall, the grand mid-Victorian pile approached by a tree-lined avenue, opening out into acres of rolling meadows and dense, mature woodlands.

It was the grand centrepiece of its own small estate situated just six miles outside of Edinburgh. It was an impressive building with its marble columns and sweeping oak-panelled staircase.

Charlie had already taken her to see it, anxious to include her in his plans for its future.

It was to be the jewel in Charlie's empire and with a diamond ring on the third finger of her left hand, Mary would be its ruling empress – only the reign of the empress was not to last for very long!

Chapter 26

Mary's marriage to Charlie was a fairly low-key affair, despite the fact that Charlie would have preferred a somewhat more grand event.

Instead the occasion was attended only by family members, but it marked Agnes's first cheek to cheek dance with Robert.

Agnes had been struck by his handsome good looks from the first moment that she saw him, when he had arrived one day to deliver Mary for a weekend away in the Borders with her father.

Willie, who worked behind the bar at the Morningside pub and sometimes acted as Mary's chauffeur, had been off sick. His employer had been anxious not to have to cancel her engagement with the man who was now courting her quite seriously, sending her bouquets of flowers and slipping Robert half the contents of his wallet to come up with a big box of chocolates for the love of his life at a time when continued rationing should have rendered such protestations of his growing affection beyond all means of expression.

With Willie ill in his bed, Mary had even allowed her immaculate grooming to be cast into windy array in the open-topped roadster, as she and Robert had zoomed out of Edinburgh along the A7 towards Hawick.

They had taken the country route, which passed through the spectacular scenery close to the Moorfoot Hills, along a twisty, winding road that allowed Robert to show off the road-holding capabilities of the little MG, amidst his mother's constant admonishments to "slow down and be careful".

'Don't worry, Mother. Just imagine that you are Vivienne Leigh in *Gone with the Wind* and don't give a damn,' he had replied.

Now, at the wedding, Agnes saw Robert in a grey morning suit and yes, he did have something of Clark Gable about him, as he led his ageing mother up the aisle, ready to give her away to the father who he still did not know was his.

Robert looked for all the world as if he had just walked off a Hollywood film set. Right now he was a leading man with no leading lady. It was a role that Agnes longed to play.

Mary, now in her mid-seventies, stood proud and erect, preparing to join herself in holy matrimony to the man who had fathered her only son fifty years ago.

It was as if their union had been planned for decades, thwarted only by Charlie's marriage to Muriel, just weeks before Mary would have been free to marry him.

If only he had waited!

Fifty years they could have spent together – as far as Mary was concerned, it was as if more than half a lifetime had been wasted, even if Charlie had loved his first wife.

Nevertheless, for a whole half century they had never come together – until this precious moment during their twilight years. Charlie and Mary – together at last.

It was Andrina's whispered remark to Anne, when Robert stood by his mother's side in front of the altar that might have created pause for thought, but was left to echo harmlessly around the chilly, unheated church.

'My God, that man that our mother's about to throw herself at looks just as I imagine Robert will look twenty odd years from now!'

It should, perhaps, have offered a clue, but Anne, who had already been "tasting" the champagne that had been put aside for the reception was hardly receptive to such comment.

Agnes too was unhearing, sitting in the front row of the opposite ranks of pews, her attention held wrapt by both Robert and her father in equal measure.

She had her nose pressed into a little handkerchief, sniffling with joy at the imminent prospect of her father's pending union, thinking too of her mother, Muriel, alternating between tears of happiness and joy. Her tear-strewn eyes flitted between her father and Robert, the fit-looking fifty-year-old, who stood tall, proud and handsomely erect by Mary's side, just as his mother did, despite her advancing years.

At the reception that followed, it was only natural that Agnes, as Charlie's daughter and Robert, as Mary's son, would be paired together.

Neither of them had ever married and although Agnes was thirteen years younger than Robert, they made a good-looking couple, even if, on this special day, Agnes had enjoyed all the help that four hours in the hairdressers' and carefully applied make-up could provide.

Agnes did not share Andrina's raven-haired natural beauty, but then nor did she share her vitriolic, viperous tongue. For Agnes, looking good, even for her father's wedding day, was an effort, whereas for Andrina, who was almost exactly the same age, a quick sweep through her lustrous hair, a dab of make-up and a swiftly applied lipstick was all that was required to complete the early morning transformation from awakening rat-haired raven to ravishing beauty.

Nanny Bapty had even been allowed to occupy the second row of pews, behind the female line up formed by Anne, Andrina and Mary's younger sister, whose arthritic hands, racked with rheumatism from years of immersion in the hot tubs of the Edinburgh wash-house, frequently caused her to lose the grip on her walking stick, which clattered on to the stone floor and made everybody turn round and look from time to time.

'Oh,' said Andrina at one point. 'I thought that was Charlie dropping his walking stick and making a run for it, but it's only my aunt and those crippled fingers of hers – more's the pity.'

Robert, slipping back in between his two half-sisters, having completed his filial duty of delivering his mother to her date with destiny, had heard Andrina's cutting remark.

'Charlie wouldn't make a run for it, even if he was capable of doing so. You really don't get it, do you Andrina? You don't see what binds the two of them together,' he said in an aside, uttering words that were truly ironic, coming from the very person who was the result of their union all those years ago and who was living testimony to what really bound the two of them together, even if Charlie still remained in ignorance of the fact after all these years, as – indeed – did his son.

In the row behind Nanny Bapty held tightly on to Jo. The child was clutching a lucky horseshoe that was to be gifted to Grandmother after the ceremony.

Jo was dressed in a little tartan outfit complete with ruffled white shirt, which made Jo complain that it looked too much like one of Andrina's blouses.

'Is it one of Andrina's old blouses?' enquired Jo.

'No, don't be silly, of course it's not,' replied Nanny Bapty. 'How on earth would any of your aunt's clothes fit you?'

'They might do,' replied Jo, who was never short of an answer.

'What are you talking about Jo?' replied Nanny Bapty.

'Well, Aunt Andrina is always complaining about Meg shrinking her clothes in the wash.'

'Yes, and how about what you did with her pearls by washing them the other day. It's no wonder she was cross with you,' said Nanny Bapty.

'I only put them in vinegar to see if they really would melt – just like they said they would at school,' replied Jo.

'Yes,' replied Nanny Bapty. 'And they did!'

Jo continued to tug at the neckline of the ruffled white shirt, scratching amongst the dark descending curls, as if suffering from a headful of nits.

'Do keep still Jo and stop fidgeting,' urged Nanny Bapty, pressing a prayer book into Jo's free hand to provide occupation, noticing that it was held upside down in the little outstretched palm – psalms, prayers and hymns rendered meaningless in the hands of an innocent child.

Anne's second husband, George, was not there to witness his mother-in-law's betrothal, claiming urgent business on the day of the ceremony.

His presence was hardly missed by anyone – except perhaps fleetingly by the raven-haired beauty, who did not share her sister Anne's love affair with a bottle of Beefeater, but who had shared the company of her half-sister's husband in bed more than once over the years.

They first slept together one cold February night, when the liquor salesman, whose wife had imbibed one too many measures of gin, had locked the bedroom door, leaving him to seek elsewhere for a bed for the night.

Yes, Andrina remembered it well – the night he had come knocking on her room at the top of the stairs in the flat above the Morningside corner pub, just as nine months later her half-brother, Robert had come knocking on Anne's door!

'Is it a boy, or a girl?' Andrina had heard her half-sister whisper from her position along the corridor, the door to her own bedroom held half ajar, so that she could spy on the proceedings.

'It's a surprise,' Robert had replied.

'Yes,' thought Andrina, newly arrived from a self proclaimed four month stint at an ammunitions factory down south as part of the war effort, 'and it would be a great surprise to the pair of you, as well as to my mother and the man who by then was ardently courting her, if the identity of its mother was known!'

* * * * * * * * *

181

Agnes's attempts to get Robert to notice her began in earnest when, six months after Mary and Charlie's wedding, Anne's husband, George was appointed to manage one of the three smaller hotels in the Borders and Nan, free of her duties there, was able to move into the Carlton Hall Hotel outside Edinburgh.

In previous years, George had helped his widowed mother run a small guesthouse on the sea front in Ayr. The clientele was mostly made up of young women whose chosen attire was loosely fitting dresses, which did little to reveal their figures – nor the impending birth of their fatherless children.

Spending most of his time working away from Carlton Hall, George soon became a stranger to Anne, returning sometimes for no more than a night at a time to the hotel, bringing with him his personal laundry, handing it into the outhouse where all the hotel washing was done each day.

Naturally, the hotel which he now managed in Hawick in the Scottish Borders, had its own laundry facilities, but he preferred the personal touch, especially on his shirt tails and undergarments and particularly on the ones that he was wearing at the time!

Sometimes he would stop for a while to chat with Meg, the slow-witted girl, who spent her days working in a wash-house, like Mary's younger sister had done before her.

Meg toiled over the hot tubs doing the washing and ironing, trailing the wire of an electric iron with which, clumsily, she would burn herself from time to time.

In return for scrubbing the collars of his shirts and sewing on the odd missing button, he would pass her a lipstick or, perhaps, a pair of nylon stockings, which Robert would supply in exchange for a ten shilling note, producing them as if from nowhere, like a magician handing him a rabbit out of a hat.

George always insisted that Meg tried them on in front of him – just in case they didn't fit!

Often in the steamy atmosphere of the little outbuilding, with its tubs of scalding, soapy water and starched white sheets squeezed between heavy rollers, he would press his hands against her white thighs, rolling her pale skin between forefinger and thumb, insisting that he had found a crease there that her hours of "ironing" had missed and suggesting that a warm hand would quickly flatten it out again.

She would giggle, as his fingers reached higher and she would arch her back, as he bent her over the hot tub, just like another much younger man, whose shirt she had washed once before, had done on a cold winter's day in the year before the end of the war.

He had been a serviceman – American she thought – staying at the Carlton Hall Hotel before it had been bought by Charlie.

He had been just 20 years old – a fresh-faced lad, who had pressed bars of chocolate and chewing gum on her, sitting out on the bench outside the wash-house, as they munched happily on the confectionery, happy and contented in each other's company.

It had been his birthday and they had sat side by side in the weak sunlight of a short February afternoon in the year before the war had finally ended.

He had found her to be an avid listener and he had told her of his arrival in Scotland and the search for the mother, who had dumped him at a Canadian orphanage shortly after his birth and who he had never seen again to this day.

Together they crammed chocolate into their mouths. In her fingers, hot and sticky from the wash-house, Meg had bitten the last two squares in two, offering him one, but missing his mouth, so that the saliva-stained slivers of chocolate ran down the front of his immaculately-pressed uniform.

She had insisted on taking him back into the wash-house, helping him out of his jacket, so that she could sponge it. At the same time, the brown chocolate stains on his shirt had been revealed.

Likewise she had insisted on him removing his shirt, leaving him stripped to the waist, as he stood shivering before her, his upper torso rapidly dampening, as his body temperature began to warm up again in the steam-filled atmosphere.

She had scrubbed away at the collar of his shirt – but only after making a minute inspection of the front of his trousers – just to ensure that they too weren't stained with chocolate.

In her own very simple way, Meg could be a very thoughtful girl!

Indeed, a year later, after Jo had been brought into the family, she always remembered to collect the soiled nappies from Anne, the child's adopted mother.

Just like Mary's younger sister, who had always had time for Anne – Meg always found time for the child that she longed to be able to call her own!

* * * * * * * * * *

Agnes's engagement to Robert on St Valentine's Night when, after many months, she finally managed to capture the wary bachelor, had all the hallmarks of a society occasion. It was one to which the rich and influential of Edinburgh's New Town were all invited.

Not only did it offer Charlie the chance to parade his handsome young son-in-law to be, but it also offered him ample opportunity to introduce the comforts that the Carlton Hall Hotel might have to offer to those who might choose to book an early morning flight on the newly inaugurated London-Edinburgh shuttle service operated from the nearby airport and who didn't wish to make an early departure before breakfast, taking a taxi from the other side of the city.

No expense was spared for the night in question. Extra waiters and waitresses were drafted in for the night, all taking their cue from Moira, who was put in charge of serving the finest selection of hors-d'oeuvres as a splendid testimony to the hotel chef's catering skills.

Unnoticed by Mary in the flummox of the occasion, Moira had even managed to get away with unpicking the hem of her black skirt the night before, stitching it back up a couple inches higher and casting her last unladdered pair of stockings to the wind of good fortune.

She wanted to look her best in the hope of ensnaring a rich husband from amongst Robert's increasing circle of wealthy bachelor friends and one who would be able to keep her in the manner in which she longed to become accustomed.

Charlie, for his part, insisted on taking care of the decorations, filling every available space with vases of red roses, inexplicably extracting a single bloom from each dozen, snapping its stem short and handing each in turn to a watchful Jo, whose task it was to strip away any last remaining thorns, wrapping each bloom in silver foil and, one by one, distributing them to the waiters and waitresses to wear as buttonholes.

Cardboard cut out figures of Cupids clung to an assortment of little red hearts, clutching their little bows and arrows and hung from every available surface.

In pride of place, at the top of the stairs down which Agnes would sweep later that evening on the arm of her beloved Robert, Charlie had enlisted the help of one of the young porters to help him erect a vast red silk heart, measuring maybe a yard across, bedecked with trailing red ribbons.

Through its centre he had struck an African spear – one which he had shipped back home to Scotland with him after he and Muriel had finally left West Africa together to settle down to the business of raising their baby daughter and developing their own business in the burgeoning hotel trade.

Along the shaft of the spear ran a bevy of little Cupid figures, each sporting a chubby belly and short, fat arms. Trailing from the spear ran a streamer of red ribbons imprinted with the words "Robert and Agnes – meant to be together".

Charlie was proud of all the effort that had been put into the occasion.

Early that evening, before the guests began to arrive, he and Mary had arrived in the bar seeking refuge from the exertions of the day.

Charlie tapped his trusty walking stick lightly on the parquet floor. It was his signal that one of the barmen should come and take their order, – which always remained exactly the same – a double scotch for Charlie and a sweet sherry for Mary.

As usual, their drinks had already been poured the minute the two walked hand in hand into the bar!

Together they toasted one another and then sat in silence, each with their own private thoughts. Charlie dozed in his seat for a few minutes, as Mary pondered how, even now – especially now – she could ever tell Charlie the truth of how, as half-brother and half-sister, in the eyes of the Law, her precious Robert and his beloved Nan were never "meant to be together".

* * * * * * * * *

It was the night of Agnes's life. At last she had successfully cast her hooks into a man of her choosing and, if looks were anything to go by, what a catch!

Throughout the night she observed how many of the other women sought his company, usually making excuses to pair her off with their husbands, or boyfriends and then enjoying long, drawn out conversations with Robert, uttering expressions of congratulations, which far exceeded the duration dictated by politeness.

Much to Moira's dismay, it was Agnes who got to dance with all the wealthy men of Robert's acquaintance, whilst the waitress busied herself serving them with glasses of champagne and offering trays of appetising canapés. For the most part, Moira remained unnoticed.

Robert, in his turn, spent more time than was strictly necessary in the company of other females. It was as if he was playing the part of a black market commodity for which someone was always prepared to pay the price.

From time to time Agnes even imagined that she was being ignored by him, but when he finally asked her to dance, she felt that he had eyes only for her – until, that is, Andrina dragged him away, suggesting that he might like to take the floor with his half-sister, before passing him swiftly into the hands of one of his many lady admirers.

Agnes felt rejected again and was not cheered up by Andrina's suggestion that she should pay a little more attention to the male guests, leaving Robert free to dance with anyone but his fiancée.

At one point Agnes found herself paired with Anne's husband, George – a man whom she had never particularly cared for, but whom she always felt she knew from some previous chance acquaintance.

Somehow Agnes could never put a finger on exactly when and where they might have first met, but it hardly bothered her that she could not remember. She instinctively disliked the man and she was pleased when he chose Andrina as his next dance partner.

As the band took a short break for refreshment, Agnes could not help but notice that Andrina and George were sat huddled together over a corner table in what seemed to be a conspiratorial conversation.

Strangely, Agnes imagined that it was she herself who was being talked about, although why she could not begin to think. What she couldn't possibly know was that it wasn't the first time that she had been the subject of gossip between George and Andrina.

Nanny Bapty put in a brief appearance, after Jo had been put to bed.

She made her excuses and left after only five or ten minutes, accepting a solitary glass of champagne, which she deposited close to where Anne was sitting, knowing that the glass would be empty when she came back from sharing a few quiet words with Agnes and taking the opportunity to press a little package into the hands of the bride to be.

'It's not very much, my dear, but it's all I can afford. I hope you'll like it and that you'll try to wear it occasionally.'

'Thank you, Nanny, I'm sure I will,' replied Agnes, pausing in the path of Moira and urging the waitress to take Nanny Bapty to the buffet table and fill a plate for her.

Moira was more intent on serving the gentlemen than feeding the mouth of the lowly nurserymaid. She began to cast an eye about for any unaccompanied man, who might enjoy an extra glass of champagne.

Throughout the night she had found herself with little time on her hands to stand and chat with anyone, as she mingled through the four hundred or so guests, all of whom had seemed to arrive with pig-like appetites for free fare and as thirsty as a troop of wild boar at an African water-hole.

At last, Robert turned his attention to his bride to be and he and Agnes disappeared upstairs together. They shared a moment on their own and a single lingering kiss, before Charlie found them and encouraged them to return downstairs with him.

First though, he urged them to join him at the top of the stairs, beneath the dark shadow on the wall cast by the speared red silk heart.

'Ladies and gentlemen, your attention please. I give you my daughter, Agnes and Robert, my future son-in-law. Please raise your glasses in a toast. A toast to Robert and Nan. 'I think you'll agree that they make a very fine couple – two people who were always meant to be together. To Robert and Nan,' he repeated, raising his own glass and smiling over the banisters towards Mary, who stood smiling up at him from below, lost in her own private reverie, as the chorus of well-wishers took up the toast, sharing the news, which was hardly a secret.

Finally, long after the midnight firework display and as the guests began to depart, Agnes retired to her room. She felt a little light-headed.

Like Robert, she wasn't used to drinking so much champagne and it had gone straight to her head.

Placing a weary, happy head on her pillow she was soon asleep – dreaming contentedly of her forthcoming wedding day, trailing her thoughts amidst lashings of confetti and sprinkled grains of rice.

She was asleep long before Robert retired to his own bedroom maybe half an hour after the last of the guests had departed.

His bachelor room was situated along the corridor from the box room where Jo slept snug and cosy in a single wooden bed decorated with transfers of Beatrix Potter characters.

Robert was not alone in his bachelor quarters.

A young woman sat on the edge of his bed in the unlit room. She was unfastening black silk stockings from a skimpy suspender belt, dragging down on the little studs, which now rested within easy reach just below the level of the hem of her short, black skirt.

'Moira!' exclaimed Robert, clicking on the light.

'Yes, Robert, she replied seductively. 'You're right, first time … or should it be second time.'

'I … I don't remember,' he mumbled in a slurred voice, making it perfectly obvious to anyone that the champagne he had drunk had done nothing to improve his memory power.

'Oh, come now, of course you do. It was on St Valentine's Night towards the end of the war. You'd arrived at a club down at the Leith Docks with a crowd of lads on a stag party night. I was one of the waitresses. I seem to remember you presented me with a couple of pairs of silk stockings the next morning. I suppose you must have thought I was worthy of the gift. Don't tell me you've forgotten?'

'Well come here and help me with my stockings now and maybe that will help to remind you,' she announced, taking his hand and guiding it down her one bare thigh.

Robert knelt down beside her, gripping the bed post in an attempt to steady himself. Unaccustomed to the copious amounts of champagne he had consumed, he nearly toppled over on top of her, losing his balance whilst, at the same time, the balance of his mind tried to address the problem of exactly what had happened that night – that cold winter's night in February 1944, nine months before Anne's baby brother had given her a baby.

Chapter 27

Growing up at the Carlton Hall, Jo's domain was the hidden acres, sheltered from the main road, past the little stone gatehouse and under the railway bridge, along whose single track the steam trains puffed out their importance on the hour every day, except Sunday.

Jo imagined them taking travellers to destinations that Jo could only dream about – exciting places like the highlands and islands, where the steam ships and paddle steamers with evocative names, such as the Waverley and the Jeannie Deans ploughed their passage through the sometimes rough waters of the Irish Sea.

Jo had ambitions to travel even further afield to places like Africa, where vast herds of elephants wandered the plains, lions stalked unsuspecting antelopes and crocodiles lazed in the murky waters of the creeks.

On dark winter afternoons, when little sun filtered through the grey Scottish skies, Jo would curl up in one of the two winged armchairs in Grandmother's private sitting room, with the two Pekinese, Mitzi and Ming sitting close by, their tongues lolling and panting in the heat cast by the open fire.

Jo would normally be engrossed in a children's encyclopedia, or perhaps thumbing through the pages of Look and Learn, eager to be educated into the ways of the Dark Continent, its tribal customs and the engrossing day to day survival tactics of its teeming wildlife.

At times, on a particularly still night, Jo even claimed to be able to hear the roar of the lions from Edinburgh Zoo, although it was nearly five miles away. It all served to make Jo's fantasy world seem more of a reality.

Most of all Jo enjoyed accompanying Grandmother on what Andrina termed her "stately visits" to one of Edinburgh's big stores, or to one of the big city auction houses.

Grandmother would summons Willie, the chauffeur, to bring the Bentley round to the porticoed front of house at the hotel and he would doff his cap, as she made her way down the short flight of stone steps to the awaiting vehicle.

Willie would defer to her and she would graciously acknowledge him when he addressed her as "Madam", knowing only too well that it was more than his job was worth to call her anything else.

Mary would look every inch the lady, with her signature diamond broach and her mink coat open just slightly at the neck to reveal her hallmark string of pearls, which she would sometimes finger with her patent leather gloved hands.

Jo would scamper into the deep, comfortable plush leather back seats, squirming with delight at the thought of sharing a whole afternoon of sheer indulgence with a beloved grandmother.

Together they would set off in style, sweeping out of the long gravelled driveway of what had once been a country house retreat for generations of the rich and influential Usher family.

Andrew Usher had set up as a spirit merchant in Edinburgh in the eighteenth century and had begun producing blended malts, going on to become one of Scotland's greatest whisky producers.

His son, John, had bought the Carlton lands in the years immediately following the beginning of Queen Victoria's reign and in 1838 he had commissioned the building of the two-storey gabled house, with its Tudor and Jacobean details as the centrepiece of the estate.

Charlie Paterson had purchased the property over a hundred years later, settling into a life of luxury with Mary – the woman he had loved for over half a century and with Nan – his beloved only daughter.

With Jo running around, it was like having his own grandchild and Charlie never begrudged Mary's total indulgence of the child.

When Willie drew the stately, silver grey Bentley up outside the main entrance to Jenners in Princes Street, a liveried doorman would immediately step forth from the shadows, ushering Mary and her grandchild into the store.

Once inside, Jo would immediately want to visit the toy department with its Pelham puppets and other delights. For Jo it was like an Aladdin's cave.

Sometimes, if it was raining, a huge black umbrella would be held aloft by the doorman, so that Grandmother would not be forced to cast the raindrops off her fur coat when she entered the store with Jo.

Shaking herself like a bedraggled beaver in the middle of one of Edinburgh's principal thoroughfares would have caused her indignity beyond words.

On wet, windy days, much to Jo's childish amusement, the doorman would be swept off his feet, as he struggled to prevent the big, black umbrella from being blown inside out.

Grandmother would sweep into the store with great aplomb, with Jo clutching her gloved hand, little legs hastening to keep abreast of the woman whom nobody would ever have guessed had spent twenty odd years stacking linen and performing other menial duties at the Queen Hotel in Edinburgh's New Town.

At this stage of Jo's life, there was little appreciation of the large part that money can play in influencing people and their treatment of those who appear to have it.

A visit to the toy department would inevitably be followed by afternoon tea. Grandmother would sip her Earl Grey from a bone china cup and nibble a cucumber sandwich, whilst Jo surveyed the tempting array of fancies with their pink fondant icing, sausage-like chocolate éclairs oozing fresh cream and scrunchy meringues, which scattered crumbs all over the table cloth before melting deliciously on the tongue.

Minding your manners came as second nature to Jo, having been brought up in a hotel where children were to be seen and not heard and even the act of running in the corridors was strictly forbidden.

In Jenner's tea room, Jo would sit demurely, quietly taking everything in, observing the pinafored waitresses, as they glided between tables with pots of tea, steaming cups of hot chocolate and silver-plated platters of daintily cut sandwiches, crispy cheese straws and, best of all, cream-filled vanilla slices, madeleines and fondant fancies neatly arranged on lacy white doilies.

Unfolding a starched white napkin and spreading it carefully on her lap was Grandmother's signal for young Jo to follow her example and for the sweet-toothed savouring of dainty delights to begin.

Grandmother certainly indulged her favourite grandchild – there was no doubt about that. For as surely as her own children had proved to be a disappointment to her, so surely did she invest in Jo a hope for the future and a continuation of the dynasty, which had so desperately disappointed her.

From an early age, Jo's destiny dictated that the child was the chosen one – the one who would eventually inherit the Carlton Hall Hotel. In the child Mary invested her time and her love.

Mary had never had the same amount of time, or money to bestow such indulgences on Andrina as the youngest of her own children which, no doubt, was the cause of much of Andrina's hatred of the child and resulted in many a harsh, vitriolic rebuke which Jo's mother did little to rebuff, even in her rare moments of sobriety.

Andrina would taunt spitefully, saying that Jo had been "bought" into the family and that it had been a "bad buy". As a child, Jo never understood the meaning of her words, but picked up on the tone of voice in which they were uttered and often used to question Nanny Bapty, or Nan about Aunt Andrina's nasty behaviour.

Sometimes too, over the tea table at Jenners, when they were alone together, Jo would attempt to question Grandmother about the sharpness and apparent cruelty that marked Andrina's every day remarks. For her part, Grandmother would simply refuse to recognize that there was any problem.

It was only Jo's imaginary friend, Georgina, who really understood how upset Jo would sometimes become and allow her friend to shed the occasional tear – something which Grandmother, for all her indulgence, refused to tolerate, with her view that any expression of grief was a sign of weakness and, therefore, not to be allowed even in someone as young as Jo.

Grandmother's answer to the slightest welling up of Jo's tears was always to organise one of their "outings" – either to Jenners, or sometimes to one of the big auction houses, where she would pick her way through the piles of bric-a-brac and musty old furniture, always on the lookout for a bargain, just as she had always been forced to do in the early days of her first marriage to Alex.

Now, however, it was not a cheap cut of meat, or a few slightly rotting vegetables that she searched for. Grandmother had developed an appreciation of art and was keen to fill the hotel bedrooms with paintings which, like Jo, she considered to be "an investment for the future".

On one such foray into a saleroom filled with the smell of dusty canvases, it was Jo whose imagination was captured by the painting of a group of highland sheep grazing contentedly on the heather-strewn hillside of a remote Scottish glen.

Its enormous gilt frame showed tiny knocks and dents where the white plasterwork was showing through but, as far as Jo was concerned, it was a masterpiece that evoked the Scottish highland landscape that Jo had read about in the tales of Ivanhoe and which had long held a strange fascination.

When the bidding started, Jo raised an eager hand in the air, much to the amusement of the auctioneer, who laughingly dismissed the young bidder, making a jovial aside to the crowd that "Little Bo Beep" upstairs in the gallery "had lost some sheep" and "not knowing where to find them" had come to the auction in the hope of a happy reunion.

Grandmother was furious at the resulting uproar, rising from the wooden bench in all her fur-coated dignity and took the auctioneer to task for his remarks.

A stony silence greeted her tirade and the gathered assembly sat transfixed at the exchange which passed between the man with the gavel and the woman, intent on making him grovel in front of his audience, shooting out her words at him, tossing expressions of displeasure at him like handfuls of gravel.

'I am sorry, Madam. I didn't mean to cause any offence. I just thought that …'

'Don't think, just listen,' Grandmother admonished. 'If my grandchild wants the painting, then you should accept the bid, for I can assure you that age is no bar to knowing what you want in life,' Grandmother asserted to the man who held the hammer.

'Go ahead, Jo,' she continued encouragingly. 'If you want the painting, then I promise that you shall have it!'

Jo's little hand shot up in the air several times more, whilst every pair of eyes in the auction room turned to watch and a cheer rose up from the crowd when the hammer finally fell and the sheep came home with Jo "wagging their tails behind them".

Andrina, of course was not amused, especially when she spotted the receipt from the auction house, in amongst the bills that Agnes was entering in the hotel ledger the next day.

'That child is totally spoilt,' she fumed, drawing deeply on her cigarette and blowing smoke rings into the air, knowing full well that her mother disapproved of her smoking and that Nan especially hated the scent of tobacco lingering in the area behind the reception desk.

'Whatever next? I suppose the first time Jo takes it in mind to play at doctors and nurses, Charles will be dispatched to purchase a lease on the Royal Infirmary.'

Andrina invariably addressed her stepfather by his proper name when she was annoyed by anything. She certainly did not approve of him being called anything other than Mr Paterson by the staff.

Similarly she hated attaching such a simple tag as the two letters that formed Jo's name to her half-sister's adopted child.

All the other children at the little private school that Jo attended had names like Arabella, Beatrice, or Clarissa and little boys were called Algernon, Benedict or, of course, Charles, as befitted their standing in life. Finding a name of suitable standing was really as simple as ABC!

Andrina had approached her mother on the subject on more than one occasion, knowing that there was even less point in approaching Anne on the matter, as her half-sister held little sway about anything which affected the family in any way.

191

Mary was pragmatic, seeing no reason to persuade her eldest daughter to impose a fresh, more formal identity, claiming that it would have been extremely bad luck to change the child's name.

'How would you like it, if someone made you change your name?' she demanded, adding that a change of attitude and a warmer heart would serve her youngest daughter well.

What was Jo short for? was the question that people often asked. Andrina would have liked to have answered with something more sophisticated, thinking of Joanna, the rather elegant young wife of an Edinburgh District Attorney, who sometimes came to dine at the hotel, or even Joseph the maitre d' at Carlton Hall, who terrified the younger waiters with his superior manner and immaculate grooming.

They were dignified with proper names, unlike the little nuisance that ran about the hotel with almost no chastisement.

What type of mother could have held her newborn child in such total disregard, as to have been not even bothered to find a more suitable name?

It was hardly a question that Andrina needed to ask, for she already knew the answer and she wasn't about to let on to anyone – not for the moment, anyway!

Chapter 28

Mary awoke to a pitch-black, uneasy silence. She had a pain in her left leg and, at first, she wondered if that was what had awoken her. She rose with difficulty from the bed, her joints felt stiffened, her tendons as taut as tightropes. Her rheumatism was playing up again and she had cramp in the calf of her leg.

She considered getting out of bed and walking into the adjoining bathroom to stand for a moment on the cold ceramic tiles in the hope that their icy cold temperature would send shock waves up her leg and alleviate the pain.

No, she didn't have the courage to throw back the eiderdown and limp across the deeply carpeted room for a brief spell of shock treatment. She felt uneasy and shivered in the darkness; a long, cold sliver of ice slipped down her spine.

She turned to Charlie, sleeping soundly by her side, snoring quietly, so that his slightly wheezing breaths snorted into the night like a contented sow suckling a litter of piglets.

She glanced across to the Victorian sash windows and heard the shutters rattle, as if caught by an inexplicable draught. She heard the wind howling outside, like the ghosts of the past, remembering another dark February night.

Glass panes, warmed on the inside and bitterly cold on the outside, had misted up from the heat emanating from the newly-installed central heating system.

The pipes gurgled, perhaps as a result of an air lock – a strange, haunting noise, seemingly from the back of the throat; it was as if they were struggling to breathe.

She would call the plumber in the next morning and get him to sort out the problem. After all, Charlie had paid good money to have the very latest central heating installed and she was not going to stand by and see him short-changed.

Still, they issued a strange, haunting noise.

Charlie continued to breathe deeply, relaxed in a comfortable dream world far away from the sounds of the night. Mary caught her own breath and stifled a cough, anxious not to disturb her husband. It must have been nearly midnight. She couldn't have been asleep for too long, as the crowd in the hotel bar had proved difficult to disperse and those who had their beds booked for the night had been reluctant to move until Andrina had uncharacteristically suggested that a free round of drinks would be supplied by Edwin, the night porter, if they transferred to the residents' lounge.

Mary found that she was still tired after Agnes and Robert's Valentine's Day engagement party just four nights before.

Nan still had her head in the clouds in a romantic dream world of her own making, spending most of her time gazing at the two carat diamond ring that Robert had slipped on her finger and, as far as the day to day running of the hotel was concerned, she was proving to be of little use to anyone.

Anne had taken full advantage of the announcement of her half-brother and future sister-in-law's forthcoming nuptials as an excuse for getting thoroughly plastered on the cases of champagne that Agnes's father had arranged to be flown over from France for the special occasion of his only daughter's betrothal, with constant cries of "More champagne, Charlie".

Consequently, she had failed to turn in the next morning to help with the task of clearing up the conference suite where last night's party had been held and the messy job had been left to Andrina and Moira.

It had been hard work for Mary too, as Charlie had been rushing around in his excitement, behaving like a headless chicken and generally leaving all the catering arrangements to his wife.

Mary had bullied the chefs and drilled the waiters to ensure that her bachelor son and his bride to be enjoyed a night to remember. She had also helped to compile the guest list, which mostly comprised Edinburgh's "crème de la crème".

The guests had come from far and wide to spend a spectacular celebration, culminating in a display of fireworks that inflamed the cold night air, filling the atmosphere with their pungent smoke and even rivalling those which had marked the New Year celebrations in Old Reekie before the war.

Mary had even had to organise the laundering of the tablecloths, as Meg, who normally worked in the wash-house behind the stables, had been off work with a bad cold and the young chambermaid who had been drafted in to take her place was slow and in constant need of supervision. Mary had even been forced to show the young girl how to make a proper job of starching and folding the napkins.

It took her back to the time when Robert had been a babe in arms, no older than Jo and had been looked after by Mary's younger sister, who worked at one of the wash-houses in the Edinburgh city centre back streets, her hands red raw and chapped from plunging them in an out of the hot water all day long and through constant exposure to washing soda.

Mary had little appetite that evening at dinner in the hotel's dining room, pushing aside her asparagus starter virtually untouched and complaining that her beef bourguignon was overcooked, when it was actually just the way she liked it. She had declined a dessert, settling for a cup of freshly brewed coffee and a couple of after dinner mints.

She was a picky eater these days, preferring to nibble her way through a selection of canapés and to sip a single glass of champagne rather than sitting down to a full meal.

The head chef and the bevy of extra kitchen staff brought in for the night of the engagement party had excelled themselves and Mary, with her normally bird-like appetite, had still felt quite full four days later.

She had also had to read Jo a bedtime story that night, as Nanny Bapty was taking a rare night off. Jo had insisted on coming to her room, storybook in hand and had fallen asleep in the rocking chair.

Mary had decided to leave the slumbering child. For some reason she felt the need to have her grandchild close by her that night.

She had taken off her dress and stored it carefully away in the closet, changing into her fleecy-lined dressing gown, before kissing the slumbering child "Good night".

Anne, not surprisingly, had only just recovered from her alcohol-induced state of insobriety following the engagement party. She had protested a bitter headache and had obviously been in no fit state to read to her child.

Mary had settled herself down in a comfortable wing-backed armchair, with Jo dozing in the rocking chair beside her. Soon both Grandmother and child were nodding off to sleep.

Mary's glasses lay on the small inlaid rosewood table by her side, with a silver coffee pot, its contents still warm, resting beside the two bone china cups and saucers, laid out on a silver tray.

Mary's cup had still been half full and when Charlie had crept quietly into the bedroom, he had poured himself a cup of the luke warm liquid, adding cream and a single cube of sugar, using the silver tongs.

When Mary awoke from her doze in the soft, velvet covered armchair, she had summoned the night porter to help her to lift the rocking chair containing the slumbering child, so that it could be rocked gently from Mary's bedside, enabling her to maintain a watchful eye over Jo, whilst her daughter, mimicking a migraine, bowed out of her motherly duties.

Mary had fallen asleep very quickly, tired by her own exertions, the excitement of the past few days and not a little by the fact that she was approaching her seventy fifth birthday.

She had slept for no more than an hour, when the spasm had shot through her leg like an arrow. Pain gripped her consciousness and something quite strange gripped her inner self. Inexplicably, she felt frightened of the darkness of the furniture filled bedroom with all its relics of the past.

Mary focussed her eyes on the carriage clock by her bedside table, as its small filigree hands moved towards the midnight hour. Jo was restless, wriggling around and murmuring in a dream world which seemed full of contentment.

Someone was rocking Jo back to sleep, with regular, rhythmic movements. Wooden rockers swayed noiselessly over the deep pile red Axminster carpet, calming Mary's grandchild and lulling the child to sleep.

Mary felt instantly apprehensive, but realised her own stupidity for not immediately grasping the fact that it was her daughter who had obviously crept silently into the room, to take responsibility for the child.

Only Anne wasn't there at all!

Save for the sleeping Charlie, no one had entered the couple's room, which was always kept locked at night, in case a wayward guest stumbled awkwardly into their private quarters after one double brandy too many.

The rocking stopped and Jo became restless, uttering soft, murmuring sobs, which spilled from quivering lips until the rocking movement began again.

Contented once more, tears were terminated, snuffed out by the gentle hand that reached out towards the rocking chair unseen in the shadows of the night.

Mary's arthritic hands began to shake, not from any vibration of the movement of the chair beside her, but in an attempt to shake herself out of the strange belief that the rocking hand was somehow not human, but a ghost-like visitor from the past.

Mary leaned down and placed a hand on the back rail of the chair, making the movement cease, but as soon as she lifted her hand, the rocking started up again.

She touched Jo's forehead. Short, stubby fingers stretched out and brushed her arm, as if informing her that her presence was not required – only that of the unseen!

Mary removed her hand in silent obedience. Apparently the touch of her hand was superfluous to her grandchild's needs.

Momentarily awake, Jo's eyelids fluttered in a last battle against sleep and the fight was immediately lost. Mary settled a blanket loosely up under her grandchild's chin, before returning to her own slumbers.

She must have imagined it. Maybe a draught in the room had caught the chair, causing it to sway on its rockers. Still she was uncertain of her own convictions and the disturbing thoughts that were going on in her head proved difficult to dispel.

She remembered a night so long ago, when her sleep had been interrupted by another baby. Her baby. Her Robert.

Suddenly, she shot bolt upright in bed, as she recalled only too clearly the exact date of that disturbed night.

It had been February 18th 1897 – exactly fifty years ago to the day, exactly fifty years to the night when Benin, the City of Blood was no more.

It was the date upon which, unknown to Mary, her first husband, Alex, had taken the queen of Benin's head from its sacred resting place.

It was precisely fifty years ago to the very night when an unseen hand had first rocked a makeshift cradle. Mary waited in the darkness, remembering Alex's tragic death, impaled upon the iron railings outside the Waverley Station by an oncoming tram.

She recalled Charlie's horror, as he had received the bloody package from a bewildered Anne. She remembered too her own subsequent revulsion at its blood-spattered contents – an unholy bronze effigy from a centuries' old past which, to Mary's mind, still held a dangerous threat to the living – a threat that Charlie had dismissed as complete nonsense.

Mary flexed her bunioned toes against the bed board, seeking its chilled coldness, as another bout of cramp affected her, this time in her left foot. She felt the cold touch dissipating the sudden pain, which gripped her in an ever-tightening vice.

Something else was gripping her too, gripping her thoughts and gripping her imagination.

That pervading presence was back in the room – not in the tiny Edinburgh attic, but here at Carlton Hall … in the bedroom in which she slept with Charlie.

Her mind began to swim, navigating the deep waters of her failing memory, until everything began to plunge back into place. Words that she had not heard for fifty years rang in her ears.

Thou taketh my head
And blood will be shed
A spear in the heart
The thief will depart

Charlie, curled up like a little boy who occupied his mother's bed, murmured momentarily in his sleep, his head poked above the soft eiderdown. He alone apparently remained unaware of the cause of any night-time presence.

Mary touched the soft, grey hairs, which sparsely covered her husband's head, barely conscious of her own gentle gesture. She was lost in her own private thoughts, trying to remember a past which was best forgotten.

Soon tumbled thoughts were interrupted once more, just as she had begun to dive headlong into a waking nightmare, which promised to drag at her arthritic limbs.

On this occasion she awoke with even more of a start. She sat upright in the bed once more. Again her left foot was spasming in cramp. She touched the cold bed frame. Instantly the pain was gone.

She shivered, despite the warm temperature of the room and against the all-pervading atmosphere that encircled her. Jo was crying now, fingers flexing uselessly and the chair rocked no more.

Queen Elizabeth's portrait hung in its bright, modern black and gilt frame above the fireplace, empty save for the electric fire that one of the chambermaids would sometimes turn on early in the morning when Mary was brought her breakfast tea, toast and marmalade in bed.

Having outlived their usefulness, both its brass fender and fire irons had long since been discarded.

The queen consort was smiling, her head tilted very slightly to one side in her habitually benign fashion that had wooed the crowds when she was more simply known as Lady Elizabeth Bowes-Lyon.

On the bedside table the hands of the little carriage clock moved inexorably towards the witching hour, like a wakeup call for the dead.

An icicle of fear flowed freely down Mary's spine – still so remarkably erect for a woman of her age. Slimy, slivering like a serpent, it settled at the base of her back, feasting on her fears, mangling her memories of the past.

She knew for certain that there was someone in the room.

Instinctively, she knew that her grandchild was in no danger – not the dark-dark haired Jo, but the grey-haired man, who slept blissfully beside her – the man who fifty years ago had carried away from the Edinburgh cobbles the Benin Bronze, as a memento of Alex – the man who had once saved his life and whose own life had been cruelly and suddenly snatched away.

Alex was the man who had taken the head of the Benin queen. He was the man who, with her beloved Charlie, had battled through the forests of West Africa to escape a massacre and who had acted as a thief, stealing what was not his for the taking. With fingers like fly paper he had helped to rob a kingdom of its treasures. Now, once again, there was a price to be paid.

Mary got out of bed and moved to the small table beside the velvet covered armchair for her spectacles. With her slightly impaired eyesight, she noted the stillness of the rocking chair swayed by no comforting hand unseen. Fearfully, the old lady snuggled more deeply beneath the bedclothes and whatever protection they might provide.

Rich red brocade curtains swayed, swirling about the bed chamber in a Devil's dance. No draught had entered the room and yet the panes of glass rattled rigorously in their tightly-fitting frames.

Jo slept soundly in tiny nursery rhyme pyjamas, whilst Jack and Jill climbed up short little legs, Little Miss Muffet sat on her tuffet and a spider perched on Jo's left buttock.

Mary took Charlie into her arms and clung to his slightly frail frame, gaining solace from his bodily warmth. She girded the eiderdown around him, as if for protection against the unseen presence, which somehow threatened only her husband.

Her bespectacled eyes searched the darkness of the large room, with its rich carpeting and pastel-coloured Chinese silk rug, whose pile sank when anyone walked across it.

Footprints clearly marked a person's passage, but disappeared again, as if no one had ever been there.

She clicked the light switch of the small bedside table lamp, with its pink silk tasselled lampshade.

The light bulb fired, instantly exploding with an audible ping. Only for a brief second had it shone its light to illuminate the darkness.

The light had lasted just long enough for Mary to catch sight of the ashen figure, its blackened features barely visible. It was black as the coal, which she no longer needed to burn in any bedroom grate.

Mary found herself wanting to cry out loud, but voicelessly no sound escaped her thin lips, rendered dry by her natural fear for her husband's safety.

If only she could locate something with which to protect them but, of course, she had a weapon.

It was propped by the side of the bed where it always was – Charlie's silver-topped walking stick that he had owned for fifty years or more. It had travelled with him to Darkest West Africa and with it he had once signalled his rescuers. Years ago it had saved his life.

She reached across him, grabbing the precious metal handle fashioned in the flames of a furnace by a craftsman silversmith.

Slowly the figure drifted towards the man who shared Mary's bed – ghosted away from the sleeping child and its grandmother. Mary simultaneously stretched out her other hand reaching for the twin lamp on Charlie's side of the bed.

It too fired once, illuminating the scene of sorcery for a brief moment before crackling and extinguishing itself with another audible ping. Plunged once more into darkness, Mary could not fathom the features of the phantom but, just like all those many years ago, she was aware that they were as dark as the night in which they sought to conceal themselves … and the blackened face was totally devoid of features.

No sparkling eyes – just empty sockets. No pink mouth, just a slash across the face; flared nostrils that had not breathed a single breath for a thousand years and coral studded ears, unhearing of centuries of sound.

It was a face where a face should have been, the likeness of which Mary had only ever experienced once before in a cold, darkened attic. Black! It was totally black!

A witch from Hell! A woman whose hand would seek to rock a cradle, or a chair and whose face would torment any tiny tot. Once again a voice began to call, but not to her.

Its listener was Charlie who, at that moment, had opened his sleep-encrusted eyes in time to catch the last flicker of illumination from the expired light bulb.

Thou taketh my head
And blood will be shed
A spear in the heart
The thief will depart
Death to the receiver
Be he not a believer

Six lines of rhyme, repeated over and over again, but no longer forming meaningless phrases. Words which mangled Mary's memory and struck terror in her very soul.

This time she knew exactly what they meant. They posed a threat – there was no doubt about that! She had heard the first four of those lines long, long ago and their significance was far from lost on her.

She had to face the witch who taunted her, face the face that wasn't a face – the one which seemed to float above the level of the floor, footless and fancy free – free of the feet that would leave rapidly disappearing footprints in the Chinese silk rug. A heathen harridan with no body and no hands with which to rock an infant's cradle.

Mary grasped her husband's walking stick which he had lent on for support and protection all those years ago, as he made his injured way through the forests of Benin – the one with which he had hailed his rescuers all those years ago.

With all her strength, she threw it across the room. It landed well short of the mark that bore no mark at all, as her antagonist wafted towards the curtained, shuttered window in a movement that was both effortless and surreal, swept away in a breeze of brocade.

The upturned face of Queen Elizabeth, mother of the two young princesses, Margaret and Elizabeth stared up from the carpeted floor. The shattered remains of the frame that had enveloped her lay in pieces in the hearth. Shards of broken glass glittered against the silver-coloured background of the electric fire.

Perhaps Queen Elizabeth recognised that this visitation was being made by no ordinary person, but none other than a ruling king's consort: an ancient queen whose existence was eternal.

Here was a queen who had been dead for centuries, not one who was destined to live for over a century. Steal the head of the Benin queen and she would strike back in vengeance at the heart of any man who cast his avaricious eyes upon her, spearing him in cardiac arrest.

Mary's third husband, Charlie Paterson had been in West Africa as a member of the Benin Expedition of 1897.

199

He was Alex's best friend: the man who had joined in the looting and pillaging of an ancient civilisation and who had stolen the head of a long dead African queen.

Right now Charlie too was heading for a life and death confrontation with the queen of Benin.

Thou taketh my head
And blood will be shed
A spear in the heart
The thief will depart
Death to the receiver
Be he not a believer

Chapter 29

Charlie Paterson sat at his desk in the brightly-lit, cluttered study, which he had made his own. With papers and books strewn everywhere, Mary often chided him that he should allow the maids in to give the little room situated behind the hotel reception a thorough clean.

He resisted all her cries for cleanliness, arguing that he would never find anything ever again, if anyone was called upon to mount a clean up operation.

It was the only room in the whole building which had not been redecorated since the purchase of the hotel. Charlie liked it that way, keeping it under lock and key and resisting dusters, damp clothes, vacuum cleaners and polish.

In many ways it was a dismal room, lined on three sides by vast floor to ceiling bookcases, stuffed full of books that Charlie rarely, if ever, read. In the middle of the one unadorned wall, was the tall door which looked straight up the stairs.

A vast partner's desk occupied most of the remaining space. It had been bought at an auction sale in Edinburgh, having emerged dusty and decidedly the worst for wear from the office of a solicitor who was closing down his practice and retiring to spend his days playing golf.

A tooled leather inset bore testimony to the marks of time, stained with patches of dark blue ink and cut into where countless paper knives had slipped and dug into the leather. One drawer was permanently locked and Charlie didn't have a key, but it didn't matter.

It all fitted in with the general chaotic appearance of the room, into which Charlie squeezed himself every morning, taking time for himself. Here he could remain undisturbed and shut away for the first two hours of the day, when the breakfast chefs threw their early morning tantrums, young waitresses, who had maybe enjoyed the previous night out on the town, arrived late for work and the chambermaids were forever complaining about the amount of time that some of the guests took to vacate their rooms, causing their duties to stretch out into the afternoon.

No, Charlie was best out of the way, locked into his own private domain, into which even Mary had ceased trying to gain entry, knowing that her husband would emerge whenever he was ready to face the day.

On this particular morning he felt strangely tired. He didn't remember waking up during the middle of the night.

Mary had experienced a restless, disturbed sleep and she had seemed peculiarly reluctant to talk about it, as they had each climbed out of bed and dressed the next morning.

Maybe her rheumatism was playing her up again, or perhaps she was just exhausted after the hectic social whirl of the previous four days.

After all, he mused, for a woman in her seventies, she really was quite remarkable, displaying a restless energy that only required half an hour's nap in the afternoon for her to be able to re-charge her batteries.

Afterwards she would emerge from her own private domain of the upstairs sitting room totally refreshed and ready to carry on her ceaseless inspections, making sure that everyone employed in the hotel was fully aware of their daily duties and that they had been completed to a standard which represented nothing less than perfection in Mary's eyes.

Whilst Mary was always happy to invite Charlie into "her" sitting room for a mid morning cup of tea and shortbread biscuits, promptly delivered there at eleven o'clock after she had completed the first of her many rounds of daily inspections, Charlie always took his early morning coffee alone in his study.

He refused even to allow Moira in to deliver it to him, making her give a couple of short raps, before depositing a pot of coffee and two slices of hot, buttered toast on a tray outside the study door.

Charlie would wait for a minute, before bending over with difficulty to reach down to the floor, leaning heavily on his walking stick and refusing any offers of help from a passing porter.

Mary had even humoured him by placing a walnut half moon table in the hall just outside the door, having ordered a member of staff to remove it from one of the bedrooms where it served little, if any, real purpose.

The following day, on her midday inspection of each of the bedrooms that the chambermaids had thus far been able to clean, she found that it had been returned, on Charlie's instructions, cast aside by a man who was sometimes as stubborn and independent as he was kind.

Mary simply gave up. 'If that father of yours wants to make life awkward for himself, then why should anyone try to make things easier for him,' she had uttered to Nan not unpleasantly, but aware of the foibles of a man, who was stuck in his ways and who, try as she might, she was never going to change.

Mary's influence over Charlie, as far as that dusty, gloomy room was concerned, was about as effective as her efforts had proved over the years to stop Robert from driving too fast, to silence Andrina's cutting tongue, or to prevent Anne from finding ever more inventive places to hide her bottles of gin.

If Charlie wanted his own private retreat, then what harm did it do?

However, she did wish he would rid himself of some of the clutter he had accumulated over the years.

On what little remained of the wall space that wasn't taken up by the tall bookcases, he had hung an assortment of African relics, tribal spears and shields covered in tightly stretched antelope skins, together with the heads of stuffed animals attached to wooden plaques under which were screwed little brass plates announcing the dates of their demise.

A photograph of his first wife, Muriel, pictured on a wooden verandah, which could only have come out of Africa rested on one corner of his desk.

Mary didn't really mind. After all, it was his past and it was from the relics of that past that Agnes had been born – his daughter, his precious Nan, his only daughter, who was about to marry her only son – his only son!

Oh God, how could she bring herself to tell him the truth after all these years? In the past he had often spoken to her of how he had wished that Muriel had produced a second child, a son to follow in his father's footsteps.

How could she possibly bring herself to tell him? What would be his reaction to her duplicity?

And, of course, how could she wreck his daughter's life? It was so obvious that Nan was head over heels in love with Robert, even if Robert's eyes were still inclined to wander.

No, Mary could not contemplate such an act of betrayal and whatever repercussions it might have in store for all of them. Besides, Charlie might hate her for the deception of all those years ago.

Robert, who had never really had a father to call his own – would despise her for keeping the truth from him and poor Nan would be totally devastated.

No, it was better to maintain her silence. Some secrets were best taken to the grave, never being allowed to assuage the conscience of the living.

Somehow that morning, Mary felt afraid, not of her own secrets being thrown to the wind, but fearful for Charlie, scared witless by the events of the previous night and remembering only too well what a similar ghostly visitation had presaged all those years ago, when Charlie's best friend, her first husband, Alex had gone to his grave.

He likewise had been kept in the dark of the truth about Mary and her relationship with his best friend and exactly how Robert had come to be born.

No, this morning she would make an excuse to join Charlie in his private study. Maybe then they would have the opportunity to talk.

Somehow she would at last find the words to tell him the truth about what had happened between them over fifty years ago.

She, and she alone, could put a stop to the forthcoming nuptials, but if Robert and Nan were ever going to learn the truth then, most important of all, she needed Charlie's support and understanding.

He loved her now, just as he had loved her then. Could her secret admission, kept from him for all these years, destroy that love?

Maybe it was a risk she had to take.

'I'll take Charlie's coffee in to him this morning,' she had told Moira, as the waitress stood at the door of the study with Charlie's breakfast.

'You get on and help the chambermaids, will you, please. There is an awful lot of extra work to do. It's four days past St Valentine's Day and we still have all the decorations up for Agnes's and Robert's engagement party.

'I really don't know what the guests will be thinking. They'll be Cupids firing with bows and arrows into the Easter eggs at this rate!'

'... but Madam, Mr Paterson always insists that his breakfast tray is left just outside the door for him. He doesn't take too kindly to anyone going into his study and, besides, no one has a key.'

'Don't you "but Madam" me young lady! Don't think either that I haven't noticed that you have shortened the hem of that skirt. And, for your information, I do have a key,' asserted Mary.

'I'm sorry, Madam, I just meant ...'

'Let me assure you, I have a key to every room in this hotel – even one to each of the gentlemen's bedrooms should I care to call on them to offer "room service" in the middle of the night!' she added, producing a gaoler's bunch from deep inside the pocket of her long skirt.

Mary bent low to the lock, scrimmaging through dozens of keys, until she finally located the right one. She inserted it into the lock, turning it quietly. Moira passed the tray into her employer's outstretched hands.

'Good morning, Charlie. I've come to keep you company. I fancied a cup of coffee this morning rather than my usual cup of ...' Mary's words trailed off. Charlie already had female company. She was sitting on Charlie's desk, bronzed and some would say quite beautiful with only the back of her neck clearly visible to Mary, but facing the man who had kept her for the past fifty years and whose presence in the study Mary knew nothing about.

'Mary, what on earth are you doing here? I ... I thought it was Moira's job to bring me my breakfast. Is she off sick?'

'No, Charlie, she isn't. I just thought you might like some company for a change. Don't worry, I haven't come to persuade you to tidy up, but heaven only knows why you've still got that wretched bronze head. I really don't know why you've kept it after all these years. I thought you'd get rid of it after Alex ...'

'Mary, Mary, don't upset yourself. I kept it because of Alex. He was my best friend. He saved my life and I suppose this is all I have to remember him by,' Charlie explained, taking the tray from his wife and shuffling some of the pile of papers on his desk to one side to provide sufficient space for his breakfast.

'If you're having coffee with me Mary, then you'll need another cup and saucer. I'll call for one for you. Now just you sit yourself down,' he said kindly, walking towards the door that she had closed behind her and calling for a passing waiter to bring another cup and saucer and an extra round of toast, which he doubted Mary would eat.

'Charlie, I've got something to tell you – something I should have told you years ago. Something that I should have said that day at the Waverley Station when Alex ...'

Her words were interrupted by the ringing of the telephone. Charlie picked up the heavy black Bakelite receiver and began discussing the delivery of that day's meat with the local butcher. He took the coffee pot, pouring out the hot liquid into the one and only cup.

As Mary took it from him, her arthritic hands began to shake, so that the cup bounced around on the saucer and the silver spoon clattered and shook.

As she reached over the table, her arm caught one of the twin silver topped ink-wells resting on the silver ink stand, spilling its ruby red contents, which seeped into the documents on Charlie's desk and puddled around the bronze head of a long dead African queen, as if she was disgorging blood from a severed neck.

'I'm sorry,' she said. 'And I do wish you'd get rid of that thing. It gives me the creeps! I'm sure its cursed.'

'Don't be ridiculous, Mary. Surely, you don't believe in all that mumbo-jumbo about ancient curses and the like.'

'No, but ... I remember it was what Alex was ...'

'Oh come now, don't be so silly,' Charlie had replied, doing his best to comfort her and to quell her inexplicable fears.

'I don't believe in all that rubbish and nor should you. I thought you had a sensible head on that old pair of shoulders of yours. You'll be telling Jo that you believe in the Loch Ness monster next,' said Charlie.

'Yes, but don't forget when Alex was killed, he ...'

'That's quite enough of that, Mary,' he replied, leaning over the ink strewn desk, staining his white shirt with the blood red liquid, as he planted a kiss on her wrinkled forehead.

'Now, here, let me clear up this mess with some blotting paper. I've told you before, you're far too old to be a waitress. You're all fingers and thumbs,' he added with a kindly smile to his wife.

'Look, you've even got the shakes.'

'Charlie, there's something I have to tell you. It's something you have to know about Robert ... about Robert and Nan before they ...'

A short tap on the door interrupted her flow once more, as a young waiter stood back and waited for his cue to enter with the second cup and saucer and a plate of toast.

'Come in!' announced Charlie, not summoning the extra breakfast supplies to be left outside the door in the usual fashion.

The door was cast wide open. As Mary turned, her gaze swept up the stairs. She caught the full view of Moira, mounted on a stepladder removing the St Valentine's Day decorations from their assorted positions at the top of the stairs.

From where Mary looked up, she caught a full view of Moira's undercarriage, clearly displayed beneath the short, black, newly hemmed skirt. Her stocking tops were in full view, as were her suspenders, together with three or four inches of naked flesh unconcealed by any underwear, for she was not wearing any knickers at all!

'Oh, my God,' uttered Mary. 'Charlie do something. Get that wretched girl down off that ladder now!'

Charlie squeezed his way round from his side of the desk, snatching up his walking stick, at the same time coming face to face with Moira's snatch.

He left the little study in a hurry, with Mary trailing in his wake. Jo came running down the corridor, almost bumping into him, as Charlie hurried up the first few steps.

'Get down off that ladder this minute and go and make yourself decent,' Mary shouted up the stairs from behind him.

Moira turned in shock, as the aluminium stepladder trembled and shook. She had just been in the process of untying the African spear, which pierced through the red silk heart, with its long trail of ribbons festooned behind it, bearing the words "Robert and Agnes – meant to be together".

As the ladder toppled, casting her to the floor, the spear fell, flying through the air towards its intended victim – the man who had just mounted the third step.

It threw him backwards, as it shot through his frail body, as if propelled by some mysterious and powerful force. He fell backwards, tumbling down the last remaining stairs, as the arrowed shaft pierced him in the heart.

Charlie stumbled awkwardly, striking the bottom stair with a heavy thud, as a pool of blood began to rise from his chest.

Jo shrieked out, rushing into the arms of a horrified Robert, who had just emerged from the dining room, sweeping up the screaming child in his arms just in time to witness the death of the man whom he had never known to be his father.

Mary rushed to the prone figure of the man lying at the foot of the stairs, whilst the son, whom he had never known was his, looked on in horror at the scene of his father's death being enacted before his very eyes, whilst Jo cried out in abject terror, clinging to him for solace.

Thou taketh my head
And blood will be shed
A spear in the heart
The thief will depart
Death to the receiver
Be he not a believer

Chapter 30

Agnes stirred in the honeymoon suite of the Paris Hotel. It was the last night of their six-week around the world honeymoon trip, which had begun as it was to end – in Paris – the most romantic city in the world.

On Monday she would return to her post behind the reception desk at Carlton Hall. She and Robert had made love until, exhausted and replete, he had fallen asleep in her arms.

She remembered how, on the first night of the honeymoon, she had feigned her virginity, just as, a short while later, she had simulated sleep, lying awake and alert for another hour, watching her new husband and listening to his gentle snores.

She had felt nervous of his tender approach on their wedding night, but he had patiently coaxed her out of the blue silk negligee, which she had bought specially for the occasion.

She recalled how she had reached for her purse and extracted from it the tiny scent bottle, with its ruby red contents. She had filled the delicately etched glass bottle carefully from the metal meat trays in the cold store adjoining the hotel kitchens on the morning of her wedding and had poured the liquid lifeblood between her legs on the first night of their honeymoon.

The next morning she had thrown back the toile bedspread and revealed the stained sheets as a testimony to her purity. Her darling Robert must never suspect that she was anything other than a virgin, although from his reputation with the ladies, she was far from certain that he could truthfully attest to his own virtue.

World War II had brought tragedy and horror to a whole generation of young men and women who knew only too well that each day might prove to be their last. Until the latter years of the war, Agnes, albeit in her mid thirties, had never known a man – not in that sense anyway!

Sheltering in a basement from the bombing raids, which rained terror over the unlit Edinburgh dockland city skies, she had clung in the darkness to a young man in uniform.

Clutching each other ever more tightly, together they had held their breath in the damp, gloomy basement, as they waited for what had seemed an eternity for the rain of falling bombs to begin, bringing with them death and destruction.

When they came, a few seconds later, igniting the night sky with a series of explosions that shattered the eerie, unnatural silence, they fell streets away.

Shrapnel pinged off warehouse walls and although the building itself shuddered and the empty milk bottles that surrounded them rattled and shook, Agnes knew that they were safe – at least for the moment.

Maybe it was this close brush with death and the relief that they had both felt, held in each other's arms, realising that no harm would come to them that night.

Maybe it was the heady mixture of a shared moment of danger. Two strangers, together in close, clammy proximity – with nothing to lose, but their lives!

As they peered closely into each other's frightened eyes, they were overcome with a raw, animal passion.

It was Agnes's first time, but she was never likely to discover whether she was just one of his many conquests, or if he had been a virgin soldier.

Afterwards, when the all clear had sounded, they had walked hand in hand back towards the Waverley Station before waving goodbye, with the certainty that, unlike the song by the Forces Sweetheart, Vera Lynn, that was a popular wartime favourite, their paths would be unlikely ever to cross again.

How could Agnes ever have known that fate had other ideas in store for the two of them? For Agnes destiny would dictate that a much older man would walk back into her life years later – one who bore a striking resemblance to the young serviceman who had once robbed her of her virginity during an act in which she was a willing participant and surely no victim, not that she had ever thought of herself as being one.

Agnes had never stopped to consider right or wrong. It had all happened so suddenly. All she knew was his name and his nationality.

From his uniform she gathered that he was in the Air Force, but she didn't know very much else at all about him.

Right now she snuggled beneath the sheets with her new husband, closing her eyes to that long ago, but unforgotten moment, cuddling into Robert's chest, her knuckles clenched tight with the memory of that very first time.

Life was lived on the edge back then and death could arrive at any moment. She had always been a "good girl" until that chance encounter, saving herself for marriage, resisting temptation at the dance halls at the top of Leith Walk.

On one occasion, she had even repelled physical abuse when a drunken English lad had tried to force himself upon her after a few too many pints of stout in one of the many pubs down by the old Leith Docks.

However, at that moment in the cold, dank, musty smelling basement, she had decided to live for the moment and had given herself and her virtue to a stranger.

All the straight-laced behaviour of the 1930s, when she had been in her twenties was rapidly changing in the sheer desperation and adrenaline pumping excitement of simply never knowing whether anyone would be alive tomorrow. Life was for the living and right then Agnes had never felt so alive in her entire life.

She had been privately educated at a convent school and even in her mid-thirties, her virtue was still intact. She had scant knowledge of the male body, not having had any brothers to share a bath with and although her mother, Muriel, had spent her early years nursing hospitalised soldiers and surely knew all there was to know about the male anatomy, she had never imparted much of that knowledge to her only daughter.

Sometimes as a teenager, Agnes and her friends had spent time scouring through books in the library, searching for any information that would serve to enlighten them about the facts of life.

An illustrated book of Dante's Inferno, complete with drawings of naked male bodies had proved to be one of their only sources of reference, but the Mother Superior, hearing their gigglings when passing along the oak panelled corridor outside the library, had burst in upon them and promptly whisked the book away and out of sight, making each girl say a thousand Hail Marys by way of penitence for her unsanctioned thoughts.

War had proved to be exciting for Agnes. Her friends were all married and had children, but for her it was a case of never knowing what she would lose first – her life, or her virtue. It wasn't at all frightening, really. It was quite thrilling, in fact.

Yes, she could have done "it" with any number of the soldiers and sailors, who hung around the bars of the hotels owned by her father, but she never did.

She had even retained both her dignity and her knickers when she was accompanied on a rare night out by some of the local girls who had joined the WAAF (Women's Auxiliary Air Force) and they had all got a bit tipsy and had been easy prey to the boys in khaki.

And as for some of the scruffy arty types in their sandals, corduroys and beards that frequented the public bars at her father's hotels in the Borders, well, they would simply never do.

What Agnes had her eyes set on was meeting a handsome young man, but it had never happened until that night in the basement … and even then their meeting had been all too brief.

She imagined that she would never have forgiven herself, if she had thrown herself at the first soldier that presented himself to her – all standing to attention, erect and ready for action! No, she would never have forgiven herself and nor would her mother or father!

'He's never been near the trenches that one! The worst he'll ever do is slip on a blob of Brylcreem in the bathroom,' her mother, Muriel, would intone patriotically whenever Agnes's attention strayed towards a young man who might have taken her eye, but who wasn't wearing a uniform.

Agnes had never found what she was looking for. She had experienced numerous brief encounters, but most of them simply made her feel unhappy until that night in the basement, when she came away with a wet patch in her drawers and a warm glow of satisfaction, which pervaded long after the initial flashlight of aroused sexuality.

In the darkness an electric shock had run through her whole body, as if, for years, she had been locked away in a dark room, which had never witnessed any development of her sexuality.

Suddenly all the lights had gone on, exploding in a bright, erotically intensive light, unlocking her chastity and awakening her womanhood. Sex was fraught with many dangers, particularly in wartime.

Illegitimacy carried a huge stigma, both for the mother and her fatherless child.

Luckily, for Agnes, her basement boyfriend had carried a packet of American army issue condoms and, as far as she was concerned, there was no chance at all that she could possibly fall pregnant.

209

She had giggled, as he had peeled one from its wrapper, exposing the coiled rubber ring, like a recumbent serpent, soon to become slippery with his own saliva, which he had used to lubricate his manhood, dribbling over his fingers and slipping them, one at a time, into her most intimate parts.

The two million or so Allied servicemen from America and Canada, who passed through Britain during the Second World War brought with them otherwise unobtainable goodies – silk nylon stockings, bars of gooey chocolate and frequent heartbreak.

In accordance with the expression of the day, they were "overpaid, oversexed and over here", and for young women like Agnes their glamour and charm proved irresistible during the long, dark years of blackout and blitz.

Agnes had only ever heard an American accent in the movies. For her meeting up with the young serviceman was like meeting a movie star, even if his accent was a little different from those she had heard on the silver screen.

She would have liked to have had dinner with him and presented her fresh-smelling, clean shaven suitor to her parents for their approval, knowing that her mother, at least, would have been impressed by the sharply pressed lines of his Air Force uniform.

Sadly for Agnes, after he had banged her up in the basement, he didn't hang around for long enough for a second "date". Perhaps it was just as well, as he was much younger than she and barely out of his teens.

Handsome he certainly was, but far too young to warrant her consideration as anything more than a brief sexual encounter.

Somehow, Agnes still retained a mental picture of him, even though she now cuddled blissfully in her husband's arms. Unlike Robert, he had been little more than a boy and his apparent expertise in making love to her belied his years.

She had kissed him openly, intimately and invitingly and everything had moved on naturally from the point that their lips had first touched and she had lowered her nimble, slightly trembling fingers, finding his fly and extracting something hard, throbbing and deliciously exciting.

She tried to put him out of her mind. Now all she thought he was to her was a distant memory although, maybe time would prove differently.

Now she had a man who had committed himself to her – a man who had placed a ring on her finger at Edinburgh's St Giles' Cathedral in front of so many friends and family.

Here was a man who loved and cared for her, whose carefree bachelor days were now a thing of the past; a man who would be both her best friend and her lover.

He had pledged himself to her on St Valentine's Day and she had waited long and patiently until this day in 1952 when they had finally walked down the aisle as man and wife.

Their marriage had taken place just a few days after the death of George VI, when a princess on safari in Africa had been told of her father's death and had learnt that she would soon become queen.

Before long they would be back at Carlton Hall, facing the world as man and wife. Agnes too was like a young princess waiting in the wings to take her rightful role as the queen of her domain.

True, her mother-in-law would probably be reluctant to step into her new role as the hotel's queen mother, but the majesty she had assumed when she had been left as Charlie's widow hardly posed any threat at all to Agnes's true position.

No, the real threat to Agnes's newly wed happiness came from a much older former queen – an African queen whose head had been lost and who would once again rise from the dead.

* * * * * * * * * *

Agnes awoke from Robert's encircling arms and faced the blackness in an unfamiliar bed, which had been bought for them as a wedding gift by the members of the local golf club for their team captain and his new bride.

The bed itself, purchased from Patrick Thompson's up The Bridges had been presented to Robert on his stag night amidst many a ribald comment about how he could now put plenty of practice into scoring a hole in one, how he should be careful not to put his new bride "in the club" on their wedding night and, how, if he had a headache, he would have to proclaim that he was unable to "bunk 'er".

After such a long honeymoon, their return to Carlton Hall was a cause for great celebration, particularly amongst the staff with whom the couple had always been popular.

Jo had spent the morning hovering around the hotel entrance, with its great marbled porticoes, anxious not to miss a moment of the impending arrival and the opportunity to see what they might have brought back with them by way of presents.

Rushing into Uncle Robert's arms, Jo demanded to know whether they had been up the Eiffel Tower and was it really taller than the massive oaks that fringed the tree-lined drive up to the hotel?

'And guess what we've brought you back from Paris, young Jo?' asked Robert, as if by magic producing a tiny replica of the famous monument from his pocket.

'Look, it's even got a little flag pole on top, with the French flag, red, white and blue,' he added.

'We've got a flag on the roof too. Look Uncle Robert. Look Auntie Nan. Grandmother got Willie to put it up there, when Princess Elizabeth was told she was going to become queen.

'It was very scary up there on the roof. I went up in the loft, but Grandmother wouldn't let me go out on to the roof. She thought I would fall and graze my knee again.'

'I think you would do more than graze your knee, Jo, if you fell from that height,' warned Robert, tussling his fingers through Jo's mop of unruly hair, at the same time placing a brief kiss on his half-sister, Andrina's cheek, as she emerged to hustle Jo indoors, in case the child disturbed any of the guests.

'And we've got lots more presents for everyone,' Robert continued, as Jo was hastened out of the way, 'but you'll have to wait until the rest of our cases have been delivered and unpacked.

'Come up to our room later and you might just get a surprise!' he added, before sweeping his new bride up and carrying her over the threshold and through the revolving swing doors.

'Don't be stupid, Robert, you'll hurt yourself at …'

'… my age, I suppose you were going to say,' he offered, finishing the sentence for her.

'Come on, let's get you upstairs and I'll show you that there's life in the old man yet!'

Andrina clapped her hands over Jo's ears, scratching the lobe with the rather ornate and flashy ring that she bore on her right hand.

'Ouch!' proclaimed Jo, struggling free of Andrina's restraining grasp, galloping upstairs ahead of the happy couple and rushing into their newly decorated quarters, which still smelt of paint.

They were situated in the private quarters of the hotel, which were occupied by the family. Jo bounced on the bed, making sure that Robert's idea of a brief afternoon coupling was to bear no fruit.

Lovemaking would have to wait until the acquisitive desires of an energetic eight-year-old had been fulfilled. After a rapid rummage through all their cases and holdalls, Jo discovered even more booty.

Agnes complained bitterly that she needn't have bothered folding her clothes neatly, with Jo delving deeply amongst her silk petticoats, tossing aside the pale pink Paris negligee that she had bought without Robert being aware, letting it fall to the floor in an untidy heap.

Now Agnes's husband had spotted what she had planned to wear that night and he turned towards her with a raised eyebrow and a twinkle in his eye.

Indeed, she did wear it that night – albeit not for long, before his eager fingers peeled it over her shoulders and up over her head, revealing a body which, although past the first flush of blossoming womanhood, nevertheless was still pretty taut and firm for her age.

Agnes felt a warm glow once again that night after another gentle, but energetic bout of lovemaking and her spine tingled with the deep satisfaction that pervaded her whole body.

She had taken a long, lingering bath, making liberal use of some of the expensive scented bath salts that Robert had bought for her in one of the perfumeries which lined the Champs Elysées, wallowing luxuriously in the hot, steamy waters, feeling herself being drawn into them like a sweetly smelling swamp.

When she finally emerged and towelled herself dry, she bent low to empty the water, returning minutes later after she had sprinkled herself with talcum powder and applied the new Morphy Richards hair dryer to her fashionably bobbed brown hair.

Leaning over to clean the bath with a soft, yellow sponge, she found a big, black spider lurking around the plughole.

She shuddered, remembering how a boy in her class at primary school had terrified her by catching spiders and placing them in her satchel, or inside her desk, making her scream, when she had opened it up for her exercise books.

She especially recalled the time when a large, hairy creature had climbed out of her inkwell and raised its two front legs at her.

In response to her shrill cries of terror, the teacher had come over to her desk and whacked it with a wooden ruler, squashing it in a horrible mess of dismembered legs, before sweeping its remains on to the floor.

She must learn to control her fears, if only to prevent installing her own fears into young Jo, but still she shuddered, remembering when, many years ago, her mother, Muriel had light-heartedly called her father "Daddy Long Legs", whenever he banged his head on a low door, before age had stooped him and the walking stick which had long since become an essential part of his every day life, had come to be relied upon more and more.

She remembered with great sadness of heart how he had died on the tip of an African spear. Tears prickled her eyes, as she recalled how he had lain at the foot of the stairs, choking on his own blood, as he died in Mary's arms, whilst Robert looked on in horror, holding on to Jo, who had rushed screaming into his arms.

She tried to dismiss such unhappy memories of the father she had loved so dearly and who, in his turn, had showed her nothing but love and affection.

She turned her thoughts to the problem in hand and considered removing one of her pink, fluffy mule slippers and giving the spider a quick thwack, but she didn't want to soil them with its unpleasant remains and so decided to let it live.

Robert rolled over, unconsciously pushing her aside, relinquishing their mutual bodily warmth and casting her into the darkness of the night, without his comforting arms around her.

She felt a slight pain in her stomach, no doubt as a result of too rich a diet of foreign food over the past few weeks, too many champagne breakfasts, too much foie gras and oysters and yet more champagne!

She got up to go to the bathroom, happy to grope her way in the dark, not wanting to awaken her bridegroom of just six weeks' duration. She was unfamiliar with the layout of the room, which had been Robert's bachelor bedroom, but which had been substantially remodelled and now had an en suite bathroom added by the builders, whilst the newlyweds had lounged around Europe and beyond.

The bathroom had been converted from an adjoining upstairs store, no longer needed now that the extra guest wing had been built on to the side of the hotel.

She blundered towards the bathroom, feeling as if she wanted to be sick, wanting suddenly to wretch her heart up, watched by the little French porcelain boy doll – another present from Robert after she had espied it in the window of an old-fashioned shop in one of the maze of side streets close to the Louvre.

She had remarked upon it, noting that, unusually, it appeared to be dressed as a boy – a boy with a wistful expression, pouting lips and an enigmatic smile – just like that of the Mona Lisa, who had smiled so secretively at them from the most popular of the portrait galleries.

Agnes knew of the controversy surrounding the sexuality of the Mona Lisa. Was she male, or was he female? What did it matter any way?

Would the figure in the portrait have been any less beautiful if she had been a man. Mona Lisa? Jonah Lisa? Who cared?

She had unwrapped the boy doll from its ornate packaging shortly after Jo had rummaged through their suitcases, fearing that Jo might take a fancy to it and claim it with those doleful eyes that Nan so often found difficult to resist.

Extracting it from its tissue paper wrapping, she had propped the china-headed figure beside the swing mirror, which rested on her dressing table, as yet unoccupied by her assortment of perfumes and lotions.

From its position, with little legs stretched out before it on the glass-topped mahogany dressing table, it stared back at her, hard and unyielding, its image trapped in its own reflection.

As she crossed the patterned linoleum floor of the bathroom towards the brand new nail varnish pink coloured sink, with its shiny chrome taps, the spider, which had somehow managed to scramble up the side of the bath, scuttled across the polished floor, its octet of hairy legs slipping on the smooth, shiny surface.

She stifled a scream.

Quietly closing the bathroom door behind her, she padded silently across the carpeted bedroom floor towards the bed, ready to dive under the eiderdown.

She nearly tripped over Robert's golf clubs, which he had left untidily propped against an armchair after the match that he had insisted on playing that afternoon on their return to Scotland from their long honeymoon.

Agnes had hardly begrudged him his late arrival back from the club house, even if, unusually, he was slightly the worse for wear. She had enjoyed his undivided attention for six long weeks, so she felt that he had fully earned a lengthy chat with his golfing pals at the nineteenth hole.

It was the swaying image of the doll's head, nodding backwards and forwards, coming towards her and backing away again, which immediately grabbed her attention, dispelling all thoughts of annoying arachnids.

The image of the boy doll, caught in the reflective glass, provided the only measure of light on that dark February night. She should have been able to have recognised its face in the mirror glass but, strangely, it didn't appear to have a face at all!

A long, cold sliver of ice slipped down her spine, replacing the warm glow that she had felt after Robert had made love to her. She didn't feel sick any more.

She felt terrified!

Agnes stood mesmerised by the movement, as the looking glass on the dressing table swung back and forth, playing tricks on her, like a series of fairground mirrors, producing images that could not possibly be.

She sniffed at the night air, catching the delicate aroma of her own perfume overlaid with a strong scent of something strange, which assaulted her nostrils. Perhaps it was the unpleasant smell of Dulux on the newly painted Victorian sash windows.

Slowly, inexplicably, their frames began to peel shards of papery paint, like shavings of cheddar slowly cascading from a cheese grater.

Slivers of paint struck the windowsill and were blown away in a draught which did not exist.

A whispering voice, that no one other than she could hear, spoke out to her like a ghost of the past, recalling other dark February nights. Minutely, inch by inch, the mirror glass began to mist over, hiding the swaying porcelain figure of the little baby boy, so that only its basic form remained visible, legs, arms and face no longer distinguishable.

Robert continued to breathe deeply, comfortable in his dream world where a hole in one victory was a feature of every golfing match and it never rained to spoil the Wimbledon tennis tournament.

Agnes gagged, swallowing a mouthful of vomit.

She inspected the pretty, but inexpensive gold-plated wristwatch that Nanny Bapty had given her as an engagement present and which she made a point of wearing every other day, alternating it with its diamond encrusted counterpart that her poor, dead father had given her on the same day.

It was a minute or two before midnight.

She and Robert had obviously been making love for longer than she had imagined, having dispersed the crowd of well-wishing staff, who had been anxious to make an excuse of their home-coming for a few extra late night drinks to be distributed from behind the bar.

Robert had finally returned from the golf club at around eleven o'clock, joining his wife and sisters at the hotel bar for an afterhours drink before the couple had quietly slipped away, allowing the staff to unwind, certain in the knowledge that his mother, Mary, had long since taken to her bed and that the coast was clear for them all to enjoy themselves after the last of the guests had been served.

Agnes's sister-in-law, Anne had, of course, been keen to encourage the would-be revellers, rushing around the bar and taking orders from the staff in a slightly slurred voice and always making sure of taking a double measure for herself.

Moira had been serving behind the bar earlier that evening and, in an aside to Andrina, she questioned where Anne found her energy from after a long day spent clearing up after another wedding party and preparing for a golf club dinner at which Robert was to preside the following evening.

'My sister would win the hundred metres hurdles at the Olympics, if she thought there was someone holding a gin and tonic for the first one past the finishing post,' Andrina had replied.

Pain shot through Agnes's stomach. She wanted to be sick again. It was as if something was lurking in the pit of her stomach, struggling to emerge, just like the large, black spider she had seen in the bath, which had finally managed to scale the slippery, enamelled sides.

She staggered back, knocking over Robert's golf clubs, spilling putters and drivers from the leather bag. They clattered together, as they fell to the floor, forcing her to pick her way between them, as if she was dancing between swords in a Scottish fling.

Inexplicably, she felt in fear of the darkness of the newly decorated bedroom which, nevertheless, still retained all the relics of her husband's carefree bachelor past.

She longed to return to her old bedroom next to Andrina's, which was safe and familiar to her, even if there was no man there to cuddle up to and luxuriate in the warmth of his body.

She focussed on the tiny gold-plated wristwatch with its enamel dial, and its miniature markings, as its tiny brass hands moved inexorably towards the midnight hour.

The boy doll on the dressing table was restless once more, its reflective image made to move by the rocking mahogany mirror, its artificial mop of golden curls glistening in the silvered glass.

Suddenly the wooden support frame of the mirror cracked and splintered, yet still continued to support the swaying mirror, finally calming the boy doll, whose lips didn't even utter a French whisper of fear.

Apart from her sleeping husband, no one could have entered the room, which Agnes had locked and bolted, suspending a "Do Not Disturb" notice from the handle on the outside, thus protecting their early morning privacy from any of the chambermaids, who sought to clean and tidy the room.

In this way, she could ensure that the two of them would be able to celebrate their home-coming with a guarantee of remaining undisturbed.

As suddenly as it had begun, the rocking stopped. Miraculously, the mirror frame appeared fully repaired. Once again the mute boy doll began to cry – soft, heart-rending sobs emitting from rosebud lips until the rocking movement began again.

Tears ran no more, dried by the gentle hand that touched the swinging mirror unseen in its reflective gaze.

Agnes's firm right hand in which she daily wrote with her steady flow of perfectly scripted handwriting began to shake – not by touching the swinging mirror, but in an attempt to rid herself of the strange belief that the reflective image was real and not made of china.

She leaned down and placed a hand on the boy doll, making the movement cease but, as soon as she lifted her hand, the rocking, which had relaxed, began all over again. She fingered the boy doll's forehead. It immediately felt cold to her touch.

She removed her hand silently, for a moment brushing against her empty breasts, fondling them with her fingers and lifting them, as if examining them for any signs of milk with which to feed the boy doll devoid of any means of suckling.

Agnes returned to bed, unable to fathom her own thoughts, incapable of offering any explanation for her own actions. She must have imagined everything. Maybe a draught in the room had caught the mirror, causing it to sway.

Still she was uncertain of the way she felt towards the mirrored reflection, at one point wanting to feed the doll and its twin image and, at the same time, seemingly disturbed by terrifying images of twins.

She almost wanted to turn and smash the coy-looking features against the wall, destroying any disturbing thoughts that the twins were alive, but somehow joined together, each held in the other's reflection, each needing her, despite her inability to offer sustenance from her empty breasts.

Suddenly, she shot bolt upright in bed, as she remembered all too clearly that tomorrow was the anniversary of her father's tragic death.

Could it be that Charlie's presence was back in the room? No, it was something far stranger, more menacing and it was right here at Carlton Hall in her marital bedroom.

Her mind began to swim, trawling through the recent past to the peculiarly hypnotic words seemingly uttered by Mary, as she had desperately clung on to Charlie in those last, sad moments, as his life had seeped away from him at the foot of the stairs.

Strange words, which seemed to have their very roots steeped in the past. Words that Agnes felt she would never forget:

Thou taketh my head
And blood will be shed
A spear in the heart
The thief will depart
Death to the receiver
Be he not a believer

Robert, curled up and sleeping like a man who had just staged a pretty good demonstration of his manhood, murmured momentarily in his sleep.

Agnes touched the soft hairs, which were just beginning to go grey at the temples, barely aware of the tender actions of a new wife, who had just returned from her honeymoon.

Her troubled thoughts were soon interrupted once more – this time by the notion that maybe Robert hadn't been taken in by the sight of the little pool of blood, which she had puddled into the sheet on her side of the bed on their wedding night.

She felt sick at the very idea that he might have rumbled her ploy to deceive him. She sat up in the bed shaking and trembled in fear at her own duplicity.

Her hand rested briefly on her stomach and she wondered for a moment if any new life could possibly be stirring there.

No, that was ridiculous! She could not possibly be suffering from morning sickness, even if she had conceived on the very first night of their marriage. It had only been six weeks ago. Surely it was too soon.

She glanced towards the boy doll and its twin reflection. For the moment they were her babies – her twins.

Princess Elizabeth and the twin portrait of Princess Margaret, occupied the shelf above the boarded in fireplace empty and lifeless for the past four or five years.

The two princesses smiled each from their separate silver frames – carefree and with the world at their feet. One was a young mother, the other had a bevy of eligible society bachelors keen to take her hand in marriage.

It was only seconds to midnight according to the hands of the little wristwatch on Agnes's arm. They crept towards the witching hour, like a wake up call for the dead.

Agnes winced and bowed her head towards the blankets. She had no time to rush to the bathroom. Now she was sure that she was going to be sick – not sick as a dog, but like a sick serpent, coiled in revulsion at herself and the thought of vomiting in the bed.

Instinctively she knew that she was pregnant.

Agnes remembered how her mother, Muriel had told her how Agnes herself had been born one of twins and how her sister had died at birth. If such things ran in the family, maybe, like her mother, she too would have twins – only her babies would surely survive, wouldn't they?

Somehow she knew that it was not just the fruit of her womb that was in danger, but also the gentle man, thirteen years her senior, who was responsible for the recent conception and whose life was now threatened.

Most of all she feared for the father of the tiny nucleus of life, which would soon swell her belly, the son of the grey-haired man who had died at the foot of the stairs at the Carlton Hall Hotel, whilst his son watched in horror.

Charlie Paterson had escaped from the Benin Expedition in 1897 and had taken the head of the Benin queen as a memento of his friend, Alex, who had been thrown against the iron railings after being hit by a tram. Charlie was her father and now he too was dead.

Robert was the son of a man who had once rifled the treasures of a long forgotten kingdom and once again there was a price to pay.

Agnes scrambled out of the bed and scuttled towards the bathroom once more. Maybe she would make it after all, before she spread vomit all over the sheets. She flung open the bathroom door. Her former fear, the hairy-legged spider, greeted her again.

She didn't care. She had to get to the sink.

Once there, she spewed into the washbasin, retching and shaking until there was nothing more that she could bring up. It left her with an awful taste in her mouth.

She quickly filled a tumbler full of cold water, tossing her head back and swilling it down her throat in an attempt to rid herself of the ghastly after taste.

Agnes returned to the bedroom, picking her way carefully through the spilt tangle of golf clubs that littered the floor and which she had felt too ill to gather up and tidy away.

Robert was still asleep.

She noted too the stillness of the swaying mirror, swayed by no hand unseen. Anxiously, she returned to her bed and whatever protection it might offer to her, to her unborn progeny and especially to her husband the would-be father of her children.

She smelt the newly gloss painted windows again and wondered if it had been them that had made her sick. No curtains were suspended from the windows, as they had not been hung up again, for fear that the paint was not completely dry. Once again, she had the vision of the newly painted frames peeling before her very eyes.

Agnes cuddled up to Robert seeking re-assurance from his body heat and the feel of his sparsely haired chest. He had grabbed most of the bedclothes in his sleep, unaware that he was depriving her of their warmth. She pulled them gently back towards her, as if seeking protection for herself and the unborn that she was nurturing in her womb.

A brief shaft of moonlight shone through the uncurtained window. It provided just sufficient light for Agnes to see. She could not believe the presence that was portrayed before her eyes – a blackened figure, with ashen features she had no hope of discerning.

Agnes wanted to scream out loud, but no sound ever came. She had to be brave, just like she had been with the spider. She tossed the bedding aside, covering Robert with a double layer of warmth.

If only she had some form of weapon with which to defend herself, to protect both her husband and the next generation. She remembered the golf clubs littering the floor.

Slowly the figure drifted towards the middle-aged man who had impregnated her with his seed, before shadowing away towards the fireplace, totally unimpeded by the obstacles scattered across the bedroom floor.

The moon, which had briefly shone through the uncurtained window, dropped behind a cloud, saturating the room once again in total blackness, so that Agnes was unable to discern the featureless face of the figure which stood before her.

No sparkling eyes – just empty sockets. No pink mouth, just a slash across the face; flared nostrils that would never inhale another breath and coral-studded ears unhearing of centuries of sound.

It was a face where a face should have been, but the like of which Agnes have never seen before.

Black! It was totally black! A witch from hell! A woman whose reflection could sway a mirror and who could persuade a voiceless doll to scream. A voice began to call, but not to Agnes.

Its listener was Robert, who had just awoken in time for his own face to be illuminated by the last rays of moonlight, before it ducked behind the sombre night-time sky.

Thou taketh my head
And blood will be shed
A spear in the heart
The thief will depart
Death to the receiver
Be he not a believer
The son of the taker
Will meet his maker

Eight lines of rhyme, repeated for what seemed an eternity, striking fear into Agnes's heart and making her want to be sick all over again.

Meaningless murmurs, but ones which filled her with a fear of the unknown. She didn't understand what it all meant.

She didn't want to know, but of one thing she was sure – their threat was implicit. There was no doubt about that!

The uttered taunts of the ghost sounded strangely familiar and somehow their significance was not lost on her.

219

Agnes had to face the evil that tormented her, like the spider with its outstretched legs. She had to face the face that was not a face – the one which seemed to float above the level of the floor, with no fear of tripping over the tangle of golf clubs.

It had no body which could be reflected in the mirror and no hands with which to sway a reflected image.

Agnes bent down and picked up a golf iron, extending it in front of her in the direction of the boarded up fireplace.

It swept across the mantelpiece taking everything in its wake – the shattered ornaments, the vase of flowers and the silver-framed pictures of the two princesses – as Agnes's adversary breezed towards the uncurtained, window in a movement unrecorded by the facing mirror on the opposite side of the room.

The upturned face of Princess Elizabeth soon to be crowned queen, stared up from the jumble of golf clubs and smashed ornaments. The silver picture frame was forever dented, as it had struck the hearth of the fenderless fireplace.

Brittle shards of picture glass speckled the golf iron that Agnes had ran across the mantelpiece. They glittered and shone amidst the broken pieces of china. A queen, who had been a queen for a thousand years, had taken flight.

Steal the head of the Benin queen and she would strike back in vengeance at the heart of the son of any man who had for years kept her sacred image, whilst his unborn sons gazed sightlessly from the belly of the woman whom he had fused with his sperm.

Agnes's husband, Robert, had watched helplessly, as his father had died at the bottom of the stairs at the Carlton Hall Hotel and right now he too was heading for a life and death confrontation with the queen of Benin.

Thou taketh my head
And blood will be shed
A spear in the heart
The thief will depart
Death to the receiver
Be he not a believer
The son of the taker
Will meet his maker

Chapter 31

Jo heard the noise of the MG's engine starting up, scampering quickly down from the hay loft above the former stables, which were used to garage Grandmother's Bentley and Uncle Robert's roadster.

Anxious not to miss the opportunity of an outing, Jo was disappointed to discover that the sole purpose of Robert's visit to the building was to start the engine of the car, bearing in mind that the two-seater hadn't been used for many weeks.

Mary's chauffeur had not thought to turn over the engine of the little red sports car once in a while, whilst Robert and Agnes had been away on their honeymoon and now the vehicle was proving reluctant to start, requiring several cranks of the starting handle before eventually spluttering into reluctant life.

A belch of exhaust smoke blew out of the open stable doors, mingling with the frosty February morning. Robert had removed the tarpaulin cover from the car, consigning it to a heap on the stable floor and was warming his hands on the rapidly heating bonnet.

'Can't we go out together? Please, Uncle Robert. Just for a little while,' demanded Jo in an imploring voice that Robert so often found hard to resist.

'No, not today Jo. It's far too cold and slippery. I don't want you catching your death of cold. Whatever would Nanny Bapty have to say if you finished up with a streaming cold and couldn't go to school next week?'

As far as Jo was concerned, that wasn't a bad idea at all. Snuggled up in bed with a warm hot bottle, a picture storybook and Nanny Bapty's undivided attention was an excellent exchange for a runny nose and a soggy handkerchief tucked behind the pillow. Sadly, Uncle Robert was not playing that game – not today at any rate.

'Why don't you take me upstairs and show me just exactly what you keep hidden up in the hay loft instead,' announced Robert in a kindly tone.

'I haven't been up there for a long time, but you seem to spend hours hiding up there all on your own, getting up to God knows what.'

'I'm not on my own,' protested Jo. 'Georgina's with me. She's up there right now. Come and see.'

'Oh, yes, silly me, I quite forgot about Georgina,' said Robert, remembering Jo's imaginary friend, who always accompanied the child on adventures beyond the wildest excess of Jo's imagination.

Slowly he climbed the ladder behind Jo, taking care to place each foot securely on the ancient rungs that he feared might be rotten in parts and which, although perfectly capable of withstanding the child's weight, might easily snap under his heavier footfall.

Reaching the top of the ladder, he was not surprised to find that Jo had created a cosy little den from musty old bales of straw, all arranged in a rough square, with a little entrance door formed by an old sheet of plywood.

The straw bales were piled just high enough for the eight-year-old child to stand up beneath the blanket, which was stretched over the top to form a roof and Robert had to duck low to follow Jo's lead.

'Welcome to Africa, Uncle Robert,' announced Jo, with a little hand that swept around the straw walls, decorated with storybook cut-outs of lions, incongruously and incorrectly accompanied by Indian tigers.

There were pictures of long-legged giraffes, elephants, with their trunks held aloft, herds of zebra and wildebeest, chimpanzees swinging from treetops and countless other creatures that Robert could barely put a name to.

With its straw walls, it resembled an African native hut. Against the far wall sat proudly on top of another musty bale of straw was a collage of African masks, shields and fly swatches, together with a couple of antelope's heads mounted on polished wooden plinths, all of which had once occupied Charlie's study – and which long ago had been consigned to a builder's skip by Mary whilst the hotel was undergoing further renovation.

In pride of place sat the bronzen image of a long dead African queen.

She had once occupied the desk in Charlie's study and now she commanded an unholy altar chiselled not out of stone but, instead, made of straw.

It was as if this was to be her final resting place. This was what she was reduced to – a little shrine of dried stems of wheat and barley from which no blood had ever stemmed.

Here she was hidden from sight, her own sight unseeing, with no sacrificial offering other than a child's imagination and with nothing to quench her age old thirst. All that was missing from the collection was the spear itself – the one which had pierced Charlie's ageing heart.

'How on earth did you…?'

'I found them,' was Jo's simple reply.

'Where did you find them?'

'Grandmother was throwing them all out after Grand-dad Charlie died,' explained Jo.

'And did you ask her if you could keep them?'

Jo's silence told Robert all he needed to know. He had remembered his mother casting all the relics of Charlie's African past into the skip, saying that she would not allow such presages of ill fortune back into the hotel again, bundling them all up and casting them amongst the builders' rubble that had occupied the inner courtyard, whilst the extension wing to the hotel had been being built.

She had threatened everyone not to touch them and had forbidden them to be brought back inside the building with words that trucked no argument.

'I thought Grandmother said that all these things were to be thrown out and not to be brought into the hotel again,' said Robert ominously.

'I haven't disobeyed Grandmother,' replied Jo with wide-eyed innocence.

'It was Georgina who rescued them. Besides, they're not back in the hotel – there here in the stables.'

'And I don't suppose for one moment that Grandmother knows anything about this, does she?'

Once again Jo's silence spoke volumes. Robert tousled Jo's head of unruly curls, despairing but, at the same time, admiring the child, who had the ability to proclaim innocence in a manner which was beyond rebuke.

'Jo, you're quite impossible. What is it worth for me not to mention this to your grandmother?'

'I'll tell you a secret if you like,' replied Jo.

'And what secret might that be?'

'Auntie Nan had an argument with Grandmother this morning.'

'And what might that have been about?'

'I don't know, but it was something that Auntie Nan said that Grandmother had to tell you about Grand-dad Charlie. Grandmother told her she should never have been allowed to marry you.'

'And why might that be?'

'Grandmother said it was because Charlie was your Daddy!'

* * * * * * * * *

Robert needed time to gather his thoughts. It all made sense. How many times had he been told, now that he was rapidly passing into middle age, that he closely resembled Mary's late husband? How could he have been taken in for all these years?

A father might lie and feign the truth, but his own mother!

How could a mother be anything other than a sparkling fountain of knowledge and truth? No, a father could somehow be forgiven for telling a lie, but a mother – no that could never be! And had Charlie ever known?

If he had have been privy to Mary's secret, then he had never let on, never breathing a word to his son. Certainly he had not done anything to stand in the way of his daughter, Nan, his only daughter, marrying his only son.

No, surely, Charlie didn't know anything. He was far too correct and upstanding ever to have allowed such a coupling, if he had been party to the truth of the matter.

Why it was Charlie who had pushed Robert into the marriage in the first place, encouraging his cautious courting of Agnes when Robert would have quite happily remained a bachelor. Robert had never been that bothered about marrying Agnes to begin with.

Why he had even bedded the voluptuous Moira on the very night of his engagement to Agnes.

It had only been Charlie's fatherly insistence that it was time he settled down that had encouraged his sporadic courtship of Agnes. She had loved him from the start, adored him from the very moment that she had first set eyes on him and, in return, he had done his best to ignore her. If only he had ignored her completely!

And how had Agnes discovered the awful truth that Mary alone could have revealed?

223

What could have caused his mother to come clean about her relationship with Charlie all those years ago? The marriage would have to be annulled. As least, at her age, Agnes was hardly likely to be pregnant!

* * * * * * * * *

Robert stormed across the frosty lawn, furious and afraid of the confrontation that surely had to follow – there was too much that could no longer be left unsaid between his mother and himself.

What possible words could he find to express how he felt? Was this why Agnes had been behaving rather peculiarly that morning? He vaguely remembered her getting up in the night to be sick.

Had she known then? How could she possibly cope with the knowledge that would rip the two of them apart without saying something to him?

How could the two of them go on living under the same roof – the apex of which Robert now looked up at. Earlier he had spotted the bedraggled flag that lay stiff and frosted on the lawn in front of him – a remnant of the jubilant rejoicing in the news of a soon to be crowned queen, torn from its flagstaff in the wind that had whipped and lashed around the Victorian building the night before.

He picked it up for no apparent reason. Its chilly, frosted surface, melted tiny icicles of pain through the tips of his fingers, as he bundled it up and stalked towards the main entrance of the hotel with the cloth remains of the flag screwed up in his clenched fist.

Right now he was intent on a confrontation with the mother who had foisted fatherlessness upon him for more than fifty years.

Jo had often expressed despair at never knowing a real father and Robert had sometimes comforted the child, explaining how it didn't really matter.

Oh yes, it mattered all right!

Robert had explained to Jo how he too had never known his "real" father, Alex and how Mary's second husband, Frank Finlay had ignored him both as a child and as a teenager, just like Anne's husband, George was wont to do with young Jo.

'I wish you were my real father,' Jo had once confided to him. 'You're kind to me. You always bring sweets for Georgina and me and take us out in your car.

'We never go out anywhere with Mummy and Daddy rarely comes to see us. Mummy's usually in bed in the afternoon and Daddy's always working. Why can't you be my Daddy, Uncle Robert?'

Such words gave Robert cause to remember the time that he had acted like a father, delivering the baby into his sister, Anne's arms – only she wasn't really his true sister; like Andrina, she was only his half-sister.

Yes, he had remembered that night, when he had walked up the stairs of the corner pub, like a proud father delivering his own spawn into a waiting mother's cradling embrace.

* * * * * * * * *

224

Now there was a score to settle – a half century spent by his mother battling with the truth forever anxious that the revelations that she had sought so keenly to avoid should never become common knowledge.

Oh God, what could he possibly find to say to Agnes? She would probably be on reception. How could he pass her by without a word?

Right at this moment, Mary was the one who mattered most, not that she mattered a jot to him right now – that deceitful mother of his who had carried with her a dreadful secret and not once thought to unburden herself to the very person to whom it concerned most of all.

Robert hated her with a degree of bitterness that he never considered himself capable of feeling. She had deceived him for more than half a century, robbing him of any opportunity of acknowledging Charlie as his real father.

God, how he despised her.

Robert longed to hit out at her with a volley of carefully chosen words – to slap her wrinkled face and watch the tears well up in her eyes and splatter down her face.

She had allowed Charlie to trap him into this marriage that he had never really wanted in the first place and with Agnes – the one woman who he should never have married.

How could she have done such a thing? How could she have stood by and let it happen? She had told him that she was happy for him. Given him her blessing. Mary had looked so proud that day in the church, watching the young woman who was already her stepdaughter (and was soon to be her daughter-in-law too) drift up the aisle on a sea of happiness.

What was even more inexcusable was the fact that she had watched her son – Charlie's son – betroth himself to his half-sister.

Mary had stood and smiled at Charlie who, after the marriage, was not only Robert's father, but also his father-in-law. It was as if with Robert's wedding to Agnes, Mary's world had at last become complete.

Finally, everything had come full circle.

Mary had married the man she had wanted to spend her life with all those years ago and now she had stood by and witnessed the marriage of his only daughter to their only son.

She had created a tangled web that just went on and on, each victim shot through and encased in a silky lair, as Charlie's spidery spouse had stood back and watched fate drumming up an appetite, ready to devour its future captives like flies caught in a Venus's fly-trap of unholy coupling.

Robert ran up the stairs, taking the treads two at a time. Agnes cried out after him and was left with nothing but the sight of his disappearing back.

He flung open the door of Mary's sitting room, only to be met with nothing more innocent than the chambermaid, who was vacuuming the lilac pink carpeted floor.

'Where is my mother?' he demanded roughly, as Agnes, rushing up the stairs behind him stood open-mouthed in the doorway. He pushed past her with no more than half a dozen cursory words.

'I shall talk to you later,' he said curtly. 'Right now I need to find my evil mother.'

'Mr Robert, please stop, listen to me … She's outside organising the replacement of the broken flagpole on the roof, with Jo,' proclaimed the embarrassed chambermaid helpfully.

'Robert, we've got to talk,' Agnes shouted at her husband's receding back, as once more he took the stairs two at a time, rushing past the empty reception desk, where he had left the bundled up Union Jack. He ran towards the swing doors and nearly toppled the doorman, sending him crashing against one of the marble entrance pillars, hurrying down the steps like a man possessed – possessed of the will to grasp his mother around the throat and throttle the very life out of her.

'Mother!' he screamed, skidding across the frosted lawn still a hundred yards or so distant from where Mary stood with Jo by her side, as a furious gust of wind cast the broken end of the flagpole into the air, sending it plunging earthwards in the direction of the patch of lawn where he stood.

The splintered end of the flagstaff hurtled downwards, like a missile seeking its victim – the son of Charlie the giver of Robert's life, the son of the man whose seed had sprouted in Mary's womb unknown to Alex who he had always thought to be his "real" father.

It struck Robert like a spear, bowling him to the ground, flattening him on his back on the grass, whose grey, frosted fringes soaked up the blood, which flowed freely from his shattered, pierced heart.

Thou taketh my head
And blood will be shed
A spear in the heart
The thief will depart
Death to the receiver
Be he not a believer
The son of the taker
Will meet his maker

Chapter 32

Agnes awoke in the hospital bed. It was night-time and the ward was quiet. She still felt the intense pain below her waistline where the knife had cut into her after the Caesarean section, as if something unnaturally heavy had been dragged from her.

The birthing had been traumatic. The cord of one of the twins had been wrapped around its neck, adding further difficulties to what was already a complicated birth.

Agnes had nearly died herself and the staff nurse had called the priest.

She had been ill for over a week and still could not fathom in her own mind the fate of the twins. Had her fatherless babies survived?

Agnes was still too ill to comprehend the ultimate outcome of their life and death struggle.

Perhaps the pain had awoken her, or maybe it was just the sedative wearing off. She struggled to prop herself up on the crisp, white linen pillows, stacked up at the back of her neck.

Her bladder weakened, she needed to visit the bathroom, but couldn't manage to reach the call button to summons a nurse to provide her with the necessary assistance. She could not even reach the pull cord for the reading lamp above her head to illuminate her plight.

Agnes felt that if only she could take a bath, she would be able to flush out the bad blood that, in her imagination, continued to ooze from her body, congealing in little droplets, as if dispensed by a dropper from a cut glass scent bottle, containing not a sweet smelling French perfume, but something far more sour and repugnant.

Something with the aroma of the ox blood which dripped into the metal meat trays in the hotel kitchen – the blood which she had carefully gathered to deceive her husband, Robert of her wholesomeness on their wedding night.

No, she lacked the strength to reach up for the bell with which to call the night duty nurse. What did it matter anyway, if she was no more able to stem her water, than she was capable of banishing the blood, which she believed still seeped from between her legs?

A rubber sheet had been laid on top of the firm mattress and it squeaked like a restless mouse with every tiny movement of her pain-wracked body.

She turned to peer behind the thin curtains used to screen her from the view of the other expectant mothers, many of whom had already experienced a painful childbirth, but who surely knew nothing of the excruciating pain and torment which had beset her.

Agnes felt uneasy. Surely there was some way that she could summons help to her bedside. She needed someone to give her news of her precious babies, the children of her beloved Robert, the man who had gone to his death, never knowing of his impending fatherhood.

If only she had woken him that night – the night before he had died, to tell him the wonderful news. If only she had been sick in the bed and he had awoken to the stench of her vomit.

He would not have minded at all. Surely, he too would have rejoiced in her first bout of morning sickness and the news that it heralded. A metal walking frame stood in the corner on its four square legs beside the hospital locker in the Western General on the Crewe Road, its light, aluminium frame reflected in the polished linoleum floor.

She could have gone into a private nursing home for the birth, but had insisted on using a National Health hospital, perhaps by way of contrition, for she felt that she didn't deserve any special treatment – not after she had duped her husband, her half-brother – the man she should never have married.

Instead, he had gone to his death never knowing the truth about his "virgin" bride and half-sister.

Maybe it was the pain in her abdomen that had awoken her. Perhaps it was just the need to go to the toilet. She struggled to control herself and to control her bladder, not wishing to awaken the other newly birthed mothers, but not wishing the further indignity of wetting the bed.

She touched the metal framework of the hospital bed with her foot, hoping that the chilling sensation would help her to forget her need to urinate.

Agnes turned towards the sleeping woman beside her and the little metal hospital cot, with its tiny infant full of breast milk and breathing softly, whilst its mother murmured gently in her sleep, cosseted and calmed by the little form, which had suckled at her breast.

In the dim light shed by the low wattage light bulb at the opposite end of the ward, Agnes could see the vase of red roses given to her neighbour by a doting husband and proud father, celebrating the birth of his first-born son and acknowledging its mother with a declaration of his love.

A single rose from amongst the dozen drooped, its neck twisted and broken by the doctor, who had passed by earlier that afternoon and caught it with his stethoscope. Agnes caught the whiff of rose-scented perfume overlaid with the disinfectant smell of the ward.

No bunch of red roses for Agnes. No doting father to celebrate the birth of his sons.

She glanced across to the metal-framed windows, rusting and corroded from lack of paint. She heard the metal fastening catches rattle.

It had been a chill autumn day, but still Matron had insisted on throwing caution to the wind, declaring that "a bit of fresh air didn't do anyone any harm" and the student nurse whose task it had been to fasten them at the end of the day had perhaps neglected to perform her duty.

No, surely no nurse would run the risk of the newly born infants catching a chill in the cold night air. It made no sense at all, but still there was an inexplicable draught from the swirling eddy of wind that blew inside the hushed, sanitised ward; a miniature hospital hurricane, which caught the curtain screen around her bed, lifting its corners like the skirts of a Paris dancer at the Moulin Rouge.

Agnes heard its soft, gentle whispering as, like a fairy tale phantom, it twisted and turned, precipitating its passage along the length of the ward, like the hushed voice of pregnant patients past.

She remembered that dark February night and her ghostly visitor. It was the night upon which she had discovered her own pregnancy but, most of all, she recalled the terrible day that had followed. Robert's untimely death had been flagged in her dream of the previous night and foretold in her imagination.

Had it really been her imagination?

Robert had gone to his death, speared in the heart in a freak accident, never knowing that he had not one, but two twin sons and heirs growing from the seed which had penetrated his bride on the first night of their honeymoon.

Agnes's near neighbour continued to breathe deeply, dreaming of returning home with her tiny bundle of joy and unperturbed by the sleepless nights which would surely follow.

A solid sounding, soporific ticking from the hospital clock marked the passage of the night. It was close to midnight.

Agnes had virtually slept for days, barely aware of the passing of time and the moment when day became night and night became day.

New life had appeared and some tiny little mites, born prematurely, had breathed their last even before they had emerged from the womb.

Agnes had been oblivious to their entries into and exits from the world, just as, right now, she was unaware of the fate of her own twins.

Visitors to the maternity ward, especially proud first time fathers, had proved reluctant to disperse. Only the thought of a few swift pints with the lads down at the local pub and the chance of drenching, rather than merely wetting, the heads of their newborn sons and daughters, had enabled the hard working day nurses to end their long shift and retire to the nursing quarters to bag a favourite armchair.

Agnes was still desperately tired after the lingering effects of the anaesthetic that she had been forced to undergo in an effort to finally evict the two little strangers from the darkness of her womb and into the daylight.

Before the operation, the doctors and midwives had rushed around, urging her to push and then to push even harder, when pushing seemed to do nothing at all. She recalled how one mid-wife had implored her to control her breathing, when it was totally out of her control.

It was only after some time that the doctor in attendance had realised that the birth would necessitate a Caesarean section.

The surgeon had drilled the hospital staff, urging them to ensure that the sterilised metal instruments that were being used to open Agnes up were readily reachable by rubber-gloved hands when she had finally been rushed from the delivery room into the operating theatre for the Caesarean.

Agnes had eaten nothing for days and had drunk little too, taking only an occasional sip of milk held to her lips by a patient nurse in one of her rare waking moments. At one point she remembered supping a tiny bowl of thin soup, which had tasted of nothing at all.

Agnes normally had a healthy appetite. She would like nothing better than to join the kitchen staff in a hearty cooked breakfast at around half past nine each morning, when the last of the hotel guests had taken their fill.

Hot, milky porridge, sweetened with a teaspoonful or two of thick heather honey, scrambled eggs on toast in fluffy yellow mounds and hot, buttered muffins, with chunky, tangy, thick cut marmalade was usually just what she needed to set herself up for the day.

It meant that she seldom had to stop for lunch, when she was busy behind the hotel reception desk.

Agnes had been conscious for a short while that afternoon, watching the new mother by her side feeding her baby and softly brushing its light sprinkling of golden brown hair with her fingertips, before tucking it up tenderly in its little utilitarian metal cot, so that both mother and child could snatch a few hours sleep before the father came a'calling, with suggestions of what to call his baby son and, of course, wanting to wake it up and cradle it in his strong, muscular arms.

Unlike her hospital companion, Agnes was yet to hold her babies in arms which sought warmth in a crocheted cardigan. She was still looking forward to closing her eyelids in contentment, as they nestled into her breasts, which felt heavy and as if no child had ever pursed its tiny lips around her nipples, growing strong from its mother's milk.

She needed a tissue to wipe away a tiny dribble of milk bursting from her nipples, but couldn't reach the box that lay on the bedside locker. She needed a drink, but could not stretch out towards the carafe of tap water and the bottle of lemon barley, which Nanny Bapty had brought in to her, leaving the hospital without even speaking to her employer, who had slept soundly throughout the other woman's visit. A bunch of grapes too lay in a glass bowl untouched, but ripe for the picking.

Agnes's unused glass perched upside down on top of a carafe of water on her hospital locker. Nanny Bapty had helped herself to a weak glass of lemon barley, carefully rinsing the glass behind her, before making her departure on the number 41 bus, which passed the top of the driveway down to the hotel.

Only the nursing staff knew exactly how long Agnes had slept. Now she was awake and alone in the tightly packed ward. Pain gripped her consciousness and her abdomen, which had been sliced open and stitched back together again and now felt as if someone had set about her with a blunt carving knife.

Pain was paramount, but something paranormal was creeping into her perception. She smelt the scent of the well-scrubbed floors, the pungent odour of anaesthetic and the sense of something sinister.

She focussed her drug-filled eyes on the Bakelite clock on the wall of the ward, as its black, plastic hands paced their way towards midnight.

The baby, born of another, lying beside her in the space between the two beds, was awake and restless, crying out for the attention that Agnes longed to lavish upon it, although the child was not hers to love and cherish.

Agnes tried hard to focus but, having been given so many tranquillisers, her vision remained blurred. She felt as if she was wearing someone else's spectacles.

Slowly the little metal cot beside her began to sway from side to side. Someone was rocking the child to sleep, with unseen hands that lifted the tall sides of the cot, so that its tubular metal legs slid gently back and forth on the glossy, linoleum floor, bringing calm once more to the hushed silence of the hospital maternity ward.

Agnes felt immediately afraid, but realised the ridiculousness of the situation caused, no doubt, by her own drug-induced stupor. Obviously one of the nurses had padded quietly down the length of the ward, anxious to comfort the child, leaving the rest of the sleeping mothers and their babies to their restful slumbers, not wanting the cries of one infant to start the others off.

Agnes expected to hear the gentle swish of a starched apron, as the night duty nurse cosseted and comforted the tiny tot beside her. No one approached the bedside. No flicker of light from a hand-held torch pierced the darkness of the darkened ward.

Save for the doctors and other medical staff, no one could have entered the ward during the night, when visiting hours were long past.

The main door to the maternity ward was kept locked in case some wayward male stranger stumbled into this strictly female domain and only Matron and Staff Nurse held a key.

The rocking movement of the small metal cot ceased. The baby started crying again. Soft, almost silent, spluttering sobs issued from its tiny, pink, toothless mouth in an attempt to rouse its mother.

Agnes's hands began to shake, the drip which had been inserted into the back of her hand, with its long, serpent-like coil of plastic tubing quivered, caught in the faint rays of artificial light from the low wattage night lamps at the other end of the ward.

She wanted to reach out and comfort the child, whose mother continued to sleep, but the ghost-like visitor from Agnes's past performed the job for her, placing an unseen hand on the little metal bed. Tears were quickly dried and once more the sobbing was silenced.

Agnes wanted to lean down and position her own soothing hand on the side of the cot to assuage its gentle rocking movement but, as soon as she lifted her hand, the tubes suspended from the plastic bag above her head tightened around the needle that had been driven into the back of her hand and even that small movement was rendered impossible.

She desperately felt the need to touch the baby's forehead to check it for a fever in an instinctive substitute action for the love that she longed to lavish on her own tiny babies, perhaps allowing its tiny fingers to fasten themselves around one of hers … maybe the one which still bore Robert's ring.

However, to her dismay, the only comforting presence that the child seemed to need was right there beside it – unseen, but so welcome and wanted and so desperately desired.

Agnes wanted to throw off the cardigan and expose her bare, aching breasts, offering them to the tiny infant. She hated their hard heaviness, so weighty and not yet pendulous, so capable of producing milk, but which no tiny mouth had, as yet, ever tried to suckle.

Quelled and quietened, the comforted child's eyelids twitched gently in a last, lingering tussle with the Land of Nod, its tearful torment terminated.

Agnes attempted to cross her legs, unable to return to her drug-induced sleep, whilst her bladder ached to discharge its contents. She must have imagined it all. It was the tablets. Nothing more!

Maybe an opened door had stirred the air in the draughty hospital corridor outside and a breeze of air had crept unannounced under the swing doors leading into the maternity ward.

Still she did not believe her own befuddled thoughts. Disturbing memories were echoing in her head and were proving impossible to eradicate.

She remembered a time not many months ago, when her sleep had been interrupted by a French china boy doll and its reflected twin mirrored image. Side by side the two baby boys had rocked and swayed, their images thrown backwards and forwards in the dressing table mirror.

Suddenly, painfully, she shot bolt upright in bed, dragging at the needle in the back of her hand.

That pervading presence was here in the maternity ward again, not in a tiny Edinburgh attic, not in Charlie and Mary's bedroom in the hotel, not in the specially prepared marital bedroom at Carlton Hall that Agnes had shared for just that one cherished night with Robert, but here tonight in the hushed hospital ward and it was ready and waiting.

Waiting for what? Waiting to bewitch her!

Her clouded mind was beginning to clear, kayaking the rushing waters of her memory until everything began to rise to the surface. Words that she had not heard since the dawning discovery of her pregnancy returned to haunt her:

Thou taketh my head
And blood will be shed
A spear in the heart
The thief will depart
Death to the receiver
Be he not a believer
The son of the taker
Will meet his maker

Agnes's drug-induced sleep was now firmly focussed on the waking nightmare that was about to begin all over again. She shivered in spite of the warm cardigan that she wore and against the chill wraith that chided her.

The baby boy beside her, the child who belonged to another, slept peacefully, rocked gently by the eerie echoes of the past, unthreatened by presence past, or present.

Princess Elizabeth, very soon to attend her own coronation, was portrayed in a poster that hung from the dado rail above where the metal walking frame had been left up against the wall beside Agnes's hospital bed.

Its corners were attached to the cork backing board by bright red drawing pins that had pricked the fingers of the orderly who had driven them into the spongy surface that morning, drawing tiny droplets of blood which, inadvertently, she had caused to spot the stiffly starched sheets which made up Agnes's bed.

It reminded Agnes of the ox blood which she had so carefully allowed to stain the sheets of her honeymoon bed; only in her case, it had been a premeditated act of deception and one for which she now hated herself for exercising.

In the photographic image depicted in the poster, the soon to be crowned queen was barely smiling, perhaps caught in a moment of sadness at the death of the old king, taken from this world just like Agnes's own father, so suddenly, so unexpectedly, so tragically.

On the wall the Bakelite hands of the clock inched steadily towards the witching hour, like a wakeup call for the dead.

A shaft of fear slew snakily down Agnes's spine, meandering, serpentine-like down the line of her backbone. It felt as if a slimy, silvery slug had slid down her cold back, finally determining its dawdling destination at the base of her spine.

She knew for certain that it wasn't the drugs that were making her imagine all manner of absurd notions. The ward had unwittingly welcomed a witch!

Intuitively, she knew that it was not her neighbour's newborn who was under any potential threat, but the tiny scraps of life, which had been taken from her at birth, like the twins born of a Benin woman – the delivery of the Devil, a demon's descendants doomed to die.

Agnes struggled again to reach the pull cord for the light above the bed, or any means by which to summons assistance. At last she cried out loud, unheeding of whoever might be awoken by her cries. She was met by the sound of silence, as her own stretched and strangled vocal chords uttered not a sound.

The thin cotton curtains, which served to screen her hospital bed, fluttered in the still night air. It was a daredevil dance, gyrating in a swirling upsurge of the draught which swept them up at the hems – only the air in the ward had remained still and silent, as the flimsy fabric lifted and drifted in a draught of air which had never existed.

No gusting whisper of chill night air had dared to enter the ward and yet the carafe of drinking water and the bottle of lemon barley on the bedside locker jangled and chinked unnervingly, rattling without reason.

Agnes longed to rush down the ward and sweep her babies into her protecting arms, but she didn't even know where to find them. Still she needed to protect them from whatever it was that placed them in such mortal peril.

Footsteps glowed in the shiny linoleum floor and backed away again, as the unseen figure pressed against the poster of an as yet uncrowned queen.

One more almighty effort and she grabbed the pull cord from above her bed, snagging the plastic tubing from the back of her hand, so that blood began to run in a little red ruby river that flowed down her arm. It dripped on to the clinically white sheet drawn up against her breasts, spreading in a puddle just like the bull's blood that had supposedly proclaimed her virginity on her wedding night, when she had deceived her husband, her lover, her half-brother and the father of her children.

The light above her head shone briefly for a moment and then broke from its mounting, dragged away from the wall in a tangle of tubing, as Agnes tugged furiously in a useless effort to free herself from the twisting, glistening, serpentine entanglement.

It shone its light just sufficiently for Agnes to glimpse the wan, ashen-faced figure, before the black metal angle poise lamp crashed on to the bed, its light instantly extinguished, as it struck the blood-speckled sheets.

Agnes heard the hurried footsteps of the night duty nurse walking briskly down the ward in her direction and towards the gruesome ghoul who grew out of the night.

She needed protection. She needed to protect her babies.

At last freeing herself from the tangle of plastic tubing, she snatched at the metal walking frame, hoping that it would support her weight, but it toppled on to its side, catching the poster of the uncrowned queen, ripping it away from the red drawing pins, which scattered on to the lino like drops of blood, sending the poster scudding to the floor, where it lay like a roll of Christmas wrapping paper lacking a present.

Agnes fell to the floor gripping herself below the waist, drugged and dazed and no longer able to determine any of the details of the demon's anatomy. She could not raise her head to stare it in the face, for there was no face to focus upon.

It was just like that time at the start of her pregnancy when the living, waking nightmare had all begun in the bedroom suite at the Carlton Hall Hotel. Now it seemed like a lifetime ago.

That night, she had been aware that the face that haunted her was as black as the night in which it was seeking to conceal itself.

No sparkling eyes – just empty sockets. No pink mouth, just a slash across the face; flared nostrils that would never inhale another breath and coral-studded ears unhearing of centuries of sound.

It was a face where a face should be and the like of which Agnes had experienced just once before. Black! It was totally black! An incantation from another world hell-bent on evil. A sorceress straight from Hell! A witch without pity, whose doings of the Devil threatened her twins and who would do her damnedest to cast them aside from their mother. A heartless heathen. A pitiless pariah dealing in damnation.

A voice began to call, but it was that of the nurse, who had just arrived at Agnes's side, bending down to pick up the fallen woman, the bride who had sought to convince her husband of her virginity with the blood of an ox.

Agnes was scarcely aware of the nurse's helping hand, as it was extended towards her. All that her mind was capable of focussing upon were the eerie words which rang in her ears:

Thou taketh my head
And blood will be shed
A spear in the heart
The thief will depart
Death to the receiver
Be he not a believer

The son of the taker
Will meet his maker
The sons of the son
By the Devil be won

Five rhyming couplets, whose verbal verses rang repeatedly through Agnes's unreasoning mind. She knew exactly what they meant – their threat had been made all too clear to her all those months ago on the night before her darling Robert had died.

She had heard the first of those four rhymes before and they had heralded the death of her dear husband – felled by a flagstaff falling from the roof, in an accident which no one could have foretold.

She had to get up off the floor, find her babies and protect them, face the fury of the faceless She-Devil, the evil enchantress, who had robbed her of the man she loved – the man who was both her husband and half-brother – the man whose chance of witnessing the growing up of a son and heir had been cruelly robbed from him, just as had been the case for his father before him, who had likewise never known that he had fathered a son.

Agnes grasped the upturned walking frame and dragged herself to her feet. It fell away from her, toppling on to the crumpled poster of the future monarch, squashing Princess Elizabeth's picture into papery pulp on the floor.

Meanwhile, her ghostly adversary sought refuge in the curtains around the bed screened from view by a billowing cascade of cheap cotton.

She was an ancient African queen whose coronation had been marked, not by the excited cries of her well-wishing subjects, but by the haunting screams of slaves put to death in ritualistic celebration of her rise to the throne.

Here was a queen whose life as a monarch had also begun in Africa, where Princess Elizabeth had likewise learnt that she was soon to be crowned queen.

The ghostly figure was that of an African queen whose terrifying hold over her people had lasted for over half a century and whose first sixty years on the throne had been marked by the presentation of a diamond – a precious stone fabled to be the biggest in the world.

Her image was destined never to be removed from its sacred resting place and her heart was supposed to beat for a thousand years.

Steal the head of the Benin queen and she would strike back in vengeance at the heart of any man who cast his avaricious eyes upon her, spearing him in cardiac arrest, piercing the heart of the son of the taker, whilst his sons by the Devil be won.

Robert's twin sons had been born as the result of an unnatural, incestuous coupling of half-brother and half-sister.

In their turn, they had entered the world not naturally, but by Caesarean section – born an unnatural, unholy twosome. Immediately after their birth, they had been taken away and separated from their mother – only Agnes's twin baby boys could not be separated from each other.

235

Horrifically, they were joined together each in a God forsaken image of its twin, forced throughout their short lives each to reflect the other. Agnes's two babies had laid together in one hospital cot; they were Siamese twins conjoined at the chest, with only one beating heart between them.

And then the beating ceased.

Thou taketh my head
And blood will be shed
A spear in the heart
The thief will depart
Death to the receiver
Be he not a believer
The son of the taker
Will meet his maker
The sons of the son
By the Devil be won

Chapter 33

Jo left school at the age of fifteen after a fairly undistinguished educational career. True, Jo could spell and add up columns of figures as well as the next person – but only when it suited and dealing with such mundane matters hardly warranted Jo's attention at all. Jo could never apply any thought to something that was of no interest.

Not that this meant that Jo was a disappointment as far as Mary was concerned, for Jo's destiny had long been mapped out.

Jo was the sole representative of the next generation into whose hands the hotel chain would eventually fall and Jo was being groomed for that role as the only heir to a fortune, which was now completely held in female hands.

Andrina had failed to find herself a husband – no doubt due to the fact that the wasp's nest upon which her tongue rested had stung so many of her would-be suitors into seeking other jam pots around which to buzz, afraid that if they slipped over the edge, the screw-top lid would come crashing down upon them, trapping them forever through her crushing remarks.

Drunkenness had been stamped upon the life of Mary's elder daughter. She was now divorced from George, who no longer called upon Andrina to share her bed and the latest saucy secrets which, in a hotel, were never in short supply.

Anne was hardly ever sober enough these days to perform any useful function around the hotel, whilst Mary's daughter-in-law, Agnes had barely spoken to her after the birth and subsequent death of her twin boys.

She was fearful of the words that she longed to lash out against the woman who had stood by and allowed her to marry in innocence and repent at leisure.

Agnes would never marry again – of that there was little doubt in anybody's mind.

Grandmother must have realised that, in Jo, all hope for the future rested, for as surely as both her daughters had proved to be a disappointment to her, so surely did she invest in Jo – her only grandchild a hope for the future and a continuation of the family dynasty, which had been cruelly robbed of so many members.

Jo now knew about the adoption which had taken place back in 1944, when a fairly large sum of money had been imparted to the owner of a private Glasgow clinic – in a deal that took no account of any adoption laws which existed during the period of the Second World War.

The then authorities presumably had more important things to think about than the actions of a black marketeer, such as Robert, whose only real interest in such deals had been in lining his own pocket.

Jo, of course, did not appreciate that a much larger sum of money had been taken out of Grandmother's savings account, allegedly to be paid over to Jo's natural mother, but which had mostly found its way into the back pocket of

Robert's trench coat, after he had deposited a suitable wad of banknotes into the hands of the less than questioning owner of the private Glasgow nursing home where Jo had been born.

Jo had figured something of what had occurred all those years ago, but had never really understood exactly what had happened, despite Andrina's efforts to drop dark, veiled hints from time to time, often referring to the child's acquisition as a "bad buy".

Jo had guessed too that it had been Grandmother, who had come up with the cash, knowing a little of Uncle Robert's chosen wartime "profession" from snippets of information gleaned from Willie the chauffeur.

Jo had fathomed that it had been Robert's responsibility to deliver part of the roll of banknotes in exchange for the tiny bundle of pink flesh that was to grow up into the person who faced Jo in the bathroom mirror every morning.

In a sense, Jo was the child that very soon nobody in the family had very much time for except, of course, for Grandmother.

Andrina never ceased her spiteful remarks, which Anne was seldom in a fit state to notice and Agnes, for all her apparent kindness, appeared to be running the hotel almost single-handedly and had little time to relax, or indulge anyone at all – least of all herself.

Anne spent most of Jo's early childhood and teenage years too drunk to realise that Jo was there at all, refusing to acknowledge any personal responsibility for the youngster, falling into an increasingly maudlin state from the moment that her second husband, George, had finally walked out the door of the hotel that he managed in the Scottish Borders and which she seldom visited. He had disappeared with a suitcase full of clothes and simply never returned.

In his wallet was a cheque for £2,000 made out to him from the account belonging to the Carlton Hall Hotel. For a sum of money like that he could keep his mouth shut and the secret that he harboured was safe from being revealed to the one person to whom it really mattered – and that person was Jo!

* * * * * * * * * *

Grandmother did her best to compensate for her eldest daughter's complete lack of interest in Jo, quelling questions about the youngster's real father and mother with bland assumptions that sometimes these things happened in wartime and maybe the mother had simply been unable to keep her child for a variety of reasons.

As Jo grew older and more wise to the ways of the world, other schoolmates would be questioned about their own upbringing.

One of Jo's classroom friends had described in graphic detail how she had been the result of a brief fling between an Italian prisoner of war and a mother she had never known, being adopted whilst she was still a babe in arms.

The girl's mother had been living in a small, close-knit community and quite how she had managed to conceal her pregnancy was beyond Jo's understanding.

'Was she married?' Jo had asked inquisitively, afterwards learning that the woman's husband had known what was going on whilst he was away fighting in

238

North Africa and hadn't cared a jot – as long as there was cash in the bank after the birth and the subsequent adoption!

It had seemed a strange thing to reveal to a daughter not yet past her fifteenth birthday, but it had been explained to Jo's school friend, when she had finally met her birth mother for the first time in details which seemed unworthy of the telling and which, probably, only served to assuage the mother's conscience.

Like Jo, the girl had never met either her real father, or the man whom her mother had been married to and who had probably lived through the experience of the years that followed the Second World War, with only the immediate prospect of having to find work and a host of bitter war memories, shattered hopes and a demob suit to prepare him for a return to civilian life.

It wasn't until some time after Uncle Robert's tragic death that Jo found that what remained of the family did not really belong to Jo at all.

On that horrible day that Andrina finally spilt the black spotted beans of discontent, Jo's whole life changed, shifting from a carefree, comfortable existence to one of self doubt – although never one of self-imposed pity.

In those moments of grief Jo had but one person to turn to – the same person who stared back from the mirror glass as Jo's teeth were brushed each morning. Quite simply Jo had been forced to learn self reliance from an early age.

Jo never quite understood why some of the other children in the playground would keep their distance, labelling their classmate as being somehow "different".

Mostly they maintained an aloofness where Jo was concerned – apart from on the occasions when one of the chefs at the hotel had sneaked a bagful of home-baked biscuits into Jo's school satchel and which new-found friends would be anxious to share.

Jo's true birthright was learnt in the back of a black hearse – from which the coffin of Uncle Robert could be seen only by leaning over the cold leather seats.

Not surprisingly, it was from Andrina that Jo first learnt that entry into the family had been by adoption. What hurt Jo most of all was the knowledge that Mary's role of "Grandmother" was not one which she was truly entitled to play.

In the funeral hearse, surrounded by darkened windows for Jo the road ahead had seemed unclear in so many different ways.

On the day of Robert's funeral, Jo's face had been wet with tears and through those sobbing tears it had hardly been possible to see the way out of that sombrely toned vehicle. Jo had climbed into the back seat, sandwiched between Anne and Andrina.

Uncle Robert had been the closest thing Jo had ever had to a father and he had died when Jo was still very much a child. Jo's paternal rock was crushed as surely as if it had been blown up with dynamite.

Jo had sought Georgina's company that day, insisting that she too occupied a place in the funeral car and Jo had cried out in shock and horror when Andrina had metaphorically slapped some sense into the child, casting the imaginary friend out of the car, whilst Anne said nothing at all in her child's defence.

'You're lucky you're allowed in this car yourself. You're not even family, so shut up and stop snivelling, you little brat!' Andrina had snapped viciously.

Jo remembered Andrina grabbing at the upper part of the black coat sleeve that Jo wore for the horrible occasion of Uncle Robert's funeral.

Jo had vowed never to wear that coat again.

Likewise, Jo had never wanted to be squashed into the back of that black monster of a car beside a mother who didn't care and an aunt whose hatred was all too apparent.

It may have been a Rolls Royce, the like of which few of Jo's school friends would ever get to travel, but the gloomy piped black leather seats were cracked and cold and offered no comfort at all on that dreadful day, which Jo would never forget.

Taking Anne's hand as the only source of solace, Jo found that it was shaking, although whether from grief, or alcoholic over-indulgence, it was hard to tell.

What had happened so tragically to poor Uncle Robert was impossible to come to terms with. Jo didn't even fully understand how he had died – only the fact that he wasn't there any more to provide his special avuncular brand of protection from the taunts of Andrina and to reassure Jo in so many different ways.

Jo didn't fully comprehend what was going on at the time, but now, years later, Jo understood only to well. Suddenly Jo was being forced to grow up and face up to the realities of a world which was full of hard work and with little time for self-indulgence. For someone used to getting all their own way as a child, it did not come easy.

For years Jo had been allowed to do virtually whatever pleased, being indulged by a whole bevy of hotel staff, who acted as additional aunts and uncles to the child and who were always ready to offer a degree of indulgence.

However, having reached the age of fifteen, Jo was expected to work in the hotel, to work hard and to set an example to other members of staff.

Jo continued to search for a father figure, for the one person who had been both father and friend was now rotting in a coffin in a nearby cemetery.

Jo would visit from time to time, taking maybe a little bunch of primroses, or daring to raid Grandmother's rose garden to place a single bloom at the graveside of the man whom Jo so sorely wished had been a father, as well as a friend.

Most of all, in this female-dominated domain, Jo longed for a father. Jo wanted someone to look up to – someone to follow and especially someone to love and be loved by. Happily, that person was just about to walk into Jo's life.

Chapter 34

Jo emerged from the back office into the main reception area one afternoon, having been employed full time in the hotel for just over a year. Jo was aware that Grandmother was speaking to a tall, dark-haired man who had just arrived by taxi.

Something about him set Jo's sixteen-year-old heart on fire. It was a feeling that Jo had never known before and there was no describing how it felt – just a very special emotion.

It was something about the way he moved that immediately attracted Jo's attention. Jo stood transfixed, unable to avert the gaze, which centred upon the stranger. Jo strained to hear the words that were being spoken, unable to catch more than half a sentence.

He was booking into the hotel with a calm air of authority. Jo was able to detect a hint of what sounded like an American accent, making the stranger seem even more mysterious – even more deliciously desirable.

Here was this man who Jo had never met before, never had the chance to speak to, yet there was something in his gracious, sinewy movements that attracted Jo like no other man had ever done before that very moment – that precious, glowing moment, when all the hairs at the back of Jo's neck began to tingle and a warm sensation settled down and decided to stay a while.

Immaculately attired in an airline uniform, he smiled at Jo over the top of Grandmother's surprisingly erect shoulder blades, as she turned the leather bound registration book round to face the newly arrived hotel guest.

Something about him was strangely familiar to her. Grandmother couldn't put her finger on it, but there was definitely something about him that reminded Mary of the past – or maybe the present. She didn't really know.

All she was bothered about was why she was having to act as hotel receptionist, with no sign of Nan, who normally stood behind the desk, all warm, welcoming smiles and cheerful, happy hospitality.

Neither did she understand why Jo, who was quite capable of booking the guest in, was lolling around in the background, as if afraid to step forward out of the shadows and take command of the situation.

Jo remained rooted to the spot, which was generally regarded as Agnes's domain. Soft, gentle Nan with her kind words and ready smile for everyone – so unlike Andrina, who resolutely stood guard over her own territory behind the bar, like a female wolf constantly searching amongst the drinkers for the right alpha male to lead a pack of which she was the undisputed alpha female.

Andrina was always on her guard, ready to match any would-be adversary with red-blooded tooth and claw and a tongue laced with acid.

It was the month of August – a whole three months short of Jo's seventeenth birthday. Jo had never known the love of a man and certainly not the physical kind. Yet here was Jo imagining this was someone very special: the object of a fantastic feeling that was beyond explanation.

Jo was confused. Totally confused.

Was it right to stick around now that the stranger so obviously knew that he was being watched by someone half his age? Did Jo risk him becoming aware that every flicker of his dark eyes was being carefully studied, every downcast shadow cast by those black eye lashes being minutely scrutinised.

Suddenly, Jo was at once fearful of just how much those thoughts and feelings were being revealed to this dark, handsome stranger and yet even more afraid to move an inch! Was it really wise to stick around any longer?

The delicious danger was all in the man's eyes, threatening and promising, tantalising and teasing, taxing and tormenting, driving Jo to new heights of pleasure, as his every movement was followed and recorded to be replayed over and over again in Jo's mind, like a LP record with its needle stuck in the groove.

Oh, yes, Jo knew all right. Jo understood with all the earnest longing of a sixteen-year-old and couldn't bear the thought of being dragged away.

Suddenly, and quite intoxicatingly, Jo believed that it really could happen. Love at first sight!

Anything was possible, if you really set your heart at it and, at that moment, Jo's heart was set as firmly as Jo's mind was resolved to captivate this attractive looking man, who was old enough to be Jo's father.

Yes, suddenly, Jo had faith – there was no reason to believe that this man could not be made to feel that he belonged to the lovestruck teenager, who simply could not avert those staring eyes.

After several heart stopping moments, Grandmother turned around to ask Jo to summons a porter, noticing that her teenaged grandchild, so normally helpful and volunteering, had not even offered a cheery "Good afternoon" to the man, who had just signed in for a week's accommodation.

Jo pretended to be busy handling the long stems of an armful of gladioli that one of the gardeners had just brought in from the walled garden, snipping at the stiff stalks and sword shaped leaves, stripping the leaves from the base of the stems, distractedly placing them, one by one, in a haphazard fashion, making no attempt to arrange them in the cut glass vase that always occupied the far end of the reception desk.

Two of the chambermaids passed by, pausing beside Jo, both pairs of eyes transfixed by the handsome guest, who stood in quiet conversation with Jo's grandmother.

'Gosh he's good looking. I wouldn't mind turning his bed covers down for him tonight,' said one.

'I think she fancies him,' the other girl confided in an aside to Jo.

'I do think he's rather good looking,' she added, almost by way of providing confirmation of Jo's own salacious thoughts.

'And what about you, Jo? I bet you've never done "it", have you? Nearly seventeen years old and still a virgin is my guess.'

'Oh, do go away and annoy somebody else,' responded Jo irritably, realising that the chambermaid had struck a chord – a virgin chord that Jo longed to be severed.

No, she definitely wasn't the only one in whom the tall, dark stranger inspired thoughts of a carnal nature, but how could she possibly understand Jo's thoughts and feelings and, most of all, how could she comprehend Jo's desires?

All agog and hinting a whiff of intrigue – scandal even, the bolder and more talkative of the two chambermaids flicked at the wooden panelling on one side of the reception desk with her feather duster in an attempt to remove a few imaginary specks of pollen dropped from the flower spikes of the gladioli and now supposedly sprinkled over the intricate carvings.

She stooped to pick up a fallen petal, keeping her head bent low to the task, as if a hint of scandal could only be enjoyed to the full from a low physical position, emanating from the ground from which all manner of life sprung, filtering upwards into the mainstream of public awareness.

If only she had known who it was who most fervently desired the dark-haired visitor.

At that moment, if Jo really cared to admit it, what Jo desired most of all was to poke the poor girl in the eye with one of the long-stemmed gladioli in an action that could only be attributed to jealousy.

Fancy him? Oh, yes, Jo fancied him. Jo was happy to admit it – but only in secret.

Who else could Jo confide in, but the one person who could be totally relied upon never to betray Jo's innermost thoughts and feelings. Jo was that person – the one person who Jo had long ago learnt to trust as the perfect confidant.

Just exactly who was he? Just one of the guests? No, for Jo he could never be just that. And to think that Jo didn't even know his name.

Jo would wait until later, flipping over the pages of the great leather bound ledger filled with Agnes's impeccably neat handwriting until the sought after entry was found, with Grandmother's hastily pencilled "Room 7" marked in the margin.

The occupant of the lucky numbered room was much younger than Agnes or Andrina. Jo guessed that he was about the same age as Moira, recognising too that he was old enough to have been Jo's father and that any relationship between them would have been frowned upon.

Jo still wanted him – longed for him even, wanting the touch of his body. Besides, Jo simply could not admit that it was just their age difference that made the very thought of what they might have done together so very wrong.

Here was Jo falling for the charms of a stranger in a time-honoured fashion. Right at that moment what Jo desired most in all the world was for Jo's own honour to be broken, defences abandoned – a virgin no more.

'Sign here, will you please,' said Grandmother, turning the vast visitor registration book around to face the newly arrived guest. 'I've given you Room seven. It's one of our nicest rooms. You'll find the door ajar and the key hanging from the lock inside.'

Jo imagined being able to trip along the hotel corridor, tap gently on the door and slip unnoticed into the room, quietly closing the door and with it closing the door on Jo's virginity.

The stranger signed the guest book, without looking at what he wrote – a long, languid scrawl of a signature that looped and curled across the page.

He turned to face the wide staircase, depositing his suitcase beside the newly arrived porter, who had appeared without Jo's beckoning.

'Would you care for a cup of tea in the residents' lounge, whilst the porter delivers your bags to your room, sir?' Jo asked, at last finding words – at last finding a way to prolong the interlude.

'I don't mind if I do,' he had replied, immediately following Jo, who had emerged from behind the reception desk – all thought of flower arranging forgotten.

The man of Jo's dreams struck out unhurriedly across the mosaic-patterned, tiled reception area. His slow moving pace oozed style and sexuality at every step.

Grandmother stopped for a moment to watch the departure of the guest with Jo, smoothing down the pleats of her immaculately pressed tartan skirt and adjusting the hook of her pearl necklace, which had slid a fraction of an inch towards the front of her throat.

Yes, there was definitely something vaguely familiar about him, but she still couldn't place her thoughts.

The glass-panelled swing doors leading into the residents' lounge swung open and closed behind the twin receding figures of her grandchild and the man, who had so enraptured the child – the child who was a child no more.

The lounge with its deep, comfortable sofas and a dozen or more armchairs stood in slight array – the untidy aftermath of a lively Masons meeting earlier in the afternoon.

Silver teapots were abandoned on a variety of small tables and cups and saucers littered every available space.

Moira, helped by Meg, who had been seconded from laundry duties, was clearing up the mess before the hotel guests began to assemble for afternoon tea, assisted by Agnes, Anne and Andrina.

Five pairs of female eyes turned away from their task and one woman stood staring in wide-eyed astonishment at the stranger, who was really no stranger at all, even if it had been years since they had last met.

A silver tea tray sprang from her hands and clattered noisily on to the floor.

* * * * * * * * * *

Later, scanning through the hotel ledger, Jo found that ten names were scrawled under the heading of Caledonian Airways Ltd – five male and five female.

Jo took no notice of the surnames, noting only the Christian names of the five male crew members: Arthur, Allen, Gerald, Thomas and, finally, Clive.

Maybe the object of Jo's longing was the captain – the one who held everything in control. Then again, maybe he wasn't in control after all – no more than Jo was in control of the mounting feeling of excitement over the next few days every time the handsome guest walked down the staircase to breakfast, or raised his dark eyebrows over his morning newspaper.

Born to lose, Jo might have been. Born to a mother, who didn't care enough to keep her baby. Born to an unknown father, who Jo longed to seek. No, this was one opportunity that Jo was not intending to lose out on. Now was a chance to awaken Jo's burgeoning sexual desires.

Here was a glamorous stranger that had swept into Jo's life. True, he sometimes regarded Nan with a strange look in his eyes and she, in her turn, met Jo's contemplative observation with a silence that suggested that something special occasionally passed between them.

Jo could do it! Jo could creep past the sheep grazing on the heather-clad moorlands in the landscape painting that hung half way up the stairs, which Grandmother had purchased at an auction sale all those years ago at Jo's bidding.

Jo could follow the course of the brightly buffed and shining brass stair rods right to his door, knock lightly and, before anyone knew what was going on, abandon everything and slip beneath the cool, candy-striped cotton sheets.

Yes, Jo would have been quite happy to have stolen quietly into Room number seven – perhaps some time a little after midnight when Frank, the night porter, was safely ensconced in his chair in the kitchen, beneath the row of brass call bells, warmed by the vast central heating boiler and the last drop of brandy in one of the hotel bar's optics that, strangely, none of the guests ever ordered for themselves!

Jo was only sixteen – officially too young for the taste of a glass of brandy, but not too young for something much more intoxicating to be pressed against tender, inexperienced lips.

As Jo was to discover, the object of such ardent desire went by the name of Clive – Clive Thompson and he beckoned Jo like a rich, mature wine. So much older than Jo, yet bright and refreshing and as effervescent as a glass of Jo's adopted mother's oft imbibed gin and tonic.

'Are you going to go out and pick some more gladioli, Jo?' asked Moira one bright, sunny afternoon towards the middle of Clive's week-long stay.

'There's not enough here for the vase on top of the piano,' Moira added, interrupting Jo's reverie, punctuating Jo's dreams, piercing through Jo's sexual awakening – that revelation about yourself by yourself.

'And while you're about it, you can do the display, as you're so much better at flower arranging than I am,' she had continued.

Summer was at its hazy height; the roses were in full, heavily scented bloom and the gladioli that had been staked by the gardeners were standing to perfection, each sharply bladed stem poking up from the virgin soil, proud and erect.

Jo observed the array of little pink trumpets – each bursting and blossoming forth, every one of them like a horn just waiting to be blown. Swaying flower heads gently unsettled by the breeze in a bed of somebody else's making, petals buffeting and shuddering.

Others, unstaked and neglected by human touch, lay flat and limp on the ground, withering without the grasp of a human hand around their stems, never plucked, but simply allowed to distribute their seed on the passing wind.

Jo had taken a pair of secateurs from the drawer where Grandmother always kept them. When she had the time, Jo's grandmother delighted in tending her roses – her deep red, heavenly scented roses, which were set aside from the rest and which she only ever cut on special occasions.

'Do remember to cut all the stems to the same length,' reminded Moira.

Jo needed no reminding.

'And don't go picking any of your grandmother's roses. You know she goes mad if anyone touches them!'

Jo could never simply walk out of the hotel and wander around the grounds with no particular task to be performed. Like the rest of the staff, Jo was never allowed a moment's respite, never permitted to be off guard for a moment and never allowed to relax. Grandmother simply wouldn't stand for such inactivity.

No, you had to be doing something. It was always the same. And if there wasn't anything to do, you found something … quickly. You found someone who needed you to perform a little task for them, or with whom you could pretend that you urgently needed to exchange a few words.

Secateurs in hand, Jo walked straight past the serried ranks of gladioli behind the old brick wall that had once formed a vegetable garden, seeing past their sprouting floral erections.

Jo went straight to Grandmother's special rose garden that lay beyond the centuries old yew hedge. Here was where all her most prized specimens were bedded down together.

It was through the gap in the tangled yew branches, in a spot where they did not lace together too well that Jo spied the canvas-striped deck chair and the person who sat there, quietly observing, as silently and as stealthily as Jo held the returned gaze.

It was Clive.

Here was the mysteriously enchanting stranger, stripped to the waist, enjoying the filtered rays of sunshine that brushed his dark, hairy chest, setting the growth of hair aglow, so that, in places, it was tinged almost blond.

From where Jo was standing, half hidden, it was not possible to see what he was wearing below waist level, but Jo guessed that it was very little – a pair of khaki shorts perhaps, revealing taut calf muscles.

Jo remained transfixed, observing a darkly forested trail to where the bush grew thicker and more luxuriant!

Here was the man who had set Jo's passions aflame and he was all on his own: smiling and waiting. Waiting for Jo to make a move?

Jo moved out of sight, deliberately choosing the path that gave access to the rose garden from behind where Clive sat. Jo gripped the secateurs and snipped at several of the rose stems, gathering an armful of them together before passing back along the path.

Jo understood only too well that it was a path towards sin and not just the sin of picking Grandmother's beloved roses! Jo knew that Grandmother would never sanction the sacrifice of her precious red roses to anyone outside the family – not least for the hotel guest who Jo had come to regard as the only man in the world.

It was a path that led to sin and temptation in more ways than one – a path that was taking Jo exactly along the route that Jo longed to go. Quite where it was leading only time would tell!

Quite how far it would go, Jo hadn't begun to consider!

Jo approached ever closer, rendered cautious by the sight of Clive's half-naked body. Jo tried – not too hard – to prevent Clive from noticing that, all the while, Jo was looking straight at him.

It was perfectly obvious and Clive shifted in his deck chair, turning completely around, until he was staring Jo straight in the face. Clive called Jo over.

Jo's pulse quickened, drumming time with an over-active heartbeat. Soon Jo was standing over him, not knowing what to say, not daring to look up and certainly not daring to look down.

Eventually Jo's eyes strayed from Clive's chest over his firm stomach and then downwards still further. There the eyes lingered.

Jo's stood entranced, loosening the grasp on Grandmother's red roses until, one by one, they tumbled out of Jo's trembling hands. One of the blooms landed on Clive's chest.

Jo leant over him to remove the single bloom, which lay across Clive's torso. A thorn had caught in the hairs of his chest. Jo couldn't extract it without touching the mass of black, curly hair, without tugging at it in an attempt to disentangle it – trying to prevent causing pain. Jo was rendered speechless.

Clive said nothing.

All Jo could focus on was the single red rose, with its cascading petals brushing gently against Clive's heart. As if in slow motion, Jo became aware of something else, as the man in the deck chair lifted his hands away from where they rested at the level of his crotch.

Fascinated, Jo detected the slight rise in the khaki material of Clive's shorts, as the fabric stretched and tautened.

Softly Clive asked Jo's name.

'It's Jo.'

'Well, Jo, is this for me?' he enquired, stooping to rescue the rose and brushing a few of the loose petals to the ground.

'I thought it was more usual for a gentleman to give roses to a lady,' Clive quietly intoned.

Jo was lost for words, especially when Clive took Jo's hand and pressed the stem of the rose into it, returning it to the giver, after carefully and methodically stripping away any remaining thorns.

'Were you picking those roses for someone special?' queried Clive.

'Oh, yes,' thought Jo. Someone very special, but decided it was best not to voice any such thoughts. 'What are you doing here?' Jo asked eventually, overcome with curiosity and the need to say something – to say anything at all. 'Is this your first stay at Carlton Hall?'

'No, I stayed here many years ago. It was being used in the war as a dormitory for convalescing airmen. I couldn't have been much older than I suppose you are now.'

'Why did you stay here? Were you hurt?'

'No, I was stationed in Scotland – up in the North East near Aberdeen. I came to Edinburgh in search of my mother. I never found her then.'

'You never found her *then*?' asked Jo.

'No, but I guess, much to my surprise, just when I had stopped looking, I found her – right in the very place that I had come to look all those years ago.

'It's strange how fate can bring you back to somewhere – somewhere you never thought eventually to find what you were looking for,' replied Clive wistfully, immediately feeling at one with the youngster who, little did he realise it, likewise knew no real mother, nor father.

'What's her name?' asked Jo.

'It's Anne. I'm her son. She dumped me on the steps of an orphanage out in Canada when I was only a few weeks old. My father was called Cameron – a good old-fashioned Scottish name I guess.

'I visited him once, not long after I found out that he was my father. He refused to acknowledge me as his son. He swore he had never even met my mother – far less did he ever admit that he had been married to her. He thought he was a smart ass, telling me a pack of lies, but I knew who he really was. I guess I just wanted him to admit it.

'He died a few years ago. I never really knew him. He certainly never wanted to know me. It was my uncle who finally told me the truth about what had happened soon after I was born.'

'And you've met this … Anne again since you arrived here?' asked Jo soothingly, remembering the afternoon of Clive's arrival and the apparent shock which it had caused.

'Yes, I've spoken to her, but how could I tell her who I really am. How does someone of my age suddenly walk back into the life of his mother after all those years? I guess she's got her own life to lead, but I see she shares my uncle's love of the bottle – my father's too by all account.'

'So that was what the clattering silver tea tray was all about on the day you arrived and I led you into the lounge for tea. I understand now,' said Jo, desperately trying to come to terms with the situation, speaking to this man who was almost a brother, a kindred spirit, but surely no relation at all.

'I doubt it,' replied Clive. 'I doubt you understand at all. It wasn't my mother who recognised me.'

'Then who did?' implored Jo inquisitively.

'That,' replied Clive, 'is another story. Maybe, one day if I ever get to know you well enough, I'll tell you. I take it that your grandmother owns this hotel?' asked Clive, attempting to change the subject.

'Yes, I guess so,' replied Jo.

'And what are you doing right now?'

'I've been sent out to cut flowers for the dining room.'

'Red roses?' asked Clive.

Suddenly Jo remembered.

'No, not red roses – not roses at all. Gladioli!'

'It's an easy mistake to make,' said Clive, laughing.

'Perhaps I can help you? I think I know the difference between the two,' he suggested, as he bent down to help gather up the fallen blooms, his strong hand folding over Jo's and noticing the strange birthmark.

As he did so, their fingers momentarily entwined.

'I should be getting back,' replied Jo. 'Grandmother will be furious, if she sees me here talking to you and if the dining tables are not all ready by six o'clock, when she makes her rounds of inspection.'

'A typical tyrant is she then?' Clive asked.

'I guess so.'

'Aren't you going to take this one too?' Clive asked gently, surveying the last of the blooms that he now held in his outstretched hand.

'No, it's for you,' Jo almost shouted, suddenly afraid of being caught out with one of the freshly cut stems of Grandmother's precious roses.

Jo was even more fearful of being seen with the Canadian and without a single stem of gladioli to justify a long absence from the necessary preparation work to ensure that the hotel dining room was ready to receive its guests.

'Then, perhaps, we shall see each other later – after dinner maybe?' Clive asked Jo, more by way of an assurance, as their eyes met in an open embrace.

'How long are you staying for?'

'A few more days.'

'Will you speak to my adopted mother again? If she's your real mother, you have to talk to her.'

'Did you say that she adopted you?'

'Yes.'

'So I guess that makes us two of a kind, you and I! Neither of our mothers really wanted us.'

Chapter 35

Jo made a point of hanging around the reception desk later that evening, pretending to be making a careful study of the guest book. Seemingly, Jo was so engrossed in studying the carefully scripted details that, at first, Clive's appearance besides one of the marble columns went unnoticed, until he began to whistle.

Jo glanced up immediately.

Clive was casually dressed in black slacks and a white shirt with epaulettes at the shoulders, denoting that it was part of his uniform.

'I've never met a pilot before,' said Jo softly as a conversational gambit.

'I'm not a pilot. I'm the navigator,' replied Clive.

'Oh,' said Jo, adding a touch too plaintively, 'you will be staying at the hotel again, won't you?'

'Maybe,' Clive replied non-committally.

'Where do you live?' asked Jo.

'I've been living in East Africa for the past two years, but I fly all over the world.'

'Will you be flying back to Africa soon?' Jo asked, once again revealing a degree of angst.

'You ask too many questions,' said Clive, without an ounce of condemnation in his voice.

'I suppose that's due to the way I was brought up. As a child, I was never allowed to talk to the guests. Grandmother didn't approve. She says I always ask too many questions.'

'So why are you talking to me? After all, I am a guest here,' Clive replied smoothly.

'Do you object?' asked Jo.

'No, I don't have any objections,' he replied.

Jo remembered how Clive had taken Jo's hand that afternoon, allowing Jo's fingers to brush against the fabric of his shorts.

'How old are you?' he asked, whilst looking straight into Jo's eyes.

'I'm sixteen.'

'A sixteen-year-old who brings a man flowers and drops red roses into his lap. Now that's what I call different!'

'Stop it!' Jo implored.

However, Jo hadn't wanted Clive to stop at all. At that moment, all Jo wanted was to do something that Jo had never done before, but something which Jo had thought about doing for what seemed like a very long time.

Jo had never done anything like this before, never reached up to a man, never looked him in the eyes – never been bold enough to … Jo suddenly felt shocked by such thoughts, at last gaining a grip on reality – the reality of what was truly happening.

'Please don't say anything,' Jo begged, feeling totally confused, suddenly experiencing a wide ranging mixture of emotions, wanting something to happen and, at the same time, not wanting it at all. 'My grandmother would kill me if she found out.'

'If she found out what?' enquired Clive flirtatiously.

'What I'm thinking right now,' replied Jo.

'And exactly what are you thinking?' asked Clive, with mock innocence.

That was enough. Jo fled back behind the hotel reception desk in terror and with a face which was flushed pink with embarrassment. Luckily, Nan wasn't around to witness Jo's discomfiture.

Minutes later Grandmother advanced upon Jo down the broad, richly carpeted staircase. She did not waste any time in summoning Jo's attention.

She was entertaining some special guests that evening and wanted Jo to serve in the main dining room, together with the new head waiter, accompanied by Moira and several of the young waitresses.

'I can't work tonight, Grandmother, it's my night off.'

'Not any more is isn't,' chimed in Andrina spitefully as she passed by. She knew that Jo would do exactly as Grandmother instructed and that she would brook no insurrection.

'You can come upstairs and help me choose what to wear tonight, if you like, Jo,' announced Grandmother, in an attempt to ward off any sharp exchange of words between her daughter and her grandchild.

'How about a shroud – quite the most appropriate thing at her age,' said Andrina, mouthing the words under her breath, for once not daring to utter her thoughts in sufficient volume for Grandmother to be able to hear them.

Mary had become slightly deaf in recent years, but had learnt to foretell most of Andrina's cutting remarks and was always ready with a quick retort.

Andrina had begun to harbour thoughts that, one day, the Carlton Hall Hotel might be hers. Anne was hardly capable of handling any such inheritance and that only left Jo between her and her ambitions.

'Come on, Grandmother, let's go upstairs and raid your wardrobe together. How about the black dress you bought in Monte Carlo when Grandad Charlie was still alive – the one with all the frilly lace around the collar. It looks good with your diamond necklace. You are going to wear your diamonds tonight, aren't you, Grandmother?'

'What's the point of you telling her what to wear?' chipped in Andrina. 'She'll wear what she wants. She doesn't need some silly sixteen-year old to tell her how to dress herself.'

'Oh, Jo, don't listen to your aunt!' said Nan from behind the reception desk. 'Go upstairs with her. Just keep her happy and out of everybody's way for half an hour or so.'

As Jo followed Grandmother, Clive passed them on the stairs. He was wearing a black leather jacket and slacks that tapered sharply in at the ankle.

He dropped Jo a broad wink which, for one horrible moment, Jo thought wasn't lost on Mary, but then Clive hurried past the flock of sheep munching their heather contentedly in the painting half way up the stairs.

Clive disappeared into the bar.

All Jo wanted to do was to stop and talk to him, but a pressing engagement with Mary's wardrobe beckoned. It was a little room situated off her bedroom, in which all her gowns were neatly suspended from wooden coat hangers.

Shortly Mary's ensemble for the evening was laid out on the brass bed and she shooed Jo from the room.

'She'll be down in ten minutes,' Jo announced, taking a cue from the Chinese lacquered grandfather clock that stood majestically in the downstairs reception hall and whose eight chimes during an evening would always herald Grandmother's regal descent down the staircase, as immaculately attired as ever.

Anne, not surprisingly, was sitting at the bar when Jo trotted downstairs, a gin and tonic glued to her right hand. She was nibbling peanuts which did little to soak up the amount of alcohol that she had already consumed that evening.

She looked straight through Jo, seemingly unaware of the teenager's presence, or perhaps too drunk to care. Jo wasn't bothered. It was Nan who bought Jo sharply back to reality.

'I hope you remembered the flowers for the dining room. You know they'll be hell to pay, if they're not there when your grandmother comes downstairs,' she warned.

Jo cursed. Mary always maintained an eagle eye over everything, bawling out any member of staff, or family member alike, who failed to perform the smallest task.

She hated anyone "letting the side down", as she termed it. She had always been the same, only recently she had begun to install her standards in Agnes too, who could be relied upon as her second sight – a back up, if ever one was needed, to ensure that everything was staged to perfection.

'Yes … I mean, no,' flustered Jo. 'They're still in the kitchen. Gladioli. I'll go and fetch them.'

Jo had lied, rushing out of reception into the kitchen and grabbing a pair of the chef's scissors from the worktop in passing.

It was a glorious summer's evening and Jo was glad of the remaining light, hacking away at the thick stems of the gladioli. Suddenly Jo was aware of someone standing by Grandmother's precious roses. It was Clive.

'Can I borrow your scissors for a moment?' he asked.

Wordlessly, Jo handed them over.

Clive stooped to cut one of Grandmother's heavenly scented blooms, stripping the stem of its thorns, before handing it to Jo, as a single red petal fluttered to the ground in the still evening air.

Clive's smile was clearly visible, as Jo stood up and faced him from amongst the gladioli.

'Jo, what on earth are you doing out there?' called Agnes from the back door. 'Your grandmother will be downstairs any minute.'

'I'm coming …' Jo replied, adding quietly to Clive standing in the shadows of the rose arbour, '… to your room tonight!'

Clive didn't reply. Instead he simply stepped to one side of the path. Jo hacked at the broad, brittle stems, hurriedly gathering a huge bouquet of bright pink trumpet-like blooms. More importantly, Jo clutched a single rose – a rose grown by Grandmother and presented by Clive.

Jo held it close for a long moment.

Clive had slipped away behind the thick yew hedge. Jo was left wondering what to do with the prize.

'I'm coming to your room tonight,' Jo repeated softly to no one other than the speaker of the words.

By the time Jo reached the hotel kitchen, Mary was already doing her rounds. Her sight might not have been what it once was, but it did not stop her from noticing the dirty cup and saucer left in the residents' lounge, nor the half empty bowl of peanuts on the bar – the remainder of its contents having been consumed by Anne as a sponge to mop up the gin.

Not for the first time it was good old Nan who took control of the situation, making sure that the crystal vase that always adorned the top of the piano in the dining room was already filled with water and sitting on one of the chef's benches in the hotel kitchen, so that Jo could plonk the floral gatherings into it and rush it into the dining room seconds before Grandmother's arrival.

'Tell Jo that the flowers in the dining room aren't arranged very nicely tonight. They're certainly not up to Jo's usual standard,' Mary informed the new head waiter.

Jo accepted the rebuke, which was rightfully due. There was still just enough time to check that Anne had been consigned to her room before Mary's special guests arrived at the appointed hour of eight o'clock and before the other guests began to filter into the dining room.

So often these days it was Jo's job to propel Anne up to her bedroom, before the guests started to fill up the dining room and in an effort to ensure that there was still some gin left to be served in the bar!

She might have been Jo's adopted mother, but Jo despised her when she got herself into one of her drunken states – something which happened all too often these days.

That night, knowing that Anne had already vacated her favourite bar stool, Jo went upstairs to her bedroom, opened the door and entered. Anne was lying on the bed, face down, fully clothed. Jo looked at the clock. It was twenty past eight. She was sound asleep. Immediately Jo smelt the alcoholic fumes which filled the room.

Anne could be such a kind and thoughtful person when she was sober but, these days, her moments of sobriety were becoming less and less. Jo leaned across the bed and kissed her on the top of her head, before retiring quietly from the room. Jo had no need to tread softly: Anne would not wake up again until the morning.

Jo began to walk back downstairs. Clive was about to enter the dining room. All Jo wanted to do was to serve him – in the dining room, or more excitingly, later in the bedroom.

That evening Jo had the unenviable task of serving a rather unpleasant group of local councillors whom Grandmother was trying to impress, for it was they who held the key to the success of the hotel's latest planning development application.

Extra bedrooms were needed to cope with the increased flow of business being created by the expanding Edinburgh Airport.

Grandmother sat in state, as she habitually did on such occasions. She always wanted Jo to be the one to serve her. Jo loved her dearly and was happy to attend to her needs, but that night Jo had needs too and they could be summed up in one word – "Clive".

He had taken the little table set for two in the corner of the dining room. Jo had assumed that he was dining alone. For a while Clive sat on his own, lingering over a single glass of red wine and declining to allow any of the waitresses to take his order.

After he had been sitting there for some time, without placing an order, Jo guessed that he was expecting company.

Still as Clive sat there alone, he managed to catch Jo's attention with every passing nod and glance.

A group of four other air crew members were sitting at the table in the bay window – two smartly suited men of about the same age as Clive and two attractive looking girls. At a guess both girls were in their early twenties. Clive appeared not to want to share their company that evening.

Once all the guests had settled down with their main course, Jo took a few minutes' break. Clive remained with his place setting intact and the waitresses seemed to have given up on the idea that he might eventually agree to choose something from the menu.

Jo grabbed the moment and slipped out to reception. Nan had just come off duty, so it was easy to search out the master key from its hiding place, unseen by prying eyes.

Jo ran upstairs past the sheep in the portrait on the halfway landing, munching their way through their own main vegetarian dish of the day, displaying total disdain, as Jo dashed along the corridor, out down the fire escape and across to the flat above the old stable block.

Jo picked up the rose – Grandmother's red, red rose that had been presented in such a light-hearted gesture, the very bloom that Clive had selected and cut with the chef's sharp scissors, before Nan's urgent call had dragged Jo back to the kitchen and to the reality of getting on with the evening's chores.

A further petal flew to the floor, the rest were drooped and curved slightly downwards, lacking water. A tiny drop of white sap stained Jo's fingers.

The corridor leading to Room seven was deserted. Most of the hotel guests were in the dining room, many of them attacking the chef's speciality of wild venison – the animal that one of the waiters claimed he had hit with his car and which had been left to hang before being butchered by the head chef.

Jo inserted the master key in the lock and hurried over to the double bed with its yellow candlewick bedspread, placing the single rose on the bed and gently turning down the corner of the sheets.

Jo slipped out of the room again, the thick carpet deadening Jo's footsteps, with only the heather munching sheep as witnesses to this feckless gesture.

Jo returned to the dining room to find that Clive was no longer alone.

It was a few minutes past nine and it was Nan, dressed in a pastel-coloured two-piece suit, who had come to take her place at the small corner table. She sat opposite Clive, relaxed now, with a ready smile dancing on her lips, her duties complete for the day.

Jo guessed they were talking about the hotel. Nan rarely shared any male company these days and it seemed strange that she and Clive should choose to dine together.

Surely she would realise that her action in taking dinner with one of the male guests would the subject of a great deal of hotel gossip the following day.

Nan wouldn't be that brazen would she? Certainly not with Grandmother sitting just a few feet away with her group of councillors and not with the young waitresses who were serving them all – too eager to listen in on anything Nan had to say to her good-looking companion.

As much as Jo tried to do so, there was little chance of hearing very much of what was being said at the corner table. However, from what little Jo could discern, there seemed to be not much more than an exchange of pleasantries about the weather, about what the local golf club had to offer and how, when she got the chance, Agnes would indulge in a spot of fly fishing, to carry on the family tradition that Grandad Charlie had taught her.

Once more, Clive's ready smile flashed in Jo's direction. He seemed to be having difficulty in listening to the words Nan spoke to him over dinner. Still, it was all too much for Jo who, stupidly, imagined them talking about all manner of more intimate subjects.

She wasn't stupid, was Nan! However much she might have wished for a few moments alone with the handsome airline navigator, she wouldn't leave herself wide open to gossip and idle tittle-tattle from the chambermaids in the morning. Besides, whatever would Grandmother have to say about it?

No, surely it was all quite innocent, but was it?

Clive was casually dressed in a manner that Grandmother would not have approved. He rose from his seat only when one of the young women from the table in the bay window walked across the dining room to have a quiet word with him.

'Clive, I have to be at the airport by no later than six thirty tomorrow morning,' said the girl, whom Jo took to be one of the cabin staff, adding, 'so I'll say "Goodnight" now.'

Nan as competition for Clive's consideration Jo could deal with, but who was this new object of his contemplation? From sitting alone earlier in the evening, Clive certainly wasn't wanting for female attention right now. Jo felt a pang of jealousy: first Nan and now this girl – all claiming Clive's attention.

Jo's concentration was no longer on serving Grandmother's guests. Instead, Jo was intent on sidling past the corner table to catch a further snippet of conversation between Nan and Clive.

Grandmother's party of councillors was beginning to become restless. Clearly they were heading for the bar and several rounds of drinks at the hotel's expense before putting an end to the evening.

Finally Nan had bid "Goodnight" to her handsome dinner companion. The remainder of the party of airline crew members had presumably already taken themselves off to the bar for one last drink, before retiring to their beds in readiness for their early start the next morning. Only Clive remained.

Once again he sat alone at his corner table, as he sipped from a goblet of brandy in between mouthfuls of a rich roast Italian coffee.

Jo was too busy helping to clear the dirty coffee cups and saucers from Grandmother's table to notice him slip away. A shiny half crown beside the empty brandy glass was the only evidence of his passing. Would he show at the bar? Would Jo's eager anticipation show too clearly?

'It's all right, young Jo, we'll finish up here, if you want to get along to your bed,' said the head waiter.

Jo didn't wait to be told twice, leaving the rest of the silver-plated trays on the dumb waiter to await somebody else's attention. In passing, Jo noted that one of the silver salvers dimly reflected the hastily arranged vase of gladioli, the clarity of its reflection marred only by the marks of past food stains.

Grandmother would have something to say about that in the morning!

Upstairs Room number seven beckoned Jo like a bee to a honeypot! A pair of dark tan brogues sat outside Clive's door, awaiting the ministrations of the night porter.

Jo tapped lightly on the door. A few seconds later the key was heard turning in the lock. Jo waited a few moments longer, before slipping into the unlocked room unnoticed, undetected and unannounced. Clive lay on the bed, with a thick, white Egyptian cotton sheet loosely pulled up to the level of his navel – it was obvious that he was naked underneath.

Jo crossed the room silently. Jo wanted so much to be shown the way that night, in that room, by Clive and by him alone.

Grandmother's red rose that Jo had placed so carefully on the bed had disappeared, with only a telltale petal still dusting the pillow.

'I … I left a rose … for you. One of my grandmother's roses. What have you done with it?' Jo asked awkwardly, filling the void that had opened up between them.

'I thought you told me that your grandmother forbade anyone to touch them,' replied Clive.

Jo undressed quickly and slid into the bed beside Clive. Reaching beneath the light cotton sheet Jo's trembling hand felt something deliciously firm and erect.

'Is that what you're looking for, young Jo?'

Chapter 36

Jo awoke with the first rays of early morning light entering the room, raising the temperature of its interior and casting a warm glow across Jo's naked back. Sheets and blankets that had been tossed aside lay in a heap at the bottom of the bed.

Snuggled into Clive's chest, Jo didn't have need of their material warmth, or their protection, for Jo had all that could possibly be desired – the warmth of a man whose lovemaking had been real and ecstatic, executed with great tenderness.

It was a special kind of love that Jo had never known before – a warmth that could only emanate from a man's body.

They had made love several times that night, first in furious passion and then, more slowly, exploring each other's bodies. The bed smelt of sweat and lust; the sheets were still slightly damp and the pillow wet, where Jo had bitten into it in the first moment of extreme pain and exquisite pleasure.

Now was the time for tenderness – not the passions of the previous night. Instead, the lightest touch, a fleeting caress of the hand, moving sensuously, tense and tingling.

At last Jo knew the feel of a man's body. It was all that Jo had longed for. Now they simply cuddled up together, with Jo feeling the warm body of the man whose head nestled into the pillow just inches away.

Jo's fingers entwined in the dark mat of Clive's chest hair, twisting and curling the little tufts around and around between fingers that had ached to reach out and touch and now wended their sensuous way through a forest of sexual desire.

Jo's searching fingertips measured in circles, slowly working their way downwards to the special place where the hair grew thicker, more luxuriant, encircling the thing which was the very object of Jo's desire, touching once more, caressing and curious, waiting and wanting it again.

Slowly, the early morning light penetrated the room, just as Jo had been penetrated the night before.

Clive moved in his sleep. Unconsciously, he took Jo into his strong, muscular arms.

Jo thought that Clive must have awoken, but the continuous rhythmic breathing told its own tale of early morning contentment – that very special part of the day balanced between sleep and wakefulness. Together they lay in the comfortable embrace that could only ever exist between two lovers, who had known each other so intimately, probing each other's bodies in every possible way.

Jo watched the little hands of the alarm clock on the bedside cabinet inching towards six o'clock, ready to press down on the button before the shrill tone awoke Clive, hoping that he might gradually come to his senses and feel the need to press down upon Jo one more tender time, before they were both forced to acknowledge the dawn and the responsibilities of the day.

Clive slept on.

He turned on to his stomach and grunted softly, contentedly, as Jo's nimble fingers ran down the length of his spine until they reached the chasm which ran between Clive's buttocks, lightly dusted with the same black hair that covered his chest.

The alarm let out its shrill, demanding wake up call and Jo's hand instantly leapt upon its metal button, with the same degree of urgency that Clive had leapt upon the button that had unleashed Jo's dormant sexuality the night before.

Clive didn't move.

Jo's hands worked their way beneath the prone body, seeking that very special protuberance, anxious to feel whether it might also have stirred, maybe growing an inch of more, just as it had extended its full glorious length, at the flicking sensation of Jo's tongue the previous night.

Nothing stirred.

Instead, like its owner, the object of Jo's intense desire remained tired, exhausted even, rendered temporarily useless by the exertions of a night of unbridled passion, during which Jo had worked it up into a furious frenzy of excitement not once, not twice, but three times, until it could operate its magic spell no more.

Jo extracted a hand that smelt of a lover's so infinitely and intimately enticing scent. Sweat glistened at the tips of Jo's fingers, as Jo slid a damp forefinger down the length of Clive's back, leaning over and kissing his broad shoulder blades.

Once more the light, caressing finger careered down a sun-tanned back, resting just short of the valley which ran between the twin mounds that rose roundly from the level of Clive's back, planting a kiss there and relishing once again the delicious taste of a man, which Jo had so longed to savour.

Downstairs in the hotel kitchen, the chefs had begun their daily tasks. A clattering frying pan hit the floor with a resonating crash, which was as sudden as Jo's aroused sexuality, splashing warm, white, slowly melting lard, in the same way as something warm and white and deliciously seductive had splashed its way into Jo the night before, melting and channelling its way forward, as if it too had eggs to fry.

Jo couldn't stay in bed any longer. Downstairs the chefs weren't the only ones for whom breakfast duty beckoned. Jo's fingers ran across Clive's buttocks one last, lingering time, as the teenage lover rolled towards the side of the bed, away from Clive, away from the love that surely should have lasted for ever. It was a quarter past six. Jo rose without awakening Clive and padded towards the bathroom.

Jo had to be ready for seven o'clock to serve any of the guests who might wish an early breakfast. Most of those who stayed at the Carlton Hall Hotel didn't come down for a first cup of coffee until a little after eight, but Jo had to be ready, just in case.

Taking Clive's toothbrush, Jo hesitated for a moment. Strangely, it seemed wrong to use his toothbrush, even when other bodily fluids had already been exchanged between the two of them. Jo's face reflected in the bathroom mirror smiled back at the person that Jo no longer knew nor fully understood, taking stock of the body that felt so different now that it had, at last, felt the cascading warmth of another person inside it.

Jo had begun to run a bath. Clive appeared naked at the door, rubbing sleep from his eyes and yawning. Jo could smell his warm breath, which mingled with the hot steam rising from the taps.

Clive stretched and yawned again, spreading his legs and thrusting out his knees, placing his clenched fists behind the nape of his neck, so that his neck muscles tautened visibly, making Jo want to touch him all over his body, especially wanting to work with hands, which dripped wet and soapy over any part of it that might feel the need to thrust forwards and take control of the teenaged body. Jo longed once more to succumb to such total abandonment. Lost again to lust.

'Why don't you shave, whilst I have my bath? You can get in after me if you like. Or even in with me, if you prefer.'

'Is there room for two?' asked Clive.

'Yes, if you squeeze in tight.'

'And why would I want to do that?'

'So that you can be close to me,' Jo replied.

'Do I really need a bath that much?' Clive responded, noting the way that Jo's eyes remained fixed at the level of his waistline, seldom looking up, but often glancing slightly downwards, as if totally mesmerised by what was to be found there.

'Yes, I do think you should have a bath. You stink of sweat.'

'Oh, thank you very much. You do have a way with words,' replied Clive.

'I could always scrub your back,' said Jo suggestively.

'Not if I get in behind you, you can't,' laughed Clive.

'I was only trying to be helpful!' came Jo's reply, as Clive took the sponge and wrung it out over Jo's head, dropping to his knees at the side of the bath, so that their faces met. Clive held the sponge aloft once more and the rivers of water flowed between them.

'You're a cheeky little …'

'… bastard?' suggested Jo, with a degree of irony, aware even at this moment that the true identity of an unknown father was a blank that had for so long remained a mystery and one which Jo so yearned to be filled.

'I wasn't going to say that,' replied Clive gently, rising to his feet and placing a tooth mug under the cold tap at the bathroom sink, without Jo noticing.

He walked over to the side of the bath, bent down, kissed Jo and then poured the tumbler of cold water over Jo's head.

'What was that for?' shouted Jo in a moment of shivering, shuddering shock.

'Because you need to cool down. And you can stop looking at my cock! You've worn it out. It needs a rest. I doubt if it will ever work properly again. I should sue you for emasculation.

'Now move over and let me get in – behind you! That way you might be able to keep your hands to yourself for a few minutes,' instructed Jo's lover, who had done so much to provide a totally different brand of instruction the night before.

'Ah, but can *you*?' asked Jo teasingly, taking Clive's hands and clutching them together, slowly allowing them to drift upwards, so that they came to rest on Jo's nipples, which immediately grew tender to the touch.

Settling in behind and tweaking Jo's nipples, it did not take long until Jo could feel Clive's manhood swelling, pushing against Jo's buttocks from behind, announcing itself like an early morning cock crow.

'Get out of the bath, right now, before I take you back to bed and fuck you again,' pleaded Clive.

'You should be so lucky,' replied Jo coquettishly. 'I've probably got at least half a dozen gentlemen guests downstairs in the breakfast room waiting to be served.'

'Just as long as you don't intend to serve them in the same way as you served me last night,' Clive retorted, casting a broad wink at Jo.

'I'm glad to have been of service to you, sir. Is there anything else at all that I can get you?'

'A towel. And then bugger off and let me dry myself and see if I can get this thing under control,' replied Clive slapping at his erect cock.

Jo extracted the toothbrush from the tooth mug, filled the white china receptacle with cold water and threw it over Clive, aiming not for his head but, instead, lower down.

'What was that for?' shouted a naked Clive.

'Because you need to cool down and stop looking at my ...'

'Piss off and go to work, will you!' said Clive, stepping out of the hot bath and throwing a final insult at the door, which Jo had already closed on last night's lover, scrambling into clothes which lay spread across the bedroom floor.

Jo was aware of the fact that it was nearly ten minutes to seven and time was still needed to rush back to the flat above the stables and change before making an appearance in the hotel dining room.

'My God, you're a flirt,' Clive called after Jo's receding figure. 'I think I've just married myself to a minx.'

'Are you going to marry me, then?' asked Jo, carefully setting the door ajar to check that no one was around and before making a swift exit.

'Don't be ridiculous,' replied Clive, unsure as to whether or not his words could still be heard.

* * * * * * * * * *

Jo slipped quietly out of the back door of the hotel, returning to the flat below which Grandmother's Bentley was garaged and which, at her bidding, had recently been renovated, affording Jo, some degree of privacy from hotel life.

At Mary's expense it had been furnished with modern formica-topped tables and a selection of spindly, chrome-legged chairs, which looked so uncomfortable to sit on, but which, Jo had insisted, were all the rage.

Jo stripped out of the clothes that had littered the floor of Clive's hotel bedroom just a few minutes earlier, standing in nothing but a T-shirt and a pair of pants, before hastily donning the hotel's uniform, which was the same for both male and female staff.

The smart attire comprised a white shirt, black tie, jacket and trousers, cut according to the sex of the wearer but, in some ways, it was unflattering and certainly did not enhance any sexual statement on behalf of the wearer.

Moira, who allowed herself to exude as much sexuality as possible at any other time of the day, particularly hated the uniform which Grandmother required every member of her staff to wear at breakfast time.

On account of her Presbyterian upbringing, Grandmother's strenuously enforced dictate was that any form of sexual stimulation in the morning was totally unacceptable.

Meanwhile, back in the hotel bedroom, Clive was also dressing. He chose casual clothing, for there was no need today to wear his uniform. From the upstairs window, Clive watched, as Jo hurried across the perfectly manicured lawns, bowling across them joyously, catching the early morning scent that emanated from Grandmother's walled rose garden and sniffing the heady perfume, which still mingled in the mind's eye with the intoxicating smell of Clive's sweaty body.

Jo stopped suddenly and ran into the rose garden, snapping the stem of a single bloom and felt the prickling penetration of a wayward thorn, which stabbed a forefinger and drew a tiny speck of blood.

Jo fitted it into the buttonhole in the jacket lapel, entered the hotel and marched into the dining room. A few minutes later, when Clive was settled down at his usual table, Jo delivered the breakfast menu, with a politely uttered:

'Good morning, sir. I trust you slept well. We always like our guests to enjoy a good night!'

Clive marvelled at Jo's composure, which bore no hint of last night's passionate lovemaking between the two of them.

'Tea or coffee, sir? And would sir care for anything cooked, or something from the breakfast buffet?'

Clive solemnly gave his order for poached haddock. When it duly arrived, he noticed that Jo was no longer wearing the buttonhole.

Delivered to his table, together with the fish, was a slim glass vase containing a solitary red rose in full bloom, which dropped a single petal on to the white tablecloth.

Clive surveyed the dining room. On every table sat a similar vase and in it was displayed a single, solitary bloom.

All the others were cream!

* * * * * * * * *

That evening when Jo walked across the moonlit lawns to the apartment above the old stable block, Clive was already there waiting. Without a word to each other, they silently went straight into the bedroom and undressed, slipping beneath the sheets.

Jo met Clive's eager embrace, delving deep between his legs and coming up with something that was already stiff and hard and which instantly began to pulsate in tune with Jo's lingering touch.

Jo threw back the bedclothes and leapt on top of Clive, claiming control, like a navigator reaching out and grabbing hold of the captain's joystick. Jo felt it swell into a rock hard protuberance, as the blood began to pump ever more greedily, coursing through the veins that lined the throbbing, stiffening shaft. Jo straddled Clive, like a naughty tomboy, climbing aboard a fallen oak tree, grasping its trunk between legs held tightly together, as if gripping the head of a mighty big acorn.

Clive entered Jo effortlessly and Jo started to move in a manner that had Clive moaning with pleasure. Jo's body moved in perfect synchronisation with every pulsating shiver of Clive's body. Such sensual pleasure was almost unbearable and Clive erupted into Jo like a bursting volcano, filling Jo with his white hot lava flow.

Extracting that part of Clive's manhood from the innermost sanctum of what, until the night before, had been virgin territory, Jo climbed off and melted into Clive's body, one cheek pressed against his torso, lips damply inviting and with one hand immersed in the fabric of Clive's chest.

Soon they were entwined in each other's arms, so that it was virtually impossible to discern just exactly where one lover ended and the other began. They remained wrapped together in an envelope of their own making, a parcelled package, soul mates and lovers, needing no stamp of society's approval.

Two more days dragged by. Two more nights flashed through their mutual consciousness, swept along in a tide of one crashing wave of intense sexuality after another.

Every morning the coolly composed breakfast routine remained the same, marked only be the daring, telltale sign that one breakfast table – and one alone was occupied each day by a rose differently coloured from the rest.

Jo was making a statement, a rather risky one, but one about which Jo no longer cared.

As the morning of Clive's imminent departure dawned, Jo rose from the bed which had become their principal love nest and walked towards the bathroom.

Clive stood naked in front of the mirror, shaving his cheeks and chin of the dark stubble that peppered his face, splashing on a fragrant aftershave, refreshing his face and stinging his flesh, as the liquid onslaught sought out the tiny nick that he had made on his ear lobe.

'Will you leave me your aftershave?' asked Jo.

'What could you possibly want with my aftershave?' demanded Clive.

'It will remind me of you, while you're away,' replied Jo wistfully. Jo had sensed a quiver in Clive's voice, before turning around and seeing that there were tears in his eyes.

No sooner had Jo noticed them, than they were gone, brushed away in a moment, just as Jo had been taught to do for so many years as a child, when Andrina's sharp retorts and stinging slaps had so often brought tears welling up and ready to descend in sadness, like a bathroom tap that no washer would ever fit.

Jo looked at Clive, whose eyes had welled up with tears – reddened in deference to his obvious masculinity.

'Don't you dare cry, Clive. Don't ever think of crying. Please, don't cry. I am finding it difficult enough as it is to see you go.'

Clive said nothing.

Like the consummate performer that was Jo, Clive too was beginning to learn that he had a part to play and play it he did, even if not a single line of dialogue had been written for him.

His was a silent part. He was like a player in a silent movie, whose actions had to speak louder than words. His was the saddest part of all – the part whose very purpose was a sad farewell.

'I have to say "Goodbye" to you,' he said finally, at last finding the words to utter. 'I won't be back in the country again for weeks. Please Jo, you've got to help me. I know you're only young. You're far too young. What we have together is … different. My Goodness, you're young enough to be my own child and I'm asking you to help me! It should be the other way round, for God's sake. Don't do anything, Jo. Don't speak. Not a word now. Say nothing – nothing at all.'

Jo remained transfixed but, ultimately, ignored Clive's plea for silence. 'Clive, I love you,' replied Jo in a voice choking with emotion.

'God help me, I love you too, Jo! When I leave here, I will become half a person again – the half that I was before I met you. I'll do my job. I'll fly that plane, but I'll just go on existing until I return. Sure, I'll go through all the motions but, believe me, that is all I will be capable of doing. I just can't exist without you. I have to go. I will see you downstairs. Remember now, not a word. Not a word to anyone!'

Clive kissed Jo, as if it was their last farewell. Quivering with emotion, Jo left the bedroom hurriedly, having finally lost the battle for composure.

Jo swept down the stairs, pausing at the door of the linen room, entering surreptitiously and dabbing at a tear-soaked face with the corner of a starched white sheet.

Only one person noticed Jo's tears. She had been looking out for any torn sheets that needed repair – a job for which the housekeeper should have been responsible. She stood unseen at the far end of the linen room concealed by racks of neatly stacked sheets and blankets.

She too would say nothing. She could not bring herself to say anything to anyone. She must remain silent – for Jo's sake, but it hurt her bitterly to see the anguish on the face of the child she had borne all those years ago.

* * * * * * * * *

When Clive's taxi arrived to take him to the airport, it was perhaps the one occasion upon which Jo broke all Grandmother's rules and walked a hotel guest to an awaiting cab.

Clive uttered just three words before shutting the door and bidding the driver to take him to his airport destination.

Just three words had been spoken and only just loud enough for Jo, but no one else to discern. They were the words that Jo wanted in all the world to hear.

Jo watched the taxi disappear down the tree-lined drive, took a deep breath, turned and walked through the main entrance towards reception, as if nothing had ever happened.

No expression of joy lingered on Jo's face. No expression of sorrow. Jo's theatre act was in full swing once more. The consummate performer was back on the Oscar winning trail. A mixture of joy and sorrow was reserved for the woman who had stood and watched Jo's tears shed in the linen cupboard and who now watched again from an upstairs window, as the two lovers had bid their fond farewells.

What mother could ever bear to see her child fall into the outstretched arms of a love affair that was doomed to die an early death?

Chapter 37

It was six weeks later. Jo knew that Clive was due to return to the hotel that afternoon and was determined to be around when he arrived.

Jo felt absolutely exhausted, having escaped into a world of work since Clive's departure when they had parted from each other's company outside the hotel and Jo had tried so hard to pretend that it didn't matter.

Since then Jo had spent every waking hour finding something to do in the hotel, willingly taking over the shift of anyone who fancied an evening off and needing someone to cover for them.

Jo reckoned that, as far as covering tracks was concerned, the task had been completed very well. As far as Jo was concerned, no one suspected a thing about the burgeoning and quite forbidden relationship that had developed.

However, Jo was totally unaware that the woman who could legitimately claim to be Jo's natural mother had watched silently over her child for over sixteen long years, not daring to speak the truth and that she alone knew of the relationship which had developed between Jo and the hotel guest.

Jo had started work at six o'clock, instead of seven, each morning since Clive had left, launching into the lunch-time shift and then taking over on reception in the afternoon to allow Nan the chance to go shopping, or take a rare trip to the hairdresser's.

When Agnes returned, Jo would move straight on to the evening shift, even volunteering to lock the bar up for Andrina, so that she could retire early.

As a final chore, Jo would look in on Anne, making sure that she was asleep and that she had a chamber pot by the bed, so that she wasn't forced to stumble blindly into the bathroom in her normal state of insobriety or, worse still, left to wet the bed, making the bedroom stink of piss in the morning and giving the chambermaids the unpleasant job of clearing up the mess.

Jo had long since lost count of the number of "mother's mattresses" which had been consigned to the local rubbish dump, stained, soiled and stinking, but sometimes providing a more comfortable night for a local tramp.

Sometime after midnight, Jo would cross the lawns to the old stable block, turn in at last to bed and try to sleep, not counting sheep, but counting the days until Clive was due to return.

Jo would invariably go through the ritual of sprinkling some of Clive's aftershave on the pillow, hugging the feather-filled comforter and shepherding the day's thoughts together like an anxious border collie.

Three weeks of lack of sleep and being physically pushed to the limits were beginning to take their toll. Jo's normally bright, sparkling eyes had dulled a little. Some of the spring in Jo's step had vanished, melting into the void that was so clearly defined by life without a lover.

Often the lonely, lovelorn lover would finally be lulled off to sleep hours later, waking at daybreak and feeling the damp embrace of nothing more than a tear-stained pillow.

Tonight would be different. Tonight they would be reunited. Tonight Jo would climb into bed and into Clive's awaiting arms, but right now that seemed like a lifetime away.

On the morning before Clive's arrival, Jo had arisen before daybreak, having had only four hours' sleep. It was too soon to go downstairs and across to the hotel, which was still all in darkness, save for the golden glow of the twin coach lamps, which decorated the entrance, providing a path of light for those who returned late and so that the night porter could identify bona fide guests.

Arthur, the breakfast waiter, who doled out his own particular brand of politics with the porridge and who bored Jo rigid, would not yet have arrived at the back entrance on his bicycle, with his black braided trousers ridiculously tucked in behind his socks.

No, the last few hours would definitely be the hardest. Clive's plane wasn't due to touch down until about half past two in the afternoon and it would be at least another hour, or more before he finally reached the hotel.

Jo was in charge of reception. Agnes was visiting the dentist that afternoon. Jo had made sure of that, volunteering to make her an appointment, steadfastly refusing all the different dates offered, until a late afternoon appointment on the day of Clive's return had been suggested and immediately approved.

It was after four in the afternoon that Jo heard the scrunch of tyres on the gravel outside, as the taxi pulled up and the doors of the hotel entrance were swung wide for a man dressed in a clean-cut uniform that Jo longed to delve into with eager hands, not caring if a shirt button, or two, flew off in the process.

'Welcome back, sir. It's nice to see you again,' uttered the concierge in polite refrain, knowing nothing of just how very welcome young Jo intended to make the tall, handsome Caledonian Airways navigator, hopefully offering to help carry his cases up to his room and indulge in a quick embrace before returning downstairs to reception.

Jo looked up into Clive's smiling face, wanting to rush round to the other side of the reception desk and run into Clive's arms.

'Welcome back, sir,' said with Jo admirable restraint. 'I've reserved your usual room for you. Is there anything you would like brought upstairs for you?'

Silently, Clive took his key from Jo, pausing just a moment more than was necessary, as the room key exchanged hands, along with a lingering look.

Clive remained silent, brooding almost, looking at Jo over the lids of dark eyes, which masked a thousand secrets waiting to be told. It was as much as Jo could bear not to lean across the desk and kiss him, lips bruising against the five o'clock shadow of a man who had not shaved and whose favourite aftershave was still locked in Jo's apartment and locked in Jo's aching heart.

It was as much as Jo could bear not to be taken against the desk and smothered with the richly masculine, musky scent of a man who needed a shower – a man who Jo longed to see stripped naked, with cascades of water drizzling down his back.

'Your key, sir,' Jo repeated, as if trying to force words out of Clive's reluctant mouth.

'Thank you,' said Clive simply. It was the voice that made Jo falter, rich tones encapsulated in a single phrase. A hint of a Canadian accent. A hint of seduction, seducing Jo in just two words. Yes, "thank you" indeed, but Jo hadn't really given Clive anything other than the key to say "thank you" for – not yet, anyway!

However, this was a key that could open the way to so much pleasure behind the locked door of a hotel bedroom.

'Shall I take Mr Thompson's bags to his room?' asked one of the porters.

'No, I'll help with Clive's ...' Jo's slight faux pas went unnoticed to everyone except the man who stood waiting at the reception desk, hoping that Jo's mistake had not been picked up on. In that split second the consummate young player had forgotten the well-rehearsed lines.

'Yes, perhaps you could take Mr Thompson's bags upstairs for him,' Jo interjected quickly, taking control of the situation once again. It was another Oscar winning performance that rarely ever faltered, prompted by the need to keep a secret that only two people should be allowed to share, but one which was already known to the woman who was Jo's mother.

* * * * * * * * * *

Clive left Jo at reception, walking upstairs to his room alone save for the porter, who pocketed a sixpence tip whilst, below, Jo lacked even a penny for the erotic thoughts that were coursing through a young mind like greyhounds running after a rabbit.

'Yes,' Clive thought to himself, as he began to unpack. It might have been for playing the leading roles in "The Hustler" that Paul Newman and Piper Laurie were being considered for an Oscar that year, but surely the Hollywood film moguls should at least have saved a walk-on part for Jo. In the role of best supporting actor or actress, no one else would have stood a chance!

Later in the early evening twilight, Jo walked towards the flat above the old stables to change, pausing beneath the massive oaks, which normally cast shadows of sombre intensity on the vast expanse of hotel lawns. A form appeared standing silently in the darkness by the high brick wall surrounding the old vegetable garden.

Dressed to impress, wearing a black tuxedo, stood Clive, now cleanly shaven and with just a hint of the musky smelling aftershave that Jo had come to recognise so well.

In his hand he held a winter rose.

Within no more than a second Jo was in his arms, crushing the rose in useless abandon: its petals bent, descending to the ground like tears of ruby rain.

Just like Audrey Hepburn rushing into the arms of Cary Grant, or Richard Burton and Elizabeth Taylor in love's embrace, now was the chance for the performance of a lifetime and all that Jo could do was cry.

Together, unseen in the darkness, the couple walked hand in hand over to Jo's apartment. Jo unlocked the door, fiddling nervously with the latch and handing the key to Clive.

'Your key, sir,' said Jo simply.

Clive sat on the edge of the bed whilst Jo washed and changed. At one point Jo came into the bedroom wearing nothing but the regulation hotel uniform shirt, standing in front of Clive, bending low in a tangle of outstretched arms and flapping shirt cuffs and kissing him on the top of the head.

'You look worn out, Jo. What have you been doing? You've lost weight too – not that you had any to lose. Have you been eating properly?'

'I'm trying to lose some weight,' replied Jo.

'Don't be stupid!' retorted Clive. 'There is not a spare ounce of flesh on you – not a tiny part of you that is surplus to my requirements.'

'Oh, so you do need me then, do you?'

'Of course I need you.'

'As much as I need you to love me?'

Jo leant in to Clive, dripping dewy tears on to the velvet collar of his tuxedo, brushing them away in an attempt to ensure that they did not stain the fabric, which felt so rich and lustrous to the touch.

'You'll ruin my jacket,' said Clive.

'I won't ruin your jacket, if you promise never to walk out on me and ruin my life!'

'I don't do much walking, Jo. I usually fly,' smiled Clive, attempting to lighten the heavy atmosphere with a flippant remark.

'Well, don't ever crash land then,' begged Jo. 'And if you do, make sure that it is on top of me.'

'Come on, brush away those tears. And you can brush my jacket while you're about it. I want to look good for you, so that you will always love me. I may be a good deal older than you Jo, but there's no need for me to look like your father – all grey hair and fusty suits. Some men can improve with age, you know!'

'I can't think of any way to improve you,' Jo replied.

'Well, come on here then, you silly little …' said Clive, his words trailing away, as they embraced.

'I love you dearly. When I'm not with you, it seems as if someone has wrenched my heart out and nailed it to the wall. I'm in a complete spin without you.

'I'm like a catherine wheel pinned to the wall, with no one to light the fuse. You're the one who makes my world spin around. You light me up with your smile, Jo. I'm completely lost without you.'

Jo finished dressing and walked back to the hotel with Clive, entering the building via the back door, whilst Clive used the main entrance.

No one saw. No one knew – except the woman who knew already.

Clive came down to dinner later that evening with two of the air hostesses who flew with him, one blonde, one brunette. He didn't bother to introduce them to Jo by name.

'Good evening, sir,' Jo announced formally. 'I can offer you Table number 12 by the window or, if you prefer, there is Table number 14, which is set for four.'

'No number 13 on offer then?' asked Clive mischievously.

'We don't have a table with that number,' answered Jo professionally, whilst taking the girls' coats.

Jo particularly noticed the blonde and noted how attractive she looked, with her straight, long, lustrous hair, which reached past her shoulders. It framed her tanned face, with its freckled nose and pink lips, which pouted, caught in the candlelight, as she moistened them with a tiny movement of her tongue.

'Then I guess it's Number 12 by the window,' Clive said, sweeping his ready smile between his two guests in a gesture, which hardly seemed to include Jo.

'Thirteen is such an unlucky number don't you think, Clive?' said Rosalind, the darker of the two girls, seeking the opinion of their male escort and not even bothering to look at Jo, who had been born on the thirteenth day of the month, but who did not figure in her appraisal of such unfortunate timing.

'Rosalind believes in Lucky Numbers,' said the blonde, speaking for the first time. 'They're her favourite chocolates. I bet she has a bag full of them in her handbag right now. She pretends she's on a diet but ...' Amanda grinned impishly, including Jo in her confidence and, for the first time since the three of them had entered the dining room, Jo felt that someone cared, even if the secret that she had just revealed was of little or no consequence.

Presenting them with the menus, Jo remained outwardly calm, but Clive noticed that the red rose that had been there when the three of them sat down, was quickly swept away, along with the extra place setting, rapidly replaced by a nondescript cream bloom that matched all those at the remaining tables.

Jo was in a rebellious frame of mind, a mood which was probably caused by tiredness and the need to go to bed – not to sleep, but to be held and cosseted by the man who had chosen to spend the first night of his return visit to Carlton Hall in the company of two females whom Jo had never even met until now.

Acker Bilk's "Stranger on the Shore" played in the background, as Clive and his lady friends took up the menus.

In that moment Clive was indeed but a stranger. Jo was unsure how to react, listening to the words of the song, as a tide of emotion washed wet and winsome.

Suddenly, horribly, Jo felt unsure of Clive. Could he be attracted to an older woman, rather than to a teenager like Jo?

Jo felt beached on the shore of an uncertain destiny.

Jo gulped back a fractious tear, hurrying over to another table with a tureen of vegetable soup and a silver ladle balanced precariously on the plate below.

Tiredness was taking its toll and Jo was forced to stifle a yawn. Sentiment remained like the sticky sediment at the bottom of a bottle of port unwelcome and unwanted, especially by Jo, whose feelings had no port of call.

Jo continued to serve them throughout the evening, watching as Grandmother glided between the tables on her customary round to ensure that all was well and to offer a few carefully chosen words of platitude to the dinner guests – all pearls and pretence, as Andrina was often wont to define her mother's nightly ritual.

Standards had to be maintained and Grandmother was always on hand with a few cheerful pleasantries to her guests and plain talk in plenty for those who delivered their plates, if ever she spotted a misplaced item of cutlery, or a smudged glass.

Service counted for everything and Grandmother counted it as her duty to ensure that the diners in the hotel restaurant never left without gaining the impression that everything was totally under control, even if chaos reigned in the kitchen.

Jo was ready to laugh and share a joke with everyone – with a constant smile and cheery demeanour for each and every client. However, tonight it was all a front, for inwardly Jo's heart ached, but no one would ever know what was truly occupying those teenaged thoughts and emerging jealousies.

As far as the guests were concerned, Jo's only purpose in life was to serve their every need. Yes, Jo was back on stage, in full command once more in what was, yet again, almost a Royal Command Performance. The show must go on. Actors and actresses must learn the part they had to play. That night Jo's part was the most difficult of all – the one that called for absolute control.

This was no walk on part: this was centre stage. And surely the evening's curtain call would bring Clive dashing from the wings into Jo's open arms.

Towards the end of the evening, as coffee was served, Clive thought he caught Jo cast a darting look across the restaurant.

It was aimed at him, like a fisherman casting a fly into the green waters of a weed-strewn Loch Ness. Oh, yes, the green-eyed monster had decided to show itself at last.

Clive was intrigued – flattered even. Let's just see how this all develops he thought to himself, allowing vanity to get the better of his judgement and to come between him and the person who really belonged in his bed. He began flirting, first with Rosalind and then with Amanda.

Rosalind returned the look he gave her, allowing her nylon stockinged calf to inch a little closer, so that it brushed against him unseen under the cover of the tablecloth.

Amanda was wiser. She had seen these games played before and she wasn't about to become a pawn in a chess match in which it was necessary to check whose mate was whose. Amanda knew to whom Clive's heart belonged. She had seen it in the fleeting glances that, from time to time throughout the night, he had cast in Jo's direction. She also knew only too well that the person to whom Clive had pledged himself was working not too far away and was watching his every move.

Clive had never really shown any interest in any of the girls he worked with – not in that way at least.

Amanda had once got herself caught up with a captain who worked for another airline and she wasn't going to make the same mistake twice, flying into the arms of a man in uniform in a momentary flight of fancy. Yes, Amanda had Clive's measure. She waited until Rosalind had left the room to powder her nose before making it perfectly clear to him that she understood only too well what was happening and that she disapproved.

'I know what you're doing and let me assure you, it won't work! You can flirt with both Rosalind and I all you like, but you know full well that nothing will become of it. Just don't hurt anyone else.

'Rosalind is quite smitten and, unlike me, she doesn't understand what's going on. And I guess that the real object of your affection doesn't appreciate what you're up to either.

'Be careful what you're doing, Clive and don't play games. It might just be you who ends up getting hurt and I think too much of you as a friend to want to see you pay the price that you may well have to pay.'

'Listen, Amanda, I'm only doing it to annoy Jo,' replied Clive.

'Gramophones used to be wound up once upon a time, Clive and look what happened to them! Nobody uses them anymore. What everybody wants nowadays is one of those fashionable portable record players, or one of those new transistor radios.'

As Rosalind returned to the table, Clive announced that they would take another cup of coffee in the lounge, beckoning for service with a click of his fingers that Jo tried to ignore, despite Grandmother's watchful eye.

Jo handed cups of coffee to Amanda and Rosalind each in turn but, when it came to serving Clive, Amanda noticed that the cup and saucer rattled slightly in Jo's hand.

'I thought that cup of coffee was going to land in your lap, Clive,' said Rosalind, nibbling at an after dinner mint.

'So did I,' replied Clive, as Amanda glared at him, aware of the antipathy which was currently passing between Jo and the man who had just paid for their meal, adding a generous ten shilling tip, which Jo made a point of putting straight into the Blue Cross box on the reception desk.

Jo didn't want Clive's charity.

Rosalind wandered over to the bar, anxious to order brandies before last orders and to prolong the night. She extracted the coins from a little leather purse, hoping that a final shot of alcohol might loosen Clive from the stranglehold that held him back and induce him to finally make a move on her.

'I think I may have upset Jo,' confessed Clive to the all too knowing Amanda.

'You do believe in living dangerously, don't you, Clive!' she replied.

'I'll be forgiven, just you wait and see.'

'Are you sure about that?' replied Amanda. 'I know what I would do to you. I'd make you suffer.'

* * * * * * * * * *

Jo worked late, helping to clear up in the dining room, re-laying the tables for breakfast and finding every last little excuse to delay returning to the flat above the old stables, hoping that Clive would re-appear from his upstairs bedroom to arrange a rendezvous, lingering downstairs beside the locked doors leading into the hotel bar.

No one appeared.

When finally Jo could find no further reason to remain loitering around the restaurant, a lonely tramp across the lawn beckoned. Jo's feet shuffled along the gravel path, kicking out at a stone and sending it flying towards the window of the residents' lounge, which was cloaked in darkness. It struck the glass with a loud crack. Jo didn't care if it had shattered the window in a thousand pieces, showering shards of glass like the remains of Jo's fractured heart.

Jo turned the key in the lock of the door to the apartment above the old stables with a heavy heart.

'Hello,' said Clive nonchalantly.

'I guessed you weren't coming. I didn't think you wanted me tonight,' Jo answered, tired and with a hint of derision.

'You know I always want you,' replied Clive placatingly.

Jo said nothing.

Clive was already partly undressed. Jo stripped out of a slightly sweat-stained uniform and got into bed besides Clive, reaching over and turning out the bedside light, settling uncomfortably on the furthest edge of the bed, anxious that their bodies should not touch.

'Are we in a bad mood, by any chance?' enquired Clive.

'About what?' retorted Jo.

'I was only teasing you.'

'Then don't.'

'I'm sorry it was just a bit of fun. You know I enjoy having fun with you.'

'Leave me alone,' snapped Jo.

'Do you really mean that?'

'Yes, I do.' Jo turned away from Clive and appeared to be sobbing into the pillow, with tears flowing through the feathery down.

'I didn't mean to offend you, Jo. I never mean to hurt you. Don't you realise, you're my world. You mean everything to me.'

'Well, you've certainly got a funny way of showing it.'

'Oh, we are touchy tonight.'

'Don't touch me. I don't want you.'

'Really!' exclaimed Clive.

'Shut up, Clive and think yourself lucky not to have had a hot cup of coffee poured into your lap earlier on.'

'And run the risk of scalding the part of me you really want?'

'As far as I'm concerned you can burn in hell!'

'Or scald in a cauldron perhaps,' Clive replied in an attempt at levity.

'Don't try to be funny.'

'Perhaps, I should put you over my knee and give you a good hiding,' replied Clive.

'I'm not a child. Who do you think you are, my father? Don't even think about it,' replied Jo from hot, quivering lips.

Clive lost his patience. Tossing back the bedcovers, he rose from the bed, dragged Jo over to a chair, forcing the sulky teenager over his knee and raised his hand over Jo's bare backside.

'Don't you dare hit me!' cried Jo, as Clive's hand slapped down on Jo's rapidly reddening flesh.

Once ... twice ... three times, the blows rained down. They were as harsh and relentless as those meted out many a time by Andrina – as sharp and as stinging as that first initial slap on a baby's bottom delivered by Nanny Bapty. Jo winced, but more from shock than anything else.

'Are you going to behave now?' asked Clive.

'I never behave,' retorted Jo.

'Oh, I think I know that only too well!' replied Clive. 'You little …'

'Little what?' asked Jo in apparent innocence, looking longingly into Clive's face.

Jo's face was now streaked and streaming with tears – not of sorrow, but tears of laughter, which cascaded down one set of glowing, red hot cheeks reflecting the same colour as the scalded, reddened backside of the mooning, moody teenager.

'Get back to bed – immediately!' commanded Clive.

Jo obeyed.

Clive awoke at around six o'clock the next morning. Jo was still asleep. He shook his bed partner awake, taking a light hold of Jo's shoulder, until sleepy eyes peered over the eiderdown, reluctant to abandon its warmth on a cold January morning, when the windows looked like the defrosting interior of one of the vast refrigerators in the hotel kitchen.

'Come on, you're going to be late for work.'

'It's Wednesday. It's my afternoon off,' replied Jo. 'I asked Grandmother. I thought we could meet up in Edinburgh this afternoon – that is, if you haven't got any prior engagement planned with either of your two lady friends.'

'I've only got one engagement on my mind right now,' replied Clive.

'Don't be stupid, we can't get married!' replied Jo.

* * * * * * * * *

Clive had arranged to meet Jo at twelve o'clock at the top of the Waverley Steps, knowing that Jo would arrive neither late nor early, for a strict upbringing dictated strict timekeeping.

Grandmother had never been late for an appointment in her life and she wasn't going to let any member of her family off with keeping anyone waiting.

As the hour hand on the clock just outside the North British Hotel inched towards midday, Jo appeared, crossing Princes Street wearing a closely fitting leather jacket, tight denim jeans and a white shirt, with a button down collar. A navy and white tie, hung around Jo's neck. Its loosely tied knot reached down two or three inches below the level of formality. Jo wore it in exactly the same way in which Clive was wont to let fly with the restrictions of his official airline attire after a long flight.

Jo's shoes had the Cuban heel that was popular with teenagers of the time. They were uncomfortable and crippled Jo's feet, but vanity was all that mattered.

However, it was Jo's hair that immediately stopped Clive in his tracks. It was no longer the usual, unruly mop, but a very short cut moulded to the head, highlighted with lighter streaks – all in the latest fashion.

Heads turned, as Jo passed people in the street and, at one point, Clive even thought he heard a wolf whistle, although whether it was meant for Jo or not, he couldn't tell.

As far as Clive was concerned, Jo was thoroughly deserving of all the admiration that those stunning good looks warranted. Jo was turning heads – both male and female. Perhaps it was the eyes, or simply the air of confidence which Jo exuded. Maybe it was just the hairstyle, or the new clothes.

Turning heads was a new experience for Jo and one which was lapped up like the cat that not only got the cream, but was being offered it from a silver salver.

'Good morning, Jo.'

'Good afternoon, Clive,' Jo replied more correctly, glancing at the Accurist wristwatch that peeked from below the level of the sleeve of the leather jacket, and noting that it was already one minute past the hour.

'Oh, I'm terribly sorry. My mistake,' replied Clive, gazing up at the clock on the front of the North British Hotel.

'Do you approve of how I look?' asked Jo, seeking compliments.

'I can't think of any objections right now,' said Clive, adding 'I take it you haven't eaten. Shall we lunch in Jenners restaurant?'

'No,' replied Jo. 'I've got a better idea. Let's eat at that new Italian restaurant at the top of Leith Walk.'

Clive ordered for both of them, noting that Jo picked at the cold meat selection, then when the pasta arrived Jo stirred it around the plate, looping the spaghetti with a fork that rarely reached upwards to the mouth.

'All right, I'll buy it. Tell me. What's wrong with you?' came Clive's questioning demand.

'I'm watching my weight,' replied Jo.

'And you chose to go to an Italian restaurant and eat pasta! God, give me strength. Jo you need to put some weight on – not lose it. Your bloody bones stick into my rib cage every night.'

'Well, it makes a change from you sticking something into me.'

'Jo, don't be coarse. It doesn't become you. Now eat up, before you send me out of my mind. Sometimes you're quite impossible.'

'No,' replied Jo with a cheeky grin. 'I'm always impossible.'

'Don't get smart with me,' answered Clive. 'You're an audacious little flirt and you know it!'

'Me?' asked Jo with mock incredulity. 'I don't flirt with anyone.'

'Oh, give me strength,' replied Clive. 'You do it all the time. You just don't realise you're doing it.'

'When do I flirt?' enquired Jo, gazing fixedly into Clive's eyes and at last forking up a mouthful of spaghetti.

'Oh, please! Give me a break,' retorted Clive. 'You've even been flirting with the waiters here. You flirt with every diner that comes into the hotel – male or female. You do it with everyone. I guess it's why you do so well on tips. It's your eyes, Jo. Your eyes always give you away.'

'What do you want me to do about it?' demanded Jo.

'Right now what I would want to do would get us both arrested on the spot,' exclaimed Clive.

'And just what might that be?' Jo asked, all mock innocence once more, with those appealing eyes that never left Clive's gaze.

'Don't tell me. You don't have a clue do you? You drive me mad with desire. Right now I would like to spread you across this table and fuck the living daylights out of you!'

'Now who's being coarse? More pasta? There's still plenty of sauce.'

'I won't dispute that,' said Clive. 'Only in your case, it's not on your spaghetti.'

* * * * * * * * *

Clive and Jo returned to the Carlton Hall Hotel by separate means. Clive arrived by taxi, whilst Jo had telephoned for Grandmother's chauffeur to bring the car to the end of Princes Street where Jo patiently waited under the shadow cast by the statue of the Duke of Wellington.

It was a chilly afternoon. Jo stood muffled into the lightweight leather jacket and welcomed the warmth of Grandmother's car when it finally arrived, plunging into the back seat in an attempt to thwart frost-bitten fingers.

When Jo arrived at the hotel, Andrina took one glance, registering a look of total disapproval, for she rarely got the use of her mother's chauffeur-driven car and here was this teenager who appeared to rule the roost, commanding attention from everyone and enjoying all the finer things in life.

'Does Jo really need a private chauffeur?' she asked, turning to her mother, making no attempt to disguise her disgust. 'Other teenagers have a bike and that one rides around the city in regal splendour. It really is quite preposterous.'

Andrina knew only too well that all the guests at the hotel adored Jo. Likewise, the staff would do anything they could to ensure that they continued to curry Jo's favour.

'Why do you maintain this absolute hatred of Jo?' asked Mary. 'You've never liked the child from the very beginning. Good grief, you even hated Jo as a baby. What has the child ever done to you Andrina, other than to be born?'

'Jo's not a child any more, Mother. Next thing we'll know is that they'll be someone hanging on the arm and, before you know it, you'll be nursing Jo's child. Only don't expect me to play the part of the doting great aunt.'

'I'm quite sure that role won't be expected of you, Andrina,' was Mary's riposte, as her daughter swept out of the room, leaving the door to smash into its wooden frame.

Jo had heard nothing of this latest argument between Grandmother and Andrina, escaping back to the flat above the old stables, stopping off to speak to the pony that grazed in the field beyond the rolling meadows of the Carlton Hall Hotel.

Polly the pony had long since been Jo's confidant, taking over the role from Georgina when Jo became too old to indulge in imaginary friends.

Behind one of the nearby oaks, Clive sheltered from the biting wind, listening intensely to the words which whistled on the wind, exposing Jo's innermost thoughts and feelings – notions that Jo would only ever have dared to express when, apparently, there was no one present to overhear them.

Nobody that is other than the shaggy maned pony, who accepted carrots and confidences in equal measure. Strangely, the pony seemed to be receptive to Jo's mood, nuzzling into Jo's outstretched hands, blowing warm arm into Jo's palms and dribbling the sleeves of the new leather jacket with a snuffling, snorting residue.

Jo was telling Polly how much Clive meant. In those moments Clive heard words that were never intended for his ears. Words of endearment. Words of love. His eyes misted over with unshed tears for a love that could surely never be.

He left without Jo realising that a single word of that ardent proclamation had been overheard, cast away on the wind that swept down the little valley, buffeting against the walls of the Carlton Hall Hotel whose residents were already beginning to gather for afternoon tea by the fire.

That night, after handing the last of the keys over to the night porter, Jo had hardly descended the steps of the hotel, when a shadow emerged from behind the overhanging portico.

Clive had been waiting … waiting and wanting, wanting to take Jo to him and envelope the love of his life in the folds of the black gabardine trench coat that he wore. Its untied belt hung loose, as if ready to lash Jo into him, like a sailor being tied to the mast to prevent the possibility of any impending shipwreck of their relationship.

'What's wrong?' asked Jo.

'I love you. That's what's wrong,' replied Clive.

'I can't live without you and I can't ever see your grandmother agreeing to us living together. You're young, Jo. I'm more than twice your age. You've ruined my life in the nicest possible way. I know I can't go on without you, but ours is not the sort of relationship that society would ever condone.'

'Sod society!' said Jo, uttering the words with a degree of venom, which normally only ever escaped from Andrina's lips. Jo's head was spinning – a fairground ride, which was totally out of control, painted horses forever chasing one another and never quite catching up with the one in front.

'You heard me talking to Polly this afternoon, didn't you. Somehow as I walked away, I knew you were there, but I could not bring myself to tell you,' admitted Jo, as if confessing sins to a priest – sins that were really no sin at all in Jo's eyes.

'Tell me now,' said Clive simply.

'Tell you exactly what?' demanded Jo.

'Tell me that you feel the same way about me, as I feel for you,' said Clive passionately.

'If we both feel the same way about each other, then what is the problem?' asked Jo.

'Oh, Jo, you know what the problem is. Don't be so naïve!'

* * * * * * * * *

That night the world seemed to move in on both Jo and Clive, as they slept, entwined in each other's arms, lost to a world of passion that was both pleasure and purgatory.

Tonight was all about love. Lust was not allowed to enter their secret world. It was as if love had posted a "Do not disturb" notice on the door handle of their emotions. Peacefully they slept together, happy to hold on to each other, contented simply to be together.

Jo had found Clive and, in his turn, Clive had found Jo. Two strangers who stood looking out upon a scrawly sea of their own making. Two strangers on the shore of an uncertain future.

Yes, by some strange quirk of fate they had found each other. At last Jo had a man, not the father that had so long been sought but, instead, a lover. Nothing else mattered in the world.

Together they could be strong. In time they would fly away, winging their way towards an ultimate destiny that would surely bring them even closer together.

Jo needed to stop thinking about the past, stop wondering about the question of a parentage that remained wrapped in mystery and instead concentrate on a future life with Clive and on making it happen.

Jo knew now of the adoption. Jo was no longer the mystery bundle that had been delivered to Anne all those years ago.

If at one time Jo had not belonged, Jo belonged right now – to Clive and to Clive alone. What did it matter if Jo's life had never included a man that could be heralded as a father? Now there was every chance that each day could begin by waking up with a lover.

Clive was scheduled to leave in three days' time – seventy-two hours remained during which they would be together – three whole blissful days spent in each other's company.

Meanwhile, miraculously, the rest of the hotel staff remained in ignorance of their secret assignations. However, one person was very much aware of the dangerous liaison that was developing between Jo and the dashing air crew member, remembering too the time when she and Clive had once been an item many years ago.

Chapter 38

Grandmother's sudden death just days after Clive's departure rocked Jo to the very roots of an existence which had not known a time when she hadn't been around. She was Jo's eternal rock and very soon Jo was to be stuck between a rock that was no longer there and a hard place to be.

Mary had died in her sleep on the first day of February 1962. She was aged eighty-nine and, apart from the fact that she had grown a little hard of hearing and her eye-sight wasn't quite as acute as it might have been for reading purposes, she remained perfectly in possession of all her faculties until the day she died.

A massive brain haemorrhage was the cause of her death. She had felt no pain. It was only those who were left to pick up the pieces who truly suffered and none more so than Jo.

More than anything else in the world, Jo wanted to be with Clive, but the Caledonian Airways navigator was probably somewhere over the Mediterranean right now, or maybe flying across Africa.

Jo had no idea exactly where Clive was at the moment that Agnes let out a stifled scream, as she walked into the old lady's private sitting room on that dreadful afternoon. Agnes had found Mary sitting erect in her armchair, her head lolling to one side and her eyes closed, as if death had shut out all the lights.

All Jo could think about was Grandmother and Clive. No one else featured in Jo's consciousness. Parting from Clive had been such bittersweet sorrow. This time Jo had remained calm in the knowledge that, unlike Grandmother, Clive was coming back.

Jo battled hard with a composure that was all but lost. Andrina seemed to accept her mother's death as an inevitable next link in the chain of events that she had come to accept.

Unsurprisingly, Anne took solace in helping herself to another bottle from the bar, staring into her gin and tonic and then gazing into the middle distance, as if she was seeking a reason for the inexplicable fact that, for Mary, death had come knocking on the door.

It was left to Agnes to hold everything together. Agnes the organiser, the woman who, since Robert's death, had immersed herself in the minutiae of everyday hotel life and to who the ordeal of arranging a funeral would come as just one more task to be added to her daily list of chores.

A few days earlier, Jo had watched Clive's black cab disappearing down the drive. Now it was time to watch the black hearse making its slow descent down the sweeping avenue of oaks, which had long since dropped their acorns, leaving them with nothing to shed in Mary's wake.

Jo took a deep breath, standing with what remained of the family, offering a last fond farewell to its matriarch before walking back into the hotel and taking over from Agnes at the reception desk with a heavy heart but, as far as the guests were concerned, acting as if nothing had ever happened.

One day, maybe sooner rather than later, Jo would escape. It had been easier this time watching Clive depart, knowing of their plans to set up home together in Africa and realising that, at last there was indeed a future for the two of them, no matter how hard it might prove to gain public acceptance of their relationship.

After Clive's taxi had disappeared from sight, Jo returned to the prison cell which was how Jo had come to regard the space behind the reception desk at the Carlton Hall Hotel – even if it did provide a very comfortable imprisonment.

It was time to return to that vast Victorian building, which had never felt more like a morgue now that Grandmother had passed away.

Andrina's hatred of Jo would never be any different. Now, at least it could be ignored. Jo had never understood the reasons for Andrina's intense antipathy, but her lack of empathy with Jo hardly mattered any more – not now that Clive and Jo had made plans to spend their lives together in a far distant land.

Clive's temporary departure had left a gaping hole in Jo's heart and now Grandmother's death had undermined the very foundations of Jo's continued existence at the Edinburgh hotel, albeit that it was planned to be short-lived – only lasting the time it took for Jo to apply to the authorities for a first passport.

Less than a week ago, Jo had felt so alive and so in love. Now Jo's heart descended along an unlit path, plunging into the pit of sorrow that would culminate at Grandmother's graveside.

Jo's bright appearance at reception on the day of Clive's recent departure, before Grandmother's death, dressed in a dark blue silk shirt that matched Agnes's blouse and a tie with big white spots had heralded comment from all quarters.

Now the black arm band defied anyone to find the right words of condolence to offer.

'Why don't you go and put something else on, Jo? Something that might brighten this place up a bit,' suggested Nan. 'I'm sure your grandmother wouldn't mind.'

Agnes remembered how Mary had even upheld Jo's choice of dress against Andrina's admonishments a few days before her death.

'Jo wears just about anything well,' said Nan quietly, like a mother eager to spring to her child's defence.

'Jo, have you any idea just how sexy you look in that outfit?' Moira had asked, with a more forward expression of what others were thinking. 'Remember what they say – sex sells!'

'Yes, and with your vast amount of experience in the matter, you'd probably claim that most men are in the market for buying,' snapped Andrina.

Immorality was far from Jo's mind. Jo believed in Grandmother's immortality and now that was a thing of the past. Nothing was going to bring her back.

Jo delivered coffee and shortcake biscuits to the residents' lounge, where the solicitor had sat pouring over sheaves of documents with Agnes. She was acting as sole executor to the will. No doubt they were discussing how Mary's estate was to be dealt with.

Anne, although the elder, had little expectations other than never to have to peer into an empty glass.

However, Andrina reasoned that the tide of fortune was about to sweep over her, for although she was the younger of Mary's two daughters, she was the only one who was capable of running the show at which, whilst she was loathe to admit it, Jo was rapidly becoming the rising star.

Although she had not been present at the reading of his will, Andrina had little doubt that Charlie's empire had surely passed to Mary upon his death and now there was a great deal at stake – three hotels in the Borders, the impressive Carlton Hall Hotel and a tidy sum in the bank.

No, Anne would never be entrusted with the business that had been built up over more than two decades.

As for Agnes, it was obvious that she stood to gain nothing from the will, otherwise she would not have been allowed to be an executor. No, Andrina would definitely inherit everything.

There was only one fly in the ointment, only one black-winged creature that had ever stuck to the honeypot of Mary's indulgence.

And that was Jo.

* * * * * * * * * *

On the solemn day of February 13th on which Mary's last will and testament was read, only four interested parties sat around the huge conference room table in the draughty solicitor's offices in Atholl Crescent.

Intended to seat twenty or more, the forlorn little party was gathered at one end, as if afraid to spread themselves out, lest the creation of any space between them marked them out as anything other than the close knit remnants of a family … and that they certainly were not!

Irrevocably, Mary's death had torn apart what had remained of the family, shredding it like the last morsels of meat on a bone over which a pack of hungry dogs would be forced to fight.

Andrina was muffled in a fur stole, which only served to enhance her self-appointed role as the alpha female, whilst Anne shuffled her feet nervously under the table and Agnes toyed with the straps of a leather case which hung from her shoulder.

Only Jo seemed unperturbed by the occasion.

As the will was read out, Andrina began to preen, first learning that she had inherited her mother's seldom used private dwelling house in Minto Street and then learning that all Anne was to receive was her mother's necklace and a few scraps of jewellery.

Agnes, of course, as joint executor, would receive nothing and that only left Jo who, at just seventeen, was surely too young to inherit the vast Carlton Hall Hotel and the smaller hotels in the Borders, which Charlie had brought with him into the marriage. Now, only Jo stood in her way.

The solicitor, a bespectacled little man, who twitched and twittered as he ran his stubby finger over the parchment documents, flashed wary looks at each member of the gathered assembly in turn, anxious to include every one of them, as he swept his piggy little eyes around, casting them in each direction with every sentence.

Mary's recently retired chauffeur was to receive £100 and various other small bequests. Her younger sister, still alive at the age of eighty-four, received a gift of £500.

A sum of money was to be set aside to pay for the weekly replacement of the flowers on Charlie's grave.

Andrina waited patiently, eager not to demonstrate her agitation as, slowly, the little man in the horn-rimmed spectacles enunciated one small bequest after another like a circus ring-master preparing a hushed audience for the main event.

Seconds ticked by on the huge clock which hung above the unlit fireplace. It would have been more in keeping with a station platform. Its sonorous chimes, as it struck the half hour, seemed to echo around the room like a booming knell for the recently departed.

No thunderbolt announcement here to rock Mary's last remaining relatives to the core. Her will was straightforward and matter of fact.

At last, the solicitor shuffled his papers together, standing up and stretching, as if his duty had been executed and there was nothing left for him to say.

'And...?' enquired Andrina, raising her eyebrows, so that they nearly touched the brim of her hat.

'And what, madam? Is there something else I can help you with?' replied the porky-eyed legal man, pushing his chair back beneath the mahogany desk.

Jo sat silent.

Surely there was more to come. More to be said. Property and possessions of far greater importance to be doled out. Money in the bank, stocks, shares, the smaller hotels and, of course, the great Carlton Hall Hotel, which had been Jo's home for as long as the youngest possible claimant to Mary's estate could remember.

'That's it ladies and er ...'

'What do you mean – that's it?' interrupted Andrina furiously. 'What about Carlton Hall? What about the other hotels? How about ...'

'How about you just sit back down for a moment and listen?' responded Agnes in a voice which Jo hardly recognised.

'My father worked all his life for everything he ever had – my mother too. I'm fifty-two years old and I likewise have worked all my life for what I own.'

'For what *you* own?' answered Andrina, incredulously, 'but, surely, my mother inherited the hotels and all Charlie's money when he died?' she asked, her voice quivering in high-pitched fury.

'That, my dearest Andrina, is exactly where you are wrong. Your mother might have behaved like the monarch of the glen, but she never owned very much at all after she sold up that little corner pub in Morningside. She just liked to act as though she did and who was I to spoil an old lady's delusions. Mary always enjoyed playing the part of the queen of her own private palace and I didn't see any reason to openly dispute the fact. She played her part well.'

'And you?' thundered Andrina, gathering up her fur stole and whipping it around her neck.

'And I, my dearest Andrina, am the owner of Carlton Hall and much more besides. I've owned everything for years – ever since my beloved father died.

'Charlie left everything to me as his only daughter. I was happy to let Mary think she was at the helm for all those years, but I can assure you that I am the real ship's captain and I have the right to control everyone who sails in her. I've tolerated you and sat and watched whilst you played the part of the wicked witch to Jo and bitched and sniped at your elder sister, who cannot help her addiction and who has never done you any harm.

'When we get back to the hotel, you can pack your bags. You can leave tomorrow morning. After all, you have a house of your own to move into now. I'll have your wages made up and sent round to you. In fact, I'll even have a taxi ready for you in the morning. Would nine o'clock suit?'

* * * * * * * * * *

Andrina wasn't the only one with packing to do. Jo had been given a thousand pounds by Grandmother just a few days before she died and was off to start a new life with Clive in Africa. Mozambique was where Jo was heading, far away from grey Scottish skies. A new life beckoned. Wherever Clive was going, Jo was heading too. Travelling to another continent. Crossing in style. Making dreams come true. Off to see the world. Off to find the rainbow's end.

Jo had hardly listened to a word of the tirade, which had taken place between Andrina and her sister-in-law. Instead, Jo sat mooning and musing over the words to the theme song to Breakfast at Tiffany's.

All Jo needed was a passport and that was a problem that would be taken care of tomorrow on arrival at the General Registry Office at New Register House – the grand Georgian building tucked away up a short cobbled street behind Woolworth's on the corner of Princes Street and Leith Street.

It seemed quite appropriate that tomorrow was Valentine's Day – the one day of the year when lovers were supposed to declare their love for each other and what finer declaration could there be of Jo's abiding love for Clive than planning their escape and starting a new life together far away from prying eyes and interfering busybodies.

Jo wasn't expecting to receive a Valentine's Day card from Clive and it didn't matter – what mattered was their plans for the future. All Jo cared about was that Clive was returning, coming to take Jo away from the only life that Jo had ever known. No there would be no St Valentine's card for Jo tomorrow. No protestation of Clive's undying love.

Jo didn't care.

What words could be contained on a simple folded piece of paper that could possibly enhance Jo's future happiness?

Instead, Jo had an appointment to view a very different piece of paper – an official document which had lain dusty and unseen by the light of day for seventeen long years and one which would pave the way to Jo obtaining a passport.

Tomorrow, on St Valentine's Day, Jo was to see a very special birth certificate – Jo's very own!

It was even ironic considering Jo's birth date of the thirteenth of November that St Valentine's Day was the likely date of Jo's conception. It never occurred to Jo that on that birth certificate would be written the names of Jo's true mother and father.

Chapter 39

Jo emerged up the Waverley Steps with a lightness of heart and a spring in the step on that cold afternoon in the middle of February. It had been one of those days when it had scarcely grown light and now dusk was already beginning to descend.

Jo had been waiting on tables both at breakfast and at the special St Valentine's Day lunch and could not wait to get away, wishing fervently that the last of the afternoon diners would hurry up, pressing coffee upon them when they had barely finished their desserts.

It was the table in the corner – the one that Clive usually occupied – that was preventing Jo from making good the planned escape to New Register House and an appointment that would shortly result in Jo receiving a passport to the world – a world in which Jo was at liberty to wander, with no one to be answerable to and with Clive there to act as travel guide and so very much more.

If only the last couple would stop staring lovingly into each other's eyes, swallow their coffee, swig back the brandies that the wine waiter had brought to their table, leaving Jo free to clear away, rush back to the flat above the old stable block and change into something more comfortable, before keeping that appointment with destiny.

'If you would care to move to the residents' lounge, we're offering free liqueurs as part of our special St Valentine's Day lunch,' Jo lied, ready to sacrifice all the tips that had been accumulated that lunch-time to pay for whatever choice of expensive drinks they might decide upon.

If only they would make their departure and leave the restaurant empty so that, at last, Jo could be free for the rest of that Wednesday, which was normally Jo's afternoon off.

'Thank you very much. That's very kind of you, but I don't think we need anything more to drink and there's still some wine left in the bottle,' announced the woman, who Jo had already guessed wasn't married to the man who sat opposite her.

'We'll just sit for a while and enjoy what we already have here, if you don't mind,' announced her partner, picking up his brandy balloon, swilling the contents around the bowl and taking a tiny sip at the golden brown liquid, before replacing his glass on the table with no discernible lowering of the level of its contents.

Jo silently cursed them.

A whole half hour later and they were still there. Jo kept on looking at the Accurist wristwatch, at first surreptitiously and then not even attempting to hide the frequent clock watching. Surely they would take the hint, but the two of them seemed so totally engrossed in each other that they were scarcely aware of Jo's presence.

'Can I get anything else for you?' Jo asked pointedly, as the minute hand on Jo's watch moved towards the hour and Jo began hovering around their table, making it perfectly clear that a polite refusal was what was expected.

'Well, since you were kind enough to offer us another drink on the house, earlier on, maybe I will take another brandy after all,' replied the man, settling back comfortably into his chair and stretching his legs out under the table.

Jo cursed them silently again.

All the other waiting staff were already gathered in the hotel kitchen for their own lunch. Jo alone was left serving and that meant that there was no one else to go to the bar to place the order. At this rate, Jo was never going to get any time off at all that afternoon.

'Is anyone still in the restaurant?' asked Agnes, as Jo swept past her, heading for the bar.

'Yes,' Jo snapped at her.

Remembering that it was Jo's afternoon off, Agnes emerged from behind the reception desk and followed as far as the twin glass panelled doors, which led into the bar.

Surely one of the barmaids could take over in the restaurant for half an hour and allow Jo a well-earned respite. After all, with Mary's sudden death, it had been an emotionally draining week for all of them and Jo deserved a break.

Jo hurried into the bar and was surprised to found Andrina topping up the optics. In view of Nan's uncharacteristic outburst the day before in the solicitor's office, when she had ordered Andrina to pack her bags and leave, it seemed strange to find her occupying her usual place behind the bar as if, for all the world, nothing had happened.

Jo didn't understand. Certainly, it was unlike Agnes to lash out in the way in which she had done so the day before, but then the last person that Jo could ever feel sorry for was Andrina, who had treated Jo atrociously for so long, lashing out physically during Jo's formative years and, now that Jo was that much older, seldom missing the opportunity to strike out verbally with a tongue that was as sharp as one of the chef's best boning knives.

'Andrina, can you get someone else to finish serving in the restaurant? It's Jo's afternoon off and, at this rate, it will be teatime before Jo gets away.' said Agnes curtly, but in a voice which seemed to harbour none of the previous day's bitterness.

'I guess Jo will continue to get away with everything even now that Mary is no longer with us,' retorted Andrina, as Jo headed for the door in an attempt to beat a hasty retreat.

'Andrina! Enough! I thought we'd decided on a truce. If you have anything at all you'd like to say to Jo, let's have it right now.'

'No, I can assure you that I won't say anything to Jo – not now that we've come to an agreement between the two of us. We do understand each other, don't we Agnes! I shall say nothing to Jo for as long as I am allowed to stay at Carlton Hall.'

* * * * * * * * * *

285

Jo had not been party to the sharp exchange of words between Agnes and Andrina, placing the brandy that had just been poured on to a silver plated tray and returning to the dining room.

At last the couple made a move to leave. Jo rushed to the cloakroom, anxious to retrieve their coats and see them on their way, quietly folding the ten shilling note, which had been proffered as a tip between nimble fingers, before ushering them out of the door.

Jo would have summoned Grandmother's chauffeur for the trip into the city centre, if the intention had been to arrive in Princes Street in style, but today Jo preferred to remain incognito.

Somehow it seemed appropriate that there should be a slightly clandestine approach to Jo's self-appointed task, for Jo was yet to reveal to anyone the carefully laid plans, which would see Jo flying off in less than three weeks' time to start a new life in Africa.

Clive was giving up his job and planned to join Air Safari, whilst Jo was going to work in one of the newly established safari lodges, which were advertising for experienced British and European hotel workers to teach the African trainee waiters and front of house staff the rudiments of providing the level of service, which the well-heeled clientele expected on their visits to the game reserves.

Clive had already written his letter of resignation to Caledonian Airways and as soon as Jo had plucked up the courage to tell Nan about the impending departure of her young charge from a life of toil at Carlton Hall Hotel, they would be off on life's new adventure.

All Jo needed was a passport and, for that purpose, it was necessary to obtain a copy of the birth certificate that Jo had never been allowed access to before and which Anne claimed never to have held in her possession. Access to New Register House was barred to anyone under the age of sixteen, but now that Jo had turned seventeen, there was no longer any such restriction.

Muffled against the cold February air and aware that the light was already beginning to fail, Jo crossed Princes Street, walking past Woolworth's where, years ago, Uncle Robert had often stopped to buy an assorted bag of boiled sweets for Jo to "share" with Georgina, or a bag of broken biscuits which, as a child, Jo would take to the field and apportion with Polly the pony, picking through the contents of the brown paper bag, saving all the custard creams and handing over the ginger nuts which, as a child, Jo didn't care for at all.

The wind blew across the narrow, cobbled street, cannoning its way down the alleyway, which ran alongside the Café Royal on the corner and bowled headlong out into West Register Street, greeting Jo with an icy blast, which seemed to frost the very tips of Jo's fingers.

The imposing looking building emerged out of the dull, cold, miserable February afternoon. As Jo ran up the stone steps. Jo counted them for no apparent reason, noting that there were thirteen in all, before the huge wooden doors beckoned Jo to enter into the hushed, quietened atmosphere of the central domed chamber, containing no less than four miles of shelving, which housed nearly half a million registers.

At the various levels the vast volumes were stacked on five tiers of ornate iron work shelving, which occupied the upper galleries, stretching towards the lofty central dome of the large circular chamber in which the registers were all neatly arranged – all in leather bindings, each in an assortment of different colours to denote the different significant stages of life – red to record births, black to denote deaths and green the colour chosen to mark a marriage.

Row upon row of dusty volumes each with a thousand different stories to tell – page after page of parchment awaiting to reveal the secrets of countless generations.

It was one of the red volumes that Jo was here to inspect and from which to extract the details of an entry into the world, which had for so long remained a mystery.

Here within this awe-inspiring circular room, into which what little light poured from above was recorded every birth since civil registration began in 1855. Here too were the details of every child in Scotland adopted since 1930.

The building itself was an amazing feat of Georgian structural engineering, whose construction had finally been completed in 1834.

In some ways the upper walkways, with their diamond-shaped grilles and wire mesh safety fencing were more reminiscent of a Victorian prison.

Above the red leather bound birth volumes occupying the first tier of galleries were the black death registers, soon to be added to with the details of Grandmother's death, and followed on the third floor by the green leather bound marriage registers in which the merger of Jo's life with Clive would surely never be featured.

In the hushed silence below, no one spoke in anything other than whisper, as if to speak of the past and question its recording was a crime in itself.

At first, Jo felt in awe of approaching the bespectacled, bookish, middle-aged woman, who occupied the light oak-coloured desk, which formed the public counter in the centre of the circular room, but Jo soon gathered sufficient confidence to make the necessary request. As her name badge revealed, her name was Margaret McKay. She smiled over the rim of her spectacles, as Jo held her gaze and launched into a short explanation.

She assured Jo that she would do her best to help, instantly being coerced into providing whatever co-operation she could by Jo's quietly spoken appeal – the plea for her assistance backed up by those dark, doleful eyes, which had always been Jo's greatest asset.

'What district were you born in?' asked Margaret.

'I believe it was Glasgow,' ventured Jo, who had once quizzed Nanny Bapty on the subject, learning a little about her background as a midwife and how it was she who had initially issued Jo with that first slap, stinging and biting on a bare backside, long before the first of Andrina's blows had rained down on her half-sister's child.

'Take a seat, while I try to establish which register I need to locate,' Margaret urged, beckoning Jo to occupy one of the tall, light oak-coloured stools, encircling the outer perimeter one each beside the twenty eight research cubicles, which afforded little privacy to those who had come to seek out secrets.

With nothing else to do but sit and wait, whilst the woman began her search for the required documentation, Jo looked up at the ceiling above the little research cubicle, with its brightly shining light, shaped like a flying saucer.

Jo's stomach was churning, turning double somersaults like a circus acrobat walking a high wire tightrope. Somewhere far, far above the ninety foot dome, which formed the centrepiece of this hushed, quietened room, Clive was up there in the skies – flying high. Within days of Jo obtaining that precious passport, Jo would be up there too – up there with Clive, treading the tightrope of public disapproval, but at last sharing a life with the ring-master of their joint future.

Jo began to feel apprehensive. What if the birth certificate could not be found? Would it ever be possible to obtain a passport without it?

'Here you are, I've found it for you – Register of Births Volume XXIX Entry number 123. I take it that you already know that ...'

'Yes,' Jo interjected. 'It's all right. If you were about to tell me that I was adopted, I already know.'

'I'm sorry, it's just that we have to be sure. It can come as quite a shock for someone seeing their birth certificate for the first time and learning that they were adopted.'

'I understand,' said Jo, adding, 'and thank you for your concern.'

'That's all right, my dear. I just didn't want you to get a shock,' replied the public counter supervisor, as she scrutinised the documentation, her eyes squinting beneath her spectacles, as she struggled to read the scrawly, handwritten entry.

'Don't worry!' said Jo.

'May I ask why you want your birth certificate? Is it for your passport?'

'Yes, I'm leaving for Africa in just over two weeks' time with ... a friend,' replied Jo.

'Oh, my dear, I'm afraid you've left it all a bit late. It normally takes six weeks to come through.'

Jo listened to her words, throwing Margaret a look of deep and desperate disappointment from across the enquiry desk.

'My grandmother died last week and everything just went out the window,' replied Jo sadly.

'I take it you already have your passport photographs and that you've had them countersigned,' asked Margaret with what seemed like genuine concern for Jo's predicament.

'Yes, I have them right here,' replied Jo, extracting two black and white prints and an application form from a buff-coloured envelope, which was already addressed to the Glasgow Passport Office.

'I was hoping to send everything by post to them this afternoon, as soon as I have a copy of my birth certificate, but I think I may have already missed the last post.'

'Look, I'll see what I can do to help you. My sister works at the Passport Office. If you like, I'll telephone her for you now and see if she can help. I shouldn't really do this, but I can arrange to send your application and an extract from the Register by courier this evening and, with any luck, you'll have your passport in plenty of time,' Margaret ventured kindly.

'Thank you. You've been most helpful,' said Jo with a genuine feeling of gratitude, flattening out the application form and handing it over the counter, together with the two head and shoulders photographs, duly signed on the back by Jo's doctor.

Jo's saviour scrutinised the application form, with its boldly printed and easily legible script, which closely emulated Agnes's neat hand with which, day after day, she filled the hotel ledgers.

'At least I can read your handwriting, which is more than I can say for what's written on your birth certificate. Elsie, can you take over here while I make a telephone call to my sister?'

On her return, Margaret informed Jo that, provided it could be collected personally from the Glasgow Passport Office, Jo could have the necessary travel documents by the following Monday afternoon.

'Thank you. Thank you so much. It's not a problem, I can arrange to be in Glasgow on Monday afternoon.'

'Don't you have to be at work on Monday?' asked Margaret.

'No,' said Jo simply.

It wasn't Jo's official day off, but that wasn't of any consequence. Jo no longer cared. In fact, with the cheque for a thousand pounds that Grandmother had written out and given to Jo just days before she died, nothing concerned Jo at all.

At last Jo was independent and even Andrina's spiteful rebukes were no longer of any importance. No, with the acquisition of the passport and the freedom that it represented, nothing really mattered any more.

In the panic of imagining that it had been left too late to obtain a passport in time for the proposed trip to Africa, Jo had momentarily forgotten all thoughts of that other official document and what it might reveal about the past and about Jo's parenthood.

'Can you read me what it says on my birth certificate?' asked Jo at last, fixing Margaret with those dark, appealing eyes and a winning smile.

Now, as far as Jo was concerned, the woman was regarded as a friend indeed.

'I'm afraid my eyesight isn't all that it could be these days. I can make out your name – Jo isn't it, but I can hardly read the names of your parents, or anything else besides. I'm afraid most of our registrars don't have such neat handwriting as yours. I have to say that some of their scrawl is worse than any doctor's,' she observed wryly, turning the book with its red binding away from Jo, so that her colleague could gain a better view of the upturned script. 'Elsie can you read this for me, please?'

'What does it say about the names of my mother and father?' enquired Jo anxiously. Suddenly all thought of obtaining a passport was forgotten – all thoughts of clear African skies instantly dispelled, as the questions to which Jo had sought the answers, for all those years leapt to the fore.

All that mattered right now was the information that had been recorded so hastily in that vast red volume. All that concerned Jo were the two names on that birth certificate. Here was the key to unlocking every question that Jo had ever wanted to ask.

Stupidly, Jo had never given a second thought to what would surely be revealed on this day – St Valentine's Day, when Jo's lover had his head quite literally in the clouds and, at last, Jo's thoughts had emerged into the real world of impending discovery.

'I think I can read it, if you give me a moment,' spoke Elsie, casting her eyes intently across the handwritten entries on the page. 'It says that the father's name is "Thompson – Clive Thompson" and under the heading of rank or profession, it says "Navigator, Royal Canadian Air Force". The mother's name is listed as …

It took a second for the horrible truth to dawn. It was maybe two seconds before Jo let out a terrible cry of anguish, turned and ran from the circular room, with its light green painted wrought iron fretwork, which suddenly, like a prison, Jo had to escape from.

Elsie, who had just read out the fateful words, turned to her colleague in amazement as Jo hurtled out of the building and out into the gathering twilight of that cold St Valentine's Day.

'What on earth did I say!' exclaimed Elsie. 'I only got as far as deciphering the father's name and occupation. I didn't even get as far as saying who the mother was.'

Chapter 40

As darkness fell on that February afternoon, a light dusting of snow had begun to cover the cobbles in the streets which surrounded New Register House. Jo had run blindly out of the building, descending the stone steps two at a time.

It seemed hard to imagine that these were the very same steps, which had led the way into the Scottish records office just half an hour ago, when Jo had been full of hope, but bringing Jo thirteen steps closer to a discovery, which now rocked Jo's world to the very core.

Not stopping to look left or right, Jo had passed through the ornate cast iron gates, painted as black as the future which now faced Jo.

Jo passed Woolworth's on the corner, with its window display full of cut out red hearts and suggestions of gifts to be exchanged between lovers.

Tragically, what Jo had received on this St Valentine's Day was not a token of Clive's affection, but an understanding of the past, which had pierced Jo's heart as surely as any Cupid's arrow, but which had brought with it only pain and despair.

Looking up towards the North Bridge stood the bronze statue of the Duke of Wellington astride his horse, now dappled with the rapidly descending snow flakes, falling in little flurries, clinging precariously to the horse's mane for a few moments before disappearing into oblivion.

If only Jo's thoughts could be so instantly dispelled, swept away like a light dusting of snow, which refused to settle. However, this news was more like an avalanche, which blotted out the way ahead and, with it, all hopes for the future. Suddenly, there was no future – not with Clive.

How many years had Jo sought to find a father?

Now that the revelation of the identity of that person had been presented how it pained Jo to learn the truth – it hurt more than Jo could ever have imagined.

As the full realisation began to dawn, it had inveigled itself into Jo's brain like a streak of thunderous lighting, arriving like a bolt from the blue – a lightning flash whose devilish tongue, like Andrina's, was capable of inflicting so much misery and mental suffering.

How would it ever be possible to pick up the shattered pieces? What hope was there of developing any form of relationship with Clive now? What they had shared together was something which would always be frowned upon and now a commitment between them on any level was rendered totally impossible.

What use was a passport to Jo now that their journey together was at its end?

Clive had already supplied Jo with an airline ticket before he had flown off on a tour of duty. Now it was a ticket to nowhere – nothing more than a scrap of paper with a few basic identifying details scribbled inside it – just like the red register book that had contained such scant information about the man who was Jo's father and the woman who was …

… Jo's mother.

In that horrible moment, Jo realised what had happened. In the shock of discovering the name of Jo's father, any enquiry as to the identity of Jo's mystery mother had been totally forgotten.

Jo was brought up with a start, halting abruptly at the top of the Waverley Steps, as a gust of air swept upwards, blowing straight into Jo's face, freckling it with snow flakes, as if the blast of cold air might serve to refresh a befuddled brain which, until then, had been capable of only one thought and one alone.

Jo hadn't stopped to consider that on the birth certificate one name would undoubtedly follow another and that side by side with the details of Jo's father would be listed the same basic details about the woman who had given birth to Jo.

A name.

Jo turned and ran back across Princes Street, dodging a number 12 bus bound for Portobello and almost being mown down by a dark green Ford Zephyr, with its shiny chrome bumpers, whose driver leant out of his window and shouted a sharp rebuke at Jo for jay-walking.

Again Jo faced those thirteen steps, which had now become slippery and treacherous underfoot. Heedlessly, Jo ran at them, losing a footing on the thirteenth, stumbling and toppling head over heels down their entire length.

Jo was unscathed in the fall and remained undeterred, brushing snow from the belted raincoat and reaching the top of the steps at the very moment that the last visitor was ushered out of the building by the concierge and the vast double doors were firmly and decisively shut.

Jo heard the bolts being slid into position and the key being turned in the lock, as Jo stood screaming to be allowed back in, hammering on the light oak coloured panelling in desperation to find out that last remaining secret – that final revelation that had to be unfolded there and then in order to be able to fit the last piece of the jigsaw into place.

Suddenly Jo wanted everything to come together – for it all to make some sort of sense. Jo had to know the truth, as much as it might hurt to do so and even if the picture that it presented would only herald further unhappiness.

Right now it was like a complicated puzzle, which was only just beginning to slot together, but which still had one all important piece missing.

Jo had to know. Jo had to know everything.

Not understanding anything of the past had been tolerable, but being in possession of only half of the story was completely unbearable. Ignorance had been better – so much better than this.

Now the future that beckoned was completely impossible. None of the pieces could ever be slotted back together again.

If Clive was Jo's natural father, then who was Jo's birth mother? Was she someone with who Clive had shared a passing acquaintance at some point during the latter stages of the Second World War? Worst still, could she possibly be someone Jo already knew?

Clive had once told Jo about how he had spent some time at the Carlton Hall Hotel during the hostilities, but that was at a time before Grandad Charlie had bought the hotel.

No one Jo knew had any connection with the place in those days … except for the one person who had worked there for years – Meg, the woman who operated the hotel laundry from the little wash-house round the back and who, by her own proud proclamation, had been employed in the same job for the past twenty years.

* * * * * * * * * *

It was already past five o'clock and Meg would have left the hotel at least a couple of hours ago. She always begun work early in the morning – sometimes before it was even light.

She would be back on duty in the little wash-house at six thirty the next morning, but how could Jo be expected to wait that long to question her?

Jo knew where she lived in the little village of Ratho from which she cycled in to work each morning on a rusty old bicycle. It had once belonged to her elderly mother, who suffered from chronic arthritis and who lived with her slow-witted daughter in a little terraced house on the outskirts of a small, down at heel council estate.

Jo had visited Meg there once or twice in the past, delivering her back home in style in the back of the Bentley, with Willie the chauffeur on bitterly cold winter afternoons, usually after a heavy snowfall when Grandmother, or Agnes had insisted that it was too slippery for her to ride home on her bicycle.

Outside the little council house, with its grey concrete rendered walls, the main feature was a row of dustbins and at the side was a dilapidated wooden shed in which Meg stowed her bicycle and in which she housed an assortment of pets, which the motherly Meg always fondly referred to as "her children".

Jo stood in the bitter cold, watching and waiting for a cab which was heading in the direction of the West End, peering through tears which mixed with the flurry of powdery white snow, as it began to settle in little drifts against the kerbside.

At this time of the afternoon, when everyone was heading home from work and on a day when the weather had taken a turn for the worse, available taxis were few and far between.

Jo stood for maybe a quarter of an hour before a black cab with an illuminated "For Hire" sign finally trundled across the North Bridge, turning left into Princes Street, where there was always a good chance of finding a fare.

Jo stepped out from the pavement, anxious to hail the cab ahead of anyone who might emerge up the Waverley Steps from the railway station.

'I'd like to go to Ratho, please,' said Jo quietly, before shaking off the worst of the snow and diving into the back of the cab, which immediately felt warm and inviting and offered some sort of sanctuary from the outside world and all its troubles.

Jo perched nervously on the edge of the piped bank seating, unable to settle back into the deep leather upholstery. All Jo's thoughts were firmly concentrated on what words could possibly be found to say to Meg, as the taxi passed first along the length of city's main shopping thoroughfare and then out on to the Corstorphine Road, past the entrance to Edinburgh Zoo and onwards away from the hustle and bustle of the Scottish capital.

Reaching Ratho, Jo immediately became confused and was unable to instruct the taxi driver which way to go. Jo had forgotten how the council estate formed a maze of identical housing, all occupying streets which looked exactly the same.

It wasn't until Jo remembered that the house where Meg lived was situated close to the one and only telephone box on the estate that Jo was finally able to give the right directions to the taxi driver.

Once the red telephone box had been located, it took no time at all to seek out the nondescript little terraced house, which was home to Meg and her mother.

Delving into a small leather purse, Jo sorted through the loose change, handing the taxi driver two half crowns and a silver sixpence as a tip, thrusting open the rear door of the cab against the wind, which raged down the narrow alley-way between two blocks of council houses, sending a flurry of snow into the rear passenger compartment of the cab.

Jo's nose began to run and reddened eyes struggled to focus and find a way up the crazy paving path, which led to the front door of the corporation house with its standard pillar box red painted door that in every respect matched all the others on the estate, except for the fact that the brass door knocker probably shone a little brighter than the rest.

Jo tapped on the door, smudging the polished brass with fingers which glistened with snow flakes. At first there was no answer.

Jo knocked on the door again, a little louder this time in order that the sound might be heard above the introductory theme tune of "Bonanza" – the television series Western, which blared out from the black and white set in the sparsely furnished sitting room.

It was one of the old televisions which had recently been replaced in the hotel bedrooms at Carlton Hall. Meg, who could never otherwise have afforded such a luxury, had been delighted when Agnes had announced that she could have one of the old Ferguson sets free of charge, as long as she arranged to have it collected.

Meg was beside herself with excitement at the thought of having her very own television set, even if it had cost her the price of two new valves when it had broken down a short while later and her mother had complained that they had been forced to listen to the Queen's Speech on the wireless, after inviting several of the neighbours round to watch Her Majesty appearing on television on Christmas Day.

Meg shuffled out of a rather threadbare armchair and crossed over to the television, turning down the volume by means of the big dial on the side of the polished wooden casing.

She was slow and ponderous in her actions, as well as being somewhat slow-witted and it was another couple of minutes before she finally opened the front door.

'Jo!' she exclaimed in obvious surprise. 'What are you doing here?'

'I'd like to speak to you, Meg. May I come in?'

'Yes, do come in, Jo,' Meg replied eagerly. 'Mother, we've got a visitor. We don't very often get visitors. Do you want to watch "Bonanza"? It's very good. Did you know that there is someone in it called Little Joe? Isn't that funny!'

294

'I guess so,' replied Jo simply.

'I remember that was what I used to call you years ago when you were very little. Do you remember? Mother's in the kitchen. We're having shepherd's pie tonight. Come in and I'll make us a nice cup of tea. Do you want to have some shepherd's pie? Have you come to see my rabbits? One of them has got babies. Do come and see my rabbits, won't you?'

Jo was immediately aware that it would prove extremely difficult to raise such an awkward matter with Meg and, perhaps, even more of a challenge to gain a straight answer.

Maintaining Meg's concentration on one subject was virtually impossible at the best of times with her scatterbrain approach to just about any topic of conversation, far less one which was going to be all too tricky to raise in the first place.

Jo reasoned that the only way to keep Meg focussed and to gain any information at all from her was to allow her to ramble on about whatever subject took her fancy, in the hope that, from time to time, she could be gently steered back to the burning question that was foremost in Jo's mind.

'Yes, I'd love to see your rabbits, Meg,' replied Jo pleasantly. 'Do you still keep them in the shed outside? Why don't you show them to me before I take my coat off and, yes, I'd love some shepherd's pie. Did you make it yourself?'

'No,' responded Meg, adding hastily, 'but I mashed all the potatoes and I'm going to make the gravy.'

Not unnaturally, Jo had no appetite at all, but it was important to keep Meg talking and not to upset her in any way, if there was ever to be any chance of learning the truth.

As hard as it was to do so, Jo had to keep every emotion in check and right now what was troubling Jo most of all was the certain knowledge that it would have been so very easy for someone like Clive to have taken advantage of Meg all those years ago.

If it had really happened as Jo had imagined, then how could Clive have forced himself upon someone as innocent and trusting as Meg? It didn't bear thinking about.

Maybe it had happened on St Valentine's Day. After all, as Jo had already calculated, the timing would have been exactly right. If what had passed between Clive and Meg had resulted in her becoming pregnant, then Jo could very easily shortly be sitting down to supper with the true mother and true grandmother whose identity had been concealed for so long.

* * * * * * * * * *

Agnes had delegated the task of manning the reception desk to one of the barmaids, whilst she went to look for Jo, who was supposed to be serving in the restaurant that evening.

It was most unlike Jo to be late for work, even if Jo's normal time off had been severely curtailed by the couple who had proven so reluctant to leave the dining room that afternoon.

Grandmother had always instilled a sense of good timekeeping into family members and staff alike. No one ever dared to be absent from duty at the appointed hour – except that was for Anne, whom everyone, including Agnes, had long since given up on, acknowledging the fact that, nowadays, the woman would often take to her bed for days at a time, seldom bothering to dress.

She greeted anyone who looked in on her attired in an unbecoming dressing gown and with blood-shot eyes, which betrayed a total lack of awareness in whatever might be going on all around her.

In the bar a lively crowd had already gathered and Andrina was busy juggling the optics, with a smile to each of the punters that was about as genuine as the freshly caught wild Scottish salmon, which was listed on the restaurant's menu that night and which had been stored in the giant hotel freezer since last September.

It was true that Andrina was popular with some of the regulars, who seemed to enjoy baiting her as much as a salmon fisherman might take pleasure in choosing the right fly with which to load his hook in the hope of landing a prized catch.

Her ready wit and acid tongue were her stock-in-trade behind the bar.

Most of those who chose to drink at the Carlton Hall Hotel on a regular basis accepted her for what she was and, somehow, seldom took exception to the squeeze of lemon with which she liberally laced any conversation.

Agnes hadn't forgotten the tirade which she had launched against her sister-in-law in the solicitor's office only the day before, when Mary's will had been read.

Now Nan had to accept that she had been given no choice but to take the woman back, employing her behind the bar at the Carlton Hall Hotel for as long as she chose to stay.

It wasn't just something that she might say to Jo that had persuaded Agnes that it was better to buy Andrina's silence. It was better for everyone's sake.

And especially, it was what she might reveal to one of the hotel's regular guests that, above all, had convinced Agnes that the only course of action to take was to welcome Andrina back, if not with open arms, at least with a false smile.

* * * * * * * * * *

Meg was holding one of her pet rabbits close to her, inviting Jo to stroke the animal, which had settled in a docile manner in her arms. It was chewing on the end of a slightly blackened carrot that the woman had extracted from a selection of somewhat tired looking vegetables wrapped in an old newspaper.

One of the hotel's chefs had left a parcel of vegetables which were no longer fit to be served to the guests outside the kitchen door for her to collect on her way home.

Some of the more wholesome looking specimens had already been chopped and diced and were due to feature in the shepherd's pie cooking in the oven in the kitchen of the little council house, filling it with an appetising aroma of the meal which Jo had been invited to share, but which Jo couldn't possibly hope to stomach.

'You're holding that rabbit just like a baby, Meg,' said Jo in a pointed effort to bring the conversation back round to the subject which, for Jo, was such a desperately important issue.

'It *is* a baby,' replied Meg defiantly, fixing Jo with eyes that would brook no argument. 'It's one of *my* babies. It's only a few weeks old. I've given lots and lots of them away to the children around here. Would you like one, Jo?'

Here was Jo's chance – a golden opportunity to steer the awkward conversation around to the burning question that was uppermost in Jo's mind.

True, Jo could have simply returned to Register House to find out all the answers, but Jo wasn't prepared to wait that long and continued to coax Meg into providing responses to the questions which had troubled Jo for so many years.

It was as if Jo had stepped on to a roller coaster of discovery. Now, there was no stopping. Questions had to be asked. At last everything about Jo's past had to be known and right now the only person who could provide the answers was Meg.

'Have you ever had a baby of your own, Meg?' Jo ventured tentatively. 'Not a baby rabbit, but a real baby – one which was born after your tummy had grown big?'

'You're grandmother always said it was very naughty to have a baby unless you were married,' replied Meg simply, but in a way which totally avoided the question.

Jo knew that it was important to tread carefully. One wrong word and Meg would say nothing more at all on the subject, leaving Jo in an unbearable state of suspense, which would result in a sleepless night in the flat above the old stables.

'I understand that you would never intentionally have done anything that my grandmother wouldn't have approved of Meg. I know that you've always been a good girl, but have you ever had a boyfriend?' Meg blushed.

'Yes,' she demurred simply.

'What was his name, Meg?'

'It was Clive,' she replied.

Suddenly, it was as if the nightmare was turning into reality. Jo could hardly bear to hear any more, but somehow there was a need to go on, a relentless quest for further information, to ask the vital questions and, at last, to learn the answers, no matter how much it might hurt to know the truth.

'Did you like him very much?' asked Jo, with admirable composure, biting back the tears, once again swelling beneath eyelids, which already felt red raw with grief.

'Yes, we spent a whole afternoon together once. I liked him very much,' she replied. 'He was very kind to me.'

'How was he kind to you, Meg?'

'He gave me lots of chocolate to eat!'

'He gave you chocolate? Was that all?'

'No,' said Meg. 'He talked to me. Nobody talks to me very much. We sat on the bench outside the wash-house and we talked and we ate all his chocolate.'

'What did you talk about?' Jo ventured gently.

'He told me it was his birthday. His friends had bought him chocolate for his birthday. Nobody buys me chocolate. Does anyone ever buy you chocolate, Jo?'

'Yes, sometimes,' answered Jo.

'I like chocolate,' said Meg simply.

'So do I.'

'My rabbits don't like chocolate. I bought Kit Kat bars for them once as a special treat and they didn't eat them.'

Trying to keep Meg's mind focussed was almost impossible with her butterfly brain, which flitted from one subject to another, back and forth like a Red Admiral seeking pinches of pollen from whichever flower it chose to land on next.

Jo was at pains to prevent the woman's mind from wandering off on to yet another tangent and, equally, had great difficulty in constantly dragging her back to the subject which they simply had to discuss.

'When was this that you first met him – your boyfriend?' Jo enquired desperately. 'Was it during the war, when chocolate was being rationed?'

'Yes,' replied Meg. 'It was nearly at the end of the war, when there were lots of injured soldiers staying at Carlton Hall.'

'Do you remember exactly when it was Meg?'

'Yes, I remember it, because it was a funny day.'

'What do you mean by a "funny" day, Meg?'

'It was February 29th.'

So it was a leap year. If Clive had been celebrating his birthday in the company of the slow-witted Meg and if there had been a brief sexual encounter between the two of them, then it was just feasible that Jo, born that same year on November 13th, had been the result of their liaison eight and a half months afterwards.

Suddenly a conversation which had once occurred between Jo and Nanny Bapty sprung into Jo's memory, in which she had explained how she had been present at Jo's birth.

Nanny Bapty! How could Jo have been so stupid never to have thought to have questioned the one woman who surely knew all the answers! Nanny Bapty had been one of the midwives, who had helped bring Jo into the world on that cold November's day in 1944 and here was Jo wasting valuable time questioning a simple woman who, through no fault of her own, could never be relied upon to give a straightforward answer.

Nanny Bapty knew about Jo being born in a Glasgow clinic, but what was far more important was the fact that she had to know the identity of Jo's true birth mother.

She hadn't worked at Carlton Hall for some years, having taken up a new appointment at the time when she felt that Jo was too old to warrant her caring attention. Now she was employed caring for a well to do elderly woman, who was in need of a lady's companion. Nanny Bapty lived in North Berwick – about twenty-five miles from the centre of Edinburgh.

It was too far to get a taxi to take Jo there tonight, but Jo had always kept in touch with her, sending her postcards and writing short letters to her from time to time, bringing her up to date with all that was happening back at the Carlton Hall Hotel.

298

Having written to Nanny Bapty so many times over the years, her address was firmly etched in Jo's memory. With any luck, the wealthy woman by whom she was now employed would be on the telephone and there was a red telephone box at the end of the short cul-de-sac where Meg lived.

Promising Meg to call again soon, Jo made a hurried departure from the dilapidated wooden shed in the back garden of the little council house, making straight for the nearby telephone box and the opportunity to speak to the one woman who surely held all the answers.

Chapter 41

Amanda and Rosalind, the two air hostesses, sat at the bar of the Carlton Hall Hotel sipping glasses of Babycham.

A crowd from the local rugby club had gathered. Two of the men had singled them out and were making a definite play for them, offering to buy their drinks and joining in the two girls' conversation at every opportunity.

Rosalind seemed to appreciate the show of attention, but Amanda was more withdrawn. She had recently become engaged to a friend of Clive's called Paul MacDonald, a thrusting young political correspondent with *The Scotsman*, who had his sights set on Fleet Street.

Amanda did not want to be seen in another man's company and especially not on St Valentine's Day, when her boyfriend was working on an assignment abroad and could not be with her.

Indeed, she didn't really know why she had joined Rosalind in the bar that night. She would readily have gone to her room after the long flight, drawn herself a long, hot, soapy bath and wallowed in her self-indulgence.

However, Rosalind had pleaded with her to at least come downstairs for half an hour and they had already been occupying two of the bar stools for over an hour, fending off some of the men who sought their company for the evening.

It was not until Rosalind accepted the invitation of her most ardent would-be suitor to have dinner with him that evening and maybe go on to a dance afterwards, that Amanda was at last free to retire upstairs, kick off her shoes and begin the process of pampering herself. She didn't intend going out afterwards and knew that if she returned downstairs on her own too soon, she would be likely to have to fight off the attentions of one or more of the rugby players.

Besides, it was a bitterly cold night and the snow was already beginning to drift. Trudging through the city centre in the snow late at night searching for a taxi was not Amanda's idea of how best to end the evening.

No, she would order a quiet dinner in her room and maybe return to the bar much later for a nightcap. With any luck, by that time, the hotel bar would be occupied only by couples sharing a quiet corner together and no one would bother her.

She swirled the last of her Babycham around in a glass which was decorated on the side with a little animal figure straight out of a Walt Disney film, stabbed the cocktail cherry and made her exit, leaving Rosalind to enjoy a more adventurous evening in the company of the man who had been making eyes at her earlier on.

As Amanda passed the hotel reception, she overheard Agnes making excuses for Jo's absence to the head waiter.

Nan was always protective towards Jo and would normally take Jo's side in any argument – no matter whether she felt that Jo had the right to rely upon her support, or not.

Agnes might not ever have had the time to indulge Jo in the way that Mary had done for so many years, but still she displayed a degree of tolerance towards Jo that belied their association.

No, as far as Jo was concerned, Nan could always be relied upon, speaking out whenever Andrina exercised her sharp tongue on the teenager and, in many ways, acting like a lioness protecting one of her cubs.

'Jo will be left in no doubt that the side has been let down this evening,' Agnes told the head waiter, knowing all the while that she would say nothing at all.

After all, it had been a traumatic week, what with Mary's death and Jo probably needed time to be alone – time to grieve privately. Jo was never usually one to show emotion in public. Always the consummate performer, few people were ever allowed to know what was going on in Jo's head which, right at that moment, was spinning cartwheels of apprehension.

* * * * * * * * * *

Jo cranked the stiff metal door of the telephone box open, squeezed inside and, with rapidly freezing fingers, began rifling through what loose change was contained in the little leather purse for the necessary number of coppers to make that call to Nanny Bapty and to have the opportunity to ask her the vital question which still gnawed away at Jo's mind.

After the death of Grandad Charlie and Uncle Robert, Nanny Bapty had always been the one person in Jo's life who was utterly dependable.

Even Grandmother, for all her sometimes excessive over indulgence, would occasionally lack the time to speak to Jo when the day to day business of running the hotel – which, Jo now knew, had never been hers to call her own in the first place – seemed to occupy every spare moment of her time.

Nanny Bapty believed in straight talking and would never knowingly tell a lie. She had long ago instilled in Jo the fact that it was always best to tell the truth – no matter what the consequences might be and right now she was about to be put to the test.

Nervously, Jo dialled for the operator, listening to the long tone and waiting for a connection, before asking to be put through to directory enquiries.

Jo gave the details of Nanny Bapty's employer's name and address, realising immediately that the short, stubby pencil which hung on a length of string from the console containing the local Edinburgh telephone directories was missing and, therefore, there was nothing to write with.

Having been supplied with the necessary telephone number, there was nothing left for it, but to begin chanting it over and over again in an attempt to memorise it.

Jo dialled and waited for an answer – waiting for an answer to the question that had troubled Jo for all those years since Uncle Robert's funeral when the subject of the adoption had first been openly voiced by Andrina, instigating the dawning realisation that, as far as Jo's parentage was concerned, nothing was as it seemed.

As soon as a female voice was heard on the other end of the line, Jo inserted four pennies into the metal slot, one after another – whilst a great deal more than four pence worth of thoughts hung heavily in the cramped space in which Jo's feet stamped in an attempt to keep warm, to maintain the circulation and, most of all, in an effort to practise the necessary patience before Nanny Bapty was brought to the telephone.

Jo had pressed Button A immediately that the voice was heard and now there was nothing left to do, but wait until the familiar voice of Nanny Bapty greeted Jo with a note of unexpected joy in her voice.

'Jo, it's wonderful to hear from you. I was so sorry to learn that your grandmother had passed away. I hope the wreath that I ...' The line crackled, drowning out the last of Nanny Bapty's words of condolence. It was probably the heavy fall of snow, causing bad atmospherics, rendering a normal, uninterrupted conversation virtually impossible.

'Yes. It was lovely. Thank you,' Jo replied hurriedly, remembering nothing of the flowers she had sent, but aware that the short stack of pennies piled up on the metal telephone console was rapidly dwindling.

'I'm so glad ...'

'Nanny, there's something I have to ask you. You told me once that ... *(crackle)* ... were one of the midwives at the clinic ... *(crackle)* ... born.'

'Jo, speak up. I can hardly hear you.'

'Nanny, you were there when I was born. You must know ... *(crackle)* ... my mother. Was it Meg who works in the wash-house?'

'Good heavens, no. Whatever put that ... *(crackle)* ... into your head?'

'It is someone I already know, isn't it? Please, please, Nanny tell ...' *(crackle)*.

'I really think that it is not my place to ... *(crackle)* ...You should ask ...' *(crackle)* ...

At that point the pips sounded and Jo hastily slid another four pennies into the metal slot, noting that only another four remained.

'Nanny, you've got to tell me. You're the only one who ... *(crackle)* ... the truth.'

'Jo, it's really not my place to ... *(crackle)* ... Why don't you come and visit me? We can't talk about this over the ...' *(crackle)* ...

'No, Nanny,' Jo begged.

'All right, Jo, if you insist. Yes, it is someone you know. I recognized her as your mother years ago when I came for an interview with your grandmother, but I never said anything, but I suppose I have to ... *(crackle)* ... It's ...'

The pips sounded again, interrupting Nanny Bapty's reluctant revelation of the truth. Jo inserted the last of the four pennies into the coin box.

'Can you hear me, Jo? I said it's ... Anne.'

'No, I know that she adopted me when I was just a baby. It can't be Anne! I know she isn't ...' *(crackle)* ...

'Can you hear me, Jo? No, I didn't say Anne – it's her sister ... *(crackle)* ...An ...'

302

Suddenly the line went completely dead, as Jo desperately tried pressing the two metal buttons, rattling the receiver rest uselessly, imagining that, by so doing, it might be possible to squeeze another precious few seconds call time from the telephone apparatus. Jo didn't really need any more time.

'It's not Anne – it's her sister … An …' Jo said out loud, repeating Nanny Bapty's fractured words. Jo was perfectly capable of completing the last, unspoken syllable.

'… drina!'

* * * * * * * * * *

Jo arrived back home by taxi, having trudged through the snow for nearly a mile before finally being able to hail a cab back to the Carlton Hall Hotel.

It was almost nine o'clock and Jo was supposed to have been working that evening. All the guests in the restaurant had finished their meals and the band, who were due to provide the night's musical entertainment for the St Valentine's Day dinner dance, were just beginning to warm up, practising their instruments on the small, makeshift stage, which had been rigged up that afternoon in the large room which usually served as the hotel conference suite.

Agnes had retired early to her room, leaving Andrina in charge of the evening's entertainment. She hated St Valentine's Day and all the associations of the past that it held for her.

She tried hard to remember the happy times – such as the year when her engagement to Robert had been announced at the top of the stairs by her father, but his tragic death just a few days later at the foot of those very stairs remained etched in her mind, overshadowing the all too brief length of her marriage to Robert and the joyful news of her subsequent pregnancy which, in turn, had been eclipsed by the death of the twins.

She would have happily not have bothered at all with any celebration, but for commercial reasons and the fact that the hotel guests expected something by way of a special occasion.

As in previous years, Nan had done her best to keep the whole affair somewhat muted and it was for this reason that Rosalind had decided to join the crowd from the local rugby club, going off into town to find a venue where the music was better suited to a younger audience.

At one of the dance halls in Leith Walk, they would be playing a totally different kind of music – "Twist and shout" by the Isley Brothers, Little Eva's "Loco-motion" or, perhaps, one of the new sounds by an emerging Liverpudlian group called "The Beatles".

Amanda had spent much of the evening in the privacy of her en suite bathroom, taking a long, luxuriating bath and ordering a light supper to be delivered to her room. She was just walking downstairs for the nightcap she had promised herself when she heard the taxi draw up at the front door.

Jo had left the keys to the apartment above the old stable block behind reception and now there was no way of escaping back to Jo's private domain, before first entering the hotel – without the chance of being seen and without the misery that was clearly written in Jo's eyes there for anyone to observe.

Jo quickly dived behind the reception desk, fumbling for the keys and ready to slip quietly out of the back entrance.

It was too late. Amanda had spotted Clive's young lover and the all too clearly visible grief that was painted all over Jo's face, which glistened from a mixture of snow flakes and tear drops.

It didn't take much to work out that Jo had been crying, sobbing in the back seat of the taxi and now fearful of bumping into the one person who most of all Jo never wanted to see ever again – Andrina!

'What's the matter, Jo? Are you all right?' Amanda asked anxiously, although the answer to her question was clearly apparent.

'I'm okay,' snivelled Jo.

'No, you're not and my guess is that you need someone to talk to. I can be a very good shoulder to cry on, you know. Why don't you get out of that wet raincoat and come up to my room? You can tell me all about it.'

It didn't take much for her to persuade Jo to accompany her upstairs – past the glass-etched double doors, which led into the bar, where Jo's aunt – no, not Jo's aunt, Jo's mother – would be ensconced, like a vixen in her lair.

As they reached the top of the stairs, Amanda placed a comforting arm around Jo's shoulders. Somehow she knew at once that all this had something to do with Clive and the trip to Mozambique that they were planning to make in early March, as soon as Jo had acquired a passport.

Amanda unlocked the door to her bedroom and ushered Jo inside.

Sitting down heavily on the end of the bed, before long Jo was pouring out an aching heart, telling Amanda everything there was to know.

'And so, you're convinced that Clive is your father just on that information?' she asked.

'Yes,' replied Jo, wiping away the tears that had now begun to flow freely down Jo's cheeks.

'Stop it, Jo. If you're basing all your fears on the fact that your father bears the same name, then you could be completely wrong.

'It's not as if Clive 's surname was " Smith" or " Jones", but "Thompson" is still quite a common surname,' said Amanda, in an attempt to offer consolation.

'Amanda, you don't understand. Clive knew Meg, They spent time together. It was his birthday – February 29th – that was why she remembered. It was 1944 and it was a leap year.'

'Oh, Jo, there you are. I knew everything would be all right. Clive's arranged a barbecue for us all on the beach in Mozambique during our stopover. His birthday is in March. I know that for a fact,' said Amanda reassuringly.

'Are you absolutely certain?'

'Of course, I'm sure and, if I know Clive, it will be one party that's not to be missed. Now come on, dry your tears and let's have no more of this nonsense,' said Amanda, speaking to Jo like a child who was in need of a mother's comfort.

Jo snivelled into a handkerchief which was already wet with tears, taking in great gulps of air in an attempt to quell those last lingering despairing thoughts.

'Come with us, Jo. Remember, I lived in Africa as a child and I learnt to love the place. I'm still enthralled by the country every time I return there. Come to Africa, Jo and be beguiled … and don't forget to collect your passport from the Glasgow Passport Office on Monday.'

Chapter 42

Arriving in Mozambique was really something quite special, particularly after all those bone-numbing hours scrunched between airline seats that gave Jo no opportunity to stretch.

It was the oppressive heat that hit Jo from the first moment of stepping off the aircraft, although it was dark and had just passed seven o'clock at night when they landed.

Even at that time in the evening, it felt like a slap in the face – stinging, yet intensely pleasurable, as the warm air burst through the open door of the cabin, once the steps had been trundled down the runway to await the alighting passengers and crew.

After a hurried passage through passport control, the party, which comprised the ten members of the air crew, deposited their suitcases and bags in three Land Rovers that stood outside the small terminal building.

They were on their way to the hotel. Jo had a separate room booked, but left it after turning back the sheets and taking a quick shower, hurrying along the narrow corridor, tapping lightly on Clive's bedroom door before quietly entering the room and slipping into bed with him, shuffling together like a pack of cards, until sleep overcame the both of them.

The next morning they left early after a breakfast of tropical fruits, cramming into the awaiting Land Rovers and heading for a beach that was miles away, but which promised white sands and crystal clear waters.

They stopped off at one point to visit a colourful Africa market where, much to Clive's concern, Jo had become lost in the crowds and had later argued with him when he had pointed out the danger of not sticking together as a group.

It was a bumpy ride and, at times, quite gruelling. For miles they had driven past small villages full of women grinding cassava. Their menfolk were huddled together in deep conversation, whilst children proffered bananas and bags of peas, packets of biscuits and roast chickens on woven platters – all in the hope that the lead Land Rover transporting Clive, Jo and Amanda would stop and dispense a few coins into eager hands.

Onwards they sped past fields of chilli peppers, sometimes trampled under foot by a herd of elephants, which might have passed by a few nights before.

Sometimes what seemed like hundreds of children would rush towards them, dust flying from their bare feet, as they charged after the vehicles, shouting, smiling and waving their wares.

'Don't the children here wear any shoes?' Jo had asked Amanda, observing that their feet had soles as thick as tyres, immediately realising the stupidity of asking such a question, for shoes were a luxury that no one here could possibly afford.

Amanda had been brought up in Africa, arriving there at an age when she had been young enough to appreciate its beauty and wise enough to understand its problems.

She had lived in Kenya during her formative years and the experience had taught her to accept just about anything that life threw in her path.

Sometimes she talked to Jo about her life as a child, free to roam over its wild expanses, careful of its dangers, constantly in awe of its ever changing beauty.

From her bedroom window she had witnessed vast herds of wildebeest wandering free, intermingled with black and white striped zebra and antelopes, which sprang and leapt from the long grass. Once she had met up with a black mamba and, on another occasion, out in the bush with her ten-year-old brother, both full of lemonade and both desperate for a pee, she had crouched in the bush filling her knickers with foraging ants, whilst he pissed up against the long leg of a giraffe concealed in the bush and whose stilt-like leg he had mistaken for a tree.

Amanda had experienced at first hand the amazing generosity of the East African people, sharing with them endless cups of chai and gristly plates of goat stew. She had walked with them for miles just to reach a shop to buy sugar and maize – amazed at the distances they would travel just to have the opportunity to buy the most basic of commodities.

When she had lived in Kenya she had been told of the beauty of the Portuguese colony of Mozambique, with its magnificent coastline, its clear, sparkling seas and its abundant wildlife.

Now she had the opportunity to admire its beauty for herself, marvelling at everything she saw and sharing the experience with Jo – to whom everything was so new and so thrillingly exciting.

Clive gripped the steering wheel of the Land Rover, attempting to avoid the worst of the potholes and content to listen to their endless stream of chatter. He appeared to be lost in a world of his own thoughts.

At one point one of the Land Rovers, containing some of the other crew members, had been pulled up in its tracks. Less resilient than the feet of the local children, it had burst a tyre driving over the rough terrain, forcing its occupants to spill out of the vehicle into the heat of an unrelenting midday sun.

It was the bumpiest dirt track in the world and after a relentless three and a half hour drive from Lourenco Marques, they reached their chosen destination on the northern tip of Mozambique. Jolted around on the rough roads, their limbs felt sore and sweaty. They longed to plunge into the sea and wash away the dirt before erecting their makeshift barbecue on the beach.

'Why has the road stopped?' demanded Jo.

'It's not a road. It's a dried up river bed,' Clive had replied, long after they had passed the last of the village outposts – a straggling collection of huts made from palm leaves and scant wooden supports.

All the villagers had come out to wave at them. Jo had waved back eagerly. In this fragile environment, its poverty-stricken community had come out to stand and stare and, above all, to laugh and cheer.

Finally, they turned down a narrow dirt track, which opened out on to the bluest sea and the whitest sand that Jo had ever seen. They all spilled out on to the pure powdery crushed coral, crashing and tumbling into the water, abandoning most of their clothes, as they ran down the beach.

The men wore only their boxer shorts and the girls stripped down to their petticoats in carefree abandon – unfettered by the rules of a society that they had left far behind them.

Before their departure Clive had announced that the lunch-time barbecue was to be celebrated as his birthday party. It was a "secret" that everyone already knew.

In that moment too he had instantly quelled any lingering thoughts that Jo might have harboured after that dreadful, depressing visit to claim the birth certificate, which had implied so much and had caused Jo such great consternation as to Clive's true identity.

Now it was March – Clive's birthday was in the third month of the year, and not in February as Jo had been led to believe by Meg.

It was not surprising really that the dim-witted girl had got it wrong. After all, she had enough trouble counting the number of sheets and pillowcases that were needed for each bedroom when she occasionally helped out in the hotel if one of the chambermaids was off sick for the day and she was called upon to abandon her normal duties in the wash-house.

No longer did Jo harbour any thoughts of gloom and despondency on account of who Clive really was to Jo.

How stupid Jo now felt! How ridiculous to imagine that this man who simply shared Jo's natural father's name, could possibly have been Jo's father.

True, they were the same age and their birthdays were only days apart, but Jo's unknown parent had been born in February and here they were at the beginning of March celebrating the birthday of the man that Jo had taken as both lover and friend. Who needed a father to love you, when you could fall in love with a stranger?

Soon a delicious smell wafted up from the old tin drums on the beach which served as a barbecue, as sizzling fish steaks and crispening shellfish began to fry in the broiling sun, which singed them from above and charred them in the glowing charcoal embers, cooking them from below.

A sweet, seductive smell of baking fish drifted over the beach, accompanied by the hissing sounds of uncapped beer bottles and of corks flying out of warm bottles of wine to land like miniature missiles in the soft, white sand.

Huge, dopey bees buzzed around them and crabs scuttled back and forth in a game of "tag" with the sea.

Jo took Clive's hand, as they ran along the beach. It was as if there was no one there, but the two of them. It felt quite magical, being virtually alone together, far from the prying eyes of a society which they had left thousands of miles behind them and with only the other crew members and the fishermen there to share this magical paradise.

They had bought their slowly singeing fish supper from the locals, who cast their nets from the beach, or who fished patiently over the sides of small, bobbing boats, which could be seen on the azure blue horizon – kingfish, jackfish and prawns. Now some of their catch languished amongst the burning charcoals on the barbecue, their skin slowly turning black and crisp in the flames.

Jo and Clive's argument during the latter part of the morning had been a real corker, but now, like the corks of the wine bottles soon to be buried in the sand, it was all in the past.

Eventually Jo had acknowledged that Clive was right, but being so stubborn had, at first, been loath to admit it.

Wandering alone along the beach, Jo had encountered a native woman with vast dangling ear-rings, who had offered to pierce Jo's left ear for a price that represented a week's earnings for the woman and which, in ignorance, Jo had rapidly agreed to pay.

Sitting in the hot baking sun with Jo, as she carried out her task, the native woman noticed the strange birthmark on the back of Jo's right hand, and explained how, according to African folk lore, Jo was destined to spend a long time in Africa and that, as one of the "chosen", Jo would always be protected.

Jo had returned to the beach camp sporting a coral stud that now decorated a slightly swollen left ear.

Clive had gone mad.

'You had your ear pierced here – in Africa? My God Jo, you're an absolute idiot! God knows what you might catch! Why didn't you have it done before we left Scotland? That would have been fine, but here in Africa! You must need your brains tested. You bloody little idiot! What did she do it with? A needle and a cork, I suppose! And not a drop of sterilising liquid available for bloody miles, I bet. God, I despair of you,' Clive had reprimanded, throwing his hands up in a gesture of total exasperation.

On returning to the privacy of their own tent, Clive had been so angry with Jo that he nearly struck Jo across the face, but stopped, looking at Jo standing there in a crumpled white shirt and khaki shorts, reached out and pulled Jo towards him.

'You're hurting me,' Jo protested.

Clive didn't reply, instead ripping Jo's shirt and then the thin cotton shorts, which tore away easily, before pushing Jo naked on to the makeshift camp bed. Clive discarded his own shorts in an instant and savagely entered Jo there and then. At first Jo tried to pull away and cried out silently in pain, but soon fell into the rhythm of Clive's hungry and lustful lovemaking.

Afterwards Jo had sulked for an hour or so, leaving Clive to talk to Amanda until, eventually, the wonder of their surroundings had at last cast Jo free of the mood that had seen the teenager remaining sullen and petulant and at odds with the world.

'Okay, you win. I'm sorry if I spoke to you as I did earlier on,' Clive had said, as they rushed into the waves together. 'I give up. You win. I won't ignore you any longer. Then again, you always do win in the end. I think Andrina's right, you're a spoilt little brat, but I can't stay angry with you for long. I love you too much. Please Jo, be more careful in future. Otherwise I'll be the one to give you a thick ear, if septicaemia doesn't do the job for me.'

'Piss off, Clive,' Jo had replied, shovelling handfuls of the salty ocean into Clive's face.'

'Remember what happened before. I can always put you across my knee again and …'

'You're just a pervert who wants to see my bare bum,' protested Jo.

'It's all right, I've seen it before,' retorted Clive, taking hold of Jo's head and sinking it down beneath the waves with both hands, so that when Jo finally came bobbing to the surface, spluttering and coughing like a submarine arising from the depths, for once there was no immediate reply.

'You could have drowned me,' Jo spluttered at last.

They ran back along the beach together, towelling themselves dry, as Amanda handed them each a cold beer. Its temperature rose almost as rapidly as it slipped down their parched throats.

Clive reached for another one from the crate of melting ice, swigging its contents from the bottle in a manner that would never have been permitted at Carlton Hall Hotel.

Together they lay side by side on outstretched towels, sprinkled with white sand from their feet. Jo's hand rested on Clive's shoulder, as they absorbed the last rays of the setting sun. Like two lovers marooned on a desert island, oblivious to all that was going on around them, Jo and Clive felt that, despite the age gap between them and the way in which society would forever view their illicit relationship, this affair was never going to end.

Clive dozed off to sleep and Jo slipped back to one of the Land Rovers, delving into a leather holdall and dragging on a fresh change of clothes, before sauntering nonchalantly back down the beach. Clive had awoken from his brief afternoon nap.

Jo stood only feet away from him. A necklace of the most wonderfully coloured coral was suspended from a sun-kissed neck, accompanied by a smaller twin bracelet of coral beads, which hung around Jo's ankle.

Jo's skin had taken on a glowing tan and Clive's heart swelled with a mixture of pride and lust. Clive took Jo's hand openly.

All of the guests attending his birthday party were fully aware of the relationship which had grown up between Jo and the airline navigator. No one thought to utter a disparaging word, for this was love, pure and simple – a love between two people. There was nothing more to be said.

The sun sunk like a pebble cast into a pond, dropping out of the sky at around six o'clock, providing the cue for candles to be lit. Soon they twinkled brightly, contrasted against the dark African sky.

Amanda had taken a shower beneath a ramshackle affair comprising nothing more than a length of hosepipe with water dredged up from a borehole and warmed by the sun.

A slow flowing trickle of water dripped into a pierced coconut shell, so that the tepid water could meander a slow stream down her naked back, which was revealed intermittently through the gaps in the rough cane screen that was all that served to protect her modesty.

Clive crept up behind her and dashed a bucket of seawater over her head, laughing uproariously and insisting that her hair also needed washing.

She had screamed obligingly and then burst into a tuneless rendition of "I'm going to wash that man right out of my hair and send him on his way".

By eight o'clock it was pitch-black, save only for the flickering candles and the dancing fireflies, which flitted in the fire-light. As the celebrations got into full swing, the other party goers began to dance, changing partners, ensuring that, from time to time, each and everyone was paired off differently, as the evening progressed.

Amanda had brought a portable tape deck with her. It weighed as much as anything in her luggage and one of the co-pilots had helped her when he had spotted her struggling down to the beach with it earlier in the day. She had even remembered to bring replacement batteries. She had selected a few songs that she liked and a special one that she had chosen for Clive and Jo. Listening to the words which had originally been sung by a young Irish girl who shared Jo's name, she had considered them quite appropriate.

It was a new version of an old favourite. Originally recorded by Jo's namesake – this new Doo-Wop version was sung by the Duprees. They had transformed the 1950s number that Amanda remembered from her teens into a lively dance floor filler, bringing it bang up to date for 1962.

Amanda had recorded it at the start of a tape, waiting for the right moment before settled into a deck chair, so that she could pay attention to the words of the song, aware that she was not the only one who was listening intently to lines which seemed to fit so well.

'Wasn't that originally sung by Jo Stafford?' asked one of the stewardesses, who had kicked off her shoes and was dancing under the flickering flames of the candle-light with one of the co-pilots.

Jo simply turned to Clive and smiled.

In the gently intoxicating smell of the open fire, burning in the night air, supper had been served. Jo crunched on a crab claw, sucking out the succulent white flesh, separating it from its large pincer, as the native singing and dancing began in earnest.

A visiting dancing troupe from a nearby village, aware of the possibility of putting a few coins in the headman's pocket, had drawn a small boat up to the beach, dispensing most of their number, apart from a young girl of perhaps no more than twelve or thirteen years of age, who was left in charge of a tiny baby, who slept soundly in the stern of the little boat.

One of the fishermen, who had sold his catch to the revellers on the beach earlier, had returned with his small entourage. All of them had crowded into the tiny boat. Now it was agreed that the native Africans would put on a performance for the beach party.

Relaxing under the stars in the candle-strewn twilight in front of the dying embers of the barbecue, fuelled by palm fronds, sitting cross-legged and quite entranced, they had watched the women and men of the group wiggle and undulate to the soft, beating sound of a drum, which was very hypnotic.

As if held in a trance, Jo had jumped up and had wiggled along with them, coral necklace and anklet shaking and jiggling in an attempt to stay in tune with the incessant drum beat, which echoed through the African night, as if evoking the spirits of past ancestors.

By half past ten everyone was ready for bed, disappearing into the tents that the men had pitched at the highest level of the sand dunes, which dipped down to the sea.

All the tents were made of thick green mesh, in order to act as some measure of protection against the biting throngs of mosquitoes and other marauding insects, which arrived in their hordes now that the candles and oil lamps had been extinguished.

Clive had taken a torch, wary of stepping on a snake, or a scorpion, although no one seemed to know if they presented any real danger on the high ridge that bordered the beach.

Having reassured the young women that nothing short of a cobra armed with a flame thrower could get in besides them, Clive had settled down with Jo in his arms. Turning over, he spotted a huge rhino beetle scuttling across the sandy floor. Jo was intrigued by the creature and watched it for a while, before it disappeared beyond the flap of the tent.

Once again they settled down, cradled in each other's arms, like tiny babies each seeking the other's comfort.

It was to be a short night, for they had to return very early the next morning, packing up their camp in what seemed like the middle of the night for the onward flight to Douala in West Africa. Their plane was due to be taxing along the runway by eight o'clock the next morning.

'Can I hear something out there roaring?' asked Jo sleepily, before drifting off into a sleep that was interrupted by a recurring dream that entered unbidden into this wonderful world of togetherness that they had longed to share.

'It's probably only the sound of the waves,' answered Clive. 'Now go back to sleep, will you. We all have to be up very early tomorrow morning.'

'I've just been dreaming that a ferocious lion entered our tent,' said Jo, waking up again a short while later. 'It had come to eat you, Clive, but I let it eat me instead.'

'You sacrificed yourself for me?' enquired Clive dreamily.

Night descended into dawn and as the first rays of light tinged the sky red, the Indian Ocean began to sparkle in the initial light of day, announcing that it was time to pack up their bags and leave, although it was not yet daylight.

'Let's go and take a last swim together before everyone else wakes up,' urged Jo.

Together they had run along a darkened beach, lit only by the breaking day and watched only by an enormous coconut crab, which had waved its massive antennae at them as if by way of a salute.

Clive spoke of another trip he had made some years ago to nearby Ibo Island. It had had once been an important trading port for ivory and slaves. Clive described it as a most eerie place, its wide streets lined with grand, but dilapidated Portuguese villas, which had once belonged to the nobility. Now they served only to support climbing lianas and rambling banana plants.

'Do we really have to leave today?' Jo had asked wistfully, looking out to sea in the hope of sighting a whale, or perhaps a school of dolphins.

'Yes, of course we do,' replied Clive. 'You know that my flight leaves Lourenco Marques at eight o'clock this morning. The time is on your ticket. You hardly need to ask.

'Just remember, you'll be with me – all the way. We're flying on to Lisbon and then I'm free. We'll catch another flight the next day and we'll be back in Africa before you know it.'

By the time that they had wandered back up the beach together, the other members of the party were sitting around in small groups on the sand. Amanda moved over to Clive with a steaming hot cup of coffee, returning moments later with one for Jo.

'I took it you'd want black coffee,' she said to Clive, who had now settled himself down besides Jo in the sand.

'Yes, that was quite a party,' asserted one of the other stewardesses, who had been on board the flight from Khartoum to Lourenco Marques.

'I think your "father" here needs to go back to his bed. These older men can't stand the pace you know and you have to realise that he's a year older than he was yesterday,' she joked in an acknowledgement of the age difference between Clive and his lover.

It was an ironic statement in view of the recent "discovery" of Clive's true identity and Jo did not find the words very amusing in the light of those thankfully unfounded suspicions.

'Come on, gather yourself together, Clive,' said Amanda. 'It's time to make a move.'

'I'm fine,' murmured Clive. 'Just let me have forty winks, will you?'

'You only get forty winks when you're forty. And how old are you, Clive? Thirty-seven? Thirty-eight?' questioned Amanda.

'I'm thirty-eight or, you could say, I'll be ten years old in two years' time, so I guess that makes me still a child. Besides, I think it was very good of me to bring forward my tenth birthday party, just to suit you lot,' added Clive from his position slumped in the sand.

'Hey, you did have a lot to drink last night – more than we all imagined,' shouted the captain.

'You're talking a load of gibberish.'

'No, I'm not,' protested Clive. 'Today isn't my real birthday, but I only ever get to celebrate that one year in four.

'What none of you realise is that I was born in a leap year. It will be another two years before I get to celebrate a proper birthday again. You see, I was born on February 29th 1924.'

For Jo that perfect world with its sparkling seas and glistening white sands was instantly blown to the four winds.

Clive – the man who Jo had been sleeping with, Jo's soul mate, Jo's beautiful man, Jo's lover was also something far, far more – something that Jo could hardly bear to countenance.

Jo's father was sitting in the sand beside his only child – the child with whom he had not only enjoyed a sexual relationship, but also the person with whom Clive had fallen madly in love.

In that awful moment Jo was absolutely certain that Clive Thompson was Jo's father.

Chapter 43

Jo walked along the beach in the half-light, as the Land Rovers were being packed ready for their departure, heading along the rough road towards the airport.

What Jo and Clive had done was unspeakable – sex with each other's own flesh and blood – an act of incest in a relationship which was already taboo.

Jo was confused beyond words. Now there was nowhere left to turn.

They had reached an almighty crossroads in which every direction led back to the same path – a track which neither of them should ever had trodden.

Jo kicked at a shell which lay on the beach. It was the discarded home of a crab, which had grown too big for its abode – a shelter to which it would never return. In the same way Jo felt that there was no going back but, more importantly, no going forward either upon that forbidden path, which had promised so much.

Along the shoreline maybe two hundred yards from the hastily disassembled camp was another little encampment.

The dancers of the previous night were all huddled into blankets against the early morning chill, waiting for the sunrise to warm their backs. Sat in a circle and gathered close together for the warmth that was no longer provided by the burnt out remains of a driftwood fire, they acknowledged Jo with sleepy nods.

Tied up to what had once been a little jetty jutting out to sea was the tiny boat that had brought them there and in which a baby and its minder had dozed the night before. Gently the anchored boat bobbed on the surface of the water, like a cork floating free of a message contained in a bottle – a message which – to Jo was loud and clear, screaming in Jo's newly-pierced ear, which now throbbed with pain, swollen up and reddened like the eyes from which tears of pain and sorrow dripped softly into the sand.

Where should it all go from here? Where was journey's end? Now that the path which had indicated the way ahead had come to such an abrupt end. What way was there left to turn?

All the signposts to the future were painted out and all the directions were now pointing backwards to a life without Clive – a life which now would be without a father, without a lover and without a friend.

How could they possibly forge a new relationship? What hope was there for Clive to act as a father to the child of his own making – the very child who had taken pleasure from his lovemaking?

Questions ran through Jo's head like a raging torrent, like lashing rain brewing up for an almighty thunderstorm.

The blackening storm clouds which now shadowed their relationship hung heavily in the air, waiting to descend in a downpour of despair.

'Jo! What are you doing? Come on we're going to be late,' cried a distant female voice from back along the beach. As far as Jo could tell, the voice belonged to Amanda.

Late for what? Everything was too late now. Certainly it was too late to pick up the pieces and glue them back together again, for this relationship lay shattered, crushed by the blow of discovery of that one simple fact that Clive was Jo's father.

Jo faced the blackness and impending gloom of a future that had been snatched cruelly away – a future that really had never offered any prospects at all.

Jo blundered along the half-lit beach with no place to go, not wanting to return to the group which lingered around the Land Rovers, padding feet through the carpet of sand which, just a few hours ago had been so warm and tingling between the toes, but now felt as if Jo was squelching through quicksand, being sucked down into the abyss of thoughts and feelings that were so totally alien.

How could Jo ever explain? How could Jo confide in Clive the knowledge that gnawed away, like a hungry maggot in Jo's tortured brain?

Life without Clive was too horrible to imagine – like the abhorrence felt by a teenager who becomes aware, for the first time, of its parents making love.

Jo wanted to be sick, wanting to deposit last night's barbecue in a heap in the sand, so that the crabs which scuttled down to the shoreline could come and feast on their half-digested brethren, whose pincers had yielded up their meat and now clawed back at Jo's stomach.

As day began to break lazily over the horizon, the child-minder who had occupied the little sailing boat awoke, dropping over the side and braving the gently lapping waters in bare feet, as she waded out of the water, caking her bare feet in the powdery white sand.

She found herself a place in the huddle of musicians and cuddled up to an older woman for warmth.

In the gently bobbing boat, the baby, whom she had left behind, swaddled in blankets, lay sleeping, peacefully oblivious of her absence. A mysterious smile settled on the child's lips, as she took hold of one corner of the woman's blanket – a smile that was aimed at Jo and one which knew nothing of Jo's inner torment.

Behind her, the boat, with its peeling, painted sides began to sway, caught in the reflective image of the sea through which the first rays of daylight had begun their descent.

Slowly the reflection of the boat began to form in the water, its image trapped in the reflective glimmer of the early morning light.

For a moment Jo considered wading out to sea, not stopping until the waves were high enough to thunder in both ears. Not stopping until Jo's mouth and nostrils were filled with a watery oblivion, drowning out all sorrow, drowning out all pain.

Spider-like, a coconut crab scampered across the sand in front of Jo, scuttling towards the sea. It ran across Jo's foot in an act of defiance against the feet that had already crossed its path and made hollowed out footprints in the sand.

Twice it fell into one of the craters created by Jo's footfall, forcing the creature to climb back out again, hindering its passage to the sea. The crusty claws of the crustacean nipped at Jo's feet, causing Jo to stifle a scream of shocked surprise, as the crab ran forward across the soft, as yet unmarked, sand which lay ahead.

Jo headed in the same direction, feeling the lapping tide tingling at bare toes. It provided a clue to the fact that Jo was still alive, still capable of feeling, when all feeling seemed numbed into a submissive disappearance from Jo's tortured mind.

Jo nearly tripped over one of the twin oars that were sometimes used to ease the passage of the little boat as it ploughed through the still waters on calm, windless days and nights. A stubbed toe shot a sharp stab of pain up the length of Jo's leg, acknowledging the fact that pain could only be felt by the living, although Jo's troubled mind carried only the dead weight of thoughts of the past, with not even a fleeting regard to the future – a future that surely had to be without Clive.

It was the image of the boat, tossing on the waves that lapped gently at Jo's sea-assaulted feet, which finally penetrated Jo's depressed thoughts. All at once the coconut crab's crimping of Jo's bare toes was forgotten.

The image caught in the reflective water provided hardly any measure of added illumination, as the sun began to rise over the far horizon. Jo should have been able to discern its face mirrored in the water but, strangely, it didn't appear to have a face at all!

Shivering in the emerging sunlight, a cold sliver of fear slid sensuously down Jo's spine, replacing the warmth of the rising ball of sun, which had begun to burst from the sky.

Jo didn't feel sick any more. Jo felt terrified!

Jo stood with feet sinking into the wet sand beneath the water, mesmerised by the movement, slipping back into the trance which, the night before, had witnessed Jo jiggling and jangling with the African dancers in a softly sounding clatter of coral.

Once more the boat began to sway, backwards and forwards on the ebbing tide that barely touched its barnacled bottom. If was as if it was being rocked by a furious flow that could not possibly exist on the unrippled surface of the water. Nevertheless, the tiny boat appeared like a North Sea trawler battling through a winter's storm.

Sniffing at the salty air, Jo's nostrils were suddenly assaulted by an acrid stench. Maybe it was the smell of a dead fish washed ashore by the tide. Maybe it was the contents of the boat itself, which still contained remnants of the previous day's catch.

On the other hand, perhaps it was caused by the discarded entrails of the fish, which were not considered fit to fill the hungry bellies of the fisherfolk, who had danced and delighted their audience, before retiring to feast in front of the driftwood fire.

Jo glanced towards the boat with its peeling painted sides, which slowly, inexplicably, began to expose its hull. Stripped bare of the last remaining flakes of brightly coloured paint, the shavings dropped into the water, like the rind of an orange, caught between forefinger and thumb, before being blown away on a sea breeze that didn't even stir the still waters of the gently lapping ocean.

A whispering voice, relayed by the wind, began uttering its secrets – but ones which Jo alone could hear, spoken in the husky tones of a ghost from ancient times, recalling the past.

A hazy mist began to lift from the water's surface, concealing the boat and, with it, the sleeping form of the child that lay asleep in its bow, so that only its blanketed body remained visible: little black face, legs and arms no longer discernible.

Jo gagged on a mouthful of half-digested crabmeat, looking towards the sunrise that was the only clock that marked the beginning of the day, guessing that only seconds remained before the burgeoning ball of fire lit up the African sky.

A sudden stomach cramp gripped Jo in a vice-like hold. Jo wanted to be sick. It was as if the crab's claw itself was clutching at the pit of Jo's stomach, dragging at the rapidly regurgitating contents, as if to draw them back through Jo's intestines, re-instating sickness and suffering into a mouth which already tasted of vile vomit.

Jo staggered back, hearing again the words of the party of Clive's group of friends, who called from the distant sandbanks that rose above the level of the beach. Jo couldn't make out a word.

The baby had become restless, its little form made to move by the rocking motion of the waves, tearing over the side of the boat, which bobbed gently on its mooring. The wooden jetty post to which it was tied suddenly cracked and splintered before Jo's eyes, yet still remained steadfast in the sand, anchoring the little boat fast by the rope that stretched between it and the stunted wooden support pillar driven firmly into the sand.

As immediately as it had begun, the rocking movement ceased and, for the first time, the child began to cry, wailing into the wind, until the rising tide, that lapped at the boat like a tiny, soft, gentle kitten licking from a saucer of milk, began to rock the boat again.

Wailing tears no longer coursed down dark, chubby cheeks, dried by the unseen hand that grasped the side of the boat like a mermaid's ugly sister arising from the deep.

Jo's hands began to shake, not by reaching out to touch the boat, but in a strange attempt to clear a throbbing head of the strange belief that the form that stood in the shallows, rocking the little vessel, wasn't capable of rocking it at all.

At once fearful and yet enthralled, Jo leant down towards the lapping waters and placed a shaking hand on the stern of the boat, making the movement cease, but as soon as Jo's hand was lifted, the tidal swell rose up again, causing the boat to rock and sway.

Jo reached into the boat, which smelt so badly of dead fish and touched the baby's head, which felt feverish, as if it had been baking in the previous day's hot African sun. Unable to offer any explanation for such motherly actions, Jo turned back towards the group of Africans gathered together on the sand.

All but the young girl, who had been in charge of the baby, continued to doze and dream. They seemed totally unperturbed by the inexplicable.

Quite simply, Jo must have imagined everything. Maybe a rising tide had caught the side of the boat, raising it up from its gentle resting point.

It was at this same time of the year that poor Uncle Robert had died, Grandad Charlie too. Jo's mind began to swim, trawling through a childhood that had been marked by one tragedy after another.

Jo touched the hairs that had began to prickle at the back of a neck which wore a coral necklace. Thoughts that were already so horribly troubled were interrupted once more by the notion that maybe Clive had already guessed the crucial part that he had played in Jo's conception.

Jo felt sick at the very idea that he might already know, that he might already be wondering how on earth their incestuous relationship could possibly continue. Surely, Clive was oblivious to the nature of his true relationship to his child?

Jo winced, tasting the crab once more. On this occasion, there was no chance to turn aside and what did it matter anyway on this vast expanse of white sand, if one small patch of it was stained with sick? Suddenly, Jo was violently, uncontrollably sick, spewing out the contents of a churning stomach, so that the vile vomit stained the white sanded beach, polluting it with the stench of half consumed shellfish. As sick as a sea serpent, Jo retched into the sand.

Unfathomably, the image of the bronze head of the Benin queen entered unbidden into Jo's consciousness – a figure which had been taken from its sacred resting place by Clive's father, who had lied about his son's very existence and whose cast image was stowed away amongst Jo's luggage.

Jo had decided that it should be returned to Africa and had packed it amongst a selection of personal belongings contained in a rucksack, which Jo had taken on board the plane as hand luggage.

Over sixty years ago it had had passed into the hands of two of Mary's husbands – first Alex and then Charlie – the man who had given life to Robert, his only son.

Now Jo was the person in charge of its ultimate destiny and the decision to return it to the Dark Continent from which it had been stolen all those years ago.

Another coconut crab scuttled forward, stopping to feast on the former life of the vomited crustacean that previously it might even have coupled with.

Jo stumbled into the pile of vomit, staining the soles of bare feet with the contents of an emptied stomach and backing away, tripping once more over the oars of the boat, which lay discarded in the sand.

Jo smelt the all pervading smell of the fishy cargo. The boat's brightly coloured sides were once more painted in stripes of vermilion and white, like oranges rolled through the snow.

A shaft of sunlight breaking over the horizon shone down on the scene on the beach, instantly illuminating the gloom and providing enough light for Jo to be able to see something which was beyond belief – a blackened figure with an ashen face that had certainly not been among those who had danced along the sand the night before.

Its face was a horrific sight and Jo wanted to scream out in terror, but no words came. Instead, Jo snatched up the oar by way of a means of defence against the unknown ghostly assailant.

Clive had come running down the beach, ready to grab at Jo and force his lover back to the awaiting Land Rovers whose engines now idled, ready for departure and waiting for Jo to join them.

Slowly the figure drifted towards the running man, the son of the original taker of the head of an ancient queen, who had so many times saturated Jo with his seed over the past few weeks.

The sun had burst through the morning sky and now, just for a second, it allowed Jo to observe the darkened face, before burying itself into the sand dunes, like a figure walking out into the desert at the break of day.

Jo was at a loss to discern its featureless face. No sparkling eyes – just empty sockets. No pink mouth, just a slash across the face; flared nostrils that would never inhale another breath and coral-studded ears unhearing of centuries of sound.

It was a face where a face should have been, but the like of which Jo had never known before.

Black! It was totally black!

A witch arisen from the past. A woman who could cause the swelling tide to toss the side of a boat anchored in still, languid waters.

A voice began to call. Its listener was Clive, who had just arrived at Jo's side in time for his own perplexed face to be illuminated by the rising sun.

> *Thou taketh my head*
> *And blood will be shed*
> *A spear in the heart*
> *The thief will depart*
> *Death to the receiver*
> *Be he not a believer*
> *The son of the taker*
> *Will meet his maker*
> *The sons of the son*
> *By the Devil be won*
> *The son of he who lies*
> *Will fall from the skies*

Twelve lines of rhyme, repeated for what had seemed like an eternity, whilst Clive and Jo had stood together on the same patch of sand, as an even more sinister thought struck fear and loathing into Jo's heart.

Jo wanted to be sick all over again.

Jo listened to the echoing words, that formed a seemingly meaningless refrain, but which filled Jo's already tormented heart with a fear of the unknown.

Jo could not understand what it all meant, but one thing was absolutely clear – the threat was implicit. There was absolutely no doubt whatsoever in Jo's mind about that!

Like the demons of an unwitting, but incestuous love affair, Jo had to face the evil threat – the one which threatened and destroyed still further any thoughts of living a life here in Africa with Clive.

Jo picked up the discarded oar and threw it uselessly up the beach in the direction of the disappearing demon.

It landed softly, uselessly in the sand.

Steal the head of the Benin queen and she would demand her revenge, striking out in vengeance through the generations.

Clive was the son of Cameron Thompson, who had originally taken the head of the Benin queen from its sacred altar. He was the deceased father who had lied about his son's birth.

And now, together with Jo, the Caledonian Airways navigator was this very morning heading back to West Africa where it had all begun. Clive Thompson was on his way for one more life and death confrontation with an ancient African queen.

Chapter 44

The sun was rising high in the African sky, as Jo looked out of the window of the Land Rover. The party was bound for the airport at Lourenco Marques and the awaiting plane that was to be flown on to Lisbon via Douala in West Africa.

It had been a long stopover – almost thirty-six hours. They had clocked up a total flying time of nearly twenty hours since leaving Luxembourg, bound first for Khartoum, before making the second leg of the trip to Mozambique.

There was to be a brief stop in Cameroon before taking off for their final destination of the Portuguese capital.

Shortly they would be arriving at Lourenco Marques, where they would be boarding the plane again for another gruelling eight or nine hour flight. They were already behind schedule, trying desperately hard to make up time on the bumpy African roads.

Having lived in Africa, Clive was more used to the roads through the bush, many of which were little more than dirt tracks and he had taken the wheel of the second vehicle, leaving Amanda and Jo alone as passengers in the back seat of the lead Land Rover.

It gave them the chance to talk in hushed whispers, as the driver, (another member of the cabin crew), was far too intent on concentrating on the road ahead to listen to anything they had to say.

Amanda knew that something was drastically wrong and immediately started quizzing Jo. At first her fellow passenger had sat in complete silence, alone with the thoughts that plagued a troubled mind.

Slowly, Amanda's gentle words coaxed Jo out of the reverie that had turned into a nightmare that would surely never end.

Amanda understood, or at least she knew everything that Jo had chosen to tell her and that was quite a lot!

She was a good listener and she tried to offer comfort but, ultimately, what really could she say? What could anyone say? What advice could she possibly offer? She knew about Jo's relationship with Clive. She had known for a long time. She understood too how Jo's love of this older man could never be acceptable in the eyes of society.

Right now the burning question was could Jo ever accept Clive as a parent – a father who desired to be so much more? Here was a man who had indeed become so much more to Jo over these past few weeks.

As far as Clive was concerned, all that Jo could think of him was as a man who had unwittingly taken his own child to his bed, not as a father might seek to cosset an infant, but as a man whose carnal desires had to be fulfilled.

And what of Andrina too?

It all made sense now and Jo wondered how all those years could have been passed in such ignorance without ever once realising the true reason for Andrina's animosity, that intense hatred with which she had always treated Jo as a child – Jo as her child!

If only Jo had thought to question Nanny Bapty sooner. She had often regaled Jo with the tale of how, as a nurse working in the Glasgow private clinic, she had once been responsible for Jo's entry into the world, even remarking on how she had first observed the strange birthmark on the back of Jo's hand.

Stupidly, it had never occurred to Jo to pose that vital question – who was Jo's real mother?

Now the truth was known – not only of how Andrina was Jo's truth birth mother, but how, unfathomably, she had once taken Clive to her bed. Had she taken him to her bed? Or had he simply taken her roughly and readily against some brick wall in a dingy side street late one night after closing time at the pub?

It was horrible – all too horrible to imagine, but thoughts floated unbidden into Jo's consciousness, conjuring up images as horrific as a headless, bloodstained and dismembered white rabbit pulled from a magician's hat.

Jo felt like a child finding out for the first time about parents who actually enjoyed an active sex life, perhaps bursting unannounced into the bedroom and finding them engaged in an act of passionate copulation. Only the difference was that most children did not have to wait until they were seventeen to find out who their real parents were!

Clive and Andrina!

It was a pairing that didn't bear thinking about. What had they seen in each other? What did they possibly have in common – apart from Jo? True it had been wartime, when passions had run high amidst the raining terror of frequent bombing raids, but Clive and Andrina!

How could they? And, especially, how could he?

Yes, Clive had been young at the time – little more than a teenager himself, Jo calculated, but still it hurt to consider it. Whatever was Clive thinking about, falling into the arms of the bitch who was Jo's aunt. No, not Jo's aunt, but the mother, who had simply given up her child with barely a moment's thought for its future welfare. A sneaking, creeping vixen, who had deserted her cub.

It was a strange quirk of fate that had brought Jo back into the family fold, for lately Jo had learnt how a beloved Uncle Robert had delivered a baby into Anne's awaiting arms.

Jo remembered the talk of how the child had been "bought". Bizarrely, it had been Andrina who had been doing the talking! How could she say such things? How ironic! How very cynical, when the one who had presumably benefited from the arrangement was the woman who had uttered such words of derision time and time again and invariably within Jo's hearing.

How ironic that she had often spoken of her half-sister Anne's adopted child as a "bad buy" when she had been the one who had provided the shopping.

Jo hated her for all those years of torture and torment. Hatred was the only emotion that Jo was capable of showing towards her – a hatred so blind that it robbed Jo of the ability to see beyond the moment of that horrid discovery.

Jo despised her now even more than all those years ago, remembering how she would wait and watch, always on the lookout for an opportunity to lash out at her own child when no one was around to witness her cruel acts.

Maybe it was because she could never come to terms with her refusal to mother her own flesh and blood that had made her the way she was. Still that was no excuse at all.

How had she stood by and watched Jo being shunned by an adoptive mother – her own half-sister? In her frequent alcoholic state, Anne was so often totally impervious to the needs of her adopted child.

How had Andrina been able to bear it? Had she not longed to take Jo in her arms, providing comfort and succour, lavishing a mother's love upon the fruits of her womb?

And what of Clive? Had he not recognised her that afternoon when he had first registered at the reception desk, signing his name in the thick leather bound ledger, walking into the lounge for afternoon tea and coming face to face with the woman he had made love to all those years ago.

Had he loved her for any longer than the time it took to perform their act of carnal lust?

Jo spent most of the long drive trying desperately not to conjure up images of the two of them together and failing miserably at each and every attempt.

Had it been love at all? Was it just sex, pure and simple? Had it just been a case of instant sexual gratification in a wartime shelter, or behind the barracks, when she had lifted her skirts just to make sure that the pair of silk stockings that he was proffering in return for her services might stretch to the very top of her long legs?

Had she just lifted up her petticoats to any man? Certainly Jo knew of the rumours that had circulated as to how Andrina had taken her half-sister's husband, George to her bed, even if Jo had then been too young to understand very clearly what acts of carnal desire might have passed between the two of them.

Was there anything special about Clive?

No, their relationship had to have been more serious, for the woman whose hand had filled in the blanks on Jo's birth certificate must have known something about her lover.

She knew his name. She knew his occupation … but what else did she know about him?

What did Clive know himself? He must have been aware that he had had sex with her. Had he enjoyed it? Had he enjoyed her? Had he ever known that she had borne him a child? Did he care?

It had probably happened when he had been stationed in Scotland during the war and had come to Edinburgh searching for his mother, leaving behind him the seed of a child, who would spend a whole lifetime, searching for the identity of an absentee natural father.

By some strange quirk of fate Jo had fallen into the arms of a lover – a lover who had made incestuous love to his own child – a father who had never had the chance to love his child in any other way than in an oft repeated act of carnal desire.

Clive, who had been raised from an early age in an orphanage and, just like Jo, had been abandoned at birth. Clive whose father had drunk himself into oblivion, unheeding of his child's plight whilst, years later, the mother who had once been his, but who he had never known, had craved another baby, feeding it from a bottle, whilst she too took to a bottle of a different kind.

Clive whose mother had simply walked out on him as a babe in arms, just like Andrina had done, after she had given birth to Jo, walking out of the private Glasgow clinic, without ever having held the child in her arms.

Clive who had made love to a woman who had borne his child and then made love to the self-same child.

Clive who, as little more than a teenager himself, had fallen into the arms of a woman, who had presumably only wanted him for sex and who had then sat in a deck chair in the garden at the Carlton Hall Hotel seeking sexual gratification from a love-struck teenager.

It all seemed to hang together in a perfect, hideous kind of symmetry. A never-ending sphere that spun around and around on its own axis, tilting this way and that but, like a circus sea lion, juggling quoits and never quite losing control.

Andrina had been banished from the Carlton Hall Hotel by Agnes on the day that Grandmother's will had been read and, mysteriously, had still been there the next day, apparently totally reconciled with Agnes, who owned the hotel and who had the right to hire and fire as she pleased.

Andrina – no longer an aunt, but a mother and one whom Jo never wanted to see ever again!

Jo couldn't face her, just as, right now, there was no facing Clive. Clive the lover. Clive the father.

What if Jo remained silent and swore Amanda to secrecy? Could they go on together in this incestuous relationship that was considered taboo in so many different ways?

What if Jo never said a word to Clive, never whispered in a father's ear, instead cuddling up warm beside a lover who had become a friend? A friendly father figure – a father who was both a friend and a lover. Yes, maybe that was the right thing to do.

The right thing to do?

No, Clive had to know.

* * * * * * * * * *

Arriving at the small terminal of Lourenco Marques Airport, the convoy of Land Rovers screeched to a halt amidst the clearing of dusty scrubland, which served as a car park. It was nearly six o'clock in the morning and they were due to fly shortly after seven.

The plane, a DC-7C on loan from a Belgian Airline, awaited their arrival on the concrete skirt, where it had been left a day and a half ago.

It was the only plane scheduled to fly out at that time of the morning and the hundred or so mostly British passengers were already filing through into the tiny area that served as a departure lounge.

Most of the forty-two British passengers had been living in Rhodesia, with almost as many South Africans on board, together with half a dozen Dutch, a small party of Germans, a couple of Danes, two Austrians and one whose broad Irish accent could clearly be heard above the crowd.

324

A solitary Italian was supping a bitter tasting cup of coffee, practising his English on a Southend bookmaker and his wife.

Many of the passengers were members of the Overseas Visitors Club from whom Caledonian Airways had already flown out a number of times from Mozambique in the wake of the mounting Rhodesian crisis, news of which seemed to be filling the newspapers on a daily basis.

Another passenger was a short-sighted, slightly stooped man, who looked like the archetypal absent-minded professor, all bustling authority. He gave the impression of being somewhat filled with his own importance. He was arguing about the large sum of money that he was being charged for what was deemed to be the hugely excessive weight of his luggage – half a dozen large wooden crates, all with their lids nailed firmly down and which were obviously so heavy that it took two men to lift each one of them.

Jo, momentarily forgetting the troubles and torments that teased a tortured mind, was curious as to the nature of their contents, watching the boxes being wheeled separately on to the awaiting aircraft, whilst the "absent-minded" professor dug deep into his wallet to pay for their transportation, before being whisked away into a small office to complete copious amounts of accompanying paperwork.

Jo was intrigued. However, what mattered right now was finding Clive; they had to talk.

Somehow Jo had to find the words to say him, to explain the reason why their relationship had to end.

Clive had run into the airport building only seconds after hastily gathering his leather satchel containing the navigator's flight information from the passenger seat of the Land Rover that he had been driving and now he was nowhere to be found. Clive hadn't had time to stop. The rest of the crew had hastened after him, shouting at Jo to call for porters to help with the luggage and to return the keys of the four-wheel drive vehicles, which had been lent to them by the airport officials, who they had come to know on previous flights into Mozambique.

'Don't forget to grab your passport out of your bag before you book it in,' was Clive's only words to Jo, tossing over a handful of change for the porters before he hurried off.

Jo was left delving into the leather holdall to extract the black bound official document, the acquisition of which had necessitated the production of a birth certificate which, in turn, had revealed so much about the past, casting a black cloud over Jo's whole future – one so fondly imagined – living together with Clive, married in all but name.

Jo clutched the passport, as all around the African porters scurried and skirmished, anxious to relieve Jo of the handful of coins, held in the hand which bore the strange leopard's head birthmark.

Relieved of all but the last few of Clive's coins, Jo sat on an uncomfortable wooden bench, watching the "professor" emerge from a small office with a sheaf of papers in his hand. He plonked himself down heavily by Jo's side, swabbing a spotted handkerchief over his heavily sweating brow.

'My God, that was an effort. A complete nightmare. I never thought they were going to allow me on board with all my luggage,' he announced to nobody in particular, but with no one but Jo around to listen to his tale of endurance.

'What's in the crates, if you don't mind me asking?' asked Jo politely, welcoming the momentary diversion from those intensely troubled thoughts.

'I don't mean to be rude, but I'm afraid it wouldn't mean a thing if I told you,' replied Jo's fellow travelling companion, adding, 'My name's Harry Cartwright, by the way and I'm sorry if I am dripping sweat.'

'My name's Jo.'

'Well, then Jo, I'm pleased to meet you. I have a son of about the same age as you. I take it from your accent that you hail from bonnie Scotland – Old Reekie, if I'm not mistaken.'

'You're right,' replied Jo. 'And I didn't wish to seem nosy ... about the boxes, I mean. It's really none of my business.'

'I accept your apologies, but there's no need of them. I just meant that if I told you what was inside the crates, you would never had heard of what I was talking about, but here, I can do better than that. I can show you a photograph.'

Harry Cartwright extracted a slightly dog-eared black and white print from an even tattier looking brown leather wallet and handed it upside down to Jo.

Turning it the right way up, Jo peered at the brown, spot-marked print in amazement. On it was depicted the bronze head of an African girl, her hair piled high towards its conical point. Underneath in a crabby hand script was scrawled the words "African princess".

Slightly less elaborately decorated than the bronze head that had stood on Grandad Charlie's desk for so long and which had then been secreted away by Jo, it almost matched the one that Jo was flying out to Africa with – the one contained in the rucksack on Jo's back that was being taken on board the plane as hand luggage.

'It's a Benin Bronze,' announced Jo, much to Harry Cartwright's utter incredility. 'My grandfather used to have one just like it on his desk and now I have it. I've brought it with me. I thought it should be returned to Africa, where I had hoped to live.'

Harry Cartwright shuffled in his seat, turning round to look at Jo in wide-eyed amazement.

'You say you *were* taking it to Africa, where you *had* hoped to live?'

'Yes,' replied Jo. 'I was supposed to be flying to Douala on the next plane, going on to Lisbon and returning to Mozambique with ...'

'... your mother and father?' asked Harry.

'No, just with my father,' replied Jo. 'And right now I don't even know if I'm getting on that plane.'

Chapter 45

Stowed in the hold of the DC-7C aircraft as it took off from Lourenco Marques were six wooden crates each containing over a hundred replicas of the famous Benin Bronzes.

Like the four-engined plane itself, they were destined for Lisbon, but Harry and his heads were ultimately bound for a completely different destination.

All 629 of them were packed neatly in rows, separated from each other by wads of straw. In their own little straw houses, the rank and file mimicked the thatched den above the old stables where Jo had taken their queen all those years ago after Grandmother had cast the bronze effigy from the gloomy, book-lined study, declaring it to be an omen of bad luck after the death of her third husband.

Jo had carefully rescued it from the builders' skip outside the hotel and enshrined it, together with Charlie's other African artefacts in the secret den above Grandmother's parked Bentley and Uncle Robert's MG roadster.

Harry Cartwright had boarded the plane again after its brief stopover in Douala, where it now stood on the runway awaiting departure. Squeezing his rather ample frame into the narrow seat, he stared out of the little porthole window, watching the sun descend into a pink sunset troubled by the brooding black clouds that were threatening a thunderstorm before the night was over.

He had flown many times, but he still felt that clenched feeling in the pit of his stomach and he drummed his fingers nervously on the seat rest in front of him. He had adjusted the seat belt to its full extent, but still it felt tight around his portly midriff.

He had been one of the first to board and now he sat observing his fellow passengers as they began cramming bags into the overhead lockers and settling into their cramped, narrow seats.

Couples argued over which one of them was to occupy a window seat and the patient air hostesses, who had seen it all before, maintained a smiling neutrality.

Harry looked around, trying to spot Jo, who aged with his own son and who had taken an interest in the heavy cargo, which Harry had arranged to be brought on board with him.

It was so strange to think that Jo also carried a Benin Bronze – or was that really the truth?

The flight had been called before Harry had been given the chance to question Jo any further about the coincidence that his fellow passenger could have likewise been carrying such an unusual item.

Obviously Jo knew what they were, instantly recognising the tribal head from the picture that Harry had dug out of his wallet, but really, what were the chances of Jo carrying on board another Benin Bronze?

Like his father, Harry's son, James had, unusually, studied African tribal art, but it was not a subject which Harry would ever have guessed would be of any interest to anyone else so young. Perhaps Jo was just trying to impress him.

Still it was a strange coincidence. Just how many people in the world could recognise the Benin Bronzes and be able to put a name to them? True, there was the display in the British Museum – but it did not belong there. Looted and stolen more than sixty years ago, in Harry's opinion, these ancient artefacts had no place in a dusty display case.

As far as Harry Cartwright was concerned, they belonged somewhere where the light shone bright – not from a rank of closely placed spotlights, but in the intense clarity of the African sunlight.

No, Harry knew exactly where those treasured museum pieces truly belonged and he was about to make an unholy fuss about it!

* * * * * * * * * *

It was two minutes after six o'clock in the evening of March 4th that Flight No G-ARUD started up its engines, following re-fuelling, when it had taken on board nearly 19,000 litres of aviation fuel.

Three minutes after the engines had first been fired, it left the apron. On reaching the end of the concrete runway, it waited for about seven minutes in order to allow an incoming Air Afrique DC-4 to land before being cleared for take off.

Preparing for take off, it opened up its engines to de-foul the sparking plugs – an operation which was essential after a period of ten minutes' idling.

One of the co-pilots set the gauge at 14psi for one minute, waiting for the cylinder head temperature to rise to 200 deg C.

Clive had helped the other members of the cockpit crew to mend the damaged HF aerial, assisted by one of the apron engineers. It was a fairly simple, routine task, involving the repair of the earthing on the fin. It was Clive's job to make the radio telephony communications between the flight deck and the ground during take off, requesting taxi clearance over the VHF radio frequency at 119.9 kilohertzs.

Lining up on Runway 12, the aircraft was still running along the ground when, for a few moments, it blocked the view from the control tower of the light emanating from the glide path transmitter.

It was an abnormal length of take off but, eventually, the plane ascended into the rapidly darkening sky, with none of its landing lights switched on to denote its disappearing passage into the African night. The landing lights should have been in use for a take off during the hours of darkness, but it was a clear enough night, although a thunderstorm was obviously brewing.

It didn't make sense for the plane's departure not to be signified by a disappearing trail of lights, which would normally be swallowed up by the yawning sky.

Take off was timed at twenty minutes past six and was observed from the control tower. The slow ascent was witnessed by the controller, as was the subsequent faltering climb made by the aircraft. It was as if the Caledonian Airways flight to Lisbon was struggling to gain sufficient height.

Harry Cartwright folded up the several days-old copy of *The Times* newspaper, which he had found himself unable to concentrate on reading.

Nervously, he glanced at his gold wristwatch, which peeped out from below the cuff of his grey three-piece suit. No amount of flying ever quelled that horrible feeling of helplessness and nervous anticipation, acknowledging that his life was in somebody else's hands.

He was seated in the second row, cursing the couple in front of him, who had beaten him to the first row with its extra leg room. He drummed his fingers on the headrest in front of him, causing the man in front to peer round and cast an accusatory look at him, which he did his best to ignore, peering out of the porthole and refusing to meet the other passenger's gaze.

It was pitch-black outside. The sun had set almost an hour ago, dipping out of the sky in a cascade of fiery crimson, clutching at the far horizon like a shipwreck victim clinging to the side of a raft in an open sea of clouds.

He could have done with a drink to calm his nerves and wished that there had been sufficient chance to visit the airport bar, instead of having to spend all his time wading through the mountains of paperwork necessitated by his extra load.

He reached surreptitiously for his hip flask, bending low across the unoccupied seat beside him and taking a large slug of brandy, unseen by any of his fellow passengers, but quietly observed by Amanda.

She was strapped into a seat facing him at the front of the aircraft, patting her blonde hair back into place beneath her hat and pretending not to have noticed anything at all until Harry had returned the hip flask to his waistcoat pocket.

She saw the beads of sweat glistening on his forehead and wondered why he had come on board the plane in Mozambique so heavily and formally dressed, when all the other male passengers sat in their shirt sleeves and their wives crossed their legs beneath thin cotton dresses, with wide skirts that provided them with a freedom of movement that Amanda's own airline uniform lacked.

Harry smiled at her, anxious to indulge in some form of human contact. She smiled back. Her hands rested by the buckle of her safety belt, revealing a diamond engagement ring, given to her by her boyfriend, Paul, back in Britain, who had once been introduced to her by Clive at a party in Glasgow nearly a year ago. He had finally summoned the courage to pop the question to her the day before she had been due to fly out of the country on a long haul trip, giving her a week to consider his proposal.

She had known her answer from the moment that he had stuttered out his words in the little French restaurant and their fellow diners had rose to their feet to applaud, when he had placed the ring on her finger.

In the cockpit, Clive felt the moment as the aircraft lifted off the runway approximately in line with the glide path transmitter. The DC-7C had travelled nearly 7,500 feet after the release of the brakes, gaining height with apparent difficulty. Its anti-collision light could be seen at a low altitude before it disappeared behind the trees.

Harry Cartwright's gold watch ticked away the seconds, like slowly descending grains of sand in the egg-timer that was measuring away the lives of the passengers and crew on board the fated aircraft. He looked at it for the umpteenth time, staring at it for a second, maybe two, as the roaring noise of the plane's engines rang in his ears, rendering him incapable of hearing anything else. He switched off the deaf aid in his left ear, enjoying the return of silence.

In the cockpit Clive adjusted his headphones and settled back into his seat, as the aircraft became airborne, noting the presence of the trees along the edge of the take off flight path area.

At one point, the controller was aware that the aircraft deviated to the left of the extended runway centre line – there was no cross wind and he put it down to the possible asymmetry of engine power, but somehow doubted his own excuse for the slight deviation along the runway.

'Man was never meant to fly,' his elderly mother had told Harry not so long ago, after the recent spate of accidents involving DC-6 and DC- 7 aircraft during their initial flight phase. One accident had quickly been followed by another – one at Orly, one at Shannon Airport and another at Bordeaux.

'Yes,' he had to agree, it was all pretty unnerving, but he tried to dispel the scenario from his mind, picking up his newspaper and reaching inside his jacket pocket for a fountain pen, with which to fill in the blanks on *The Times* crossword. Striking off the first couple of clues, as he began to fill in the spaces, he settled more comfortably into his seat, regaining some of his composure, lost in a world of cryptic clues, which teased his brain and took his mind off the noise of the propellers and the deafening roar of the engines which he could no longer hear, but whose vibrations he continued to feel.

Out of habit he always started in the top right hand corner of the puzzle, reading the clue for Number 9 Down – " Daughter of Noah goes boating". Harry scribbled down the letters that formed "Joan of Arc", causing him to wonder if she had ever simply been known as "Jo" just like the curiously appealing youngster that he had shared an airport bench with and who, strangely, seemed to share a little of his own son's knowledge of African tribal art – a subject which Harry had studied since his days at university and about which he was now an acknowledged expert.

Most people had never even heard of the ancient civilisation of Benin and here was a chance acquaintance, whom he had met thousands of miles from home, who was claiming to be carrying a Benin Bronze that, unlike the replicas in the hold of the plane, had to be worth a tidy sum of money, if it were genuine.

He had to talk to Jo again and find out if the youngster was telling the truth about what, supposedly, was being carried in a rucksack on board the plane. It couldn't be a genuine Benin Bronze – could it?

How on earth had Jo come by it? So intent was Harry on learning the answer, that he unfastened his safety belt and rose in his seat.

Immediately, a tannoy announcement told him to sit down but, with his hearing aid switched off, Harry was unable to hear the words of warning.

At that very moment, the aircraft began to descend progressively into a precipitous dive, throwing Harry off his feet, as he plunged headlong into the gangway, bloodying his nose and smashing his spectacles. Stunned for a few moments and unable to pick himself up off the floor, he sensed the terrifying jolt, followed by a resounding roar, as the aircraft went down on its port wing.

As he plunged face first into the gangway, a rush of air swept through the passenger cabin. Harry could not see what was happening, but in that split second he knew that they were about to crash. Before the final impact – before the exploding ball of fire which ripped through the aircraft and lit up the African sky in a thunderous outburst, G-ARUD plunged into the forest trees at the edge of the runway, snapping them off, one by one, at their trunks, as the left-hand side of the fuselage and the port wing scythed through the tall trees, striking them at a height of just over seventy feet above the elevation of the threshold of Runway 30.

Chopped down like rows of matchsticks over a distance of maybe 130 metres, G-ARUD swept through them like an airborne bulldozer, crashing through Nature's timber yard, before entering the creek, impacting on the surface of the water at an angle of dive of some twenty-five degrees.

Harry never heard another word!

It was the impact with the forest giants that caused the first of a series of explosions, which ripped through the aircraft; bouncing a ball of fire which flung itself through the pressurised cabin like a demented pinball wizard, shooting backwards and forth intent on quenching its thirst by swallowing up great mouthfuls of the living, turning its captive audience into corpses, as it swept along the rows of aircraft seats.

It was like a dragon breathing fire, scalping some as they sat, sweeping along the aircraft's tubular structure at a tremendous rate, not stopping to count the numbers of the dead.

What was left of the Caledonian can of victims, plunged into the treescape, clearing a path before it, as its velocity swept it across the forest floor, demolishing everything in its way until, finally, the movement of the greater part of the wreckage of the wings and fuselage, was arrested by the left bank of the creek, whilst the tail came to a halt on the opposite bank.

Oil and water spreading over the surface of the water ignited instantly, ripping its way through the tangled metalwork in a flashing flood of flames, exploding in a series of almighty thunderbolts, like a subterranean volcano erupting from the deep, sending huge, explosive cascades of fire leaping into the sky with all the fury of a Devil's dance.

A scream rang out from one of its last victims.

It was high tide and rapidly parts of the fuselage began to sink into a swampy grave from which there was no escape for those still trapped in their seat-belts, inhaling their last breaths of noxious fumes, their nostrils assaulted by the dreadful smell of burning flesh.

The thermometer had measured twenty-nine degrees centigrade in the cooling night air before takeoff. Now the temperature around the shattered remains of the aircraft leapt off the scale.

The threatened thunderstorm had brewed up, scattering heavy drops of rain, doing nothing at all to dampen the flames that swept through the tangled, rapidly submerging wreckage on that moonless night, which had been marked only by heavy static in the southwest.

In the control tower the alert was raised but, almost at once, it was realised that little could be done. Army officers located at the aerodrome were summoned to their four-wheel drive vehicles within less than a minute of the accident, joining the fire service trucks, which raced across the runway, whilst others attempted a more direct approach via the road along the extended runway centre line, which ended only five hundred yards from the point of impact.

In the nearby town doctors and nurses from the local hospitals were alerted to the possibility of casualties being rushed into their care.

A hastily summoned military aircraft took off and flew over the wreckage on a given heading, switching on its powerful lights, as it passed over the scene of the crash.

Members of the first rescue team headed for the glow of the fire, arriving quickly at the creek, but soon lost their bearings, as the flames began to extinguish themselves and the would-be rescuers were forced to act without the aid of any portable lighting to illuminate the plight of what remained of the stricken aircraft, its passengers and crew.

Another team of rescuers succeeded in making their way through the gap in the forest made by the aircraft as it had crashed, picking their way through the debris, some of which still burned and glowed bright in the night.

Sometimes, they would stumble over a suitcase, or burnt and charred body parts – an arm, or a leg, or even, on one occasion, a completely dismembered body, blackened and torched like the remains of a Bonfire Night Guy, dressed only in the singed, tattered fragments of whatever he or she had been wearing.

Mostly they found nothing at all – not a single survivor rose phoenix-like from the ashes.

Struggling though the creek, the rescue teams encountered parts of the aircraft rapidly becoming bogged down in the gurgling swamp, often disappearing before their very eyes, with glugging noises, like the sound made by a bath being emptied.

A cracked pair of spectacles crunched underfoot.

Most of the time it was impossible to make any headway at all, impeded by the exposed tangled mass of mangrove roots, which twisted their tortuous way through the trail of wreckage.

The first obstacle that had been encountered by the descending plane was an isolated tree, which now stood bare of its branches, snapped in two like a mere twig. Devoid of any foliage, it rose up like a stunted dwarf of its former self, the jagged remains of its trunk jutting eerily skywards. It had been sliced through at a level of about half its original height.

A child's teddy bear lay face down in the dirt, its furry back singed and blackened.

As the rescuers plotted their way towards the mass of rapidly disappearing debris, they found the shattered remains of the reduction gear, a propeller truncated of its blades, the tips of the starboard and port tailplanes, part of the instrument panels and the pilot's control column.

Another propeller, its casing cracked and broken wide open, was suspended from a tree, caught up in a mass of branches, threatening to topple to the ground by dint of its sheer weight.

A woman's vanity case spilt its charred contents across the forest floor. Lipsticks had melted in the ensuing heat and a little pink powder puff had burned like a bonfire of the vanities.

Another engine, which had parted company with its propeller, had lodged itself up against the left bank of the creek, the two parts separated and divorced from their power sharing by the force of the initial impact.

Only the fourth engine remained virtually unscathed, with its reduction gear casing intact. The propeller spider was still attached to the shaft, holding in place the rear half casing of the propeller, like the sails of a windmill which were no longer capable of spinning.

A leather handbag swung from a tree.

The left-hand side of the cockpit and the forward part of the fuselage were lodged hard up against a massive forest tree. By the time that the remaining part impacted with the waters of the creek, there was a very large opening in the front of the cockpit.

The throttle and mixture controls rested in what remained of the cockpit wreckage, ripped off from their pedestal. The co-pilot's control column, complete and still connected by the torque tube lay, uselessly, alongside.

A peaked pilot's cap hung from a twisted mangrove stem.

Large parts of the heavily damaged port wing were still attached to the fuselage. The starboard wing was still integral with the fuselage, but it too began to disintegrate when the bulk of the plane struck the waters of the swamp.

A major section of the port wing, together with one of the engines, continued on its trajectory, finally coming to rest on the right bank of the creek. The other three engines and the starboard undercarriage unit and nose wheel, together with the main part of the fuselage had continued on their course, heading for the left bank of the creek, which marked their final resting place.

The sheer strength of the impact had caused the wreckage to disintegrate into a huge number of scattered parts, most of which had become twisted and deformed by coming into sudden contact with the trunk of a tree, or by crashing into the mangrove roots with such violent velocity.

A leather briefcase had spilt its paper contents, whose wispy, charred remains danced over the surface of the muddy waters of the creek, before becoming waterlogged and descending into the murky depths.

Fire had ripped through the scene of the crash, instantly incinerating fuselage and flesh, engulfing engines, burning human lungs and exploding the very air that had been forced through them, blasting clothes from their bodies, flaying flesh and exposing bone, blackened in a sticky, sooty sprinkling of charcoaled skin, as the excess pressure inside the passenger cabin had wrought one explosion after another.

A blackened arm hung from a tree; what remained of the fingers pointed downwards in the direction of Hell!

Further explosions followed, as the plane hit the surface of the water, caused by the hydrodynamic pressure, due to the penetration of the inside of the fuselage by the water flooding in at high speed, through the large opening in the front of the aircraft, where the commander, his two co-pilots, the navigator and three flight engineers had sat.

At the front of the aircraft, Amanda and two other stewardesses remained strapped to their seats, descending helplessly into the swamp together. Three friends who had shared so much time together, now shared an untimely death.

Parts of propeller blades, like discarded paddles, lay scattered along the path that had been burnt through the forest, as if a circus flamethrower had swept along the path.

One of the aircraft's still inflated tyres, ripped from the undercarriage, had bounced through the forest undergrowth, wheeling a path for itself, crashing through the dense foliage, before toppling on to its side, where it languished smouldering in a stench of burning rubber.

A fire extinguisher bobbed momentarily on the surface waters of the creek, like a lifebuoy to which there was no one left alive to cling.

Its light weight bore testimony to the fact that its discharge heads had been torn off on impact, allowing its fire quenching contents to spurt and hiss uselessly against the furious rampage of the rapidly spreading flames.

Swept up amongst the tangled web of mangrove roots, which crept along the creek, a body lay face downwards, peering through sightless eyes into the murky, muddy waters. In places a film of ignited oil continued to glow.

Clive's airline uniform had been stripped from his burnt back, his black head of hair had been scalded from his scalp, revealing the charred remains of flesh that had been turned the colour of coal.

Not a single bubble arose from the water that had seeped into his scorched lungs, distending them, so that they brimmed with the brackish contents of the creek, whose murk and mire seeped into his nostrils, filling his mouth and washing over the hands that had clutched one of the now empty fire extinguishers, whose last spluttering contents he had aimed full in the face of someone who had to survive this holocaust.

With his lungs bursting with water and little of his handsome flesh still adhering to his bare and blackened skull, he resembled a death mask of himself.

The bronze head of the Benin queen was no longer contained in the overhead locker. Escaping from the rucksack that Jo had carried on board the plane, it now lay close to another blackened body.

At last the Benin queen was back on West African soil – but still a long way from the sacrificial altar that, for a thousand years, had been her home. Now the Devil queen was back where she belonged. Her bronze face was scorched and blackened, but she remained virtually unharmed and only part of her hardened waxen plug had melted in the white hot heat.

Unlike Clive, whose face had literally exploded in the intensity of the searing heat, the metal head of the Benin queen had survived the burning temperatures.

Over a hundred passengers and crew members had boarded flight GARUD at Douala and now every one of them was missing – presumed dead.

A total of 630 Benin Bronze heads had been taken on board the Caledonian Airways flight and now all but one of them lay submerged in the depths of an African swamp.

And Clive was dead.

Thou taketh my head
And blood will be shed
A spear in the heart
The thief will depart
Death to the receiver
Be he not a believer
The son of the taker
Will meet his maker
The sons of the son
By the Devil be won
The son of he who lies
Will fall from the skies
He who commits incest
Is not allowed to rest

Chapter 46

Agnes had come to a decision. It was all becoming too much for her and particularly now with the shock announcement that Jo no longer wanted any part in the running of the hotel, it made sense.

She had contacted a firm of estate agents specialising in the sale of commercial properties and had spoken at length to the senior negotiator, who had told her that spring was the best time to sell.

Carlton Hall Hotel was to be marketed for sale at the beginning of March. The estate agents were already working on an impressive looking brochure and a full page advertisement was to appear in *The Scotsman*.

Agnes had gathered all the members of staff together in the conference room. She thought that it was only fair to let them know of her intentions, as soon as possible, affording them ample opportunity to start looking around for new employment. She promised them all that she would provide good references for those who had worked to build up the hotel into the well-renowned establishment that it had become since her father had purchased the run down property shortly after the end of the Second World War.

Meg met the announcement with an outburst of tears and even Moira had to wipe a tear from her eye. Mostly the staff had enjoyed happy times at Carlton Hall, in spite of the strict regime which Mary had imposed and Agnes had to admit that the decision to sell was tinged with sorrow, even if, on a personal level, the last fourteen or fifteen years had been marked by such frequent tragedy.

Mary had always fondly imagined that, over the coming years, Jo might take over much of the day to day running of the hotel – a natural inheritor of all the hard work and toil that had been put into building up the business by the three women who, until Mary's death, had worked together, despite the many rows and the bitterness of Andrina's spiteful remarks.

Now that Mary's will had been read and Andrina knew the truth of who had really owned Carlton Hall for all these years, there would be little co-operation from Agnes's sister-in-law.

Charlie had added a specific clause to his own will all those years ago that, whilst his daughter inherited his estate, she was not free to sell any part of it whilst Mary remained alive, as Charlie's second wife had come to regard Carlton Hall as her home and would never have chosen to leave it willingly.

Now that Mary had gone to her grave, Agnes was free from all burdens bar one – that of her other sister-in-law, Anne.

Until then the task of tending to Jo's adopted mother had mostly fallen upon those young shoulders. Now with Jo off to seek a new life, Anne was one responsibility Agnes could well do without.

Anne rarely emerged downstairs before the middle of the afternoon these days and even then it was usually only to take tea and while away the time until Andrina opened up the bar for the evening.

Agnes had already made enquiries at a local sanatorium, which specialised in patients who had a drink problem. Anne was now nearly seventy years old and her addiction to the bottle was never likely to improve.

After a great deal of consideration, Agnes had convinced herself that moving Anne into a private nursing home, where she could be cared for by a professional team of medical staff, was in everyone's best interest – including Anne's.

Now all she had to do was to persuade Andrina that it was the best course of action and that didn't promise to be an easy task – especially since Agnes had been forced to re-instate Andrina for fear of what her long-term adversary might reveal about the past!

* * * * * * * * *

Moira handed in her notice the next day. She wasn't going to hang around for however long it might take for the Carlton Hall Hotel to be sold – especially not whilst she had a better offer on the table.

Anne's husband, George, had lately re-appeared on the scene, looking for his wife to sign divorce papers. He had been reluctant to officially terminate their marriage until now, hoping that Anne might be due to inherit considerably more from Mary's will than a few pieces of jewellery.

He had kept in touch with Andrina over the years and now that she had revealed the contents of Mary's will to him ahead of probate, he knew that any expectations that he might have harboured of some sort of financial reward filtering down to him through his estranged wife were completely unfounded, there was nothing to be gained from maintaining the sham marriage.

George had arrived at the door of the Carlton Hall Hotel about ten days after Mary's death. He didn't even bother to offer any condolences to Agnes, as he swept past the reception desk, causing Nan to recall the fact that, likewise, he hadn't attended his mother-in-law's funeral. He had disappeared upstairs to Anne's room, clutching a handful of papers and bore a rare smile on his face when he came back downstairs a few minutes later.

He didn't even bother looking in at the bar to speak to Andrina – any relationship which they might have shared was something which he considered to be very much a thing of the past.

Andrina was over fifty now. Her once raven-black hair was beginning to turn grey and her looks had started to fade. Why bother to kindle an old flame, when there might be a younger, more fiery and flirtatious woman with whom to strike a match?

Moira had just emerged from the residents' lounge with a silver tray full of used cups and saucers. She had noticed the smart grey Rover draw up on the gravel outside and she had observed the well-dressed man, who had emerged from the driver's side.

He had cast a pair of kid leather gloves on to the seat and pocketed a packet of Benson & Hedges cigarettes in his overcoat before marching into the hotel, as if he owned the place and as if he had never left.

At first Moira had not recognised him, with his posh new motorcar and a style of dress that was infinitely superior to anything that she remembered him wearing in the past. Yes, it was obvious that he had come up in the world.

Moira had guessed what he had come for – the possibility of his re-appearance had been the subject of rumours circulating within the hotel for days.

Now that it was common knowledge amongst the hotel staff that Agnes held all the trumps, that Andrina's sole inheritance was a fairly insubstantial pile of bricks and mortar on the south side of the city and that Anne had been left holding only a few diamonds, speculation had been rife that George would re-appear and show his hand.

When he emerged from Anne's bedroom after only five minutes or so spent in his ex-wife's company and brandishing a pile of official-looking documents, Moira made a point of bumping into him at the foot of the stairs, inviting him into the staff quarters for a cup of tea before he left.

It had been Moira's tea-break not half an hour since and she had already enjoyed two cups of tea in the company of the other waitresses.

As usual, the chef had disappeared for his afternoon nap, so she knew that the little room behind the hotel kitchen would be empty, affording her the opportunity to renew an old acquaintance and to catch up with what it was that had happened in his life, which had resulted in this outward show of increased affluence.

He had told her that he was now managing the hotel attached to one of Scotland's top golf courses and when Moira learnt from him that there were vacancies for additional waitressing staff, she made her decision there and then.

It didn't take her long to pack her few belongings later that afternoon, after announcing to Agnes that if the Carlton Hall Hotel was going up for sale, then she had no intention of hanging around to see if there was a job for her under the new ownership.

Packing the three suitcases into which she had crammed her clothes and a few personal possessions into the boot of the Rover, it had been no problem to persuade George that he should offer her a lift back up North with him that evening.

It took even less effort on her part to encourage him to write her a glowing personal reference to produce at her interview scheduled to take place two days' later, after she had allowed his hand to stray from the gear knob on more than one occasion during the long journey up the North East coast of Scotland and after they had arrived back in St Andrews far too late at night to book her in for bed and breakfast anywhere!

* * * * * * * * * *

The first weekend of March had been extremely hectic. All the rooms in the hotel were fully occupied and the restaurant had been booked out on three consecutive nights, catering for a full complement of dinner guests on the Friday, Saturday and Sunday.

With both Jo and Moira having announced their resignations so suddenly, each heading off in different directions to start a new life for themselves, the restaurant had been short-staffed and even Agnes herself had been forced to lend a hand on the Saturday night.

By late on the Monday afternoon it had all began to take its toll and she felt quite exhausted. Most of the weekend guests had departed and there were no air crew members from the nearby Edinburgh Airport booked in for the night, so the fact that there were only half a dozen or so guests staying at the hotel provided a welcome relief after such a busy weekend.

Agnes retired to what had been Grandmother's sitting room. She still had a lot of Mary's papers to sort through and the job of tidying out her large wardrobe and bundling up her clothes for Willie, the chauffeur, to take to the Red Cross.

Virtually every polished surface was littered with silver-framed photographs and every one of them brought back a memory for Mary – a yellowing snap shot of Anne as a child pulling a Christmas cracker, Charlie enjoying a Sunday afternoon picnic in the country with Mary, Robert proudly sitting behind the wheel of his MG roadster and, of course, a whole selection of photographs of Jo taken over the years.

Agnes selected one of her own particular favourites – a recent photograph taken by her from the door of the private office behind the marble-topped reception counter which had once led into her father's study. In the foreground stood Jo booking in a long line of guests, who had just arrived at the Carlton Hall Hotel. At the head of the queue stood Clive, resplendent in his airline uniform.

For no apparent reason, Agnes took the photograph from its place on the small side table, placing it on the mantelpiece in full view, where she could sit and observe it more clearly.

She settled down with a well-earned cup of tea, picked up the copy of the Edinburgh Evening News, which had just been delivered to the hotel, with the intention of putting her feet up for half an hour and relaxing, before she set about the task of clearing out Mary's belongings.

She switched on the radio for Mrs Dale's Diary. It had been weeks since she had last tuned into the programme and she had lost track of the story line.

Agnes couldn't really be bothered with it anyway. She got up to switch the radio off, just as the programme was being interrupted for a news flash. Apparently, there had been a big air crash, but the announcement was swallowed up by the sound of another crash, as the framed photograph of Clive and Jo, which had been perched on the end of the mantelpiece, rent the air with the sound of tinkling glass, as it dropped to the tiled hearth below, the glass shattering into a multitude of tiny fragments.

Agnes had failed to hear all but the basic details of what had happened. She decided to switch the radio off anyway. So seldom was there any good news these days – it really was all so very depressing.

She had enough of her own problems to deal with anyway what with the pending sale of the hotel and the likely prospect of a very stormy confrontation with Andrina over the need to place Anne in a private nursing home for treatment of her alcoholism.

She arose from what had been Mary's favourite armchair and viewed the splintered remains of the shattered picture frame, but she didn't have the energy to get up and clear it away. Instead, she bent down and extracted the photograph from the debris.

She settled back down in front of the fire, clutching the photograph to her bosom. She picked up the newspaper, which had been laid on the coffee table and for which the newspaper boy had pocketed his usual tuppence-halfpenny.

Nan glanced over the front page which, as usual, was full of classified advertisements – clearance sales offering "genuine bargains" a billing for the Capitol Bingo Hall in Leith, proclaiming a top weekly prize of £2,000, various cooking demonstrations and "sensational" sales of carpets and rugs, together with an advertisement offering refrigerators, washing machines and spin driers all available on "easy rental terms".

None of it was remotely of any interest to Agnes. She was tired. She didn't really know if she could be bothered to turn the newspaper pages, idly flipping over to the beauty column on page three headed "Eve's Beautiscope", proclaiming that the "relaxed perm" was the latest trend and extolling female readers to invest in a "permanent wave", which would at least give their hair "body" and "bounce".

In the advice column, one reader was seeking advice on how to remove perspiration stains from her husband's navy blue jacket, whilst another sought guidance on how to remove custard from a green woollen coat and "Mrs G" was advised on the merits of a cold water cure for removing egg white, which had been allowed to stain a camel coat.

Really, how did these people get into such a mess! Had no one ever taught them how to look after their clothes!

It was only as she turned her attention to the fifth page, that Agnes was brought up with a start.

In horror she read the glaring headline, echoing the news, which had been on the radio earlier and which she had scarcely been able to hear.

111 FEARED LOST IN
WORST SINGLE
AIR CRASH
Scots Among Crew Of
Charter Airliner
BLACKENED WRECK
IN AFRICAN SWAMP

Agnes began to read the dramatic news story that followed, concentrating on every word that was written beneath that attention-grabbing headline.

It was a Caledonian Airways plane which had been involved in the crash, that had taken place out in West Africa.

And Nan knew who was on board that flight!

She picked up her reading glasses from the table beside her, anxious not to skip over a single word. She felt instantly fearful for the safety of the two people whom she was sure were on board.

She focussed her eyes on the text, as tears of grief swelled her eyelids and a single teardrop began to course its way down her cheek.

All 111 persons aboard a Caledonian Airways
DC7C airliner were believed killed when the
plane crashed into a swamp and caught fire
soon after taking off from Douala, Cameroon,
last night. It may be the worst single crash in
the history of civil aviation.

The airliner, on a flight from Lourenco Marques,
Mozambique, to Luxembourg, for Trans-African Air
Coach Ltd, of London, carried a crew of ten, five of
them Scots, and 101 passengers.

Planes flying over the crash scene reported that they
saw no signs of life. Half the fuselage, burned and
blackened, lay in a swamp, accessible only by boat.
Wreckage was scattered over half a square mile. The
plane crashed just over a mile from the end of the
runway. Rescue workers were hampered by the deep
bog and used inflatable rubber dinghies, being guided
in the darkness by the flames. But the heat prevented
them getting near the wreckage.

There were 42 Britons, many living in Rhodesia, and
40 South Africans among the passengers. There were
also six Dutch, four Germans, two Danes, two
Austrians, one Irish, one Italian and three of unknown
nationality.

Passengers with British addresses were named as Mrs
P I Ellis and Mr and Mrs R L Hart, 193 Elm Road,
Leigh-on-Sea, Essex. Mr Hart was a Southend
bookmaker.

Another person thought to have died in the crash was
the prominent African historian, Professor Harry
Cartwright, who has recently been in the news for his
efforts to persuade the British Government to return
the famous Benin Bronzes, now displayed in the
British Museum to ...

Agnes could not bear to read another word. Instead, she let out a piercing
cry, bringing Andrina rushing into the sitting room. Agnes sat, simply pointing at
the newspaper, which had fallen on to her lap.

'Agnes, what on earth is wrong?' demanded Andrina.

'There you are. Read it. Are you happy now?' she cried. 'It's Jo. It's all in
the newspaper. There's been a crash out in West Africa and it says that there are

341

no survivors. You always hated Jo. Well, now there's no reason to display your hatred any more. Jo's dead … and Clive too!'

In a rare moment of pity for her sister-in-law, Andrina crossed the room and flung her arms around Agnes, hugging her tightly, as the other woman began to sob uncontrollably.

'Agnes, you've got it all wrong. I never hated Jo. Really, I didn't. You've got to believe me!' exclaimed Andrina.

However, Agnes heard nothing of Andrina's uncharacteristically comforting words. All she could think of was the child that she had given birth to seventeen years ago in a private Glasgow clinic, whose entry into the world she had never been able to admit to and who was now probably lying dead submerged in an African swamp.

Chapter 47

Jo regained consciousness maybe an hour or more after the crash, drifting in and out of a state of wakefulness. Awareness came and went like the tide, ebbing and flowing. From time to time a sea swell of realisation filled the rock pool of Jo's mind.

Jo tried to move, but movement was too painful. Jo was trying desperately hard to cling to reality, trying to hold on, trying to clutch at something tangible with burnt hands which felt that they shouldn't still be attached to broken arms and with fingers devoid of any feeling.

Jo was almost blinded, barely able to see through flickering eyelids, which cast everything in a blur. Jo's eyes were stuck with blood, glued together by the seeping wound on top of a head from which the hair had been singed and burnt.

Jo's hairless scalp was now traversed by a long, meandering cut, caused by a piece of burning metal, which had been driven directly into Jo's skull. It had been a massive blow to the head. Jo didn't remember being blown free of the shattered fuselage. Jo didn't recall reaching up to the overhead locker for the rucksack shortly after take off. Jo didn't remember the sharp rebuke from Rosalind to "sit down at once".

Jo didn't remember settling back down in the narrow seat. Jo had taken the bronze head that had been cradled in the rucksack, standing in the aisle, extracting its contents, staring at the ancient bronze effigy of the Devil queen at the exact moment of impact.

Jo tried to recall what had happened.

Jo remembered nothing at all. No, there was something – a memory of holding the cold, metallic, bronze image of a face, which now seemed faceless in the swimming currents of Jo's confused mind.

Jo could see her clearly – not literally, but in the mind's eye. No sparkling eyes – just empty sockets. No pink mouth, just a slash across the face; flared nostrils that would never inhale another breath and coral-studded ears unhearing of centuries of sound.

She was staring back from those fearful eyes. She cried out to Jo. She who was unheeding of a descending oxygen mask with which to breath during those last fateful moments before the crash.

She snorted, but inhaled no acrid stench of burning human flesh. She listened intently but, like Harry Cartwright, she was incapable of hearing the roar of the aircraft's engines – such an alien sound to a centuries dead African queen.

Right now she had a role to play – a life to protect, if she was ever to be returned to her sacred altar and bask once again in the midday sun. She was Jo's protector in this struggle with life and death – just as Jo was the one intended to be her saviour!

All but one of the one hundred and eleven passengers and crew on board G-ARUD were dead. She had performed another act of retribution. Clive, the son of he who had lied about the very existence of his own flesh and blood, had met his death, falling from the skies and taking with him all but one person – that one very special person, with whom he had unknowingly committed an act of incestuous love and who bore the birthmark that signified a future rendezvous with an unforeseen destiny.

Jo bore the mark of the leopard's head on the back of a burnt right hand. It denoted the only person who had been aboard the plane, who yet lived. It signified someone who was yet to awaken to the calling.

Jo's burnt, broken fingers flexed desperately and uselessly in the oozing mud, stretching towards a bronze head, which had rolled perilously close to the all enveloping swamp – a sticky, oozing landslide, which had already claimed 629 bronze replicas of past Benin kings and queens. They had been swallowed up in the effluvium and were now never destined to tell their tale.

When the plane had crashed, its fuselage skidding towards the swamp, deaf to the world, Harry Cartwright had been the one person whose death had been merciful, blacking out on the floor of the passenger cabin as he fell. He never regained consciousness, as the licking flames began to lap furiously at his prostrate body.

He was a friend of a long dead African queen – a protector even! Yes, his death had been merciful. An ancient queen had made sure of that! One person and one person only had been thrown clear of the wreckage – the choice had been all hers! Jo was that choice – the choice of royalty – the chosen child marked out upon entry into the world by the leopard's head birthmark placed by a Devil queen.

Clive had rushed back into the passenger cabin from the flight deck seconds before the plane had crashed, seizing a fire extinguisher and aiming it fair and square into the face of the one person who was standing in the aisle – Jo.

At that moment Jo had been holding the effigy of a queen who had died centuries ago, but whose life-giving heart continued to beat from within.

Jo could not be allowed to die!

The impact of the crash had sent Clive hurtling back against the door of the cockpit; the force was so great that it broke his back as quickly and as suddenly as the flames began to engulf his body.

It was a horrific death, but it was all over in seconds. Clive was a lamented lover now forever lost, but he who had committed incest would not be allowed to rest until his only child had learnt to love the Dark Continent and be awakened by a ghostly calling.

Clive had never known all that he was to Jo – a lover one minute – a father now tragically fried and flambéed in an all consuming ball of fire. His battered, bruised body, had been engulfed in flames, but even that had not been enough to purge him of the incestuous acts in which, in ignorance, he had indulged with the child that was his own.

Clutching uselessly at the red metal fire extinguisher, Clive's last thoughts had been of Jo – a lover laughing and smiling. Jo showering him with rose petals. Jo sitting up in bed. Jo running along the beach in Mozambique. Jo happy, Jo crying. Jo, his stupid, darling, beautiful lover.

Clive's thoughts were vanquished in an instant – in the very second that the raging furnace took possession of his body, racing up his broken back and exploding in a mind, which considered only one thing and one person – the one who really mattered to him during those last seconds of his life.

Most of the passengers were killed instantly in the furious fire which swept along the cabin's corridor, hungering for flesh.

The man who had sat in front of Harry Cartwright remained strapped to his seat, incapable of any consideration of his own fate. No thoughts passed through his head. Nothing dawned in his brain. He no longer had a head!

Badly burnt, but still alive, most of those who had not been killed in the first rush of flames, dropped into the swamp and drowned. Others fell into the muddy waters of the creek – food for the hungry crocodiles.

It was the screams of one particular victim that had awoken Jo from a state of semi-consciousness.

Jo was still alive, even if a feeling of total numbness pervaded a body scorched and aching, hammered and broken, charred and agonised, blackened and burnt.

Jo tried to crawl further away from the edge of the swamp. Movement caused agony beyond belief, which surged through every part of Jo's battered and bruised body.

Jo was wracked with pain. Jo wanted to die.

Surprisingly, for someone so young, Jo was not afraid to die. In fact, Jo longed for death during those fleeting moments of awareness. A life without Clive seemed pointless – lost without a lover and now unfathomable without a father.

It was pitch-black; everything around was in darkness. Both the brooding sky above where Jo lay and Jo's thoughts – everything was the colour of witchcraft.

It was early evening, but here in the Tropics there was really no twilight – just daylight and darkness – like the consciousness in and out of which Jo drifted on a perilous raft cast adrift on a stormy ocean sea.

Would anyone rescue the person who clung to that raft?

Jo became aware of a strange grating, groaning sound of fatigued metal being sucked into the swamp, as the last remaining parts of the shattered fuselage and its cargo were sucked into the depths.

It was like a giant sink plunger unblocking a waste pipe. A metal cylinder that had once contained human life was being squeezed into its final resting place, like an empty tube of toothpaste.

Jo tried to move to see what was happening – the sole surviving mourner at a mass burial that needed no digging.

Along with a hundred or more others, Clive was sinking into an unmarked grave, as further parts of the plane he had helped to fly began to sink beneath the surface.

Jo squinted through barely seeing, blood-caked eyes, horrified by the vision of the giant metal coffin sliding slowly into a muddy grave amongst the mangrove roots, which traversed the dark-stained, murky waters of the creek in a tormented tangle, taking Clive to a cold, wet, watery grave. It was a place in which his soul would not yet be allowed to rest.

A last piece of the boxed cargo stuck out from the swamp. Cradled amongst the mangroves, it was yet to descend into the sucking sands.

Instead, what remained of the crate bobbed up and down in the water. Most of the box had been broken open, with a large hole gaping from its side as, one by one, its contents had descended into the swampy abyss.

On its side it still bore the letters which spelled out the name "CARTWRIGHT".

Strategically placed around the wooden box were the fragments of black and red coloured stickers bearing the instruction: "HANDLE WITH CARE".

Inside, in their sodden straw packing had lain the serried ranks of the replica Benin Bronzes like a large family of Victorian children all sharing the same bed.

One by one, they had spilled from the crate, dropping to the depths, until a single figure remained trapped between the side of the box and the mangrove roots.

* * * * * * * * * *

In Jo's heart there was no doubt that Clive was dead. Never again would Clive scold Jo for being childish. Never again would Clive whisper words of affection to Jo, as they lay locked together in a lover's embrace.

He would never take Jo in his strong arms again. He would never kiss Jo again in public – not even when he was sure that no one was watching them. Never again would Clive take Jo's firm body in the middle of the night.

Jo would never have the chance to explain to him that their incestuous relationship had been doubly dangerous and totally taboo.

Unshed tears rushed to Jo's eyes, somehow incapable of escape through the blood-matted eyelids. Jo's sobbing rang out in the darkness, before those eyes finally closed, as Jo lay alone in the African night … waiting for death to come.

Death the merciful reliever.

Moments later, maybe minutes, maybe hours, Jo let out a shriek of anguish, as a shuddering sensation took hold of a burnt, blackened body, which trembled and shook uncontrollably.

Jo called out. Words that no one could hear. Calling out for Clive. Calling for someone to come. Calling out for a friend. Calling for a rescuer. Calling out for a father. Calling for help. Calling out for a lover now forever lost. Calling out for the dead to rise again!

Shock was taking its toll. A long, cold glistening of ice sliced through the burning, scorched flesh on Jo's back. It felt almost sensuous, relieving Jo of the pain that was both physical and mental.

For a moment – for a horrible moment, Clive was forgotten, the pain of his memory burnt out like a snuffed candle that had been the only light of Jo's life.

All around the smouldering fires that had sprung up from the surface of the water with its clinging film of aviation fuel had died down, extinguished by their own initial intensity.

Jo lay on a bed of muddy clay, drifting in and out of consciousness every few moments, occasionally catching sight of the wooden crate containing the last remaining replica bronze heads which continued to bob just above the surface of the swamp.

It was a wooden box not unlike the one that Alex had used nearly seventy years ago to construct a roughly-hewn cradle for his baby daughter, Anne – the mother who had adopted Jo unknowing that the child really belonged with someone who she was soon to know only too well!

Someone who lived and worked at the Carlton Hall Hotel and whose identity had never been revealed to Jo.

Jo had no idea what time it was – how long it was since the plane had crashed. Squinting through blood encrusted eyelids, Jo endeavoured to focus on the Accurist wristwatch, which still clung to an arm that was barely capable of movement. Its leather strap had melted in the heat, moulding itself into Jo's flesh.

The bottom section of the watch glass bore a star crack that rendered any observation of the passing time all the more difficult. Luckily, both hands rested in the top half of the little watch face – the small hand stood resolutely to attention pointing due north. Whilst its larger companion crept inexorably towards it, waiting to denote the midnight hour.

The gurgling swamp glugged and slurped in an attempt to release the last remaining crate from the stranglehold of the mangrove roots, waiting to cradle its contents in its own all consuming embrace, dragging the last remaining replica bronzes to a final resting place.

Jo felt uneasy – waiting for death's tight, all enveloping embrace. Waiting for the last of life's shutters to be drawn, as the final curtain descended upon a life that had already been touched so many times by tragedy.

Perhaps this was what death was all about – a final recall of all the most poignant moments of a past life. Jo attempted to dispel the strange thoughts that were piercing through a brain which throbbed and ached and scarcely seemed to be attached to Jo's burnt body.

Was death a friend? Certainly it was no foe.

Yes, a friend was coming – a strange friend, one who would walk beside Jo, a friend that Jo had never known before. Jo was not afraid.

No icicle of fear flowed down Jo's back. No coiled serpent fed on Jo's painful emotions.

No, Jo was not alone!

Was it Clive who had arrived in a dim light, which had suddenly grown in intensity?

Was it Clive who was standing there, smiling at Jo?

Who else could it possibly be?

It had to be Clive – there was no one else out there. Clive had come back. Clive was waiting to take Jo with him. Together they would arrive to meet the Holy Father – Jo and the father, Jo and the Holy father. Jo with a natural father. Jo with a lover and a friend.

347

Jo extended a hand that could barely move, eyes reluctantly prised open, searching for Clive's familiar face, but there was nothing there – only the slight movement of the bobbing crate that was caught in Jo's line of vision, cradling its last remaining African princesses in a bed of straw.

Jo cried out, gripped by further feelings of anguish, as the storm which had threatened the balmy African night whipped itself into a chilling fury and the pain that Jo felt became totally intolerable.

Jo's impaired eyesight searched the blackness and again only caught the swaying, bobbing motion of the wooden crate, as it struggled to remain afloat.

It was a moonless night upon which the torches of the searching military rescue party had little effect, as they shone their penetrating light through each of the patches of mangroves, little hoping to find any sign of life.

A torchlight beam escaped from the surrounding forest trees for a moment, allowing a ray of light to stab through the darkness. For a few seconds its piercing, incandescent light struck at Jo's fleeting consciousness, illuminating an ashen figure, burnt and blackened, its features barely visible, like the charred remains of someone who had recently been burnt to death.

Clive had returned!

Jo summoned every last ounce of waning strength and stretched towards the cascading light, seeking Clive's hand, seeking assurance, as the figure receded into the blackness.

Jo waited.

'Come back, Clive. Oh, please, Clive do come back!' Jo whispered.

Jo wanted to scream, but no further sound would escape from a burnt, fractured throat, rendered hoarse by the smoke and fumes of the burning aircraft.

It was a cry of happiness that Jo so desperately wanted to utter, for this person, this presence was surely beckoning and posed no threat at all.

As if reading Jo's thoughts, slowly the figure drifted towards the sole survivor of the air crash, but didn't immediately arrive at Jo's side. Instead it rested for a moment on the sandy bank, stretching a ghostly hand towards the crate that bobbed amongst the mangroves, casting its worthless contents free from the entangling roots, with one effortless movement, leaving the final replica bronze heads free to join their companions and sink into a watery grave.

Ghosted away from the swamp, slowly the figure drifted back in the direction of the injured Jo. A torch light shining through the trees brought its features into focus.

Jo could barely discern the face that was peering down, as if with compassion. It had to be Clive – Jo's lover with a face as black as burning coal. No, this form was different, its face so unrecognisable from that of the man whom Jo had come to know so well.

It was a face as dark as the night in which it sought to conceal itself. Its hair was piled high, but the blackened face was apparently devoid of features. No sparkling eyes – just empty sockets. No pink mouth, just a slash across the face; flared nostrils that would never inhale another breath and coral-studded ears unhearing of centuries of sound.

It was a face where a face should be, but the like of which a dying Jo had only once experienced since arriving in Africa.

Black! It was totally black!

In the dim glimmer of light cast by distant torches, the friendly face which had come to rescue Jo remained the colour of witchcraft, but its owner was not intent on any evil.

A voice began to call to Jo. It was a voice which seemed to resonate around the thick canopy of the remaining trees, which had not been flattened in the wake of the Caledonian Airways flight, as it had fallen from the skies.

Thou taketh my head
And blood will be shed
A spear in the heart
The thief will depart
Death to the receiver
Be he not a believer
The son of the taker
Will meet his maker
The sons of the son
By the Devil be won
The son of he who lies
Will fall from the skies
He who commits incest
Is not allowed to rest
Until his only child
By Africa is beguiled
The child of the falling
Awakens to the calling

A total of eighteen rhyming lines which should have meant nothing, but somehow were all too easy to understand. Even in such a confused state of mind, Jo knew what they meant.

Were they a threat? No, not at all.

Still Jo could not see the face of the witch who seemed to be extending welcoming arms. Maybe this was the way that she appeared to the dead and dying.

She seemed to float above the ground in a shroud of cloth, enveloping a body which bore no legs with which to traverse the last remaining steps to the edge of the swamp and no hands with which to scoop up the last remaining Benin Bronze – the head of a long dead African queen.

Suddenly all was brightness, as a dozen or more torches penetrated the darkness. At a minute past midnight the rescue party in their dinghies, who had but one living sole left to save, had arrived in the muddy waters of the creek.

With their flashlights they searched through the clearing, which had not existed until G-ARUD had come crashing through the sky, blazing its devastating route through the jungle.

Torches shone around on all sides, illuminating the aviation graveyard, which was yet to claim its final victim.

In the light which no Devil queen could bear, she was forced to make a hurried departure, without the very thing that she had come for – the head that she was incapable of carrying away with her.

Instead, she knew that she had to rely upon the child that had been born with the birthmark of the leopard's head to return her head to its sacrificial altar, placing it upon the sacred stone.

Jo had a destiny to fulfil.

Jo had to live!

Book III

1997

Chapter 48

It was the last Saturday in February, as James sat at a corner table of the small café, which looked out on to Amsterdam's bustling flower market.

Short in stature and aged in his mid-fifties, he had spent his youth living in different parts of East Africa, before settling down in Holland with his Dutch mother, who had divorced his father when he had been only five years old – a father who James had never even been allowed to speak of, because of his mother's intense hatred of the man with whom she had once shared a bed.

James had intended to have a haircut before opening up the gallery, knowing that there would be little hope of doing any serious business with the weekend sightseers, who were coming in simply to escape from the dismal weather.

However, he found the prospect of sitting in the barber's chair, watching grey hair dropping into his lap too depressing on this cold, damp, miserable winter's day.

It had been drizzling with rain since daybreak and James was happy to sit with a steaming mug of hot chocolate, before summoning sufficient courage to brave the outside world with its dismal, dreary skies, which threatened another cloud burst at any minute.

He clasped the hot, steaming mug of liquid in both hands, drawing solace from its warmth.

Outside the rain began to lash against the wide expanse of window, causing the owners of the flower stalls to launch into a scurry of activity, removing the galvanised metal buckets bursting with blooms away from the pavement into the protection from the elements, which was provided underneath the multi-striped awnings.

Meanwhile, the weekend tourists began to scuttle into the cafés, which faced out on to the canal to find a place to sit, order coffee and evade the rain.

He would definitely stay where he was for a while longer, maybe order a plate of fried eggs on toast and linger over one of the several days-old British and other European newspapers, stuffed untidily into a rack above the coffee machine, whilst he waited for the rain to ease off.

If he left right now, it would probably soak him to the skin, before he reached the little gallery specialising in the sale of African tribal art, living alone above the shop in an apartment, which was within walking distance of Anne Frank's House on the Prinsengracht.

He hadn't seen an English newspaper for weeks. Normally he preferred to read The Guardian, or The Independent, but today he took the slightly tattered copy of one of the other British broadsheets, thumbing through its pages in the hope of finding something which would interest him.

One of the corners of the newspaper dipped into the yolk of his fried eggs, as he flipped idly through the pages in between mouthfuls of his breakfast.

James folded the unwieldy pages in half, peering over the top of his reading glasses for a moment at the heavy rain, which continued to beat down on the path outside.

James stopped at a regular column written by a prominent British journalist. Under the strap line: "It matters to MacDonald" he began to read the lead article:

> As a Scotsman, I have sometimes worn the tartan of the MacDonald clan when returning north of the border for special occasions, such as the recent christening of my first grandson and one day I hope that he will follow suit and be proud to do his bit to maintain Scotland's national identity by donning a kilt.
>
> Now, with the announcement this week of the cloning of Dolly the Sheep by a research team at the Roslin Institute in Edinburgh, twenty or thirty years from now my grandson could be wearing a tartan woven from the wool of what, to all intents and purposes, is the very same sheep.
>
> The work of the Edinburgh Institute raises the question …

James wasn't really interested in reading any more. He had spent enough of his life counting sheep on sleepless nights, when his thoughts had been troubled by memories of his father's tragic death.

He drained the last of the sweet sediment, which had settled in the bottom of his mug and was wiping his mouth with a paper napkin, when he was interrupted by the waitress asking him if he minded sharing his table with the rain-coated figure, who had been searching in vain for an empty table in the crowded café.

James gave a cursory nod of consent and returned to his newspaper, without really taking very much notice of his new table companion. As he was about to turn the page, his attention was caught by another of the columnist's comments on a completely different subject – one that interested the Dutch born African art dealer very much indeed!

Under the heading "Heading back to Benin?" was an article which claimed to be a re-appraisal of a little known outrage, which had taken place out in West Africa a hundred years ago.

He began to read avidly:

> Britain's first black council leader and one of our three first black MPs, West African born Bernie Grant is backing a campaign for the looted treasures of a little known former African kingdom currently on display in the British Museum to be returned to their country of origin – a small city state in what is now southern Nigeria.
>
> It was in 1897, whilst preparations were being made to celebrate the Diamond Jubilee of Queen Victoria and exactly 100 years ago to the day, that a British led imperial rampage resulted in the seizure of the famous Benin Bronzes now displayed in the British Museum.

Their theft occurred after the invasion and destruction of the state, the burning of innumerable villages, the torching of the royal palace and the show trial of its king, who was required to kneel down and to literally bite the dust before the orchestrator of the events which had led to his capture by the British. Throughout the fighting, which culminated in the sacking of Benin City, African troops were placed in the forward ranks, whilst the British by and large remained protected by the steady deployment of machine gunfire.

Now on a half landing of the main staircase of the British Museum is a unique display of Benin Bronzes looted from the royal palace in what can now been seen as a typical atrocity of the British colonial era.

Nowhere on the accompanying wall notice is any mention made of the manner in which these treasures were taken, nor the number of lives of black Africans which were lost in their acquisition, during an advance into Africa, which can be likened to Hitler's march through mainland Europe.

Now the author of the article had James's full attention. He already knew something of what had happened when Benin had been conquered by the British and the City of Blood had been set ablaze by men acting under Rear Admiral Harry Rawson – a long time admirer of Queen Victoria.

James read on avidly, not even stopping to bid a cursory "Good morning" to the sodden stranger, who had just joined him at his table, propping a rain-soaked rainbow-coloured umbrella by the side of the overcrowded umbrella stand, which stood against the brown painted wall of the café.

He read on:

In the wake of the burgeoning global rubber boom, which had followed on from the invention of the rubber inner tube by John Dunlop, the need to control the virgin forests of Benin was essential to British interests.

It was therefore not surprising that the British were endlessly plotting to overcome the protectionist zeal of the Benin king who had, for so long, sought to keep his kingdom independent and mostly isolated from the rest of the world.

At a time when Queen Victoria's subjects would happily turn out en masse to witness the hanging of a murderer, or a traitor, Benin was portrayed as the "City of Blood" on account of its sacrificial beheadings and hangings of convicted criminals, who had already been sentenced to death and the British chose to

355

exploit such lurid tales of human sacrifice to justify the destruction of the small West African kingdom and the seizure of its vast treasure trove.

James paused in his appraisal of the narrative, dredging his mug for the very last dregs, before adjusting his reading glasses and summoning the waitress to order another mug of hot chocolate before he continued to read the text:

Benin City was finally captured on February 18th 1897 and today marks the centenary of the torching and looting of its palaces and compounds.

As the fires raged out of control, igniting what was left of the city, much of its centuries old wooden carvings and other artefacts were lost to future generations.

Miraculously, its extraordinarily diverse collection of bronze sculptures mostly survived the holocaust and were subsequently removed by British troops to be auctioned off to defray the cost of the expedition.

Most of the 900 or so bronzes were purchased by museums in Germany, but a handful found their way to the British Museum, where they remain to this day. Having disposed of most of the loot to German collectors, it may seem ironic that less than twenty years after British troops had trained their machine guns on the Africans of Benin City, they too were to be given a taste of their own medicine in the trenches during the First World War.

James took a sip of the hot chocolate, which the young waitress had just delivered to his table. It was too hot to drink and he began to stir it absent-mindedly with his spoon, before he began to read on, concentrating on the words, which formed the conclusion of the article:

Meanwhile, the British Museum is adamant that it has no intention of returning the Benin Bronzes. As its curator was keen to point out: "We're not in the business of redressing historic wrongs".

Perhaps it is never too late to attempt to put things right. What happened in West Africa a century ago is just one example involving the wrongs of Britain's imperial past, which now surely need to be redressed.

356

And it is for this reason that the Labour MP, Bernie Grant deserves to triumph in his campaign to witness the famous bronzes heading back to Benin.

James put the newspaper down, suddenly aware that the stranger, who had shared his table, seemed to be attempting to read over his shoulder for the past few minutes.

Now his unknown and uninvited guest was staring into middle space and, for the first time, James took in those piercing brown eyes, whose normal sparkling animation was right now clouded by thoughts of the past and a difficult decision which had to be made.

It was as if the written words of the British newspaper columnist, Paul MacDonald, who had lost his then fiancée, Amanda almost exactly thirty-five years before out in West Africa in what, at that time, had been the world's worst ever air disaster, had struck a chord of recognition.

* * * * * * * * *

It was nearly eleven o'clock that morning when James arrived back at the narrow ground floor gallery, depositing a bunch of black tulips purchased from the flower market on the counter top, before taking his coat off and disappearing into the little downstairs kitchen to find a vase, filling it with cold water and carrying it back with him into the shop.

It had finally left off raining and James had been forced to splash through the puddles, muddying the bottoms of his new pair of corduroy trousers, whose purchase had been necessitated earlier in the week by a spreading waistline.

At least the rain had washed away the dog dirt, which habitually littered the streets bordering the canals.

He turned the sign around on the shop door to announce that he was open for business, observed by the dozens of carved wooden African masks, which lined the white painted walls of the showroom.

At night, when most of the spotlights were extinguished, they lent a somewhat eerie atmosphere to the premises, watching over it with hollowed out, expressionless eyes and bone and ivory teeth, which protruded from gaping mouths.

James settled himself behind the counter, flattening out the British newspaper which he had taken from the café, spreading it before him, ready to read the article which had so interested him once again, anxious to absorb every last detail. However, before he had the chance to do so, the telephone rang.

It was Johan, his friend, who worked as a porter at one of the city's auction houses, which sometimes held specialist sales of African tribal art.

James was often wont to leave a bid for certain articles of antiquity to augment his own private collection displayed in the upstairs apartment or, maybe, to sell on at a profit to one of the wealthy American collectors, whose names and addresses were listed on his computer.

'Hello, James, how are you?' Johan greeted his friend, with whom he would sometimes go out for a few beers on a Saturday night. 'Can you drop round to the auction rooms on Monday morning. I think there may be something coming up for sale, which may interest you. It doesn't have a very high reserve price, but …'

'What is it?' James asked, interrupting the caller, as the bell above the shop door rang and a rain-coated figure entered the gallery and gazing up at the massed ranks of African masks arranged above James's head.

'It's being catalogued as a Benin Bronze. It's in the form of a woman, with a conical-shaped head. Our valuation expert reckons it's a replica. I heard him speaking to the person who brought it in yesterday.

'Our chap says that there were hundreds of them being produced in the early 1960s, but I'm not so sure that it isn't a great deal older than that. Come and see what you think. And while I'm on the phone, do you want to come out tonight for …'

'Yes, I'll see you tonight. Shall we say around seven. Usual bar,' James replied hurriedly, recognising the person, who had just walked into the gallery, as his table companion with the rainbow-coloured umbrella from the café earlier on that morning.

'Can I help you?' James asked, placing the telephone receiver back on its hook.

'Yes, I saw you reading that newspaper article in the café in the flower market,' said the visitor mysteriously, pointing to the slightly damp pages of dog-eared newsprint.

James listened to the boldly spoken words, intrigued by the blatant admission that was being made – all the while searching into those poignant dark brown eyes as if, somehow, they held the key to the identity of their owner and the reason for the unexpected visit.

'I followed you back here. I take it you know a little bit about these things,' said the stranger, diving into a black leather bag and extracting a photograph of a Benin Bronze head from amongst a number of documents, which included a passport bearing the name of Jo Paterson.

* * * * * * * * * *

James had never been married. He had never really been interested in any girl since an early engagement when he had been in his mid-twenties had ended in disaster for reasons which James had since always been reluctant to talk about.

Often, after they had enjoyed a few beers together, his married friend, Johan would try to pair him off with someone at the bar, but James would invariably protest that it wouldn't work and that he simply wasn't interested.

No, if James was ever to become involved with anyone again, it had to be with someone special – someone like the person, who had arrived at the gallery that Saturday morning, dripping water on to the polished floor and who had had the audacity to follow James half-way across Amsterdam, dodging cyclists riding rickety old bicycles, crossing over the countless canal bridges and being careful not to step into the path of an oncoming tram.

It was those eyes which so enraptured James; they were the most beautiful eyes he had ever seen. James had imagined what they would look like when the person laughed. The stranger began to tell the tale, which had resulted in James being unknowingly followed along the rain-glistened cobbled streets running alongside the canals on that cold, wet February morning.

Shutting up the shop again, James found himself sitting in another café next door to the gallery, ordering two cups of espresso and delivering them to the little table against which the rainbow-coloured umbrella was firmly propped.

James held the tiny coffee cup between two fingers, reaching over the table with his other hand and took the photograph to inspect it once more.

It had been sandwiched between two postcards depicting scenes of one of the brightly-lit canal bridges at night. Each was addressed in a scrawly hand to a different destination in Scotland.

One of them bore a Dutch stamp, which was already peeling off at the corner, leaving a sticky patch by which it now attached itself to the back of the photograph.

James sat and listened to the story of how the stranger who, as yet, had not thought to offer a name, had originally come by the Benin Bronze, which was depicted in the photograph, the subject of which was now sitting on a shelf in the store-room of the auction house awaiting James's unofficial appraisal on Monday morning.

James had explained about the telephone call he had received from Johan and how his friend wasn't sure whether the item in question was a cheap replica, or something much, much older and, therefore, far more valuable.

If it had been dismissed by the auctioneer as a mere worthless reproduction and if ... just if ... it really was something completely different, then he stood to make a great deal of money on such a rare piece of West African artwork.

James couldn't exactly recall the last time that a genuine Benin Bronze had been offered for sale. He thought that he remembered one coming up for sale in New York and that it had fetched several thousand dollars.

Strangely, the thought of possibly losing out on such a money-making venture didn't prevent James from inviting the owner of proposed Lot No 213 to accompany him to the auction house on the Monday morning ... and from suggesting that, afterwards, they might take lunch together.

'Do you mind if I keep this photograph in the meantime?' James had asked. 'I'd like to carry out some research on it over the weekend. I'll return it to you on Monday. If you like to give me the name of your hotel, I'll meet you there – let's say at ten thirty.'

'It's all right, I'll meet you here at the gallery,' came the quick response, as if the speaker was reluctant to reveal the whereabouts of the hotel accommodation.

Swallowing the last of the dark liquid, James's visitor had seemed anxious to go, resisting all attempts to encourage any additional discussion ... or a further chance for the two of them to get to know each other over a second cup of coffee.

'How long are you in Amsterdam for?' James asked, in a final, desperate attempt to prolong their meeting.

'Only until late Monday afternoon, when I'm catching the train down to the Hook of Holland and then taking the overnight crossing to Harwich.'

'I didn't think many people used that route these days. I take it you don't enjoy flying then?'

'No, not when I'm a passenger,' came the simple answer.

'I understand,' replied James. 'I don't like airports very much myself. I try to avoid them, if I can. I've always had a fear of flying. My father was killed in an air crash out in West Africa when I was a teenager but, of course, that was a long time ago,' said James, twiddling with the ends of his grey moustache.

'Look, call me, if you feel like going out for a quiet drink on Sunday night. Here, I'll give you my business card. Give me a ring any time!' On the printed business card in bold script above the Amsterdam address and a telephone number was printed the name: "JAMES CARTWRIGHT".

* * * * * * * * * *

James awoke quite early on the Monday morning, after yet another troubled night's sleep, during which the recurring image of the photograph of the bronze head had haunted his dreams.

Similarly, the person who had presented the picture to him was proving impossible to eradicate from every minute of his wakening thoughts throughout the remainder of that weekend.

James sat eating a breakfast of thinly sliced cheeses and a selection of cold meats, washed down with several cups of strong, black coffee, as he planned his day – a day which would be dominated by the pleasant thought of having lunch with the owner of the Benin head which now, more than ever, he was convinced was the genuine article and which he guessed could be hundreds of years old.

Normally, he didn't open the gallery on a Monday morning and as the clock ticked towards the time of their appointed rendezvous, he began to grow anxious, glancing out of the window, which looked down on to the narrow street every few minutes, waiting for his visitor to ring the door bell.

No one came.

James continued to wait in vain, as the hands of the clock moved inexorably towards eleven o'clock. He began to think that no one was *ever* coming and realised that he had no way of contacting the person who had walked into his life so unexpectedly and without whom James felt sure that nothing would ever be the same again!

He didn't understand his own feelings – they felt strange and alien to him – an emotional tugging of the heart that he had not experienced since the dawning discovery of his own …

No, he wasn't going to go there.

Annelies had only ever figured briefly in his life. She had accepted an engagement ring from him shortly after his twenty-first birthday, at a time in his life when James hadn't really known his own mind.

Their relationship had floundered on the day that she had let herself into his student flat and found him in the arms …

No, don't go there James!

It was now past eleven o'clock. He poured himself a cup of coffee, which he didn't really want. He would wait until midday and then make his way to the auction house.

Maybe he should go now! Perhaps there had been some sort of misunderstanding and the person he was to meet was already standing outside in the cold waiting for him.

James went to the cloaks' cupboard and reached inside for his overcoat and a woolly scarf, muffling himself up against the biting north wind, before emerging on to the narrow pavement and locking the door behind him.

He hurried along the side of the canal, as a tourist barge ploughed its way through the murky waters, causing a swell, which sent the coots scurrying across the surface in a clumsy, skittish fashion – like awkward ballet dancers all dressed in black.

James reached the auction rooms just before half past eleven, but no one was waiting for him! Perhaps it was too cold to wait around outside. He entered the building, running up the steep staircase to the upstairs reception desk, behind which sat a rather bored looking young woman, who tried her best to look busy, as soon as she saw him.

'Is Johan around?' he questioned her in Dutch.

'One floor up. Second door on your left,' she answered him in a desultory voice, adding, 'but I think you'll find he has someone with him at the moment.'

James didn't wait. He reached the second floor room in question, just as his friend, Johan was struggling to open the door with a large packing case. James grabbed the door handle and held it wide.

'I'm afraid you've just missed your friend. Left a couple of minutes ago,' announced Johan, pre-empting James's obvious question.

'And the Benin Bronze?'

'Withdrawn from sale. Wrapped in newspaper and carried away rather unceremoniously in a plastic carrier bag,' Johan offered by way of explanation.

'I don't understand ...' James responded.

'Apparently there was an article in one of the British newspapers. It was saying that all the Benin Bronzes should be returned to West Africa where they belong and that's where that little beauty is heading off to. I'm sorry to say that you're too late, James.'

Leaving the building without another word, James sought refuge in the nearest bar and ordered himself a beer, as he sat lamenting the loss of both the bronze head and, more especially, regretting the fact that he would probably never meet up with its owner again.

All James Cartwright was left with was a colour photograph of the withdrawn lot. No name of the owner. No address. No telephone number. Just a photograph with a picture postcard glued to its back.

He sat on the bar stool for a long while after he had drained his glass, gazing uselessly at the photograph, as it lay on the bar top in front of him.

Eventually he ordered himself another beer. It arrived with its frothy head spilling over the sides of the glass, soaking the print, which lay in a little puddle of the barmaid's making.

As the girl behind the bar picked up the photograph and the postcard which had been glued firmly to its back, the two sodden elements began to separate. She peeled them apart and handed them both to James with an apology and an offer to buy him another beer.

Now the script on the back of the postcard was exposed, revealing the blurred handwriting, which was still just about legible. On it was written the address of a woman living in North Berwick, who was apparently known by the unlikely sounding name of Nanny Bapty!

And the postcard also bore a smudged signature, which seemed to read simply "Jo".

Whether James Cartwright particularly feared flying or not, at that very moment he decided to catch the first available flight from Schiphol, arriving at Edinburgh's Turnhouse Airport, where he would surely be able to find a hotel for the night.

The next morning he would hire a car and set off for North Berwick and the chance to call upon the one and only person in the world he was able to contact who he imagined might be able to reveal to him more about the mysterious "Jo" – the owner of that precious Benin Bronze ... and those mischievous, dark brown eyes!

He picked up his mobile telephone and booked a flight, using his credit card and then sat down at his computer to compose a long letter, which he could fax to the newspaper office where Paul MacDonald, the journalist, who had written the article about the Benin Bronzes, occupied a desk.

In it James detailed everything he knew about the air crash in 1962, which had claimed his father's life.

For a long time James had suspected that there was something not quite right – something that was not being told in the Civil Aviation Authority's report about that fatal air crash and exactly why the Caledonian Airways plane had failed to lift off properly from the runway at Douala.

Chapter 49

James Cartwright arrived in Edinburgh in the latter part of the afternoon of the following day. His flight had been delayed for well over an hour leaving Schiphol Airport and for lunch he had only eaten a sandwich, whose filling was hard to distinguish from its cellophane wrapper, helping it down with a tasteless cup of lukewarm coffee served up in a cardboard cup.

He had no idea where he would stay for the night, as he hadn't booked anything in advance, relying on the taxi driver to recommend somewhere not too expensive and within a short distance of the airport.

'You could always stay at the Carlton Hall Hotel. It's not too far away. It used to be quite grand once upon a time, but I'm afraid that it's a bit down at heel these days. Still, it won't cost you a fortune and at least you'll find that the place is clean, even if it is a little bit threadbare at the edges.'

'Thank you,' replied James. 'I'm not sure how long I'm intending to stay, but I'm sure that it will do.'

'My name's Bob, by the way. I have a cousin who works there, helping to serve breakfast in the morning. Mention by name and I'm sure it will be good for an extra rasher of bacon.'

James watched out of the window of the cab, as the taxi swept up the driveway, with its majestic oak trees. Throughout the journey the driver had kept up a non-stop monologue, extolling the virtues of the Scottish capital.

However, his passenger wasn't listening to this garrulous outpouring, which seemed to include details of every recommended port of call for the visiting tourist and which didn't interest James one little bit.

As the cab drew up in front of the porticoed entrance, it hardly made a sound on the pebbled driveway, which was pitted and potholed in places. It was a long time since any vehicle had been capable of making scrunching noises on the scant amount of gravel.

Most of the flower beds looked empty and neglected, with no sign of early spring primroses, or bursting buds of daffodils poking through the bare earth.

Arriving outside the huge doors which led into the hotel, James couldn't help but notice that they were in need of a coat of paint and that the ornate brass knob could have done with a polish.

He rang the bell on the unmanned reception desk and had to wait for a couple of minutes before a young girl of maybe sixteen or seventeen, who clearly doubled as one of the chambermaids, emerged from a downstairs room and asked if she could help in a bored voice.

'Do you have a room for the night please?' James asked.

'Just one night, is it? Yes, no problem. That will be £45, including breakfast, payable in advance. Cash or credit card?'

She hadn't even had to check the hotel register before confirming the availability of accommodation. It was an ominous sign that the hotel was probably half empty.

'Will you be wishing to take dinner with us?'

James declined to book a table at the hotel dining room, which looked sad and seemed to be closed, anyway. Instead he toyed with the idea of calling for a taxi to transport him back into the city later on and find a restaurant of his own choosing, but he couldn't really be bothered, deciding to order a meal in his room, although what the uninteresting menu had to offer, he had no idea.

After his "plastic" sandwich, which was already repeating on him, whatever culinary delights that the Carlton Hall Hotel could provide had to be an improvement on the "cardboard cuisine" that he had suffered on board the short flight.

'I'll maybe order something in my room,' he replied.

With no sign of a porter to offer assistance with his small amount of luggage, he accepted the key to an upstairs room, taking the flight of stairs at the end of a long corridor, whose walls had been heavily scuffed by suitcases.

It led to a part of the building, which clearly formed an extension. It was probably built in the late 1950s and lacked the elaborate plasterwork and high ceilings of the main part of the hotel.

James inserted a key to unlock the bedroom, which proved to be almost entirely bereft of character. He threw his bags on to the bed, with its studded velvet-covered headboard. Once it had been a rich rose pink in colour, but now it was faded to a light, sickly shade of puce, which almost matched the background colour of the swirl patterned carpeting, which felt slightly sticky underfoot.

He clicked on the two twin lamps, one on either side of the bed, discovering that the light bulb in one of them had expired and that no one had bothered to replace it.

Now he regretted his decision to have something to eat in this dreary hotel bedroom. Perhaps, he would summons a taxi into town after all, find himself a little restaurant and afterwards go for a few beers.

James wandered over to the window and pulled back the net curtains, looking out on to the vast expanse of lawn, which had missed its last autumn cut.

On one side of the lawn was a large flower bed containing a sparse selection of evergreen shrubs interspersed with a few of last year's puny-looking perennials, which still sported dead growth from the previous summer.

In the middle of the lawn was what appeared to be a bare flower bed, surrounded by a picket fence with white peeling paint. On closer inspection, James noticed a number of little white crosses implanted in the soil – a cemetery in miniature and perhaps that of a child.

One section of the grounds housed a walled garden containing a selection of old roses, which were no doubt in need of pruning. Beyond a raggedly clipped yew hedge was an old stable block from which a warm, welcoming light shone out like a beacon – a lighthouse which drew James's line of vision towards it, like a hibernating animal seeking a warm lair.

James felt strangely drawn to the source of light, which cast a warmly, inviting glow over what was obviously living accommodation and whose rich interior seemed to bear no resemblance to the depressing ambience of the hotel bedroom.

In the failing afternoon light, he observed a figure cross the room in front of an open fire and draw the curtains.

Whoever it was reached up, failing to completely close the curtains, so that a chink of light escaped from the blanketed lattice-work window, permitting a continued view of the shadows cast by the flames, as they ate hungrily into the sweetly-scented logs, which crackled and burned on the open fire.

James could not stand the thought of staying cooped up in this characterless box of a room any longer. He didn't even bother to unpack properly, extracting a few toiletries from his bag and leaving his fresh clothes still folded in his suitcase.

Instead, he turned on his heel, scooped up the room key from where he had laid it on the glass trinket tray on top of the shabby mahogany dressing table, with it damp spotted mirror. He locked the room door and began his descent down the more ornate staircase at the opposite end of the corridor.

It emerged on to the original part of the Victorian building in to what had once been a very impressive entrance hall, with a mosaic patterned tiled floor and walls which were sorely in need of new wallpaper and a fresh lick of paint.

James paused as he passed an oil painting depicting a small flock of sheep munching heather in a highland setting, observing their apparent contentment with the patch of canvas moorland that they occupied.

Once again, there was no one manning the reception desk and James went outside to take a gentle stroll down the driveway, in order to gain a breath of fresh air in the hope of ridding himself of the headache, which he always seemed to suffer after flying.

He stopped for a moment under the bare, leafless, spreading branches of one of the massive oak trees, which bordered the mile-long drive.

Once or twice, he glanced back towards the welcoming shaft of illumination, which shone from the apartment above the old stable block as if, somehow, mesmerised by the source of light.

A car's headlights swept up the tree-lined avenue, blinding him for a moment, as James stood, like a frightened rabbit caught in the glare of the head lamps of the advancing vehicle, which swept round the curve in the driveway and came to a halt outside the old stable block.

Its woman driver, a tall, angular looking girl in her early twenties emerged from the driver's side, crossing round in front of the bonnet of the car and opened the passenger door.

She held it open and leant in, offering her arm to support the frail-looking, elderly woman, who emerged with the aid of a walking stick.

'I'll be here at two o'clock next Tuesday to pick you up for your hospital appointment at the Western General, Agnes. You've got your pills, haven't you? Now don't forget your handbag, like you did the other week. Do you need a hand up the stairs?'

'No, I'm perfectly all right. I'll manage quite well on my own, thank you. I may be nearly ninety years old, but I haven't reached the jumping off point yet and I still intend to be around to receive my telegram from the queen,' answered Agnes independently.

As the car drew away, the old lady struggled with the walking stick, gripping it tightly in her right hand, as she delved into a voluminous black leather handbag for her front door key, scrummaging around inside with her arthritic left hand, before she eventually found it and inserted it awkwardly into the lock.

As she struggled with her various belongings, she dropped the white paper pharmacy bag on to the ground and disappeared inside the half-timbered building leaving the little package where it lay, obviously unaware of the loss of her medication for her ulcerated legs.

James observed the little incident from afar and, guided by the light which shone from the chink in the curtains hanging in the second floor window, he walked over and picked up the paper bag, shaking it as he did so and hearing the rattle of the tablets in the little brown plastic container inside.

He knocked sharply on the front door, listening for the sound of movement. He knocked again – louder this time and waited for a minute or two before he heard the muffled sound of footsteps treading on the creaking stair treads.

'Good afternoon, can I help you?' asked the stooped woman, who opened the door to him.

'Excuse me for disturbing you, but I couldn't help noticing that you dropped these as you arrived just now. I see that they're from the hospital, so I guess they must be important,' announced James, proffering the paper bag.

'Let me assure you that I do not require any pills to maintain my health. I'm as fit as a fiddle. I think you must be talking about the old lady who lives here with me, who has just arrived back from her hospital appointment. I'm sure she will be grateful to you for finding these for her,' Andrina informed James, adding confidentially, 'I'm afraid she is inclined to drop things, you know.'

'Then I'm glad to have been here to pick up after her,' replied James.

'Why don't you come upstairs and have a cup of tea with us. I've just put the kettle on. We don't get too many visitors these days,' said Andrina, extending an invitation, which James hardly felt that he could refuse.

'Yes, thank you. That would be very nice,' he replied politely.

'You go on ahead of me. I'll follow you upstairs,' said Andrina, anxious not to betray the fact that, at her age, she too was a little unsteady on her feet and sometimes found the stairs a bit of an effort.

At the top of the stairs there was nowhere else to go, but straight into the warm, inviting little sitting room, with its chintzy armchairs and elaborately embroidered cushions and there sat Nan!

She occupied a winged armchair, which protected her from any draught from the door. She sat nibbling a rich tea biscuit and clutching a bone china teacup and saucer in hands, which shook a little from time to time.

James was immediately aware that the "old lady" to whom Andrina had referred a few moments ago, appeared likewise to be in her late eighties and was probably no older than her companion, who had opened the door to him.

'Here, Nan, let me take that cup from you, before you drop it,' said Andrina out of kindly concern and in a manner that spoke volumes of the way in which, unbeknown to James, she had mellowed over the years.

Andrina placed the delicate, floral patterned Aynsley cup and saucer on the richly polished rosewood tripod table besides her sister-in-law's chair next to a framed black and white photograph.

James recognised that it had been taken from the door of the private office behind the marble-topped reception counter at the Carlton Hall Hotel.

In the foreground stood a young, attractive looking seventeen-year-old booking in a long line of guests, with a radiant smile – which was so directly opposed to the indifferent greeting that James had received earlier that afternoon from the young girl on reception, who was probably the same age as Jo had been when the picture had been taken all those years ago.

At the head of the queue stood Clive, resplendent in his airline uniform. Here was the man who had once been in love with the teenager depicted in a silver-framed photograph.

Staring at it intently was the man who was now equally besotted by the stranger whose name was simply Jo.

* * * * * * * * *

James took the photograph from its place on the small side table, as he peered at the image, concentrating on those mischievous, dark-brown eyes and at once he was certain that he recognised them!

It couldn't be – it couldn't possibly be and yet there was something about the youngster that bore the same look of the person who had walked into James's gallery just a few days ago and about whom James knew nothing more than a name!

'I see that you're quite taken by one of my photographs,' observed Nan, almost knowingly, whilst Andrina busied herself in the kitchen, noisily rattling an assortment of biscuit tins, in an effort to find the last of the chocolate bourbons, which were Nan's favourite and which she knew that she had hidden away somewhere, in order to offer their guest something more than a plain biscuit.

'I'm sorry. I didn't mean to be rude. It was just that it reminded me of someone. I take it that the photograph was taken some time ago. In the 1960s I shouldn't wonder, if the women's fashions are anything at all to go by.

'Who is the teenager in the foreground, if you don't mind me asking?' enquired James, his heart racing, as he felt almost afraid to learn the answer.

Agnes leaned back in her armchair, resting her head heavily against the embroidered cushions, as tears began to course down her deeply furrowed cheeks. She gasped out loud, throttling a little cry, wiping away the tears which flowed freely down her face with the back of a liver-spotted hand, whose fingers were crippled with arthritis.

She reached over the side of her chair, pulling a tissue from the little fabric-covered box and dabbing it at her eyes, before crumpling it into a loose ball, which her crooked, bent fingers were incapable of jettisoning into the wicker rubbish basket, standing on the richly carpeted floor a few feet away.

'I'm sorry. I didn't mean to upset you,' James interjected quickly. 'It was really quite stupid of me. It was just that someone in the photograph reminded me of …'

'… Jo?'

'Yes,' replied James, 'and do I take it that you're Jo's mother?' he asked, at the same time mindful that persistent questioning might cause the old lady to revert to silence on the subject of her child, which was surely no business of this person who had walked into her life out of the blue and who could hardly expect her to reveal secrets of the past.

'Yes,' replied Nan simply. 'You're looking at my child – my only child.'

James could not believe the words he was hearing. What had seemed like an impossible search for the stranger, who had visited his shop in Amsterdam just three days ago had led him straight to the one person who could surely provide all the answers. It was as if it were ordained by fate!

Andrina entered the room with freshly brewed cups of tea and a plate containing a number of rich tea biscuits, on top of which were a couple of chocolate bourbons, both slightly crumbled at the edges.

She handed James his cup of tea and a small plate, together with a dainty linen napkin and then pressed the plate of biscuits upon him. James picked one of the chocolate bourbons.

'Take two,' instructed Andrina, with a hint of glee, purposely reaching over for the second chocolate biscuit and placing it on his plate, before passing the rest of the biscuits over to Agnes to make her choice, when the best had already gone and really there was no choice at all.

'Tell me about Jo,' urged James, fixing Agnes straight in the eyes, as if, by looking directly at her, he could dry her tears. He was afraid that one false word would prevent her narrative flow and frightened that she might choose to say nothing at all in front of her companion.

'It's all right, Andrina knows everything,' said Agnes, as if reading James's thoughts.

Nan was strangely drawn to their unexpected visitor. She immediately felt that she could confide in him, acknowledging the need to pour out the grief that had bothered her for all these years to this person who now sat opposite her and who seemed all too willing to listen to what she had to say.

Sometimes it was easier to talk to a stranger. Over the years she and Andrina had ironed out most of their differences. It had all begun at Anne's funeral about fifteen years ago.

With Anne's death from liver disease, Agnes and Andrina were the only two remaining members of "the family" and both were struggling to live on their old age pensions, so they moved in together into the apartment above the old stable block after Andrina had sold Mary's house in Minto Street and depositing the money into a savings account, this allowing the two of them to live a little more comfortably off the interest.

Agnes had made some unwise investments with the money she had obtained from the sale of the Carlton Hall Hotel back in 1962, gambling on the stock exchange and getting her fingers burnt on more than one occasion.

What had begun as a strictly financial arrangement between the two women had blossomed into a grudging acceptance of each other and whilst they may never have been friends in the true sense of the word, constantly bickering and goading each other over trivial matters, it was their point-scoring matches, which seemed to keep the two of them going.

Now they were living out their twilight years in a state of amicable disharmony together in the apartment, which had once belonged to Jo and which

Agnes had refused to sell even when the Carlton Hall Hotel had been put up for sale.

'Would either of you care for another cup of tea?' asked Andrina, exercising a rare display of diplomacy and giving her the excuse to busy herself in the kitchen once more even before she had received a reply.

She sensed that Agnes needed to unburden herself and if she should choose to do so to a complete stranger, well that was her business. For years Andrina had threatened to "spill the beans" about the identity of Jo's natural mother, blackmailing her sister-in-law with the promise that she would tell all, until there had been no point in doing so.

Now it would do Agnes good to talk to someone about it, even if it did mean painting Andrina as the villain of the piece.

'Jo was my child,' Agnes began, 'but one which I couldn't ever consider raising. You see I wasn't married to Jo's father. It was in 1944 – the year before the end of the war that I met Clive. He was serving in the Canadian Royal Air Force. I was a good deal older than him at the time. I guess that he was only about twenty years old. I remember it was St Valentine's Night. We were sheltering together in a basement in the Edinburgh docklands during a bombing raid.

'You have to understand. I had never done anything like that with a man before. He promised me that he would be careful, but soon afterwards I discovered that I was pregnant.

'I knew for certain who the father was. I had never done "it" with anyone else. He even wore one of those … condoms,' she explained, finding difficulty in expressing the last word to this man whom she had never met before, but with whom she had felt so strangely at ease.

'I understand,' said James soothingly. 'It couldn't have been easy … during the war I mean. I suppose everyone learned to live for the moment, but if your boyfriend was wearing … something, how come …'

'I don't know. I really don't understand. I suppose he simply wasn't "careful" enough. What I did know was that I couldn't tell anyone, especially not my father. I was his only daughter and he idolised me. It would have broken his heart. I just couldn't bear to tell him.'

'And what about the child's father, did he not want to know you afterwards?'

'No, it wasn't like that. We only met the once. He never knew that he had fathered the child. I never got the chance to tell him. By the time I knew that I was pregnant, he had flown back to Canada and I was left on my own. I didn't know what to do. I couldn't tell anyone. My mother had died during the war.

'I joined the Women's Land Service in the spring of 1944. We were known as land girls. I was posted to a remote farm in Ayrshire and everything was fine for the first six months of my pregnancy and I would return to visit my father, but then, of course, I began to show.

'I knew that I couldn't go on working and I certainly couldn't return home either, so I really didn't have much choice.

'I had some personal savings in the Post Office – enough to see me by for a while, but I knew that I would have to go into a National Health hospital to have the baby. I didn't have enough money for private medical treatment.'

369

'And your father never guessed anything?' asked James.

'No, by that time I had booked into a guesthouse on the seafront in Ayr ... along with a number of girls who were in a similar position.

'One of them was a farmer's daughter. We became friends and we used to spend a lot of time together just talking about our lives. She used to tell me stories about things which had happened on the farm.

'Every night, I would write a long letter to my father telling him about what had been happening at the farm where I was working but, of course, none of it was true. All the time the tales I was telling him were the ones that my friend had been relating to me. I don't think he ever suspected a thing.'

'And so you had the baby in a local hospital?' prompted James.

'No, in the end it wasn't necessary. I gave birth in a private clinic in Glasgow – all paid for by this man who was running a black market racket during the war.

'At the time I had never met him but, when he was introduced to me years later, it turned out that Robert was the man I was destined to marry. He was killed shortly after we returned from our honeymoon.

'Apparently during the war he was running a lucrative black market operation and he could obtain just about anything anyone ever asked of him – and that included finding children for childless women, who chose not to go through the usual adoption channels. No questions asked – no questions answered.

'His mother owned a corner pub in Morningside. It was where George used to drink from time to time – mixing in all the wrong company, I suppose you could say.'

'Who was George?' asked James, anxious not to lose track of the conversation, now that this old woman had decided to pour her heart out to him and intrigued to learn where all this was leading.

'George's mother owned the guesthouse where I was staying with all the other young women who had got themselves into trouble. She was a kindly woman and she did her best to help us girls.

'I don't think she ever knew that it was her son, George, who offered to put me into a Glasgow clinic when my time came and to pay for my treatment, as long as I immediately gave up the baby for private adoption.

'I didn't take a penny from him, I promise you. As long as I kept to my part of the bargain, I never had to pay for the time I spent in the maternity clinic.

'It seemed like a pretty good deal at the time. I wasn't the only woman whose illegitimate baby, he had helped to farm out – all for his own personal gain, of course.

'After I returned home to my father's hotel in the Borders, I never thought I would meet up with George again, so I figured that my secret was safe, but that was where I was wrong.'

'What happened? *Did* the two of you ever meet up again?'

At that moment Andrina had entered the room with a tray containing a hot water jug. It had been filled from an electric kettle, which had obviously taken an extraordinary length of time to come to the boil!

James suspected that she had been listening at the door.

'Yes,' said Andrina, taking up the story. 'It was my fault, I was working behind the bar at the Morningside pub and I was the one who introduced my half-sister, Anne to George.

'Anne had returned from Canada after the break up of her first marriage. She was pretty unhappy at the time and I introduced her to George. Agnes and I didn't know each other then. We never met until her father started courting my mother, Mary.

'Shortly after they met, Anne married George and then my mother married Agnes's father. After that we all became one ...' Andrina hesitated '... happy family.'

'And what happened to the baby?' asked James, now even more intrigued by the story and impatient to learn its outcome.

'That was the strangest thing of all – quite the most remarkable coincidence,' replied Andrina.

'My sister, Anne had produced a child whilst she was living out in Canada – nobody knew anything about it. When she paid for her passage back to England, she didn't bring the child with her. She simply abandoned it on the steps of an orphanage.

'By the time that she remarried, she was too old to have another child and so my brother arranged to "adopt" a newborn baby for her – little knowing that the child he had delivered to her had been born to Agnes, who was to become his future wife. George knew who was the child's real mother. He told me at one point and I'm afraid that I ...' Andrina's words trailed off and it did not take much for James to guess that, like George himself, Andrina had at one time threatened to reveal the truth about Agnes's baby, but little knowing that, years later, Agnes had even had to pay George off, presenting him with a sizeable cheque written on the account of the Carlton Hall Hotel in order to buy his silence.

'How long was it before you had to give the baby up?'

'As soon as it was born,' admitted Agnes, with a sigh, reaching into the little box of tissues, extracting a paper handkerchief and making no attempt to hide the fact that she was wiping tears of grief from her face.

'I never even got to hold my own child. I never had the chance to give it anything but a name,' she spoke through quivering lips, as she picked up the silver-framed photograph that had attracted James's attention earlier and clutched it to her bosom.

'I felt so very tired after the birth and I wouldn't even have bothered to have named the child, if one of the nursing staff hadn't been so insistent that I should do so,' concluded Agnes.

James didn't have to ask what she had decided to call the baby. Somehow he already knew. It was the same simple name that was signed on the back of the picture postcard of Amsterdam, contained in the inside pocket of his jacket.

'When the child was about four years old, I persuaded my mother to employ a nanny and, by some quirk of fate, the person who turned up to the interview and was given the job was the midwife, who had brought the child into the world,' chipped in Andrina, settling herself down into another one of the comfortable, squashy armchairs, after she had poured the tea.

It was as if she was relishing the opportunity to finally tell the whole story and to reveal her part in it all. It was as if, at last, the two women had gathered sufficient inner strength to unburden themselves.

'Yes, and why was that?' asked Agnes, at last turning towards Andrina, with a hint of venom in her voice.

'The only reason Jo needed a nanny was because Anne was never sober and you were always so horrible and refused ever to look after the child. You always hated Jo. Why be afraid to admit it now?'

'Oh, Agnes, you've never really understood me, have you? I never hated Jo at all. I was just so jealous. You see, I've never been capable of having a child of my own, not since my father, Frank Finlay, came into my bedroom one night.

'I was only about five years old at the time. I didn't understand what he was doing then, but I certainly understood that it hurt. I know now, of course, what he was doing to me.

'He raped me and afterwards he threatened me with a thrashing of a lifetime, if I told my mother. I suppose it's why I've never been able to have a successful relationship with any man and it's the reason why I have never been able to have children of my own.'

'Oh, my dear, I never knew,' said Agnes, reaching for Charlie's old walking stick and rising from her chair unsteadily. She walked across the short space occupied by the woollen rug in front of the fireplace, took her sister-in-law in her arms and hugged her warmly, reassuring her like a nanny would seek to comfort a distressed child, as the two old women clung to each other and began to sob in each other's arms.

James had another question that he longed to ask, but figured that the two elderly women were too upset to provide him with the answer. It didn't really matter. He was pretty sure that he already knew the answer anyway!

He was certain that he knew the identity of Jo's nanny and the fact that her address was written on the postcard in his pocket. He reckoned that he knew too how important a part she had played throughout Jo's life.

It didn't take much to work it out for himself that, for years, Jo had been kept in the dark about Agnes's identity as Jo's mother. More importantly, how much of this story did Jo know now?

What mattered most was finding Jo and who better to ask where Jo was than Jo's own mother. James sat quietly for a few minutes, gazing into the flames of the open fire, trying to absorb everything and endeavouring to choose the right moment to pose the vital question as to Jo's present whereabouts.

'Can you tell me one more thing, please,' he begged. 'Where is Jo, now?'

It was Agnes who regained her composure sufficiently to answer the question, withdrawing herself from Andrina's grasp and gazing straight at James, as she broke into floods of uncontrollable tears.

For a while, she stood regarding James in silence, just as she had done when she had observed Jo from the linen cupboard at the Carlton Hall Hotel, when Jo had been upset by Clive and again watching from an upstairs window, when Jo had bid Clive "Good-bye" before Jo's lover had departed for the airport in a taxi.

'You see Jo died in 1962 in a plane crash out in West Africa. It was reckoned to be the world's worst air disaster in those days. There were no survivors!'

Chapter 50

As far as James was concerned, it made no sense at all. It was as if the Devil was demanding his dues, playing mind games with his tortured brain.

As a teenager James had been traumatised by his father's death, suffering nightmares for years afterwards and now everything was coming back to haunt him.

In 1962 James had been due to fly out of Mozambique to meet his father. He was supposed to have been on that plane, which had crashed at Douala and for years he had imagined that he had no right to be alive.

His parents had gone through a messy divorce and his mother had resented any time that he spent out in Africa with his father, visiting the tribes and learning about their cultures.

When James had announced that he was flying out to Mozambique on his own to accompany his father on the onward flight to Douala and then on to London, via Lisbon, she had refused to sign the parental consent form for him to obtain his first adult passport.

At the time, James had been living in England with his mother and, unlike in Scotland where even a sixteen-year-old was free to marry without parental approval, under English Law, as a seventeen-year-old, James hadn't been able to do as he might have chosen for another year.

It had meant that Harry Cartwright had flown from Mozambique to Douala on his own, but now the question that was haunting James and preventing him from falling off to sleep was whether another seventeen-year-old had really been on board that flight – someone who had been proclaimed dead and buried in the very same swamp, which had presumably swallowed up the body of James's father.

Someone whom James believed to be alive and well and free to wander the rain-soaked cobbled streets of Amsterdam just a few days ago had just been proclaimed dead.

James tossed and turned in the uncomfortable bed in the shabby room in the Carlton Hall Hotel with its soft mattress, which meant he was constantly rolling into the middle, tormented by the demons of the distant past, his mind twisting and contorting and playing tricks on him just as it had done so many times before.

Was he going mad?

Had he simply imagined the rain-coated figure, who had sat beside him in the little café looking out on to the flower market in Amsterdam.

On their first meeting, they had never spoken a word to each other. In fact, now that James began to think about it, he didn't even remember Jo at all from that morning when he had ordered his breakfast and his two mugs of steaming hot chocolate.

He didn't even recall the stranger who had shared his table ordering a cup of coffee, remembering only the person who had visited him in the gallery! Surely he hadn't imagined that visit too! Was he going completely mad?

True, that morning he had been more intent on reading the newspaper article on the Benin Bronzes, written by the British journalist, Paul MacDonald, urging them to be returned to their place of origin. Yes, the bronze heads – he remembered them well enough!

His father had commissioned the reproduction bronzes specially from an accomplished West African sculptor, who had settled in Mozambique.

It had taken almost three years before they had finally been delivered to Harry Cartwright – all 629 of them destined to be brought back to Britain – each with a definite purpose to be served. Each one was fashioned in the form of a Benin princess, with her hair piled high in a conical shape above her head. Packaged individually in a wooden box containing a bed of straw, one was destined to be posted to each Member of Parliament, with the exception of the two which Harry had intended to deliver in person —one to the British Prime Minister at the time, Harold Macmillan, and one to the then Foreign Secretary, Sir Alec Douglas-Home.

Accompanying each of the bronze heads was a letter signed by the prominent proponent and lecturer on African tribal art, Professor Harry Cartwright, in which he sought support for his personal campaign to have their genuine counterparts removed from the display in the British Museum and returned to the then fledgling independent African nation, within whose boundaries lay Benin City – the place of their original creation.

Only Harry never got to deliver his message and Harry's heads now lay submerged in a West African swamp this past thirty-five years after the tragic accident involving the Caledonian Airways plane, which had crashed in 1962, claiming the lives of everyone on board.

Everyone on board?

Had there really been no survivors? Right now, Harry's son, James Cartwright was beginning to wonder, as he tossed and turned throughout a sleepless night.

* * * * * * * * * *

James had collected the hire car early the next morning, foregoing breakfast at the Carlton Hall Hotel and the chance to inveigle an extra rasher of bacon out of the waitress, as the taxi driver had suggested, in his eagerness to make an early start before the rush hour traffic clogged the city bypass.

It was no more than twenty-five miles to North Berwick and he found himself arriving in the attractive little coastal town shortly before ten o'clock.

Driving along Dirleton Avenue, turning first into Fidra Road and then turning left into Cromwell Road past the majestic looking Marine Hotel on the right, which overlooked the West Golf Course and out towards The Craig – an island shaped rather like a sleeping African lion guarding the gateway to the harbour.

Immediately he was struck by the faded, old-fashioned air of the town, with its plethora of guesthouses jostling for position in their mostly Victorian sobriety.

James parked the car close to the sheltered little harbour, which was set on a headland, with two crescent-shaped sandy beaches radiating out from the centre of the town.

Resembling a giant's tooth, the massive Bass Rock could be seen clearly rising over three hundred metres above the level of the sea a few miles to the northeast. In the summer it provided nesting sites for a vast colony of hungry gannets and the smaller, clown-like puffins.

Now on this cold February day, when a biting north wind cut into James's shoulder blades, apart from a few circling terns, the massive chunk of basalt was virtually bereft of life and with only a light covering of bird's droppings which, from the distance, looked like a dusting of icing sugar.

In its time the foreboding rock that jutted out from the sea, had served as a prison, a fortress and as a monastic retreat. The last lighthouse keepers had departed almost ten years ago and now it was left, quite literally, to the birds.

Small parties of marauding gulls stalked the empty streets devoid of tourists at this time of the year, squawking and arguing over the meagre pickings to be found in the rubbish bins.

In the summer they would grow fat on the remains of discarded fish suppers, but now they wandered along Beach Road like ravenous schoolboys waiting for the tuck shop to open.

Overlooking the town, the extinct volcanic crag of North Berwick Law rose high above the nearby red sandstone ruins of Tantallon Castle, set on the cliffs on the Firth of Forth.

Surrounding the small coastal enclave, were many of the finest golf courses in Scotland, ensuring a steady trickle of visiting golfers to the town throughout the winter months.

James turned his collar up against the cutting wind, which drifted in over the North Sea, buffeting the masts of the expensive sailing yachts moored in the harbour.

He reached inside his jacket pocket for the postcard addressed to "Nanny Bapty", which he had no intention of simply dropping through her letter box when he finally located the posh residential street, where she lived in a detached, double-fronted house, with a neat front garden full of burgeoning spring bulbs.

Apparently, the woman he wanted so much to find lived in Fidra Road, the next turning up from Strathearn Road, which he had driven past earlier.

She lived in one of the better class residential areas of the town, typified by the pinkish-red East Lothian sandstone, which afforded the stonework a warm glow, even on this chilly February morning.

Had it been high summer, James would not have been able to glimpse the magical Fidra Island, which had provided the inspiration for Robert Louis Stevenson's novel "Treasure Island".

However, on that cold February morning the trees had long since given up their protective green mantle, becoming the dark, brooding guardians of the windswept coastal town.

James walked up the pathway bordered by neatly clipped boxed hedging and rang the door bell of the brightly painted door, stepping back to wipe his feet on the thick coconut matting, for fear that the resident would not allow him any further than the front door on account of his dirty feet.

He did not have long to wait for an answer, even if the woman who greeted him was probably only a few years younger than the two elderly women, who had invited James into their home in the old stable block at Carlton Hall the previous afternoon.

James stood in the doorway, holding the picture postcard in his hand, with its scene of Amsterdam uppermost. He had no idea what to say to the woman whom he hoped fervently was known as "Nanny Bapty".

'Have I come to the right address?' he began awkwardly. 'I'm looking for a Mrs Bapty.'

'It's Miss, actually,' replied the old woman, a trifle stiffly.

No doubt her caller was one of those interminable canvassers, conducting some survey and seeking her views on one subject or another which, undoubtedly, was of no interest whatsoever to her.

'I'm terribly sorry. I'm trying to find "Nanny Bapty". Have I come to the right house?' asked James contritely.

'You have indeed, young man. My name is Miss Nancy Bapty. It's many a long year since anyone has addressed me as "Nanny". How can I help you?'

And it's many a long year since anyone has ever addressed me as "young man" mused James privately, but choosing not to voice his thoughts.

'I have a postcard to deliver to you … by hand,' he offered by way of an explanation, hoping that it would serve as an introduction – one which would act as a pass and allow him to enter the house for a chance to sit down and talk with its owner.

Nanny Bapty accepted the postcard from the hand of her unexpected caller, turning it over to see who it might have come from. She wasn't wearing her glasses and the scrawled signature was smudged where it had been glued to the back of the photograph of the Benin queen and from where the barmaid had upset James's beer all over it.

She couldn't read the message, but she was still sufficiently astute to notice that the back of the postcard bore a stamp and a correctly printed address, so there was no reason why it couldn't have been delivered to her in the normal way.

'It's from Jo,' James announced, desperate to capture her full and undivided attention, before she simply accepted the postcard, thanked him for delivering it and closed the door again.

'I beg your pardon, but how on earth did you come by this?' Nanny Bapty demanded, clearly flabbergasted by James's explanation as to the identity of the sender.

'Jo left it behind in Amsterdam. I thought I would deliver it to you in person.'

'And you've come all this way to do so?' questioned the woman standing on the doorstep incredulously. 'I don't know who you are, young man, but I think you had better come in,' she added, regaining a modicum of her previous composure.

'It's a very nice house you have here,' said James conversationally, as he entered the large lounge, which was almost completely furnished with antiques, including an inlaid display cabinet crammed with Chinese porcelain and elaborately carved ivory figures.

One wall was covered with exquisitely embroidered Japanese silk pictures. Finely filigreed cloisonné and giant Imari plates were displayed on every polished surface in the immaculately presented sitting room.

'Yes,' replied Nanny Bapty, 'I'm very lucky to live here. I inherited the property from my former employer a few years back. She was very good to me. She died after a long illness. It was all very distressing.'

James was invited to sit down. He chose a comfortable looking low armchair, upholstered in a fabric decorated with Chinese dragons. Having not stopped for breakfast, he would have welcomed a cup of coffee, but Nanny Bapty didn't offer him any form of refreshment, pressing him to continue with his story, listening intently and hanging on to every word, with the grim expression of a sumo wrestler.

At last, when she had heard everything he had to say about his meeting with Agnes and Andrina, she too began to open up to her unexpected visitor, explaining how she had come to be working in the private Glasgow clinic where mothers rarely got to care for their newborn babies for very long.

'I was very naïve at the time. It was my first job after training as a student midwife. All my friends, who had been taught alongside me, were earning very poor wages and the Glasgow clinic promised to pay me almost double what I could have earned elsewhere. At first I had no idea what was going on behind the scenes and when I eventually found out, I was horrified, but the money was good and I'm ashamed to say that I stuck with the job for two or three years.

'I had been brought up by my grandmother. She died when our home was bombed in the Blitz. At the time, I literally had the clothes I stood up in, together with a silver St Christopher. Its chain had broken and my grandmother had put it in to the jewellers for repair. I collected it a few days after the bombing raid. It was all I had left – that and her little dog that was buried in the rubble and was dug out alive by the Home Guard.

'I was left on my own with nowhere to live. Hundreds of houses had been bombed and so many families had been left homeless that rented accommodation was expensive and in short supply and I needed every penny I could earn.'

'So what happened after you left the clinic?' asked James carefully, having practised his patient-probing techniques the previous afternoon.

'I advertised for a posting as a nanny in the Edinburgh Evening News. I only received one reply. It was from the child's grandmother. 'I was terrified when I arrived for the interview and I couldn't understand why I wasn't allowed to meet the child's mother, although I soon learnt that she was rarely sufficiently sober in the afternoon to entertain any visitors.

'When I was introduced to the child, we seemed to strike up an instant rapport. I was appointed on the spot. Jo was three years old at the time and quite a handful by all accounts. 'I remember that it was quite a sunny afternoon for February and I was taken outside to meet the child for the first time. Jo's pet hamster had just died and Jo was burying it behind a little white painted picket fence.

'I had no idea that I had been one of the midwives, who had helped bring the child into the world and when I recognised the child's mother standing at the French doors to the hotel restaurant, which looked out on to the lawns at Carlton Hall, I could scarcely believe my eyes.'

'And how did you know that Jo was her child?' demanded James anxiously, trying to maintain a soothing note in his voice.

'It was the birthmark on the child's right hand. It was most unusual. I remembered it from when Jo was born. I had never seen anything quite like it before.' explained Nanny Bapty.

'I don't suppose you ever met the child's father. I gather he was in the Canadian Royal Air Force when he … met Agnes.'

'Ah, yes, poor Nan. She never expected to meet up with Jo's father again and she had no idea that he was her sister-in-law, Anne's child, abandoned at birth and left to make his own way in the world.

'I met him once at the Carlton Hall Hotel. He must have been in his late thirties by then – quite a dashing looking chap, if I recall and, of course, no one, least of all Jo, ever suspected that he was Jo's father until …'

'… until what happened?' asked James, now hardly able to contain his curiosity, which was mounting steadily like a tower of children's building blocks, waiting to be demolished the moment that one brick too many was piled on top.

'Jo found out,' replied Nanny Bapty. 'I remember that dreadful telephone call. It was on St Valentine's Day in 1962. I begged Jo to come and see me.

'I couldn't bear the thought of not telling Jo everything face to face, but Jo couldn't wait, forcing me to reveal the identity of Jo's real mother over the telephone. It had been snowing heavily and it was a very bad line. I remember that Jo kept thinking that I was saying that it was Anne.'

'And what were you saying?' James prompted.

'I was trying to tell Jo that it was Agnes, but I probably called her Nan. It was the nickname by which her father had always addressed her. She was very fond of her father was Agnes and after he died so tragically, it was the name that she insisted on being called.'

'Oh,' replied James, 'I imagined that when you spoke of Nan earlier, you were referring to Andrina. I thought that you had just shortened her name.'

Suddenly, a look of horror swept across Nanny Bapty's face. She recalled all too clearly that snowy winter's night when the telephone line had been so bad, crackling and spitting, like chestnut logs burning on an open fire.

It was the last time she had ever spoken to Jo and it wasn't difficult to imagine that Jo might have misheard her, believing that the last syllable had been missed from Nanny Bapty's voicing of Andrina's name.

Jo might have inferred that it was Andrina, the hated aunt, rather than the kindly Nan who was the woman who had enjoyed a brief relationship with Clive on that St Valentine's Night, when the bombs had rained down on Edinburgh's dockyards.

Now there was no way of correcting the false impression that she had inadvertently created all those years ago, for she had no way of contacting Jo.

It was true that there were all the postcards that had been sent from foreign lands and which she kept bound together with a thick elastic band in the drawer

379

of the dresser, but never once had she received another telephone call, nor a single letter from Jo to reveal the whereabouts of the child she had once helped to raise.

Nanny Bapty sat in silence for a few moments, scrutinising the picture postcard which James had given her. She had never received any postal communication from Amsterdam before. Indeed, all the cards she had ever received had been posted from the same place.

What was Jo doing there in Holland – just across the North Sea – so near and yet so far? And why, oh why had Jo never spoken to her, or come to visit her?

It was strange the way that Jo chose to keep in touch with her, sending her picture postcards from time to time, but never anything more.

It was as if there was a need to maintain contact with the past, whilst still fearing that any revelation of an exact address would drag a tortured mind screaming back into the present and the reality of having to face up to the truth of all that had gone before.

Yes, it was her fault. If only Nanny Bapty had made it clearer to Jo all those years ago that Andrina was not the mother that Jo imagined her to be.

Now all she had was a drawer full of postcards, which bore nothing more than a scrawled signature just like the one that she held in her hand.

'I need to contact Jo,' said James, with a note of urgency in his voice, but as if no further explanation was needed.

Somehow Nanny Bapty knew. She understood. She knew of Jo's past relationship with a much older man and here was this stranger sitting in her lounge, who would be about the same age as Jo and who was obviously willing to do anything to discover Jo's whereabouts.

'If I help you, will you promise me one thing?' she asked.

'Yes, of course, replied James, 'anything, anything at all!'

'If you ever find Jo, make sure that I receive a visit one day. Bring Jo to see me. I'm an old woman. We need to talk – just the two of us alone together. We've never spoken properly and there is something which I need to explain.'

'Here take one of my business cards in case you ever need to contact me,' said James, extracting an embossed card from his brown leather wallet, containing his address in Amsterdam, together with a mobile telephone number.

Nanny Bapty crossed to the oak dresser and pulled open one of the drawers, extracting a thick bundle of postcards from a perished rubber band, which snapped in two, slapping her in the wrist, stinging and biting – just like the very first blow that she had delivered to Jo's bare backside fifty-five years ago.

'How will I ever know that whoever I might find is the same person you cared for all those years ago?' James demanded.

'That's easy. Remember what I said about the strange birthmark on the back of Jo's right hand. Here take this!' urged Nanny Bapty, feeling around the back of her neck and unfastening the catch on the silver St Christopher, which had once belonged to her grandmother. On the back you will see the City of London hallmark. It is in the form of a leopard's head and the birthmark on the back of Jo's right hand looks for all the world just like it. Perhaps Jo will return and give it back to me one day.'

'I really don't now where to begin my search,' said James sorrowfully. By way of a reply, Nanny Bapty handed James the little pile of postcards, each one of them depicting some scene of African wildlife.

James immediately started flipping through them, before turning them over to the reverse side. Every picture postcard simply bore a scrawled signature.

Every one was signed simply "Jo" and each bore a stamp that had been issued in Mozambique!

Chapter 51

Paul MacDonald sat at his desk in a small cubicle on the tenth floor of the office tower block in London's Canary Wharf. He had just received a telephone call, informing him that his visitor had arrived and was waiting downstairs in reception.

The meeting had been pre-empted by the fax that had been delivered with his mail first thing on Monday morning.

He had never met James Cartwright, but it was a rendezvous he was looking forward to now that he had been given the chance to absorb what the other man apparently knew of the circumstances surrounding the crash in which Paul's fiancée, Amanda, had died, along with rest of the crew members and passengers on board Flight G-ARUD.

He drummed his fingers on the desk impatiently waiting for the tinging noise of the lift bell, which would announce its arrival on the tenth floor, followed by the gentle whooshing sound of air, as the metal doors were opened and the lift was summoned to another level.

Paul would have got up and greeted the visitor, as soon as he stepped out of the lift, but that would have meant walking past Jean, his secretary, who always made a point of being there to cast a beady eye over anyone who made it to the tenth floor of the building, as if it was her appointed task to sanction every visitor.

Paul stood up promptly from behind his desk, as soon as the grey-haired man appeared in the open space serving as an entrance to the little cubicle, with its partition walling, which lacked both permanence and privacy.

'Welcome,' he said simply, extending a warm hand, but making no effort to bid his visitor to take a seat.

'It was good of you to agree to see me at such short notice,' replied James.

'I'm glad you could come. I hope you didn't mind me contacting you on your mobile phone, but after I received your fax, I felt that we had to talk. When you told me that you were passing through London on your way to Heathrow, it seemed like too good an opportunity to miss,' said Paul MacDonald.

'I would happily have flown over from Amsterdam just for the chance of speaking to you and I still have a stupid, irrational fear of flying, even after all these years,' replied James.

'I have to say that I found what you wrote in your article in the paper very interesting.'

'I have a feeling that our conversation may be mutually illuminating,' responded the journalist.

'Yes, I gather that we both have a vested interest in learning what really happened out in West Africa all those years ago,' replied James.

'I've always had my speculations as to the real reason for the plane crash and somehow I think it may have something to do with my father ... and someone else who, until last weekend, I didn't know had been on board,' James added.

'Look, this is probably not the easiest place for us to talk,' replied Paul, sensing the presence of Jean, rummaging around in the filing cabinets housed in the adjoining cubicle, with its paper thin walls.

'Would you care to join me for a cup of coffee downstairs in the staff canteen? It's only out of a machine, I'm afraid, but we should be able to grab a quiet corner now that it is well after lunch.'

Foregoing the lift, the two men walked downstairs, exchanging banal pleasantries about the duration and comfort of the short flight down from Edinburgh, which James had boarded early that morning after another sleepless night spent at the Carlton Hall Hotel.

Clutching two polystyrene cups of coffee, Paul made his way over to the table where James had already taken up position, with his travelling bags gathered around him in a little circle on the floor.

'I'm sorry about your father...' Paul began.

'I'm sorry about your fiancée, too...' James replied.

'It was a long time ago. I'm married now with two grown-up children and my son and his wife have just produced my first grandson, but I still think of Amanda sometimes. She was a beautiful girl and always had a concern for others.'

'Yes, you mentioned the birth of your grandson in your newspaper column last week. I guess I'm speaking to a very proud grandparent,' said James.

'Do you have any grandchildren of your own?' asked Paul.

'No, I'm not married,' James replied, anxious that the polite turn of conversation should finish right there, extracting the beer-stained colour photograph of the Benin queen from the inside pocket of his jacket and placing it on the table in front of the newspaper columnist.

'I take it that this is not a photograph of one of the reproduction bronze heads that your father was carrying on board the plane,' said Paul, turning the print upside down for a moment and observing the fact that neither the word "Kodak" nor "Ilford" was printed on the reverse.

'Yes,' replied James. 'It was taken quite recently by someone I met in Amsterdam – someone who is apparently in possession of one of the original ancient Benin heads – one which is quite valuable by all accounts, if it proves to be the real thing.'

'I thought that all the Benin Bronzes were on display in museums – either here in London at the British Museum, or in Germany. As far as I know, there hasn't been any left in private hands in this country for many years. I take it you know the person who it belongs to?' questioned Paul.

'We only ever met the once,' replied James simply, adding 'and that is what is so very strange about it. Apparently the photographer was the one and only survivor on board that flight – not that the name will mean anything to you. It's Jo Paterson.'

It was hearing that name after so many years that caused Paul to upset his polystyrene cup of coffee, sending the murky brown liquid cascading over the photograph to mingle its stains with the beer, which had already permeated the print.

'I recognise that name. Amanda used to stay at a hotel near Turnhouse Airport and I remember her introducing me to someone called Jo Paterson.

'I believe Jo used to confide in Amanda and she knew about Jo's affair with Clive Thompson – the navigator, who was also killed in the crash. It was a dangerous liaison from the very beginning and one which could only result in tragedy for both of them.

'Jo was only a youngster and Clive was old enough to be Jo's father. Jo was working in the hotel and was sixteen or seventeen years old at the time, I would guess and a member of the family who owned the place, if I remember correctly. What was the hotel called now?'

'It's the Carlton Hall Hotel. I was staying there just last night. And, yes, you're right about Jo. That was who I met in Amsterdam last weekend,' replied James, swabbing the table with a paper napkin in an inadequate effort to clear up the mess.

'I don't believe this. It was always claimed that there no survivors and now you're telling me that someone walked away from that crash!'

'Maybe Jo didn't exactly *walk* away from it but, as far as I can gather, all that Jo suffered was a few broken fingers,' replied James, remembering the scrawly signature replacing the neat handwriting, which Nanny Bapty had proclaimed to James that Jo possessed as a child.

'Yes, and I think that, like you, I am beginning to believe more than ever that it wasn't an accident,' James continued, staring at Paul, as if the two of them were bound together by some sort of conspiratorial alliance.

'I also think that you might know a great deal more about this than has ever appeared in any newspaper article. Please, Paul, tell me more!'

'I don't know what to say. It's only a theory, but it is one which I have held since I began investigating the whole story back in 1962 and with what you wrote in your fax, it all begins to make a lot more sense. I believe I know what happened back then and it was no accident, let me assure you. It was the world's worst airline disaster in its day – I don't need to tell you that. Amanda's death … your father's … they all died unnecessarily. It was a Government cover up. I'm certain of that now.'

'What exactly is your theory, Paul?' demanded James anxiously, leaning across the table, failing to notice that the surface was still damp, as he deposited both elbows in the small remaining puddle of spilt coffee.

'I gather that, like Harry, you have studied African tribal customs, but you would have to know a little about what was happening on the political scene in West Africa in the early 1960s in order to understand why the British Government might have had a vested interest in making sure that your father never got to deliver his message.'

'Paul, you understand far more about politics than I do. I've always been more interested in the people rather than the politicians. It's contemporary culture and ancient folklore than normally inspire my curiosity – not parliamentary plotting.'

'I take it you've never read the Civil Aviation Authority report on the crash. It recommended that all multi-engined transport aircraft should be equipped with flight recorders, but even then I doubt whether that would have revealed anything of the truth.

'The Commission of Enquiry was never able to eliminate instrument failure as a possible cause of the crash, as none of the instruments were ever recovered, or they were too seriously damaged to allow for any valid expert examination.

'What was more, the state of the wreckage and its position in an inundated forest area prevented them from determining with absolute certainty the cause of the crash.'

'What are you trying to say, Paul? Was it sabotage?'

'Yes, I believe so and from what you put in your fax to me, I think I understand the reasons why.'

'Could it ever be proven?'

'I very much doubt it. You could say that it was the Lockerbie disaster of its day and I doubt if the truth will ever officially be told about that either, even if it was put down to the work of Libyan intelligence agents.

'Incidentally, I understand that the trial is due to take place next year and that it is to be conducted under Scottish Law somewhere in the centre of Holland – but you didn't here that from me!

'I doubt if there will ever be a similar trial of those whom I suspect were implicated in the case of G-ARUD and most of them will be dead now anyway. Sometimes it is all too easy to forget that it happened thirty-five years ago.

'It said in the report that on takeoff from Douala the Caledonian Airways plane deviated to the left of the extended runway. Neither the cross wind, nor the possible asymmetry of engine power were sufficient to explain the deviation, which was observed from the control tower.

'If the pilot and navigator had followed the indications made by faulty instrumentation, without checking them and without confirming the altitude, heading and pitch, then the cockpit crew might have been sufficiently misled into making that deviation, which could have led to the crash.'

'And what do you possibly suppose that this had to do with my father?'

'As I say, you have to understand something of the political situation at the time. In the early 1960s it wasn't only Rhodesia, which was moving towards independence.

'Nigeria is one of the largest countries in the world and it was a pretty poor one at that until 1958 when large deposits of oil were discovered in the Niger Delta, which flows out into the Gulf of Guinea close to the estuary which served Benin City in its heyday during the late nineteenth century.

'Nowadays the revenue from oil and petroleum provides the Nigerian Government with its chief source of income. Even in the early 1960s, profits from Nigeria's rapidly expanding oil industry were beginning to bring about immense prosperity and, prompted by this new-found wealth, the call for independence from British sovereignty was gaining pace.

'Foreign oil companies began drilling for petroleum and opening up most of the oil wells, ploughing almost half their profits into the Nigerian Government and, of course, Britain and America were poised to serve as two of Nigeria's most important trade partners.

'In 1960 Nigeria was finally granted its independence. The African nation was on the brink of proclaiming itself a Republic and during the early 1960s various ethnic groups were competing for political power.

'It was a potentially explosive situation and, with its oil interests at heart and those of its American cousins, the last thing that the British Government would have wanted was to inflame old memories of a colonial rampage and the looting of centuries old West African art.

'And I'm afraid to say that, with his campaign to shame our Government into returning the Benin Bronzes on display at the British Museum, that was just what your father was about to do.

'Britain and Nigeria had ended their joint defence agreement in January 1962, just weeks before the air crash at Douala Airport. Harry Cartwright had to be silenced and my guess is that there was a good reason for that Caledonian Airways flight being brought down in an area covered by swamp.

'It was all too convenient for most of the wreckage to become quickly submerged and with it the crates placed on board by your father and for there to be no survivors!

'Bar one – by the name of Jo Paterson, who is the only person who might be able to flesh out your theory, Paul!'

'Yes,' replied Paul MacDonald. 'If, indeed, there was a survivor! Have you any idea where this Jo might be living right now?'

'If what I'm told is correct, it's in Mozambique and that's where I'm off to as soon as I leave here. Now, if you'll excuse me, I have a plane to catch,' announced James, getting up from the table, adding, 'thanks for the coffee. I'll be in touch.'

* * * * * * * * * *

James Cartwright sat in the cramped economy class seat on board the flight whose destination was Mozambique's sprawling capital of Maputo (formerly Lourenco Marques), after the long wait for the transfer flight from Johannesburg.

Now, they were coming into land, James could just make out the offshore island of Inhaca, renowned for its fascinating maritime museum and historic lighthouse, as he sat fingering the silver St Christopher medallion, which had been given to him by Nanny Bapty.

He hadn't spoken to her of his unfounded fear of flying and it seemed strange that she should give him a talisman depicting the patron saint of travellers.

Maybe she was trying to send him safely on his way and perhaps the journey he was setting out on would lead him to his goal, even if James had no idea of the exact direction that he had his sights set on. He couldn't bear to entertain the personal penalty of failure.

Mozambique was an enormous country, extending over eight hundred thousand square kilometres – almost four times the size of France and somewhere in that vast, mostly barren land was the person he had come to find.

It had been ravished by civil war during the 1970s and 1980s and when peace had finally returned, the once proud capital city was in terrible disrepair. Now it was trying to rebuild and was slowly recreating some of its former glory.

Once the rich and famous had flocked to the five-star Polana Hotel, with its grand views over the harbour and its old-fashioned tea gardens, after arriving at the imposing Central Station – a palatial structure, which looked more like the home of royalty than a railway siding for commuters.

Somewhat rashly, James had promised to return with Jo for a reunion with Nanny Bapty, who obviously still cared very much for the child that she had helped to raise and who had still kept in touch with her in this mysterious manner after all these years.

What was he doing chasing half way across the world on this fool's errand?

What was he hoping to find? Was it a valuable bronze head, or the body and soul of a stranger whose brown eyes sparkled in such a mischievous manner and whose hair was bleached fair by the sun that he was really looking for?

Was he a fool to have fallen in love?

It was a rough landing at Maputo and James would have nervously clenched the arms of his seat, if the instructions had not long since been given to fold them away.

Instead, he dipped into his pocket, retrieving Nanny Bapty's St Christopher and fumbled around the back of his neck to fasten the little catch, mindful of the need for the safe keeping of the hallmarked silver keepsake.

In the overhead locker was the holdall containing the few clothes that he had brought with him and none of them were suitable for a tropical climate far removed from the February frosts that he had left far behind him.

He would have to stop off somewhere and buy himself a pair of lightweight cotton trousers and a couple of T-shirts.

He could have raided one of the retail outlets within the terminal building at Heathrow before bidding his farewell to a bitingly cold British winter, but he hadn't stopped to think.

No, there was just one thing that occupied James's mind at the moment – more than the chance to stretch his legs after nearly fifteen hours' flying time – and that was his search for Jo, if only he knew where to begin!

Soon the sun would disappear from the afternoon sky, descending in a glowing red ball of fire, as James made his way into the recently war-torn city, full of classic colonial Portuguese architecture and the occasional building still riddled with the bullet holes of the past conflict.

From a stream of garishly lit streets Maputo's night-life beckoned with a heady, seductive Latino beat, but all James could think about was finding a hotel for the night at one of the popular beach resorts.

He had allowed himself to be guided by another garrulous taxi driver, hoping that, this time, he would arrive at a more alluring place to rest his travel weary bones than the shabby Carlton Hall Hotel.

His beach front hotel was adequately furnished and perfectly clean and James couldn't wait to peel off his clammy clothing, diving into the shower and taking a gentle stroll along the white sandy beach before seeking somewhere simple for supper – feasting on dog-tooth tuna and succulent peri-peri prawns, which peeled from the shell so easily after they had crackled and crispened on the oil drum, which doubled as a makeshift barbecue at one of the cheaply-priced beach shacks roofed over only by an incendiary sunset.

Along the way James was propositioned by a plethora of prostitutes, who thronged the infamous Fere de Populaire, with its lively bars and late night discos, thumping their music out into the night, but he wasn't interested in what they had to offer.

Instead he headed for a quiet bar, where he could gather his thoughts and plan the day ahead. Perhaps he would start off by visiting the Government-owned building where it had been suggested that he try his luck by the helpful, cheery woman he had spoken to at the Mozambique High Commission in London the day before.

It was the only place that he knew Jo would have had to have visited over the years to renew an annual work permit. Maybe someone there would be able to furnish him with a clue as to where to begin his search.

Anyway it was a start!

A small group of Danish tourists occupied the bar and spoke to him in English, urging him to join their party and share a beer with them.

They were due to make an early start the next morning, planning to visit the Maputo Elephant Reserve about eighty kilometres south of the capital in the southernmost province of Mozambique.

After the brutal civil war only two hundred elephants had remained and in 1975 huge numbers of animals had been relocated there from South Africa's Umfolozi Game Reserve.

Now they were being re-established in what had become a conservation area, occupying the coastal plain between the Lebombo Mountains and the sparkling iridescence of the turquoise blue ocean, where rolling green hills met the sea.

One particularly affable Dane, by the name of Mads Mørtensen, had urged James to join them, explaining that the small party had chartered a light aircraft and that there was one spare seat on the plane.

James refused their invitation politely, but regretted it the next morning as he awoke to a tranquil dawn when the glowing fireball of an African sun rose high over a clear blue sky, reflected in the calm, limpid waters of the Indian Ocean.

It promised the arrival of flocks of pink flamingos, sifting the silt in the river mouth of the Limpopo and a picnic of freshly caught fish grilled in the flames of a driftwood fire, funnelling its smoke into the fronds of the palm trees which fringed the beach.

Sunny skies, endless beaches and clear waters teeming with marine life darting in and out of the coral reefs – but James wasn't here for a holiday. He had but one purpose in being here and that was finding Jo!

James ate a breakfast of tropical fruits and drank strong black coffee whilst sitting on the slightly wobby, slatted wooden verandah of his beachside hotel. Afterwards he exchanged a few traveller's cheques at the reception desk where he ordered a taxi to take him to the administrative building where he intended to begin his search.

He stood listening to the squabbling weaver birds, dropping beakfuls of dried grasses looted from a nearby nesting pair with which to fashion their own untidy, conical-shaped brood chamber, trail blazing their brazen-coloured breasts like fire crackers flashing through the fronds of the palm trees, which provided welcoming shade outside the sheltered lobby of the hotel.

James waited in vain for the cab that never came.

'Hey, can we give you a lift anywhere?' asked the cheerful Dane, as he chivvied his little party into the back of a tourist minibus.

'We're on our way to the airport to pick up our charter plane taking us to the elephant reserve. Sure you don't want to change your mind and come with us?'

'No, thank you, but I wouldn't mind a lift to the airport. At least there I'm bound to stand more chance of finding a taxi looking for a fare. I could be standing here all day.'

'Climb aboard then!'

Arriving back at the airport, James was the first person to climb out of the back of the minibus, scurrying across the blistering, baking hot tarmac, heading for the taxi rank.

If he had only been a few minutes later, he might have bumped into the pilot of the eleven-seater Piper Cheyenne light aircraft, dressed in khaki shorts and a light-coloured T-shirt, wearing dark sunglasses, whose bronze-coloured frames poked back into a head of shoulder-length, sun-bleached hair.

It hid the sun-kissed neckline decorated with the most wonderfully coloured necklace jiggling and jangling in a softly sounding clatter of coral and a single coral studded ear!

Chapter 52

It had been a fruitless day, mostly spent tramping from one government building to another in the baking heat of the day. James had made the British Embassy his first port of call, but had drawn a complete blank.

Arriving at the front reception desk, he was greeted by a middle-aged man in a long-sleeved white shirt, which was clearly unsuited to the climate.

Immediately James was quizzed as to whether he had his full complement of vaccinations before arriving in East Africa.

The official seemed only to be interested in ascertaining that James had obtained a full course of preventative treatment, citing the risk of polio and typhoid and regaling him with lurid accounts of outbreaks of rabies and the prevalence of falciparum malaria – the type which carried the highest risk of mortality.

What seemed to be a well-rehearsed patter of "welcoming" conversation proved difficult to interrupt and James left the air-conditioned building, emerging into the sweltering February heat none the wiser as to where he might seek any further information.

Setting off on his own initiative, he eventually located the government offices responsible for issuing work permits, but was unable to find anyone there who had a reasonable command of any European language other than Portuguese.

He was advised to return the next day by a lean-looking young man from Lisbon, who was applying for a visa and who spoke a little English and was able to translate for him.

Hot and weary by the end of the afternoon and dispirited by his lack of success, James retired to the same small bar that he had occupied the night before with the party of Danish tourists, drinking his beer straight from the bottle and swigging it back far too quickly in the urgent need to assuage his thirst.

He had just settled into his second bottle, slugging it more slowly this time when Mads, the leader of the small Danish contingency, walked in and settled himself on to one of the high, woven wicker-back bar stools.

'Hi! Did you have a good trip? Can I get you a beer?'

'Cheers,' replied the Dane, depositing his new digital camera on the counter top.

'You should have accepted our invitation. It was a great day and I've got some superb photographs. Here would you care to see some of them?' he asked, picking up the camera and placing the viewfinder to his eye, as he began to flick through the day's images.

'Yes, that would be great,' replied James courteously, handing his drinking companion a cold beer and digging into his pocket for a few meticals with which to pay for the two beers.

'It's a great camera – cost me a small fortune, mind you, but you can see what you've taken instantly. Not like the old days, when you wasted so much money on developing a whole lot of useless negatives and, even then, you couldn't really see how the pictures would turn out when you had them printed.'

Mads handed over the Canon camera. James accepted it reluctantly, imagining having to sit there making a polite appraisal of his newfound friend's photographic endeavours, flicking through a whole series of exposures of elephants and other wildlife wonders, which would undoubtedly bore him as much as his recent visit to Amsterdam's Artis Zoo had done the other week, when he had accompanied his niece and nephew there on a chilly Sunday afternoon.

James ordered himself another beer by way of consolation, accepting the invitation to peer into the little viewfinder with a barely concealed sigh.

He scrolled through a series of photographs, which began with the assembled party all lined up in front of the Volkswagen minibus, where it had deposited them at the airport.

They were followed by pictures of the airfield with its assortment of grounded private planes and then one of a small, eleven-seater plane, with the rest of the party depicted one by one, as they ascended the short flight of steps, paused and, with a beaming smile, looked straight into the camera.

In the last of this little series of pre-boarding pictures was a photograph of the pilot and co-pilot – one male, one female.

It made James stop in his tracks, choking and spluttering on his third beer, which slurped from his wide open mouth.

Turned towards the camera was a face that James immediately recognised. Without the dark glasses, those mischievous, dark brown eyes were clearly visible, as was the coral-studded ear.

Mads was peering over James's shoulder, urging him to scroll on to the wildlife, which was the main subject of his photographic aspirations, but the attention of his drinking companion was glued to the little viewfinder.

'What's the matter, Old Man? Does she take your fancy? Quite a looker, isn't she, wouldn't you say?

'Like the pilot she certainly seemed to know how to handle that thing. A woman who was perfectly in control, if you ask me,' said Mads, adding, 'and please don't mention to the wife that I said that.'

James wasn't listening to a word. He couldn't even begin to explain to the Dane what he was thinking about at that moment and how he couldn't believe his extraordinary luck that the search for Jo was already nearly over before it had even begun.

* * * * * * * * * *

Two days later James was standing on the edge of the airstrip at the same time of day as the now departed Danish holiday-makers had gathered for their short flight to the game reserve, watching as the light aircraft taxied towards a small group of tourists, whose turn it was to marvel at some of Mozambique's remarkable wildlife.

Jo stepped down from the cockpit, dragging a pair of dark sunglasses into position, so that they hid those dark brown eyes and provided some measure of protection from the bright sunlight, which seemed to radiate from the tarmac.

In Jo's left hand was a small holdall, which was not much larger than the one with which James had flown out to Mozambique, with his few clothes and scant amount of personal belongings.

Both the pilot and co-pilot were heading across the scorching tarmac towards a little thatched roofed kiosk serving ice cold cans of Coca-Cola. If James moved quickly, he could cut the two of them off and reach the oasis of refrigeration before them.

James stood facing the small boy who was "manning" the kiosk. He couldn't have been more than ten, or eleven years old and stood grinning happily at the prospect of another customer.

The boy asked him what he would like, switching effortlessly from what James took to be Portuguese to fractured English.

James rifled through the pocket of his newly purchased shorts and pulled out a small handful of centavos, handing them to the boy, without counting the coins.

From the broad smile that immediately broke out on the boy's face, James gathered that he had handed over far more than the cost of a can of Coke, but he wasn't bothered at all.

Indeed, he would have emptied the whole contents of his wallet in exchange for the moment when he had turned round, squinting slightly against the dazzling sunlight and came face to face with the person he had pursued across two continents.

'Somehow, I knew you'd try to find me,' spoke the coolly composed co-star of the film production that, for years, had been Jo's life, speaking the words softly and without a hint of self-importance.

James was momentarily at a loss for anything to say, staring at the actor who, more than half a century ago had began rehearsing the part that had to be played in life and who had learnt the lines so well.

'Are you surprised to see me?'

'Not really!' replied Jo in a matter of fact manner, which suggested someone full of their own self-esteem but, in reality, simply spoke volumes about Jo's approach to life in general.

'I thought you told me that … you didn't like flying,' stammered James, finding words that almost seemed like a condemnation and immediately cursing himself for what he had chosen to say.

'Only when I'm the one who is in control! Besides, I never fly without my protector,' replied Jo, squatting on the ground and unzipping the top of the canvas holdall, which had been deposited on the ground between Jo's feet.

James remained standing and from that advantageous position the back of Jo's right hand was clearly visible. It bore the strange birthmark of the leopard's head, which so closely resembled the tiny hallmark on the silver St Christopher given to him by Nanny Bapty!

Inside the holdall nestled in a bed formed from a cushioning of a change of clothing and a garishly coloured beach towel, lay a sculpture fashioned centuries ago in beaten bronze by a master craftsman.

James immediately recognised it as depicting the head of a long dead Benin queen!

Unlike the trinkets brought on board the ill-fated aircraft in their crates thirty-five years ago by his father, James was in little doubt that this was the real thing – the effigy of the Great Witch Queen Oba Eeeni!

* * * * * * * * *

Taking time off work, Jo spent much of the remainder of the week with James, giving them a chance to get to know each other whilst, unbeknown to Jo, the Dutch born art dealer had made contact with various private collectors in Germany and in New York in an attempt to place a value on the priceless treasure that was Jo's good luck talisman.

As a good luck charm, which served Jo and Jo alone, it had foretold of Jo's survival, virtually unscathed, save for a few broken fingers, a loss of memory and fears which continued to haunt Jo to this very day!

Jo was the sole survivor from the plane crash, which had killed both their fathers and which James now firmly believed had been caused by an act of sabotage.

Had the British Government known of the sole survivor! Had the front page newspaper headlines, which had appeared all over the world, told the truth?

James doubted it very much, but he had no more way of knowing than the journalist, Paul MacDonald had of proving his theory. Now what was important was gaining Jo's trust and that wasn't going to be an easy task.

It was obvious that Jo desperately needed the money, otherwise surely the thought of selling what Jo regarded as a precious talisman at auction in Amsterdam could never have been entertained, but for what purpose was Jo in such desperate need of the money?

James's enquiries soon established that, just as he had thought when he had been first been shown the photograph of the Benin Bronze, this was indeed the effigy of the Great Witch Queen Oba Eeeni – the Mother of all Damnation.

He had once heard his father relate the tale of the ancient curse that had been inscribed upon the sacred stone that was her sacrificial altar … and slowly, little by little, James began to recall the often cited indictment of his father's namesake, another Harry – Rear Admiral Harry Rawson, who had led the Benin Punitive Expedition a century ago and whose real reason for doing so was yet to be revealed!

* * * * * * * * *

It was their first row – it broke out early one morning when James had told Jo how he had been in touch with an old friend in New York, with a view to gaining the best possible price for the Benin Bronze.

Jo had screamed that the head was not for sale at any price, arguing furiously that having read Paul MacDonald's persuasive article and now knowing of Harry Cartwright's efforts to right the wrongs of the past that, no matter what sum of money was at stake, the head of the Great Queen Oba Eeeni should be taken back to where she belonged.

Jo had stormed off, visiting a nearby market alone. It wasn't the first time that Jo had walked unaccompanied through an African market place.

It had happened once before in Mozambique when Clive had chided Jo that it was not a safe thing to do, explaining that three Europeans had been hacked to death a few months previously – killed for the sake of what was in their wallets and the price of a cheap lady's wristwatch!

Jo had claimed that this was rubbish and had later backed up the argument by telling Clive that upon seeing the leopard's head birthmark on the back on Jo's right hand, the old woman, who had pierced Jo's ear on the beach had explained in simple words that, according to ancient folklore, this marked Jo out as someone who would always be protected for as long as they remained in Africa.

Jo didn't return to the hotel that evening, choosing instead to spend time walking along the moonlit beach, seeking solace and companionship from the dark coloured rocks, which jutted from the sand like termite mounds.

Jo wandered aimlessly in bare feet, feeling the white, powdery sand squeezing gently between toes, which sometimes dipped into the sea at the water's edge.

Jo's brightly coloured necklace, which James had already imagined placing a hefty price tag on, jingled and jangled in a clatter of softly sounding coral, as its owner shuffled through the sand, sinking into the soft substance, so that it came up to the height of Jo's ankles.

Grains of sand rubbed against the individual beads of coral forming the matching anklet, which Jo had worn ever since that day on the beach in Mozambique with Clive. Now it almost seemed to be an integral part of Jo's sun-kissed anatomy.

A clear coloured fishing float had washed up on to the beach, being cast out to sea again, as each gently lapping wave invaded the shallows.

Captured in the moonlight, it bobbed on the surface of the water and then rested still again each time it was thrown up on to the sand.

Slowly, the reflection of the fishing float formed itself in the limpid waters, its image encapsulated in the creamy glow of the moonlight.

A discarded fishing net caused Jo to trip, as one bare foot became entangled in its folds strung together with a loose length of twine, which now twisted around Jo's toes and knotted itself around the string which held the coral bead anklet together, trapping Jo on the spot at the end of a line of footsteps that Jo had hollowed out in the sand.

Jo bent down to untangle the ties, carefully unknotting the twisting twine, with fingers which had once been smashed and broken. Jo made a conscious effort not to snag the anklet, for fear of casting the coral beads free to lose themselves in the enveloping sand.

A fish hook dug into Jo's big toe, sending a sickening stab of pain across Jo's right foot and a tiny trickle of blood began to flow into the sand, like the seeping signs that a virgin had been taken for the first time.

Jo's ears drummed with the memory of the recent row with James over the question of selling the Benin Bronze, before shifting to another argument which had taken place long ago in the dead weight of a distant past, when Clive had fought with Jo over the unwise decision to have that coral ear stud implanted without so much as a dab of disinfectant.

Jo waited for a dark cloud which had been sent scudding across the crescent moon to disappear and for the moon to shed its light once again on the darkness of that African night.

As a sliver of moonlight appeared, Jo resumed the task of trying to free a foot held fast in the torturing twine and waited for sufficient light to determine the direction in which to twist the fishing hook and free it from the bloody flesh without causing further pain.

The reflection of the moon captured in the fishing float provided a tiny measure of extra light. The clear glass ball wrapped around with rope, tossed gently back and forth in the lapping oceanic flow, as a figure drifted towards Jo, initially hidden from view, as the moon ducked behind another dark cloud.

At first, Jo imagined that it was James who had come out to make his peace and apologise for their stupid argument, which had caused friction between the two of them for the first time, but clearly the tall figure was not that of the Anglo/Dutchman, who was much shorter in height than Jo had initially thought.

Jo should have been able to discern the features, as a crescent of moonlight appeared once more but, strangely, it didn't seem to have a face at all!

A shiver of fear shot through Jo, as the memories began flooding back and the full horror of what had happened when the Caledonian Airways plane had fallen from the skies began to crowd in on Jo's thoughts, causing waking nightmares about what had happened under another black African sky.

Jo didn't feel the sickening stab of pain any more.

Jo didn't feel any fear.

Jo stood with feet trapped in the twine, sinking slowly into the wet sand held spellbound by the stranger, who was really no stranger at all!

Slowly, she drifted across the sands, just as she had done after Clive's birthday party, which hadn't proved to be his real birthday at all and Jo had danced under the moonlight with the troupe of African dancers.

Once more the fishing float began to bob up and down, cast momentarily upon the waves, before being tossed back on to the beach again on the ebbing tide.

If was as if it was being swayed by a soft, gentle flow that barely rippled the surface of the water, before it bobbed up one last time and was carried out to sea on a sea breeze that never stirred the surprisingly still waters roused only by the gently lapping tide.

A whispering, rhythmic voice, relayed by the wind, began to chant its secrets – ones which Jo alone could hear, spoken in the hushed tones of a mother rocking her child back to a world where nothing could possibly harm it.

Jo pulled the fishing hook free from where it had sunk deeply into the skin, releasing a fresh, more abundant flow of warm blood, as slowly, inexplicably, the encircling twine began to unravel itself from Jo's foot.

Jo was free!

Jo was free to live and love again!

Mindful of the moon, which now shone in all its bright intensity, Jo faced out to sea, as if hypnotised, looking for any signs of the fishing float bobbing on the surface of the water, but it seemed to have sunk without trace.

Inscrutably, the image of the bronze head of the Great Queen Oba Eeeni permeated Jo's thoughts like a warmly welcome guest.

Once she had been stolen from her sacred resting place and now she longed to be returned by Jo and by Jo alone!

Jo was the child of the falling, who bore the special birthmark. Jo was the chosen child and it was Jo who had to answer to the calling!

In the moonstruck atmosphere, which cast deep shadows along the deserted beach, the phantom seemed to arise from the sand, instantly illuminated in a cascade of dazzling white light, which allowed Jo to see something which was beyond all understanding – a blackened figure with an ashen face, which slowly began to glow in the moonlight.

James came running down the beach, ready to make amends and wanting nothing more than to hold Jo in enveloping arms, which spoke volumes of their growing feelings for each other.

Under a full moon which cast its guiding light through the night sky, at last Jo was able to view the once fulsome features – no longer cast in shadow and no longer a featureless face!

Bright dancing eyes formed a window to the soul. Full, lustrous lips filled a friendly face; gently breathing from a scenting nose, savouring the aromas of a thousand years and coral studded ears listening to every soothing sound.

It was face where a face should be and totally unlike the one that Jo had once seen before.

Black and beautiful! It was blindingly bright!

A beaming sorceress who yet lived again! A woman who could sink a fishing float deep beneath the still waters of a tranquil ocean.

A voice began to call. Its listener was James, who had just arrived at Jo's side in time for the crescent moon to light up his face in the milky moonlight.

Thou taketh my head
And blood will be shed
A spear in the heart
The thief will depart
Death to the receiver
Be he not a believer
The son of the taker
Will meet his maker
The sons of the son
By the Devil be won
The son of he who lies
Will fall from the skies
He who commits incest
Is not allowed to rest
Until his only child
By Africa is beguiled

The child of the falling
Awakens to the calling
Upon the sacred stone
Place the head alone

Twenty lines of rhyme, repeated for what seemed like an eternity, whilst James and Jo stood together, embracing each other with a love that was now deemed acceptable and which knew no boundaries.

Suddenly, Jo understood the meaning of it all. At last, Jo was free to live and love. No evil curse threatened to destroy that love and the only price that was still left to pay was that of an airline ticket to a destination in West Africa where Benin beckoned.

Return the head of the Great Queen Oba Eeeni and she would reward the person responsible for her happy home-coming.

Jo was the offspring of Clive Thompson, who had committed incest with his only child.

Clive was the son of he who had lied about the existence of his only son, and who had tragically fallen from the skies.

Clive who was not allowed to rest until his own child had awoken to the calling.

Jo had fallen in love with Africa and at last Jo was free to love another man.

In that instant, Jo had made a decision which would certainly please the ancient queen. On the next available flight, accompanied by James, Jo would be flying back to Benin City where it had all begun a century ago.

Soon Jo Paterson would be en route for a long awaited reconciliation with the Great Queen Oba Eeeni.

* * * * * * * * *

With no scheduled flights between Mozambique and Nigeria available the next day, there was no chance of carrying out the plan to fly directly to the capital of Lagos and from there to make their way by road to Benin City, but James had another idea – one which would lay a few more ghosts of the past and which, hopefully, would help him to finally conquer his fear of flying.

With the discovery of the existence of a direct flight from the city which had once been known at Lourenco Marques to Douala, they would follow the very same route, which had been navigated by Clive back in 1962, with both Harry Cartwright and Jo on board as passengers.

James booked their tickets, using his already overstretched credit card and the two lovers boarded the plane to West Africa.

Their plane touched down just as twilight was descending over the place which, for James, held so many memories of sleepless nights following the death of his father.

Now that Jo's mind had finally been unlocked, the arrival in Douala, after an interval of thirty-five years, represented a steep mountain which had to be climbed. If there were to be any recurring nightmares, then Jo would endeavour to hold them in check.

Switching his mobile phone back on and registering on to a new network, as they stood in the queue at passport control, James noted a total of three missed calls and every one of them was from an Edinburgh telephone number.

As soon as they had cleared the terminal building, James pressed "Redial" and waited to be connected.

After a short series of ringing tones, his call was answered by a woman, who proclaimed herself to be a hospital almoner working at the Royal Infirmary in Edinburgh.

'Is it possible to speak to Jo Paterson, please?' she asked.

James handed the mobile phone across to Jo, somehow sensing that this was bad news.

'I understand that you are a relative of Miss Nancy Bapty,' the woman said in a calm, matter of fact tone.

'Well, not exactly a relative, but I've known her virtually all my life. She used to be my nanny years ago.'

'I'm afraid that I have some bad news for you. She's had a stroke. It's quite bad. It has left her with a severe speech impediment, but she's asking for you. I understand that she is a Roman Catholic and she has asked if she can see a priest to be administered with the last rites. If you do decide to come, I wouldn't leave it too long, if I were you.'

'Listen I've just flown into West Africa. I don't know how soon I can get back to Scotland, but I'll do my best. Please tell Nanny Bapty that Jo will be coming.'

In that moment, all thoughts of Benin City and the imminent return of the Great Witch queen to her sacred altar stone were instantly forgotten.

She could wait. The Great Queen Oba Eeeni was not pleased!

Chapter 53

The taxi drew up outside the main entrance to the Edinburgh Royal Infirmary opposite George Heriots School in Lauriston Place. Jo scrambled out of the back, as the driver slid back the glass partition. James leant over and paid the fare.

It was a cold, wet, windy day and the two weary travellers already felt chilled to the bone, after the tropical heat. They had spent just the one night in Douala, catching the first flight back to Britain the next day.

Whilst there they had chartered a small boat, which had weaved its way through the mangroves, permitted them a brief visit to the unofficial graveside to pay their respects to Clive, to Harry Cartwright, to Amanda and to the hundred or so other crew members and passengers who had died that day.

Sentimentally, Jo had insisted on buying a dozen red roses at an enormously inflated price from the boutique in the lobby of the African city's one and only five star hotel, which was able to provide them with accommodation for the night.

When they had been delivered to the room, there were just eleven blooms – all of which were already beginning to wilt in the heat. Their number was made up by the inclusion of a single pink rose, which stood proud and erect, as if unaffected by the soaring summer temperature.

Jo extracted the single pink bloom from the bunch, snapping off its long stem and stripping it of its thorns before presenting it to James in an action which, for Jo, held poignant echoes of the past.

'I thought that it was usually a gentleman who presented a rose as a love token to the lady of his life and, besides, it should really be a red one,' said James teasingly.

'I guess you got it wrong,' replied Jo simply, in an attempt at lightheartedness, with thoughts solely occupied by Nanny Bapty and whether or not the two of them would arrive back in Edinburgh in time to fulfil her last dying wish.

In the metal hospital bed she had laid, propped up by a plump selection of pillows in their bleached white pillowcases. She was clearly dozing off to sleep when Jo entered the antiseptic smelling ward.

James had remained downstairs in the lobby with a cup of plastic tasting coffee, giving Jo the chance to have time alone with the dying woman, whom he could hardly claim to really know.

She awoke sleepily, as Jo placed a gentle hand on her forearm. At first there was no spark of recognition but, then again, Jo was now fifty-five years old and no longer the fresh faced teenager that Nanny Bapty had last held a conversation with on that nightmare night in February, just two short weeks before the air crash, when Jo had spoken to her from a telephone call box and shivered in the snow.

'Nanny! Can you hear me? It's Jo. I've come to see you.'

One side of her face was almost completely paralysed. Slowly, she opened her eyes, unfolding the blurred vision of the person who stood by her bedside and who now spoke words of tender comfort to her.

'Is that you, madam?' she asked in a slurred voice, which was barely comprehensible.

'Are you looking for Jo? You'll find your grandchild on the lawn, tending the little flower bed with the white painted ... Her words trailed off and Jo could only just make out what she was saying – words which probably would have made no sense at all to anyone other than the small child, who had once insisted on installing a pet's cemetery in the middle of the wide expanse of rolling lawns at Carlton Hall Hotel.

'Nanny. It's not Mary. It's me, Jo. I'm here right beside you.'

'Jo, go and wash your hands at once. You're not coming to the tea ...'

'Alright, Nanny I'll wash my hands,' replied Jo in an attempt to humour the old woman, as she began to drift off into an other worldly existence occupied only by small children and her former employer, who had been dead for more than thirty-five years.

'Please Nanny, speak to me. I've washed my hands,' replied Jo placatingly, adding, 'they're perfectly clean now. Here smell them.' Jo's knuckles were balled up tight and the strange leopard's head birthmark was clearly visible on the back of Jo's hand, as Jo ran the inside of a perfumed wrist gently past Nanny Bapty's nostrils.

It allowed her to sniff the mixture of aromas and scents, which the girls in the duty free shop at their stopover in Lisbon had insisted on spraying over Jo's wrists.

Nanny Bapty had virtually no control of her movements, especially on her left side. She tried to free her right arm, with which she could still manage a little movement from the bedclothes, eventually succeeding in doing so, lightly brushing the side of Jo's face.

'Is that you, Jo?' she enquired faintly, as a single tear began to course down the right side of her cheeks, whilst the opposite side of her face remained spasming in a constant stream of convulsions over which she had absolutely no control.

Her mouth twisted into a surreal smile. She obviously had difficulty in swallowing and she began to drool and dribble from the corner of her thin lips.

Jo took a Kleenex from the box on the bedside locker and gently wiped away the spluttering liquid flow.

'I've just been speaking to your grandmother,' she spoke a little more fluently.

It was clearly an enormous effort and Jo had to strain to hear her, resting a coral-studded ear close to her lips, so that her soft, hesitant flow of words could penetrate through the swooshing sound of the curtains surrounding the next door bed being drawn across to protect the patient's privacy.

'She says that you must forgive Andrina ... and forgive your mother, too,' whispered Nanny Bapty after another gargantuan effort to make herself understood.

It was Jo who was the one who didn't understand, as James had not yet related the tale of his unexpected meeting with Andrina and Agnes in the flat above the old stable block at Carlton Hall and the revelations that had subsequently been made to him by Nanny Bapty.

Why, Jo had not even thought to question how the hospital almoner had come to be in possession of James's mobile telephone number in the shock of learning about Nanny Bapty's hospitalisation and the unlikely event that she would ever be going home again after such a massive stroke.

'... and forgive your mother, too!'

Jo mused over the words, as Nanny Bapty closed her eyes again, struggling particularly with the left one, which continued to flicker like the faulty shutter of a camera.

'... and forgive your mother, too!'

'Who is my mother, Nanny? Who is she? Please tell me her name,' pleaded Jo. 'Is it not Andrina – just like you told me all those years ago?'

At that moment the bed-ridden woman regained consciousness.

Perhaps Jo's questioning words had got through to her after all – Jo couldn't be sure!

'Jo I had to wait for you. I had to set things right. I should have been brave enough to tell you the truth all those years ago,' she said drowsily stammering with her words.

Jo helped her up into a sitting position, so that she could see Jo a little more clearly through her rheumy, bloodshot right eye through which she still maintained a degree of vision.

Reaching out gently with a trembling, shaky right hand, she took hold of Jo's, gripping it as tightly as her last feeble amount of failing strength would allow and clutching it, as if she felt the need to hold on to something tangible.

Jo responded by taking hold of Nanny Bapty's hand, acknowledging that there was little power left within her and grasped her small, bony hand in a tender action, which only slightly tightened the tendons on the back of Jo's damaged right hand, stretching and contorting the image of the leopard's head marking.

Nanny Bapty had been the first to observe that blemish in a private Glasgow clinic over half a century ago and she had remembered it after all those years, citing it as the means by which James could be certain of Jo's identity.

'Who is my mother?' Jo repeated quietly a second time, inclining a listening ear even further towards the wrinkled lines on Nanny Bapty's face in an effort to hear her softly spoken reply.

'Why it's Nan, of course. I told you on the tele ...'

Nan ... Anne... An ... drina. Three sets of names, all of which began with such similar sounding syllables. An interrupted conversation just like the one they were having now ... a crackling phone line ... and a mind which had been racing towards a conclusion and a final answer to the questions which had troubled and tortured Jo's mind throughout a childhood marred by tragedy and those turbulent teenage years.

'I never knew whether you were alive or ... dead. Something told me ... the postcards. I was so proud of you. I knew about your ... with Clive. I knew all the time, but never ...'

Once again her words trailed off and a stream of milky, bubbling saliva drizzled from the corner of her mouth.

'I reckoned ... were happy ... all that mattered. Let me go, Jo. Tell your ... friend that he must look after you. Learn to live again and learn to love ... and let me die in peace.'

Now it was Jo's turn to cry – big, swollen fat tears, which flowed down Jo's face in rivulets, dripping on the hospital sheets, like huge rain drops in a tropical rainstorm.

Jo remembered the Saint Christopher, which James had imparted to Jo shortly before they arrived at the hospital and which now jostled for position with the coral necklace that Jo wore around the neck.

With both hands Jo felt for the clasp, which held the two ends together, loosening it and bending low, tenderly lifting Nanny Bapty's head off the pillow, fitting the medallion around her neck, returning the silver talisman to its owner.

'My house in North Berwick. Look after it. There's a small amount of money too. I've left it to you in ...'

Jo was still holding Nanny Bapty's hand when the Staff Nurse, who had been attending to the woman patient occupying the next bed, came and asked Jo to leave for a while, noticing the tears which Nanny Bapty's visitor made no attempt to hide.

'You can come back in about ten minutes, if you wish. It's just that the doctor wishes to examine her now,' she announced kindly, as Jo arose from the uncomfortable wooden chair, pushing it away from the bedside, as it scraped across the polished lino floor.

Jo joined James downstairs for a quick cup of coffee, reporting briefly the news that he already knew about Agnes being Jo's mother.

James said nothing of his prior knowledge, reasoning that Nanny Bapty had told Jo all that his lover needed to know.

'Is she sleeping?' Jo asked of the Staff Nurse, on returning to the brightly-lit hospital ward and not wishing to disturb the woman who had clearly cared so deeply for her charge.

Jo was full of regret – not just because Nanny Bapty was clearly slipping away, but mourning the lost years, when an occasional postcard had been the only contact with this woman who obviously cared so much – enough even to leave a home for Jo to go to now that the advancing years made it imperative for Jo to leave Mozambique and settle down to a more sedate way of life.

North Berwick wasn't a bad place to live – just twenty-five miles outside the Scottish capital and within easy commuting distance of the city centre if only James could be persuaded to leave Amsterdam and, perhaps, re-establish his business selling African antiquities and tribal art in Edinburgh.

If they looked around, maybe there would be an empty shop to rent in Dundas Street, with its art galleries, antique shops and little cafés, or perhaps in Howe Street somewhere up the hill from the Laughing Duck, where the broad cobbled street stretched down towards St Stephen's Church. Here James could probably find a ready market for his African art, carved wooden masks and ...

Yes, with somewhere to live and the promise of money in the bank, now there was no longer any pressing need to find a buyer for the Benin Bronze. Now Jo could afford to return the head of the Great Witch queen to her chosen resting place …

Jo's thoughts stopped right there.

How could Jo be so insensitive as to be planning the future, at a time when Nanny Bapty's life was slipping away and she was yet to be taken to her own chosen last resting place?

She had suffered a massive stroke and it was plain to see that she was close to death. All she had been able to think about was seeing Jo one last time and ensuring that her own good fortune was passed on, thus guaranteeing Jo's future welfare.

Tears of shame welled up in Jo's already reddened eyes, dripping their salty sorrow on to the highly polished linoleum, just as years ago, after an early admonishment by Andrina, a single tear had escaped from the corner of Jo's eye unbidden and had dripped on to one of the highly-burnished brass stair rods at Carlton Hall Hotel, leaving its salty mark.

'Her condition is quite grave. The doctor's just left. She is very weak. I'm afraid you should prepare yourself for the worst.'

Jo took the last few paces over to the hospital bed, which still had the cotton curtains drawn around it, drawing back the thin fabric forming a screen protecting the patient from the outside world.

'She's gone!' proclaimed Jo simply.

'What do you mean – she's gone?' demanded the Staff Nurse gently, as if Nanny Bapty had just popped down the hospital corridor for a short afternoon stroll.

'She's passed away. Hopefully she's gone to a better place.'

'No, she's probably just dropped off to sleep again and breathing shallowly,' replied the Staff Nurse, adding, 'she was perfectly all right a minute or two ago.'

Jo was one step ahead and had already taken lightly hold of Nanny's Bapty's wrist, feeling for a pulse that wasn't there, listening for a heartbeat that no longer sounded in Jo's coral studded ear.

The Staff Nurse placed her fingers gently on the side of Nanny Bapty's neck, feeling for the patient's pulse and noticing the silver St Christopher, which hadn't been there before.

'I'm sorry, my dear, she has passed on. How did you know she had gone?' asked the Staff Nurse adding, 'I didn't notice the St Christopher before.'

'I've just given it to her,' replied Jo. 'After all she's embarking on a long journey. I wanted to send her safely on her way.'

Afterwards Jo stood with James who had just entered the ward.

'How is she?' James asked.

'I'm afraid she gone,' replied a grief-stricken Jo. 'I knew she would wait for me and now she's gone.'

'How did you know?' asked James.

'I always know when it is time for someone to go,' replied Jo, taking James's hand and holding it very tight, with no attempt to hide their actions.

Chapter 54

It was December 21st 2005 – a very special day for James and Jo, who had been living together for nearly eight years in the house in North Berwick that had once belonged to Nanny Bapty.

Jo had given up a life living with animals and so much more when the time had come to leave Mozambique. In some ways Jo felt cheated – not because of the adoption of a very different lifestyle, living with James in the small Scottish coastal town, but simply due to the fact that Agnes had never had the inner strength to raise the child that she had brought into the world, nor even allowed herself to tell Jo the truth years later.

It was mainly for this reason that Jo had never returned to Carlton Hall and visited her. Besides, James had related how the once grand Victorian building had fallen into disrepair and Jo preferred to maintain a store of memories of its former splendour.

Indeed, even when Andrina had died peacefully in her sleep on a cold January night earlier that year, Jo had refused to attend her funeral, despite James's gentle coaxing.

It had been left to James to wrestle with his conscience – did he attend the burial ceremony, or even put in a brief appearance at the graveside on Jo's behalf?

In the end, he had settled for the less contentious option of sending a wreath made up of cream-coloured roses and orange blossom, accompanied by a simple tag, which bore the words: "Andrina, may you rest in peace".

Underneath he had signed his own name and had mimicked Jo's scrawly signature copied from that last postcard, which Jo had written to Nanny Bapty in Amsterdam and which had provided James's one and only clue to discovering Jo's whereabouts.

James had squirrelled it away as a keepsake, along with the photograph of the Benin Bronze, which stood incongruously in the middle of the mantelpiece amidst the splendour of antiques gathered from the Far East, which filled the spacious sitting room at North Berwick and which Jo had inherited, along with the house.

Jo had spoken about one day taking a trip to Nigeria and returning the precious bronze to its place of origin, but somehow it had never happened.

Initially, James had struggled to re-establish his business in Edinburgh and money had been tight. Throughout the last remaining years of the previous millennium, they had struggled to survive financially, being able to afford to live mostly on account of the few thousand pounds that Nanny Bapty had left to Jo in her will, which paid the bills.

Jo had accepted the need to take a part-time job working long hours at a small restaurant in North Berwick in order to be able to put food on their plates and leaving James to look after the shop on his own during the day.

For the first few years any thoughts of taking a holiday, or a costly trip to West Africa had been pushed to the back of Jo's mind by the need to work six and sometimes seven days a week at the harbourside restaurant in North Berwick.

It had been Jo's birthday on the second Sunday in November. It was the thirteenth day of the month – a day regarded as unlucky by some, but one which Jo had always thought of as bringing good fortune, unlike the fourteenth day of the month, which had often been overshadowed by the dark secrets of the past.

It was the one evening of the week that Jo was not forced to work and James had insisted on a simple celebration – just the two of them at Stac Pollys – an expensive Edinburgh restaurant opposite the New Town Bar on Dublin Street.

Here they had enjoyed a light supper of succulent lobster and monkfish salad, served with ripened mango and a frissée of lettuce and rocket leaves, drizzled with a piquant dressing of lime and chilli, followed by a honey glazed fillet of wild-caught Scottish salmon from Loch Fyne, which had left no room for dessert.

Extravagantly James had ordered champagne, although it was not a drink which Jo particularly cared for … or normally could afford!

As they toasted each other in a gentle chink of champagne flutes, James extracted the tiny velvet-lined box from his inside pocket and "popped" the question to Jo in a way which seemed quite casual and as if the whole occasion had not been planned at all.

'It makes sense for the two of us to get hitched,' said James hastily, before Jo was given the chance to reply.

'After all, we're both over sixty years old now and what if anything should happen to either of us?' James reasoned in an attempt to take a practical approach to the matter.

'With the shop, the house in North Berwick and the rapidly rising property market, our joint assets will push us over the threshold for Inheritance Tax and if we never bother to formalise our relationship, whoever dies first may be forced to sell up just to pay the taxman,' said James, explaining the proposal in a matter of fact manner.

'You make it all sound so romantic, how could I possibly refuse!' replied Jo grinning, in such a manner that those mischievous brown eyes began to sparkle even more than the bubbles in the champagne glasses.

'Well you know what happened to Agnes after Andrina died. It was Andrina's money from the sale of your grandmother's house in Minto Street that kept them and she made Agnes put the deeds in her name many years ago.

'Without Andrina's money they wouldn't have been able to have afforded to live there. And now look what's happened. Agnes has been impelled to leave the grounds of Carlton Hall, which had been her home throughout so much of her adult life.

'Now she's been obliged to sell up and move into a tiny ground floor flat in Stockbridge – just to settle the account with the taxman!'

'And you feel sorry for her, of course!' replied Jo unsympathetically.

'Oh come now, Jo. Learn to forgive and forget. She's ninety-five years old. She once told me that she was intending to be around to receive her telegram from the Queen, but she may not live that long.

'She is your mother after all. I know that what she did all those years ago wasn't right, but surely you can find it in your heart to forgive her and ...'

'... invite her to the ceremony, I suppose you're going to say next.'

'Well, at least promise me that you will think about it,' replied James, as he removed the gold band with its small half carat diamond from the enveloping folds of blood red velvet and passed it across the table to Jo.

'I'll think about it, but I'm not promising anything,' replied Jo, adding, 'Thank you for the ring.'

* * * * * * * * * *

It was a small number of invited guests who gathered outside the registry office in North Berwick on that early morning just before Christmas when the sun shone unusually bright from a clear blue sky, which was to herald a beautiful day in more ways than one.

At Jo's insistence James had worn a hired kilt of navy blue, black and white tartan, displaying a pair of legs, lightly dusted with greying hair, with long, cream-coloured socks folded over at the knee and decorated with twin dark blue flashes – one on either side. On the right, tucked into his sock was a silver skean dhu shaped like a dagger.

On his feet he wore a pair of black brogues, which had been polished to perfection and nestling below his spreading waistline was a sealskin sporran, with silver tassels in the shape of thistles.

Above the sporran was a thick leather belt, with a large silver buckle and, to complete the Scottish regalia, he wore a black dress jacket and a tartan tie, which matched his kilt.

Jo hadn't worn tartan since the occasion of Mary's marriage to Charlie when, as a child, Jo had complained bitterly to Nanny Bapty that the accompanying ruffled white shirt had been one of Andrina's blouses that Meg had shrunk in the wash.

For the ceremony Jo had chosen instead a rather plain, but obviously expensive black velvet outfit, which had likewise been hired.

As the small party, led by James's Dutch friend, Johan, disappeared behind the entrance doors leading into the registry office in Quality Street, an Edinburgh taxi cab drew up on the kerb beside the Ship Inn opposite.

James held the doors open for the guests to move inside the somewhat unimposing red sandstone building.

It bore a slight resemblance to a Scottish kirk, although the stonework around the windows had, at some point, been painted a garish colour.

Dipping into his sporran, he extracted a small bundle of Scottish five pound notes with which to pay the taxi driver.

Passing in front of the bonnet and scurrying round to the rear door, he thrust it open wide enough to allow the frail-looking woman, who sat huddled alone on the passenger seat, the chance to gather up her walking stick and, with a determined struggle, emerge to accept James's outstretched hand, as she climbed awkwardly out of the black cab.

Taking her arm in his, the two of them stood for a moment in silence, as James planted a kiss on the old lady's forehead, before escorting her into the municipal building at which the ceremony was due to take place.

Walking slowly down the middle of the room, along the space created by the two sections of separated chairs, they arrived at the place of honour in the front row.

Jo turned and blinked in surprise, at once battling against the tears, which began to flow freely and abundantly down Jo's face, which looked strained and quivered with emotion.

Soon those tears found their destination amongst the beads which formed the coral necklace that Jo always wore and which glowed brightly below the collar of a white shirt, which had been left open at the neck.

After the registrar began her welcoming speech, she asked for the witnesses to step forward. Immediately Johan took up his position on the far right, beside James, where he stood as the sole witness.

'Do we have another witness, please?' asked the registrar.

'Yes,' replied a softly spoken voice, before the scraping sound of a chair was heard and Agnes struggled to her feet, supported by the walking stick which had once belonged to Jo's grandfather.

'I will stand witness to the occasion,' said Nan proudly, as a gentle smile broke forth, radiating over her time-worn, aged features.

* * * * * * * * *

After the ceremony, Jo emerged with James to discover a battery of television cameras and newspaper reporters gathered outside the little registry office in North Berwick, as clouds of confetti and lucky horseshoes were thrown at the happy couple.

The appearance of the press and a BBC television crew had drawn a large crowd, which had gathered in an attempt to find out exactly what was going on and what was special about this particular ceremony!

In high spirits James's Dutch friend, Johan, had bought tins of Quality Street as a joke and had distributed handfuls of the chocolates amongst the local children, who were now on school holidays.

The plan had been that the children should bombard the couple with the sweets, as they emerged from the registry office located in the street which bore the same name as the popular brand of confectionery, being free to gather them up for themselves afterwards but, like a gang of wily street urchins, the children had quickly disappeared, taking their unexpected bounty with them.

Nan had been taken warmly into Jo's arms after the ceremony, at which she had elected to act as a witness, signing her name in a hand which shook and trembled, as she gripped the fountain pen with her arthritic right hand and signed her name in a crimped, crabby style of handwriting, so unlike the neat hand with which, day after day, she had once filled the leather bound ledgers at the Carlton Hall Hotel.

She had pressed an envelope containing a cheque into Jo's right hand, which bore the strange birthmark that both she and Nanny Bapty had observed over sixty years ago.

It was made out for £2,000 and it was every penny that she could afford. It was exactly the same sum of money that she had given to Anne's husband, George, when she had bought his silence all those years ago and prevented him from "spilling the beans" to Jo about the true identity of Jo's natural birth mother.

It was a tidy sum of money and one which was to come in especially handy to the couple a year later, when they departed for a belated "honeymoon" in West Africa, where they planned to visit Benin City.

At long last, Jo would be given the chance to fulfil an obligation to a long dead African queen, returning her effigy home and placing the bronze effigy of her head upon the sacred stone on the day of the summer solstice, when the sun's rays would shine directly overhead.

Chapter 55

In celebration of their first year of official union and for the first time in many years, Jo and James were planning to return to Africa together – not to Mozambique, but to Nigeria and to the City of Benin where it had all begun!

They planned to arrive on the night before their first anniversary and Paul MacDonald, the journalist, was due to join them the very next day, having sensed that there might be a story here for him, which he could recount in his newspaper column.

Agnes's cheque had been sufficient to pay for their flights and would probably even cover the cost of their hotel accommodation.

What had once been a permanent suntan had now completely disappeared, wiped clean by years spent enduring the Scottish climate. On the following morning it was good for Jo to feel the heat of the sun once more.

Jo had awoken at dawn, as the first rays of sunshine broke over the horizon, promising a blisteringly hot day, which would see the temperature soaring to its zenith on this midsummer's day.

James was still sound asleep and Jo decided to leave him snoring lightly underneath the covering of the light cotton sheet.

Alone Jo walked out into the lush tropical gardens, which surrounded the hotel swimming pool, fringed by the gently swaying palms, occupied by a small troop of vervet monkeys, which squabbled and fought playfully, as they swung through the tops of the trees.

In the bright early morning sunlight an inflatable plastic dolphin floated on the surface of the crystal clear water in the swimming pool.

It had a stupid grin on its face and it immediately made Jo smile.

Apart from the chattering monkeys and the iridescent, jewel-like superb sunbirds, which flapped and fluttered amongst the palm fronds, the pool area was completely deserted.

Jo stuck a testing toe in the water, finding it warm and inviting. Jo wondered whether or not to return to the hotel bedroom and change into swimming gear, but decided against it for fear of awakening James, who would undoubtedly sleep on for another couple of hours following the long flight.

Jo's brightly-coloured necklace jangled in a clatter of softly sounding coral, as Jo walked barefoot along the walkway strewn with bright pink and purple petals of bougainvillaea, which littered the sandy path, showering their discarded blossom in a riot of colour, each paper-thin petal remaining exactly where it had fallen untroubled by the slightest rustling wind.

Gently the smiling dolphin – the protector of the seas – bobbed up and down in the slipstream created by the overflow in the clear, turquoise blue water contained in the swimming pool, which reflected the deep azure colour of the tiles.

From time to time, it was cast out into the middle of the irregularly shaped pool, carried there quietly, like a real live dolphin, but cresting the non-existent waves, its bright blue back ready to hold afloat the next child who chose to seek its safety.

Captured in the first rays of early morning sunshine, the dolphin dipped momentarily, immediately rising again out of the blue on the calm, untroubled surface of the water, as if afraid of being left high and dry at the water's edge, should a passing gust of wind force it to become beached on the sandy path.

Slowly, the reflection of the plastic dolphin formed itself in the light blue, limpid waters, its image duplicated in the depths of the swimming pool, like a porpoise with no definite purpose.

Distracted by the dolphin, Jo tripped over a sun lounger, stubbing a toe on one of its metal legs. Jo sat down heavily on the canvas-covered cushions, wrapping a clean white handkerchief around a bloodied big toe and tore the cotton, as it became entangled with the coral anklet and beads of ruby red blood began to drip on to the sand.

Jo bent down to free the anklet, noticing that a few of the coral beads were stained with blood and cursed at the prospect of a blackened, bruised toe, which would look unsightly in sandals.

As the sunlight began to intensify, Jo sat watching the dolphin riding the surface of the water in the swimming pool, its patches of clear plastic reflecting the rays which pierced through the palms.

At first, Jo imagined that it was James who had awoken earlier than expected and who had come out to savour the sunshine, but the height of the approaching figure was a certain indication that it was not James who had come to join Jo.

Jo should have been able to recognise the face, but the summer sunlight dazzled Jo's vision, making it necessary to squint and peer with difficulty from those dark brown eyes at the fulsome features.

No fearful memories came flooding back. Instead it was just like the time nearly ten years ago when, after a stupid argument with James, Jo had walked along a moonlit beach alone and the phantom had made its ghostly appearance.

Jo didn't feel the sickening stab of pain in that bruised big toe any more. Jo was not afraid. Fear wasn't necessary, for this was no longer a stranger that stood there in the blinding light.

Slowly, the female form drifted across the path which led around the perimeter of the swimming pool. She had appeared twice before – once on the beach in Mozambique when Jo had danced under the moonlight and again after Jo had discovered that it was possible to be in love again.

Once more the plastic dolphin crested the still waters of the swimming pool and began to bob up and down, before being beached on the well-trodden path for no reason at all.

If was as if the dolphin was being cast up on to the dusty, dirt path by a soft, gentle wind that barely rippled the surface of the water in the swimming pool, being carried there on a breeze that barely swayed the fronds of the palm trees, whose coconuts remained resolute and unready to drop.

In a soft whisper, soothing words whistled gently on the wind, like the chant of a heavenly choir of angels, which held no heathen overtones.

410

Words of worldly wisdom began to wend their way through Jo's meditating mind.

Jo alone could hear them, listening to their almost silent whisper, uttered like a mother reluctant to awaken her sleeping child.

Jo stood up, limping slightly, as blood oozed from the damaged big toe around which a white handkerchief had been hastily bound. Now it was stained bright crimson like a bandage pulled from a First Aid box and used as an emergency dressing.

Somehow the pain had disappeared.

Jo was no longer free! Jo had never wanted to be free – wanting to live and love again!

Now Jo had James and together they could be strong. At last their union was officially recognised and they could go on together in a way that Jo and Clive could never have dreamt of being able to do.

Sizzling in the sun, which now shone in all its bright intensity, Jo knelt at the edge of the swimming pool, as if kneeling at the altar in readiness to receive the Holy Sacrament, delving into the deep and looking for the plastic dolphin, which no longer rode the calm, flat expanse of crystal clear water.

The image of the bronze head of the Great Queen Oba Eeeni bubbled up to the surface, like a basking shark, which had never had any teeth with which to bite, no insistent incisors with which to slice through flesh and bone.

Once she had been stolen from her sacred resting place and now she was about to be returned by Jo – the chosen one!

Jo was the one who bore the special leopard's head birthmark – the one who would be protected upon entering the inner sanctum.

No serpent's serum would ever harm the chosen child, who had at last answered to the calling!

In the sunlit atmosphere, which began to cast its shadows through the overhanging palm trees, fringing the dirt paths in the hotel gardens, the phantom figure seemed to arise from the serene, settled surface of the water, instantly showered in a bright, blinding light, again allowing Jo to see something which was beyond all understanding – a blackened figure with an ashen face, which slowly began to glow in the early morning light.

Paul MacDonald had just arrived at the hotel from the airport. Having deposited his bags in his room, he had changed, intending to take a refreshing early morning dip in the inviting swimming pool.

He stood in a pair of black swimming trunks, with a towel draped over his shoulders.

In the full sunshine, which reflected off the surface of the swimming pool finally Jo was able to gain a proper view of the fulsome features – no longer cast in shadow, but now a beautifully sculpted face!

Bright dancing eyes formed a window to the soul. Full, lustrous lips filled a friendly face; gently breathing from a scenting nose, savouring the aromas of a thousand years and coral-studded ears listening to every soothing sound.

It was a face where a face should be and even more radiant than the one which Jo had once seen before.

Black and beautiful! It was blindingly bright!

411

A beaming sorceress who yet lived again! A woman who could blow away a plastic dolphin without the slightest breath.

A voice began to call. Its listener was Paul MacDonald, who had just arrived at Jo's side in time for the sun to light up his face in the golden glory of early morning sunshine.

Thou taketh my head
And blood will be shed
A spear in the heart
The thief will depart
Death to the receiver
Be he not a believer
The son of the taker
Will meet his maker
The sons of the son
By the Devil be won
The son of he who lies
Will fall from the skies
He who commits incest
Is not allowed to rest
Until his only child
By Africa is beguiled
The child of the falling
Awakens to the calling
Upon the sacred stone
Place the head alone
In the heat of the sun
The wax will run

Twenty-two lines of rhyme, repeated for what seemed like forever, whilst Jo and Paul stood together, somehow sharing a knowledge of what was to come.

Suddenly, Jo understood the meaning of it all. Jo was about to receive the greatest reward of all – a prize fit for a monarch.

No evil curse threatened to destroy the chance to become the recipient of that great prize and the only price that was still left to pay was that of standing naked before an ancient queen!

* * * * * * * * *

It was essential that they made an early start, as Benin City lay some two hundred miles east of the Nigerian capital on a branch of the Benin River.

They had to make their chosen point of arrival before midday, aware of the fact that, for Jo at least, it was a destination deemed by destiny.

They were travelling by road, driving along the hot, dusty main highway, which threatened another asthma attack for Paul MacDonald, sitting and suffering in the back of the four-wheel drive vehicle.

The air conditioning in the hired car wasn't working properly, forcing them to open the windows occasionally to provide a change of air and enveloping them in a fine layer of dust, which swirled up from the tarmac like a miniature desert sandstorm and immediately penetrated Paul's nostrils.

Paul sat miserably clutching his inhaler, as they swept out of Lagos – one of the largest and most crowded cities in the world – where skyscrapers and modern high-rise blocks of flats intermingled with open market stalls from which women dressed in garments of brightly coloured dyed cloth were selling yams and sweet corn and children carried heavy plastic canisters of palm oil.

In the back of the Jeep with Paul sat Felix Abati, a professor at the Benson Idahosa University in Benin City, who had studied ancient West African culture.

He had been contacted by Paul MacDonald and had readily agreed to meet the small party and act as a guide to take them to the Oba's palace.

'You will find that there are still a few good pieces at Okada House and in the National Museum in Benin City, but nothing like as good as those in the British Museum and certainly nothing of the huge historical importance of the head of the Great Witch queen,' Felix explained to his travelling companions.

James was driving and Jo was sitting in the front passenger seat, with the small wooden crate held tight in both hands. It had been taken on board their flight to Lagos as hand luggage – perhaps the most precious item ever to be carried on board an aircraft!

Passing through Heathrow, the Benin head had been revealed briefly in all its glory after being scanned and then scrutinised by the customs officer in charge of the conveyor belt at passport control.

Eventually, Jo had been allowed to pass in to the departure lounge, but only after the customs officer had insisted that the bronze effigy should be lifted from its bed of straw, poking and prodding at the solidified plug of wax, which might have concealed a stash of drugs, but which hid so very much more!

* * * * * * * * * *

After a dusty journey, which lasted for nearly five hours, they finally arrived at Benin City, passing through rural villages, comprising clusters of houses with walls mostly made of mud and covered by a thatched roof.

A selection of ramshackle outdoor market stalls were strung out along the side of the road, where an assortment of fruit and vegetables were displayed in woven baskets.

Forty years ago the city had been occupied by the secessionist Republic of Biafra, during the Nigerian Civil War and Felix remembered the heart-rending images of starving refugees and malnourished children, with pot-bellied stomachs and bones protruding from their breasts.

Occasionally, in a more prosperous little neighbourhood, they would encounter a group of houses with rough wooden walls and roofs fashioned from cement asbestos, or corrugated iron – the highly prized roofing material which the Oba had demanded from the British Government back in 1897, when he had asked for no less 20,000 sheets of the stuff.

The bustling West African city was surrounded by moats, which had taken over three years to dig and, like the Great Wall of China, had involved the labours of countless thousands of workers.

Once they had acted as a defence against enemies of the ancient City of Blood. Now they simply served to enhance the spectacular beauty of the modern city.

Here, unlike in Lagos, where Western style clothing prevailed, many of the people still wore their traditional garments – long, loose ethereal, white robes, which swept the dust, as they walked along the roadsides, like a gathering of ghosts, whose faces were anything but wan.

However, all was not a dazzling array of purity, as the advancing avalanche of white was sometimes interspersed by an array of brightly coloured fabrics.

Many of the men wore short, full jackets and sported small round caps and their womenfolk hid their hair beneath scarves tied in turbans.

Emerging from the driver's seat into the blistering heat, James envied their head gear, as he felt the scorching sun begin to bake his balding head and wished that he had thought to bring a cap along with him to perform the task of protection, which could hardly be provided by his scant amount of greying hair.

Following Felix's instructions, they had parked not far from the Oba's palace. It was late morning and they had drunk the last of their bottled water more than an hour before. Now their lips felt cracked and crusty as the result of a constant application of saliva.

Paul MacDonald suggested that they stop for a drink before entering the king's palace, with its mud relief sculptures of ancient gods and goddesses, which decorated its walls.

However, Jo was aware that it was nearly half past eleven and Jo was in a hurry!

Jo had an appointment with destiny – and Jo was determined that the ancient queen should not be kept waiting. In Jo's hands was the small wooden crate, which held her head nestled comfortably in its bed of straw.

Its lid had been prised open with the aid of a screwdriver by the customs officer at Heathrow and one of the protruding sharp metal staples had pricked Jo's thumb, causing a tiny droplet of blood to form like a ruby red gemstone.

Felix walked alongside Jo, explaining how traditionally entry into the inner sanctum of the palace was only ever allowed after a special initiation ceremony, usually lasting seven days.

Today they were to be met by two descendants of the Iwebo – the most senior society whose job it was to take charge of the royal wardrobe, making and repairing the splendid coral bead garments worn only on ceremonial occasions.

Since the death of the thirty seventh Oba, Akenzua II in 1978, the Iweguae (the Oba's private residence) had been unoccupied.

Located in a central position within the palace, only after the coronation was the Oba himself allowed to enter the Iweguae and stay there.

Now it was only the chosen child who would be taken this far into the inner sanctum. James and Paul would be made to wait outside, whilst Jo was ushered through by the Ighogbe (the worshippers and recorders of the departed Obas) and then passed on to those whose task it was to sanctify and purify.

Jo had no idea of what was to come, accepting the fact that now the bearer of the precious head of the Benin queen was in the hands of those who had learnt the ancient ceremonial rites, as they had been passed down from generation to generation.

In a darkened room hands stretched forth like the gently groping tentacles of a mild-mannered octopus, as slowly Jo's clothes began to fall to the floor.

Hands reached out of the darkness. Jo was guided to a short wooden ladder and lifted into a chair with gleaming white ivory arms by unseen soothsayers, who loosened the laces of Jo's shoes, revealing dusty, dirty feet, which they began bathing in warm, scented water, just as the juju priests had done by way of welcoming the members of the British Benin Expedition over a century ago.

Out of the darkness two candle-bearers arrived with the Emehe of Urubi – the royal carrier who, by tradition, had always to carry any load on his head and who bore the wooden box containing the bronze effigy of the long dead Queen Oba Eeeni.

He raised the box high above his head, lowering it again, so that it could be balanced perfectly. His hands were encased in thick leather gloves, so that there was no fear that mere mortal flesh would be allowed to touch the container in which the queen was enthroned on this midsummer's day.

In the flickering candle-light one of the juju priests took each of Jo's hands in turn, making a careful inspection – first of the left hands, which bore no mark at all and then taking hold of the right hand, turning over the palm to reveal the leopard's head birthmark, tenderly touching it and nodding solemnly to the other priests.

The juju priests promptly welcomed their very special visitor with traditional salutations, making three circles with their right hands, bowing and nodding their heads, as they began to anoint Jo's body with palm oil.

Jo stood completely naked save for the ear which held the coral ear stud, the anklet and the necklace, jiggling and jangling in a softly sounding clatter of coral, as unseen hands glided their way sensuously over Jo's body.

Glistening and gleaming from the use of the lubrication, they gently worked their way backwards and forwards through Jo's fingers, deploying their mysterious magic in a manner which left Jo's whole body tingling to the touch.

In any other circumstances, Jo would have felt embarrassed at strangers' hands searching sensuously, but with no hint of sexuality, over Jo's bare buttocks, slightly protruding nipples and that part of the anatomy that was the base of all desire.

With hands that glowed with the slippery residue of palm oil, Jo was rendered incapable of holding anything. Lifting the bronze bowl, which had once held sacrificial blood, to Jo's lips, the chief priest offered Jo the drink that Paul MacDonald had begged that they should stop for – but this was no ordinary form of liquid refreshment!

At first, it simply tasted strong and bitter – like the palm oil wine that few Europeans ever developed a liking for, but this was totally different!

It was laced with a pungent potency that soon had Jo's head rolling from side to side, working up the softly sounding clatter of coral into a furious frenzy.

With one white robed juju priest on either side supporting Jo's weight, the naked figure was led forward through the great wooden gates into the inner sanctum.

Following in Jo's wake was the royal carrier, who bore the box containing the head of the Great Witch queen on his shaven head and who continued to maintain a respectful distance a few paces behind the chosen one.

Now Jo was alone in the inner chamber with only the royal carrier who never spoke a word. Like the child of Oromiyan – a former Benin king, who had been responsible for the building of the first palace, he had been struck dumb at birth and was therefore incapable of voicing any fear.

As Jo's eyes began to focus on the candle-strewn altar stone, they also took in the poisonous snakes, which slithered around on top of the stone table and the pair of guarding leopards at one moment cast in bronze and then immediately seen as the animals they really were – bloody in tooth and claw, snarling and baring their teeth at the intruder.

Jo's head continued to spin like an exploding catherine wheel, whirling in unexplained circles, which a drugged, hallucinating brain could do nothing to bring under control.

Holding the oily palms of both hands in front of a pair of eyes, which were struggling to focus, the back of Jo's right hand was clearly displayed, revealing the leopard's head birthmark to the hungry beasts and, just as the native woman in Mozambique had predicted all those years ago, Jo was instantly protected.

The Great Witch queen was standing above the sacred altar stone, which writhed with a sea of serpents slithering down its inscribed sides.

Bright dancing eyes formed a window to the soul. Full, lustrous lips filled a friendly face; gently breathing from a scenting nose, savouring the aromas of a thousand years and coral-studded ears listening to every soothing sound.

It was face where a face should be and even more radiant than the one which Jo had seen before.

Black and beautiful! It was blindingly bright!

A beaming sorceress who yet lived again! A woman who could tame a seething snake pit, silencing their hissing and blowing a kiss upon their forked tongues without even pursing her fulsome lips in order to quell their venomous strike.

A voice began to call. Its listener was the royal porter, who had been struck dumb at birth, but whose hearing was acute to the merest whisper.

Upon the sacred stone
Place the head alone

The royal carrier stepped forward, placing the wooden box in the centre of the stone altar, deliberately toppling the surrounding candles as he did so, causing their hungry flames to begin consuming its thin wooden sides, igniting the straw bed and illuminating the bronze head, which glowed bright in the reflection of the firelight.

Sparks drifted up towards the thatched roof of the inner sanctum, like a myriad of dancing fireflies reaching upwards towards a last tango, as they were ignited and united in death.

Within seconds the straw roof was ablaze, torched in a thunderous explosion, as drifts of burning straw, caught on a gently uplifting breeze, brought about the conflagration, which soon saw the whole building engulfed in furious flames.

Pockets of air trapped in the flaming thatch exploded like the repetitive gunfire of the Maxim machine guns, which had wrought their deadly harvest of so many innocent lives over a century ago.

In the midst of it all stood Jo, protected under the canopy of two sheets of corrugated iron, which had been used in the construction of the roof.

Not a single spark dared to land on Jo's naked flesh.

As the flames began to die away, it was as if a mythical sun god had arisen from the slumbers of a thousand years, bursting down upon the scene from directly overhead, bathing the sacred altar stone in all the glowing luminosity of the midday sun on this the summer solstice.

One piercing ray shone directly on to the bronze head of the Great Queen Oba Eeeni, bathing her in a light of dazzling intensity, as slowly her waxen plug began to melt, puddling itself in a series of deep crimson splashes around the base of her neck.

Like blood, the molten liquid began to flow, seeping into the narrow channel cut into the sacred altar stone and dripping down the front of the inscribed stone, blurring words written in a strange tongue, but which that Jo already knew so well:

Thou taketh my head
And blood will be shed
A spear in the heart
The thief will depart
Death to the receiver
Be he not a believer
The son of the taker
Will meet his maker
The sons of the son
By the Devil be won
The son of he who lies
Will fall from the skies
He who commits incest
Is not allowed to rest
Until his only child
By Africa is beguiled
The child of the falling
Awakens to the calling
Upon the sacred stone
Place the head alone

In the heat of the sun
The wax will run
The head is returned
The reward is earned

Two dozen lines of rhyme, repeated for what seemed an eternity, whilst Jo stood with the royal carrier, who appeared to know exactly what he had to do next.

In one deft movement, the shaven-headed porter lent forward and with his leather gloved right hand, lifted the burning hot bronze head of the Great Queen Oba Eeeni to reveal her heart, which had been beating for a thousand years!

Chapter 56

James booked their tickets for Antwerp at Amsterdam's Central Station after spending the night sharing a narrow bed with Jo in Johan's flat somewhere close to the Red Light District, populated by ladies of the night, who besported themselves in shop windows in the narrow streets bordering the Singel.

On the previous cold, foggy November's night the mist had risen from the surface of the canals and they had wrapped up warm and gone out with Johan for what had promised to be a few beers, but which had rapidly become a drunken, albeit much belated, celebration of their home-coming from West Africa.

A few days before it had been Jo's sixty-third birthday, which had given the three of them yet another excuse for a "night on the town" and now James and Jo were both suffering from blinding hangovers.

James had been anxious to tell their story to his Dutch friend before the news broke in the national newspapers, prompted by Paul MacDonald's exclusive article, which had made the front page, together with a photograph of Jo holding the prize now wiped completely clean of the last remaining traces of wax.

Now that the story had broken worldwide, a constant stream of reporters and television news crews had beaten a path to Nanny Bapty's old house in North Berwick all anxious to hear at first-hand the account of the discovery of what had quickly become known as "The Benin Bronze".

As Paul MacDonald had explained, this was what Sir Harry Rawson had been seeking over a century ago, when the City of Benin had been looted of its treasures in the year of Queen Victoria's Diamond Jubilee.

And what better to give to Her Majesty as a token of Sir Harry Rawson's abiding love for the British queen than the biggest uncut diamond in the world!

It had been the beating heart of the ancient Benin queen. In its roughly heart-shaped form, it had weighed nearly four thousand carats and was of almost flawless colour and clarity.

It was the largest gem diamond ever to be found, exceeding the famous Cullinan Diamond by almost a thousand carats.

Nicknamed "The Star of Africa" when first discovered in 1905, the world's former biggest diamond had borne signs that it might have been part of a much larger crystal, but until Jo had returned the head and earned the reward, the missing major "half" had never been found.

Now the experts were unanimous in their opinion that "The Benin Bronze" was indeed the larger part of the original stone, which had yielded a pear-shaped cut diamond, with no fewer than seventy-four sparkling facets.

It was set in the royal sceptre housed with the other Crown Jewels in the Tower of London and now it had a rival.

In 1908 The Cullinan Diamond had been cut by Joseph Asscher and Company of Amsterdam. It had been Mr Asscher himself who had the self-appointed task of making the first cut, after he had spent almost six months examining the enormous crystal before determining exactly how best to divide it.

According to popular legend, when Mr Asscher had struck the steel cleaver's blade to make the first cut, the blade had broken, leaving the diamond intact.

On his second attempt, it had split exactly as planned but, for a while, the master diamond cutter had remained oblivious to his own success, having fainted on the spot, as he had made his mark.

Further cuts had yielded three principal parts, including the Cullinan II – a cushion-shaped stone weighing over three hundred carats, which was subsequently set into the British imperial state crown, together with an additional nine major gem stones.

In the early years of the twentieth century, the mine superintendent, Frederick Wells, who had been responsible for the find, had received $10,000 by way of payment.

Now Jo Paterson was set to receive a figure which could run into many millions, if the recent sale in October 2006 had been anything to go by.

Sold in Antwerp to a South African company the "Lesotho Promise" was lauded as the world's fifteenth largest uncut diamond and had sold the previous year for over $12 million.

It was cut into a single gem stone of over sixty carats in addition to other smaller stones and altogether it had been reckoned that they would eventually achieve a sales price of in excess of $20 million!

Now Jo stood to gain an unbelievable fortune and had arrived in the Belgian city with James to witness that first all important cut at the Antwerp Diamond Beurs – the world's most important diamond trading centre, responsible for the importation of over eighty per cent of the world's rough and polished diamonds.

The Antwerp diamond centre was located just a hundred yards or so from the main railway station and there a multitude of diamond merchants traded in both rough and polished diamonds worth billions of dollars.

With over two hundred and fifty diamond cutting factories located in the area, guaranteeing an army of highly skilled cutters and craftsmen renowned the world over for the quality and perfection of their work, it had been a difficult task to choose the right man for the job.

It was Jo's call and Jo had chosen to employ the services of a Dutch craftsman who, in some ways, possessed the same striking good looks as Uncle Robert and who seemed full of confidence about being able to perform the task.

"The Benin Bronze" had already been in his possession for many months, whilst he scrutinised it from every possible angle, taking minute measurements, before finally contacting its owner to confirm that he was ready to wield the steel cleaver in a breath-taking moment watched over by Jo and James.

It was why they had travelled to Antwerp and why they now stood together in the main hall of the Antwerp Diamond Beurs, which formed the focal meeting point for all those involved in the diamond industry and where a special work-table had been set up for the purpose.

Watched in hushed silence, the craftsman prepared to make his first cut in an attempt to break the uncut diamond exactly along the intended line.

If he got it right, a legend would be born – one which would see the world's royalty and leading heads of state clamouring to become the owner of a diamond, which would rival that contained in the royal sceptre used on state occasions by Queen Victoria's great great granddaughter, Queen Elizabeth II.

Queen Victoria had occupied the throne for sixty-three years – exactly the same number of years since the time that Jo had been born back in 1944 when the world had been at war.

Now Jo was on the brink of acquiring a fortune and Jo didn't have a clue what do with it!

In the hushed silence the master diamond cutter took hold of the steel cleaver, ready to make the first incision.

James held his breath.

As the steel cleaver cut the huge uncut stone, fracturing it exactly along the line that had been intended, Jo held tightly on to James's hand, their two sets of fingers totally entwined.

In that defining moment, at last Jo felt able to openly celebrate *his* life-long sexuality.

THE END …

… is only the beginning!

421

Epilogue

James went behind the bar at the Carlton Hall Hotel and poured two generous measures of scotch – one each for himself and Jo to be taken by the two men with the traditional Hogmanay black bun, which had been made several weeks in advance to allow it to mature properly.

It was over a year since their return from West Africa, and Jo was sitting in the upstairs room, which had once been Mary's private sitting room.

Jo had switched on the wide plasma screen television and had inserted a disc into the DVD player, as the two men sat down together to watch the recording of the news item, which had first been televised just over two years before and which Jo never tired of watching.

On the plastic casing was a sticker which bore nothing but the date – December 21st 2005. Pressing the "Play" button on the remote, Jo settled down in one of the comfortable modern leather armchairs, resting his legs on the matching footstool.

He concentrated on the screen in front of him, as the smartly dressed BBC television newscaster announced his next news item:

'Now in sickness and in health gay and lesbian couples across the country have been tying the knot today, as same sex partnerships became legal.

'Sir Elton John and David Furnish said "I do" earlier on and our wedding gatecrasher, Alison O'Neil has been at another ceremony,' he stated, before the scene switched to a scene being enacted outside the registry office in North Berwick.

'To love, honour and share the happy times, today Jo Paterson and James Cartwright made a public pledge to be with each other forever.

'It was an emotional service as the couple formed a civil partnership in front of close friends and family in North Berwick.

'Dame Shirley Bassey's "Thank you for the years" summed up the day for the pair, who had waited years to make their union formal,' announced a smiling Alison O'Neil.

The camera panned across to the scene outside the the registry office, softly focussing on Jo, as he stood hand in hand with James, with the two witnesses flanking the happy couple on either side.

I thank you for the years
I thank you for the good times
As we go on together
I just want to say I'm glad you're here tonight
Thank you for the way you've touched my life
I thank you for your love
It helps me through the hard times
And the joy we share together
Gives me all I need to make it through the night

Thank you for the way you hold me tight
I thank you for the years
I thank you for the years
I thank you. It's been so wonderful
And through all the good and bad times
I just want to say I'm glad you're in my heart
Loving you was only just the start
Holding on
When we're down and we are hurting
Holding on
To the precious things we have
We'll carry on
We'll carry on together
Our love's the reason we are strong
As we grow old together
I just want to say I'm glad you came my way
Thank you for the love you bring each day
I love you now and all I have to say
Is thank you for the years

'It's been a long time coming,' said James, during the televised interview, which had taken place outside the civic building, brushing confetti from his shoulders, as the camera panned in on the two men.

'We've always felt that we have a great deal of pride in each other and, at last, this has enabled us to demonstrate that.'

'We live together, we share each other's lives and this should have happened a long, long time ago,' continued Jo.

'The twenty-first of December has been an historic day for same sex couples,' proclaimed the female interviewer, as she continued:

'Many hope that the new laws will help stop discrimination, allowing them to have the same rights as other couples.

'In North Berwick the locals wished the newly weds well,' she concluded, as the camera switched to the crowd of well-wishers, who had gathered to offer their congratulations and to shake hands with James and Jo.

'They have the right to get married if they want to. It's their life,' said one of the women who had stepped forward to offer her best wishes, adding, 'I'm not against it, as long as they're happy together – that's the main thing.'

'A new era in gay rights dawned this week, with the floodgates opening for other couples to take a walk down the aisle,' said the announcer speaking directly into the camera.

'James's and Jo's ceremony is one of hundreds taking place across the UK in the coming months. It has been a historic week for gay couples and, for better or for worse, civil partnerships are here to stay and to be very much a part of our society. Alison O'Neil reporting from North Berwick for the BBC.'

* * * * * * * * *

Jo had purchased the run down Carlton Hall Hotel and had at once began the task of restoring the once grand building to its former glory.

In the spring of 2007 the work had begun on converting the Victorian building back into a private residence into which James and Jo moved into later that year, selling the house in North Berwick, but transporting with them many of Nanny Bapty's antiques and other treasures.

It wasn't only items of old furniture that were being moved into Carlton Hall with Jo and James!

Living with them was a very old lady, who was now ninety-seven years old and determined to live long enough to receive her telegram from the Queen.

Slowly, Agnes walked down the stairs, past the oil painting of the highland sheep contentedly munching their moorland heather supported on one arm by James, as her son, Jo stood arranging a vase of red roses in the hallway.

At her neck she wore a diamond pendant – one of the smaller gem stones cut from "The Benin Bronze" and given to her on the day that she had moved from the ground floor flat in Stockbridge to come and live with her son and his lover at Carlton Hall.

Jo made a tiny adjustment to the flower arrangement, knowing that "Madam" would arrive at the foot of the stairs at any moment to inspect this handiwork.

A blast of cold air seemed to come from nowhere and, as Jo looked down, a rose petal as red as a drop of newly shed blood landed at his feet. Jo bent down to pick it up, only to discover that it had completely disappeared!

'Jo!' Agnes announced sternly. 'Are you going colour blind in your old age? You've got one pink rose in amongst all the red ones!'

'No Nan, all the red ones are for you and the pink one is for James!' replied Jo, turning towards his mother and smiling at her gentle rebuke, remembering how his grandmother, Mary would have re-acted in exactly the same way.

It was all just a little bit of history repeating!

Author's Notes

Separating the fact from the fiction

Book I

The characters of Mary, Muriel, Alex, Cameron and Charlie are fictional and entirely the work of the author's imagination, although every possible effort has been made to place them in a factually accurate historical background.

Captain Boisragon, Ralph Locke, James Phillips, Rear Admiral Harry Rawson, Miss Slessor (and others portrayed in less detail) are true historical figures, all of whom figured largely in the life and times of the Benin Massacre and/or the subsequent Benin Punitive Expedition and every effort has been made to portray them as accurately as possible.

Whether James Phillips ever experienced the company of the redoubtable Miss Slessor is open to conjecture and whilst it is true that Rear Admiral (later Sir) Harry Rawson certainly enjoyed a lasting friendship with Her Majesty Queen Victoria, any further association between them is the work of the author's imagination.

Whilst the author does not condone the violence and atrocities portrayed in this part of the novel, the fact is that they did occur and he has attempted to write about the nature of such human suffering inflicted both by and upon black West Africans in the manner in which it truly occurred at the time.

In 1897, and throughout its earlier history, Benin City and its people were very much controlled by their beliefs in the ancient spirits of their ancestors, although the part played in this novel by the Great Queen Oba Eeeni has no basis in fact.

Book II

The central character of Jo is loosely based on the life of the person to whom this book is dedicated and many of the events that occur in the novel at the fictitious Edinburgh hotel are inspired by true life happenings.

Some of the characters in this part of the novel are likewise very loosely inspired by persons who featured in the life and times of the person who, in this book, is called Jo but, wherever appropriate, names have been changed in order to protect their true memory.

The accident involving DC-7C Aircraft Flight Registration No. G-ARUD at Douala on 4th March 1962 really did occur and that part of the book detailing the crash has been written with due reference to the Report of the Commission appointed by the Government of the Federal Republic of Cameroon and transmitted to the British Foreign Office by the Cameroon Embassy in London on 29th November 1963 and with due reference to the findings of the Civil Aviation Report of that time.

The exact reasons why the Caledonian Airways DC7C airliner crashed on take off that day in what was then claimed to be the world's worst single air crash have never been accurately and definitely ascertained and remain open to conjecture.

All 111 persons on board died in the crash, including five Scottish crew members although, for the purposes of this book, the characters of the navigator, Clive Thompson and the stewardesses, Rosalind and Amanda are fictitious.

Book III

Much has been written in the press about the need to return the famous Benin Bronzes to their country of origin, especially in 1997 – the year which marked the centenary of the Benin Punitive Expedition but, at least for now, many of them remain displayed in the British Museum. See http://www.arm.arc.co.uk/ for more information.

The lyrics of the Dame Shirley Bassey song: "Thank you for the years" are reproduced by kind permission of Andrew & Elizabeth Neve ©1998 Neve Music info @ nevemusic.co.uk and a suitable donation to a children's charity has been made.

Tribute

The author is indebted to the Civil Aviation Authority for supplying detailed reports from its archives, to the Edinburgh Evening News and to the Cambridge University Library for providing access to various historical works chronicling the Benin Massacre and the subsequent Punitive Expedition.

Thanks also go to two Edinburgh ladies, Irene Peebles and Freda Satow, for providing free access to their personal libraries and for help in researching this book.

And most of all to the person to whom this book is dedicated, for the love, life and happy times and for providing the necessary inspiration for simply getting on with the job and getting it all down in the first place.

Zanzibar

by John L. Emslie

To be a man
One of the clan

The heartbeat of a lion
A sword must die on

Escape across the water
With the Sultan's daughter

Freedom from chains
On the African plains

You'll go to your grave
No white man's slave

Following fortune's star
From the island of Zanzibar

A painting in oil
Of a princess royal

The image reflected
Will remain undetected

Until all the pretence
Begins to make sense

Revealing the relationships
Whispered on everyone's lips

And murderous intent
Will have to be spent

Before those family ties
Reveal the ultimate prize